Stone upon stone
On stone a stone
And on that stone
Another stone

(from a folk song)

Wiesław Myśliwski

STONE
UPON
STONE

Translated from the Polish by Bill Johnston

archipelago books

Library of Congress Cataloging-in-Publication Data
Mysliwski, Wieslaw
[Kamien na kamieniu. English]
Stone Upon Stone / Wieslaw Mysliwski ;
translated from the Polish by Bill Johnston. –
1st Archipelago Books ed.
p. cm.
I. Johnston, Bill, 1960- II. Title.
PG7172.Y8K3613 2010   891.8'5373 – dc22
2010038451

Archipelago Books
232 Third St. #A111
Brooklyn, NY 11215
www.archipelagobooks.org

Distributed by Consortium Book Sales and Distribution
www.cbsd.com

Cover art: Nikifor
Jacket design by David Bullen

This publication was made possible by the generous support of
Amazon.com, Lannan Foundation, The National Endowment for the
Arts, and the New York State Council on the Arts, a state agency.

This publicaton has been funded by the Book Institute –
the © POLAND Translation Program.

Manufactured at Thomson-Shore, Inc. in Dexter, Michigan
Visit Thomson-Shore on the web at www.thomsonshore.com

CONTENTS

STONE
UPON
STONE

THE CEMETERY

Having a tomb built. It's easy enough to say. But if you've never done it, you have no idea how much one of those things costs. It's almost as much as a house. Though they say a tomb is a house as well, just for the next life. Whether it's for eternity or not, a person needs a corner to call their own.

I got compensation for my legs – a good few thousand. It all went. I had a silver watch on a chain, a keepsake from the resistance. That went. I sold a piece of land. The money went. I barely got the walls up and I didn't have enough for the finish work. It's another thing that if Chmiel hadn't gone and died, I probably would have gotten it done. Maybe not right away, but bit by bit. I would've put something aside, found something I could sell. In any case there would have been someone to keep at me and not let me give up. Chmiel never liked starting a job then leaving it half done, like workmen these days. What he began he always had to finish. Except that after he did the vault he never even came to ask for his money. He took to his bed the same day, and a week later he was gone.

And before then I couldn't find any extra cash so he could wrap the job up before he died. Because even when something came along, there were more urgent needs and the tomb had to wait. Luckily no one's dying, I'd say to myself. Plus there were taxes and taxes. I ended up having to borrow some. Then the time came to repay and I had nowhere to get the money from.

Kubik, my neighbor, he'd come by almost every day and straight from the doorway, without so much as a good morning he'd start in with, "When are you paying me back, when are you paying me back? I was supposed to get it last Christmas, and now it's almost December again. My lad has to get married. There's a baby on the way. He needs a suit, a shirt, shoes. Music, vodka. The groom has to foot the bill for the whole thing. Don't think it's like weddings in the old days. Back then you wore your dad's suit and your mother made you a linen shirt. And it was only local people from the village, all you really needed was the priest's blessing. These days you have to invite everyone from the town. And you can't give them homemade hooch – it has to be the fizzy stuff from the store. And the wedding has to last three days, cause if they've taken the trouble to come all this way they have to eat and drink their fill. Otherwise they'll bad-mouth you and say the hosts were bums. And on top of everything they manage to sober up every few minutes, the bastards. The food isn't so much of a problem as the booze. Then at the end you have to give every one of them a bottle for the road, so they'll remember you well."

So I borrowed from Maciołek and repaid Kubik. I reckoned that since Maciołek lived all the way past the mill, he wouldn't be there every day like Kubik was. But Maciołek turned out to be a pain in the ass as well. He didn't come visit. But every time I met him in the village, he'd start hollering from way off:

"Give me my money back, you son of a bitch! You borrowed it fast enough!"

I was afraid to go down the co-op to buy bread, because I might run into him there. I was even afraid to go to church on Sunday – sometimes he wouldn't even wait till we got out of the churchyard, he'd start right in on me in front of everyone while we were still on hallowed ground.

In the end I said to myself, why should I let some old fart push me around. I put a rope on the heifer and walked her down to the purchasing center to sell her. Ever since she was a calf I'd planned to keep her, but what could I do. I just made sure not to meet anyone in the village on the way. I didn't want people feeling sorry for me and saying what a pity it was I had to sell it. Luckily the weather was good and people were working in the fields. There was only old Błach sitting on the bench outside his place warming himself in the sun. His eyes were closed, either from the glare or because he was dozing, so I was counting on being able to pass by without him noticing. The heifer wasn't making much noise, and I was walking softly as well. But all of a sudden something flashed in those eyes of his, like they'd flipped over.

"You taking her to be serviced?"

"No, to sell her."

"It'd be better to have her serviced."

"That it would."

"Then you'd have a fine cow. You could milk her on all six teats. You wouldn't have to drink water during the harvest. You could drink sour milk. You'd just have to buy some jugs. Back in the day, at the fairs there was every kind of jug you could want – clay ones, earthenware ones, tin ones. You could make cheeses. You could hang 'em up in your attic in straw baskets and let 'em cure there. They can cure for years. War comes, you've got cured cheeses. You can eat 'em with noodles or with bread. You can even take a hunk to the fields with you. You can plow and mow and seed all day long and you won't go hungry. Or you could tear bits off it and toss 'em to the rooks. They'd follow you all day long. This way, they'll just slaughter her and eat her and shit her back out again."

"Cows don't last forever either."

"But while they're there they give you milk. Besides, what lasts forever?"

I had to bite my lip to stop myself saying something harsh to the old man, he was driving me crazy. I knew full well I'd have had a cow. I didn't need to be reminded. Her coat was dense as thatch. She had a nice small-sized head and broad shoulders. Her hind legs were set wide apart, she almost looked like she'd have grown a double udder. Also, when I went to lead her out of the shed she wouldn't let me put the rope over her horns. She wouldn't have it, she shook her head left and right to stop me. In the end I had to take her by the muzzle, stroke her, and say:

"Come on, I have to build that tomb."

And now the tomb's standing there unfinished and going to waste. It needs timbering on the outside. There needs to be a separate slab for the entrance, so you don't have to wall it up after every casket. And an inscription saying this is the tomb of the Pietruszka family. Maybe it could even be gilded. These days everyone has a gilded inscription. At the Kłonicas' they don't just have an inscription that says Kłonica Family, but each Kłonica is written separately in gold – Baltazar Kłonica, Jędrzej Kłonica, Adelajda Kłonica, Zofia Kłonica, née Cholewka, when they were born, when they died, and in addition, "Lord, what is man, that thou takest knowledge of him!" There must be a hundred letters in all. But then the Kłonicas sow eight or ten acres of flax alone every year, so they can afford gilding.

People have been trying to convince me to grow flax as well. Flax is gold, they say. An acre of flax is worth five acres of wheat, seven acres of rye, and potatoes, God knows how many. And it's no more work than with rye or wheat or potatoes. You sow it, pick it, dry it, thresh it, and take it to be sold. As for seed, if you contract for a supply they'll provide it. They'll even give you a loan so you can pay them. And if there's a wet year for flax? Then it'll be a wet year for rye and wheat too, to say nothing about potatoes. When it's wet, everything's wet. The rain doesn't choose to fall only on wheat or potatoes or flax. On your field or on mine. Is any of us more pleasing to God? The flood covered the whole world. Only Noah was left, and he took two of every animal and two grains of every grain. And if there's a disease? Don't rye and wheat and potatoes have their own diseases? With potatoes it's even worse, because they have the potato beetle. And even pheasants won't get rid of the potato beetle. One time they released pheasants into the fields, to eat the potato beetles, they said. It got quite colorful out there. You'd be mowing and a pheasant would fly up from under your feet. But did it last long? There was one group of hunters after another, and now you can't find a pheasant to save your life. So they're sending people out again to look for beetles. And turnip, carrots, cabbage – don't they all have their own diseases? What doesn't?

If you look closely enough you'll see that even diseases have their own diseases, and those diseases have diseases of their own. Everything in this world is up against everything else, and it'll be more and more that way. So grow flax, because flax at least pays. Quickly even. What about sparrows? Don't be stupid, in the country you can't get by without sparrows. Put up a scarecrow, put up a couple of them, one in each corner of the field. It's no big deal to nail a couple of poles together and dress them in some old pants, jacket, shirt, hat. Everyone has old clothes lying around that are good for nothing. You save them up over the years because it's always a pity to throw them out.

With flax the straw and the grain both pay. With rye and wheat only the grain pays. Look around the village. You can tell right away who grows flax. Or go to high mass on Sunday. Paper money comes fluttering down into the collection tray like feathers from angels' wings. When there's a rattle of coins once in a while, people look round as if you'd done something wrong. When I was in the hospital, from spring to fall there were two guys here painting the church. One of them got drunk and fell off the scaffolding. But the other one kept on painting. Now the ceiling is blue as the sky. On the walls there's a new stations of the cross. Before, Jesus's head was in a crown of thorns, but now you can just see one of his eyes. When people are better off, the Lord God does better too. And that new bell in the church tower, where did that come from? From flax, my friend. When it rings you can hear it up hill and down dale. Folks come from all around to buy salt and oil and matches, and they say they can hear it ringing everywhere: *Ding-dong, ding-dong*.

But then if everyone grew flax, who would grow rye and wheat, what would they make bread out of? Though I often think to myself, I've got ten acres, maybe I could plant at least one acre of flax? It'd bring in a few pennies if there was a good year for flax. And maybe I'd finish that tomb, because it's gotten embarrassing. It looks like a bunker, with no statue, no cross. There was a guy made a cross for Malinowski's tomb. He offered to do one for me. But I didn't care for it. It looked like a fence post, without a Lord Jesus. What kind of cross is that? Though I can't say I think much of the more expensive ones either in our cemetery. Sometimes I drop by there to take a look and see if one of them might be good for my tomb, but they're just getting fancier and fancier.

The Kowaliks' cross you can see way before you even get to the cemetery. It's almost on a level with the trees. It looks like a tree that's been snapped in a gale, like two unstripped tree trunks nailed together. It even has knots from sawn-off branches like on a real tree, and bark that's cracked with age. And it's all carved in stone. The Lord Jesus is no great size, but his crown of thorns is like a crow's nest. When you stand underneath it it's like standing at a gallows, and you have to tip your head way back like you were looking at a hung man. What does it have to be so high for? You can't look at death high up like that for long. Your neck goes stiff. Looking up is something you can only do to check the weather or when the storks are flying away. Death draws you downward. With your head craned up it's hard to cry even. The tears get stuck in your throat when it's stretching up, and they trickle down into your stomach instead of into your eyes.

One time the Germans hung someone from the village on a high cross like that. When you looked up at him from below he seemed to be laughing at it all. But when they took him down and he was lying at our feet you could see his face was twisted and his tongue was poking out. You could imagine he'd choked on some word that had gotten stuck in his throat when he was trying to shout it out. Though in those times, at moments like that people usually shouted out something short, mostly the same kind of thing. In the time between the trigger being pulled and the bullet entering your body.

If he hadn't run away into the fields but in the opposite direction, toward the river, he might have gotten away. The river's no great depth or width, it's just a river, like you find in any village. When you water your horse its muzzle almost touches the bottom. Old buckets stick out from the surface with mint growing in them. When the women go down to rinse their laundry they wade out into the middle and the water barely comes up to their knees. There are willow trees and bushes along the banks. And he was closer to the river than to that cross. Though maybe they happened to chase him in the direction of the cross, and you run away in whatever direction you're being chased in. Or perhaps he thought the cross was the edge of the wood.

They shot him, but he somehow managed to crawl to the cross. He put his arms around it with all his strength. Afterward his fingernails were full of splinters and the skin on his arms was scraped all the way up to the elbows because they couldn't get him to let go however much they tried. They had to break his fingers. And he was already almost dead when they hung him on an arm of the cross. Later there was no way to get him down and they had to cut down the cross.

Or Barański's daughter. She hadn't even turned three, but Barański had a tomb built for her that made it look as if the Barańskis had been burying their people there since time immemorial. On that tomb, as well as the Lord Jesus being gigantic, the stone was kind of gray, or covered in something, so he looked a hundred years old. And how old was he actually? Thirty-three. And he could have walked into any cottage without having to bow his head at the lintel. I'm not exactly on the short side myself – as a young man I was the tallest in the village. When there was a dance at one of the villages farther away there'd sometimes be somebody taller. In the resistance, in our whole unit there were only two or three men taller than me, though every one of us was straight as an oak. If we'd been lined up in double rank, Lord Jesus would have been somewhere in the middle. I even said to Barański, for a little child like that an angel would be better. But he wouldn't listen. Angels can intercede but they can't save you.

He's standing as if he was on a hilltop, his hands folded on his chest, his head lowered, thinking. There's a lot for him to be thinking about. God or man, it comes to everyone. Even a three-year-old child. You could think and think what might have become of her. Barański used to brag that she would've been a doctor. But can you boast about the dead? Better just say a prayer for them. Barański always was a blowhard. One time he bought a horse and he claimed it was only four years old. You could tell from looking at its teeth it was at least twice that. She might have become a seamstress. Or like the other women, she would have gotten married, and she and her man would have worked the land till they died.

Or take Partyka. On his tomb he put up a Jesus carrying his cross to Golgotha. His shoulders are as wide as three Partykas, and each foot is the size of three human feet. On top of that the end of the cross reaches over above the Ciepielas' tomb next door, and Partyka and Ciepiela always get into a fight on All Souls'. When Lord Jesus is so big, you don't get the feeling that he's suffering even when he's carrying his cross to Golgotha. Even if you wanted to help him, what can you do with your little strength next to his. God ought to be like a person, so you can see that whatever's painful for people is painful for him as well. So you can be troubled when he's troubled. And feel sorry for him the way you'd feel sorry for yourself. And understand when there's nothing he can do, just like a person. And even switch jobs with him awhile. Give me your cross, I'll carry it for you, and you do some of my thinking for me.

Pity I wasn't an airman, or I'd have put up a propeller like the Króls' lad Jasiu has on his tomb. I really like that propeller. But a person's neither fish nor fowl. As for Jasiu, the last time he visited he'd made captain. His jet crashed when they were practicing for a flyby. They brought him back in a metal casket in a separate van. His pals were in another van. There were twenty of them, every one an officer. Each of them had silver cord on his shoulder, there were medals on their chests, bayonets at their sides. They carried him six at a time all the way from the house to the cemetery. They wouldn't let anyone else do it even for one shift, though Jasiu had friends here in the village too. They'd minded the cows together and been at school with him.

The whole village came to the funeral. The fire brigade turned out. Schoolchildren. Two older gray-haired colonels walked behind the casket and gave their arms to Jasiu's folks, Król and Mrs. Król, one on each side. Old Król wasn't that tall to begin with, and he seemed to have shrunk, either from being on the colonel's arm or from his son dying, though he didn't cry at all. Afterward people said no one would have cried at the compensation the Króls got from the government. But it could have been that when he walked next to the colonel old Król felt like a soldier too.

Mrs. Król didn't look like she'd been crying either. But at the cemetery, when everyone was standing at the graveside and one of the colonels said he'd died like a hero, she collapsed into the arms of the other one and they had to bring her round. She only started crying the day after the funeral, when everyone had gone home. Since then it's been all these years and she's still crying away.

Then some guys came and brought sheet metal. They cut it and bent it and welded it, and it turned into a propeller. Some people didn't think a whole lot of that propeller, they said that the parents were Christians and Jasiu himself was christened, and here there's a propeller instead of a Lord Jesus on the tomb. If you ask me though, that propeller is sadder than a good many Lord Jesuses. Aside from anything else, it's designed so that when the wind blows you can hear something in it, as if a plane was flying across the sky. Maybe it's the one Jasiu crashed in? And when you stare at it for long enough, you even think the propeller's spinning. Except it's going so fast you can't see it. You can just see a blur of light over the tomb. If someone wanted, that propeller could stand for a crucifixion.

I wonder what a propeller like that might cost? Even the labor alone. An ordinary tinsmith couldn't make one. Covering a roof is one thing, making a propeller is a whole other business. The men that put it up on Jasiu's tomb kept checking some papers they had and measuring lengthways and widthways and from a distance, like the guys that merged land together for the big farms. Except that at government prices it probably wasn't that expensive. But then you have to die for the government first.

When I worked in the district administration, whenever one of the office workers died the administration would at least send a wreath for free, with fir and spruce branches and a few flowers woven into it, and on the ribbon it would say, from your friends at the district administration. And at the graveside someone would always say a few words about how he was liked, how he was good with people, farewell, may the earth weigh lightly on you. But when a person's on their own they have to pay for the whole thing on their own, with their own money. Even if you borrow from someone, they'll suck the blood out of you afterwards, anything to make sure you don't accidentally die before you've paid them back.

Actually, the tomb alone might not have cost me all that much. But I'd a yen to have a vestibule as well. And a vestibule is almost a third the size of the tomb, and of course that means the cost is one third more. On the other hand, with a vestibule you can go in and turn around properly. The casket can be put in like it should be, not just shoved in there like a barrel of cabbage. The deceased isn't being tugged about and twisted and shaken. That way people aren't distracted from their mourning. And you can tell just from their behavior that this is for all eternity.

Also, I had partitions built to make separate compartments, broad ones because I can't stand being cramped for space, even in a tomb. Not like other people's, where they're all on top of each other like beetroots in a beet pit, on rails. Then they rot and collapse onto each other. In my tomb the deceased is slipped in like bread into an oven, and walled in, and at least in the next world no one's going to come poking their nose in there. Because let me tell you, there's no lack of people who'd be snooping around in there if they only could. There are eight compartments, four on top, four below. That's how many I counted there ought to be in our closest family. Mother, father, Antek, Stasiek, their wives, Michał, and of course me.

I didn't include our grandparents either on mother's side or father's. They say grandparents are close family too, but it's been so many years since they died. And they were buried just normally, in the earth, so the earth will have worked them over long ago. On top of that, the war mixed all the graves up in our cemetery, so it'd be hard to even find where they are. Today there's probably someone else in their place.

Besides, on mother's side I never even knew my grandfather Łukasz or my grandmother Rozalia. Way back in the last century grandfather killed a farm overseer and had to run away to America. And he stayed in his new land. Apparently the overseer was a brute and he would make passes at grandmother, while grandfather wasn't the type to take any nonsense even from the lord of the manor himself. One time when they were in the fields during harvest, the overseer patted grandmother on the backside. Grandfather grabbed him by the throat and squeezed him against the sheaves till his eyes almost popped out. To get his own back, the overseer counted two days less work when grandfather was mowing the barley. Grandfather couldn't count, but he remembered every day he'd worked. He got furious. He grabbed the tally stick that the overseer wrote the days of work on, tore it from his hand, snapped it over his knee, and tossed it aside. How do you like that, you son of a bitch! Grandfather thought he'd taken revenge on him big time. But all the overseer did was laugh so loud the field rang. And after he was done laughing he said to grandfather, get the hell out of here! Without a second thought grandfather swung his scythe at the other man's neck, and the overseer's head went rolling all the way to the horses' hooves. The horses took fright and tipped over a cart full of grain, and one of them broke its leg and had to be put down. The Cossack militiamen came; they turned the house upside down and combed the village from one end to the other, but grandfather was already on his way to America.

For a long time he gave no sign, no one even knew he was there. It was only a few years later, when everyone thought he was dead, that he sent Grandmother Rozalia a few dollars and a letter. He wrote to say he wasn't ever coming back to the village, and that he didn't regret what he'd done, because at least there was one less villain in the world, so it was a little bit of a better place. Though it wasn't easy for him over there. For days on end, in the heat and dust, through the wilderness they drove cattle to the town to be slaughtered. They traveled farther than it took when you had to go to the war back home. And once they were done driving one herd, there was another. Sometimes when there was a drought they had to drink their own piss, because the rivers had all run dry, and the cattle would drop like flies. And even when there were clouds the rain would dry up in the sky before it reached the ground. But he would cut the overseer's head off all over again if he tried it on with grandmother. One time he turned the food table over in a pub in America because he suddenly saw her kissing the overseer. "Get down on your knees before Lord Jesus, Rozalia, swear on His Passion. Maybe you've got some other feller now? Then hope the good Lord is watching over you, Rozalia, and may your brother Felek look out for you. And you, Felek, brother-in-law, keep an eye on her, because if anything happens, remember we'll meet in the next world and we'll have to settle our accounts there." And he said the next time he'd write he would tell grandmother when she should come and join him. And it wouldn't be soon, because this letter cost him five dollars, and five dollars, do you know what a fortune that is,

Rozalia? The letter to grandmother was written by Blume the tailor, that he went to to get his pants patched when they were driving cattle, and he turned out to be a good Christian even though he was a Jew.

But grandmother was just as much of a hothead as grandfather. Without waiting for him to write again like he promised he would, she left mother and mother's brother Sylwester – the one that died later of dysentery – with her sister, even though they were both still small, and off she went to join grandfather over in America. People advised her against it, they said it was halfway around the world, that it was farther away than where the sun goes down, and people over there walk on their heads. Someone from Podleśna had come back from there and he was all upside down, he slept during the day and got up at night, and the dogs wouldn't stop barking at him. He plowed in the night and mowed in the night, and one time he even went to market in the night. He didn't sell anything or buy anything there and he never came back to his house. Eventually he washed up on the bank of the river. But grandmother ignored all the advice and the warnings.

People said afterwards that God punished grandmother for abandoning her children and chasing off after her man. Because when she was already on the sea a huge storm blew up. The sky was full of thick clouds, and it went as dark as the darkest night. The gale howled like a pack of starving wolves. Lightning cracked the sky in two over and over. And there were thunderbolts the like of which no one had ever seen, that smashed holes in the sea all the way to the bottom. And the waves crashed over the ship with all their might. People were pulling their hair out, calling on God and Our Lady and all the saints, and strangers were saying goodbye to strangers. There was a priest on the ship, and some folk rushed to him to make their confession, but others just jumped into the sea. Grandmother knelt down and started shouting out, "Łukasz, Łukasz, I swore to Lord Jesus on His Passion just like you wrote me to! I never went with that pig of an overseer, or with anyone! You're the only one, Łukasz! If I could count the tears I've cried! If the priest could only pass on the holy secrets I told him at confession! Don't believe my brother Felek! He's a bad man even though he's my brother! All he did was keep asking if you'd sent him any dollars! And saying that if you didn't send him money he'd write to you and tell you things so you wouldn't want anything to do with me. The key to the house is over the lintel on top of the door, if you ever want to go back! I left the children with my sister Agata, she'll be good to them. I gave her a cow and all the chickens and some bed linen. If you say you're their father they'll know you. I wanted to tell you all this when I got there, but I'm not going to make it, Łukasz. God doesn't want it. So I'm at least sending these words to you through Him, so you'll know." At that very moment a wave the size of a building hit the ship and the ship broke in two and sank, and grandmother with it. They say she always was a giddy one and that she liked to enjoy life. She never missed a church fair, or a wedding, or a christening, and she'd dance three nights in a row. And in the end she never even got her own grave, but instead she was eaten by the fishes.

Though if you ask me, eternity's the same whether you're eaten by worms in your grave or fishes in the sea. When the Day of Judgment comes, the folk in their graves and the ones from the sea will have to rise up just the same. And it's a lot less trouble in the sea than when you have to build a tomb.

My grandmother on my father's side, Paulina, died when I was still a kid, and I don't remember her that well. Her husband, Grandfather Kacper, outlived her by a good few years, but what kind of life did he have. When he had to go to the outhouse, mother would send me out to keep an eye on him.

"You go, Szymuś honey, I've got pots on the boil here. Take grandpa behind the barn. If he wanders out onto the road again it'll be embarrassing. And pull up a couple of parsnips for me."

It's hard to believe grandfather was supposedly the first person in the village to think up a hoop on the handle of a scythe. He either thought it up or saw it somewhere, people said different things. Some folks reckoned he must have seen it on his way back from the war. Someplace the people mowed with hoops on their scythes, and so when he got back he started mowing like that with his own scythe. I mean, what was there to think up. A length of oak rod, two holes in the grip, anyone could have thought of it. Besides, there are some things that nobody has to think up because they're just there. A horsewhip for instance. It's there and you crack it when the horse won't pull. It must have come with the horse. Or the roof on a house, wheels on a cart, soles on boots.

Grandfather was supposed to have also started the fire brigade. Before, when someone's place was on fire people would just run up each with their own bucket of water and when they'd emptied it onto the fire they thought they'd done all they could to help. The women would start their wailing, Lord Jesus, Lord Jesus! And the men would take out their tobacco and light up. Here something's on fire, and they're all sitting around wondering if it was God's will or if someone set it deliberately. Because if it was God's will there was no point trying to put it out. Though the fact was, there weren't any pumps in the farmyards and you had to go down to the river to fetch water. And the houses were made of wood, with thatched straw roofs. One time half the village went up in flames, including our place.

Also, grandfather had gotten papers to say he had a right to some land, because he'd given refuge to a group of insurgents in the uprising. He didn't remember how much land it was, but he said it was a whole lot. He could have been lord of the manor. Except that he buried the papers somewhere and he couldn't for the life of him remember where. It was hardly surprising, for more than fifty years there'd been no need to show them to anyone or even admit he had them. You could be sent to Siberia at the drop of a hat, so the papers could just have gone and lost themselves somewhere. On top of everything else, that was the time half the village burned down, so it wasn't just people's memory that got muddled up, but even their land, and now the papers were gone, because they'd been buried when the land was arranged differently.

Father would beg grandfather by all that was holy to remember, because it was already going around that Poland was going to be reborn. There'd be an end of servitude, obviously people would be grabbing land, and whoever grabbed it first, it would be theirs for good. They even tried to remember together. They'd get up at the crack of dawn, say a prayer, then father would lead grandfather around the farmyard and they'd go step by step, ever so slowly, staring at the ground, and at each step father would say, maybe here? They'd pause, grandfather would think and think and think, father's eyes would start to light up with hope, but mostly grandfather would say, no, not here. Though sometimes, as if he'd gotten some kind of inspiration, he'd say, you know what, we should dig here. And father would dig. He'd dig a hole, then fill it in afterward. Later he'd get mad at grandfather, and start going on at him about how the devil must have clogged up his memory, that grandfather was a freeloader, because he never forgot how to eat, and if he hadn't drunk so much back then his memory would be fine now, that he remembered all sorts of things he didn't need to. What a song and dance there was about grandfather's memory. Some days my mother even defended grandfather, saying what was father getting so hot under the collar about, we didn't have that land before and we didn't need it now to keep us healthy. Perhaps God didn't want grandfather to remember, and there was no point getting angry at God, because God knew what he was doing. And grandfather was all timid, his bad memory weighed on him like some great wrongdoing, he was afraid to even look father in the eye. It was only when father reached for his tobacco pouch, which was a sign he was through being angry, that grandfather's words also got their courage back:

"Dammit, I remember everything, but not that. I could even tell you who died when the epidemic came. Go on, ask me. They said it was Bolek Koseł brought it from somewhere else to Górki. Right after he came back from the army people in Górki started falling ill, and soon the whole village was dead. After Górki there were other villages, though people weren't allowed to travel from one village to another, and everything was bleached, houses, fences, trees, shrines. And all those crosses they put up! There was a cross in every direction. And there weren't just four directions, like now. Everywhere you turned there was a cross. And at every one of them people would be praying, Lord have mercy, Lord have mercy, Lord have mercy. Luckily it only reached the edge of our village. The Powiślaks died, and Kasperski the miller. The Powiślaks were bandits, they got what they deserved. And Kasperski used to mix low-grade flour in with the regular stuff and he never gave you back all your bran. He was a straight-up crook. But there weren't as many mills back then as there are now. There was the one here, then the next one was all the way over in Zawodzie. Sometimes it'd take you three days to get the job done. But people rode all the way to Zawodzie, though they cheated you there as well, even if it wasn't by so much. There never was a world without cheating and there never will be. Once I bought some boots at the market. They looked like leather. When you spat on the sole it didn't soak in. They were supposed to be for rain or shine, for church and for working in the fields, but they barely made it through the spring. I rode back over there to make the bastards give me my money back, but the people I bought them from weren't there anymore. There were other people and they were saying the same thing, that their boots were the real deal. And do you know how much those boots cost? Go ahead, ask me. Just about the boots. Why shouldn't you. Three rubles. I remember. I could even tell you the names of all the horses we ever had, in order. Ask me. At the very beginning we had a roan. Ruffian was his name, because he'd bite you and kick, he was a son of a bitch. He wasn't a good workhorse so father sold him. But he didn't tell the merchant the horse's name was Ruffian. He said he was called Kuba, not Ruffian, and that our family name was Kapusta, not Pietruszka, and that our village was Oleśnica. Oleśnica was three miles in the opposite direction. And he never found us. You see, I remember. So I'll remember about the papers as well. I'll not die before it comes to me. Can I have a smoke?"

And though father was still acting like he was mad, he'd pass grandfather the tobacco. Then the next day he'd lead grandfather round the farmyard again. Step by step, and at every step: "Maybe here?" If you'd counted all those steps together they would have gone halfway around the world, though our farmyard isn't that big at all. They walked the area behind the barn as well, and around the pond, they went into the cattle sheds and the barn itself, and father even carried grandfather down into the cellar, because our cellar's a deep one with a couple dozen steep steps, and grandfather wouldn't have been able to make it down there on his own. But it was always, not here. And just once in a while, we should dig here. And father would dig. He'd dig a hole then fill it in afterward. And once again he'd get mad at grandfather.

Father tried every possible way to get at grandfather's memory. In the morning he would make grandfather tell him what he'd dreamed about the night before. But old people don't have much to dream about anymore, so grandfather hardly ever had dreams. Father got angry again. He really didn't have any dreams? So sometimes grandfather had dreams, but it was never what father wanted. Because either he was wading in the river and picking mint from the buckets that were stuck there, and as if out of spite the water was murky. Or he was dancing with Karolka Bugaj at Karolka's wedding, and Karolka strokes grandfather's cheek and whispers in his ear, "Oh, Kacper, Kacper, how come you're so old?" Or father and him were walking around the farmyard and father asks, maybe here, and grandfather says, look at that worm coming up out of the ground. That means the soil is sick, nothing'll come from it anymore.

So then father changed grandfather's bedding, and instead of straw he filled the mattress with pea stalks, because if he wasn't going to dream anything, at least he should sleep less soundly. If he twisted and turned more in the night he'd wake up more often, and his thoughts would come to him more and maybe he'd remember. He explained to grandfather that there'd been too many fleas and he'd had to refill the mattress, and there was only enough straw left for chaff. To begin with grandfather complained that he was stiff all over. But eventually he got used to it and in the end it was the same as straw for him.

Then father heard somewhere that wormwood was supposed to be good for bringing back memory. He gathered it all summer long from the edges of the fields and dried it; people thought he had something wrong with his stomach, because wormwood is good for your stomach as well. Grandfather wouldn't drink it because it was too bitter, he said. So without telling mother, father bought some sugar and sweetened it. But grandfather still couldn't remember.

Another time father took grandfather to the pub and got him drunk. He was hoping that when grandfather was drunk his soul would open up and let on where he'd buried those papers. But grandfather got all merry, as if he was fifty years younger. All of a sudden he felt like singing and dancing, he even almost got in a fight. And he bought drinks for anyone that happened to be at the pub, all on father's penny it goes without saying. And when father tried to get him to go easy, saying he'd had enough, that they'd be left stone broke, he started calling him names, you little idiot, I'd never want a kid like you again! Not on your life!

Afterward father had to sell off a calf to pay back what he owed at the pub. The only good to come of it was that the next day, when grandfather sobered up and he just had an awful headache, he promised father that when Poland got its independence back he'd remember for sure. There was still time. The fighting was still going on. Because without an independent Poland those papers weren't worth anything anyway, and that was why he couldn't remember where he'd buried them. But Poland got its independence and he still didn't remember.

Then he swore it would come to him when he was dying, because in the hour of death a person remembers their whole life. The person's life stands by their bedside with a great book and says, I am Kacper Pietruszka, see all you've forgotten and all the sins you've committed, it's written right here. You got crushed one time by that cart loaded with grain, you'd forgotten about it, but here it is. You never returned the sack of oats you borrowed from your neighbor Dereń, here it is. You wouldn't give the Lord God your money that one time on Palm Sunday, here it is. And here are those papers you buried, right here on the first page. Written in the biggest letters in the whole book. But there was no way you could have remembered before the book was opened. Shall I read it to you?

Father watched over him like a dog for three days and three nights when grandfather lay dying, he didn't have a moment's sleep, because for some reason grandfather wasn't able to die. It even seemed he might get better, because that had happened once before, he got better after he'd been given last rites. Goddammit, he'd said back then, there I was thinking I was already dead, and I was just dreaming it. On the third day father dozed off for a minute and that was when grandfather died. Ever so quietly, as if a little fly had flown out of the house. So when father woke up he asked grandfather one more time:

"So then, does it say in that book of yours where you buried them?"

It wouldn't have been right for father to be mad at a dead person, but he put on a funeral for grandfather that wasn't the kind a father should have. The casket was made of pine boards that weren't even painted, just varnished over. And the priest didn't lead the body out of the house, but only from the church. And at the cemetery all he did was sprinkle the casket and the family with holy water, throw in a piece of earth, and leave, because father didn't even want those few words said over grandfather's grave, that's how bitter he was. And for years afterwards he never once looked in on grandfather, though grandfather and grandmother were in the same cemetery and close to each other, and he visited grandmother, but it was only mother and us grandsons that visited grandfather. He never gave money for a mass to be said for grandfather, mother had to do it on the quiet. And he never said grandfather's name out loud. He would just give a sigh from time to time and say we could use more land than we had, because what was he going to leave to his four sons.

And he kept digging. He dug at random, wherever he felt he should, because there was no one left to say to him, Not here. He dug in the barn, in the grain bins, in the cattle sheds under the mangers, round the wagon house, by the front door. He even wanted to dig inside the house, but mother wouldn't let him. One time he dreamt that the papers were buried under the dog's kennel, so he moved the kennel to the other side of the yard, then he moved it somewhere else, then somewhere else again. He must have moved it ten times or more, and he dug in each of those ten places, as if we had ten kennels and ten dogs. But we only had the one. And from having his kennel moved around the whole time the dog stopped knowing what he was supposed to bark at. So he barked at everything, people, horses, cows, chickens, geese, ducks. He even barked at father. In the end, one night he broke loose from his chain and disappeared. People said they saw him running across the fields like a mad dog.

And father kept digging. When the mood struck him he wouldn't even go out plowing but he'd dig holes instead. War came, the planes flew right over the thatched roofs, people ran away into the fields with their cattle and their bedding, and he just seemed to get more single-minded with his digging, and he'd make bigger and bigger holes.

He kept digging after the war too, though he seemed to have lost faith, because often he'd just walk round and round the farmyard not knowing where to start, and all of a sudden he'd toss his spade down and go off to do the threshing or cut chaff. When he got old and his strength began to fail, once in a while he'd still go and do some digging. Sometimes he'd dig a pit as deep as half a man right in the middle of the yard, and it'd have to be filled in straightaway because the wagon couldn't even drive in.

When I wouldn't let him dig in the yard he'd go into the orchard and dig there. From all that digging my russet tree withered up, and my *masztan* sweet plum. The plum tree used to bear plums like cow's eyes. Some years there'd be so many that its branches were weighed down to the ground. I had to keep an eye on it the whole time to stop the local boys pulling the leaves off with the fruit. They were the best plums of all for fruit soup.

Then, when he was dying he gave me a sign that he had something to say to me, and in a croaky voice that already seemed to come from the next world he told me I should keep digging, because although he never found the papers, I would for sure. Now, now he would know where to dig. But now it was too late for him.

Father and mother were both buried in regular graves in the ground, and they're lying there now waiting for me to finish this tomb. There's probably not much left of them, it doesn't take long for the earth to make them over. There may be more of father, because he was buried a lot later, but mother, after they brought Michał back she only lived another six months or so, that was all those years ago, and she first fell ill soon after the war. Maybe they even think I've forgotten about them. They've been lying there all this while, the earth working them over, perhaps they reckon I've turned to drink. "Szymek, Szymek, think what you're doing." Soon there won't be the littlest bone left of them. But I made myself a promise that as soon as I finish that tomb I'll have new caskets made for them and I'll move whatever's left of them. They'll be in there next to each other, on the left lower side, that's what I decided, because the bottom right is for me and Michał, and on top there'll be Antek and Stasiek and their wives. In that way we'll all be together and none of them'll be able to say that I got the farm and they were left with nothing. If it wasn't for that I wouldn't be building a tomb, I wouldn't have gone to all that expense and all that effort. I mean, when it comes down to it is it all that much better in a walled tomb than in the ground? If it was just me I'd actually rather be in the ground. So long as I had a mound of earth smoothed over with a spade, some kind of cross stuck in there, and the thirty years of eternity a person's officially entitled to, I'd be fine. Then someone else could come lie in my place. And after them there'd be somebody else, and somebody else, and so on till the very end, as long as there are people in the world. Because there's no point separating yourself from the earth with a stone wall after you're dead. A person lives from the earth, and they should give their eternity back to the earth. The earth deserves something from people too.

One time in the resistance I spent three days alive in one of those walled tombs and I won't say it was all that comfortable. I tried imagining that I was a corpse myself, but it didn't help. On top of everything else, probably to keep people out they'd made the entranceway small as a rabbit cage, you couldn't even stand up or turn around. There was two of us, me and this other guy, Honeybee was his resistance name, and we had to squat facing each other the whole time. Our legs were all tangled up, his next to mine, mine next to his; it was like they all belonged to both of us at once, because there wasn't room for us to each have our own legs. And we kept asking each other, is that your leg or mine? I've gotten the worst goddam pins and needles in it. I kept thinking it was yours. When one of us needed to stretch, he'd slide over into an empty space where there was room for a new body. Three of the places were still free and three had coffins. They weren't even walled in, they'd just slid the caskets in there. But you couldn't lie for long in those slots, you got stiff from the lack of room and from the concrete.

We'd been on a recce to this one village and we'd gotten caught in a manhunt. Before we knew it the place was crawling with Germans. There was no woods and no river, and the village was right in the middle of a flat plain. Plus it was autumn, the crops had been harvested and the fields were bare. There were just a few orchards behind people's barns, that was it. Luckily there was an old man sitting outside his house, and when he saw us running away he shouted to us:

"Go to the cemetery! The cemetery! Over there!" And he pointed with his stick at a stand of trees that looked as though they'd popped up in the middle of the flatness just to give us shelter.

We ran there and crawled into the first tomb we found. We pulled the cover over and stayed there. They must have buried someone in it not that long ago, because on the top there was still a wreath made of fir and spruce and flowers, all dried up. Over the whole thing there was the most beautiful Lord Jesus I think I've ever seen. He had one hand on his heart and the other stretched out in front of him like he was checking whether it was raining out in the world. Inside, it was dark and smelly, but you just had to say to yourself, tough. Though it was actually hard to say anything at all, words just left a bitter taste in your mouth. Besides, what can you talk about in a tomb. You let out a fuck it or whatever and that's pretty much all you have to say. Even when we tried to talk to pass the time, the only thing that came to our lips were more cusswords, like we'd forgotten all the decent words. But there are times when all the decent words in the world won't do the job of a single fuck it. It's like they're all hollow and blind and lame. And too stupid for the whole situation, however decent they are. Decent words are good for when life is decent. But in there the lice were biting like there was no tomorrow, it was all we could do to just keep it together. Once they got properly going there wasn't an inch of our bodies that didn't itch. We were a paradise for them in that tomb. And in addition, it was like we were sharing the lice and our bodies were shared as well. When his body started to itch, mine upped and started to also. I'd scratch my belly or the back of my neck, and he'd start scratching in exactly the same place. Though it was hardly surprising. We were crammed in there, bent double, and they could hop about on us to their heart's content. Besides, if we hadn't had lice we would have itched anyway. When a person isn't talking or thinking or moving, they have to at least have an itch.

I was tougher, I'd scratch and for a while it would go away. But he was a town kid and he'd probably never had to deal with lice before. He'd start scratching his head and all you could hear was *scrit, scrit, scrit*, like someone was planing a casket nearby.

"Cut it out," I'd say, because I was starting to hurt from his skin. But he'd just keep on, *scrit, scrit, scrit*.

"Cut it out for chrissakes, you hear?"

And he'd just be *scrit, scrit, scrit*. He was going to scratch himself to death, or give us away. At one moment I got so mad I pulled my gun on him.

"If you don't cut it out I'll shoot you, I swear to God I will."

"Fire away. Makes no difference to me whether I die from a bullet or from lice."

That same day, in the late afternoon, the old man that had pointed the way to the cemetery came to visit. How he figured out which tomb we were in I couldn't say. First we heard this light tapping on the cover. Our hearts stopped and I grabbed the other guy's arms in case he felt the need to scratch himself. Then all of a sudden there's this banging noise, and when you're in a tomb it sounds like you're inside a drum.

"Hey there, say something. I know you're in there. It's me." I moved the cover aside a bit and I saw it was the old man from outside the house. He was kneeling with his hands together as though he was praying.

"Because of you I gotta kneel at the Siewierskis' tomb, and they're a right bunch of good-for-nothings. One of those bastards in there with you stole my heifer, the crook. But what can I do. I brought you some moonshine and some bread and lard. You ought to eat something."

"God bless you," I said. "How are things in the village?"

"Not good. There's going to be hangings. They gathered all the men outside the firehouse and picked out ten of them that haven't provided a levy like they were supposed to. The carpenters are building a gallows. When they're gone I'll let you know."

The moonshine was strong – not at all watered down. We each tried a mouthful to begin with. He was going to refuse, said he didn't drink, but I made him. Then we took another mouthful. It was supposed to just warm us up and help with the lice, because when you've got vodka in your system they don't bite so bad. But would that work from two mouthfuls only? Your blood has to be properly drunk, so there's not a single drop left sober. And if you could measure it, two mouthfuls wouldn't even be enough to get your finger tipsy. So we had another drink. In addition, we didn't want to waste the food, because who knew if the old man would come back again. So we drank without eating, like we were drinking to the dead, on empty bellies. He started saying no, he couldn't drink any more, that it stank of beetroot.

"Drink," I said. "You see, the lice aren't biting. If you were sober you'd already be scratching away."

So we drank, him a mouthful, me a mouthful, and so on in turns till the bottle was empty. Nothing was biting, nothing was itching, and the tomb seemed less cramped. You even felt you could have stood up and stretched. In the end we fell asleep.

Except that when we woke up, then the lice really started in. Once he got to scratching himself I thought I'd lose it. I gave him some of the bread and lard. He ate it with one hand and with the other he just went on scratching. Plus he started whining about whether there wasn't a little drop of hooch left. There wasn't. I could've used a drink myself. I felt sorry for him. I was itching like hell myself, but you could tell it was worse for him. In the end I pulled my belt out.

"Give me your hands, I'll tie them."

He started begging me not to do it because he'd itch even more. True, I thought.

"Then get a goddam grip!"

"I can't though, it itches so bad."

"Then eat sunflower seeds."

"Sunflower seeds? Where would I find sunflower seeds?"

"Don't ask questions, just get on with it."

"I would, but how can I do it without a sunflower?"

"It's easy. It's so dark in here you can't see a thing anyway. Just imagine you've got a big sunflower dial on your lap and you're picking out the seeds. You're putting the seeds in your mouth and biting out the insides. Don't you remember? You found the sunflower at the edge of the village outside that one house. The one that was painted blue, with the pots drying on the fence and the cat sunning itself by the wall and chickens pecking in the dust. You slipped into the yard and tried to twist off the head of a sunflower but it wouldn't come off. Then this girl came out of the house and said, I'll get a knife. And she did. Take that big one, she said. Or you can take all of them if you want. And she kept smiling at you. What about that one, see, it's got nice big seeds. You got it there? Just don't spit the husks out on me."

"It's good and ripe, did you try it?"

"Sure it's ripe. It's fall, this time of year everything's ripe."

"You want to pick some seeds with me?"

"I'm not the one the lice are bothering."

So he picked away. He'd only scratch himself once in a while, the rest of the time he picked seeds. You could hear them crack in his mouth and then he'd spit out the husks. I was already thinking he'd forget about the lice. Even I was itching less, though I wasn't picking sunflower seeds. Then all at once he ups and says:

"At the edge of the village, outside that blue house? That was where they were growing?"

"Keep picking," I said. "Why've you stopped?"

"I'm going out to get more. Maybe they're still there." And he starts getting up to go.

"Where are you off to? Sit the hell down, you're fine here."

"I'll bring some more and you can have some."

"What are you, nuts? The Germans are out there."

"So what? You heard the old man – they already chose the ones they're gonna hang. Maybe they already hung them."

"They'll kill you," I said, trying to stop him. "There weren't any sunflowers there. I was making it up. The sunflowers were in a different village."

"You weren't making it up. I remember them. And I remember the girl. She brought me a knife. She told me to take the one with the big seeds. And I did. But now I'm out of seeds."

I buried him in the same cemetery, in the bare earth, without a casket or a funeral. I patted down the mound of earth, made him a cross. I took the wreath from the tomb we'd been hiding in, from the Siewierskis – if they were bastards they could do without a wreath – and I played him a tune on my mouth organ, because I always had my mouth organ with me. Honeybee, you damn fool. You should've stuck to picking sunflower seeds.

That was mostly how we buried people in the resistance, wherever they fell. Without a casket, in the bare ground. For the cross you'd cut down a birch branch. You wouldn't even strip the bark off, just fasten two pieces together with a bit of wire or a strip of leather and you had a cross. And you didn't leave any information, no first name or last name. The person just lay there and they didn't know who they were. Anyone who stopped by on their way wouldn't know either. The Lord God himself might not have known. Though every one of them had some kind of name. Grzęda, Sowa, Smardz, Krakowiak, Malinowski, Buda, Gruszka, Mikus, Niecałek, Barcik, Tamtyrynda, Wrzosek, Maj, Szumigaj, Jamroz, Kudła, Wróbel, Karpiel, Guz, Mucha, Warzocha, Czerwonka, Bąk, Zyga, Kozieja, Donda, Zając, Lis, Gałęza, Kołodziej, Jan, Józef, Jędrzej, Jakub, Mikołaj, Marcin, Mateusz. There wouldn't have been enough room in the calendar of saints. And all of them had to deny their own names and rot like carrion.

Sometimes you'd just hang a forage cap on the cross, if the man had one.

And it was, Sleep beneath the earth and dew, May you dream of Poland true. But not many of them had a forage cap. They mostly had caps with peaks, berets, ski caps. There were a few hats, a handful of four-cornered army caps, and once in a while someone would have a sheepskin hat or a fur hat. Some of them had hats that you didn't even know what to call them, because they were whatever they'd brought from home or had come by during their soldiering. Mikus and Łukasik even had balaclavas like mothers make their children wear in the winter, with earflaps and a strap buttoned under the chin. But those two weren't even sixteen, we'd found them sleeping in the woods in a clump of juniper, because the Germans had burned their village and killed their fathers and their mothers, they were the only ones from the whole village that had managed to escape. And if you didn't have anything else you just wore a plain goddam cap. You just had to give it a good wash first, not to clean it so much as get rid of all the bad thoughts from the cap that might have taken root in the dirt. And you pinned a little eagle on the front, and under the eagle a tiny strip from a white-and-red flag.

To judge by the caps you might have thought we were a bunch of riffraff and pansies, not an army. A rabble that was only good for digging ditches, or building dikes, or beating game when the masters go hunting, not an army. But inside each man there was a devil, and each one of them had a heart of stone. They forgot about God and they forgot how to cry. And even when we were burying one of our own, no one shed a tear. It was just, Ten-shun! Because sometimes tears make bigger holes than bullets. No one dared so much as let their stomach rumble, even if they hadn't had a bite to eat in three days and were hungrier than during Lent. Or even swallow loud. Or even sniff. And no one was allowed to whisper amen. I'd just look at everyone's eyes to make sure none of them were wet. Because in my command, attention didn't just mean feet together and hands at your buttocks. It meant attention in your mind, and standing up straight in your soul. Everything was at attention. I had a voice like a bell, I sang bass in the church choir and sometimes the priest even had to ask me to sing quieter, our church isn't that big, you don't want the Lord God to go deaf, do you? Remember you're singing right in his ear. He doesn't like it to be too loud, he even prefers it when someone's feeling the hymn more than singing it, just like he prefers humbler people over greater people. So when I called Ten-shun! even a hunchback would have straightened up. But then, in the resistance my name was "Eagle," and the difference between attention and at ease was the same as the difference between life and death. People might find it hard to believe that one word could have so much power. But it did. Like the power of fate when it settles on someone. Like the power of hell and heaven together. At attention a person can do anything, however much he doesn't want to, or it's beyond his strength. Like they say, he could knock over mountains and turn back rivers. At attention the heart beats slower and the mind thinks straighter. Who knows, maybe at attention you could even die without regrets. I sometimes wonder how so much power can fit in a single word like that. Whoever thought up that word must have known life through and through. Because there are times when you have no other choice than to say to your own self, attention!

If I died they were forbidden the same to shed a tear, they had to just stand at attention. At most someone could play a song for me on the mouth organ. "Stone upon stone, on stone a stone." Because if I had to choose only one tune to take with me to the next world, that would be the one. Of all the tunes in all my life.

Sometimes I regret it didn't happen that way. I'd have had it all over and done with, I wouldn't have had to struggle with everything like I do now. Like with the tomb for instance. On top of that the district administration folks are always telling me how much grain I have to sell them, how many potatoes, how much beet, how much of this, how much of that, and every year it's more and more. I'll sell however much grows. A bitch won't pup ten times a year, she'll do it twice at the most. Likewise the earth'll only give birth to what it can. And from you it'll only buy the same shit. Though when I die you'll take my land away anyway, it's not like I have anyone to leave it to. You'll be able to sell it and buy ten times as much. But while I'm alive it's my land, and it's just as well I feel like working it, because otherwise it'd be standing fallow. Yet you won't get those folks to understand. They've never worked the land in all their lives, though they know all about it because they went to school. But you can only learn about the land from the land itself, not from any books.

For years they went on at me to get rid of the thatch on my house and put up tiles or tar paper, because there was an ordinance against thatched roofs. But it's in perfectly good shape, it's not leaking or anything. They say it's an eyesore. If you ask me, though, that thatched roof of mine is handsomer than any amount of tile or tar paper or even sheet-metal roofing. Besides which, I've got the attic. Come take a look, goddammit, you've probably all forgotten what an attic looks like. Where are you going to find an attic like that under tiles and tar paper and sheeting? Those aren't attics, they're boxes. Crates. When it's hot they're hot as hellfire itself, and when it's cold, up there it's even colder. In my attic it's warm in winter and cool in summer. Grain, flour, onions, garlic – it can all be kept up there without going moldy or without freezing. You can dry cheeses there, or hang clothes up to air. Or just go take a nap, when you've been working like a dog or you've had enough of everything it's cozier than downstairs, there aren't as many flies and it's as if the thatch keeps the rest of the world at bay. What the heck have you got against thatched roofs? You know, you'd be better off building a road to the mill, because in springtime a pair of horses isn't strong enough to pull a wagon out of the mud that's there. Or find a blacksmith for the village, so people don't have to go all the way to Boleszyce to get their horse shod. There's not going to be an ordinance against horses any time soon. Have you heard the sound of rain on thatch? You won't ever hear that sound under tiles or tar paper or metal sheeting – those make it sound like gravel falling from the sky. Under thatch it sounds like pure white grains of semolina pattering down. You can lie there forever listening to the rain making that sound. And if you need to gather your thoughts, you won't find a better place to do it than under thatch. Not in the fields, not in the orchard, not by the river or in the church.

Also, I've got swallows under the eaves. When the little ones hatch they start chirping for food right from first light, and I wake up with them. There's fewer and fewer swallows in our village, ever since people started getting rid of their thatched roofs. Because swallows won't just build their nests again when you change your roof. They won't take to any old roof. For instance they can't stand tar paper, metal sheeting the same. With the metal sheeting, when it's hot the heat makes their nests all sticky, while tar paper stinks. Storks, now, they're more likely to get used to a different roof, so long as you mount an old wagon wheel up there for them or a handful of sticks woven together. Doves can be lured back too, you just need to put down some grain for them. Not to mention sparrows – to them it's all the same what kind of roof you have, as long as they've got food to eat. But swallows, even if they've lived under the same roof as humans for years, they're constantly afraid. The fear of God, human fear, trembling like aspen leaves. And they're forever in flight. Forever on the wing. Close by one minute, way far away the next. Up high and down low. One minute skimming the ground, the next up a height. Like they were always on the run from something. From what, though? Sometimes you look at them up there, and it's as if they're a blade of grass making the eye of the sky water. Other times, seems they feel hemmed in by the world and they're bouncing about like they're trapped in a cage between the sky and the earth. Like they're losing their senses from all that flying. They keep chasing, chasing. Chasing what? Because even when they fly ever so low over the house they make such sharp turns that they almost cut your eye, it's like they don't want you to even remember them at all. If it wasn't for the fact that they're half black you'd be forgiven for thinking it was the sun glinting up in the sky. It's only when they're high up that they get a bit calmer. Though even then they're nowhere near as calm as storks, or doves. There are times the whole world is broiling, the heat's so sleepy even the dogs are too tired to bark, they just doze in their doghouses. Even the chickens move over to the shade and put their heads under their wings. There's not so much as a leaf moving. The flies can't be bothered to bite. There's nothing but the swallows trembling high up in the air or plunging down close to the ground. You wonder how they have the energy, what they're doing it for. Then the next day there's either a storm or there isn't. Because swallows know no peace.

People have one swallow's nest, maybe two, but under my roof there must be ten of them. We got so used to each other that even in the hospital they'd wake up with me. It would usually start with a noise that sounded like a drop of dew falling on something soft. That was the first hungry nestling waking up. I'd open my eyes and look out the window. Dawn through the window looks like an empty tin pail. After the first drop there'd come a second, though this time it was like it hit the pail, it was hungrier. After that a third, a fourth, a tenth, each one hungrier than the last. Then the dawn would start to grow brighter. At first it was like someone was rinsing out the dark blue of the pail. Then after a bit someone else would bring milk in the pail from the milking and put it in the middle of the room. Right away the beds would start creaking. Someone would say something. Someone would give a sigh to God. Someone missing a leg or an arm would turn over on his other side and the whole ward would turn with them. After that you couldn't sleep any longer.

It might even have been one of those dawns when I got the idea of maybe having a tomb built, so everyone would have a place they could be buried in. Because your thoughts after you've been asleep are like swallows at dawn. And in the hospital wanted and unwanted thoughts come to you alike. Even thoughts that would never have occurred to a healthy person.

Because healthy people only think on this side of the world. When you try and think on the other side, your thoughts slip like they were on glass. Because if you're going over there you need to go body and soul with your thoughts. For good.

It's not surprising really. You're lying there confined to your bed, you've got more time than there are flies on shit and you don't know what to do with it. You don't feel like sleeping any more, how much can a person sleep anyway. There's nothing to talk about either, because it's always about the same thing. An hour seems as long as a day, a day as long as a month, a month as long as a year. I doubt you'd have so much time even in eternity. And that kind of empty time is worse than the sickness itself. On top of that, you've got twelve beds on the ward. And in each one of them there's either an amputated leg or a crushed arm, someone run over by a tractor, someone that broke their back, or someone else with a pipe in their Adam's apple making this whistling sound, here someone's had half their stomach cut out, next to them someone's head is wrapped in bandages, and over there it's hard to know exactly what's wrong with him. Every day the whole place is sighing, hacking, groaning, dying. And everybody's going on and on and on about his illness and all. There's nowhere to run, so you run away in your thoughts, though it's not much better in there.

I never did as much thinking in my whole life as I did during those two years in the hospital. When I got out I felt as if my head was twice as heavy. It kept buzzing like a beehive. But you couldn't not think. Even if you didn't want to, your thoughts thought themselves on their own. If you shooed them out of your head they just flew around you like a flock of crows driven out of a poplar tree. Cawing and squawking. There was no way you could stop them, even though they were your thoughts.

If someone had said to me before that I'd be the one to have a tomb built I'd have laughed them out. Me build a tomb. I wasn't either the youngest or the oldest. And I had no intention of running the farm. I wasn't drawn to the land. I did what I did because father told me to, but in my thoughts I was always somewhere else.

Of us four brothers Stasiek was the one most likely to take over the farm, he looked like a farmer ever since he was small. Father even used to imagine how Stasiek would probably have a new house built when he grew up. And Stasiek and him would discuss it back and forth, because Stasiek wanted it to have stone walls, with cellars and a verandah and rounded windows, with sheet-metal roofing and laid floors in all the rooms. While father wanted to leave an earthen floor at least in the kitchen, because how could you walk on floorboards in muddy boots when fall comes. And sometimes you needed to spit or stamp out a cigarette butt. Stasiek wanted three rooms. Two downstairs, one for him and his wife when he got married, and a separate one for father and mother. And a third one upstairs so that when one of us brothers came to visit we'd also have a room of our own to stay in. Plus a storeroom and a larder. You were supposed to get to all the rooms separately from the hallway. Father tried to convince Stasiek that at least him and mother should be able to go into their room from the kitchen. Their whole lives they'd lived like that and it would be hard to change. But Stasiek wouldn't budge, it had to be from the hallway only, because he'd seen it done like that at the presbytery and at the miller's, where you went into each of the rooms separately. You were supposed to take your boots off in the hallway and put slippers on, because he'd seen that at the presbytery and the miller's as well. Though before he built the house, father would probably have persuaded him to let him and mother get to their room from the kitchen. They were old and they wouldn't have used that doorway long. Then afterward he could've altered it. Or maybe he would have changed when he got older himself, and he'd want to get to his room straight from the kitchen just like father and mother.

And if he'd had a house built he probably also would have put up a tomb. Because a real farmer ought to have his own tomb too. The house is the trunk and the tomb is the roots, and it's only house and tomb together that make up the whole tree. Besides, if father and mother had died he wouldn't have just buried them in an ordinary grave. Even just for when you visit the cemetery on All Souls' Day it's nicer to stand at a stone-built tomb where everyone's all together than at separate graves in the earth. It's nicer to pray and to light candles there, even your grief feels better. And when your tomb is better looking than the other ones, you feel like you're not just master of your own however many acres but that you've worked a decent piece of land in the next world as well.

Michał or Antek, not to mention me – none of us could compete with Stasiek. Though by the time Stasiek was starting school Michał had already left to seek his fortune in the outside world. Antek, on the other hand, he was a madcap, you never knew what he'd come up with next. Whereas me, I never dreamed of ever building a new house, let alone a tomb. I was always more interested in living than in dying. Living and living, as long as I could, as much as I could. Even if there was no reason to. Though does it matter all that much whether there's a reason or no? Maybe it actually makes no difference, and we're just wasting our time worrying about it. Who knows, maybe living is the eleventh commandment that God forgot to tell us. Or perhaps everyone has it written in their stars or in some other book that they're supposed to keep on living, and that has to be enough. People don't need to know everything. Horses don't know things and they go on living. And bees, for instance, if they knew it was humans they were collecting honey for, they wouldn't do it. How are people any better than horses or bees?

In any case I couldn't have said whether I liked living or I just felt I had to, so much so that I felt closer to being born than to dying. And death counted for little with me. I was only interested in life. It goes without saying that death came after me a good few times, probably more than the next man. There were moments it followed right behind me and even lay down to rest beside me, because it thought it might take me in my sleep. Other times it already had its bony hands on me. But it never got the better of me. Sometimes, at those moments it would weep with rage. Weep away, you dark bastard. I'm going to keep on living awhile, because that's what I feel like doing. You'll never take me when you want to. I'll come to you myself when I've had enough, I'll say I'm done with living, I can die now.

How so much life got into me I couldn't say. Sometimes it's destiny, and sometimes a person's born that keeps on living however much everything gangs up against them. It's as if life itself picked them to stand up to death.

I wasn't quite three when the neighbor's turkey-cock strayed into our yard. It was big as a young cow and all covered in dangling red wattles, like it had a cherry branch instead of a neck. The wattles made everything around go red, like a red glow from a fire. The barn, the cattle shed, the fence, the ground, it all suddenly turned red. The dog dashed out of its kennel and started yapping at the turkey, it was filled with red anger. The cat came out of the house, here kitty kitty, its fur was gray, and all of a sudden now it was red. The geese, it seemed like someone had taken their white covers off, as if they were pillows and they were waddling around in the red linings. And even the scythe leaning against the barn started to drip with red blood, drip, drip, drip.

I set off toward the turkey to pull off those wattles of his that had turned the whole world red, and hang them around my own neck. He probably thought I wanted to play with him, and to begin with he started running away. Then all of a sudden he came to a stop, bristled up, gobbled, and spread out like a whole cherry tree, and the blood almost burst from his wattles. I reached for his neck, and he ups and jabs me in the hand, jabs me in the head. Then he gobbles again and jabs me again. But by this time I'd already gotten ahold of his neck with both hands, and I held on like it was a fence post. He tugged and jumped, but I wouldn't let go. He started hitting me with his wings, and with his head caught in my hands he jerked me one way and the other like he was trying to leave me his head and get free even if it meant going headless. He didn't manage to, though, because in my little hands I could feel the strength of four grown-up hands. He dragged me all the way across the yard and back. In the end he must have decided there was nothing else for it. He stood still, spread his wings like two clouds, and tried to fly. He flapped and flapped, he thrashed and he twisted and turned, but for some reason the air wouldn't lift him up. We both fell to the ground. We were covered in dust. You couldn't have said what was turkey and what was me, we were just one big tangle.

I thought my eyes were covered in red from the wattles, and I didn't mind one bit. But it was blood that was blinding me. I started to feel weak. The turkey was on his last legs too, he was just barely moving his wings. He tried to peck me again, but what could he do with nothing but his head sticking out of my grip like it was poking out of a hole. He didn't peck any harder than if he'd been picking up grain from the ground. Besides, he might not even have been able to see what he was pecking, because his eyes were popping out like pebbles. He opened his beak wide and began hissing like a punctured tire, but he was weaker and weaker. I passed out and he collapsed on top of me. Father and mother came running out of the house. They thought we were dead. And that more likely the turkey had pecked me to death than that I'd strangled the turkey. I was a child, after all. And the turkey weighed twenty-two pounds even after it was plucked and dressed. Father carried me into the house. He was crying up a storm and all covered in my blood.

A whole horde of neighbors gathered. They sent to the village for holy water to splash on me before my soul left my body and it went cold. Some of them already began to say the prayers for the dead, others were comforting mother, telling her God wouldn't let any harm come to me in the next world, and he might even make me one of his angels, because I'd not done any wrong in this world. And they waited for the holy water. But before it arrived I came to of my own accord. Except that when I saw the crowd of people over me I burst out crying and mother had to hold me in her arms for the longest time before I calmed down.

It was the same when I was older and I'd go caroling with the other boys, no one would agree to be King Herod, because death cut Herod's head off and no one liked to be killed. So I was always Herod, because I preferred being king to being afraid of death. We had a real scythe, one that was used for mowing, not a fake one with a wooden blade. When death cut your head off with a real scythe you felt death was real too, and not Antek Mączka dressed up as death in a white sheet. Especially because each time I was killed the blade of the scythe had to touch my neck, not just knock my crown off. But I never once flinched. Though death cut my head off and I was a goner as many times as we visited houses in a night. The farmers we caroled for sometimes couldn't even watch, and their wives would scream and cover their children's eyes. But in the houses where they were most frightened, afterward they'd give us each an even bigger serving of pie, and a piece of sausage, and a glass of vodka. They always turned to me and said, you want a top-off? They'd check whether the scythe was honed and whether I didn't have a cut on my neck. And they couldn't get over it. He's a brave one, dammit. That's for sure. He's a proper Herod. The real thing. There was just that one time Antek Mączka brought the scythe down and nicked me till I bled, so I took his scythe away from him and kicked his ass and he didn't play death anymore.

Or in the resistance, seven times I was wounded. Once I thought I was already in the next world. I got hit in the stomach. When I opened my eyes I was actually surprised it was exactly the same woods, the same sky, that a skylark was singing somewhere up above. A skylark, okay, why shouldn't there be skylarks in the next world. Except that not far away there was a village in flames. Cows were lowing there, a baby was crying, someone was wailing, Jesuuus! And way far away in the distance a farmer was plowing. He didn't look like a farmer from this world but like the soul of a farmer, because he wasn't looking in the direction of the fire, he didn't hear the shouts or the howling and moaning, he was just bending over his plow and plowing. I didn't know which world to believe in, this one or the next. Truth be told, I didn't really feel much like coming back to this world. But the next one just seemed like a continuation of this one. Till I felt that I was lying soaked in blood, and that the lark above me was a lark from earth. Though I wasn't glad about it at all. It felt like I'd died in the next world and I'd come to this one to live.

I figured it'd be almost fall before I got out of the hospital, maybe I'd be home after the potato lifting. Because I wasn't in any kind of a hurry. For what? I was just a bit worried about Michał. But they told me he was getting by more or less. One day this person would bring him something to eat, another day someone else. The people from the farmers' circle were supposed to take in the harvest for me, or if not them, the neighbors. As for the potatoes and the beets, someone would agree to do them in return for a third of the harvest, that was what I was offering.

Except that one day the doctor came. He told me to get out of bed and walk up and down across the ward, with sticks and without. He said he ought to keep me in till the fall, but he knew, he knew I'd want to be getting home for the harvest. So they discharged me, I just had to come back for checkups. I was going to tell him there wasn't anything I particularly had to rush back for, that the farmers' circle would take in my harvest for me and if not the neighbors would do it, like they'd done the previous two years. It wasn't as if I was about to pick up a scythe myself from the get-go. When you're working with a scythe your legs need to be as healthy as your arms. Mowers even say that with proper mowing, you use your legs and your back, that all your arms do is swing back and forth. But I didn't say anything. I thought, you've been through umpteen harvests and now all of a sudden you're going to try and get out of one, and here in front of a doctor. There were plenty of men on the ward who dreamed of getting out for the harvest, at least one last one before they died. Just to touch the spikes of wheat with their living hand, maybe see the mowing one last time, take a look at the fields, breathe in the earth. For a good many of them it'd be easier to leave for the next world if they knew there were harvests waiting for them there too. It's common knowledge, a person lives by the earth, so they ought to be drawn to the harvest like a dog to a bitch.

And so I came home. And right away on the third day I headed out for the cemetery to take a look around. I took a tape measure, a pencil, and a piece of paper, because I wanted to measure some of the graves to see what would be best for me.

Our cemetery is just outside the village. You pass the last houses, hang a left, and walk uphill a bit. When they're taking a dead person in his casket from one of the houses you can make it all the way with three changes of bearers, four at the most. Even from the farthest places, from the mill or by the school. I've been a bearer many a time, always at the head. The head is a lot heavier than the legs, because from the stomach up you've got the back and the shoulders and the head, while what is there to carry at the legs, just thighs and shins and ten toes. But I could've gone the whole way without being spelled, except it wouldn't be right not to have a change of bearers. And that's probably what made me think the cemetery was close. Besides, I'd forgotten that my legs weren't the same legs they used to be, and every step was like a hundred steps before.

I looked to see if there wasn't someone driving that could give me a ride part of the way. But I'd picked the wrong time – it was noon, everyone was in the fields. My hands went numb from the walking sticks, the uphill part at the end was the worst. So the moment I made it past the cemetery gate I plopped down on the nearest tomb. I was staggered, my eyes were blinded with sweat.

Kozioł Family, I read on the stone I was sitting on. It didn't look that big. No one would have believed you could've gotten more than three or four people in there. But when they buried old Kozioł here a few years ago there were already five of them in the tomb and he was number six. Though the fact is they barely managed to squeeze him in there. The coffins were squashed next to each other like barrels in a cellar. There wasn't enough room to go inside and set the casket on its rails. They looked for the smallest farmer to climb in, but no one wanted to be the smallest one. Each one they asked said no, it wasn't him, so-and-so was smaller. Anyway, how can you tell who's the smallest in a crowd of people like that. You'd have had to take out a tape measure and measure them. In the end they found someone, maybe he wasn't the smallest one, but he went in there. Except afterwards he couldn't get out, because the casket was blocking his way and they had to pull it out again. So then they lifted it up because they thought it might be easier to get it in from the top, but this time the coffin lid got in the way. When they took the lid off, it came out that they were burying their father in resoled shoes. Another time I went to the firehouse to watch the farmers playing cards. The Kozioł' kid Franek was playing with Jasiu Bąk and Marciniak and Kwiatkowski. Jasiu Bąk had gotten a full house, Marciniak had a straight flush, Kwiatkowski was carrying a pair, and Franek didn't have a thing, but he was the most fanatical of all of them. In the end he bet the whole pot, and in the pot there must have been ten pairs of shoes, a suit, a shirt, a tie, maybe even a coffin. And he lost the lot, because Jasiu called him. Franek didn't bat an eyelid. He even took another two hundred from his pocket and sent Gwóźdź out for a bottle of vodka.

I measured a dozen or so of the tombs. I didn't just measure them, I looked them over carefully and sounded them. From what I could see, the tombs that Chmiel built were way sturdier than the ones the Woźniaks had made. Also, in comparison with Chmiel's, the Woźniaks' ones were tiny, even when they were for the same number of coffins. And even the oldest tombs Chmiel had built, from before the war, were still good, it was like they were part of the earth. Because Chmiel had been building tombs for donkey's years. The Woźniaks only started during the war, when Chmiel couldn't keep up with the work.

Some people told me to go with the Woźniaks, they were a lot younger and they worked the two of them together, while Chmiel was old and took his time. And that with the Woźniaks I wouldn't have any trouble getting lime or cement, because they bought it directly off the people that filched it from the trains. It was just that I didn't like the Woźniaks' work, and on top of that they like to eat well and at each meal you have to buy them a bottle, because otherwise they'll go work for someone else and leave your job unfinished. Chmiel didn't drink. Also, whenever he ate too much or he had food that was too greasy he'd get the bellyache and he'd have to squat down a bit to put pressure on his stomach. He said that in the last war he'd eaten some bad herring and ever since then he needed to squat like that whenever he ate too much, or he ate greasy food. But it wasn't anything he couldn't live with.

And you didn't need to keep an eye on Chmiel, he'd check everything himself and remember about everything. When I bought cement it wasn't enough that I had it, he had to come and see what kind it was. Actually he pissed me off, because it was like he was looking for problems. First he wet his finger, stuck it in the cement, and put it on his tongue. Then he took a handful from the sack, poured a thin stream of it onto his hand, and blew to see how light it was. Then he took another handful on the palm of his hand, spat on it, and rubbed and rubbed. And if he'd at least smiled. But no, his face was crooked as a dog's tail the whole time.

"What are you even checking it for, Chmiel? It's all written on the sack."

"Sure, be a fool and believe what's written. Then later on the roof of your tomb'll collapse. You won't feel a thing, but me, they'll say I'm a lousy craftsman."

Besides, if you go to the cemetery you can tell just by looking which tombs are Chmiel's. Each one of them is solid as a boulder. While the Woźniaks', scratch them with your fingernail and they start to crumble, because they never put in as much cement as they should. On some of them there are whole cornerstones broken. On some the sides have started to cave in. Or the top plate's cracked, and rainwater gets in and drips on the deceased.

On All Souls' Day you don't see it, because the tombs all look the same. The whole cemetery's decorated, flowers and wreaths and candles, and crowds of people, so all you can see is mourning. But on a regular day, when the next All Souls' is far off and the last one's even further, and the cemetery's like a tract of fallow land that hasn't been plowed in a long, long time – at a time like that every crack comes to the surface, every chip is like an unbandaged wound, and each tomb is different from the next like each person is different from the next one, and all together they're like people that are dog-tired and they're taking their rest, and none of them has the strength to be embarrassed. The menfolk scratch themselves, the women spread their legs and you could even sneak a look, it's just you don't feel like it.

Before the war Chmiel built a tomb for the schoolteacher's daughter, Basia was her name, she used to sit in the front row at school. She was pretty as a picture and because of her, one or other of the boys was always getting distracted during class and being sent to sit in the corner. In sixth grade she suddenly went away and she was gone the whole year. Then when she came back she didn't come to school anymore, but instead she sat around in the shade the whole time. It would be summer, bright sun, and she'd be in the shade by the wall or under a tree, with a little umbrella. She got paler and paler, and her eyes were bigger and bigger, those eyes of hers that were blue as cornflowers.

I wasn't that good in Polish, and our bitch had just had puppies. So I took one round for her.

"Basia, if you have to sit in the shade you should at least have a little dog."

"A puppy, a puppy!" She started hugging and kissing it like it was the best thing that had ever happened to her.

I didn't know what was so good about a dog, especially a black-and-white one that was still blind. Father had told us to drown them before they got their sight, or maybe leave just one, because what use were all those dogs. They'd just have to be fed the whole time they were growing up. Then later they'd start chasing after bitches, and get beaten by folks around the village and we'd end up having to look after a cripple dog. You could chain them up of course, but think how much chain you'd need to buy. It was bad enough the cow's chain broke and no one had the time to take it to the blacksmith's to get the link mended. And can you even imagine if all of them started howling? The racket would be unbearable. You wouldn't sleep a wink all night, then how could you get up in the morning and go to work? Let alone wondering who's died to make them howl like that. Lord, let's just hope it isn't any of our relatives. It wouldn't be so bad if they were just howling to the moon, but the moon's not always in the sky, while death is always there.

"Hey, little puppy. What's its name?" she asked.

"It doesn't have a name yet. I brought you one without a name so you can name it yourself."

"You name it," she said. "I want you to name it. I'll call it whatever you decide."

"Name it yourself. I gave it to you, it's yours."

"Please, give it a name."

"What's the big deal about naming a dog. You just call him the first thing that comes into your head."

"All right, then he'll be called Szymuś. Would you like that?"

"Don't ask me, ask the dog. Makes no difference to me."

"Szymuś, Szymuś." She started cuddling it again, and blue tears flashed in her blue eyes. "It's a pity I'm going to die soon."

I moved up to the next grade, while she spent another six months dying in the shade. The white angel on her tomb has gone gray now and the tomb itself is all rough like old thatch, but there's no sign of any cracks. The gold's worn off the inscription, but you can still read the letters as clear as in a schoolbook. "My home stands gaping empty now and drear, My sweetest Basia, since you went from here. Your mother." What was she, no more than twelve, but when you read it you'd think the whole world had died. I asked Chmiel if he'd made it up or if someone else wrote it for him.

"Who could have made it up," he said. "It just goes from one tomb to another."

While on the tombs the Woźniaks built it's always the same thing, born on such and such a date, died on such and such, rest in peace.

Or the tomb of the young squire. That's from before the war also. Maybe even from before the schoolteacher's Basia. He died in his automobile. He'd drive it around the villages and the fields, frightening people and animals, and the dust he kicked up! There were times when after he'd driven by there was a cloud hanging over the village half the day, and people would be gasping like they had the consumption. You had to close the windows in your house and shoo the chickens and geese off the road, and if anyone was heading out into the fields they'd turn back as fast as they could. Because the horses were afraid of it the worst. The moment they heard it droning in the distance they'd rear up. The farmers would have to climb down off the wagon and hold them by the bridle. With horses that were already skittish even that wouldn't work, they'd break the shaft, snap the reins, then turn the wagon over and run away. Some people said it was a sign of a coming plague. On top of everything he'd be wearing a leather pilot's cap, and with those big goggles on his eyes he looked like Lucifer himself. That was what they called him. Lucifer's coming! Lucifer's coming! Every soul on the road would run for their life. And the old people would cross themselves three times and spit behind them, get thee behind me, Satan.

So one evening the cows were coming back from the pasture. And as usual with cows in those days, the road was all theirs. Also, they'd eaten their fill so they were moving slow and sleepy, you couldn't have gotten them to go faster even with a stick. They wouldn't let so much as a wagon get past them, let alone an automobile. They weren't like the cows these days, that walk along with their ears pricked up and their skin twitching the whole time. The minute they hear the slightest noise behind them or in front, they move to the side of the road of their own accord. They've even learned to walk on the left. But back in the day cows were the masters of the road. Except that the young squire thought he was master of everything. And instead of stopping and waiting till they went their way, he started honking his horn and flashing his lights, he didn't even slow down. And the cows just moved even closer together. He smashed one of them to pieces and broke another one's legs, and he ended up a corpse himself.

I moved my finger across the inscription. It was even as a ditch, first name and last name, and, died tragically, you could read it all, and in front of the last name Count. The manors didn't survive, though you'd have thought manors were a whole lot stronger than tombs.

When the front passed through, of all the tombs Chmiel's survived the best then as well. And there's no harder test for tombs than a war. For six weeks there were two German artillery batteries stationed at the cemetery, firing to the east day and night. And they were huge guns, every one of them. On top of that they were half dug into the ground so only their muzzles were poking out from among the graves, and with every round the whole hill with the cemetery on it would jump, and each time the crews working the guns had to open their mouths so as not to go deaf. And all those trees they cut down to make room for the guns.

And from the east the Russki guns fired day and night the same, for six weeks. It looked as though the cemetery hill would turn into a valley. It was so hellish even the worms couldn't take it anymore, let alone the dead. It was like the earth itself was turned inside out, and all of eternity was flung to the surface.

There were skeletons, bodies, coffins, all over the place, like death had suddenly gone on the rampage all on its own because it had run short of living people and it had dragged the dead out of their graves so it could kill them all over again. Like even though they were supposed to already be dead, they were part of the earth now, some of them had rotted and some were nothing but dust – still they had to die a second time. And without even knowing they were dying. So when the front moved on they had to be buried again, like real dead people. And for years later the cemetery looked like a battlefield.

Any time you went there you'd see ruins and stumps of trees, the place was empty and silent, there was only the odd tomb or tree that had survived intact. As for the birds, it was like they'd vanished, you wouldn't see even the lousiest little sparrow. And for the longest time afterward, even though there wasn't any danger or anything for them there, they avoided the place like it was infected. They didn't even perch there on their way to someplace else and sit and chirp. They didn't even turn up there by accident. Or visit their old nest the way birds will do.

Before, the cemetery had been a paradise for birds. There were cuckoos, blackbirds, goldfinches, titmice, orioles, bullfinches, woodpeckers, crows, doves. Who could have even counted them all. The trees just about shook with them. They'd sing and chirp all day long, and cuckoo and caw. The moment you went into the cemetery you'd find yourself right in the middle of a hullabaloo of birds, before you even got to the graves. When you prayed, the words of the prayer would sometimes get lost in the din. Every so often Franciszek the sacristan would climb up into the trees and knock down the nests of the noisier ones, because he thought it was too cheerful for a cemetery. Though they didn't just nest in the trees, but on the crosses and the

Lord Jesuses and in the grass on the ground. But after the front had passed through, whenever a bird happened to fly over the place it would rise up higher in the sky, sometimes as high as its wings would carry it. As if it was suddenly hemmed in by something and its only escape was to climb higher and higher.

Franciszek the sacristan, who used to think that because of the birds the cemetery wasn't sad enough – now, he'd make bird feeders and put them up here and there where a tree was still standing, or even just a branch, or even on the crosses and the Lord Jesuses and angels, he'd hang them wherever he could. You'd see a cross over a grave and on its arms there'd be two bird feeders hanging, as if Jesus was holding them in his crucified arms to attract the birds. Or in the place where there'd been the head of an angel that had gotten blown off by a shell, the angel would have a feeder for a head. He put up so many of those feeders that when you saw them you'd be forgiven for thinking there were all kinds of birds at the cemetery. But there wasn't a single one, they wouldn't touch the feeders.

He also set out water in old tin cans from army rations, so the birds would have something to drink if they came. People kept removing the cans to put flowers in for the graves, so he put new ones down, luckily there was no shortage of tin cans. The front had been stationed there for months and the soldiers had emptied piles of cans. They were lying about all over the place along the roadsides, in ditches, in dugouts and trenches. People used them as containers for sugar and salt, if need be you could make a bowl or a mug out of a can like that. Boys even used them for goalposts. Sometimes you'd read the label in Russian, *svinskaya tushonka*, and that would be the closest you'd get to eating all day.

Some days you could find Franciszek at the cemetery at the crack of dawn wandering like a spirit with his pockets full of millet, flaxseed, wheat, poppy seed, bread crumbs. He'd be scattering it all among the tombs and calling to the empty sky: cheep-cheep, cheep-cheep. Every few steps he'd drop his eyes from the sky to the ground, stop, and look to see if there wasn't some starling or bullfinch or waxwing he'd managed to attract, pecking the grains and skipping about. Then he'd move on his way like someone sowing in the fields: cheep-cheep, cheep-cheep.

Some folks reckoned Franciszek was scattering sand instead of grain, and that the birds weren't stupid and they wouldn't let themselves be fooled by sand. I mean, think how much grain you'd need for a cemetery the size of ours. People didn't even have enough to bake bread with. The fields were all churned up and trampled, and how could they harvest anything from under all the shells? But the birds must have been hungry too. And a hungry bird'll be tempted even by sand. Besides, when you're a bird and you're flying way up a height, from up there you can't see who's scattering what down on the ground, whether it's sand or grain. And if he's going cheep-cheep and looking up at the sky, why shouldn't you trust him?

Franciszek would teach the new altar boys how to serve at mass. The old ones had grown up because of the war and they preferred spending their time defusing mines and unexploded bombs. But anyone who had a yen to be an altar boy had to make a trap to catch starlings. And Franciszek would take his altar boys over to the hill along the edge of the woods. Then for days on end they'd try and trap starlings there. Whenever they caught one they'd bring it to the cemetery and release it there.

It sometimes happened that Franciszek would be lying there in the grass and bushes, with the ends of the strings from the traps in his hand and his altar boys all around him, and he'd forget about the church. Because trapping starlings is easier said than done. You can spend the entire day and not catch a single one. All it takes is for someone to whisper to someone else right at the moment the starling's getting close, or even to just give a louder than usual sigh, and the bird'll get spooked and fly away. And altar boys are altar boys, they see a starling coming close and their heart immediately starts pounding, and with starlings, they can even hear your heart if it's beating too loud. But anyone who scared a bird away wouldn't be an altar boy any longer.

"Clear off, you little imp. You think you can serve the Lord God when you don't have the patience for a starling?"

And it wouldn't do any good to cry or say sorry, or that you'd get a hiding from your parents. Franciszek could be stern as they come. Though really he was a good person. When I was learning to be an altar boy we mostly spent our time just scraping wax off the candlesticks. Whenever anyone asked what *saecula saeculorum* or *Dominus vobiscum* meant, he'd claim it was a divine mystery.

"You need to know when to turn the page in the missal, and when you're supposed to pour the water and the wine into the chalice, and when you have to ring the bells. The rest, you just need to be able to mumble along."

There were times people would come to mass and it would be so stuffy in the church it was like a holy cattle shed, because there was no one there to air the place out. The priest himself would have to fetch the long pole and open the windows, because Franciszek was out trapping starlings. Or folks would start to arrive for the service and the church door would be locked, because Franciszek had been out after starlings since early morning and wasn't back yet. Or mass was already supposed to have begun, the church is full, the priest's in his chasuble and he keeps popping his head out of the vestry to see if the candles are lit, but here the candles aren't lit and the altar's not prepared either, the organist is playing on and on, and Franciszek's nowhere to be seen.

Sometimes one of the parishioners who could remember his altar boy duties would throw on a surplice and carry in the missal behind the priest. Franciszek wouldn't turn up till the priest was raising the chalice. He'd be all flushed still from the starlings. His gray hair would be full of grass, and his shoes and pants wet and muddy from the dew. It wouldn't have been so bad if he'd been embarrassed and knelt down quietly. Nothing of the kind – he'd plonk himself down on his knees so loud it would echo all round the church. And the guy that was taking his place, he'd push him aside and be all angry he was in the way. And he'd shout out *et cum spiritu Tuo* or at the very least amen like he'd been kneeling in front of the altar the whole time.

But it wasn't anything to be surprised at. Starlings are best caught in the morning, especially on a Sunday, when they're hungry from the night and everything's quiet out in the fields. And from the hillside by the woods it was a good mile and a half to the church, Franciszek was getting on and it might only have been those starlings that were keeping him among the living. Or maybe the Lord God had said to him, trap some starlings before you die, Franciszek. And so the priest went easy on Franciszek too, and he never told him off. He'd even ask him when Franciszek was helping him off with his chasuble in the vestry after mass:

"So how was it with the starlings today, Franciszek? Do we have any more at the cemetery?"

Besides, Franciszek was too old to do any heavy jobs around the church. Trapping starlings on the hill up by the woods and bringing them down to the cemetery – that was all he could handle.

One time he brought a nest of blue tits with the young birds still in it and he put it in a tree in the cemetery. Adult birds would probably have flown away, but the young ones grew up and stayed there. Then someone brought him a squirrel from the woods and he let that loose among the graves as well. Someone else brought a woodpecker. Someone brought a blackbird. Someone a dove. And gradually life came back to the cemetery.

THE ROAD

There was a road ran through our village. It wasn't the best of roads, like most roads that go through a village. It had bumps and potholes. In spring and fall there was mud, in the summertime it was dusty. But it did okay for people. Every now and then they'd level it out here and there, fill it in with gravel, and you could drive on it just fine. You took it to get to market in town, or to other villages around here, and whether you were going off to war or headed for the outside world, the road would lead you there just the same.

As well as the road being for everyone, each person had a bit of it that was their own, depending on where their farmyard was. And before every Sunday or holiday in the summer they'd sweep it, in the fall they'd scrape the mud off it, in the winter they'd clear the snow and put down ash so nobody would slip and fall in front of their house. On Whitsun it'd be spread with stalks of sweet flag. The sweet flag would crunch underfoot when you were on your way to church, it smelled like in the woods, and people said it was the road that had that smell. And almost everyone had a bench or a big rock by the roadside. They could go out and sit there of an evening, chat with the neighbors, have a smoke, or just stare up at the dark sky over them. Ask God about this or that. And see nothing but the lights of the fireflies.

People, cows, geese – they'd all walk down the middle of the road, there was no left or right side. You could leave your horse and wagon by the side of the road and go to the pub for an orange soda or a beer, or sometimes even a half-bottle of vodka. You'd have your drink and your horse would just stand there. Or if you were on your way back from the fields with your crop and someone was coming from the opposite direction, you'd stop the wagons next to each other, like standing shoulder to shoulder, and no one would honk their horn to say you were blocking the road. And you'd take the same road on your final journey, because there wasn't any other. Except the women would hurry out of their houses and shoo their chickens and geese into their farmyard. The farmers would keep the dogs in their kennels to stop them from barking. Wagons would pull over to the side. Mowers would take the scythe off their shoulder. Mothers would bring their babies out in front of the houses. And even drunks would take their cap off and sober up a bit.

On both sides there were acacia trees. When you walked down the road and they were in bloom, the smell would almost choke you. At night you'd have to close your windows or you'd wake up in the morning with a head-ache. When the farmers smoked on their benches or rocks in the evening, it was like the acacia was smoking. Watchdogs would lose their sense of smell and just lie there outside their kennels. If you had a young lady with you under one of those acacias in bloom you didn't even have to do much talk-ing. Today there's maybe three or four of those trees left in the village. They cut them down when they were building the new road. Time was, acacias were planted for their wood that was used in making wagons. If you had an acacia, you'd have a wagon. Well, maybe not the shaft or the sides. For the shaft the best thing was young oak, and one-inch pine planking for the sides. But you'd have the perch, the bench, the tapers, the clouts, the futchel, the bolster, the weight, the singletree, the stanchions, the reach, and of course the wheels. For wheels there was no better wood than acacia. Even oak ones couldn't match them. They were too hard, they were prone to crack. And the wheels are the most important part of a wagon.

Except these days it's all rubber wheels. They're trying to convince me to switch to rubber wheels. It'd be less work for the horse and you can carry a lot more on your wagon. Or at least reshoe him and put rubber linings on his horseshoes, because the asphalt is sharp. At harvesttime the farmers can carry four layers of sheaves in one go on rubber wheels. Before, even two horses together wouldn't have been able to draw that much, now one of them can on its own. You sail down the road. Some of them barely have any land at all and they still have rubber wheels. Or the old folks, you'd think all they'd want would be to pray for a peaceful next life, and here they are swapping out their wooden wheels for rubber ones. Karpiel's going to be headed for the next world too before long, and there won't be any more wheelwrights. There'll only be mechanics left. Then who's going to even change a felloe for you when it goes bad? Who'll turn a hub? And out of what? Back in the day there were acacia trees and you had the material. But back in the day there was the road as well.

True, it was winding. Roads often are. They have to go around one thing or another. A shrine, a pond, a house. They straightened the whole thing out and asphalted it over. They made long rounded curves so it doesn't really bend at all, you just drive straight. A good many of those curves took up a whole field. Albin Mucha had a field next to the road where he grew buckwheat and serradella, now there's a curve there. Sometimes on a Sunday he goes out onto the curve and knocks his cane on the blacktop and he shouts, this was my field! They buried it, the sons of bitches! Or he'll sit by the ditch and make a list of the cars that are driving on his field.

There's no denying the new road is three times wider than the old one and smooth as a tabletop for driving on. And you can see something of the world on it. Especially on Sundays. Though it's a pity roads like that don't have names like rivers. Because for our village, being next to the road is like being next to a river in spate. You stand there watching, and it just keeps on flowing and flowing. It even sort of divided our village into two villages. One on one side, one on the other. Mothers won't send their children to the store if the store isn't on their side. Neighbors would rather walk farther to borrow another neighbor's horse or plow or scythe, just so as not to have to cross the river. When the cow minders take their cows to pasture, some are on one side and some are separate from them on the other side, when they used to all go together. Even at village meetings, the people from each side stick together. Or when two farmers that live opposite each other come out in front of their houses, they don't go up to smoke and talk together like they used to. Instead, each one smokes on his own side and from his own pack of tobacco. And the way they talk to each other, it's like they were deaf. Though how much can you say when one of you's on one bank and the other's on the other, and there are cars forever driving through your conversation. The little ones you can at least shout over, but the big trucks won't even let the words out of your mouth.

It was a pity about those acacias as well. It made you want to cry, to see those old trees come toppling down like sticks under the saw. You were born with them and grew up with them, and you thought you'd die with them too.

It happened in the spring, if I remember rightly. It was cold, wet, muddy. There was still snow in the fields in places. They came with their machines and saws and started cutting the trees down. And the people came out and watched – what else were they supposed to do? Old folks, young ones, kids, mothers with babies, the way everyone goes down to the riverbank when the river's about to flood. Or when there's a glow on the horizon at night and all you know is there's a fire somewhere, but it's too far away to go help. There were a good few tears, a good few people calling on God, a good few wailing babies in their mothers' arms, because for the kids it was like their world was being cut down before their eyes.

Except that afterwards, when it turned out the trees were going to be sold, everyone miraculously got over it and they all rushed to buy them. There were quarrels and bribes and accusations. Some people kept watch over the trees round the clock for days on end. Some guys sent their daughters out to wiggle their backsides in front of the workmen. Whoever didn't have a young girl in the family showered them with vodka and sausage and whatever they had. Someone even nailed a picture of a guardian angel on one of the trees to mind it for him. Someone else hung a length of red ticking on another one to mark that it was his. Boleś Walek tied his dog to one because he was planning to make a wardrobe out of it. But in the night someone knocked the animal out and tied it to a telegraph pole instead. Mikus, in turn, he had his boy climb up in a tree and sit there till they cut it down. And they went on like that, competing with each other the whole time.

I admit, I picked a tree out for myself as well. It stood half a mile beyond the village and I figured that before they got to it I'd have time to buy it. So I go there one time, and all that's left of my tree is a stump. And every tree the entire length of the road is already sold, whether it's already been cut down or not. They were using mechanical saws. They'd put the blade to the tree, and *bzzzz*, that was the end of the tree. Then they'd move on to the next one and the next one. And here was I fool enough to think they'd be using a regular saw. All along the road the only thing left was the old willow by the footbridge beyond the church, that no one wanted to buy because the place was haunted. It was so rotten inside it was just one big hole, and the trunk was only what was on the outside. It was amazing the branches at the top still grew back green in the spring.

People said the devil had used to live in it. They said he'd show himself to people, though never in his own form, always disguised, as a stray sheep, a rider on a horse, a hooded monk, as someone looking for a bed for the night or who didn't know the way. He appeared to Pięta that lived beyond the mill as a bride in a long white veil, and the veil trailed across the whole width of the road. Pięta tried to pass her, because something seemed wrong from the get-go, a bride in the middle of the night, and by the old willow. But he accidentally stepped on the veil, and all at once the veil fell off and she stood there naked as the Lord God made her. And she says to Pięta, now you have to marry me. Come with me, I'll take you to our wedding. But Pięta's a smart one, he says, sure, just wait a moment while I go take my ax and finish off my old lady. All right, she says, hurry!

Then my grandfather would tell how when he was a young man he was coming home one night, and here there's a gentleman in a top hat and overcoat with a cane, walking by the willow. He thought it must be the squire that was having trouble sleeping and he'd come out for a stroll. Though he was a bit surprised he'd chosen such a rough road, like he didn't have the grounds of his own manor. He might twist his ankle in a pothole or step in some cow dung – for a gentleman that would be embarrassing. So he bowed like you do to a gentleman and he asked him:

"Are you not taking a walk in the grounds, your grace? You need to be careful here, there's lots of potholes and bumps."

The other man says to him:

"Oh, it's you, Pietruszka."

Grandfather felt like someone had put a slice of honey on his heart, that the squire had recognized him in the dark and remembered his name. Then, when he even took grandfather's arm and said he'd walk him back to his house, grandfather thought to himself that maybe bad times were coming for the masters.

First he started asking grandfather what was going on in the village, how life was treating everyone, whether there weren't any complaints. Just some old chat. But they evidently enjoyed talking to each other, because when they reached our house grandfather said that now he'd walk the squire back to the manor. And they chatted and chatted some more. And they walked each other back and forth like that half the night, first him walking grandfather back to his house, then grandfather walking the squire back to the manor. Then, at a certain moment he suddenly turned to grandfather and asked him:

"Have people never thought about attacking the rich folks' houses?"

Grandfather realized right away, so that's what this is about, you old son of a gun, and he said:

"What for?"

"You know, to burn and steal and kill!"

"Not at all, the village people are God-fearing, they're quiet, hardworking. We live fine with the rich folk."

"How's that?" said the squire, his hackles rising. "Don't you want to be the masters?"

"Being peasants is good too," said grandfather cleverly. "That's how things were set up, evidently it's for the best." So the other man gets even more upset, and starts banging his cane on the road and saying people ought to attack the manors. That the rich folk have done them so much wrong, and they're still at it. And he starts going on about what they could burn, how much blood could be spilled, how much weeping there'd be, it'd be like the whole world was crashing down, not just the rich folks' houses. Grandfather's legs began to shake and he crossed himself out of fear. At that moment the wind blew up and knocked the other man's top hat off, and grandfather saw he had horns on his head.

"Let me go, Satan!" he shouted, and all of a sudden no one was holding his arm anymore.

But was I going to be scared of a devil? I bought the willow. I put it down by the barn, and it's been lying there ever since. Because truth be told, it's no good either for chopping up for firewood, or for making something out of. Though at least I have the willow, after I missed out on an acacia. I can't say I've seen the dog bristling at it or the cat giving it a wide berth. The chickens like it the best, they roost on it all the time. If there's a devil in there let him come out and we'll square up. Later on I tried to buy an acacia off Józef Winiarczyk, I offered him double the price. He'd bought six of them and I said to him, what do you need so many for. I could have used it to have a new wagon made. Or if not a wagon then a new table. Actually I need a table even more. The one I have now I got way back when the front came through and it's barely standing. You can't put anything heavy on it or lean on it. If you move it, it creaks and sways like it was in the wind. Not long ago I had to put a new leg on it. The dog rubbed against the old one and it fell off. Before that I had to replace the middle board. I put a bowl of cabbage on it and the next thing I know it's crashing to the ground. I sawed off a piece of an old sideboard from the wagon. It was rotten as well but I didn't have anything else. When I hammered in the nails they went in like it was butter. The leg I made out of the plum tree that had stood there dead for a good few years, I just hadn't had time to dig it up. It doesn't match the other three legs, but at least the table's standing. I mean, how can plumwood match when the other three are carved oak. Each one's got a sort of wreath around it at the top, while at the bottom they're slim as horses' fetlocks and they have these funny paws that stand on the floor.

Right after the front passed through and I was doing a bit of work as a barber, when a bunch of farmers would gather together here on a Sunday they'd always argue about those legs. There were even bets about whether they were lions' feet or if they were some other monster. No one managed to figure it out, but we got through a good few bottles while we were trying. And it wasn't just about the legs but also who'd sat at the table, what they'd eaten and drunk. There were times they got so excited when they were guessing that it turned into a feast. You'd hear nothing but laughter and shouts and cheers. Even popping corks and clinking glasses. The table would be groaning under the weight of the food. And they'd keep bringing more and more dishes. The smells would make your head spin. Till finally one of them would come to his senses and say:

"Come on, get on with shaving us, Szymek. All those bastards are stuffing themselves, and we're walking around like Moses with these beards."

But back then the table still had all four legs, and there was this sort of bindweed twirled across the top. There was a drawer with a gilt handle. It was a good place to keep your pliers and hammer, screws, nails, shaving equipment, receipts, mother's old rosaries, because she had four of them. One of them was even from the pilgrimage my mother took me on one time when I was a kid.

But when I came home from the hospital the drawer had disappeared. Someone must have taken a liking to it. From that time on there was a hole in the table, like it had no soul. Also, the top had long lost its shine, and it was covered with woodworm holes that looked like freckles on a freckly face. What can I say, a person's time comes and so does a table's.

I found it the day after I came back from the resistance. Father had told me to go check whether our fields weren't mined, because spring was coming and we'd have to plow and sow. Though really it was nowhere near springtime, there was still snow on the ground. Not far from our land I was just poking around and I saw something lying on manor property in the unmown rye, under a sprinkling of snow. A body? No, it was a tabletop. So I started to look for the legs. I found one straightaway close by, then two others way over by the woods. Then the fourth one turned up in a ruined potato clamp when I was looking for shoes for Stasiek. The drawer I spotted around Easter at our neighbor's. He was feeding the pigs out of it.

"Karol," I say, "I think that drawer might fit my table. You could take my trough. It makes no difference to the pigs what they eat out of, and we could share a bottle together."

"Sure, why not," he says. "But if you give me the trough so the pigs'll have something to eat out of, what'll you give me for the drawer?"

"What do you mean? I just told you."

"Sure you did. But what'll you give me?"

"You'll take my trough and we'll have a bottle together."

"We can have a bottle together. But you'll have to throw in a half-bushel of rye. Your folks managed to gather it in before the front came through, on my field they dug trenches. And for the handle you can lend me your horse for plowing for a day or two. It's no ordinary handle. It's a bit dirty, but if you clean it up with ash it'll shine. You could make a nice door handle out of it. And never mind that I found it on my land. Or how many mines there were. My kid spent a week getting rid of them. Day after day we were terrified he'd get blown up. Bolek, the Szczerbas' kid, was clearing mines over there, and that was the end of him. There wasn't a body left even. An arm here, a leg there. That way you get your drawer practically for free."

And that was how the table ended up back together.

Mother even killed a chicken and made broth to celebrate. We sit down at the table, me opposite father, Stasiek and Antek opposite mother. We cross ourselves and start to eat. Father says:

"Finally we're eating like human beings."

Mother sighs:

"Lord, if only Michał was with us. All these years and no word, no sign. Who knows if he's even still alive?"

"He's alive, he's alive," father reassures her.

And Stasiek tries to change the subject and says:

"Can you imagine if someone came to visit right now, with the chicken, and the table."

And it was like he'd said it in an evil hour. The door opens and in comes Mateja from across the river.

"Christ be praised."

"Forever and ever." But I can see there's something about him. He's smiling, but there's a fox in his eyes, you can even see its teeth.

"You're having chicken," he says. "Lucky for you."

"We got a new table so I killed a chicken," mother explains.

"I know you do. That's what I'm here about." And without so much as a by-your-leave he starts checking the table from every side, tapping it, rapping it, tugging at the legs to see if it isn't wobbly, patting it like you pat a horse's rump, and in the end he says it's his table.

"Have you got a certificate?" I ask him.

"What certificate?"

"You know, to say it's yours."

"I can see it's mine. It was on my land."

"What are you talking about, your land, you moron! It was on the manor's land!"

"It was the manor's when it was the manor's. Back then I wouldn't have taken it. But after the land reform it's mine, so the table's mine too."

"The hell it is! What kind of table did you have before the front came through? You forgotten? A bunch of planks nailed together, the wood wasn't even planed. You were always getting splinters under your fingernails. Your fingers were bandaged so often, people made fun of you for picking too many blackberries. The table's from the manor, so get the fuck out of here! How many of you are there at your place? You, your woman, seven kids, the grandfather. As many as you've got fingers. And do you know how many people sat at this table? As many as there were apostles at the Lord's Supper. You couldn't even have counted them. If a thirteenth came along there would've been room for him too. How is this supposed to be your table, you old fool? Look, you can still see the stains from the candle wax. They had candles when they ate. You all couldn't even afford kerosene. Your eyes would be shining in the dark like wolves. And what, you want to eat *żurek* and potatoes at a table like this? They ate capons. Do you even know what capons are? Roosters with no balls. When they ate, all you could hear was knives and forks clinking against the plates, like bells during the Elevation. When you lot eat, you can hear the slurping noises all the way out on the road. They had napkins tied around their necks. And what's left of them?

This table. And even that, all the parts got scattered and it had to be put back together after the war."

As chance would have it, after they built the new road Mateja was the first person to get run over by a car. He was crossing to the other side because he'd remembered his woman told him to buy salt and the store was on the other side. Not only did he not buy the salt, it also turned out it was his fault. Here he was in his own village and he was to blame. He was going to buy salt and he was in the wrong. He didn't die right away. They carried him to the side of the road. The whole village came running. I went too, though we'd been mad at each other all those years because of the table.

"I'm not angry at you about the table," he whispered when he saw me. "Yours or mine – either way we'll end up sitting at the same table."

I gave the speech at his funeral. I even mentioned about the table. I said to his wife and children, don't cry, don't cry, Wincenty's sitting at the Lord's table now.

Then some time after Mateja, Mrs. Pociejka was run over. She was going to high mass, and she was trying to cross the road just like Mateja, because the church was on the other side. She was really scared of the cars, so she waited till the road was clear. But it's never going to be completely clear. She waited and waited, then she hears the bell ringing for the Elevation. So she ups and starts shuffling across. The nearest car's still way in the distance. And if she hadn't looked to the side she would have made it, because she didn't have far to go. But she saw the car coming towards her and she was so frightened she dropped her walking stick. Some folks said she bent down to pick up the stick, others claimed she knelt down to pray that the driver wouldn't kill her. But he did.

Then Kacperski's stove cracked from the cars. The thing is, the new road passes right by his wall. They're sitting eating dinner, and whenever a car drives by, the spoons shake in their hands. Thick soups they can usually lift to their mouths, but if it's a thin broth they sometimes spill half of it before it gets there. Kacperski says he's even tried eating standing up, or sticking his mouth right in the bowl, or taking his food out into the orchard. The only time he has a proper meal is when his woman brings him dinner in the fields.

Then Barański's dog got run over. Then Mrs. Waliszyn's calf. One Sunday it was one of my chickens. In the morning I'd taken the horse down to the river to water it. The sky was cloudless, the river glistened, the air was warm and fresh, the birds were singing, who would have thought anything bad would happen. I fed the cows and the pigs. I tossed some hay out for the horse, brought the dog's bowl out, poured some milk into a saucer for the cat. Then I started to shave. I was halfway done when Mrs. Michała runs in:

"Oh dear Lord, Szymek! One of your chickens has been killed!"

I run out onto the road with my face half lathered up, still holding my razor, my shirt unbuttoned. I see a crowd of people standing in the road, and in the middle my chicken that's been run over. It's still flapping a bit. I pick it up by the legs. Is it yours, they ask. Of course it's mine. You don't think I know my own chicken? What's one life worth for those cars?

"Which one did it?" I ask, not because I want to know, but it seemed wrong not to say anything at all when it was your chicken.

"He's gone now," someone says.

"It was a green one," somebody else adds.

"Not green, blue."

"What am I, blind? It was green!" They start arguing.

What was I supposed to do? I took it home and it had to be eaten.

There's no more peace to be had in our village. Nothing but cars and cars and cars. It's like they built the road for the cars alone and forgot about the people. But are there only cars living in the world? Maybe a time'll come when there won't be any more people, only cars. Then I hope the damn things'll kill each other. I hope they have wars, worse ones than human wars. I hope they hate each other and fight and curse each other. Till one day maybe a Car God will appear, and it'll all make him angry and he'll drown the lot of them. Whoever he spares will have to walk on their own two feet again. Like when the Man God appeared among people.

Because these days anyone who goes around on their own two feet is nothing but an obstacle to the cars, on the road and everywhere else. Even when you're walking at the side of the road you feel as if all the cars are driving right through you. Your heart's in your mouth. Not that you're afraid of dying. It's just that dying from a car is no kind of death. Even the memory of a death like that, it's as if someone had just spat on the road. Yeah, he got run over. But does that mean the same as, he's dead? Is there eternity after that kind of death? Plus, they honk and make gestures and wave their arms from behind the windshield, and a good few of them wind the window down and call you every name under the sun. As if you were the lowest of the low, because you're on foot. A person's legs don't mean anything anymore. Time was, whole armies went to war on foot. And they won. And people said, there's nothing like foot soldiers. Or if there's a pool of rainwater on the road they'll even deliberately try and splash you. Then the guy that's done it laughs at you from his car, the jackass. If his woman's with him she laughs too. If he's got kids, the little bastards have a ball at your expense.

You know, if you could get ahold of one of those sons of bitches, you could grab one of those cars like a sheaf of hay and hoist it off the road into the field. But do you think any of them stop? They're only strong when they're speeding by. And where are they rushing off to? The sky's the same everywhere, and no one can get away from their own destiny, even in a car.

These days there's no telling how you're supposed to walk on the road. They say on the left. But push comes to shove, all that means is you're looking at death face-on instead of having your back turned. Otherwise no one would even know you're walking there, that's how low you've fallen, man. They can see you or not see you, it's up to them. A car's lights aren't eyes.

There you are swinging your lantern in front of every car like a fool, like you were begging it not to kill you.

And to think that when we were young men, after a dance it'd take us all night to get home along that road. The rooster would crow once, twice, three times. The cows would be hungry and lowing in the cattle sheds. Buckets would be clanking at the wells. And here someone was still on their way home. Sometimes till it was broad daylight. Till morning. What was the hurry? The dance was still spinning in our heads, the music was still playing, and we'd cut a step on the roadway like it was the floor of the barn and sing the first thing that came into our heads. "Stone upon stone, on stone a stone!" And the road never let out a word of complaint that you were waking it up. And it never dared hurry you. It'd go step for step under your feet, alongside you, like a faithful dog. When you stopped it stopped also. You could go one way or another, any direction you wanted, you could even turn back to the dance and it would turn back with you. From one edge to the other it was yours. Like a girl on a bed of hay, underneath you.

The night could be black as pitch, and you'd be three sheets to the wind. One moment you had the sky over your head, the next the earth, then the next nothing at all, maybe not even God himself, because why would God want to watch over a drunken man. But the road never left you. The whole world would rear like a stallion under you, try and throw you off. Sometimes a tree would hold you up, sometimes a post or a shrine. Or you'd just fall over, pick yourself up, and continue on your way. If not on your feet then on all fours. Or you didn't get up at all. Till you got woken in the early morning by the birds singing like a heavenly choir in the acacias. And if you didn't know where you were, the road itself would lead you home like a guardian angel. Unless you got a ride from Szmul when he was taking the milk churns into town of a morning. But Szmul was just as much a part of the road as the acacia trees.

I never missed a single dance, not just in our village but anywhere in the neighborhood. There were times we'd go five and ten villages away when we heard there was going to be a bash. And since I knew how to have a good time more than most folks, I was always greeted with open arms and they knew me far and wide. Hey look, Szymek Pietruszka's here! Then they knew the party would be a blast. When I'd show up in the doorway it'd be, in with the band! in with the dancers! Musicians, play a march for Szymek Pietruszka! And the band would play like wild horses. And I'd enter dancing the march.

The first thing you'd do was go to the buffet in the middle of the room. Like bride and groom walking up the aisle. Stand aside, everyone! At the buffet you'd meet people you knew and people you didn't, but they were all friends. Szymek, Szymuś, you're here, greetings, friend, buddy, pal. Somebody's pouring a drink, someone's handing you one already poured, a third person gives you an even bigger glass, someone else a piece of sausage and a pickle. Drink up, Szymuś! Here's to being single! We're gonna have fun tonight! Long live us! And when on top of that my watch chain would be dangling from my belt, the whole dance shivered in anticipation. Now there'd be a party. Because on my watch chain I carried a knife.

Oh, that knife of mine was famous. It looked like just a handle. Anyone who didn't know might think I was only carrying it for good luck, like a keepsake. And having it on a watch chain like a watch, it seemed almost innocent. But all you had to do was press a button at the side and the blade would pop out like a wasp stinger. Often they'd come at me with sticks, and all I'd have was my knife. A whole mob of them, from every side, and me in the middle all on my lonesome, with nothing but the knife. But even a sword wouldn't have matched it.

Sometimes I didn't even have to take it out. All I needed was to unbutton my jacket and flash the watch chain, fear did the rest. It was the same at the buffet – because of the knife I barely spent a penny. Anyone who wanted to see, it cost them a half-bottle of vodka. If you wanted to see it with the blade open, it was a half-bottle and a beer. And to handle it, a half-bottle, a beer, and something to eat. And if some wise guy pretended to want to know what time it was, you told him it'd be eternity when he found out, and he preferred to stand you a half-bottle as well.

Four strings of garlic that knife cost me. I bought it off this guy that went around the villages selling needles, thread, safety pins, head-lice lotion, various stuff. They called him Eye of the Needle, because he could talk all day about the eye of the needle, who'd passed through it and who hadn't. Afterward mother went on and on about how someone had stolen some of her garlic from the attic. I told her to count again, that maybe she'd made a mistake. But each time she counted she was missing those four strings. It was only when she was dying and I wasn't young anymore, and it had been so long ago that those four strings had shrunk to four heads of garlic, as you might say, that I confessed it had been me. By then the knife was long gone as well, missing or maybe stolen. There was no shortage of folks that had their eye on it. A good few tried to buy it off me. But at that time I wouldn't have sold it for all the tea in China. I could have gotten ten strings of garlic for it, or a hundredweight of rye, a necktie or a pair of gaiters. One of them even offered his watch. No one had a knife like that in those parts. They usually fought with regular bread knives, sometimes a butcher's knife, most often with penknives.

But a penknife, at the most it's only any good for killing frogs or whittling a pipe while you're minding the cows. You can't even cut tobacco with it. Its blade is weak as a willow leaf and the handle's like a twig. When you're up against someone in a leather jacket, what use is a penknife, it won't even cut through the leather. Also, every dick in the village carried a penknife since they were knee-high to a grasshopper. You could buy one at any church fair or win it at one of the stalls with a fishing pole or an air gun. But as for taking it to a dance, you'd be better off with your bare hands.

So then, after you'd been to the buffet you went and danced. To begin with you were nice and polite. You'd take a young lady that was free and sitting on one of the benches or standing with her girlfriend. You'd bow to her and kiss her hand. And you wouldn't hold her too tight, because what you'd had to drink was only enough for first courage. Besides, it was still light out. The sun was only just setting, it was shining straight in through the windows. And all the old women were sitting like crows on the benches around the edge of the barn with their eyes burrowing into all the couples like woodworms. There were small kids all over the place like it was a nursery. The band hadn't had their supper yet and they were only playing slow numbers. All the dancers were still following the emcee's instructions. In pairs, form a circle, one pair to the left, one to the right, make a basket, girls in the middle, girls choose their partner! And the firefighters in their golden helmets would still be sober as judges, standing there by the door like it was the entrance to Christ's tomb, making sure no one drank too much. And if anyone did get drunk and went looking for a fight they'd haul his ass out the door. So a young lady could easily tell you you were a pig.

It wasn't till later. Once the sun went down and the ceiling lamps were lit. When the old women round the edge of the room went off for the evening milking, and the mothers took their kids and put them to bed. When the first dew broke out on the foreheads of the band, and the party really started to get going. Then, sure, you could drag a young lady to the buffet. And at the buffet it would be a first and a second and a third and, what's your name, honey? Zosia, Krysia, Wikcia, Jadwisia. I'm Szymek. So listen, Zosia, Krysia, Wikcia, Jadwisia, will you have a drink with Szymek? I've been going to one dance after another looking all over for you, and finally I've found you. Are you lying? Why would I lie? Come on, they're playing our number. And in that dance she'd let herself be held close. You could run your hands over the embroidery on the back of her blouse. Some of them had blouses like a flower garden, covered in cherries and rosebuds and raspberries and rowan.

A good many of them would like it so much they'd show their teeth when you tickled their cherries and rosebuds and raspberries. Others would look at you reproachfully, like you were trying to pluck the fruit off of them.

Then it was back to the buffet. Then back to the dance floor. And not for a kujawiak or a waltz this time, but for the oberek! That was a dance and a half! You'd tap your foot, and spin faster and faster. To the left, to the right. Hey! And your partner would be clean off the floor, with only you holding her up. And you'd throw her way up to the ceiling. Her skirt would be flying and her blouse would be bouncing. And her braided hair would spin around as you danced across the room. Oh my Lord! Szymek! My head's swimming! She falls into your arms all out of breath. This time she's the one holding you tight. The devil's in her eyes by now. Szymek, I have to take a break. You're something else, Szymek. Come on then, Zosia, Krysia, Wikcia, Jadwisia, let's go get some fresh air. Or maybe she'd suggest it even, come on Szymek, let's get some air, it's hot in here. And once you were outside you'd go as far as you could away from the dance. Not here, Szymek, farther away or someone might see us and afterwards there'll be talk. And you might come to the next dance, but then again you might not.

Because the dance meant that all sins were forgiven. Even if one of them asked, will you take me for a wife? You could promise you would, sure, why not, but not right after tonight's dance. Come on, get up, the music's playing again.

If you took a liking to one of the young ladies, then whoever she was dancing with it didn't matter, you treated her like she was yours and you didn't ever have to apologize for cutting in. Hey, come have a dance with Szymek. Szymek'll show you what dancing's all about. And you, beat it, loser! If he was meek he'd go sit on a bench and watch or get drunk at the buffet. If he put up an argument the watch chain would get dangled in front of him. And if that didn't do the job, he'd get a fist in his face.

Quite often that was how fights would start. Someone would shout, they're beating up on our guys! The young lady would scream. Someone would jump forward. Someone would step in, try and separate them. Someone would charge up waving a stool. Someone would already be reaching for his knife.

Though real fights usually started without any reason. When the dance was in full swing, and everybody was well watered. And whoever was going to stay had stayed. Whoever still had the strength to sing was singing. And whoever had lost their singing voice was reeling about and yelling. The young ladies would be squeaking like mice in the corners, and everything would have gotten good and mixed up. Dresses and shirts, souls and bodies, sweat and blood, and the ceiling lamps were hidden in a dark mist. And there was nothing but noise and crush from wall to wall. And no one knew anyone anymore. People's feet would be making merry all on their own, the entire barn felt like an apple tree that someone was shaking with all their might. It was dusty as a dirt track in summer. Because by then every dance was a fast one. Obereks and polkas, polkas and obereks.

The musicians had had their supper, and the vodka was playing in their veins. They'd taken off their coats, they were playing in shirtsleeves. Some of them even unbuttoned their shirt down to their belly button, and loosened their belt, and took off their boots because they were pinching. And all for the music. Because it was only now the musicians' souls would come out. And man, would they play! They couldn't feel their lips or their hands, they'd play with their gut, like their fathers and their fathers' fathers before them. They played like they were about to die. Till lightning flashed, and armies marched to war. And a wedding party rode on drunken horses. And flails flailed in barns. And earth fell on a casket. And there wasn't any shame anymore in feeling up a young lady here and there, you could even put your hand on her backside. And reach under her blouse. And pull her legs to yours. And young ladies would find themselves between your knees of their own accord, like chickens coming home to roost. And they'd fly around the dance floor breathless. They'd forget their fathers, their mothers, their conscience. Even the Lord God's ten commandments. Because at those dances heaven and hell mixed together. Chest squeezed against chest, belly against belly. They'd giggle and faint their way into such a paradise, you could feel it flowing out of them even through their dresses. And the band would be filled with the devil, he'd have them waving their bows like scythes cutting off nobles' heads. He'd put a storm wind in the clarinet. He'd set the accordion spinning. And hurl rocks at the drums. And if on top of everything else it was a hot close night outside, there was nothing for it but to let some blood.

By that time it could be over anything at all. Someone would suddenly stagger as if the room had been tipped on its side. And right away there'd be screams and shouts, Jesus and Mary, Staś, Jaś, goddammit, the sons of bitches! Over here, boys! They're coming for us! And your legs weren't even done with the last dance. Your girl was stuck on you like bracket fungus on a birch tree. It was like you had to cut her off with a knife. She wouldn't let go of you and she'd be crying and begging you:

"Szymuś, let's go outside. Don't go over there! I'll do it with you. I want to. Do you hear, Szymuś? I want to. I do! For the love of Christ, they'll kill you! Szymek!"

But someone nearby is already whacking people on the head with a bench. A couple of swings of his bench and he goes down like his legs have been swept from under him. The crowd heads for the door or jumps out the windows. Someone hits a ceiling lamp with a bottle. And the band is playing louder than ever, it's not obereks and polkas anymore but a full-blown thunderstorm. They play loud, louder, as loud as they can, to drown out the shouts and squeals and the you sons of bitches.

Then someone tips the room the other way. And back again. You don't know whether you're standing up or lying down. The girls are grabbing you by the jacket and the shirttails and the arms and neck, pulling you by the elbow, whimpering, screeching, crying. But what do you care about girls now that the knives are out. Somewhere the emcees's roaring, stay in your pairs! One pair after another! Now form a circle! All the pairs dance! Then suddenly there's a groan, and all that's left of the emcee is his colored ribbon. Someone's trying to swing a chair. They spin it around once and twice and they're swallowed up by the crowd. Because chairs are no use when it's knives up against knives. Blood up against blood.

And the room is rolling down a big slope. There's clattering and wailing and curses. The sound of breaking glass. There's only one lamp left hanging from the ceiling. A second one is turned on somewhere. Probably over by the buffet. But someone quickly puts it out with another bottle. Glass flies everywhere. And the room goes back uphill through darkness and dust. All you can hear is panting. And the swish of knives like scythes at harvesttime. Then downhill again. All the way over to near the band. The musicians' arms are dropping off. Keep playing! Keep playing! Play a march now! The fiddler leads off on the march, when all of a sudden someone bumps into his side. There's blood on his white shirt. The fiddle comes flying down like it's dropping from heaven to earth. And the drum stops in midbang because someone else has taken a knife to it like it was an exposed belly. The accordion's been ripped open. And the clarinet is smashed over the clarinetist's head. The hell with the band! It all started because of them.

And there's no more band. There's not a single pane of glass left in the windows. The buffet's been turned upside down. The decorations hanging from the ceiling are all in tatters. Your jacket's in rags. There'd be times you could wring the blood out of your shirt – your own blood and other people's. Then after the whole thing was over you'd sing all the way home.

One night, after one of those dances some farmers took us back home in their wagons. We were drunk as lords. That time I spent three weeks or so hiding out in the loft over the cattle shed, because there'd been a dead body and the police were poking about the villages looking for the guilty party.

But you might as well go looking for the wind in the fields. When you're having fun like that there is no guilty and innocent. Everyone lashes out left, right, and center, you could stab someone to death and you wouldn't even know who. Or he'd get stabbed and he wouldn't know who'd done it. Only the Lord God alone could know who was guilty, not the police.

I had three cuts, one in my side and two on my back. I could only lie on my stomach. Mother made compresses with different herbs. But it wasn't healing up properly. The knife must have been rusty, because the wounds kept bleeding and bleeding, and mother was all teary:

"Szymuś, son. Think of your mother. One of these days they'll kill you. I couldn't take that."

"They're not going to kill me, mother. No way. Stop crying. I'm not that easy to kill. Look – I've got three holes in me, and did they kill me? You see yourself. And I'll get even with them. Even if they do kill me, better it be sooner than later. There's no point clinging to life, mother. Just living from one harvest to the next – what kind of life is that?"

As it happened the harvest was beginning, so at least those cuts got me out of mowing the rye and the barley. And more than half our land was barley and rye. On top of everything, that year there were rains, it rained and rained without stopping. Everything was flattened and mowing it was the hardest thing. One acre of flattened crop took as much work as three regular ones. You couldn't feel your arms afterwards, your back was agony, your head felt like it was made of stone, and your legs would barely carry you home. What were those three holes in me in comparison.

I often tried to convince father to buy a harvester, because I was sick to death of all that mowing. Was it some punishment from God that the harvest had to be taken in year after year? Couldn't it have grown some different way, so it didn't have to be mowed and tied up and transported, then after that threshed and winnowed and driven to the mill, and only then you could have bread? Bread could grow right from the start, you'd go out and collect the loaves straight from the field. They could even be small ones the size of heads of cabbage. Not tiny little seeds that you have to sweat over.

But father wouldn't agree. We can't afford it, and besides, the hay stays straight when you mow it, but harvesters mess it up so it isn't any good either for mending the thatch, or making chaff, or stuffing mattresses. And Antek and Stasiek there, they're growing up. They wouldn't have anything to do, they'd have to sit around idle if we had a harvester. And when the crop's been flattened by the rain, you need to mow it by hand anyway, a harvester's not up to the job.

I didn't get back on my feet till the wheat was ripe. But we only ever grew a half-acre or so of wheat. So as to have cake for Easter and Whitsun and Christmas, as a base for *żurek*, and from time to time, mostly on Sundays, for dumplings. As well, the crop hadn't succeeded that year. It had been overgrown a bit by thistle and gotten lodged by the rain. The police had given up on looking for the culprit. Searching at harvesttime wasn't the best idea anyway. The farmers were all carrying scythes and the blood was hot in everyone's veins. And whatever happened the dead man wouldn't be brought back to life. Besides, he'd been killed among his own people, it was none of the police's business.

I did a bit of mowing, but I started to feel dizzy and mother told me to go home. She even went after father, saying he should be ashamed of himself, sending me out to work like I was his stepson or some foundling instead of his own son. The poor thing ended up in tears. Because father had been trying to get me out to work since the third day. He came up to the loft where I was hiding while I recovered.

"Are you not getting up? We need to make a start on the rye tomorrow. The spikes are beginning to ripen. You're not hurt that bad. Looks like flesh wounds. If you could use a knife you can use a scythe. You're going to come to no good. You'll end up in jail. We never had a bad seed yet in the family, but it looks like we're going to now. Grandfather Łukasz killed a man, but that was for the sake of justice. And he ran away to America. You, where are you going to run to? Stach Owsianek only has one leg, the other one's made of wood, and he mows like no one's business. Or Mielczarek, his body's twisted like a tree root, but when he picks up that scythe you'd never know he was deformed. He stands there straight as a fence post and the crop lies itself down in front of him. See, when you're mowing rye you forget whatever's wrong with you, whatever hurts. I mean, it's not like they killed you to death. And if something hurts, it's best to walk it off. You got cut in the side and the back, but your arms are fine. Your legs are fine. And for mowing all you need is your arms and your legs. If someone's a good mower they don't even need to twist. They walk forward like they were going down the road, and their arms swing to and fro in front of them all on their own. The man and his arms are separate. And it's just legs and arms. You ever see the priest walking along saying his prayers? It's exactly like that – step by step, slow as can be. Sure, it hurts. But once you've mowed a swath it'll pass. After the second swath you'll forget you're injured. The Lord Jesus was stabbed just the same as you, and he's been hanging on the cross all these thousands of years. His wound isn't healing. And he has to keep looking at all the badness. Don't you think he'd rather be mowing than hanging there on the cross? But how can he come down if that's his lot? The worst part is getting started. Even if you've not been stabbed, after the first day it feels like you have. In your arms, your legs, your sides, your back, everywhere. But once you get going your scythe won't let you rest. Only enough to sharpen it up. Or cross yourself when they ring the Angelus bell. After that it'll pull you back to work, and on, and on. Till the very end. That's how it is with a scythe. Wounds'll often heal quicker when you're mowing than if you'd gone to church. Wounds of the body, wounds of the soul, wounds in the family, in the village, out in the world. It was thanks to the peasants mowing all those hundreds of years that they could stand having masters. Once you've done some mowing, you can put up with all sorts of things, and forgive even more. And how someone mows will tell you whether they're good or bad, mean, or false. And even when death comes, it's like he just took the scythe from your hand at harvesttime when you were getting tired, and he took your place and finished what was left of the rye and the wheat and barley. Depending on what you were mowing. When you mow in wartime, it stops death being so terrible. And you, you didn't get stabbed in wartime, it happened at a dance. You and your pals were having a party, not crying. Holding young girls, not the dead. Drinking vodka, not bitterness."

And though I'd been a fool to let myself get stuck that time, the harvest came and went and my wounds healed and it was off to the dances again. And boy, did I like to have fun! I didn't think the world was all that well set up, but if you got even a little bit scratched up in a fight, after the dance you somehow took a kinder view of things, you were more in the mood to work. One time I got a job for the railways building an embankment they were going to lay the track on, and with the money I earned I bought a brown suit with white stripes. Another time they were digging a pond at the manor and paying half a zloty per cubic yard. I bought a gabardine coat, a shirt, necktie, socks. I even thought about getting a watch and a cigarette case, I probably would have if the war hadn't broken out. But even without the watch and cigarette case I was better dressed than many a rich man. I had a handkerchief that some people, they didn't even know what it was for. You'd have had to look far and wide for another young buck like me. And so there wasn't a single girl at the dance that didn't want to dance with me. I could take my pick. Sometimes it happened that I wouldn't come home from a party till the evening of the next day. Father would treat me like I'd just gotten back from hell. Have all the fun you like, damn you. You'll see, before you know it you'll have wasted all your life on fun. Then what'll you say to God when your time comes – that you were busy having fun?

But what did I care about father. All he ever talked about was work and

God. He never gave me any money for my ticket. So I'd sneak a quarter-bushel of rye from the attic and sell it to the Jew at half price. Or take a few eggs and then tell mother afterwards the hens didn't seem to be laying properly. One time I shook almost every last pear out of the pear tree and took them to the railway workers for two groszes apiece. Another time a dogcatcher came through the village buying dogs. I untied our Reks and quietly, round the back of the barn so no one would see, I led him all the way to the end of the village, and I sold him to the catcher as he was already heading out. He was a fine dog, but there was a dance over in Boleszyce that Sunday. It would have been a pity not to go, though it was a pity about the dog as well. He kept rubbing against my leg and whimpering, like he knew what was going on. I started talking to him to make him feel better. This isn't much of a life for you, Reks. From now on no one's gonna make you watch out for housebreakers. You'll be working in a better world. Dogs go to heaven too. Afterwards father went about in a daze, asking everyone in the village if they hadn't seen our Reks. Because he liked him like no other dog before him, and Reks was fonder of him than of anyone else.

One time there happened to be no dance. So a bunch of us guys were standing around outside the pub on a Sunday afternoon. The young ladies were still all at home for some reason. They had to wash the dishes and clear up. The old women were on their way to late afternoon mass. We would have gotten something to drink, but none of us had two pennies to rub together. The Jew wouldn't give credit, because each of us already had a tab with him. The sun was all hazy, like it was going to rain. And it was still a long ways till evening. If someone would at least have shown up and bought us a beer. Or gotten into a fight, except there wasn't even any ragging going on, the boys were all kind of sleepy.

All of a sudden, far away down the road there's a cloud of dust and three horses, and on the horses three riders. Who the heck could be riding to the village on a Sunday? They looked like they were in military uniform. They ride up to the inn, rein in their horses, and we see it's a captain, a lieutenant, and a young lady. The captain just looks like a captain, the lieutenant the same, but the young lady takes my breath away. She's wearing riding breeches and tall boots and spurs, a kind of black skull cap with a peak, she's got a riding crop in her hand. She looks like an angel in riding clothes. The captain speaks up from the saddle:

"So then, boys! I see there'll be no shortage of fellows ready to fight for their country if need be! Is there anything to drink in this inn of yours?"

"Sure there is!" The guys livened up, they were talking over each other. "Beer! Kvass! Lemonade!"

I had my eyes glued on the angel, I was staring at her like she was a picture. You'd meet good-looking girls in the village too from time to time, but I'd never seen a beauty like her ever before. Or was it just because of what she was wearing and the fact she was on horseback? In any case I must have been looking real hard, because the angel looked back at me and smiled. Then she slipped down off her horse light as can be, like a cat jumping down from the stove corner. The captain and the lieutenant dismounted as well.

"Mind our horses then, boys, while we go get a drink."

The guys all rushed forward to hold the horses. Holding horses like those ones meant something. But wait up! I pushed them all aside. They gave them to me to hold.

"Out of my way, all of you, or you'll be seeing stars!"

I gathered all three sets of reins together and wrapped them around my hand. The three riders went into the inn. After a short while they came out again. The captain mounted up first.

"Thank you, young man!"

The lieutenant followed. Then the angel put her foot in the stirrup. Whether she wasn't lifting her other leg strongly enough or what, she tried once and twice, but it seemed the saddle was too high for her. And she looks at me. So I grab her under the backside with my right hand, my left still holding the reins, and I hoist her up into the saddle. And then, as if of its own accord my hand ran down her thigh and her boot to the spur, and at the spur I squeezed her foot. She closed her eyes for a second, then she smiled, though kind of sadly. At that moment someone lashed me on the head with a riding crop. The angel exclaimed:

"Oh!"

I turned around. It was the lieutenant.

"Save your hands for your pitchfork, you peasant!" he hissed furiously. "Here, so you don't feel wronged." He threw a coin down at my feet. I gave his horse a mighty whack on the rump that made him jump in the saddle. Then they rode away.

The guys ran forward to pick up the coin. I was going to head home – I couldn't drink with that kind of money. It would have been like selling your soul to the devil. But they grabbed me and forced me into the pub. And before I knew it there was a glass in front of me and it was, down the hatch, because it's thanks to you. Pity he didn't hit you twice and give us more. Then, when we'd had a few drinks we started a fight and smashed the place up. Benches, tables, beer mugs, glasses, whatever came to hand got used. One of them picked up a barrel of beer, and when he slammed it down on the floor we all got covered in foam. The Jew hid under the bar shouting:

"Police! Police!"

Every window in there got shattered. The door came off its hinges. And I broke a bottle over my best friend Ignaś Magdziarz's head so hard he fell to his knees and wept:

"Why, Szymuś? Why?"

I didn't know why either, and I wept with him, because he looked like someone had dipped his head in a bucket of pig's blood.

"I don't know, Ignaś. I don't know. Maybe if you'd gone for me I wouldn't have gone for you. Someone had to go for someone. Don't cry. Next time we go to a dance you can smash me over the head with a bottle. I won't say a word. I'll even buy you a drink afterwards."

But we were young. When we were enjoying ourselves we did it with all our might, with all our soul, as if we were going to be gone from the world the next day. And I had youth enough for two inside, it was bubbling out of me. There was no right or wrong moment, if there was a chance to have fun you did. There were times when inside you didn't feel like doing anything at all, but outside you were having a ball, drinking and dancing like nobody's business. Inside you'd be sad, but you could cheer up the saddest person. And the young ladies thought I was the best fun of all the guys in the village.

"I'm telling you, Szymek, you know how to make people laugh. Even more than Błażej or Łukasz. It's like you had the devil in you. Hee, hee, hee!"

Because girls like it when you make them laugh to begin with. Making someone laugh is like forgiving their sins. Then it's easier to persuade them to do the rest. You'd meet one or another of them as she was taking dinner to her folks in the fields, you'd keep her company a ways, joke a bit, put your arm around her, and by evening you'd be lying next to her by the river or in the orchard. And she wouldn't be afraid it was a sin, because when young people sin it's honest sinning. If you wanted a peek at this or that she'd show you, even let you hold it in your hand like a dove. Or in church at high mass, you'd sidle up to a girl and whisper in her ear:

"Sleep in the barn tonight, Wikcia."

And no dog would bark at you, the barn door wouldn't creak, and the ladder to the hayloft would already be in place. And the hay had just been brought from the fields, so it was like the girl had made you a bed in the meadow, and she was bursting with sunlight like a meadow warmed in the sun. And her blood was buzzing inside her so loud it was like you could hear grasshoppers when you laid your head on that meadow.

Or you only had to go down to the river at noon when the girls were taking their bath. They mostly went in naked, only the odd few would keep their blouses on. The river water was so clean it sweetened their bodies, so what did they have to be embarrassed about. The horses were always watered down there and they never once got the mange. The geese and ducks would go down to the water all on their own, they didn't need to be driven. Fish swam about almost on the surface. And the bottom glistened from all the different pebbles. You could sit on the bank and gaze at the river to your heart's content, think about how it flowed just like your own life. It was clean as clean can be.

And all the screaming and squealing! You could hear from way off where the girls were bathing. The river only came up to their belly buttons. Not many of them could swim. So they were more splashing about than bathing. They'd splash and stumble and push each other over, and run upstream and downstream, taking the river in their arms, or lie on their backs and daydream and let it carry them. They wouldn't even notice me standing on the bank, behind a willow tree or a bush, staring at their breasts and bellies and thighs and backsides swirling around in the water. Till one of them would snap out of it and shout:

"Hide, girls! Szymek's behind that tree!"

"The dirty so-and-so! Has he no shame!"

"The priest'll never forgive you for this!"

"Like he doesn't know what girls look like! They look like this – stare all you want!"

"Come on, Szymek, get lost now."

"Sure, I can go away, but I'm taking Zosia's things. Come behind the bush, Zosia, I'll let you have them."

"Give them back, Szymek! If I tell my mother she'll have your guts for garters! I'll never look at you again. And for sure I'll never dance with you again! Come on, Szymuś, give them back. At least give me my skirt, or I'll cry."

"Go to him, Zośka, if he only sees one of us it won't be such a big sin."

And Zosia pouts and fumes, but she comes to me. And once she comes behind the bush she'll go farther.

"Come over here, Zosia, under this alder, and I'll give you back your clothes. A little bit farther and I'll give them back to you. Almost there. I'll give you them over there. In that patch of sunlight. In that shade. Don't be embarrassed, there's no need to feel embarrassed in front of me, and the girls are out of sight. You can hear them in the river."

And Zosia would come closer and closer.

In the winter I'd go where they were plucking feathers and husking beans. They'd all gather, the girls and young men and old folks. The evenings were long, there was nothing else to do, and you could at least hear your fill of ghosts and devils and witches, because back in the day there were all kinds of them in the village, they lived alongside the people and the livestock. Then when it got dark it'd be time to head off back home. And it was common knowledge ghosts and devils and witches only ever went around at night, and that their favorite thing was to go after young women. The ones that lived close by, it wasn't such a problem for them. The farmer or his wife would come out in front of the house with a lantern and wait till they heard their neighbor's door creak. But the girls who lived farther off needed to be walked home. And I'd usually choose the one that was most afraid or lived the farthest away. Actually I never had to choose. They knew me, that I'd walk to the ends of the earth in the darkest night, because I didn't believe in any ghosts or devils or witches, though I liked hearing about how other people had seen them. So either the girl would come up to me herself:

"Say, Szymek, will you walk me back? I won't be scared if you're with me."

Or the farmer's wife would say:

"Szymek, take Magda back, she lives way over near the woods and she's frightened to go on her own."

And since nothing brings people closer together than fear or a long journey, it often happened that the girl would cling to me the moment we set off, squeezing against me, leaning her head on my shoulder, and me with my arm around her. The snow would be creaking underfoot. The road was quiet and deserted, not a living soul to be seen, and after a few steps she'd let herself be kissed. Also, there were more stars in the sky than pears on a pear tree, so we'd stop and look up at the stars. Which one is yours? Because that one there is mine. How do you like that, they're right next to each other. Then we'd kiss again, like the two stars. And we'd follow the stars all the way to her house. And if her old folks were sound asleep, we'd end up under her quilt.

Though I preferred summer to winter. In the summertime the world is wide open, orchards, meadows, fields, woods, haystacks, sheaves, bushes. You didn't have to have a house, all you needed was the sky over your head. In the summer the girls' blood was hotter from being warmed up out in the fields. In the summer you didn't need to chase around after them, they fell into your arms by themselves. There'd be times you were mowing barley in your own field, and she'd be cutting wheat with a sickle in the next field, and all you had to do was cross from your barley to her wheat.

"Let me give you a hand, Hania."

Or she'd start it herself:

"Could you help me out, Szymuś? I've still got so much to do."

And in a wheat field you don't have to worry about talking her into anything. Wheat is like a turned-down bed. The wheat's hot, the sun's shining above it. The girl would lie down and you'd take hold of her among the spikes and seeds like you were taking bread from an oven with your bare hands.

It must've been the devil tempted me to sow wheat on the other side of the road. I was going to plant potatoes, but Antek Kwiecień came to lend me a spade and we got to talking, what are you sowing, what are you planting, and how it was a waste of that land across the road to plant potatoes. Potatoes you can plant any old where. Over there, that's the perfect place for wheat. It's flat as can be, it'll be no work at all, and this is going to be a good year for wheat. You can tell, the storks aren't even thinking about flying away yet. Sow wheat. If it grows well you'd have to plant twice as many potatoes to equal it. And I won't deny it, it did grow well. The stalks were as tall as me, every spike as thick as my finger, and the grains were fat and oily. Everyone that came past would say, that's some fine wheat you got there, you'll have grain like gold from that. It was a pleasure to mow. Even the weather helped out, like it was trying to live up to the wheat. It only rained once, and even that was nothing to speak of. I'd already started figuring out how many sacks I'd need once I threshed it, how much I'd leave for myself and how much I'd sell. Antek Kwiecień deserved a drink. I just had to finish bringing it in.

I spent all Saturday bringing in the sheaves, till late at night, and I counted on finishing Monday. The horse could rest up on Sunday, eat its fill of oats, then on Monday he'd work like a machine. And I'd be fresher after Sunday as well.

On Sunday there happened to be a church fair because it was the Feast of the Assumption. I've always liked fairs ever since I was a kid, so I went. But fairs aren't what they used to be. Two or three wagons, other than that it was all cars and motorcycles. More outsiders than locals. There was no knowing where they'd all come from or why. Pretzels with no taste, nothing but water and baking powder and flour; back then you could have any kind you wanted. And there wasn't half the stuff for sale there used to be. Back then there'd be two or three rows of stalls around the church wall, and every one loaded with things, especially all kinds of candies. Even the grown-ups would be watering at the mouth. And you could buy whatever your heart desired. Every animal that ever lived under the sun. Every saint there ever was. Our Ladies, big ones, small ones, with veils or wreaths on their head, crowned, with an Infant Jesus and without. Lord Jesuses on the cross and fallen under the cross, on Golgotha, with the lamb, risen from the dead. Armfuls of rosaries, beads, all sorts of trinkets. And on every stall, piles of mouth organs, swords, trumpets, pipes, whistles, everything a child could wish for. There was bunion cream, shoe polish, whetstones. You could listen to adventures from wartime, from plagues, from the wide world. People played and sang songs about bandits and rebels and bad children who threw their parents out of the house, and about evil stepmothers. There were people prophesying what would happen in a year's time, in ten years and a hundred, and a good few things even came true. You could play black-and-white, hoops, dice, fishing, or try the shooting gallery. You could have a tooth pulled on the spot if you had the toothache. Or get your boots patched. Or have your picture taken in an airplane, on a camel, in a general's uniform, or with your girl in a cutout heart.

But today? Today it's all about conning people out of their money. And people are daft as monkeys, they'll let themselves get taken in by any old thing. They buy and buy, whatever's put in front of them, you can barely push through to see what's at the stalls. Though even if I wanted to buy something, who would I buy it for?

The only thing I bought was an Our Lady in a blue dress. Years ago I'd broken one like that of mother's. She'd gotten it on a pilgrimage way back when she was still single. I'd been swatting flies, the house was so full of them they wouldn't let you sit in peace, and they were biting especially badly, the way they do before a storm. Mother was getting dinner ready and the Our Lady was up on this little shelf. One of the flies landed on it, and I swatted at it, but I missed the fly and the Our Lady came crashing down onto the floor. I froze, and mother burst out:

"Oh my Lord, he's broken it!" And she looked at me as if I'd done the worst thing in the world. Then she took a clean white cloth from the chest and gathered all the broken pieces in it. She might even have been crying, though I couldn't see because she was bent over.

"I'll buy you another one," I said after a bit.

"You won't buy one like this," she answered sadly. "I always prayed to her about you. She knew everything."

Afterwards I looked around at different fairs, but I never did find one just like it. Then the war came. After the war I went less and less to the fairs. And the fairs seemed more and more timid somehow, it was hard enough to get an Our Lady at all, let alone one like the broken one. But even after mother died I carried on looking, because the thing kept gnawing at me.

Then I went to the shooting gallery to see if I still had a good eye. Ever since I was a boy I used to like to go shooting at the fair. Turned out I hadn't lost it. The first five shots were spot on, then the second five too. I almost didn't even have to take aim, just bang bang bang, and hand over the flowers, because you shot at tissue-paper flowers, or rather, at the string they hung by. There was a target as well, that had a black ring like a saucer in the middle, but any idiot could hit that and you didn't get a prize. But with the flowers, every one you shot down was yours. All the people gathered around the gallery, kids, young men, girls, adults – they were all gobstruck. And the shooting gallery guy tried to take the gun away from me.

"Come on there, mister, let the young folks try their luck."

But just out of spite I bought five more shots. Again every one was a hit. I gave the flowers to Irka Kwiatkowska, because of all the young girls in the village I thought she was the prettiest.

"Here, Irka, take this. That young fellow of yours isn't going to hit anything for you. That's young men these days for you." Irka jumped up and down she was so pleased, and she gave me a kiss on the cheek, because her and that Zbyszek of hers had been watching me shoot.

Toward the end I bought two strings of pretzels, because that afternoon I was supposed to go watch television at Stach Sobieraj's, and his Darek called me uncle and whenever I'd go there he'd always badger me to tell about the resistance, even if it was the same stories over and over. Sometimes I'd say to him:

"Darek, I really don't remember any more."

"Then tell what you remember."

Or:

"I already told you that story."

"Then tell it again." And he'd sit there openmouthed. It was mostly whether I'd killed anyone, and what that was like. So I had to at least take him some pretzels.

For lunch I made cabbage soup and served it with bacon. It was good. We had two helpings each, the soup in a bowl and the bacon and bread on a plate. I could tell Michał liked it too.

"You like it?" I asked him. As usual, he didn't answer. I washed the dishes. Saw to the animals. Then I started to get ready for the television.

But I go outside and I see the farmers are starting to drive out to the fields. There's Stach Partyka, Barański, Socha. More and more of them.

"What are you doing standing there?" says Heniek Maszczyk. "Put your work clothes on and get out into the fields. Can't you see, there are storm clouds coming, it's gonna rain. We can at least get a wagonload or two in."

I look at the sky and I think, what's he talking about, rain? The sun's bright as anything, sky's blue as a cornflower. There's a little dark spot over in the west, but that can mean good weather. Or it'll pass us by.

"What do you mean, rain," I say. "Look at the sky."

"Never mind the sky, they said on the radio. Gee up!" And off he went.

I stood there and thought, it'd be a pity if the crop got rained on. The wheat had come up like never before. And here you couldn't tell if it'd just be a few drops or whether the rain would set in. If it did set in it could rain and rain. And I'd be standing there staring at the sky, looking out the window, and worrying about not having brought the wheat in. For a moment I'd think it was brightening up a bit over there. But then Maszczyk's rooster would crow and that would mean the rain would keep up. When the chickens ruffled their feathers you could tell the rain wouldn't stop. And if the cat stayed over in the stove corner, it would all go to hell in a handcart. And my wheat would get so wet it'd make your heart ache.

On top of everything else, recently I'd had a dream about mother. She was kneading dough to make bread, but she had this kneading-trough that was half the size of the entire room, so there was no space for anyone and we were all standing around the walls. Mother was half the age she was when she died. She was in her nightshirt, barefoot, she was so hot the sweat was pouring off her, and she knelt at that trough and kept pushing her hands up to the elbows in the dough. But for some reason the dough wouldn't knead properly. She kneaded and kneaded, but the water and the flour were still separate.

"Maybe we should all knead together?" I said. "Then it would go quicker."

"But it's my punishment," said mother.

Then father spoke:

"That's how it is in the next world. Whatever you did down here, you do there as well. I have to go water the horse." And he went out. Someone was standing by the window with his back to the room, and everyone thought it was Michał, though no one could see his face. We couldn't tell if he was old or young. He was wearing a brand-new suit and patent leather shoes, and a ratty old hat father used to put on when he was threshing so the chaff wouldn't get in his hair. And it was only the hat that made it look like Michał. But no one had the courage to ask, is that you, Michał? And he didn't seem to know either that he was with us, he just kept staring out the window. Then finally mother spoke again:

"Take the hat off, son. Don't hurt your mother's heart. See, the bread's baking."

Then Antek said in a soft voice:

"Ask him if he likes biscuit, mother. Do you, Michał?" All of a sudden a baby wailed in its cradle. Where had the cradle come from? There hadn't been any cradle in the room. Mother stood from the kneading-trough and took the baby out of the cradle, and it was like it was Michał when he was tiny, though the figure by the window was still standing there and if it had been Michał he might have turned his head at his own crying. You know your own crying even from long, long ago.

"Oh, the poor little thing's peed itself," said mother, and she took a firm breast like a young girl's from her blouse and put it in the baby's mouth.

Right then father came back in and said:

"So, it's Christmas Eve. We'll need to bring the bread down from the attic. You go get it, Szymek."

I harnessed the horse and it was, gee up!

With the first wagonload I didn't even wait that long to get out onto the road from the field. One car came by, a second, a third, then again one, two, three, then there was a longer gap with the next cars quite a ways away. I flicked the whip and we made it up onto the blacktop. True, they honked like mad dogs because I'd gotten in their way, but you can kiss my ass, use your damn brakes, the road is for horses and wagons just the same.

Things didn't go so well with the second load. The afternoon was getting on, there were more and more cars and the gaps between them were shorter and shorter, and here I had a wagon loaded up with sheaves. With just the one horse it was no easy matter getting out quickly from the field onto the road. The road is higher than the field, and you have to make a sharp left turn. I got down off the wagon, took the horse by the bridle and moved him forward. It was like walking in some deep place. I'd take one step, then it would be, whoa! And the cars would be zooming past, honking their horns and flashing their lights. The horse strained, he was trying to move forward but the wagon pulled him back because the rear wheels were still down in the field. I was holding him back then pulling him forward, I was bathed in sweat. The horse was foaming at the mouth. But in the end we made it across. Though if the road had been clear, in the time I waited I'd have been able to take a whole other load.

So I come up with my third load, and here old Kuś is parked by the road, loaded up with sheaves and waiting. And the cars are speeding by one after another after another, both ways, there's not a single gap between them. It was like a cloud had opened up and it was raining cars, and there they were pouring down the road.

"What, are they not letting us across?" I asked the old man.

"Sure aren't."

"You been waiting here long?"

"Sure have."

"Did you try to drive out?"

"Sure did."

"And?"

"Sure didn't work. I'm still here."

"You could wait here till you goddam drop dead!"

"Sure could. What can you do?"

"Drive out!"

"Sure, then go."

"Goddammit! We should just take the shaft out and give them hell!"

"If waiting doesn't work, you won't do any good with a shaft either. You've got a rosary there, pray awhile and you'll stop being angry. Always works for me. Whenever I need to get anything done, at the district administration or the co-op, I take my rosary along and say it one bead after another, and however long I have to wait, it's like I didn't have to wait at all. How about it?"

"You know where you can put your rosary!"

"Don't blaspheme or you'll turn God against us as well. And he's all we have left."

I was madder at old Kuś than at the cars. For getting to the road before me. He was sitting there now without a care in the world, up on his sheaves, his whip between his legs, saying his rosary with his hands, and he probably felt like he was sitting on the bench outside his house. And when you're on your bench outside your house, time lies like a dog at your feet, warming itself in the sun or thinking about the next world. Besides, he was over eighty, his woman had long since died and his sons had gone off to the town, where did he have to hurry back to. Me, on the other hand, I was planning to make another trip after this one, even two more if I managed. Since I'd already given up my Sunday, let there be a good few loads to show for it. And the sky looked more and more like rain. There were twice as many dark clouds over to the west.

After a bit Wicek Marzec came along, his wagon was full also.

"You're waiting?"

"Yep."

"Whoa!" He pulled his horse up, the shaft almost poked into my sheaves. "Looks like we'll be here awhile. Where are all those damn cars going? People don't even know how to sit on their asses these days. Sunday's no good for a day of rest anymore, evidently – they'll have to pick another day."

"Then there'd have to be another God," said Kuś, bristling.

"Let there be, if that's how it has to happen!"

Then Heniek Maszczyk drove up with his Terenia. And he says the same thing:

"You're waiting?"

"Yep."

I liked that Terenia. Couldn't I have been born twenty years later? I felt sorry for her that all that beauty was going to waste in the harvest. When she saw us all waiting there she slipped down off the sheaves.

"Heniek, I'm gonna walk back, the kid needs feeding. There's no telling how long you'll be here." She set off on foot across the fields.

There was no break in the cars. It was one long string of them. Syta and Barański and Franek Jędrys came along and each of them repeated:

"You're waiting?"

"Yep." It was like they were saying a greeting, "God bring you fortune," and we were answering, "God give you thanks."

In the end there was a line of maybe ten wagons, with Kuś at the front like a lookout.

"Bartłomiej, keep your eyes peeled! The moment you can, whack your horse on the backside and get out there!"

"I am keeping my eyes peeled," he said, annoyed. "Can't you see the cars keep coming and coming? Is it my fault they've had enough of staying home?" Then a moment later he says in a good-natured way: "Hey there, Szymek! Any idea why those cars are all painted? Green and red and heaven knows what all else? I mean, horses are different colors as well. But horses are born that way. Though one time, you know, thieves stole four horses from the manor and they colored two of them black and two of them chestnut. They went to market and they might even have sold them, they already had buyers. But it began to drizzle. People saw a miracle, a horse changing color. The black ones become duns, the chestnuts turned into grays. On a fair day like today they surely would have sold them. But tomorrow, who knows. Looks like rain. Though in one of them cars it makes no difference whether it's raining or not, they're all nice and cozy in there. They're just riding along seeing the world. Not like when all you've seen of the world is when you were in the wars. Or when you went to market. But back then you'd have to wait till your cucumbers grew. You'd pick a whole lot and your woman'd put on her fancy clothes, and you'd be off to Karasin, cause the money was better there. And if you sold what you had you could go to the pub. That Waleria of mine was quite the lady. You'd never catch her drinking plain old vodka. It was always only rum. The Jew knew her, he didn't even have to ask. Then when she'd had a bit to drink she'd start singing. She had a lovely voice. There were times everything we made on the cucumbers would go. And you know, she could cook cabbage like nobody else. She'd chop up black turnip and garlic and onion, sprinkle on some caraway, then she'd chuck in some lard or bacon fat. Then once it was cooked on the stove, in the wintertime she'd put it out in the frost for the whole night.

Next day she'd light the stove and put it in the oven. We'd be eating it the whole week. When she died she said to me, all your clothes are washed and ironed, Bartuś. I even whitewashed the inside walls for you. I was going to cook you up some cabbage as well, but God didn't let me. You'll have to do it yourself."

"Don't talk so much, Bartłomiej. Watch the road," I said, but in a way that wouldn't make him take offense.

He stopped talking and kind of hunched over, and from behind you couldn't tell if he was watching the cars closely, or he was praying.

"Hey, Bartłomiej! Are you asleep?"

"Why would I be sleeping," he said angrily, turning toward me. "You think I've never done guard duty? Let me tell you, I was a soldier long before you were even a twinkle in your mother's eye."

But a moment later he pointed to the road with his whip and shouted almost pleased:

"Szymek, look how that green one's chasing the red one. And the red one won't let him past. He's a feisty little devil, even if he's small."

All of a sudden Franek Jędrys called from behind:

"Hey, you there up front! Watch out! There's a gap after the red one! The second he passes, Kuś needs to get out there. And you after him, Szymek!"

You could already see the first bigger gap from around the bend. Behind a black car the next one was only just entering the curve, and the black one was almost on a level with us. I tightened the reins on the horse and lifted my whip, all ready to flick it and shout, gee up! and follow right behind Kuś. I called to the old man:

"Look out, Bartłomiej! Come on, now! Off you go! Gee up!"

But instead of tugging at the reins right away he had to sit himself up straight, switch the reins from his left hand to his right, and he didn't even give a decent tug, he just twitched them like he was setting off from home, and at first his mare didn't even know what he wanted. It was only when he said, "Gee up!" But even the gee up was like when you start plowing. So there was only time for the horse to strain forward a bit, the wagon jerked and he had to stop because it was too late. The car from the other side of the gap was almost there, and behind it there was a snake of cars so long you couldn't see the end of it.

"Goddammit!" I said, furious at Kuś, especially because I'd moved off quicker than him and my shaft got stuck in his load and twisted my horse's neck. "The hell you were in the army! You wouldn't have survived a day in the war at that speed! You'd have been pushing up the daisies long ago! Why you had to be at the goddam front of the line instead of the back I don't know. All you needed was to get your horse's front legs on the blacktop and you'd be on your way! You should've used the whip, not the reins! Give her a good lash instead of being gentle on her!" I was so furious I yanked my horse back as hard as I could, and the trace almost ripped the creature's head off. I used the whip on both sides, it's not easy backing up with a loaded wagon.

"Fucking hell!"

"Shit!"

"He had to go and straighten himself up!"

"He forgot to cross himself as well!"

"You get a guy like that up there and all he'll do is wait! You can't go around him, you can't go over him!"

"He ought to be saying his goodbyes to the world, not bringing in the crops!"

"Or haul his sons' asses back from the town and let them do the job!"

"He's got one foot in the grave and he can't leave the earth alone! You'll have enough of it when you're six feet under!"

"He should give his land to the government, let it be!"

"The countryside's supposed to be moving forward, but how can it with old farts like him standing in the way!"

Curses and insults stormed down on Kuś's head. All he did was hunch up, his head tucked in, and wait till it all passed. Or maybe somewhere there in his lap he was saying his rosary, like he was waiting his turn at the district administration or the co-op. In the end I felt sorry for him. I'd stopped being angry, because what was the point of being angry at the wrong person, and I called out to him:

"Hey, Bartłomiej! Maybe you could take my wagon and I'll drive yours?"

I had no idea he'd be so upset.

"Why should I take your wagon? What's wrong with mine? I've been a farmer longer than you have. I've got more acres than you. No one plows or sows for me, and no one else needs to drive my wagon for me either. Eighty-two years it's been, that's long enough to know how to farm."

At that, one of the other men shouted:

"Eighty-two years and he's still clinging to life, goddammit!"

Someone cracked his whip and it made all the horses twitch. Kuś turned around oh so slowly to the other wagons, gave us this strange look, and said:

"It's not my life I'm worried about, it's the horse's."

Everyone suddenly felt foolish. No one said another word one way or the other. Someone tugged quietly at the reins, whoa! but not because his horse was uneasy, the reins were maybe just stinging his hands. No one even reached into his pocket to have a smoke. And that's always the best remedy when you can't think of anything to say or you've got a bad conscience. But Kuś seemed to be kind of overcome by bitterness, maybe not at the other farmers but just in general:

"She's eighteen years old, you know, and it's good she can still pull. Because that's like a dog being ten, or a person, however old they're meant to get. Only ravens live longer. But you won't find any ravens these days! It's all crows and rooks, though people call them all ravens. You know, she already almost died on me one time. I was plowing the potato field and she started playing up, so I give her a flick with the tip of the whip and I shout, gee up! All of a sudden, you know, she goes down on her knees, then she falls on her side. I run up, I think, maybe she's got a touch of the colic. I grabbed her by the bridle and pulled, get up now. I think, I'll try with the whip. I gave her a good crack, but you know, I look and I see it's death, not colic. She turned her head but she couldn't get back up. What could I do? Tell me what to do, Lord, my mare's dying. But not a peep from up there. All you can hear is crows and rooks cawing away. So I squatted down, I took her head on my lap, I held it and I said to her, get up, are you going to leave me with the potato field half done? We can die together. You know it won't be long. Get up. We've worked so long together, why should we die separately? We'll plow this field next year again, maybe the year after as well, and that'll be that. Or maybe God'll only let us finish this field, nothing more. Get up. And she did."

He sighed and coughed so hard he had to hit himself in the chest with his fist because something got stuck, then he coughed it up and spat it out and he turned back around to the wagons and carried on:

"One time, you know, my grandfather Mikołaj told me how long ago God was handing out riches. He called all the people that lived on earth because he wanted to give things out fairly. But first there came the princes and judges and merchants and other rich folk. They arrived in all different kinds of carriages. And, they were racing each other, the drivers were lashing the horses so hard their whips snapped. And the peasants, like you'd expect, even if some of them had a horse they didn't want to tire it out if they didn't need to, so they came on foot. And even though it was God they were visiting, it was still a ways. So when they got there God had already given everything away to those other folks. God was really upset that there were still some other people, because the rich men had told him that was everyone. Also, he could see the peasants were dressed in rags. They had shoes made of linden bark, and coarse shirts with rope belts. They didn't even have caps to take off when they came into God's presence. And so God was even more troubled.

"'What have I got for you, my little golden people?' he says. 'I've given everything away. All I have left is the crown of thorns on my head and this cloak you see me in. I'm as poor as you are.'

"He sat there, he rested his chin on his hand, lowered his head, and thought and thought. The peasants reckoned nothing would come of it and one of them says:

"'All right, we'll be on our way, God.'

"But God says:

"'Just a moment. I'll give you a little of my patience. If you take it, you'll be able to put up with anything. Because people are going to have more need for patience than for riches.'"

Kuś fell to thinking and stared at the passing cars. All of us on our wagons followed suit and stared at the cars like he was. And maybe they were even a bit less mad at them. All of a sudden Kuś pointed at the road with his whip and shouted:

"Hey, two hundred!"

"What about two hundred?"

"That's how many have driven past."

"What are you counting them for? It's a waste of time. They're not worth it."

"Well, when there's nothing else a fellow can do, he can at least count. My old father, God rest his soul, he'd always tell me, count, son, keep counting, you never know when it'll come in handy. One time, you know, in the summertime we were lying under this apple tree in the orchard of a Sunday. I was already grown up. Father wasn't saying anything and I wasn't saying anything either. Father let his hat slip down over his forehead, I thought he was asleep. So I closed my eyes a moment too. Then all at once he says:

"'Three thousand five hundred and eighty-three.'

"'What do you mean, three thousand five hundred and eighty-three, dad?' I ask, I thought he was dreaming.

"'That's how many apples there are on the tree.'

"'How do you know?'

"'I counted them. I always count things when something's bothering me. You should too. Start with raspberries. There aren't that many raspberries on a bush, so it won't be too hard. After that, try counting the sloes on a sloe tree. Then break open a poppy head and count the seeds. Go up on a hill and count the fields and meadows and field boundaries. Count whatever you see in front of you, pigeons, clouds, people at funerals, posts in a fence, rocks in the river. Just never be idle. And if one time you can count all the stars in the night sky, then you'll be able to say you have patience and you can overcome anything. I never was able to, but you should try. Maybe you'll manage it.'"

"Hey there, Bartłomiej!" someone called from one of the wagons down the line. "I think there's a gap, get going now!"

But there wasn't any gap to be seen. The cars were closer and closer together. They were starting not to have enough space, they were honking at each other and flashing their lights and braking.

"The bastards won't even let you take home a wagonload of sheaves!" said Wicek Marzec behind me. "Not that it'll stop them eating the stuff. They can't get enough of it!"

The men on the wagons started getting riled up again.

"They're breeding like reptiles!"

"You know what, Wincenty, they're not reptiles, they're germs!"

"Can't God do something?"

"What can God do? God made the world without cars! Cars must have been made by the devil."

"Never mind the devil. I wish a big tree would just fall across the road and kill them all, damn them."

All of a sudden Stach Brożyna, who was standing up astride his sheaves, started waving his whip in the direction of the road.

"Hey, you there! Stop for a minute, you sons of bitches! We'll get across and you can all be on your way!" He was jumping about so much his horses took fright. They jerked forward, and Stach toppled over and landed on the sheaves. Everyone roared with laughter. Stach didn't let up though. He got back on his feet. "Hey, you!" But he realized shouting at the cars wasn't going to do any good, and he started firing up the other men:

"Come on, guys! Are we sheep or what? Someone ought to go up onto the road and wave his arms. Maybe they'll stop!"

"That's not gonna happen. Now if we all went out, maybe we could block their way."

"What are they, water, that we have to block their way? What we should do is take our scythes and pitchforks to them! With them folks that's always the only way!"

"Or throw rocks at their windshields!"

Anger swept along the line of wagons. Even Kuś got carried away and shouted:

"A cross is what you need! A cross would stop them! No one can stand up to the cross. Nip over to the church, you know! It's a hop and a skip. Bring a cross and go out on the road with it! The priest won't mind. Tell him we can't get over the road with our wagons."

"That's bullshit! A cross? You might as well just spit on the ground in front of them."

"Don't you blaspheme now! The cross is bullshit?" His voice even got hoarse. "You'll be begging at that cross yet, damn you. Why do you think people put crosses and chapels and shrines by the roadside? So nothing bad will happen when you're walking or driving there. Or at a crossroads? So you'll know which way to go when you're lost! You know, one time in the first war we were marching down a road just like this one. We were soldiers, not civilians. And it was a whole lot narrower. There was no blacktop back in those days, just dirt. From the other direction there was a funeral procession with the cross at the front. We'd barely heard them saying the 'Eternal Rest' when our CO gives the order, Don't kick up dust! Pick your feet up high!"

At that moment Stach Brożyna, who'd been standing taking a piss by his load, ran up to Kuś's wagon, buttoning himself up as he came.

"You're talking crap! Goddammit!" And just like that he lashed out once and twice at Kuś's mare. "It's because of you, it's because of you we're waiting here! Gee up! Gee up!"

The mare took the strain and jerked forward. Kuś pulled back on the reins with all his might till the animal's head twisted, and he didn't let go.

"Whoa! Stop! What fault is it of hers, you son of a bitch!"

Stach was in a rage, he took the whip in his right hand and struck out at the mare's back and sides and legs.

"Giddyup! Giddyup! Come on now, move!"

From the beating she probably would have moved out in front of the cars, there was nothing else she could do, but Kuś lay down flat on the sheaves and wouldn't let go of the reins, holding on with all the strength in his old body. The mare tossed her pulled-back head, pressed against the shaft, shifted left and right, and in the end she squatted with her hindquarters on the ground, but she didn't move.

"Leave her alone, Stach!" I shouted.

But it was like Stach had gone crazy. His cap fell off. His shirt came out of his pants. And he kept hitting. Suddenly the mare lurched sideways and something cracked in the reach. The shaft rose upward and it looked as if the wagon would tip over.

I jumped down off my sheaves, grabbed Stach by the shoulders and forced him back into the field. He twisted clear and hit me on the head with the whip. He tried to do it a second time but I dodged out of the way, then I grabbed him by the throat. His eyes almost popped out, his tongue poked out, he fell to his knees. The guys on the wagons were shouting:

"Christ, he's gonna strangle him! Let him go! Szymek!" When I freed him he was gasping for breath.

"Don't you raise your hand again!" I said to him. "The next time I won't let go."

Kuś came down off his sheaves, straightened the shaft, straightened the harness on the horse, patted her and stroked her and mumbled like he was talking to himself:

"How could he have beat her. Honestly, how could he have beat her. Her skin's all trembling. And for what? For what? Come on now, stop shaking."

"Bartłomiej," I said, "get back up there and stop fussing with your horse. We're gonna have to be going, we'll miss our chance again. We've been waiting here long enough already."

"How do you know, maybe the Lord put us here and he's making us wait as a punishment. And the cars just keep coming. You know, there's no point hurrying. It's Sunday. Either way we're sinning against God with every wagonload. The fewer loads, the fewer sins. The seventh day shall be a day of rest, that's what it says. And it was God that said it, not people. And he reckons everything up, he does. If not on his own, then through his reckoners. And they're just as careful as human ones. Pity I didn't bring her feed bag. She could have had a bite to eat the while."

He started clambering back up onto his sheaves. It wasn't easy.

"Shall I get down and help you?" I said.

"Why would I need your help. You're no spring chicken yourself. Time was I could shimmy up a poplar tree in the twinkling of an eye. And without anyone's help."

In the end he managed to climb up there. He got settled, took his whip and reins in hand.

"See, I could climb a tree even now."

"Just keep your eyes open," I said.

"That's all I am doing."

The men had quieted down on their wagons again. Nobody even felt like cursing, all you could hear was the cars roaring past, screeching and honking, then from time to time one of the horses would give a snort.

"Why so quiet, Bartłomiej?" I said, because everything seemed too silent to me. All those furious wagons and no one saying a word.

"You told me to watch out so I'm watching out. Where are they all driving to, damn them? Are they running away or something? From what? They can't drive forever, though. They'll get sick of driving before we get sick of waiting. Sure, not waiting would be better than waiting. But getting mad won't do any good either. Think of all the things people have to put up with that are worse than waiting. Sometimes they think they can't take it anymore. But they do. And you can never say they couldn't take anything worse. Because in this world there's no limit to how much worse things can get. And all people have is patience. So they have to just wait it all out. They're like trees, just standing there, for years, for centuries. Wherever they were planted or wherever the wind sowed them. They don't choose their place, they just stand there from the moment they're born. Oaks stand the longest of all the trees. Poplars the shortest. Poplars are crap trees. You can't even make a scythe handle out of their wood. But oak is like rock, you know. You can use it for anything. A doorstep, a wheel hub, a barrel, a cross, whatever you like. And all because it doesn't get angry, it doesn't curse, it just stands there. There are times when shouting won't do you any good, nor tears, nor mowing. Neither God nor people will help you, only that patience of yours. And even when your time comes to die, it won't seem so terrible, because you know, death is patience too. So we'll outwait them, we will. We've outwaited all kinds of things with nothing but our patience to help us."

I wasn't thinking what I was doing. It was like someone had jabbed me in the side with a knife. I jumped down off my load.

"Back up, boys!" I shouted. "I'm going out there!"

There was alarm among the wagons.

"Are you nuts, Szymek?!"

"What's gotten into you now?"

"You'll never make it across!"

"There's one car after another!"

"Think what you're doing, for heaven's sake!"

I straightened the traces and bridle, patted the horse on the neck, checked the straps. I didn't feel upset, I wasn't mad at anyone.

"Szymek, for the love of God!" Kuś leaned down all the way from his load. "I ought to be the one to go, you know. I'm the first in line. I'm only a few steps from death anyway. And my mare's ready to die as well."

I took the whip and reins in hand, but I could see the farmers standing there like the cat had their tongues.

"Come on, back up! Otherwise I won't be able to get out from behind Kuś!"

And all of a sudden it was like the fear got into them, one after another they started backing up, pulling their horses' heads up, snapping their whips, shouting, "Whoa, back up!" The reaches and axles creaked and goddammits were flying, because reversing a loaded wagon is no easy task.

I jerked back, pulled the horse to the right, and first of all drove into the field. Then, as I passed Kuś's wagon I tightened the reins and it was giddyup! toward the road.

"Dear God, he's going to kill himself! Stop! Wait up! Szymek!"

Kuś's hoarse voice rang out through the air:

"Cross yourself at least!"

I leaned my shoulder against the wagon. The whip was burning my hand.

The horse was trotting along at a decent pace, maybe he sensed what he was up against. The front of the shaft was almost at the road when suddenly he hesitated and tossed his head. That part happened to be uphill. I flicked the whip across his back and legs. His whole body tensed, all the way to his hind hooves that were steadied against the ground. Gee up! Gee up! He was already coming out in front of the moving cars. Then the wagon sort of jerked him backwards, or maybe he just got scared of the cars. I braced my shoulder with all my strength against the load and took the whip to his legs once and twice again, till the horse arched. He moved forward. His front hooves were already clopping on the blacktop. The front wheels were on it too. I leaned back and whipped him again, like I was knocking the cars away from in front of him. By now my legs were coming out onto the road as well.

All of a sudden something flashed in front of my eyes. There was a terrifying honking sound right close by. I heard the squeal of tires. There was a crash and I came down like a felled tree. To begin with I couldn't see a thing, like a fog had fallen all around me, I couldn't feel anything either, I only heard voices and shouts somewhere far away. Then the fog began to slowly clear, and nearby to my left I saw a big hole, and in the hole a light-colored head covered in blood and looking like it was sleeping. I tried to get up. But it was as if I didn't have a body, all I had was my will. Right in front of me on the blacktop my legs were lying all twisted like tree roots, and they were covered in blood. It seemed like my blood was flowing out of them, spilling far and wide. Though they weren't hurting. I had the vague feeling they mustn't have been my legs after all. And the whip I was holding in my right hand also didn't seem to be mine, or the hand itself. Where could a whip have come from? I couldn't for the life of me remember what I'd needed it for. It was like I was dreaming it all. It was only the road I knew was real, because I could see there weren't any acacias growing alongside it anymore.

People were gathering around me. I couldn't figure out why. They were shouting, their heads were bobbing like turkeys' heads, they were waving their arms about. There were more and more of them. They shouted louder and louder, waved their arms faster and faster, and all of them were staring at me like crazy. Someone kicked my legs as they lay there on the blacktop. But it didn't hurt at all. Someone else leaned over me, he was wearing a checkered shirt and he had eyes like a fish.

"He's alive," I heard him say, his voice was so loud it felt like it was boring into my ears.

He started to tug at my shoulders. And he must have woken me from my dream, because I saw I was sitting hunched over among the sheaves, and the people standing over me were real. Right next to me stood my horse, tangled in the traces, the shaft forcing his head all the way up to the sky.

"See, peasant like him, still alive."

At that moment I felt it was my hand holding the whip, and I sensed a huge furious force gathering in that whip. I started lashing out blindly at all those screaming faces, and eyes, and shirts.

"You bastards!" I felt I was shouting at the whole world, though the sound might not even have passed my throat. Because the fog covered everything back up. As if I didn't have a body again. Someone pulled the whip from my hand. Then when the fog rose again a moment later, I saw Kuś kneeling over me.

"You're alive. Thank the Lord, you're alive."

BROTHERS

I decided to write a letter to Antek and Stasiek about the tomb. I went to the co-op, I bought paper and ink and a penholder and a nib. Because when was the last time I wrote anyone a letter? I don't even remember. No one in the house went to school anymore so those things weren't needed. All we had was an old dried-up inkpot lying around from back when mother was still alive and she still wrote to them. I never wrote after they left home, even though they were my brothers. And they never wrote to me. It just worked out that way. They were in the city and I was in the village. They had their lives, I had mine. What was there to write about? Was I supposed to tell them what was happening in the village, when they maybe weren't that interested in remembering the village anymore? What was the point of forcing myself on someone else's life, even if it was my brothers'? Besides, one or other of them would swing by for a visit every two or three years so we more or less knew what was going on with them. One of them traveled abroad, one of them bought a car. One of them got an apartment, three rooms and a kitchen, the other one split up with his wife and got married again. One has a daughter and a son, the other one only a son, but he's not that interested in school. As for my news, well, when mother died I sent them a telegram: "Mother died. Come." Then, a few years later another one: "Father died.

Come." That was all my news. Though even if there'd been more, would they have wanted to know?

While mother was alive she'd always have to write a few words to them every Christmas. And each time it was the name day of Saint Stanislaus or Saint Anthony. And sometimes when she'd suddenly miss them or when she had a dream about one of them. When the flour was bolted she'd send them a packet, and a letter to go with it. Then they'd write a thank-you for the flour and send their regards to everyone at home, "and Szymek as well." That was enough. I mean, we didn't stop being brothers.

But a tomb is a tomb, you only build one in your whole lifetime, so I had to ask them if they wanted to be buried with everyone else, because I'd planned eight places so there'd be room for them as well. Or maybe they'd rather be buried there, where they live – that way I wouldn't have to spend more money unnecessarily, I'd have a smaller tomb built. Of course, I hope they live as long and as happily as possible, but sooner or later they have to die, because all of us that are alive are going to die. And please answer right away, because I've paid for the plot and gotten the cement, and I'm all set with Chmiel. They probably remember Chmiel, he built tombs even before the war, half the tombs in our cemetery are his work. He'll make us a solid, comfortable tomb. I just have to let him know that my brothers agree.

I spent the whole evening on that letter. Not that I said a whole lot. The entire thing came out to less than one page. But I wanted to write something more than just about the tomb. I was embarrassed that it was the first letter I'd written to them in all those years, and it started with "Dear Brothers," and the paper wasn't that big, plus it was folded in two and not even written on to the end. But I couldn't think of anything else to say. I thought and thought, I even had a drink. That reminded me I hadn't milked the cows. I lit the lamp, took the pail, and even in the shed, as the milk was squirting between my fingers, I was thinking what else I could write to them about. But I couldn't even make it to the end of the page, so the Love and the God bless, Szymek would at least fall on the next side. After a whole room's worth of thinking there was no more than a handful of words. I guess I could have written how much the tomb was going to cost me, the plot and the materials and the labor. But I thought, they'd only get offended and write back that they just want to be buried in the city.

It was like I was writing an official letter, not to my own brothers. And when you're writing an official letter you don't just have to be careful not to say anything against yourself, you also need to make sure the words all agree with each other, that they're not making nonsense of each other, because otherwise you'll have the whole office laughing at you. And it shouldn't be too long, because who's going to read a long letter. I worked in the district administration and I know. You'd read the beginning and the end, but the whole middle was like it was written to God alone. Though the middle often contained the most pain.

On top of that, one of them's got a degree and the other one's an engineer, and I couldn't just write the way you talk. Out here no one pays any attention to how they talk and they don't talk that much anyway, because on a farm work comes before words. Plus, truth be told, who is there to talk to? The plow, the scythe, the pitchfork, the hoe, the field, the meadow? If I have a real strong urge to talk I can talk to the horse or to God, but most of the time I just talk to myself in my own thoughts. And in the evening at home, after work, sometimes to Michał. Though talking to Michał is like talking to your horse or to God, or to yourself in your own thoughts. I ask him, so how are things, did you go anywhere in the village today, or, did you eat the dumplings I left for you, or, did anyone come by today? As usual he doesn't answer, and that's it for the day. Some days I don't feel like saying even that much, I'm fit to drop and I just want to go straight to bed.

Though there isn't always work. In the fall, sometimes it rains and rains, there's no way you can go out into the fields, or to the village, and it'd be the perfect moment to talk like brothers, not just, When is this rain ever going to let up. But I don't want to ask him any more questions. Because the most he'll do is raise his eyes at you, and there's no telling whether he's heard you or not. And often those eyes look as if they've gone far, far away from him. What would be the point of asking him anything else. Though sometimes I feel sorry for him, he's my brother after all, and at those times I want to at least ask him, Michał, tell me, who hurt you? But even if he told me, it wouldn't help either of us. So maybe it's better I don't know.

It was the same when I was writing the letter, I wanted to ask him, shall I say hello to Antek and Stasiek from you? But I didn't ask, I just wrote, Michał says hello as well.

The next evening I took the letter over to the Kuśmiereks' next door. Their Rysiek goes to technical school in the town, I thought it'd be good for someone young to read it through. Maybe there are different ways of writing these days, or maybe I'd made some mistakes, even though they're my brothers I didn't want them laughing at me.

"Christ be praised."

"Forever and ever."

"Is Rysiek in? Listen, Rysiek," I say, "take at look at this letter. I'm writing to my brothers. Put it right if there's any mistakes. When I was young they taught us to write different than they do now. I'll buy you an ice cream one Sunday as a thank-you."

Kuśmierek was sitting by the kitchen stove. Through this cough that was choking him, because he has asthma, he says:

"What are you talking about, ice cream? Buy him a half-bottle. All he thinks about is vodka and whores." He got such a bad coughing fit that his wife had to thump him on the back. "Yesterday he comes home from school rolling drunk. He's lost all his notes and his books. So of course he needs new ones. Plus I have to write him a note to excuse him, say I needed him for the threshing. The little worm only got up a short while ago. The whole night his mother had to sit holding a cabbage compress to his head, he had such a bad headache. You see how his eyes are still all gummed up? He must have drunk a bucketful of water by now. I wish he'd go about his studying the same way. But he's thick as two short planks, him. It's a waste of money. The thing is, they say they have to go to school because otherwise you won't be allowed to hand down your land." Then all of a sudden it was like the helpless father sounded in Kuśmierek and he shouted hoarsely: "You ever come home drunk again and I'll show you what's what, you little shit! I'll kick you out like a dog!" But he was stopped in his tracks again by his cough.

Rysiek muttered something back to his father, rubbed his eyes, and started reading.

"Read it out loud!" roared Kuśmierek, barely able to catch his breath. "Reading quietly's no kind of reading."

Rysiek did what he was told and started to read out loud. He must have been a bit afraid of his father after he'd gotten drunk, because otherwise he wouldn't have let himself be ordered around like that. But the reading didn't go too well. He cleared his throat, stammered, stumbled like someone walking across uneven ground. It felt like every word stabbed me, because I thought I'd written it that way. I was about to say to him, here, give it back, I'll write it again. But I thought to myself, he mustn't have sobered up yet, so I encouraged him:

"Keep reading, Rysiu, keep reading."

He even stood under the lightbulb as if the light was too dim. But it was too dim for him there as well. He started complaining about the lightbulb being covered in fly droppings, and was it too much to expect someone to wipe it clean once in a while, he couldn't do it because he had to study. And that his father needed to stop all that coughing, it was distracting him.

Kuśmierek made a big effort, he even clapped his hand over his mouth. But it didn't help the reading much, he was still staggering through the words like a drunk. All of a sudden he stopped and, as if he was thinking, he began scratching his head. He thought and thought till in the end I asked him:

"What are you thinking about?"

"Tomb," he mumbled.

"What about tomb?"

"I think it's spelled wrong. I think it's with a *u*. An open letter, not a closed one."

"It always used to be written with an *o*," I said. "Unless they changed it."

That worried him a bit. And Kuśmierek, who was about to collapse from holding in his cough so as not to bother Rysiek, straightened up and said in a loud despairing voice:

"See what that damn kid doesn't know! He's going to fail his exams again! That'll be the third time he's taken the same class! Dear God. Then he comes back home and he's a know-it-all, dammit! Tells me to sow corn instead of rye. What do you know, you dope, when you can't even spell tomb! Can you imagine leaving the farm to him. He'd throw it all away in the blink of an eye. All he'd do is lie on his back watching his belly grow. An open letter. Go to the cemetery, do you see anyone in an open tomb? Everything's covered in earth and stone slabs. The dead are apart forever from the living. That world from this world. Even closest family isn't allowed to see what happens to someone after they die. Cause just like you have to be alive to know what's going on here, you have to die to know what's going on over there. Your time'll come as well one day, damn you, it comes to everyone. You'll see how you'd feel in an open tomb. No one would even come visit your grave, cause you'd be rotting, you'd stink like a dead dog. You'd be begging for someone to take a shovel and cover you with earth." Kuśmierek was so bitter he'd gotten carried away, but all of a sudden his bitterness turned to anger. "And here he is, the little bastard, getting two hundred zlotys a month for his supper, and a hundred for bus money, that's three hundred! Where are his notes and his books?! And there's always something else he needs, this thing and that thing! And for what?! For what?!" He wound up in such a coughing fit it was a good while before he got the better of it. His eyes stared ahead like he was gone from the world.

"Jesus and Mary! Józef! Józef!" squealed his wife. I jumped forward as well to save him, though I didn't exactly know how. Rysiek was yelping also:

"Dad! Dad!"

Luckily Kuśmierek came to and breathed a sigh of relief. Except he looked at us like he didn't recognize us. That short moment had tired him out as much as if he'd been mowing on a steep slope.

I felt sorry for him. Any father wants the best for his kid.

"Don't be mad, Józef," I said. "He's young, he's got time."

"Am I telling him to rush, damn him? I'm telling him to study!"

"There's nothing you can do. That's how it is with young folks – they're in no hurry to study," I said, because I was feeling sorry for the boy as well. Was it his fault he was bad at school? I just regretted bringing the letter. I told him not to bother reading any more.

"Leave it be, Rysiek. It's fine as it is. If you change it you might make it worse." I took the letter back. At this, Kuśmierek took offense as if for Rysiek.

"I mean, who even writes to their own brothers like that. You need to begin, In the name of the Father and the Son and the Holy Ghost. That would remind them right away about their family home. They might even give you something towards that tomb of yours."

All of a sudden Rysiek started saying it wasn't fashionable anymore to start letters with God. They'd had a lesson about how to write letters and he knew. It was like Kuśmierek was struck by lightning:

"You little bastard, you're telling me God isn't in fashion? That's what I'm paying for you to learn?!"

But Rysiek had gotten over his fear and he snapped back at his father that he didn't give a damn about studying. Give him what was his and he'd get married.

I got up and left, because what business was it of mine. Let them argue among themselves.

The next day I wrote the letter out again because it was all dirty from Rysiek's fingers. I added that if they were planning to visit they should bring bags for flour, because as it happened I'd been bolting and I had some good flour. I was just saying that, because I didn't at all think they'd come, but it made the letter a bit longer.

It must have been a month or so later that a letter came from them saying they were going to visit the following Sunday. I didn't know whether to believe it or not. But I cleaned the house. I got fresh bedding ready. I brought mother's quilt down from the attic, because it was the biggest one. And though they were going to sleep in the same bed, I gave them two pillows so their heads would be apart. I changed the straw in the mattress. I threshed two sheaves with the flail so it wouldn't be lumpy. Though it was hard for me to stand for long on those legs of mine. I had to pull the chaff-cutter up behind my back and lean on it, otherwise I couldn't have done it. I even put some dried thyme under the sheet to keep the fleas away, like mother used to do.

I bathed Michał and shaved him, and I gave him a fresh shirt and a necktie. He's their brother too, after all. There was an ash bucket stood in the room that was old and full of holes. For some reason I'd always been reluctant to throw it out, but because they were coming I tossed it without a second thought. I put in a brighter electric bulb. Let it be lighter while they were here, after they left I'd change it back again. I killed a rooster and made chicken broth. I was going to make noodles, but I decided to buy some instead. They're used to the store-bought stuff, they might not like homemade. I also bought a bottle of vodka, because you have to have a glass with your brothers. I even took down the Lord Jesus with the apostles and put it in the other room, because I remembered Stasiek isn't that big on God. He might get annoyed. And I won't know how to defend him, because on the one hand it's God, on the other hand it's my brother. Oh well. What people won't do to keep the peace in a family.

They came. But they'd barely crossed the threshold and said their hellos when they started in on me. That there wasn't anything to sit on here except the same old bench and a single chair. That the table was the same one from the war. That why don't I have a proper floor put in? Why don't I plant an orchard? Why don't I get married? I need a housekeeper! Am I waiting for a princess? One thing after another. Why not this? Why not that? And not a word about dying. It was like I'd never even written them the letter.

I was stunned, I barely said a word. I even forgot to ask what was new with them. And I didn't let on about the bottle I'd bought. I mean, what for? So we could drink while we were arguing? Maybe a better opportunity would come along. Then we'd have a drink and we'd talk like brothers.

Because when brothers only get together once in such a long time they ought to have something to talk about. Talk all day and all night. Even if they don't feel like talking, because what are words for? Words lead the way of their own accord. Words bring everything out onto the surface. Words take everything that hurts and whines and they drag it all out from the deepest depths. Words let blood, and you feel better right away. And not just with outsiders, with your brothers also words can help you find each other, feel like brothers again. However far away they've gone, words will bring them back to the one life they came from, like from a spring. Because words are a great grace. When it comes down to it, what are you given other than words? Either way there's a great silence waiting for us in the end, and we'll have our fill of silence. Maybe we'll find ourselves scratching at the walls for the sake of the least little word. And every word we didn't say to each other in this world we'll regret like a sin. Except it'll be too late. And how many of those unsaid words stay in each person and die with him, and rot with him, and they aren't any use to him either in his suffering, or in his memory? So why do we make each other be silent, on top of everything else?

Though perhaps it was my fault. Because when I saw them I didn't really know what to say and I just said in an ordinary way:

"Oh, you're here."

As if they'd just gotten back from the fields, or from market in town, or from the next village. When actually they'd come from the outside world. And when had we last seen each other? At father's funeral. Stasiek was still at the university then. He was wearing a ragged old overcoat and shoes with worn-down heels. He didn't even have any gloves, he was skinny and hollow-cheeked. I slipped a few zlotys in his pocket as he was leaving and he was so grateful he even tried to kiss my hand. I wouldn't let him. Now, he was on the stout side, ruddy, his chin spilling out over his collar. The front of his head was completely bald, it was only at the back and on the sides he still had some of his old shock of hair left. At first I wasn't even sure if it was Stasiek or not. But I pretended he hadn't changed at all and I didn't say a word about him being so bald. I welcomed him like you welcome your brother.

Antek had just gotten married back then. He even had a photograph of his wife. We'd barely buried father when he took the picture out of his wallet and asked if I thought she was pretty. I didn't much like her, but what could I say. Yes, she's pretty.

And I didn't tell him off either for not letting me know, so I could have sent best wishes.

That time too we didn't talk at all among ourselves. First because it was a funeral and the right thing to do was talk about father, because it was his day. He deserved at least a few words from each of us for his whole life. Second, Stasiek had some important examination the next day. So we just drank a bottle to mark our sorrow, and ate some sausage. Then they left.

Actually, when father and mother were alive it was the same thing, whenever one of them would visit it was always in a rush. They'd arrive and spend the night then in the morning they'd be gone. Or even the same day, they'd say hello in the morning and goodbye in the afternoon. One minute they were there, the next they'd vanished. Like the crack of a whip. You didn't even notice they'd been.

The next day already mother would start missing them again, when will Antek and Stasiek visit, she'd say. She was always worried that something had happened to one of them because they hadn't been in so long. When father reminded her that Antek or Stasiek had just been the previous Sunday, she still wouldn't stop worrying.

"That's true, he was here. But what kind of visit was it. There wasn't even time for the cheese to be pressed dry, or he could have taken it with him."

Or when someone in the village asked if Antek or Stasiek had been, you didn't know whether to say they had or they hadn't. To say they'd been but they were in a hurry was the same as saying they hadn't been at all, but they'd be coming, they would.

When they left for the city it was the same – like they were here a moment ago but now they were gone. It was as if they'd just popped down to the village or gone out to the fields and they'd be back soon. Father kept forgetting for the longest time, he was always wanting one of them to give him a hand or do a job for him.

"Maybe Antek could do it . . . Maybe Stasiek could . . ."

Then he got used to it, and it was only before going to bed sometimes, he'd be sitting there fit to drop, like an ox that's been working all day, and out of the blue he'd pipe up:

"It's been such a long time since they wrote."

And mother would mention their names more and more often in her prayers.

Antek was the first to leave. He was those few years older than Stasiek, maybe it was his due as the eldest. Stasiek was still a little kid when Antek was already off chasing after the ladies. True, he always was a bit of a hothead. But to leave all of a sudden like that? It's not right even to die that way. In the morning he was still plowing the potato field by the wood, then in the afternoon Kulawik brought him a letter from the post office. He came back from the fields, opened it, read it, and said:

"I'm going."

"Going where?" asked father.

"Away." He was so pleased he actually danced around the room.

"Away, you say?" Father thought he'd misheard.

"Away, that's right. Away! Away!"

"When's this?"

"On the five o'clock train tomorrow morning."

"I won't even have time to iron your shirt for you!" Mother was in despair.

"What do I need a fresh shirt for? The one I've got on will do just fine."

"You might at least take a bath. I can bring the bathtub and put water on to heat."

"I'll take a bath there. Wojtek said in his letter they go to the bathhouse there."

"But you haven't even got a decent pair of shoes. And I could make you some new clothes."

"They'll give me shoes there, clothes as well."

"We could sell the heifer, you'd have a bit of money to take with you. I could bake you a cake."

"What are you talking about, bake him a cake," said father, though he was more upset than angry. "His train's at five, didn't you hear? And the heifer's still growing. It'll be another two weeks or so."

"So he could wait. The world's not going to run away. Instead of rushing off the minute he gets back from the fields." The poor thing started to cry.

"And what exactly are you planning to do there?" Father could be tough when he had to be.

"What am I going to be doing? You'll see!" He waved the letter. "Wojtek says they go to the cinema every day. As for work, they only work eight hours a day, and they get paid for it as well."

"Perhaps you should go to confession, son," mother started to beg him through her tears. "When people used to go away they'd always go confess their sins before they left. There might not be anywhere you can go confess when you're there. Or they won't let you."

"They go to the cinema, you say?" said father as if to himself, because he didn't really know what a cinema was.

The cinema even came to our village soon after that. The day it was supposed to arrive, a crowd of people went out to the edge of the village in the morning and waited for it. Someone even drew in the snow with a stick, "Welcome to our village, Cinema." People thought it would be a car or at the very least a carriage drawn by two horses. No one believed at first that it was the cinema. Two men on a wagon and some bundles. Plus, the horse was so skinny its ribs stuck out. Instead of a proper seat there was just a sheaf of straw covered with an old cloth. The sides of the wagon were all smeared with something as if they'd been transporting manure. And the wagon driver and the other guy were so drunk they could barely see straight. They tried to nail up a poster on the firehouse but neither of them could even hit the nail on the head, the guys had to do it for them. But almost the whole village came to the cinema, because it was wintertime, there wasn't much work, and also the watchman had gone around beating his drum to say the cinema was coming. So there were almost as many people outside as in the firehouse, because there wasn't room inside. People blocked each other's view, but they stood there anyway. It spoiled it a bit, but they still stood there.

Father went down there as well to see what it was that was taking Antek away from the village. He didn't say what it had been like, but afterward from time to time he'd burst out:

"It's because of the cinema, it's all because of the cinema. Who's going to do the work around here when you leave? Your mother and I are getting on. Stasiek's too young to plow or mow. It'll be another three or four years before he's ready."

"What about Szymek?" Antek started up like he'd been stung by a horse-fly.

"True," said father. "But it's like he's not here. He's not drawn to the land and the land's not drawn to him."

"The land! The land! I'm sick of that land of yours! Out there I'll at least learn something! What can I learn from the land?!"

"The land can teach you if you only want to learn from it. But you go, you go. I just hope you won't come crawling back on your hands and knees."

And he left, in a huff at father, mother, Stasiek, me.

Though at that time I was away from home. I was in the police and we were going around the villages searching the farms for guns. He slammed the door so hard whitewash came down from the ceiling. Father jumped up and shouted after him:

"Don't you go slamming doors when it's not your house anymore!"

I came back a week or so later, soaked to the skin, frozen to the marrow of my bones, covered in mud up to my knees and more exhausted than after the hardest plowing. On top of all that, father greeted me the moment I walked in the house:

"Oh, it's Mr. Policeman. He's been chasing so many people he can barely move his legs. We wanted a priest in the family and God gave us a policeman. What did we do to deserve that?"

I didn't say a word. I stood my rifle in the corner by the door and flopped down on the bench. I didn't even have the strength to pull the cap off my head. Water was dripping down my face. Mother begged me, come on now, take off your cap, take off your jacket, pull your boots off, but I could feel sleep wrapping around me like a rope, round my body and my eyes and my will. On my back, underneath my shirt I could feel the lice starting to itch from the heat. But I couldn't even be bothered to reach back and scratch.

We'd been searching all sorts of barns and cattle sheds and wagon houses and cellars and attics, not to mention the houses themselves. And as it happened the harvest had just been taken in and the barns were filled to the roof, in the cellars there were potatoes and carrots and beets, the attics were packed with hay, and on top of everything else it rained day and night without a break as if the flood was coming. And wherever you went it'd be:

"You got any guns?"

To which everyone would answer meek as lambs:

"Guns? What would we need guns for, officer? What are we, soldiers? We don't even know how to use a gun. We work with plows, scythes, rakes – those are the tools the Lord meant for us. Not guns. Who would we even shoot at? The enemy's all gone. There's nothing but our own people everywhere. When you're among your own, even if someone gets mad at someone else they just call them names, get even with them, threaten them. Maybe go after them with a fence post. But a fence post isn't a gun. Besides, the war's barely over. We've had enough gunfire to last us a lifetime. These days, you hear a bee buzz close to your ear and you think you've been hit. All we did was cry and pray for it to stop. So when it did, were we going to keep on shooting? The land was waiting for us. The land suffered too. It was tired out as well like everyone else. That Lord Jesus or Our Lady up there in that picture, they can be our witness – we don't have any guns."

But you only needed to reach behind the Our Lady or the Lord Jesus and pull out a pistol. You'd look in the stove, and inside there'd be a rifle. Have them open the chest, and there under a pile of headscarves, rounds and grenades. Or go up to the attic. Their Sunday suit was hanging from a rafter like it was just waiting for mass, but you'd nudge it and there'd be a clank of metal. Not to even mention what was in the hay, among their clothes, in with the onions, in the thatch, in barrels full of grain, in old shoes – everywhere you'd find stuff. Where did they not hide things. In dogs' kennels, in chaff-cutters, in cows' and horses' mangers, in holes up in old trees.

At one guy's place, under the grain in the barn we found an entire arse-nal. He had everything you could imagine. Rifles, pistols, regular ones and automatics, all of it oiled and wrapped in rags. There were helmets, belts, mess kits, backpacks, Russian and German maps, over a dozen ammunition belts, a couple dozen pairs of boots.

"Where did you get all this?" It was a stupid question, because you knew where he got it, but we were staggered, we didn't know what else to say.

"Off dead bodies, sir. You know – they were all over the place out in the fields. Was it all supposed to go to waste? And it didn't feel right to bury it."

"There was an order to turn in weapons, right?"

"That there was."

"So why didn't you hand them over?"

"Well, what if we have to fight again?"

"Fight who, for God's sake?"

"Whoever. They might invade us again."

At another guy's, in the barn as well, we found four heavy machine guns and several cases of ammunition. Another one had a motorcycle and sidecar, and a whole pile of guns in the sidecar. They most of them hid the stuff in their barns, like they reckoned the crop was the most innocent place for it. You sometimes had to dig down through three or four layers of sheaves. And on your own, because the farmer would claim his back had suddenly gone out. At another farm we had to muck the place out ourselves, because the farmer ran away the moment he saw us.

There was one house we went to, all we find is this little old lady in bed. She's got her cat with her, there's no one else around.

"What a good thing you've come to save me! That Judas son-in-law of mine, he's put so many rifles under my bedding my sides are all sore. I'm afraid to even move in case they go off."

We took five wagonloads away from that place. You even felt envious there were so many guns, when in the resistance any old pistol could cost you your life.

Not many people got fined, because what were you going to fine them for. It was the war that brought folks all those guns, the war was the one that should have been punished. But how can you punish a war? Besides, there was enough to do fining the ones that got caught with guns actually in their hands. Even if you just went into the fields you'd always catch two or three of them that were out hunting hares. No one bothered setting snares anymore, there was no point when they had rifles, handguns, automatic pistols. And how many hares could there be left after that long of a war? When you saw one hopping by somewhere it was like seeing a miracle. Look, a hare, a hare! And it didn't even look much like a hare, it'd have its ears shot away or a missing leg and it'd be peg-legging it along more like an old man than a hare.

Those days almost everyone went hunting with a gun. Not to mention when they were driving their wagon to market or to a wedding, or to gather wood in the forest, they'd always stick a pistol under the seat or in the horse's feed bag.

One time we had to search a school because the teacher told us the boys were chasing the girls with pistols during the break. Another time Tomala comes rushing into the station all white and shaking and shouting, help! What is it, Wojtek? Turned out his wife is waking their Tomek saying it's time to go to school, and Tomek pulls a gun from under the pillow and says he'll shoot her if she doesn't leave him alone. He needs his sleep, and he's not going to go to school anymore. Or the boys grazing the cattle, every one of them would have a gun stuck in his belt. And day after day there'd be shooting out in the meadows like the war was still going on out there.

And some parent would come running to the police to say their cow had a gunshot wound or it had come home with its horns shot away, because the little bastards had been using the cows' horns for target practice like they couldn't think of anything else to shoot at.

And if it had only been in the meadows. But sometimes it was in the middle of the village. Anyone that bore a grudge against someone else, before, they'd have just shouted at them and called them names, or at the most set fire to their place, but now they'd take out their gun and start firing. It could be over women, debts, field boundaries, anything. Wrongs from the time of their fathers or grandfathers. And even if they didn't shoot directly at each other they'd fire over the guy's head, at his windows or his roof if he had a tile roof or metal roofing, or they'd put a hole in his wagon or shoot his dog.

Or like it happened once at Rędzinówka. One farmer runs into his neighbor's yard with an automatic handgun and shoots all his geese and chickens and ducks, then to finish he shoots up the stable door. So then the other guy takes revenge on the first guy's orchard. He ties a couple of blocks of TNT with a fuse and a detonator to each of the trees, then he lights the fuse from his cigarette. He goes up on the hill and watches the trees blow up one after another. We went to take a look and it was like the worst war you could imagine had passed through that orchard. We had to put both of them away. Though some people said they were just crazy. But you can't claim they were crazy when everyone was shooting guns left, right, and center. And it wasn't just one person against another, there were whole villages fighting each other. One time we even had to call in the military because we thought we were being attacked by an army.

After a few months I'd had enough of the police. All I'd done was ruin my tall boots. They were the kind they call officer's boots. I'd brought them back almost new from the resistance, but after the police you wouldn't have known they were the same boots. You had to wade through manure and mud and water in them. And those were boots that should only have been worn to church. Plus, you'd think you wouldn't work as much as when you're working the land, but there I was, day and night, chasing, looking, searching like the worst bandit, and on top of that everyone was out to get their revenge on me. And instead of the number of guns getting smaller, it was like people were growing them in the fields.

Worst of all was at the dances. People stopped fighting with knives, now it was only ever with guns. There wasn't a single dance without any shooting, and every second one someone got killed. And there were no culprits. No one could say who'd been shooting, who the killer was. Butter wouldn't melt. They'd all been dancing and singing, they couldn't hear anything over the music. Maybe the guy was already dead when he came to the dance? And you lost count of the number of shot-up windows, lamps, beer barrels, bottles, drums, fiddles. And when a fiddle gets shot there's no more playing it. A drum can be patched up and it'll still work. But when you put a gunshot in a fiddle it's a goner, it's dead. Like a person.

People really had fun in those days. They were happy because the war was over. There was one dance after another. Not a Sunday went by without one. Sometimes there were two or three dances on the same Sunday in different villages. Musicians even came by train from far away, because there weren't enough local ones for all those dances. Besides, the local musicians played the way they used to before the war, but who danced like before the war now. Now different dances were in fashion.

There were times you didn't know which dance to go to first. You get word from one here and you get word from one over that way. There's shooting here and shooting there. And at the station there's only five of us officers and one bicycle. And of course you can't leave the station unmanned.

"You were asleep," said father, not on my case anymore.

"No I wasn't," I answered, though I don't know, maybe I was.

"Look around the house."

I looked, but I didn't notice anything in particular.

"What about it?"

"Antek's gone," said father in a painful voice.

"Where is he?"

"He left."

Then a few years later Stasiek followed Antek. Though you'd have thought that of all us four brothers Stasiek was the one God intended to stay on the land. And that no force on earth could have torn him away from it. Ever since he was tiny, come rain or shine, heat or cold, he'd always be out in the fields with father. If father was plowing, Stasiek would walk alongside him holding the whip. Give her a flick, Stasiek, the damn creature's stopping and starting. And Stasiek would flick the whip just like father told him to. When father was sowing, he had to at least tie one of mother's shawls around Stasiek's neck and give him a handful of grain so he could sow too. When father mowed, every time he stood the scythe upright and sharpened the blade with a whetstone, Stasiek would hold the handle for him. When he grew up a bit, one day he took the scythe himself and straight away he started mowing like he'd been doing it all his life. Me and Antek and Michał, father had to teach us for a long time, first how you had to stand, how to grip the scythe, how to take short, even steps, how to move the scythe back and forth, how to do it with rye and wheat and barley and oats, how to lay it down and how to keep it straight. And did he ever used to get mad while he was teaching us. He was forever having to tighten the handle and sharpen the blade. Our hands would be covered in blisters from those lessons. But with Stasiek, it was like he'd come into the world knowing how to do it. He just picked up the scythe and mowed.

"Stasiek now, he'll be a proper mower soon as he gets his strength up." Father would watch Stasiek mowing like he was gazing at the sunrise. "None of you is as good as him. He'll probably end up better than me. I've been mowing all my life and I never move that evenly. He doesn't jerk the scythe, he doesn't leave too much stubble. If you look at his arms it's as smooth as if he was scooping up water. And the way he walks forward, it's like the earth itself was moving along under his feet. That's how it is when God means someone to do something. You can see right away, even though he's only a child. Take a break, Stasiek! Sit for a while! Drink some water! Or throw pebbles at sparrows a bit! You'll do your fill of mowing yet!"

Or another time father was getting all worried about how little land we had, and how would he ever be able to divide it up between the four of us sons, and Stasiek pipes up like a true farmer that can find a solution to any problem:

"We can buy some more land, daddy. You said Kaczocha was looking to sell his two acres because he was going to the mill to be a miller. That would be two more acres!"

"He's taking over the mill, you say." Father fell deep in thought. After a moment he said: "Well, two acres is a lot of land, that's for sure. And it's right next to ours. All we'd have to do is plow over the field boundary." And he cheered up right away. He slapped his knee and said to mother: "So? Maybe we could have a slice of bread each? Can you go bring us the loaf?"

"It's the last one," mother reminded him.

"Never mind that. Even the last one has to be eaten sooner or later." Father was all cheerful, like he'd just had a drink, he was so pleased about those two acres of Kaczocha's.

Mother went and brought the bread. She cut each of us a good thick slice, not a crumb more or less for anyone, we all got exactly the same. She only hesitated when she was cutting father's slice, but she went ahead and gave him one too, though his was much thinner. She left herself out.

"What about you?" father said. "If we're celebrating, everyone should. Or take mine. I'll do fine without."

He reached into his pocket and took out his tobacco pouch, then slowly, his mind somewhere else, he started rolling himself a cigarette. And when father rolled a cigarette it meant something good was happening inside him. Because he rarely felt like smoking when he was down. As he puffed out clouds of smoke, he said to mother:

"Cut Stasiek another slice. Why should we skimp on bread for him if he likes it so much. Szymek and Antek have done all the growing they're going to, Stasiek's only just starting. Or give him mine if you don't want it."

Another time he fell to thinking about something or other, and lost in his thoughts he suddenly started bad-mouthing Kaczocha:

"Damn fool decides out of the blue to be a miller. He thinks wheat rolls are gonna come falling from the sky just like that. In that job you have to carry sacks. Him, he spends his whole day staring into space and cooing at the pigeons. Out in his fields anything grows that wants to. You'd need to not have a conscience to let land go like that. One year he was cooing away so long he didn't notice the fall was over, and he forgot to sow. Though whether he sows or no, all that grows there is wheatgrass and other weeds. His father was the same, but at least he'd mend people's shoes. But him, he just sits there making pigeon noises. The land would need to be cleared of weeds first of all. Plow it over in the fall, then again in the spring. And early, before the soil loosens up. Because once wheatgrass takes hold, afterward nothing can stop it. It'll eat up the grain and eat up the land. We'd need to borrow a plow with a deep share from someone and dig that sickness out by the roots. Then go over it with the harrow. But even the harrow won't get rid of all of it. After the harrow we'll all have to go and pick it out by hand. Then we'd lay down manure and leave it awhile. Plow it over again. And then we could plant lupin."

"For the love of God!" exclaimed mother. "How much do you think that land's going to give you! And what do you need lupin for if you already have manure!"

"Well, did the bastard ever even muck his fields? The land's starved to death, if we get a drought it'll be like walking over dry bones out there."

"Never mind lupin." Mother refused to be convinced. "You should sow rye right away, or wheat, put some potatoes and cabbage in there!"

"I'm telling you, lupin!" said father, getting annoyed. He stood up from his chair and walked to and fro across the room, richer by those two acres of Kaczocha's. "Dammit, she's going to tell me what to do with land. All you think about is what's on the surface. But land is what's underneath as well. There's nothing you can do about wheatgrass if you don't get it out by the roots."

"Though for a plow with a deep share we'd need another horse, daddy," Stasiek put in. "One horse wouldn't be enough."

"That's a good point." Father's eyes lit up with admiration for Stasiek. "Good you mentioned it, Stasiek. We could maybe borrow Kuśmierek's. He could borrow ours afterward. Or we could help him out at harvesttime."

"I'm not helping with anyone else's harvest!" Antek burst out. "Ours is work enough for me! I'm not gonna be someone else's farmhand."

"Just the once," said father good-naturedly. "It won't do you any harm. No one's going to lend us their horse for free. If you don't want to mow you could help with the binding. We're not always only going to have one horse. If we get two extra acres we should think about getting another horse as well. There's plenty of people have less land and they've got two horses. We'd find the money."

"And where would we do that exactly?" asked mother, bridling up. "Our bedsheets are one patch on another and we can't afford new. Antek needs a new jacket, his elbows are poking out. Stasiek's shoes are falling apart. Plus, I'd rather have another cow than another horse. At least that way we'd have more milk."

"Another cow we can rear from a calf. A horse, we need to buy. We'll never be able to work all that land with just the one. We won't borrow any more – just this once. Do you know what it means to have two horses in farmwork?" Father was completely lost in his fantasies by now. "All you'll need to do is crack the whip and they'll be off! It'll make no odds whether the plowshare's deep or they're going uphill. And when you bring in the crop you can stack three layers of sheaves in the wagon. Or on your way to market, you'll pass everyone, leave them in a cloud of dust. When you get invited to a wedding, if you go there with two horses you'll be like a proper lady. With one horse it'd be like going in clothes with holes in them. Because on the other side of the shaft it's like there's a hole there. Having two horses is like having two healthy arms. With one it's like you've got one healthy arm and the other one's withered, or you lost it in the war."

"Let's buy a chestnut mare, daddy!" Stasiek shouted, all excited.

"Shut up, you little twit!" Antek suddenly went for Stasiek. "Don't listen to him, father. Everyone in the village has a chestnut mare. We should buy a stallion – a black one! A black stallion, that's a proper horse."

"The thing is, son, a mare's better for farmwork," father explained to Antek. "More manageable. It won't balk, however much you put on the wagon it'll pull it. However tired it is. With a stallion, once it gets an idea in its head you can beat it dead, it'll turn your wagon over but it won't budge an inch. Plus, with a mare you can raise a foal."

"But a stallion would go like the devil, father. Especially a black one." Antek had gotten all excited too. "You put the whip to him and he'd go like the wind. We could call him Lucifer."

"Jesus and Mary!" objected mother. "Calling a horse Lucifer! And our horse too. What are you thinking, Antek?"

"A mare, dad!" Stasiek kept on. "We'd have a little foal."

"A stallion!" insisted Antek, he was all worked up. "Otherwise I won't lift a finger! You can do the harvest and the potato lifting on your own. I'll leave the village!"

"A mare, dad." Stasiek was almost in tears. But all of a sudden mother bursts out:

"Have you all gone completely crazy? Mares and stallions! I have to scrimp and save just to buy salt and lamp oil, otherwise you'd all be sitting in the dark eating unsalted food. For goodness' sake, I just brought you the last loaf of bread! We're running out of flour! There's barely any potatoes left! And you're all set to call a horse Lucifer! For the love of God! That Lucifer must've gotten into you! Tell them, Szymek, you're more sensible than that! Why aren't you saying anything?"

The reason I wasn't saying anything was so father wouldn't start in again about the mare I had when I was in the resistance. One time I'd made the mistake of boasting to him about it, and ever since then he wouldn't let it go.

"You should have brought it home! At least you'd have had something from all that soldiering."

I couldn't convince him it wouldn't have been any use for farmwork. Besides, the animal died on me, how was I supposed to bring it home?

"Because you didn't look after it properly, dammit. Why would you take a creature like that into the line of fire. As for farmwork, we could've trained it. To begin with she could be harnessed to an empty wagon. You'd have to wrap the shaft in rags so it wouldn't rub against her. Or we could borrow the priest's chaise. She could pull that for a bit. Then she could be harnessed along with our bay. He's old, he wouldn't let her get carried away. Then we'd harness her to the harrow so the work wouldn't be too hard to begin with. If she bucked you'd give her a lash once or twice. And you'd see, after that she'd be just fine with the plow."

He'd have put anything to work on the farm. But the first time I got on her back I was afraid she'd collapse under me. Her legs were half as long again as your regular horse. Her muzzle was small and slim, and she had a long neck like a swan. When she walked, however rutted the road was, or whether she was walking over fields or tree roots or in the woods, you never felt anything except a slight swaying, like you were riding on a cloud, or on cushions in a fine carriage, or when a baby's rocked by its mother in the cradle.

They gave us the horse at one of the manor houses, along with a saddle and a sword, because they wanted to help out in the war but they didn't have any sons, only daughters. And what can daughters do in a war? They dressed our wounds and washed our ragged clothes, they played the piano for us a bit, had a laugh with us, and then when we were leaving they ran out after us into the courtyard and started crying. I must admit it's nice to be going away when someone's weeping for you and waving a white handkerchief wet with tears, and you're on horseback with a sword at your side. I felt like that uhlan from the picture on the firemen's calendar. All that was missing was for me to say, Don't cry, I'll be back to marry you.

The squire himself led the mare out and said:

"I chose the best horse from my stables. Let it serve its country."

I looked at the mare and I had the feeling I'd seen her somewhere before. I went up to her and patted her on the face. She tossed her head and whinnied.

"Easy there." I took hold of her fetlock. It was no thicker than my wrist, and it rose straight all the way to the knee. I'd often dreamed of taking a ride on a horse like that, instead of it always being the horse pulling the wagon, pulling the plow, the harrow, the lister. The horse with its head bowed to the ground. The horse in its suffering. And the man standing over it with a whip.

When I was a kid I'd sometimes take our bay down to the river to water him. I'd try to imagine I was riding a slim-legged steed fast as the wind, and I was galloping at breakneck speed through the village, across the fields, into the distance, so fast I could hardly breathe. But our bay was a long way from being swift as the wind. His legs were all cut up, his hooves were like millstones, his head hung down to the ground. And he would just plod along, because he was like any farmer's horse, he took farmer's steps and you couldn't make him go any faster either with your whip or with your heels. As well, most of the time he was worked so hard all he thought about was eating his fill and flopping down. He probably reckoned splashing about in the river was just another scourge for horses.

I often used to think and think about how at least one time I could turn him into a proper horse. Because maybe he used to be a proper horse once, before he came to work for us. You read in books about those kind of horses.

One time father wasn't at home, some neighbor had given him a ride to market in town. I whittled myself a lance out of a hazel stick. I stuffed a sack full of chaff and got the saddle ready. I made some spurs with wire from an old bucket handle and fixed them to my heels with straps. I led the bay out of the stable, stood him by the wagon, and from the wagon, because I couldn't have done it any other way, I put the saddle on his back, climbed on, and with one hand holding on to his mane, the other gripping my lance, I headed down to the village. First at a walk, like the horse wanted. A whole bunch of boys gathered, they followed behind me and started shouting and egging me on. Women, men, whoever happened to be on the road, they all stopped and stared like it was some kind of show.

"That's the Pietruszkas' bay. I'd never have recognized it if it wasn't for the crazy kid that's riding him."

"Where are you off to, seeing a young lady maybe?"

"Has he gone completely nuts or what?"

"It was just last spring he fell out of a tree. They've got their hands full with that one, the Pietruszkas."

"Because they don't smack their kids. You gotta smack them, otherwise they grow up bad."

"What the heck is that, are you the cavalry or what? Wait till your father comes back, he'll give you cavalry, you little pip-squeak!"

I was still riding at a walking pace, but in my mind the horse was stretched out like a blur he was going so fast, his hooves weren't even touching the ground. We were hurtling above the village, and everyone down below was tiny as ants. They were shouting something or other and waving their hands. Let them. I was bursting with pride.

"Come on now," I whispered in the bay's ear. "You show them."

And lightly at first, just to test, I jabbed his sides with the wire spurs. He seemed unsure whether to stop or carry on. No one had ever prodded him in the flanks like that before, how was he supposed to know what it meant. They'd always just use the whip on him. I poked him a bit harder, but he didn't change his pace, he just kept plodding along. His head was drooping like it always did over the shaft, and it was all I could do to reach his mane. I kicked him again so at least it'd make him shiver. Nothing. By now the boys were helping me out with louder and louder shouts:

"Faster, Szymek! Off you go! Charge! Hurrah!"

All right, if you don't want it that way we'll try something else. I started pricking him in the belly with my lance. But all he did was flick his tail like he was waving off a bee, and he kept on walking. He probably thought it was just a bee stinging him, and he was strong as anything when it came to bees. Bees, cart, whip, plow – that was a horse's life.

"Come on now. Faster. People are watching us," I began begging him. "I'll give you oats afterward, on their own, without any chaff. You can eat as much as you want. Just jump at least a bit off the ground." And I poked him again and again with my spurs. I could feel the spurs digging into my heels till they bled, like when your shoes are too tight on the way to church. But I prodded, prodded and begged in turn, because the embarrassment hurt ten times worse that the pain in my heels.

The boys had already begun to lose faith in me when they saw my spurs weren't working on the horse. They were still walking alongside but their shouts got quieter. They gave advice, they said I should sharpen the spurs maybe, or make some others out of thicker wire. Some of them offered to get the horse going with sticks.

Some of the grown-ups watching were starting to laugh and make fun of me:

"Stick a needle under his tail, make him run!"

"Or pour vodka in his mouth, that'd do the trick!"

"Don't waste the vodka, drink it yourself! The best thing for the horse'd be cowbane – that'd make him fly!"

"You have to spit in his ears or he won't obey you!"

"Stop jabbing him like that, you damn fool! His sides are bleeding! What's the horse ever done to you!"

All of a sudden the bay shook in an odd way, like it was coming from deep in his belly. He lifted his head, pricked up his ears, he even seemed brisker in the way he was walking. I thought he'd finally gotten it.

"All right," I whispered gently to him, and I gave him a soft nudge with the spurs. The horse suddenly kicked up his hindquarters so high that I was thrown forward from his back onto his neck. The moment his back legs dropped, he flung his front hooves high in the air and jerked his head. I grabbed on to his mane with both hands. My lance fell to the ground, and there was a burst of laughter from the road. The horse threw up its hindquarters again, higher even than the first time. I almost came tumbling down like I was falling out of a willow tree into the river. Luckily I managed to hold on to his neck. He lifted his front legs way off the ground again – he was nearly vertical this time. He opened his mouth, bared his teeth, and neighed like he was full of bottled-up rage that had been gathering for centuries, for all the peasants' horses that had been as meek as him. The saddle slipped from under my backside, my feet with their spurs flew out to the sides, and for a second I hung there in the air, clinging to his neck alone. He dropped back down, but not for long. He turned around, dropped his rear almost to the ground, then jerked it upward again, higher still. And he neighed, even louder than before. I could feel his guts churning inside him. Blood and rage and pain – it was like a dam had broken. The people on the road were shouting. The horse was leaping upward yet again, his front legs were clawing at the air as if he was trying to climb even higher, it was like he was trying to tear off a piece of the sky with his teeth. He was running amok, tossing his rear and his head in turn, he hardly seemed to come down to earth at all.

Suddenly, with a sort of furious tug he freed his neck from my grip and I fell to the ground like an apple falling from a tree. He kicked again to check I wasn't still stuck to him like a burr. Then once and twice he spun in a wide circle, scaring all the people. He gave a great whinny of relief. And off he ran like a storm, leaving nothing but a cloud of dust.

People ran up to me and started to help me up. I didn't want their help. But I couldn't straighten my back or turn my head to the side, and I could hardly see out of one eye. Plus, the spurs were covered in my blood and the horse's. On top of that, Michał had somehow shown up, even though he'd not been there when I led the horse out of the stable because he and mother had gone to the fields to do some weeding. He stood over me and burst into tears, as if I wasn't embarrassed enough as it was.

"Szymuś, are you all right? Szymuś, are you all right?" he sniveled. He even kneeled by my feet and tried to untie the bloody spurs. I was so angry I almost kicked him.

"Leave me alone. I'm fine. Stop blubbering."

Father came back from market and gave me a hiding and a good talking to, and it was only then we went off to the fields to look for the bay. He was feeding on someone's clover near Boleszyce. When he saw us he neighed and ran a couple of fields farther off. Father told me to stay back and hide behind a field boundary, and he went to try and get close on his own. But whenever he came near, the horse rose up on his hind legs and kicked at father with his hooves. In the end we brought the wagon. We took the horse-collar and a full feed bag. It was only then he let himself be harnessed to the wagon.

And so father probably imagined my chestnut mare would have been like the bay. I didn't ride her for long. We got ambushed and she was hit by machine-gun fire in the legs. I had to finish her off with a shot to the head.

We took the saddle off her. It was all decorated with brass studs. The stirrups looked like they were made of gold. And there was so much leather in it you could have resoled who knows how many pairs of shoes. It would have been a shame to leave it. I even thought about finding another chestnut mare for the saddle. We searched around in the villages. But all the horses there were in terrible shape, overworked and worn out. We might have found one at a manor house somewhere. But there didn't happen to be any manor houses on our way.

That saddle traveled with us almost the whole summer. Through the villages and woods and fields. No one knew what for. Everyone got sick of lugging it around. They had to be ordered. You carry it a bit. Now you. Now you. Now you take it off him. They cursed and complained. The hell do we need this for, sir? I wish I knew. We should have just dumped the damn thing somewhere so someone would find it. But what if the wrong person found it? And so on. Sometimes I'd rest my head on it. Sometimes I'd sit on it and think for a bit. Because thinking's different in a saddle like that than on a tree stump or on the grass. In the end a farmer came along the road and we threw the saddle in his wagon. Maybe you'll find a use for it, if not now then after the war. In return, if we find ourselves in these parts again we'll come by for some sour milk.

Likewise, I never did much fighting with the sword. I mean, what can you do with a sword in the woods – cut branches? The squire had said his great-grandfather had thrashed the Turks with it. That may have been the truth, because whenever you wanted to take it out of its scabbard, one man would have to hold it between his knees while the other one pulled with all his strength to get it out, it was so rusty. Out of respect for the squire I wanted to at least cut one of the bastards' heads off or chop off an arm, so the squire would have something to be pleased about, so he could say the sword had fought for its country during his lifetime as well. But they were always too far off and you could only reach them with bullets. I just took it out a couple of times so it could tell me about the Turks. But it was iron after all, and when you ask iron a question it doesn't answer. Then once in a while I'd do the present arms with it when we were burying one of our own. But when the chestnut mare fell I wasn't really able to keep walking with the sword, it kept rubbing against my boot. I thought to myself, maybe you were good against the Turks, but in this war you won't be doing any cutting or slicing. If all I ever do is present arms when someone's being buried, I'll end up burying the lot of them. So I hung it on a tree in the woods. It could be dangling there to this day for all I know.

But father didn't hold the sword against me, because what use is a sword on a farm.

"They fought the Turks, you say? That would have been for our faith. You should have taken it to a church, it could have hung there instead of on a tree."

But the chestnut mare and the saddle, he couldn't stop thinking about them. With the mare at least I had the excuse that they'd killed her. But the saddle hadn't been killed.

"Do you know how much a saddle like that is worth? All that leather and studs, and you said the stirrups were gold. You could have bought any amount of land. To have a saddle like that. But you're not interested in land – all you care about is girls and dancing and fighting. You can't spend your whole life gallivanting around the countryside playing your harmonica. You sure lucked out with that war – anything to get out of working."

"I wouldn't exactly say I lucked out, father. We worked ourselves into the ground, we gave our blood as well."

"Fine, but what am I supposed to do when it comes time to divide up the farm among you all?"

"You don't need to give me any share. I'm going away," I'd snap back at him when he really got on my nerves.

The truth was, I'd thought about doing that right after I came back from the resistance. I wasn't drawn to the land, and after those couple years of freedom I really couldn't see myself plowing or mowing. I even regretted coming back. I should have done what quite a few of the guys did and gone straight into the army or to the city, anywhere so long as it was far away. But not going back home after the whole thing to see father, mother, my brothers, the village, it would have been like the war hadn't finished at all, with its filth and lice and sleepless nights and killing. Besides, I was thinking I'd stay a month or two, catch up on my sleep, forget what needs to be forgotten, rest up, and then head out, instead of leaving right off the bat.

But I'd barely crossed the threshold and kissed everyone hello and sat down, when right away father starts in with his, we've been watching and watching for you, we didn't think you'd come back, and here spring's right around the corner and there'll be plowing and sowing to get done. I didn't say a word, I pulled off my tall boots, mother poured water into a basin and she didn't say anything either, she didn't even ask, how was it there? She just stood next to me, letting the tears roll down her cheeks. Then she kneeled down by the water, stirred it and started washing my feet.

And father went on and on. The plow would need to be hammered out because the share had gotten damaged on a rock. You'll need to find another blacksmith to take the horse to, because the Siudaks' smithy was blown up by a shell and now there's no one in the village that can shoe horses, but maybe there'll be someone in another village. One shoe's completely fallen off and the other ones are worn down to the hoof. When he walks he slips around like he was on a sledge. There was so much fighting around here we didn't even have time to muck out the pig sheds. But we should at least take some manure out to put down on the potatoes, and it needs to be done while the frosts last, because once the earth gets wet you won't be able to drive the wagon onto the field. It doesn't matter if the manure gets frozen, it can just lie there. There's no need to plow the fields right after you've mucked them. And look up there – the ceiling's leaking. It can't just be whitewashed, the plaster'll need to be scraped off. There's a hole in the thatch from a piece of shrapnel. Whenever it rains your mother has to put a bucket under it. If we can rustle up a ladder from somewhere you could shin up and fix it. And we lost our table. We'd stay down in the cellar, so anyone could do whatever they wanted up here. They took stuff for firewood, not just tables but doors, wagons, barns. They cut down all the orchards. They needed the wood to build potato clamps. Now people are going around looking for what's theirs. Maybe you could go look as well. You've got a decent pair of boots. Course, we can eat in our laps just as well, but not having a table in the house, it's kind of like the middle is missing. Or maybe you'll find something else. These days anything'll come in handy. That was quite a war. And it hung around in these parts for the longest time. It owes us something back, instead of just bringing us bad luck. Our pig sheds burned down. Did you see? A shell hit them, they caught fire and that was the end of them. At least we got the animals out in time. Stasiek and Antek took turns minding them. The wind was blowing in the other direction, thank God, otherwise the barn and the house would have gone up and we'd be sleeping under the stars. The damn dog got loose from his chain and ran off. On a farm not having a dog is like not having an arm. You have to keep your ears pricked the whole time so thieves won't sneak up on you. When he was still here he'd bark and run them off. Or at least wake you up if he couldn't see to them himself. You could ask around if someone's bitch has had puppies. Dogs, they don't care if it's wartime or no, the damn things still go around mating. The Lord alone knows what we've been through here. We stuck windows together from little pieces, then we had to board them up. What are you sitting there thinking for? You're only just back and already you're thinking."

"I don't know, maybe I'll go away?"

"Where to?" Father was stopped in his tracks.

"To the army maybe?"

"Have you not had enough of soldiering?"

"The war's not over yet, father. And I was made lieutenant."

"By who?"

"It was in the woods."

"That doesn't count, being made an officer in the woods. That's not a proper promotion. I mean, making a farmer an officer. Farmers are made to work the land and nothing else. This is your place."

"What am I supposed to do here?" I said, losing my temper, because it all seemed somehow foreign to me. The house. Father. And what he was saying.

"What do you mean?!" Father's voice trembled like he was about to get mad, or burst out crying. "Are we short of work here? We barely know which way to turn first. We need to start from the beginning. But go! Go! All of you, go! Let the land die!"

And father wouldn't have kept me back no matter what. Except they'd just opened the school, and Stasiek's shoes had fallen apart and he didn't have anything to wear on his feet. Outside, the boys would whistle and call, are you coming, Stasiek? It's late! And Stasiek would be sitting there in straw slippers, crying. And it was seventh grade, it would have been a pity if he hadn't gone back and finished. True, he was kind of in seventh grade during the war. But what could he learn at a school in an occupied country? He'd forgotten everything. I asked him who the first king of Poland was, and he didn't know. He didn't know who the king of the peasants was, and he thought Kościuszko was a king.

So I headed for the fields one day thinking I might find him some boots. People said there were bodies everywhere. So there had to be boots also. There was no point being squeamish. Is a dead person any worse than a living one? At one time he was alive as well, and now he's dead, just like the people that are alive now are also going to be dead in their turn. Though it's a bit rude taking things off a dead body, you can't ask them is it all right if I take your boots, since you don't need them yourself. But if they were only going to rot away, it'd be better if Stasiek wore them to school, and if the dead guy knew he might even be glad someone else was still using his boots.

There was a good number of them, Russkies as well as Germans. But none of them had boots on. I plodded around the entire day, and I only found one with his boots still on. I was all set to congratulate myself, I even said "*zdravstvuytye*" to him, because he was Russian. But when I got closer I saw there were holes in the soles and the heel on the left boot was completely missing. On top of that, he was barely older than our Stasiek. He lay face upward, his mouth open, as if some word had frozen in it, maybe "mama." I pulled his blanket out from behind his back and covered him up so at least the wind wouldn't blow in his face.

Some of them were lying in piles of two or three, like they'd been clinging to each other for warmth. Some looked as if they'd only fallen asleep, as if they'd gotten tired of the war the way you get tired at harvesttime, and they'd slipped their boots off to ease their feet. Everyone knows that war is worst of all on the legs and feet. Many a time, from the waist up you'd be raring to fight but your feet wouldn't budge. You'd be shouting hurrah, but your legs had no life in them. And many a time the war would be won not so much by bullets as by feet. Because war and feet are like half sisters.

When I was at war we didn't do a whole lot of fighting. Instead, we just walked and walked, and if we went in the wrong direction we'd walked in vain. And you didn't even hope for the end of the war so much as for a chance to take your boots off, even for a moment, and cool your feet in a stream.

The bodies that still had socks or footcloths maybe didn't feel the cold so much. But the ones with completely bare feet, it hurt to even look at them. One time I was made to walk across snow barefoot and I know how painful it is. You could read from those bare feet like from a book. They were swollen from the frost, cracked till they bled, and rubbed sore from marching and from the boots. They were blue and dead. Though living feet also, you could read all sorts of sufferings from them, even more than from a person's eyes, their face, or their words or their tears.

With some bodies the snow had covered their legs and all you could see were toes poking out of a snowdrift. Other ones were lying on their bellies with their bare heels jabbing at the sky. Or they'd be sticking out of the snow from the waist up, or from their belly button or their private parts, while their legs would be growing deep down in the snow like the roots of their body.

I found one under a sloe bush. He was some kind of officer – his epaulettes were all decorated with gold braid – so he ought to have had decent boots as well. Except his legs had been blown off at the knees, and it wasn't even right to wish I could have had those boots, even though they'd probably been made of chamois leather, with stiffeners and pointed toes. All I did was pick a few sloes from over his head, because sloes taste best when they're frozen.

Another one I found, I thought he was still alive. He was sitting outside a potato clamp leaning against his pack, his rifle in his lap, helmet on and playing his harmonica. I even thought I recognized the tune. But when I leaned over him I saw the harmonica was covered in dried blood, like he'd been blowing blood instead of air. He didn't have any boots on either. Though if he had, I still wouldn't have taken them. How could I do that – there he was playing the harmonica, and I come along and take his boots instead of listening? I used to play myself and I know, when you're playing you get so carried away, someone could even steal your body and you wouldn't notice, because at moments like that you're pure spirit. There were times I could barely straighten my back from work but the moment I came home from the fields, instead of flopping down and sleeping, I'd go out in front of the house and play. Often the lights would go out in the village and the dogs would be chasing bitches, and I'd just play on and on.

The snow was trampled down everywhere and there was a path to each corpse. You could tell a lot of people had been there before me, like mushroom pickers in the woods, from all the local villages.

I even met a guy I knew from Łoziny. Łoziny is two and a half miles from our village and the front passed through there as well just as bad as here, and he'd come all the way from there.

"A decent greatcoat's what I'm mostly after," he said. "But everything's all cut up from the shrapnel, either that or it's German."

"You haven't seen any boots, have you?" I asked.

"Boots? You're wearing boots. Nice tall ones too."

"It's not for me, it's for my brother. He hasn't got any shoes to wear for school."

"You're a bit late for that." He pulled out a bottle of moonshine. "Here, take a swig – you're blue with cold. If you're gonna go looking around here you need vodka. First off, you could freeze to death, and second, you might dream of these poor guys afterwards. Right when the front moved on, then there were boots. You could pick any kind you wanted, find a pair that fit. Wide ones, narrow ones, lace-ups, tall boots, ones with buckles. Black, yellow. Hobnailed or with rubber soles. There were even some fancy ones like yours. But now they've all been taken. You might still find some, but you'd have to go off the beaten track. And a shovel would be a good idea, 'cause some of them are buried up to their neck and you have to dig down to get to their boots. You need to get a move on though, because when the weather eases off they'll be burying the bodies. The village chairmen have announced it already. Maybe if you went up by the woods there'd still be some with their boots on. Thing is, though, there are mines up there. You might end up losing a leg or an arm instead of finding boots. Or even lose your life for a pair of boots, after you've made it through the war. Here, have another drink."

There was nothing for it, I lent Stasiek my officer's boots, because I mean he couldn't not go to school. School was like first communion. Everyone went. People who'd only finished second or third grade. People who'd never even started school before. People that couldn't read or write, bachelors, married guys, folks with kids. He looked like a stork in those boots, they almost came up over his knees. But who was interested in whether your boots were too big or too small, the important thing was they were in one piece. To begin with he walked around like he was on stilts, he even fell over a couple of times, but then he got used to them, he started walking in long strides without really bending his knees, and he looked pretty good, even though it's not that easy to walk in tall boots when they're the wrong size. I mean real officer's boots, of course. Because people say officer's boots whenever their shoes have any kind of uppers at all. Or any boots that an officer's wearing. But real officer's boots you can tell not from the uppers, not even from someone's rank. Real officer's boots have to be made of chamois, the toe caps and straps and stiffeners need to be leather that's hard as metal, and the boot has to be the exact same shape as your leg. And not just around the foot, but at the instep, the ankle, the calf, everywhere, like it was your own skin. You might have been walking around like you had two left feet your whole life, the Lord God himself might have decided that's how you're supposed to walk, but the moment you put on officer's boots it's like you'd been given new legs. Because it's not just that you're wearing footwear that goes all the way from your toes to your knees, also the straps hold your heel like it was in a vise, and the stiffeners do the same for your calves, and you have to walk the way the boots tell you to.

Kurosad, the guy in Oleśnica that made those boots for me, he measured each leg separately, and in different places. On the calf alone he took three measurements, by the ankle, in the middle, and under the knee. And he did it both on bare flesh and in breeches. And by the way, you won't find another shoemaker like Kurosad for love nor money. He made boots for "Eagle" that was my resistance name – and he wasn't the only one that knew who Eagle was. When you went into his shop you'd never know it was a shoemaker's – there was a carpet and armchairs and mirrors, and Kurosad behind the counter with his, how can I help you, sir. He only made boots for SS officers, resistance fighters, and the gentry. And when it came to officer's boots, he had no equal. When I tried them on, stood in front of the mirror and clicked the heels, I felt as if even dying in those boots would be a different kind of death than dying in ordinary shoes or barefoot. And Kurosad was licking his lips he was so pleased:

"All you need now is a pair of spurs and it'll be: Mount up! mount up!"

I stayed in every morning with my feet in the straw slippers, waiting for Stasiek to come home from school and give me my boots back. It was only in the afternoon I could go down to the village. In the mornings I thought I'd go nuts with boredom. I couldn't even watch the road from the window because the window was forever iced up and you had to breathe a hole in the ice to see out at all. Though father didn't let me get too bored. He'd come right in with the horse-collar.

"If you're just going to be sitting around doing nothing you can mend this."

This, then that, then something else. Every day it was the same thing. I even got kind of depressed, to the point where I didn't feel like talking to anyone. Someone would come by and ask, so how was it in the resistance, but I didn't even feel like talking about the resistance, and father would speak for me:

"Well, since he came back he's just been thinking and thinking. But thinking's no good. I mean, you're not going to think something up unless you actually do it. People thought and thought, and what did they come up with? The world's still the way it was, and all thinking does is make you want to think more and do less."

There were times all I wanted to do was jump up, slam the door, and head out wherever. But how could I go without anything on my feet? So in the end I started cutting the farmers' hair and shaving them. Luckily, from the resistance I'd brought home my razor, my scissors and brush and shaving cream, and I started cutting hair and giving shaves. Right after I came back I cut father's hair and Antek's and Stasiek's, because their hair was so long they looked like sheep, and I did a pretty decent job of it. Then one day I met Bartosz down in the village. He was over seventy, but he was a soldier to the marrow of his bones, he'd served way back in the tsar's army, and he always wore a crew cut. But this time I see his hair's so long he looks like Saint Joseph, and he's scratching away at it.

"I didn't know you, Bartosz," I say.

"I'm not surprised. I used to cut my hair the army way. Now look at me."

"What are you scratching it for?"

"Lice, son, lice. The blasted things bite so much they won't let you sleep, they won't let you live. They bite when you're praying. But in a mop of hair like this, of course they're going to bite. Plus our house burned down and we're sleeping with the cattle in the shed. Maybe you could cut my hair for me, I'd give you a rooster?"

I felt sorry for the man. I used to like listening to his army stories, he served with the heavy cavalry all the way over in the Caucasus.

"Come by tomorrow morning," I said. "I'm at home then, because Stasiek wears my boots to school. Just bring a cloth I can wrap around you."

I was never taught how to cut hair, but it's no big deal. You can do harder things than that without being taught. Besides, the important thing wasn't how you looked but feeling comfortable. If anyone doubted that, they could have told by looking at Bartosz what a relief it was to him. His eyes were brighter, he breathed more easily, and he held himself straight as a ramrod, like I'd taken twenty years off him. He looked at himself in a piece of mirror and he was so pleased his old soldier's blood stirred in him.

"You've done a fine thing, young man. You weren't in the resistance for nothing, I see. Anyone that can succeed at being a soldier can succeed at anything."

Afterward one guy or another who saw Bartosz would come, and anyone that bumped into me in the village, then they started coming by of their own accord. It wasn't surprising really, every farm had lost something to fire, if it wasn't the house it was the barn or the cattle sheds. If their horses hadn't been requisitioned they'd been killed. The cows' udders would dry up from lack of feed. In the fields there were mines. Anyone would have been glad to at least get rid of the shock of hair they'd grown, to feel freer. But there was no barber in the village. Under the occupation there'd been one, an newcomer. Jan Basiak they called him. He told people he'd been resettled, and he seemed to fit in. He made a decent living, rented a room at Madej's place on the side next to the road and hung up a sign: Jan Basiak, Ladies' and Gentlemen's Hairdresser, Permanent Waves, Water Waves. All the women in the village went crazy, the young girls, the married women, the ones with small children – everyone. They cut off their braids and they all started getting those perms.

The first one was the Siudaks' Gabrysia. She had braids like ropes of wheat straw, but with her new hairdo she looked like a scarecrow and right away she started sleeping with a German corporal from the police station. One time Siudak beat her, in fact he cut her till she bled, because he used a whip handle, so she told her corporal and the corporal beat Siudak up. Siudak couldn't get out of bed for a month or more. On top of that he had to pay a fine for being disorderly. Ever since then he was scared of Gabrysia like she was the devil himself, though she was his own daughter. She had them all wrapped around her little finger.

Once she started sleeping with the corporal she even learned to be picky, she got as finicky as a fine lady though she was just a regular girl. She made them buy her a fur coat and knee-length boots, and Siudak had to sell a cow to pay for it. As for the hairdresser, she could spend half the day there.

The thing that upset people even more than the corporal was the fact she had her hair washed at the hairdresser's. Whoever heard of such a thing – a man washing a woman's hair. The hairdresser fussed around her like he was dancing on eggshells, he'd do anything he could to satisfy her and it was always yes, Miss Gabryjela, no, Miss Gabryjela. In the end, as well as doing all those perms he became an informer. When the front got close, all of a sudden he disappeared overnight. And Gabrysia, she left for the West and married some official over there. She came back one year to visit her mother and father's graves, but no one mentioned what she'd done when she was younger. What was there to mention? It was a different world, a different village; more than half the people from those times were in the cemetery. They were just lying there, what did they care about Gabrysia. From the other world it didn't mean a thing that at one time, in this world, some Gabrysia used to sleep with a German corporal.

Me too, when I go to the cemetery I sometimes think it's strange so many people are buried there that back then I shaved and cut their hair, and now they don't remember anymore. Stanisław Kiciński. When he sat down and I told him, don't move, he virtually turned to stone. Later I couldn't turn his head either to the left or right. I had to squat down, twist and turn one way and the other. I asked him, I got annoyed with him, just turn a bit Stanisław or I won't be able to finish cutting your hair. See, look over at that apostle at the Last Supper. The third one from Jesus's left. Come on, look. Though on the other hand, when he finally stood up and passed his hand over his head, he said:

"It's like a fellow was born a second time. God bless you, Szymuś."

"Here, take a look in the mirror."

"I don't need to look, I can feel it."

Or Wincenty Mitręga, may he rest in peace. He looked at himself in that scrap of mirror, ran out the house without a word, then a short while later he came back with a milk can full of moonshine.

"I was going to buy myself some new pants and a new dress for the old lady, but have a drink, lads, because that goddam war finally finished today. Your health, Szymek!" He tipped the can back and took the longest swig you ever saw. When he finally set it aside he didn't even have the strength to pass it to the next person, he just hunkered down on the stoop and fell asleep.

There were days so many men came by that Stasiek would get back from school and I still hadn't finished. They'd sit around the place wherever they could, on the beds, on the doorstep, some would stand or squat by the wall. They'd smoke till the room was black with smoke. Mother would complain she couldn't breathe, and every so often she'd air the place out. But father was in seventh heaven, because everyone would give him a smoke and he could at least have his fill of cigarettes. I brought two logs and laid down a board to make a bench, because people even started coming from other villages.

To begin with my hands were a bit stiff when I worked. But anyone sitting there with hair that hadn't been cut for months, that was dirty and sometimes full of lice, their mind was on other things and so what did they care about my hands. They could only feel themselves. Some folks would shudder like a horse being stung by a bee when I'd pass the comb through their hair. Some of them, the skin on their heads would stretch tight as sheet metal. Some of them shut their eyes as hard as they could. Or they'd grip the chair with both hands like I was about to cut their head off, not their hair. Or they'd clam up and not say a single word the whole time, till it was over and they could relax. Some of them even let other people in line go ahead of them just to put off the moment. You'd have been forgiven for thinking I was baptizing them, not cutting their hair.

I got better and better at it from one head to the next. I stopped doing everyone the same, instead I'd ask do you want it longer, shorter, to the side or to the back. I learned to do shading. I'd shave necks till they shone. And I did sideburns in two different ways, straight and angled.

Later I bought an electric razor from a Russian guy for a half-gallon of moonshine. He'd worked as a barber as well, but the war was over and he was heading home. Another time a traveling saleswoman sold me a bottle of cologne, and after that I'd ask, splash of cologne? Naturally cologne was more expensive, so not everyone wanted it. I bought a sheet and mother made me cloths to put around people's necks. I was going great guns. All I needed was to hang out a sign. And as I worked I'd tell stories about the resistance, so no one got bored even if they had to wait the whole morning.

I probably would have stuck with being a barber, because winter passed and spring came, Stasiek gave me the boots back since he could go to school barefoot now, but I was still cutting people's hair and giving shaves. I even thought about renting the room at Madej's that Basiak had used. Luckily Madej's place survived the war except for the roof got damaged and the windows were broken. But Madej had already more or less repaired it. Maybe one day I'd learn how to do perms. Szymon Pietruszka, permanent waves, water waves. No worse than Jan Basiak. Hairdressing's a decent trade, and it's a whole lot easier than working the land. At the most I'd just go take a course. Or I might not even have to do that. The war had done away with a good number of hairdressers as well. In town there used to be three of them and now only one was left.

Plus, harvesttime was getting close. And harvesttime was a curse. From dawn till night you worked like an animal. Your head's pounding from the mowing, your eyes are blinded by sweat. Instead of crossing the sky, the sun just keeps moving to and fro across your back, all the time from when it rises in the east till when it sets in the west. It's like its claws were sunk into your skin. Because it's not even the sun, the sun is what shines over the river and the meadow and in the reeds, this thing is a huge bright bird that's got it in for you. The moment you feel like straightening up a bit, it jabs you in the back of the head with its beak. Like it was reminding you your life belongs down below, not up above, that your life is this eternal unmown field that you keep moving across, swinging your scythe. And you don't even know if you'll ever finish mowing it. You'll only be done when death takes you.

It was the same when I went to war, I was glad to be missing the harvest because it had just begun. Father had gone out into the fields with his scythe at the crack of dawn, I was supposed to follow with mine and we were going to mow, the two of us. It was right then Gunia brought me the letter with my call-up. I was so pleased, I forgot to take the scythe with me, I just grabbed the letter and ran out to the field to tell father:

"It's war, father."

Father looks at me surprised and says:

"Where's your scythe? You were supposed to bring your scythe."

"I just said, it's war." I waved the letter in front of him. "Read this."

"I don't need to read anything. If there was a war we'd be hearing it. Can you hear anything?" He tipped his head back as if he was listening, but the only sound was larks singing in the sky. "There's nothing but larks. It's probably just talk. I mean, how long has it been since the last war? And there's going to be another one? What are they fighting about? When there's a war, first there has to be a sign in the sky. When the last one started there was a burning cross up there in the south at night. Come on, get to work. You can mow with my scythe, I'll bind the sheaves."

He pushed the scythe into my hands, then he laid out some straw rope, gathered an armful of crop, held it down with his knee, tied it up, and the sheaf was ready. It was a good-sized one as well, because father liked his sheaves to be man-sized.

"What are you still standing there for? Job needs finishing."

He bound a second sheaf and a third. Then all of a sudden it was like he'd gotten exhausted, he sat himself down on one of the sheaves and fell to thinking. He thought and thought, he could've tied a good few sheaves more in that time, and it was only when he'd sat through eight or nine sheaves that he said:

"So you're going to go?"

"I think I have to." I sat down next to him on another sheaf. "Everyone's going. The Dudas' Franek, Kasperek, Jędrek Niezgódka, other guys."

"Maybe you could be the only one not to go. When it's war you don't see the one man, just the war. Plus, once they shave your heads and stick you in uniform you'll all look like sons of the same mother. You'll all get mixed up like leaves, like trees, no one'll be able to tell you apart."

He lost himself in thought again. The sun was climbing into the sky and getting hotter and hotter. The cool of night was gone from the crop and it was warming up too. A stork flew across the sky.

"Oh look, a stork," I said for the sake of saying something.

"Who's going to do the work around here," he said, "before Antek and Stasiek grow up? Four sons and no help. I mean, we might at least finish the harvest, there's a whole lot still needs doing. Maybe it's not our war, this one?"

"Whose war could it be?"

"What do we have to fight about? We plow and plant and mow, are we in anyone's way? War won't change the world. People'll just go off and kill each other, then afterwards it'll be the same as it was before. And as usual it'll be us country folks that do most of the dying. And nobody will even remember that we fought, or why. Because when country folks die they don't leave monuments and books behind, only tears. They rot in the land, and even the land doesn't remember them. If the land was going to remember everyone it would have to stop giving birth to new life. But the land's job is to give birth."

"Maybe that's what the war is about, father, so the land can give birth. If that's what it's about then it *is* our war."

"The land gives birth, war or no war. Only God can stop it giving birth."

"Even Romcia the thief is going," I said. "He ran over to make confession first thing this morning. Now he's drinking at the pub. He says, I'm drinking my own tears, pal, no one can stop me doing that. But at night he's gonna go rob someone one last time. He says he couldn't go killing people if he was all holy."

I thought father would get worried about Romcia and say:

"Maybe it'll be us he robs? You should've sounded him out a bit more."

But he didn't pay any attention, he just said:

"What if you get killed? My hands and your mother's, that's not enough for all this land!" He threw his arms open wide like we had fields all the way to the horizon, when there was barely one acre where we were.

"Morning!" someone called from the road. It was Ginger Walek with his scythe over his shoulder. "Father and son together, a sight for sore eyes! Your rye's looking good."

"God bless you."

"I won't get killed. I won't, father. Romcia's more likely to get killed. He says it's going to be his last thieving, after that he's going straight."

Father calmed down a bit, he lowered his eyes from the fields and looked at his feet. He plucked an ear of rye, crushed it against his hand, blew away the chaff, and stared at the glittering grain as if he was telling the future in his mind, even numbers for good luck, odd numbers for bad.

"Even if they don't kill you, who knows how long this war could last. The other one went on four years."

"That was when we had a tsar, this one'll be shorter. We'll win and we'll come back. There's a whole ton of men going, from our village, from others. Back then, who wanted to fight for the tsar. He was foreign, no one cared one way or the other about him."

"Foreign he might have been, but you could draw lots and have a chance of staying home. If you were well off you could even pay for someone else to go in your place. And if some guy was really stubborn about it, even the draw couldn't make him go. Before the Cossacks came for him he'd already be hanging from a tree. He was damned by the church but at least he got to stay among his own. Though those kind of men, they weren't in any hurry either to go to war or to do much of anything else. Or they'd put their leg under the wheel of a wagon and let it run them over, and afterwards, even though they limped, they were limping on their own land, not all around the world. Or they'd put their eye out, because the army wouldn't take a one-eyed man. When you're at home you can see just as well with one eye as with two. Besides, what's to see, you know everything by heart, you can find anything you need in the darkest night. There's that saying, blind as a bat, but bats find their way around just fine. You can sleep just as well with one eye as two, you can cry just the same. Back then people obeyed their parents more than you all do these days. Or you just needed to lose your trigger finger. You'd cut it off and they'd not take you. You'd dress it with bread mixed with cobwebs, it would hurt a bit, then you'd say you lost it in the chaff-cutter when you were cutting chaff for the horses. There's many a farmer missing a finger to this day, and they never went to war, they just cut it off in the chaff-cutter. What's one finger out of ten. A tailor needs it to hold his needle and thread. A rich man, cause he has to keep counting his money. A priest when he has to point at sinners from the pulpit. But when you work the land you use your whole arm, up to the elbow, not just your fingers. One more or less, what's important is to want to work."

I remember one time, I'd not yet properly learned to mow, we were mowing rye, father was in front and I was behind him, and I deliberately hit the scythe against a rock and it broke the whole thing. But he didn't even get mad at me. He just looked at the notch in the blade and said:

"You've not quite got the trick. But one or two more harvests and you'll be there. I had trouble too at the beginning."

And it was always like that, even when I'd gotten the hang of it and we'd both be mowing, him in front and me behind, it was like he was always watching over me to make sure I didn't lose patience during the harvest.

"You don't have to cut a whole swath in a single swing! If you lived the way you're mowing you'd run out of steam halfway through your life. And you'd lose the will to work even sooner. Slow down a bit, we're just getting started."

Because with me the first swath was always angry, like I was getting my own back. I'd often send the earth flying from under the scythe. And it'd be as wide as I could swing my arms. And though I was strong as a horse in those days, by the second swath the anger and spite had gone, by the third my eyes were filled with sweat, and by the next one I had to stop for a moment and sharpen up the blade with the whetstone so I could catch my breath. Because you can't keep mowing for long out of anger and spite. To mow well you have to start like you were in the middle of a swath and finish as if you were just beginning. That was how father mowed. He wasn't a big man, and when it was a good year and the rye or the wheat had grown well it was as tall as him, but when he mowed it was like the field was moving him along of its own accord, evenly, step by step. And he'd finish the whole field like that, step by step, evenly. And whole harvests the same way. It looked like it wasn't him swinging the scythe through the rye or the wheat, the scythe itself was moving his shoulders back and forth, and he was only letting it.

Even now, when I'm mowing I sometimes feel that I'm following behind him. And I even compare myself, whether I'm mowing like he did when he was alive. Is the field moving me along the same way, evenly, step after step. Is the scythe swinging my arms back and forth, and I'm just allowing it to. But I don't think I'll ever match him. You have to be a born mower to mow like him. I don't know if Michał or Antek or Stasiek would have matched him either, though they were better sons than me. But it's hard to say what would have been.

Michał was the smartest of the four of us and he was supposed to go into the priesthood, he left the village before he'd done a whole lot of mowing. Though before the war he'd come home almost every harvesttime to help out. Except that father usually wouldn't let him mow, instead he'd have him do the raking or sweep up the loose ears. Leave it be, Michał, what's the point in you mowing, you'll only get blisters on your hands. Szymek, he's another matter, he's built like a cart horse. He could mow with one arm if he felt like it. So Michał never even had a chance to learn to mow properly.

Antek was pretty good, he didn't mow as evenly as father yet, but it was like he moved the scythe even faster and drew it back even shorter. The thing was, though, he'd get mad at the slightest thing. It was enough for the crop not to be standing up straight, or he'd prick himself on a thistle. He never had the patience to get to the end of the swath in one go. He'd always have to take a break even if just for a minute, look around at the field and the sky, or go get a drink of water from the standpipe, because he was always too hot. But for whatever reason, father never hurried him up. The only thing he'd say occasionally was:

"Don't drink so much water, it'll take away your strength." Or when he heard from the sound Antek's scythe was making that it had gotten blunt, he'd tell him:

"Sharpen it up a bit."

This played into Antek's hands. Because even though he never knew by himself when the blade needed sharpening, he liked sharpening just as well as drinking water or staring at the field and the sky. He was better at sharpening than he was at mowing. The whetstone moved in his hand like he was whipping a cut branch, and sparks would fly from the scythe. Father's face would light up when Antek was honing his scythe. He'd act worried and warn him in a good-natured way:

"Don't let those sparks fall on the hay, Antek. We wouldn't have time to stomp them out. And other fields would go up after ours. Field boundaries don't mean a thing to fire, what's mine and what's yours."

Maybe Antek was pulling the wool over father's eyes with all the sharpening. Or father was waiting till Antek grew up and got as strong as he could, then he'd tell him if he'd gotten to be a better mower than me, or the other way around, and what kind of mower he was going to be.

For the while it was obvious the best mower one day would be Stasiek. The first time Stasiek picked up a scythe, right away he planted his feet apart like father did. He spat on his hands like father did. Just like father, he moved evenly, one step after another. He didn't take a break till he got to the end of the swath. And he was no taller than the rye.

Though what's the sense in wondering which one of us would have been the best mower. You'd have to live your life and then see. And there never was a harvest all four of us worked together. There's no telling how it would have been if one of us had been mowing right behind the next one, then the third and the fourth. Michał, Antek, Stasiek, me, and if we'd all mowed the rye or the wheat on the same day, at the same time, under the same sun. Father could have been the judge.

"What was my life even for," he'd sometimes complain. "Four sons, I thought when death comes I'd ask to be carried out onto the land and you'd all be standing there with your scythes ready to mow together. And I'd say, I've had a happy life. Thank you, God."

Because one Sunday afternoon Stasiek came home from the village and like Antek a few years back, he said he was leaving.

"Where to?" asked father. He thought maybe Stasiek was off to a dance in Bartoszyce or Przewłoka. Maybe he had a girl and he didn't know how else to say it.

"I'm going away," he said.

"You're going away as well?" Father sounded surprised, but he didn't fully believe it yet. "Away to where?"

"To Poland," Stasiek answered rudely, though he'd never spoken to father that way before. He always liked spending time with father, going places with him and talking with him.

"Poland," father repeated, like he couldn't quite figure out where it was.

"That's a big place. It's easy to get lost there if you've never been. How will you get back?"

"I'm never coming back."

"Never coming back?" Father was still calm. "So what are you going to do in this Poland of yours?"

"I'm going to build it." Stasiek's hackles were up.

"We were supposed to build new cattle sheds," said father, not giving up. "We already got nearly all the materials. The bricklayers are coming in."

"Never mind cattle sheds. These days Poland's more important. You should go read about it, father. There's an announcement on the firehouse wall. They talked about it on the radio as well. We've all signed up, the Tomalaks' Antek, Bronek Duda, me . . ."

Father didn't let Stasiek finish. He jumped up and ran to the door. He stood on the threshold, spread his arms, took hold of the door frame, and in a trembling voice he shouted:

"You're not going anywhere! I won't let you! I'll kill you before I let you go! I'd rather get sent to hell! I'd rather die than let you! Why I am being punished like this, God?"

Stasiek burst into tears. Mother was already in bed, she started snuffling as well. And father just stood there blocking the door with his arms, furious, his hair all messy, his face screwed up, shouting:

"I won't let you! I won't allow it! You were supposed to be a farmer! We were supposed to buy more land! God meant for you to stay! Your Poland is here. Nowhere else! Nowhere!"

His hands slowly began to slide down the door frame, though he seemed so angry he was about to rip it out of the wall. Maybe he'd bring the whole house down with it and bury his misfortune. His voice softened. The words came with more and more difficulty, it was like they were getting more helpless. He wasn't shouting now, just moaning. In the end he sank down on the threshold, lowered his gray head to his chest, and cried.

Mother dragged herself out of bed and slipped her skinny feet into her clogs. She tied her apron on and started busying about.

"You'll need a couple of new shirts. But don't wear one longer than a week or it'll be hard to wash. Maybe you could take your father's sleeveless jacket. Otherwise you'll get cold. Away from home a sweater would be better. But you've grown out of yours, and there are holes in the elbows. Or we could buy something for you and send it on. You'd just have to write and tell us where you are. Here, you can have Antek's old winter socks. They're perfectly fine, I'll just darn the heels for you. They might laugh at you if you wore footcloths. I'm giving you this little pillow so you'll have something to lay your head on. Maybe you should take half a loaf of bread? Your own bread is always your own. You never know what you'll get out there. Here's a couple heads of garlic. If you catch cold, chop it up fine and spread it on a slice of bread. And here's some onion, if you get hungry you can fry it up or just eat it raw with some bread. There's a piece of bacon fat in the pantry, you can take that too. We'll be fine. I ought to give you a pat of butter, but I haven't got anything to make it with, one cow's calving and the other one's not giving milk, we barely get enough to add cream to the soup. I'm giving you some sage in case you get the toothache. Here's horsetail for if you get a nosebleed, it'll stop it right away. Here's some linden flower. And chamomile for your throat. Make an infusion and gargle with it if it gets sore. We can't give you any money because we don't have any ourselves. Unless we borrowed some. Or Szymek, you give him some if you've got a few zlotys. We'll make it up to you. And here's a prayer book. Pray once in a while if things get bad for you. Always go to mass on Sunday. I'll pray for you here as well. Write to tell us how things are for you out there in the world. And come back when I die."

It was a good six months before he wrote. We were already thinking something had happened to him. Mother was so worried her health got even worse. Father was all dejected, he didn't have the will to do anything. When

Stasiek finally did write it was only a couple of sentences, that everything was fine, he was working and studying, how was mother's health, and that he'd visit soon though he didn't know exactly when. But he never did visit. He just sent a photograph. He looked gaunt and skinny, he was wearing a cap like a forage cap. He hardly looked like the old Stasiek at all. Mother had me wedge the picture in the frame of the Our Lady that hung over her bed, and she gazed at him as she faded from day to day.

Him and Antek, the two of them only came back for mother's funeral. And they left the same day, after the burial, because they didn't have time. And after that it was always the same. One of them or both of them would visit, but there was never time to sit and talk or ask them how things were, what they were up to, they were always in a hurry. And right away they'd start arguing with me about any little thing, that the table was still the same one from the war, that I'd not put a wooden floor in, even that the lightbulb was covered in fly droppings, one thing on top of another, as if their old home was somehow painful to them. Yet it was still their home.

It was the same when they came about the tomb. They shouted and protested, and I didn't say a thing. In the end I took the sacks they'd brought for the flour and went to the pantry to fill them. I didn't have anything to give them except for flour. Then they left.

I didn't know how to tell Chmiel that we'd be putting up a smaller tomb now. We'd already settled on eight places. Chmiel had measured it all and done the calculations. I'd even given him a down payment. I'd been holding off on the final decision just in case, till they wrote back and said yes. I didn't want to go ahead without their say-so. The tomb was for them as well. If they were going to be buried in it they had a right to decide. I only had to go and tell Chmiel they'd agreed.

Whether they say yes or no, they have to be reckoned with, I'd said to myself. They were good boys one time. Maybe the outside world had just gotten to them a bit. When they came they were wearing suits and overcoats and hats, it all looked brand-new. Stasiek even had an umbrella. Antek was wearing eyeglasses and he had a little leather case. It was no surprise they weren't in any hurry to die. But if not now, then maybe another time, or maybe when they got old. Because when people get old you can never tell. When death's staring you in the face even a college graduate becomes a person again, so does an engineer. At those times everything falls off life like leaves dropping from a tree in the fall, and you're left like a bare trunk. At those times you're not drawn to the outside world but back to the land where you were born and grew up, because that's your only place on this earth. In that land, even a tomb is like a home for you.

So I went and told Chmiel they'd agreed.

THE LAND

Sometimes I think to myself, what does the land actually care about me? What does it know about me? Does it even know I exist? Does it know how long I've traipsed around it? If you counted up all the steps together I might even have gone all the way around this world of ours. Or maybe I'd even have made it into the next world, and I'm still walking along. Over ridges and furrows and ruts, over stubble fields, in rain and cold and swelter, in agony, spring and summer and autumn, with scythe or plow. And for what?

On top of that, does it know how much you've quarreled over it, how much you've hated? To the point that you were amazed where all that hatred inside you came from. Did you enter the world with it already in you? And the hatred only later turned into the land?

In any case, before I was ever born, father had a law case with the Prażuchs over our field boundary. He didn't believe in earthly justice, but he came back from the field one time shaking with anger, saying:

"Whether there's any justice or no, that crook Prażuch needs to be taken to court. The land can't take it anymore."

What had happened was, Prażuch had yet again plowed over our field boundary. And so it began. One time father sued Prażuch, then Prażuch sued father, and so on in turn, depending on whose land happened not to be able to take it any longer. It went on for years, because the courts weren't exactly in any kind of hurry to make a final judgment. Judges have to earn a living too.

Maybe you couldn't even say who was in the wrong, maybe the Lord God himself couldn't have decided. Because when it comes to the land there aren't any guilty or innocent folks, only those that are wronged. And everyone knows what courts are like, it's all about being guilty or innocent. But that wasn't the right measure. And so the courts took their course, while father and Prażuch doled out their own justice. Where Prażuch would plow over a strip of our land in the spring, father would plow it back in the autumn, and add at least another half-furrow from Prażuch's field to make up for the wrong he'd suffered. That bandit shouldn't think he can get off scot-free.

Then one day, after yet another time in court that hadn't resolved a thing, father met Prażuch out in the fields. Father was harrowing his land, Prażuch was mucking his. Prażuch ups and says, when you need to sell that field to pay for the courts, I'll buy it off you. Wishful thinking, answers father, because if the courts don't finish you the Lord God will. One way or another you'll get what you deserve, and then maybe you'll finally drop dead, you crook. It turned into a terrible argument between the two of them, you could hear it way off, like two whole villages were at each other's throats, or two whole manor houses, or the sky and the land. Anyone who was out working the fields straightened up, stopped their plow or their harrow, stood for a moment, and looked around to see where the quarrel was. They argued so loud the larks vanished from the sky. And even the sky, that had been clear, clouded over and there were flashes of lightning in the distance.

In the end father had had enough, he ran up to Prażuch and landed him one with his whip. Without thinking Prażuch pushed his pitchfork at father. Father fell down, there was blood, and the other man stood over him, leaned on his pitchfork, and jeered:

"Who's dying now, you bastard? Who's getting what they deserve?"

Father was barely conscious, but he threatened him back:

"You just wait till my Szymek grows up, you crook."

And so when I did grow up there was nothing for it. One time I was plowing the same field, and Prażuch was in his field sowing wheat. A flock of crows landed on his field and mine, and they walked about pecking at things, the way crows do. All of a sudden the old guy bent down, grabbed a clod of earth, and chucked it, supposedly at the crows that were on his field. But the ones on mine flew up as well. That made me mad, because I like it when the crows follow behind me when I'm plowing. I stopped the horse and shouted:

"Leave the crows alone, you old fart! Scare them off your own land! Keep the hell away from mine!"

Not only did Prażuch keep throwing clods of earth at the crows, he also started cawing, caw! caw! caw!

"Shut it, or I'll shut it for you!"

But on he goes with his, caw! caw! caw!

I ran up to him and landed my fist right between his eyes. He flipped over and all the grain scattered from his canvas sheet. I kicked him where he lay on the ground.

"Who's getting what they deserve now?" I said. I went back and plowed half my field and he still couldn't even get up, he just lay there grunting and cursing. People even said I'd done something to his back, because he was stuck in bed almost till the spring.

Then autumn came again, and Antek was grazing the cows one day among the potato stalks, and Prażuch was plowing his land. And somehow or other one of the cows strayed onto his field. Antek ran over to drive it back. Prażuch left his plow and horse and set about Antek with his whip. He beat the kid so bad he had purple welts all over. Then he whipped the cow that had strayed. And as if that wasn't enough, he ran over onto our land and whipped the other cow, that hadn't done a damn thing to him. Antek came back home crying, it wasn't even close to midday, and the cows were flogged so bad their skin was covered in ridges.

That finally did it for me. I grabbed an ax and ran out into the fields, I was going to kill the old man and be done with it. After that I could rot in prison. But he saw me coming from far off, he quickly unhitched the horse from the plow, jumped on the horse, flicked the reins, and galloped off down the road by the mill toward his house. I ran after him, but his place was all bolted up. I started hammering at the door.

"Open up, you son of a bitch, I'm gonna kill you! Open up, you hear! This world's too small for the both of us!"

But I couldn't even hear the slightest peep from behind the door – it was like no one was there. And they all *were* there. I looked through the window, there was a tin crucifix standing in it. I could have smashed the window, but it somehow didn't seem right to clamber in over a crucifix. I just hacked the corner post of the house with my ax.

From that time on he avoided me like the plague. I never ran into him down in the village. Or at the store. And whenever I'd go into the fields, his land would already have been worked, like the devil himself had done it in the night. In the end we bumped into each other one time at the pub. He mustn't have been expecting to see me, because it was still morning, the weather was perfect, and it was harvesttime. He'd come for tobacco, I was at the bar and I'd already had a bit to drink.

"So it's tobacco you're after, granddad?" I said. He shrunk his head in and didn't utter a word. "What's wrong with smoking clover? Or chop yourself up some cherry leaves!" Then I said to the Jew: "Chaim, give him a glass of anis vodka, let him drink to my health since we've finally run into each other."

The Jew poured the drink, but Prażuch acted like it wasn't meant for him.

"What, you're not gonna drink to my health?" I grabbed his head in one hand and the glass in the other, and I was about to pour the stuff down his throat by force, when he ups and spits in my face. "That's the thanks I get, you son of a bitch? I buy you a drink and you spit on me?"

I lifted him almost as high as the ceiling and threw him down on the floor so hard the place shook. He gave a moan like it was his last breath. I got scared I'd maybe killed him, he was getting on and his old bones could have been smashed to pieces by a fall like that. But he managed to stand. The Jew helped him some. He staggered out of the pub almost on all fours, meek as a lamb. It was only when he was outside, when he'd climbed up on his wagon and taken the whip and reins, he started cussing me out:

"You bastard! You piece of shit! Antichrist!"

I ran out after him, but he whipped up the horse. And once he'd gotten a good ways away, he turned around to threaten me again:

"Just you wait till my boys grow up!"

He had three sons, Wojtek, Jędrek, and Bolek. And so when they grew up, though the oldest one, Wojtek, had barely come of age, they waited for me one time. I was coming back that night from a dance in Boleszyce. It was like everything conspired against me that evening. I'd had the urge to walk a girl back to her place, she lived almost at the edge of the village, and I stood with her outside her house for a while. But she wouldn't even let me kiss her, she was stubborn as a mule, she squeezed her lips shut and kept turning her head away. And afterwards I had to walk back home alone because the guys had gone off somewhere. The night was black as pitch, there wasn't a star in the sky or even any moonlight, just dogs barking in the distance. On top of that I'd taken a shortcut through the dense woods in this hollow, and there was one bush after another, hawthorn, juniper, hazel, you could barely see the path that led through them. But it wasn't the first time I'd gone home on my own, and often it was from a lot farther away, so what did I have to be afraid of. I whistled as I walked, O my Rosemary, and, My darling war, and, Duckies and geese in the water clucking, run away girl or they'll come pecking. All of a sudden the Prażuch boys jumped out from behind the bushes waving sticks. Before I had time to reach for my knife I was already on the ground half dead. All I could feel was them kicking me from every side, but it only lasted a moment, after that I didn't feel a thing, I couldn't tell whether I was alive or dead. It wasn't till the morning that a farmer came along the same path and went to tell people in the village there was a corpse in the hollow.

For two weeks I couldn't get out of bed. Though everything hurt even when I was lying down. Mother kept making compresses for me, sobbing over me the whole while:

"Dear Lord Jesus, Szymek, how many times have I begged you! How many times have I prayed to God! Are you trying to send me to my grave? Promise me this'll be the last time."

But how could I make any promises, even to my mother, when I'd sworn to myself I wouldn't forgive them. I'd burn their house down, I'd kill them, but I wouldn't forgive them. Except that soon afterward, the war began and I had to go to war. True, before you could say Jack Robinson, the war was lost and I was back home before the potato lifting was even done. But after the war, all the things that had happened with the Prażuchs seemed like they'd been in a different world. Because losing the war bothered me more than the Prażuchs did. And I probably would have forgiven them. But father went on about Prażuch plowing over the field boundary again while I was away at the war, because the old fart was counting on me not coming back. And he kept telling me, you need to do something about it, you really do, the land can't take it any longer. At the very least go take him to court. I couldn't get him to understand that there was no court to take him to anymore. What court? Poland was gone, so the courts were gone as well. He just kept repeating:

"You lost the war, and on top of that I'm supposed to lose to the Prażuchs as well?"

So one day I threw the plow into the wagon, and although our field and

Prażuch's were both sown already, and the crop was starting to come up, I plowed over what was ours so the old fart would know I was back.

The following year there was a church fair in Lisice for Saint Peter and Paul's Day. Normally I might not have gone, but there wasn't anywhere to mill rye for bread because the military police were minding the mill like guard dogs, and you needed to have a chit to say you'd provided a levy. Though even when you had the chit, they'd still sometimes requisition part of your crop and smack you in the face into the bargain. Plus, the mill in Lisice belonged to a guy called Pasieńko that had a daughter he was trying to marry off. She was an old maid already, Zośka was her name. I knew her from different dances and she'd often invited me to come by. But first off, Lisice was a fair ways from us, and second, she was a plain, dumpy thing, her back was level with her rump, she had teeth like a horse, on top of which all she did was laugh. All the same, what won't a person do for bread. I thought to myself, I'll go over there, take her to the fair, and her old man'll grind at least a quarter bushel of rye for me on the down low. I can even spend a bit of time with her, let him think I'm interested in marrying her, maybe the war won't last that long. At most I'll buy her a puppy or a kitten at the fair, or a string of beads, so she won't bad-mouth me later.

Luckily people were crowding round the stalls like bees on honey, and there was no way we could elbow through. Though as it happened I didn't feel a whole lot like pushing anyway, and for Zośka it was enough that she was on my arm. She would have given anything to be seen around the fair with a young fellow like me, never mind puppies or kittens or beads. Also, even though it was wartime the fair was grander than many a one before the war. The rows of stalls stretched all the way to the cemetery. There were as many wagons as on market day. And the crowd was so big the place was stifling, it was like processions moving this way and that, you couldn't even tell which one was going which direction, because they were all squeezed together. And all the squeals and shouts and laughter, and trumpeting, and whistling, and roosters crowing, like there was no war and the whole world was one giant fair. Plus, I told her I liked it when she laughed, so she kept laughing the whole time.

All at once the three Prażuchs are standing there in front of us like three pine trees. They're eyeing us like bandits. Uh-oh, I think to myself, this could turn nasty. I tried to go around them, because I had rye flour and bread-making on my mind, not fighting. But on the right there happened to be a stall with a crowd of customers, and on the left a wagon that some-one was selling cherries off of, and I wasn't about to turn around and beat a retreat. I let Zośka go ahead first, thinking it might be easier if we passed them one by one. They let her through, though as she passed Bolek, the youngest one, he said with a sneer:

"He's found himself a genuine dwarf girl."

The three of them snickered, and I was sure they'd let me past too, at Zośka's expense. Then suddenly the oldest one, Wojtek, blocks my way with his shoulder and he's all, Where the hell do you think you're going? Can't you see we're standing here?

"Of course I can see," I answered. And without a second thought I punched him in the mouth as he stood there still grinning. He didn't even have time to duck. He swayed, I straightened him up with my other fist and he rolled backwards onto the wagon with the cherries. His head hit the wheel and after that he didn't get up. Bolek jumped forward and grabbed me by the shoulders, and we struggled for a moment. There was a commotion. Some folks got out of the way, but others pushed forward so they could see. There were even some wanted to join in. Someone called out like they were selling candy:

"Fight! There's a fight!"

Someone else shouted:

"Jesus and Mary! Isn't it enough there's a war on, damn them!"

"Get the priest! Have him spray holy water on them, the goddam fools! Get the priest!"

Zośka was tugging at my jacket.

"Szymek! Szymuś! You're the smart one! Let the stupid idiots have their way!"

At that exact moment a massive weight hit my head from behind. I reeled, and my eyes went blank. But I managed to stay on my feet, and I swung my fist blindly into the darkness in front of me. I missed. It made me stagger, and so as not to fall over I lurched after my arm. My head landed in someone's belly and there was a grunt. I got my sight back. I saw Bolek, it was his belly, spin back against a stall and knock it over. Plaster figures flew every which way. The stall owner let rip with a stream of curses, he took Bolek by the shoulders and pushed him back toward me. I held up my fist, and Bolek smashed into it with his nose like it was a wagon shaft. His eyes spun. But he was a strong one, even though he was the smallest of the three of them. He just shook his head like someone had thrown a bucket of water over him. I gave him a left hook, he rocked but stayed upright. If I'd punched him one more time that probably would've done it. But by now Jędrek, the tallest one, had pushed all the people aside and he was reaching his arms out toward me like he wanted to put them round me and crush me. I leaned back a bit and with all the force I could muster I hit him halfway between those arms. They opened up like wings. It was almost like he was suspended by them. All at once he clapped his left hand to his eye and gave a terrible howl:

"Jesus!" He swayed for a moment with his hand to his eye as if he didn't know whether to fall or not. I helped him out with a pretty gentle blow under the elbow and he dropped down at my knees, moaning: "My eye! I can't see! My eye! You fucking bastard!"

I wondered whether I should keep fighting, most of all I'd have liked to stomp him into the ground. I just pulled his hand away from his eye and I said, Look at me with that bloody eye of yours, you son of a bitch, I want you to remember this. He thought I was fixing to keep at him and he burst into tears:

"Don't hit me anymore! Leave me alone! We're from the same village!"

Except that while Jędrek was begging for me to spare him, Bolek had recovered and was coming at me from the side with a knife. I might not even have seen it, but there was a sudden flash, as if the sun had glanced off the gold cross on the church steeple. Plus, a well-wisher in the crowd warned me at the last moment:

"He's got a knife!"

It was too late for me to knock the knife out of his hand because he was already swiping it at me. But I managed to dodge, and I gave him an almighty kick between the legs. He folded in two, and the knife flew out of his hand like a little sparrow. I lifted his limp body from the ground. With my left hand I held him up by his lapels, and with my right I started hitting him as payback for the knife, slowly, with pauses, because I could barely keep on my feet myself. Though maybe I only thought I was hitting him because of the knife, and really it was for that damned field boundary that had been plowed over so many times. I pulled him up every time he started slipping back down, and I kept hitting him. He came round and passed out again in turns, as if he didn't even feel he was being hit. I was running out of strength, but I still had so much rage in me it probably wouldn't have been satisfied even if I'd killed him. In the end blood welled up out of his mouth.

"Let him go. He's had enough," some angel said to me from the side. And I let him go.

He dropped like a lump of earth, but my legs buckled as well and I almost fell down with him. For a moment I stood there like a drunk, afraid to take even a single step, it was like someone was striking sparks in my eyes. Then I heard the angel's voice again:

"Come sit here, young falcon."

I turned my head, and right by me I saw a stall, and the owner sitting behind it. She was a plump old woman, her face was all pitted with the smallpox, but the angelic voice was hers. She gave a kind of strange smile, as if two different smiles were competing on her face, maybe it was because of the smallpox, or maybe I was just seeing double. I suddenly remembered I was supposed to get the rye milled with Zośka. I looked around, but there was no sign of her.

"Don't waste your time looking for her," said the stall owner in her angelic voice. "She squealed and squealed, then off she ran. That's young women today for you. Come over here and rest up." She put a stool out for me in front of the stall. She even took her headscarf off and laid it down on the stool. "Szymek's your name? I heard her calling you that. Nice name. Pull your jacket off and I'll sew the buttons back on, they've all gotten ripped off."

She came out from behind the stall and removed my jacket. She took it to the neighboring stalls, and a moment later she came back with a handful of buttons.

"Here. These'll look even nicer than the old ones."

She squeezed back behind the stall and started sewing. As I watched her worn, swollen hands at work, she picked a string of pretzels from a pile in her stall and tossed them into my lap.

"Here, have something to eat, young falcon. You've been working hard. That you have. There's still strength in this country. They can't put us down so easily. It was only the first one you didn't do enough to, the wagon wheel was what finished him off. That last one, he'll have had enough for the rest of his life. It was quite a show. People were running away like they were being blown in the wind. A couple of the stall owners even closed up shop. They must have had something on their conscience, they still had merchandise and they could have done business till evening. Today there's no more selling to be done. But it was worth coming. There'll be something to remember. Cause usually fairs come and fairs go, they're alike as peas in a pod, what's there to remember? How many pretzels you sold? Selling on its own, that doesn't make a church fair. A real church fair is either when the bishop comes, or there's a fight. Back in the day there was more fighting. One year in Radzików, on Saint Vincent's Day, they started scrapping right after morning mass and they went on all through high mass, they were still at it after it ended. People were beginning to gather for the evening service and the fight was still going on. One of them fell on my stall, he had a knife wound from ear to ear and he spilled blood all over my pretzels. I had to go through each bunch one by one and wipe all the blood off. Half of them I had to throw away. And it had all started from nothing. First one guy with another guy. Then there was no telling who was fighting who, they were all scrapping together. You couldn't even tell which side was against which, all the sides got mixed up. It was just one big free-for-all. The priest came out with holy water and a sprinkler, the organist came, the verger brought a cross, and they started ringing the church bell. But they only got as far as the edge of the tangle, they couldn't go a step farther. The organist sang for a bit, the priest sprayed them with holy water, and off they went. And the boys just kept on fighting. Here." She threw me another string of pretzels. "Eat. I'm not going to sell them today anyway. That way I won't have to cart them all back home. Look – with this one a piece of the cloth's been torn out as well. But I'll patch it up for you. With the dark color and it being next to the button, it won't show. That suit's good on you. But you'd look even better in brown. With a light blue shirt, and a spotted necktie. You needn't have any regrets with that young lady of yours. It's just as well she ran off, she wasn't meant for you. All she did was cling to your coattails instead of cheering you on. With a girl you have to feel like she's part of you, then you can get hitched. That one, she just stood there squealing. If it were me, I'd have at least bitten one of them on the hand or kicked him in the leg. She wouldn't have been any kind of wife or housekeeper for you, nor a mother to your children. You could tell from how she walked she wasn't the one for you. And she'd have been a downright quarrelsome one. After the first baby you'd have had a real shrew at home, then in the years to come she'd be an absolute she-devil. All you'd be thinking about was where you could go so as not to have to be at home. God wouldn't call you to him yet, because God only calls people when they get old, so you'd either have to find another woman or turn to drink. Sometimes the pub can help, but that's no good in the long term either. It often happens the road from the pub leads straight to the noose. Though truth be told, with a young falcon like you no woman's going to last long, however rich or good-looking she might be. She can lock the doors and the windows, close the chimney vent, tie him up with a rosary even, he'll still get away. And all those things he swore before God, it'll be like he spat them out, all his oaths will come undone. Because he's not made for the happiness of one woman, but to bring unhappiness to many. Besides, why should you be in any hurry to wed. Marriage isn't so sweet. Enjoy yourself while you feel like it. Because as long as you're enjoying yourself, death's going to stay far off too. I've lived through all sorts of things and I know. I've had three husbands. Life was good and bad with them, though with each one of them it was different. But I recall more raising them like children three times over, than them marrying me three times. It was lucky I had my pretzel stall, I'd barely buried one and the next was wanting a wedding. They flocked to me, that they did, like it was easier to die at my side. But after three of them I said to myself, enough. What am I, a graveyard? I've got my pretzels, I'll go sell them here and there, I'll be content if the guys fight over me once in a while. Because fight they did back when, young falcon, they'd fight till the ground ran red with blood, like the earth itself was bleeding. They fought with knives, iron bars. Whatever came to hand. One time, one of them smashed the other over the head with a figure of the Virgin Mary. The one that got the Virgin Mary over the head, he was my first. I would have preferred the other guy, but I felt sorry for the first one. He sold saints, I had my pretzels and our stalls were always next to each other. But he didn't live long. The second one I got from a fight as well. He made this huge ruckus at a Saint Sabina's Day fair in Wojciechów, and at some point it just popped out of my mouth, you'll be mine. And he was. Till a policeman shot him. He went for the policeman when he was being taken to jail. The third one, he stopped for a moment right there in front of the stall, where you are now, and he said, I'll buy all these pretzels, and twice as many more again, but you have to be mine. I was. Except he could never get over the fact I'd had two men before him, and he'd get drunk every day. And whenever he was drunk he'd grab an ax and start in with, Throw them out, throw them out, you bitch, or I'll cut you up as well as them. And he drank worse and worse. Till I came back from a fair one day and I see my third one dangling from a rafter. From that time on I never wanted them to marry me." She tossed me another bunch of pretzels from the pile. "Dig in, they're made from good flour. And there I was thinking nothing was going to happen. High mass was already over, and there was nothing but people asking, How much a bunch, how much a bunch. And they were all so polite, they were more like nuns in disguise than young men. I'm not complaining, I did decent business, but I was thinking it wouldn't be a good fair. Did you not have a knife? You should have used a knife if he went for you with one. The Lord would have forgiven you, he could see it was one against three. But you shouldn't have kicked him between the legs. You can smash people up any which way, but you have to respect between the legs, young falcon. However much of a bandit the other guy is, what's between the legs is sacred. It's like you were kicking God himself, who gave birth to all of us and told us to give birth to others. Even him, though he's God, he didn't have any other way of coming into the world. He supposedly came from the Holy Ghost, but what could the Holy Ghost have done without the Virgin? What's between your legs is life, it's death, all sorrows and joys, from it one man is good and another bad, one is one way and one the other. It gives us treachery and wars, kings and do-nothings and saints. All that was and all that will be comes from there, young falcon. And do you know where dreams lie? Between your legs. It's from there that they come out to you at night so you can dream them. Whatever's between your legs is in your heart and your head too. Because what's there stands above it, the way eternity stands over a split second. Without his head a man is nothing but a fool, and without his heart he's a stone. But kill what's between his legs and it's like you drove him out of paradise all over again. After that he's got no interest in either sin or salvation. Once in a while a nightingale'll appear in his throat and sing. But it's like it was singing about how he was driven out."

I must have eaten a dozen strings of pretzels, but she wouldn't take a penny from me. She just wanted me to promise I'd come to the Assumption Fair in Milejów. I promised. As for the Prażuchs, since that day it was like they'd gone underground. Though once in a while someone would tell me they'd been making threats, because everyone in our village heard about the fight. Apparently they even needed to get a doctor out for Bolek. The old man supposedly said I'd have to pay for the doctor. But soon after that I joined the resistance and stopped giving a damn about the Prażuchs. I thought I was done with them, that at most the field boundary would get plowed back over after the war.

But one time I went to pay my folks a visit in the night. The journey went well. It was quiet and deserted, there wasn't a soul about, the houses were all asleep and not even any dogs barked. It was kind of like in the old days, when I'd often be coming back home from some young lady at that hour. You almost felt like asking the sky, So where's this war I hear about?

I was almost halfway through the village, I just had to pass Dereń's place and Maszczyk's and it was our house. Then all at once, out of the darkness, from only a few yards away I heard in German: "*Halt!*" And a flashlight gets shined in my eyes. Without a second thought I dodged sideways into Oryszka's yard, I knew every lane around here. There were shots and a clatter of boots. I vaulted the fence into Niezgódka's farm. Niezgódka's dog started woofing furiously. Behind me, again I heard: "*Halt, halt!*" More shots rang out. From Niezgódka's I ran behind Kwiecień's barn. Luckily Kwiecień's dog didn't have time to wake up, or maybe it was just too lazy, in any case it never even barked. Then I crossed Gawil's farm and took the hollow behind the firehouse to Barański's. I thought about maybe climbing into Barański's wagon house and waiting things out there. Barański's place was set back a bit from the road and he was well off, maybe they wouldn't go looking for me there. Plus there was a German lieutenant that had been seeing Irka Barańska, maybe he still was. Except I forgot that the Barańskis had a devil of a dog. The moment I squeezed between the lilac and jasmine around the edge of their place, the dog starts up like a fury and comes at me from way the other end of the yard. On top of that it was dragging its chain over some wire, and the wire and the chain made a barking noise along with the dog, like they were mad too. Over on the road, right away there was the stomp of boots. *Halt! Halt!* And a burst of gunfire from the orchards in the other direction.

Things weren't looking good. I decided to try and make it down to the river, it wasn't far and maybe I could beat them to it. I crept around the backs of the fenced yards to Siudak's smithy. I squatted there for a moment, listening whether I couldn't hear any suspicious noises, then I snuck over to the other side of the road. I slipped into the passage between Żmuda's place and Gabryś's. Then I followed the edge of the pond through the alder thicket and came out behind Zdun's barn. I thought I was safe already, because from Zdun's place the river is just across a meadow, and over the river there's a slope then woodland, and they could kiss my ass. I even sat down a moment to catch my breath. Then all of a sudden there's a rustling in the bushes, I reach for my pistol, and this tiny little mongrel pops out like a sprite and starts sniffing at me. I felt all warm inside, I thought to myself there's dogs and dogs. So I tried to stroke him, and the damn thing bites me on the hand

and starts yapping. So that's the kind of dog you are, you little bastard! I kicked him away, he gave a yelp and barked even louder. I thought, there's nothing for it, I'll try and be nice. I wanted to appeal to his doggy logic, make him calm down:

"Good dog, good, good dog. You're not silly like the other dogs. Come on now, cut it out. You hear those shots? It's me they're shooting at. You'll have plenty of time to bark once the war's over. After the war we'll all have it easier, people and dogs both. Are you a dog or a bitch? Something tells me you're a dog. A bitch wouldn't yap so much. A bitch would have puppies, she'd be lying with her puppies. Who do you belong to, the Zduns? Do they at least feed you decently? Cause they're sneaky ones, they'd take food from each other and never give it to the dog. You'd have it better at Jamróz's or Stajuda's. Stajuda trades in pigs. And the Jamrózes are always praying for God to give them a baby. What's your name now? Maybe Rattles? Come here, Rattles, let me pet you, just stop yapping for chrissakes. The Zduns don't give you any affection because they don't give their own children any, they just send them out to work. Come on, come here."

But he was having none of it, he was barking away as if what I was saying made him even madder.

"Are you a Polish dog or a Kraut dog? They're after me, goddammit, how can I get it through to you? Am I not talking plain Polish? Are you trying to give me away? Do you know what they do to dogs that do that? The same thing they do to people. A bullet in the head. A Polish dog wouldn't bark at a Pole like that. You must be a mix, or a stray. Go on, get the hell out of here, you dumb piece of shit."

I got up, and the dog must have decided I was a burglar, it started biting my boots and yapping louder and louder. Suddenly, over the yapping I heard someone running across the field, more than one man. Over the river there was the glint of a flashlight beam, then another.

"See what you've done, you little bastard? Now I'm surrounded."

At this point the only way out was through the upper fields. But to get there I had to circle the entire village so as not to cross the road, because they were probably lying in wait there. I set off through the willows down the path that led to the mill. The dog stuck to me like a burr, it came right after me yapping its head off. Wait, goddammit. There wasn't a moment to lose, but still I bent down and grabbed the creature by the head. Normally I'd never have hurt a dog, a cat sooner than a dog. When I was a kid I even used to think dogs came from people. It bit me and scratched and yelped. I held it to the ground and smashed my heel down on its head till there was a crunching sound. Right at that moment, from a dozen yards away I heard: "*Halt!*" A burst of gunfire whistled right overhead.

I dashed into Jamróz's orchard. The branches whipped at my face, my eyes. Bullets struck against the leaves like hail. They must have hit apples too. One knocked my cap off. I tripped over a stump and fell. I stumbled into Mikus's field. As if out of spite, Mikus happened to have sowed alfalfa. And it had grown well, it was up over my knees. It took all my strength to lift my feet up at each step. It was like in a dream, I was all in a rush, and here my feet were being held in place, and the guys chasing me seemed on the brink of catching up. I felt my strength beginning to fail. I fell again. For a split second I thought about not getting back up. Let them capture me and shoot me, let the whole dream finally come to an end. But I jumped up, and a dozen or so steps later I came to the end of the alfalfa. In a couple of leaps I was at the ravine, and to make my trail harder to follow I scrambled up the side. Then I made a big loop around Karwacki's farm so I wouldn't attract his dog's attention. At the statue of Saint Florian I turned toward the Prażuchs' house, since the cutting to the upper fields happened to lead that way.

I even slowed my pace a bit. I looked in at the Prażuchs' windows, but without any hatred, and I just thought normally, the way you do about people in the night, that they were probably in there snoring away. The night had lightened a little, and a good many stars had disappeared from the sky. Suddenly, from across the way I heard a muffled jabbering. I moved quickly behind the corner of the Prażuchs' house. I poked my head out, and at the place where the cutting dropped downward, I saw three figures coming out of the darkness. They were moving slowly, but I could tell they were coming in my direction, because they were getting bigger and bigger and their chatter was growing clearer. It was too late to run back into the night, with the growing light I would have been in plain sight. But there wasn't anywhere to hide there either. The Prażuchs didn't have a fence, there weren't any trees or bushes. The house and barn and cattle shed were virtually in the middle of open ground. The worst thing was that at any moment their dog might smell me. I was even surprised it wasn't already barking. They had a dog, after all. Maybe it had gone looking for bitches? Either way, it'd be back any minute now, and when it came, everything would be over.

I moved nearer to the door and tapped lightly on the window. I stuck my face close to the pane, trying to see in the darkness whether there wasn't any movement inside. But the window was covered with a cloth. I tapped again, a bit louder. The chatter of the three men was almost by the farmyard. Finally, behind the door there was a creak no louder than the squeaking of a mouse. I tried the handle. There was silence. But I felt someone was standing behind the door, because it was as if the whole house was leaning up against it. I pressed the handle down again. Then I heard the fearful voice of the old man:

"Who's there?"

"A friend. Open up," I answered, more breathing than speaking. He would have expected someone from the next life sooner than me, so he didn't recognize my voice. He unbolted the door, poked his shaggy head out, his eyes suddenly looked like an ox's eyes, and he started to close the door again. But I'd expected that, and I put my foot in the jamb. He pressed his whole weight against the door, but I pushed back so hard he staggered across the hall.

"What do you want?" he hissed.

"Shut the door," I said hurriedly. "There're Germans outside."

I moved quickly into the main room. I was struck by the stale smell of sour cabbage. There was a barely smoldering lamp on the stove that had obviously just been lit, because the oldest son, Wojtek, was putting the glass over it. He looked at me like he was about to reach for an ax, but he didn't say anything. Jędrek and Bolek poked their heads out from under their bedding and stared at me, uncertain whether they should jump out of bed or stay there.

"Christ be praised," I greeted them, catching my breath.

None of them responded, they just scowled at me like wolves, expecting the worst. Finally Wojtek finished with the lamp and sat at the table, but he was still on edge, because he even put his hands on the table, and there was bread and a knife on it. Then their old mother got out of her bed in the farthest dark corner and, like she was the most unforgiving of all of them, she said:

"What's that fiend doing here?"

"I tried not to let him in, but he pushed the door open," Prażuch said, trying to explain it wasn't his fault. And as he stood there, barefoot, in his long johns, he dropped down on the bench and rested his arms helplessly on his knees, as if they were broken.

Then the two that were still in bed, Jędrek and Bolek, got mad and raised their voices at their father:

"Couldn't you at least have grabbed a poker and let him have it over the head? There's one standing right there!"

"You should at least have asked the bastard who he was before you opened the door!"

"They're after me," I said. "If you want, you can just turn me in."

They lowered their heads, and none of them said a word. Wojtek suddenly grabbed the knife and cut himself a big slice of bread. He started biting off mouthfuls like he was about to starve to death. The two in bed got sleepy again. They fell back and pulled their quilts up under their chins. The wick of the lamp guttered and started to fizzle, and the faint light got even dimmer. But no one moved to turn it up. It even seemed that everyone was waiting for it to go out and plunge them in darkness again. And just when it seemed about to fail, the old woman spoke again from her corner:

"Turn the lamp up a bit, Wojtek."

Wojtek stood, turned the lamp up, and sat back down at the table. He cut himself a second slice, but this time a smaller one, that he could have fit in his mouth in a single go. This time he picked at it with his fingers like he was eating sunflower seeds. The old lady spoke again:

"Sit yourself down. There's some cabbage left over from dinner. I'll heat it up for you." She dropped her feet from the bed, slipped her clogs on, and tying on her apron she sighed: "We oughtn't to be born if we don't know how to live."

Not long after that all three of them, Wojtek, Jędrek, and Bolek, joined my unit. All three of them died. Jędrek fell in an attack on a train outside Dębowa Góra. Wojtek was taken wounded as we were trying to escape from an encirclement at Maruszew. They hung him from a tree along the Kawęczyn road. As for Bolek, he was covering our retreat from the Olechów woods. He got hit in the legs by submachine-gun fire and he couldn't get away. He'd fired every last round he had and he didn't have anything left to shoot himself with, so he wrapped an old MPK submachine-gun strap around his neck and kept twisting it till he died.

Their old lady passed away not long after the war, when she finally realized none of them was coming back. She knew they were dead. But while the war had still been going on it was like she was holding out hope they'd be home. When Jędrek, the first one, died she started having problems with her heart and she couldn't do much work around the farm, old Prażuch had to do everything. Then when Wojtek was lost, and after him Bolek, and the war went and ended without them, her heart couldn't take it.

Prażuch, though, he just kept on living. And he never got funny in the head, and never let the farm go, though he had a right to and people would have understood. His land was always plowed on time, always sowed when it needed to be, and mowed and gathered in. And his house, whenever you went over it was clean and swept, there was fresh water in the pail and milk in clay pots souring for cheese, or already made cheese being dripped dry. The pillows on the bed were so white they shone. Every spring there'd be a brood hen in a basket under the table hatching eggs. Come Easter, he'd whitewash not just the hallway and the main room but the whole outside of the house as well. He even wove a wattle fence around the farmyard, though all those years they'd never had a fence. When he did the laundry he'd wash everything however clean or dirty it was, whatever there was lying around the room, whether it was his or his sons' or his old woman's. When he hung it all out to dry in the yard, you'd have thought an orchard had just bloomed at the Prażuchs'. On top of that he learned to read and write, because teachers were going house to house around the villages and teaching old folks to read and write.

From time to time I'd swing by and visit him, and I'd have to sit and listen how his reading was coming along, or check whether he hadn't made any mistakes in his writing. The only thing he had trouble with was addition. But even with young people, not everyone does well at addition. You have to be born a good adder. And none of the animals at Prażuch's – horse, cow, dog, cat, anything else – none of them could complain they had it bad there or that they had to lie in crap. Nor him himself, you couldn't tell from look- ing at him that anything was bothering him except for just old age. Though sometimes a lust for life like that can also be despair. And it can happen that because of that, a person lives longer than their age ought to allow, longer than they'd have wanted to.

He even looked after my farm when I wound up in the hospital after my accident, and he did just as good a job with it as with his own. I didn't have to worry about what was happening while I was gone. The animals were always fed. Michał always had enough to eat and he was properly dressed. Prażuch would sweep the house out every so often and clean up and light the stove. And most of important of all, the fields would be seen to. He didn't do everything himself, he wouldn't have been able to look after his own land and mine with just one pair of hands. But he'd at least watch over the work and make sure it was done well. Once a month, on a Sunday or a market day, he'd visit me in the hospital. And he'd never come empty-handed. He'd always bring something in a basket, some cheese, a dozen apples, cigarettes, an egg blessed at Easter time, or at Christmas a Christmas Eve wafer and a length of sausage. Then, when he was going to die he also came, and he said he wouldn't be able to keep an eye on my farm anymore, because it was time for him to die. Every night he could hear his sons calling him and his woman weeping for him.

It was a Thursday, and on Saturday he went to the priest to have him give last rites, because he'd decided that he'd die on Sunday afternoon, and he didn't want the priest to have to trek all the way to the other end of the village just for his death. Actually he could have managed fine without the priest. For a long time already he'd had an oak casket, a black suit, elastic-sided boots, a shirt and tie, all set. In the morning he saw to the livestock, fed the dog and the cat, swept out the house, swatted the flies, poured the sour milk into a muslin sack to make cheese. Then he took a bath, shaved, dressed, and called Strugała to come light a funerary candle for him. His last words were:

"Staś, my will is under the picture of Jesus. Everything's written there, who's to get what, and when the cheese stops dripping you can have it."

And in that way my farm was left to the mercy of fate. Because even with my closest neighbors, if any of them did any work there it was only in their own interest, so they could take as much as possible for themselves. When I came back the place looked like a battleground. I didn't know where to turn first. The main shaft of the wagon's chassis was cracked, and the side panels had been stolen. All that was left of the dog was its kennel, even its chain must have come in handy for someone else. When I went into the barn, the mows were almost empty, though there was no shortage of sparrows. It sounded like I was standing under the sluice-gate of a mill and water was pouring down on me from above – the noise was deafening. They'd run so wild they weren't even that afraid of me. Only the ones on the threshing floor rose up, though to the last moment they weren't sure whether they needed to be scared of me or not. I threw one of my walking sticks at them, but you're never going to hit a sparrow, they just flew up under the roof. And my walking stick bounced off the boards and into a mow, and I had to clamber over the partition to fetch it. I was so furious I tipped my head back and started cursing them and calling them names, you damn this and that! But they couldn't even hear me. You'd have needed the trumpets of Jericho to be heard over that racket. Besides, sparrow talk is different from people talk, and they wouldn't have understood anyway. You just wait, you little buggers!

I hurried out to look for my whip. But try finding your whip when you've been gone two years. I went to the neighbor's.

"Franek, lend me a whip, will you."

"You in a hurry to get out into the fields? You only just got back from the hospital."

"It's not for going to the fields, it's for the sparrows."

"What the heck use is a whip, with sparrows?"

I bolted the door, stood in the middle of the threshing floor, and leaning on a walking stick with one arm, with the other I started waving the whip and cracking it way up to the rafters, shouting, "boo! boo!" at the top of my voice. There was a swirling confusion of birds. It was like a sudden whirl-wind was blowing them out of the mows, out from under the thatched roof, who knows where from, so they all gathered in a huge swarm that was frantic with fear, with the beating of thousands of little wings. Sometimes when a storm wind blows through the orchard the leaves on the trees make the same sound. They weren't sparrows, they were a gale, a blizzard. The entire barn was shaking. And I kept going "boo! boo!" and cracking the whip. The birds were thrashing about, flying this way and that, up above, down below, I even had to duck because they were flying around me as well. They moved toward the door, but the door was bolted, then up toward the sky, but there there was the roof, then against the walls. In fact the walls had fist-sized holes in them, because the barn was a good old age, plus it had been hit by shrapnel in the war, and even a pigeon could have squeezed through those holes, never mind a sparrow. But the sparrows were so confused that one sparrow was a flock of sparrows, and a flock of sparrows can't get through a hole for one sparrow. You could actually smell overheated feathers in the air, like the stink of chaff when the wind is in the grain. But it wasn't chaff, how could it have been chaff? It was the fear of the sparrows that stank like chaff, as they rose up in a swarm to try and escape their sparrowy death.

My walking stick fell out of my hand, but it was like a miracle had happened, my legs stood on their own. I didn't even feel any pain, because I didn't feel I had legs at all. I just hobbled this way and that around the threshing floor, and, boo! boo! My throat was as dry as a well in a drought and my arm was about to fall off from waving the whip. But the birds up by the roof were evidently also getting tired, because they started looking for somewhere they could perch even for a second. They weren't that frightened anymore, either by the whip or by my shouting. I am not giving in to you, I said to myself, not if it kills me. I grabbed the flail that was standing in the corner by one of the mows, and I started smashing it against the threshing floor, the doors, the partitions, the pillars. This set the storm in motion again. They weren't flying in a single dense cloud anymore, but in little groups, in tatters, birds on their own. They flapped about every which way, even bumping into each other. They didn't look like sparrows so much as sparrow dust, sparrow fear, sparrow death, fluttering around the barn. And in that dust, that fear, that death, they crashed against the walls and rafters and beams and came tumbling down to the ground like rotten apples falling off a tree. At moments it was like someone had shaken the trunk of the barn, and there was an absolute hail. Though the others kept trying to get away, maybe they thought they'd already made it out of the barn to freedom, that they'd managed to pass through the walls and the roof like sparrow ghosts and they were soaring through the air farther and farther away from my flail. Because in a state of panic like that, even sparrows can think goodness knows what. A couple of them even fell on me, but what's a sparrow, even a dead one. Just a little bundle of feathers. Besides, I was in a rage, and I'd gotten so carried away with the flail that even if rocks had fallen on me they would've felt like sparrows.

I began to run out of strength, the flail got out of control and I hit myself on the head with the swingle. At that exact moment it felt like someone had kicked my legs from under me, and I had to grab hold of a pillar so I wouldn't fall over. I dragged myself to a sack of bran and plumped down on it, exhausted and gasping like a dog that's been rushing around. The sparrows were still flying all over the place and killing themselves up above, though the cloud wasn't so dense now, it was like the last drops of rain. And even after they'd stopped flying, every so often one of them would still rise into the air then thump down into a mow or onto the threshing floor.

My rage was through and I was even starting to feel bad about what I'd done. I mean, what had the sparrows done to me. But how could I help it if the sparrows had been on the receiving end? I could just as easily have turned the house upside down or taken an ax and cut down the orchard. Because I'd obviously needed to do something to come to terms with myself. What was I now? It wasn't enough that I had to learn to walk from scratch, I also had to learn how to live all over again. Yet how could I live when everything here was in ruins. One of the cows was at least calving, but with the other one you felt bad even milking her. When you pulled her teats she twisted her head around to see why you were tormenting her. And she gave no more than a cupful of milk in the morning and the same in the evening. As for the horse, if I hadn't known he was mine I'd never have recognized him. His ribs were poking through his skin. He only stood when I took him by the halter. And even when he was only harnessed to an empty wagon he staggered like he was about to collapse. He'd need to be fattened up on oats for at least a week to get his strength back a bit. But where was I supposed to get oats from when the bins were gaping empty. He had to eat chaff, and from borrowed straw at that. And on top of everything, the harvest had begun.

I'd had about twenty chickens. Mrs. Makuła was looking after them for me, and that was a lot of eggs for her, minimum one egg every other day from each chicken. In return she was supposed to water the flowers in the window boxes. There was nothing left of the flowers except dry stalks, and she claimed the chickens had gotten fowl cholera and it happened to be my chickens that all died. She gave me two of hers to replace my twenty, and she promised me a brood hen in the spring.

As for the fence along the road, no more than half of it was left, though there hadn't been a single post missing before.

I had a chaff-cutter, I'd thought about motorizing it one of these days, but someone had borrowed it. I went around almost all the neighbors near and far, and eventually I found it all the way over by the mill with Przytuła, he even tried to convince me I'd lent it to him myself before I was taken to the hospital. I didn't have the strength to argue. It might have been true, it might not have, so be it.

My scythe had always hung under the overhang of the barn, now there was no sign of it. The rake had lived next to it, that had disappeared just the same.

I went to Stajuda's because he'd been the last one to look after my land, all I wanted to know was whether he'd mucked my fields, because the muck stall was completely empty. Sure, he'd gone and mucked the fields and plowed them over, he swore he had. Except his eyes were darting about in this odd way and he didn't look at me once, he just kept squinting at the walls the whole time. I had to believe him. I mean, I couldn't go ask the land, tell me, did the bastard muck you or not?

The floor in the house was so covered in mouse droppings it was like walking over spilled buckwheat, *scrit scrit scrit*. I grabbed a broom and started sweeping. All at once I hear a scratching sound in the pail. I look in, and there's a mouse. Where did you come from? It made me think, because a bucket for a mouse is like a well for a person. There's no way to either get in or get out without a ladder. So I had to think it had been born from the water. The water had dried up and the mouse was left behind. I set it free, why should I go blaming a stupid little mouse for everything and killing it.

When I looked at the Our Lady over the bed I saw the glass was broken. There were umpteen empty vodka bottles under the bed. The lightbulb had been removed. It was just as well I'd come back during the day, I managed to go buy a new one. Except that when I screwed it in it turned out there was no light, because there hadn't been anyone to pay the bill and my electricity had been turned off.

I'd had an alarm clock. Admittedly it was broken, it was stopped on nine o'clock. But at least it showed nine o'clock. You looked at it and you knew you had to do this and do that, go here, drive there, bring such and such, take something down, throw it out, feed the animals, milk them. And everyone has the time inside them anyway, they don't need a clock to tell them. But someone had found a use even for a broken clock.

Someone else had taken a liking to the calendar, though it was a good few years old. It hung on the wall under the crucifix and I got so used to it being there that I'd been reluctant to throw it out. Plus, once in a while I'd write something on it, maybe someone died, or there was a big hailstorm, or the cow was taken to be covered. Maybe they'd liked the sayings, because there was a different saying for each day. And if someone doesn't know how to live, a saying like that can often be good advice.

I'd had a bucket I took the food out to the pigs in, that had gone too.

I'd had two stools, only one was left.

What I missed most were my haircutting things. Whoever took them, I cursed him to high heaven. I wished him a lingering death. I'd been counting on maybe beginning to offer haircuts and shaves for the local men, though there was a barber in the village now. Olek Żmuda was his name. But they'd come to me as well, if not the young folks then the older ones, and I'd earn a bit of money to help get me started again.

Or my fireman's helmet, these days you won't find a helmet like that anymore, all gold, with a crest and a peak and a studded chinstrap. It had hung on a nail in the main room. The bastard who took it couldn't even wear it, I mean where would he go in it? To a fire? Everyone would stare at him instead of putting out the fire. There aren't any more parades, and the firemen don't guard Christ's tomb at Easter anymore.

Or my prayer book. I got it from mother when she was dying. She had four prayer books, the same as her number of sons. She prayed for each one of us from a different one. From one she prayed for Stasiek, from another for Antek, a third one for Michał, and the one she prayed from for me she'd gotten from her own mother. That was all I had of hers. It was in the drawer in the table. I mean, how can a son of a bitch like that pray from a stolen prayer book? Will God listen to him?

I had a saw used to always be propped up in the hallway. Someone took that as well.

I had a raincoat. It had holes in it, but I'd still always put it on for going out into the fields when it was raining, or taking the animals down to the river to water them. That was gone.

The hoe for weeding, it was almost brand-new, I bought it the spring before my accident, someone even stole the handle.

Then there were all kinds of things I only remembered later.

The basket I always used to take food to be blessed, I didn't remember till Easter when I'd already boiled the eggs to take them to be blessed.

Or the masher for mashing potatoes up for the pigs. It stood by the door in the passageway, I remember well, twice a day I'd take it and twice a day I'd put it back in its place. And not just for a year or two, but even when mother and father were still alive. Mashers would come and go, but they were always kept in the same place, behind the door in the passageway. But what use was a memory. Sometimes it's best not to remember at all, because when you remember something it ought to be there.

When I went up into the attic, there'd used to be a sack of feathers hanging from a rod, an old cloak of Michał's, some other old clothes, half a dozen strings of garlic, a horse-collar, two lengths of rope. Only the rod was left.

I'd had an almost full sack of bolted flour, one and a half hundredweight, yellow as the sun, I didn't even need to add eggs when I was making noodles. There was no sign of flour or sack.

There'd been two cheeses hanging from a rafter in wicker baskets, I thought they'd be just what was needed when the cow stopped giving milk before it had its calf, but someone had cut the baskets down and left just rag-ends of cord.

Wherever I looked there was something missing. I didn't want to look anymore. But on the way back from the attic to the main room I noticed the sieve was gone, though there'd always been one hanging on a nail by the ladder. This was gone, that was gone, and two of the rungs of the ladder were broken.

I threw myself on the bed to try and gather my thoughts. Though that's easier said than done, gathering your thoughts. There are times a man would much rather scatter his thoughts to the four winds. Then turn into a table or a stool. And just be that stool or table till his time came. Because it was like pouring sand from one hand to the other, back and forth, endlessly. You could pour it there and back again all your life, you'd never make it into a whip. And even if you did, who would you use it on? Szymon, Szymon – I thought I heard someone calling me. But I didn't want to hear who. I stared at the room, or the room stared at me, and there was nothing but a dead reflection in my eyes. And then the cat appeared.

It stood on the threshold, meowed, and jumped up onto my lap. I'd forgotten all about it. I couldn't remember everything. Besides, truth be told, I never liked it. It was lazy as the day is long, and you had to force it to go out mousing, it would hardly ever go of its own accord. And when it came back it would be all hungry and bedraggled like it had been the one being bitten by the mice, and it would look at me to get me to toss it a crust of bread at least. It would have just laid there by the stove and slept all day. There were times it drove me mad when the mice were running wild in the barn, and the cat's in here sleeping, maybe even enjoying a nice dream. Though I don't think cats have dreams, because if cats do then other animals must, horses, cows, dogs, pigs, chickens, geese, rabbits – why would a cat be any better than them? If all of them had dreams every night on the farm, with all those animals and on top of that all those dreams, a man would go mad. It's enough that people dream, sometimes even that's too much.

Often it would sleep all day and all night, and still not want to wake up in the morning, not until I'd lit the stove and it felt warm enough. And even then it wouldn't hop down right away. It would stretch and arch its back, stick its tail up in the air then curl it underneath, till I lost patience, I'd grab it by the scruff of the neck and force it to get up. Or I'd take it straight to the barn and bolt the door, this is where you belong, damn you. Can you smell mice? Then go catch some. But sometimes it'd be less than half an hour before it was back scratching at the door again. And how could I not let it in. Sure, it was an idle one, but without a cat the place felt somehow empty, just like a farmyard feels empty without a dog and cows, fields without a horse, the sky without birds. Come evening, it's nice just to hear purring from something that's alive. You listen to the purring and it's like someone was sleeping in the other bed, or like mother was kneeling way over in the corner saying her prayers.

I thought it would have disappeared in the two years I was gone. I wouldn't have minded much. And here it'd even grown fat. If it wasn't for the fact it was a tomcat, you might have thought he was about to have kittens and that was why his belly was so big. Even his meow was deeper. And his tail had gotten all bushy, like a fox's. His head had almost become one with his body. It was hard to even believe it was my old cat. But how could I have not known my own cat? He was dark gray with green eyes and half his tail was white. No one else had a cat like that in the whole village. I stroked his back, and it was like stroking sun-warmed grass.

He sat in my lap like a loaf fresh from the oven and I could hear the mice playing inside him. He must have had a good bellyful, because I could feel beneath my hand how they were stirring in him, jostling about, running amok. His big stomach was just swelling and settling, swelling and settling. And he was purring somewhere deep down. You could have been forgiven for thinking his stomach was the only living part of him, while the rest of him lay in my lap, lifeless and contented. And the hand I was stroking him with was like the sky over that dead contentment of his.

He even stank of mice. Maybe he'd had so many of them for my benefit, to make up for all his years of idleness. And I felt bad that when I was in the hospital, whenever anyone asked if I had a cat I'd said I used to, but it was so lazy I'd put it down.

Though there wasn't that much talk about cats. What kind of a creature is a cat that you'd want to talk about it. It's gray or black, a hunter or a lazy-bones, that's it. There's more to say about dogs, or pigeons. And most of all about horses. When it came to horses, if one person started talking about them, all of a sudden everyone was talking. This kind and that kind, old ones, young ones, workhorses, horses gone bad, black ones, grays, bays, sorrels, chestnuts, tows, dapples, roans. Sometimes we'd talk all day about horses. Because everyone had more to say about horses than about themselves, more than about their own children and their wives and their farms, more than about the rest of the world. Made no difference whether it was all true or not. You didn't have to believe it, you listened along with everyone else. Because when you're stuck in bed, and in some cases you've got one foot in the next life, it makes no difference whether you believe what you're hearing or not. There were times they'd turn the lights out for bedtime and people would carry on talking about horses in the dark, as if the horses were lying down for the night between the beds, each one by his owner.

There was one guy that was a lawyer on the ward with us, other than him it was all farmers from the country. But he liked listening too. Not just about horses, about any animals. Even if he was reading his book, when someone started talking he'd set it aside and listen as if what was being said was more interesting than what was in the book. His bed was next to mine, to the left. He had something wrong with his spine, and he was visibly going downhill. But he never complained of being in pain. It was just that he couldn't sleep much, and he'd wake up way early in the morning. Then he'd wait for me to wake up as well. If I so much as reached my hand out of the sheets in my sleep, I'd hear a whisper, muffled like it was coming from inside the earth:

"Are you awake, Mr. Szymon?"

Ever since I was in the resistance I've been a light sleeper, plus I had plenty of sleep in the hospital, so I would have heard a mouse. Besides, I used to wake up early myself, before everyone else. I'd just lie there with my eyes closed, but my head would already be full of thoughts. I sometimes even thought about him, how his breathing was so shallow, how that was death breathing inside him.

"Did I wake you up?"

"Not at all. At home I'd be up and about already."

"What would you be doing?"

"There's no shortage of things to do. The animals will need feeding. They'll all be squealing and lowing and neighing and cackling so loud you never know who to see to first. The worst are the pigs, they won't eat things raw so you have to cook it for them, and they're the biggest eaters of all. On a farm, Mr. Kazimierz" – because that was his name, Kazimierz – "the day doesn't begin with the sunrise but with the animals being hungry. The sun's only just starting to come up when the animals have already been fed. In here, we don't do anything but laze around. It's neither living nor dying. There's no telling why we need to go to sleep, or why we have to get up."

I knew that he liked hearing about the animals, and I often brought the subject up deliberately, because I felt it helped him. So he would ask right away:

"Do you have a lot of pigs?"

"There's a good few of them, Mr. Kazimierz. Sows, I've got two of them. With a good litter there can be as many as twenty from one of them and twenty from the other, and I don't sell any of them, I raise them all myself. When you go in to feed them there's no room to even put your feet. It's all white as can be, like the floor was covered with lilac. And once they latch on to the teats, all you can hear is sucking, suck suck suck. Sounds like someone was threshing corn far off, or like rain dripping down the walls. And the sow just lies there in the middle of all that lilac doing nothing, you'd think she was dead. Her belly's wide open, her eyes are half closed, and she's barely breathing. And the young ones, they're squealing and scrambling all over her and jockeying around her teats. They're stubborner than puppies. But you need to know that not all teats are alike, even though they all belong to the same mother. Some have more milk, some less. Some are firm, others are limp. And the piglets aren't born equal either, there are sickly ones, fussy ones, greedy ones. The greedy ones can feed from three teats in one sitting. And they fight for the teats like no one's business. It's just as well they don't have claws, cause they'd be covered in blood. And the sow is just a big heap of flesh, meekness itself. The most she'll do is kick one of them if it tickles her too much, but otherwise she'll just lie there till they've sucked every last drop out of her."

"Do you have much in the way of poultry?"

"Sure I do. Chickens, geese, ducks, other things. Loads of them. But I like poultry. In the early morning, before you even open the door of the coop they set up a racket, as soon as they know it's you. Then when I open the door for them it's like opening a sluice-gate in a water mill. They rush past you, under you, over you. One big cloud of feathers. The whole yard is filled with feathers, earth and sky. If the dog tries to bark it's choked by feathers and it sounds like it's barking behind a wall. And even more than the feathers, there's all the cackling and quacking and honking and gobbling. And once they all start pecking at the ground, the whole place quakes like in a hailstorm. If the calf pokes its head out from the cattle shed, it hurries back in again right away. If you need to harness the horse, you have to drag him by force through all the hullabaloo. I've got turkeys, guinea fowl. But guinea fowl are something else. They're calm as anything, timid, it's like they're lost among all the other birds. They're not pushy, they don't get in the way. Because chickens, they're ragtag and bobtail. All they're good for is laying eggs. Though come wintertime, eggs are expensive and things even out. I even have two peacocks. I hold on to them because people in the village have gotten used to saying, the house with the two peacocks. Sometimes one of them will spread its tail, and I have my own rainbow. It's lovely to look at. The truth is, though, I don't know how many birds I have. I don't count. Besides, how could you count even if you wanted to? They're always moving around, hopping and pecking and fighting, you'd need a hundred eyes to keep track. Plus, when the sun comes out in the yard everything's all glittery. Sometimes, if I get to a hundred I can't be bothered to keep on counting. What's the point, I ask myself? Will there be more of them if I count them? Let them live uncounted. If I knew how many I had, I'd need to worry whenever one of my geese or ducks or chickens went missing. Though when that happens, try searching other people's farms and orchards, in their yards and behind their barns, try asking if they haven't seen anything anywhere. In the village there isn't even anywhere to look. There's one house next to another, all in a row. You'd have to look to the neighbors, because when something goes missing, they're the likeliest suspects. Though maybe that's why people are neighbors? And if you're at odds with your neighbors, then all the more they're the likeliest. Or you could set traps for polecats, and catch a neighbor in one of them from time to time. Though polecats can do their fair share of damage too."

It was a Monday, and he asked me right away if I could give him a shave along with the other guys. Because Monday was market day, and from early morning everyone on the ward would start getting ready for visiting hours. Dawn would barely be lighting the windows, and already they'd be whispering and sighing and saying their prayers. Some of them woke up much earlier even, as if it was time to feed the animals. So if anybody felt like sleeping in, Monday wasn't the day to do it. One bed would creak, and right away every bed in the place would start creaking. Though whoever woke up first generally woke everyone else up right off:

"Hey everybody, wake up! Today's Monday!"

Right away there'd be a commotion and comings and goings. Even when someone was stuck in bed because of illness or injury, and they couldn't get up, on a Monday it was like they were expecting a miracle to happen and they'd get ready as well. Everyone washed, shaved, combed their hair, and those that couldn't do it by themselves, someone else would shave them and comb their hair and wash them. Eventually, when I could get up myself, I was the one that shaved everyone. I had my work cut out for me on Mondays. Because every man jack of them needed something special doing. One of them had to at least have his sideburns evened up, someone else wanted his mustache trimmed so everybody would know he was expecting someone.

And though some of them never had visitors, Monday was the kind of day when you might finally get one. They might come to town to buy a horse or sell some suckling pigs, and while they were at it they'd come visit.

That was all people talked about from the early morning, will they come or won't they. Will they come or won't they. They might come, they've got a bullock they need to sell, why keep it any longer than necessary. It'll eat more than their cow, and it's not going to give them any milk. They've already plowed and sowed, what else do they have to do. They don't have that many apples in the orchard, no, not like last year, the branches were almost breaking under the weight. I told them they ought to spray one more time. Damn aphids ate all the blossom. So I think they'll come. They didn't sow any beet or carrots this year, they only had to lift the potatoes, so they probably already did it. Why should they need to do the threshing now? It can wait till winter. I'll do it when I get back. Working the fields with only one leg would be harder, but you can do the threshing as long as your arms are healthy. Really you can, though it'd be easier with a threshing machine. I told her, just get a hired hand if you can't manage on your own. I bet she did. With me, whatever I say, goes. Though where am I going to get a hired hand these days? You think it's like it was before the war? She might not have found anyone. They were supposed to come right after the harvest festival. They didn't come last time, or the time before that, or the time before that either, ever since you've all been in here. Because the land won't let them go. In the winter they'd come for sure. What work is there in the winter? You feed the animals and then you sit and warm yourself in the kitchen. What, you don't know what the land is like? It'll grab you by the legs or the arms or round the waist and hold on. If it ever popped into that head of hers to collect a few eggs, some cream, even just a little cheese, she'd have something to bring to market. A bit more money never goes amiss. To buy salt, or sugar, or vinegar. The bus comes to the village now, they've surfaced the road, all you have to do is sit and stare out the window and you're there.

Maybe they'll at least come let me know whether it's a bull calf or a heifer. Ask me if I think they should keep it or not. I mean, the priest isn't going to give them any advice, what does he know about calves. I'm telling you, it's a poor story when the head of the house is gone, that's for sure. I even said to them, the moment I'm gone, then you'll cry. Who's going to drive the geese down to the pond, who'll look after the grandson, who'll put the water on to boil when you come back from the fields. Who? I won't be able to hear you anymore. Cry all you like. They'll come, they'll come. Why wouldn't they? She was going to buy herself a new pair of shoes, and an overcoat for Jaś. She sure dresses up a lot. When he married her she was dirt poor, now she's the lady of the village. They're wanting to build a new house but they can't get sheet metal for the roof anywhere, maybe they'll come buy it in town. They've promised to give me my own room, with curtains in the window and a carpet on the floor. They're going to paint flowers on the walls. What do you think, will flowers look nice? My whole life I lived with whitewashed walls, I'm worried flowers'll give me asthma. Maybe they'll come to buy wedding rings. Christmas is on its way, and at Christmas they're planning to get married. They could get my blessing at the same time. Cause there's no telling if I'll ever make it back home. And without a blessing life can go wrong. Last Monday I sent word by the neighbor, come as soon as you can, me, I could wait, but death might not be willing to. Death's like an emperor. However much you beg him, he won't wait even just one more week, till the next market day at least, because something must have held them up. He's actually not that bad of a farmer, but man does he drink. If he wasn't drinking yesterday, he'll for sure come today. He needs to pick up supplies for the cooperative. They canned him three times already, but they don't have anyone else to give the job to. I told him, I said, it's my land, my inheritance, my everything, the mutt and the rake and the stork on the roof. And you, you Johnny-come-lately, what's your contribution? Ten lazy fingers and a lazy arm. And those glazed eyes of yours that are only interested in sleeping the whole time. And on top of that you disrespect me? I'm not giving you a thing. I'll give to the church, I'll give to the poor, but you, you're not getting one red cent from me. So he beat me up so bad the dog was yowling over me. You old fart, you belong in the cemetery. That's where your land is, your inheritance, your everything. And all she says is, Miecio, don't hit daddy. Daddy! Daddy! But I guess I'll forgive them if they come. Why not. I can't take it with me after I'm gone. So maybe they'll come. God'll tip them the wink and they'll come. I never was much of a one for revenge. It's all because of the land. The land's run wild. The land isn't what it used to be. Evidently the land's going to die with us, Wojciech. You'll have enough of it in your hands, in your feet, under your back, in your eyes, in your gray hair. Last year I had a dream that I was standing on a field boundary and the land was coming toward me. There were oats and barley and wheat and rye coming, and fallow fields. There were farmers' fields coming alongside the squire's. They were coming from somewhere on the other side of the sky and marching like regiments, armies, battalions, companies, one field after another was marching past me and going on, moving away then disappearing. There were the neighbors' fields, my brother-in-law's, mine. I recognized them all from far away, of course I knew my own fields, they were all blue with cornflowers. I spread my arms. Where do you think you're going? Stop! Stay there! I shouted. I grabbed fistfuls of crop, but it slipped out of my grip like eels. I fell to my knees. Come back! But they passed by and they vanished, and then I woke up. Why shouldn't they come today. I bought them a car, all they need to do is hop in, vroom vroom, and they're here. If the Lord would just send some rain, then they'd come. When it rains people remember the most forgotten things. And when the rain really sets in, it rains and rains and you keep remembering things. Long rains, people call it. You can't send the cows out in weather like that. You can't go plow. You sit at home, the windows are running with rain, it's pouring down like it was coming from the sky to the earth and then back from the earth to the sky. All the houses are in a row but every one of them's apart, every person's apart. Course, you could mend the chair, the one that the leg fell off of. Or visit your neighbor. But it's raining over there just the same, it's raining everywhere in the village. And it's raining in Sąśnice, in Walencice, the whole world. Cut it out, what's gotten into you with that rain. If it's potato lifting time let folks dig their potatoes in peace. The thing is, when it rains it gets at you inside so bad you'd even make up with your worst enemy. One time I actually did make up with my enemy when it was raining. For twenty years we'd been at each other's throats. But I'm sitting at home, I couldn't even go look outside cause it was cats and dogs the whole time, and my conscience started nagging me. I'll go see him, I thought, why should we be angry with each other. I go by there, and he says, I'm surprised you could be bothered in this weather. I would've made up with you anyway before I died. Sit yourself down, since you're here. Look how misty it is over the way. Take a look, your eyes are better than mine. Mine don't see too good anymore. In the village I'd be able to tell. There'd be smoke lingering on the rooftops, and my bones'd be aching. This could be my last Monday? Lord, let it rain.

It had never happened that anyone had died on a Monday. They died on a Tuesday, a Wednesday, Thursday, Friday, Saturday, sometimes even on a Sunday, but on Monday they were always alive. The afternoon passed. The market was at its busiest.

"Are you not reading your book today, Mr. Kazimierz?" I asked. There was a book lying open on the bedside table and I was a bit surprised he wasn't reading, because a day didn't go by without him reading. His cupboard was full of books, there were even some on the windowsill. Often he'd read a whole book in a single day. When he lost himself in his reading he didn't hear what people said to him. We couldn't get over the fact that he kept wanting to read. Because on the whole ward he was the only one that read. Didn't it hurt his eyes? Didn't it give him a headache? And after all, what was the point? You read and read, and in the end it all went into the ground with you anyway. With the land it was another matter. You worked and worked the land, but the land remained afterwards. With reading, not even a line, not a single word, was left behind.

Evening had begun to set in. The nurse came in, she gave him a sort of funny look and hurried out. A moment later the doctor arrived, held his arm for a moment then left again. The nurse came back and gave him an injection. She asked if he wasn't thirsty, and she brought him some compote. Someone wanted to put the lights on but I said no, it wasn't time yet. No one was reading, and it was far from dark.

You couldn't tell anything from looking at him. Though people say that when someone's going to die, you can tell two days before. But truth be told, what were you supposed to be able to see? He was always pale as can be, he couldn't have gotten any paler. He was skinny as a rake and he couldn't have gotten thinner. As the dusk fell his eyes grew sort of dim, and you'd have needed to lean over him for him to see anything. Only that open book on the bedside table that he didn't feel like reaching for even just to close it – that might have been the only sign he was dying.

I sat on the edge of his bed and it seemed strange to me that you couldn't tell anything from looking at him, but that he was dying. Things went quiet on the ward, though there were twelve of us in there. No one said a word, no one coughed, no one sighed, and if anyone was in pain, they kept it to themselves. Though more than one of them could have died right after him. But it was always the way that when someone on the ward was dying, everyone else died a bit with him, and they set their own deaths aside. Someone started whispering the rosary in the corner, though it was so quiet every word could be heard all around the ward like pebbles falling on the floor.

"Don't pay any mind to him," I said. "In the country they always pray in the early evening."

And I took him by the hand, the way you take a child's hand to lead him across a footbridge over the river. His hand was actually like a child's, it was so small and scrawny both of them would have fit in my one hand. At one moment he squeezed my hand so hard and so desperately it was like he was falling off a cliff, and I felt my hand and my arm were dying with him.

"Mr. Szymon" – his whisper reached me like something moving down a bumpy road – "you've been in the next world. What's it like there?"

"That was a long time ago, Mr. Kazimierz. And it was in the war. In wartime things might be different in the next world as well as in this one. Besides, war doesn't distinguish between one world and the other. Maybe I just thought I was there. Shall I tell you about rabbits? What kind do you like better, angoras or lop-eareds? Me, I prefer angoras. Lop-eareds are big, but if you keep them it's for the meat. Angoras are white as can be, they like to keep clean, and their eyes kind of shine red. When you touch an angora's fur it's like touching the daybreak, or touching a cloud, or the sky. And I've been thinking, I'm going to start keeping rabbits when I come home from the hospital. To begin with I'll only need a single pair. After that they'll breed. One pair can have three litters a year, six or seven little ones each time. Then the next year the same. Because rabbits, once they start breeding there's no stopping them. And as for food, they'll eat anything, grass, peelings. Come visit sometime and you'll see. When they eat, their jaws make a noise like they were talking to themselves. Though grass makes one noise, peelings a different one. With grass it's a tiny sound like autumn drizzle, but with peelings it's deep like warm rain in May. You could listen to it till the cows come home. And if you listen harder, you can even hear the rush of spring-water, bees collecting honey, clouds rubbing against the sky. You can hear the earth turning, and people turning with it. Even though it's nothing but rabbits making a noise while they eat. But you often have a yen to just lie down on the ground among them like you were lying on hay, in the meadow, by the river, in the shade of a tree, and just melt away in that noise, among the springs and the bees and the clouds, and let yourself be carried away by the tired, tired earth around you. Because there's something about rabbits that makes everything get softer all around, and inside you as well. Maybe it's their whiteness. Have you ever seen anything whiter than a rabbit's fur? Nothing's whiter than that – not an orchard in bloom, not an eiderdown airing in the sun, not geese swimming on the water. It looks like something that isn't even born yet and that's why it's so white, because it hasn't yet come into contact with the world. When you pick up one of those rabbits, pull it out of the mass of them and put it on your lap, it's like you'd taken it out of a warm womb. It trembles, it fights, sometimes scratches, as if it's afraid to come out into the world. Then when you stroke it, you can feel the fear through your hand, that its whiteness is going to forever be dirtied from your touch. Though on the face of it it's no big deal, you're sitting stroking a rabbit and the rabbit's trembling. You just have to hold it by the ears with your other hand, or else it'll hop off your lap and there'll be an emptiness in your hands, it'll be emptier on your lap than before. And you won't be able to catch it again. It'll mix in with the other rabbits and you'll lose it in all the whiteness. White mixes with white like water mixes with water, sand with sand. When there're all those white creatures, how can you pick out one of them? Has anyone ever picked a drop of water out of a pool of water, or one grain in a handful?"

I felt a strange chill in the hand that was holding his hand. It was a bit like the chill of freshly plowed earth, or an apple picked when the dew's still on it.

"I think he's dead," I said unsurely, as if it were him I was asking whether he'd died. Everyone on the ward held their breath a short while, like they'd died with him for a moment. Or maybe they were waiting to see if he'd answer me. In the end someone couldn't take it anymore and they said as if they were surprised:

"He's dead?" He probably said it not because he didn't believe it but because you ought to be a bit surprised by death, that's death's right.

"Then he's dead," someone said almost with relief.

"So, he's dead," someone else sighed at the other end of the ward, as if he was saying, "so, it's evening."

"Then it's evening," someone agreed, because what else can you do with death except agree, "then he's dead."

I freed my hand carefully from his and sat back on my own bed.

"Turn the light on maybe," someone said as though he was suddenly afraid. "Turn on the light."

"What for, he's not going to be doing any reading."

"Well, so we can at least close his eyes."

"Maybe he's not dead? Maybe he's not dead." Old Ambroży jumped up from the bed right in the corner. No one had come to visit him that day. He'd had his leg amputated at the knee. He grabbed his stick and hobbled over, close to tears, as if he were still trying to keep death back. "Maybe he's not dead. Look closely. Having cold hands doesn't necessarily mean he's dead. Nor having cold feet. Death's a whole lot more than that. It's not enough to just say he's dead. You can say all manner of things, it doesn't make them so. You can say it's day, but it'll still be night. Just like Jesus, he was supposedly dead, but he hadn't died at all. Give him a shake! Now how am I supposed to get Stolarek back for the wrong he did me? Stolarek, Stolarek. Half my land is gone almost. Skin and bones, that's all my land is. A dried-up branch. Give him a shake. Lawyers don't just up and die like that. Maybe he's sleeping only? When death comes, your tongue has to die as well, and the things on your conscience have to die, everything has to die. When you're dead you can't even blow your nose. He promised. Sure as he's lying there now, he promised. Some people just can't catch a break. Why? Because they're fools. Stolarek's land is rich as you like, and he's still filching other people's, the crook. All he does is flick his whip at his horses, and they're just horses, they're not worried about whose land they're plowing. His father used to steal land from my father. But what could my father do when his father was backed up by lawyers. All my father had was a head full of anger and a mouth full of prayers. So all he did was pray and curse, pray and curse in turn, while that guy took his land. Plus the other guy had a pair of horses, father only had the one horse, and with one horse there was no way he could have plowed back land that two horses had worked. He kept plowing his land back and his land kept getting smaller. Then one time he got riled up and took a whip to Stolarek. So Stolarek's lawyers set on him like ravens, and it wasn't long before he died. Besides, what kind of a life would it be anyway to live and watch your own land shrinking. I'll leave it all to you, son, my father said, though you'll need to take an ax with you one of these days. Me, I somehow didn't have the strength to defend what was mine. You know, I let him have it with my whip, though I didn't even hurt him that much cause he was wearing a thick cape, and now I have to die already. But you, don't use a whip, take an ax. All a whip is, is anger and a strip of leather, and there's nothing you can do against lawyers, it's like beating a bull with a little twig. As for them, it's not enough that they're the law, they're in with the devil to boot. And there's no greater power on earth than the law and the devil in cahoots. All you can do then is grab an ax and kill the other guy. Even if you have to die in the slammer afterwards. It's better to die than to live when you're up against the law and the devil. God'll forgive you, because when it's about the land, he always forgives. He was born on the land, he lived on it and died on it, so he knows what it is. And God wasn't one of the masters either, he was just a regular carpenter. Same as Kosiorek or Bzdęga in our village. Kosiorek built our cattle sheds, and Bzdęga made wagon wheels for us. And if God doesn't forgive you, the land will. Because sometimes God doesn't always see everything from up in his heights, but the land feels every hurt. Though even better than using an ax would be if you had enough to buy your own lawyers. Sell a few acres, sell the horse or a cow, go take a loan, but buy some lawyers. Then you can face Stolarek and his lawyers like an equal. Cause a guy like that, even if you cut him to death, his sons'll rise up, their sons'll rise up, their grandsons and great-grandsons, and they'll be plowing your land over till kingdom come. But you need to find lawyers that are in with an even bigger devil than Stolarek's. With devils it's like with people, there's bigger ones and smaller ones. Don't keep with the small ones. A small devil is the same as a small calf, small boots. Not much of anything. Always keep with the big ones. However much they ask for. Even if you have to sell your soul. What do you need a soul for if you don't have any land. A soul on its own, without land, it's like its body didn't want it and God's driven it away. Take the religious pictures off the wall, smash the cross with a mallet and leave it there broken, pour the holy water into the night pail, then go get drunk and curse for all you're worth, and the devil'll come find you of his own accord. Prick your finger for him, he'll do the same, and Stolarek'll be quaking in his boots. Pity I won't live to see it, we could have gone together. You'd knock at his window, hey there, Stolarek, I got my own lawyer now! Now we'll see what's what! Now we'll see who's stronger! We were like two brothers, our beds were next to each other in the hospital! He's in with better devils than you are! He knows Lucifer! He knows Beelzebub! He knows the Antichrist! He knows all the important devils! He knows all of hell! Your devils are pisspots! He knows all the laws! A hundred times more than yours know! He knows every law there is! And he knows the right law for you, you thief! They cut my leg off, but I don't care. I'd let them cut the other one off if it meant getting even with you. Come here, Stolarek, come outside, I've got more to tell you! He's visiting Sunday! Come take a look through my window! You'll see us drinking vodka, eating sausage together! My old lady'll cook him some chicken! And we'll laugh together. Ha, ha, ha! Hee, hee, hee! And it's you we'll be laughing at! It's curtains for you, Stolarek! God is slow but just! And you know what he said to me? He said, there's no reason we should lose against a guy like Stolarek. We don't even need the devil on our side, Ambroży. All we need is regular justice. That's what he said. He even laughed, he said those lawyers of Stolarek's, they're no more devils than fleas are wasps. When we're done with them, all that'll be left of them will be their farts. Ha, ha, ha! He laughed and laughed. Hee, hee, hee! He just kept laughing and laughing. You could see the devil flashing in his eyes. I asked if I should pay him, I said I could pay him, but please stop laughing like that. I can't afford it, but I'd sell a few acres, the horse, a cow, take a loan, and I'd pay. If Stolarek could pay for a lawyer I could too. But he should stop laughing, cause it was frightening. The only thing left for Stolarek to do will be go hang himself. Pick your tree, Stolarek. And he asked me, Stolarek's his name? Stolarek. Same as his father! And his father before him. As soon as we get out of here. He promised. But it looks like there's no law for Stolarek, no God, no devil. That's for sure."

"Easy there now, don't cry."

Right off, two big brawny auxiliaries came in and took the lawyer away. Then Jadzia the orderly came in and changed his bed. She said, "So, the poor guy's gone." She checked around to make sure he hadn't left anything behind. There were a few small things, like there always are after someone dies, so she gathered them in her apron. There was the glass of compote he'd not finished, she asked if anyone wanted it. But no one did so she poured it down the sink. She wiped the top of the bedside table with a cloth. She took down the old temperature chart and put up a new one. She was going to take the books as well but I told her to leave them, that maybe I'd read them.

At one point I even took the book he'd left open by his bed and started to read it. It was about this guy that went around asking about a carpenter. It wasn't really a carpenter he was interested in, but he didn't know what he ought to ask about so he asked about a carpenter. Was he nuts or what? You ask about a carpenter when you need someone to make a door or a table or a chest. If he'd come to our village any little child would have told him where the carpenter is. Józef Kalembasa, on the way to the mill, third house after the roadside shrine, the one with the acacia in the yard.

I only read a few pages. I couldn't get any further because his bed was taken by a damn kid that wanted to be my best buddy right from the get-go and talked my ear off from morning till night. His head was all wrapped in bandages, both his legs were broken, he'd crashed his motorbike when he was drunk, and he was all pleased because he was getting out of doing jobs for his father. He never shut his trap once, whether anyone was listening or no. Most of all he liked to go on about his girlfriends, though it was mostly just dirty stories. Which one he'd been with, and where, and when, and how. Lying down, standing up, from the front, from the back, kneeling, squatting, straight up, and upside down. You really felt sorry for the girlfriends.

One time one of them visited him, she was a nice, good-looking young lady. She brought a basket of apples and gave one to each of us, she even had me take two, and she picked another one out herself and put it on my table. She gave you the impression she was visiting her father and grandfather and uncles, not the kid. She even took her basket around the beds like she was embarrassed at being the only girl among all those men. Though they weren't much in the way of men, they were all wrinkled and feeble and gray and bald, their teeth falling out, their eyes failing, some of them with one foot in the grave. But they were kind of embarrassed as well, they were supposedly just taking apples from her, but everyone lowered their eyes so as not to look at her without her clothes on, because it was like she was giving out her breasts instead of apples after that animal had undressed her in front of us all.

Not only did he undress those girlfriends of his, he laughed at them as well. He laughed so much sometimes he slapped himself on the thigh, on his cast. He laughed the way a fool laughs at the slightest thing. He laughed to himself. And though it was none of our business, everyone looked at him as he laughed like he was on his way to his own funeral. How could you laugh like that on a bed that was still warm after someone else had died. Maybe he was so stupid he didn't even know that through all that laughter and all those undressed girlfriends he was just continuing the other man's dying. Old men can see straight through the world, and they could see that too.

Besides, is it true that there're so many different ways? Stallions don't do anything like that with mares, nor dogs with bitches. Why would people? And what for? After all, whichever way you do it the result's the same. I was a young man too in my day and I may even have had more girls than him, but I always did it the way you're supposed to.

The only one to laugh was old Albin in the corner by the door, he'd squeal with delight whenever the kid would put his hand between his girlfriend's legs, or she'd do the same to him. But Albin's back was broken and he just lay there like a tree stump, and his arms and legs lay next to him like chopped-off boughs. He could only dream of sleeping with a woman one more time before he died. He was forever cursing his life, cursing his injury, his children, everything. He promised an acre of land to the ward orderly, Jadzia, if she'd only put her hand under his covers, it could even be right before he died. Jadzia laughed and said death was probably a lot nicer than her hand, her hand was all work-worn and chapped and not exactly young. Because Jadzia was able to laugh at even the saddest things. Another woman would have given him an earful, but she laughed. Another woman would have burst into tears, but Jadzia laughed. Often it'd be quiet as the grave on the ward, then Jadzia would come in and say something and everyone would be laughing.

It wasn't surprising really. To be surrounded like her for so many years by misery and pain and death and moaning, and it was constantly, clean up shit and piss, tidy the place, change the beds, take this out, bring this in – after all that you'd learn to laugh at anything. Plus, everyone was always trying to marry her, old, young, widows, married men, though all of them had half a foot in the next world. A good few couldn't even stand up on their own, or turn over in bed by themselves, they were armless, legless, they shat their pants, their faces were all crooked, they ached everywhere. But the moment Jadzia came on the ward, every one of them was all set to marry her. Some of them would have married her one day and died the next. And she never turned anyone down, she never said no, she just laughed.

Often one of them would set about marrying her in a way he'd never have done with his own wife, because she'd have knocked his block off. But Jadzia the orderly let anyone try to marry her as much as they wanted, and she laughed with each one the way she would have done with her own man. She was never sad, never angry. It was just that when one of them would try to arrange a wedding with her, she'd ask:

"How am I going to get to the church? Are you planning to take me in a regular wagon with the boards all dirty with manure? Cause I'm not going unless it's in a carriage drawn by four white horses."

One guy would promise she'd be a fine lady when she lived with him.

"Then you'll have to become a fine gentleman first."

One of them would swear she'd never lack for caviar in his house.

"Caviar maybe not, but I'd lack for everything else."

One tried to tempt her by saying he had gold rubles buried under a mow in his barn, and when he got back home he'd dig them up and they'd all be hers.

"Best go home first and dig them up, your kids might have gotten there first."

Another one kept pestering her about getting together in the morning when everyone was still asleep.

"In the morning there's no moonlight and your breath smells."

One guy sighed and said that if the Lord let him get well even just for a moment from being with her, he'd buy a new bell for the church.

"Then buy the bell first so I can hear it ringing."

Someone else boasted that though he was old, if he went with her he'd get his youth back.

"You should get your youth back first, because afterwards it might be too late and we'd both be embarrassed."

One of them asked if he could at least feel her breast.

"What good would that do you? You're not a baby anymore, you won't get any milk from it."

Another one complained he wanted her so bad it hurt, but he couldn't move arm or leg.

"So you see yourself. No moving, no loving."

Another guy would grin at her when she was putting a urinal in place for him, though he couldn't ever go.

"You need to take a piss first, cause otherwise later it could be a problem."

When one of them was dying she'd sit by him and say to him:

"You were supposed to marry me, and here you are dying. I laughed just because, but I would have gone with you even in a regular wagon with dirty boards."

Maybe that's why she never took a husband, because they were forever marrying her and then dying, and it was like she was constantly being made a widow. I laughed myself a good many times that if it wasn't for my legs, or if I'd met Miss Jadzia earlier, she would have had to be my wife. I'm no spendthrift, Miss Jadzia was a sensible woman too, we'd have made a good couple. But nothing was lost, when I got home I'd come visit her one day, bring her a chicken, some eggs, cheese, and we'd talk it through. The house would have a housekeeper, I'd have a wife, because my brothers had been on at me about getting married. There was no point even talking about it right now with these legs, who knew if I'd ever walk again, and Miss Jadzia wouldn't have been able to carry me, even though she had strong arms.

One time at the very beginning, when she was changing my sheets she saw the scars on my body and she was horrified:

"Heavens almighty! Who gave you all those wounds, Mr. Szymek?"

"Different people, Miss Jadzia, some of it was at dances, some was in the resistance."

"And you survived all of them? Lord have mercy!" And she asked me to tell about one of the scars at least.

"Then you decide which one, Miss Jadzia," I said playfully. She chose the scar on my shoulder, a small one though it had gotten bigger over the years. And so I had to tell her how it got there.

I was spending the winter in hiding at the house of a guy I knew in Jemielnica. The village was a long way from any main road. To the south there were woods. And it was no ordinary winter either, there was snow everywhere and you could only travel by sleigh. The animals came out of the woods right up to the house. You'd step outside and there'd be a deer poking about in the yard, a hare hopping around, and partridges flying in like snow suddenly falling from the roof. What was there to be afraid of? I even moved my bed from the attic to the main room. Then one night, bang! bang! they start hammering on the door and shouting, open up! And before anyone could even open the door they smashed it in with their rifle butts. They virtually took me from my bed – I just had enough time to put my pants on when they started knocking me in the back and on the head with those rifle butts, and it was, forward march! Like they were in some kind of big hurry.

They'd come in two sleighs. But three of them stayed back to escort me on foot, while the rest went ahead in the sleighs. They didn't even let me put my boots on – for them I was probably already a corpse. So they pushed me along barefoot in pants and shirt, following the tracks made by the sleighs.

The snow stuck to my feet, and from time to time I tried to rub one foot against the other. But right away one of them would thump me in the back. Though they kept hitting me the whole time anyway, probably to warm themselves up in the cold. Or they may have felt even colder than me, because every couple of yards one of them would bat his arms against his sides. They were wearing greatcoats and boots and balaclavas under their helmets, and gloves, but if you're not used to it, you'll be cold even if it's not that cold. Plus they had their hands on metal the whole time, and metal is even colder than the ground.

To begin with I walked as if I was on burning coals, and I felt I wouldn't make it very far. I wanted to get beyond the village, at that point I was planning to jump them, let them kill me where I chose for it to happen, not them, especially since there was no telling where that might be. Besides, why go farther when it was all leading to the same thing. But once we got outside the village I started feeling sorry that it was about to happen right now, and I thought, I'll keep going a little ways farther at least. Why should I worry about my feet, they're going to be dead either way, and it would be good to go on even a little bit. The sleighs with the other men were farther and farther away, it looked like they were sinking into the snow, and in a minute they'd be out of sight. The guys behind kept prodding me for walking too slowly.

Eventually, to make me forget I was walking on snow I started imagining to myself that I was walking over stubble. Stubble pricks and hurts just as bad, but at least your feet are warm. Though if you know what you're doing, walking on stubble is no big deal. All you have to do is shuffle your feet along instead of picking them up. If you do that you can move as fast as you like, and you can run away when you're being chased. And so I felt less and less that I was walking on snow, and more and more I could feel the stubble under my feet, I could feel the earth warm from the sun and dusty dry. I could even hear the chink of a whetstone against a scythe blade. The heat from the crop stuck in my chest. For a moment, way up overhead I heard a lark. But one of the bastards behind me must have heard it as well because he fired a shot over my head and the lark stopped singing.

My throat started to feel dry, as if from the baking heat from the grain and the earth, and I stooped down to take a handful of snow. At that moment one of them whacked me as hard as he could on the side of the head. I went sprawling and I thought about not getting up. I even wanted them to finish me off. But with them it's never that easy. They don't like it when someone chooses his own death. They have to take him to where they've decided he's going to die. Even if it's the same death. They started yapping like wolves, beating me and kicking me, and I got up. But it was harder and harder for me to walk. My ankles were aching. Every step felt like I was treading on a nail. So I started to imagine the grain must be full of thistles, and it was because of the thistles that it hurt so much walking through the stubble. Or maybe it'd been cut with sickles. Stubble that's been cut with sickles feels like it's packed with nails. Then I imagined my father was calling me from the far end of the field to bring him his whetstone, and I was on my way to him. Or that my cows had wandered onto the squire's land and they were eating his beets, and I was hurrying towards them across the stubble, heart in mouth, as fast as I could, to shoo them out of there. At a time like that, who'd be thinking about whether their feet hurt when you can barely breathe, you're so afraid that any minute now the squire's steward is going to confiscate the cows before you get there. Or that I was racing the other boys across the stubble field, seeing who'd make it to the field boundary first. I won.

Those sons of bitches probably thought I was exhausted, because how could they have known that the whole way I'd been walking on stubble, at the height of summer, the height of the harvest, since they were leading me over snow. In the end they evidently got real cold themselves, because they started clapping their hands and blowing on them, and stamping their feet. On the left-hand side, right by the track there was a slope overgrown with juniper bushes, and at the bottom there was a deep twisting ravine. But they were so convinced I wouldn't go an inch farther without being beaten that one of them even dug out a bottle and they all took a swig. They must have been telling dirty stories as well, because all of a sudden they all hooted with laughter as if on command. One of them opened his fly and took a leak. Right at that moment I ran for the slope. Before the first shots sounded I was rolling down through the junipers. Then I dropped like a sack into the ravine. For them it was too steep to chase me. They just stood there shooting. But only one bullet got me, right here in the shoulder. The rest hit the snow, the junipers, the trees. I didn't even feel anything at the time, only later, when I was already safe.

From that moment on, Jadzia started giving me special treatment with the meals. She'd bring me a bigger piece of meat for dinner, or more potatoes, or a second bowl of soup. Whenever she came onto the ward she'd always ask if I was hungry or thirsty, or if I'd run out of cigarettes, she could go buy me some. A few times she even got me a pack with her own money. Every so often she'd come onto the ward seemingly for no special reason, and while she was there she'd straighten my blanket, because it's gone and fallen on the floor, Mr. Szymek. She'd plump my pillow, because you'll get a headache, Mr. Szymek, from lying on a pillow that's all squashed up like that. And she'd always slip something to eat under the pillow.

"Just make sure you eat it during the night, when everyone else is asleep, Mr. Szymek," she'd whisper, as if to the pillow. "And watch out for that guy by the window, because he sleeps with one eye open."

Or when she was bending down for the urinal under the bed, she'd murmur in my ear:

"Tomorrow it's chops for dinner. You'll have one on the outside like everyone else, but there'll be another one hidden under the potatoes. Just don't pull it out or people will see. The old guy in the corner has eyes like a hawk. He lost his leg but there's nothing wrong with his eyesight. He watches everyone else's plates while he's eating his own dinner. But it won't do him any good. And you, Mr. Szymek, you need to live so you need to eat. I'll bake a plum cake for Sunday because my sister's coming, and I'll bring you some too."

One time she brought me an orange. It was the first time in my life I'd eaten an orange. Those wounds of mine came in useful after all.

MOTHER V

They happened to be looking for someone to run wedding ceremonies at the district administration. In theory the district secretary was supposed to do weddings, but since the end of the war no more than three or four couples had gotten married in the registry office, mostly people still had a church wedding. Though legally a registry office marriage was just as valid as a church one, and you could be just as happy or unhappy after a civil wedding as a church one. Also, when you had a registry office wedding it was easier to get a horse through UNRRA, or building materials, or grain for sowing. And you could get divorced, the next day even, if things didn't work out. Not like in the church, where that was an end of it, because what God hath joined together let no man put asunder, so you have to stay with some awful bitch for the rest of your life. Quite a few of them lived exactly like that, cat and dog, they'd fight, have running feuds, when one of them pulled left the other would pull right, but they'd have to keep on living together all the way till one of them died before the other. Though if you ask me, a life like that is actually against God and God ought to break it up. I mean, it can happen that the wrong two people end up together, no one can know ahead of time who's meant for who, because destinies get mixed up as well, destinies are like days, you should only say they're good after the sun's gone down. That was another reason people preferred registry office weddings.

The first ones to have a civil wedding, right after the front passed through, were Florek Denderys and Bronka Makuła. The district administration gave them a better wedding than a lot of rich folk get, even the ones that have a church wedding. They put a flag on the administration building, they decorated the walls with fir branches, they laid down a carpet a good ten yards long leading up to the entrance, and over the doorway they hung a sign in cutout letters saying: The District Administration Congratulates the Happy Couple. On top of that they were awarded several thousand zlotys. Florek was given a length of material for a suit. Bronka got cloth for a dress, she got a horse, a cow, and baby clothes, because there was one on the way, and an alarm clock to wake them up for work if they ever overslept. Except they had to leave for the West soon after, because people in the village wouldn't leave them alone, they kept calling Bronka a whore and saying the kid was a bastard, though it hadn't yet been born. So after them, for a long time there weren't any takers for a registry office wedding.

The mayor or the district secretary even visited anyone that they heard was getting married and tried to persuade them to do it at the registry office, they'd say that at the registry office you didn't need to announce the banns, you didn't need bridesmaids and veils, you just write it in the registry book and that's that. Also, it was easier to get a horse, building materials, everything was easier. In the church the priest charged the earth. True, wedding vows were supposed to be before God. But has anyone ever seen God? Only in a picture. How can you be sure it's him? Even before the war there were a few unbelievers in the village. Kruk for instance, he'd never taken confession in his life till his old lady and his daughters made him. And at the manor houses there was always a strike going on somewhere or other. Mostly at harvesttime, or sometimes during the potato lifting. Wicek Chrząszcz from over in Poddębice even did six months in prison for agitation, because he got drunk at the harvest festival and threatened the village elder he'd get hung from a tree the moment justice would arrive. But now it *had* arrived, what next? The folk from the county offices came asking how many couples had tied the knot at the district administration. And the answer was, none. What do you mean, none? Aren't people getting married in your district? Well, sure they are, but everyone's doing it at the church. So then, this district of yours is going to have to pony up if people there are refusing to understand the new times. The taxes'll get upped, or they'll maybe stop supplying coal. There's always something you can stop giving.

And on the other side, every Sunday the priest would rage against those registry office weddings from the pulpit, he'd say they were godless, threaten folks with hellfire and eternal damnation. And anyone that was thinking of getting married at the registry office, he'd tell them, don't you dare, otherwise you'll get expelled from the church, and the Lord God would expel them from humankind. The worst part was that he poked fun at the district administration all he could, he said it was no house of God, that ever since the district administration has been there it was the place you go to pay taxes, and that wedding vows are a sacrament, not taxes, one of the seven holy sacraments, that they were established by God, not by earthly powers, because earthly powers come from Satan. And a good many pig sheds are cleaner than at the district administration, they haven't had their walls whitewashed since before the war, and when you go in there the floor's so dirty your shoes stick to it, and the officials there do nothing but smoke cigarettes and chase around after the secretaries. So then, young man and young lady, try going and swearing to be true to each other in that Sodom and Gomorrah. What will a vow like that really be worth?

It might have been because of what the priest was saying that they prepared a separate room in the administration building, they whitewashed the walls, decorated it with flowers, cleaned the floor, put in a new desk and chairs, laid a carpet, and started looking for an official whose only job would be to give those weddings. Though some people said an order had come down from above.

I ran into Rożek one time when I was transporting cabbage home from our patch. He was mayor in those days. He asks me:

"How would you feel about working at the district administration? You could be the one to give weddings. You'd hardly have any work, because no one wants to get married at the registry office. You'd get a regular salary. And you were already in the police once, you'd be one of ours."

I thought to myself, why not, I'd rather sit behind a desk than cart cabbage. I wasn't sure I believed in God either, so what did I care about the priest trying to scare people. And at least I'd be able to wear decent clothes, because all my clothes were starting to get ragged. When there was a dance I didn't have anything to wear. Not to mention I had no money to buy drinks, or sometimes even for admission. My officer's boots were still in okay shape, but not many people wore officer's boots anymore. The war was further and further away, and now everyone wore shoes and suits, and the fashion was for pants as wide as skirts and coats big as sacks, as if people were getting as much freedom as they could after the war. Me in my britches and officer's boots, I was like something from a different world. To the point that after I left the police I started wondering what to do with myself. Because father spent every penny he had on building new cattle sheds, and even when he gave me money for cigarettes he'd always complain, you smoke like a chimney.

I'd left the police because I was supposed to become the commanding officer, but instead they chose this snot-faced kid that hadn't even been in the resistance, he'd just finished school. Plus he thought he could fix the world's problems in the space of a week. But it's easier to create a world in a week than fix it. Especially a world that's been through a war. And instead of carrying on looking for guns, because people were still shooting at each other, or at least guarding the freight trains carrying cement that would stand in the sidings till half their load had been thieved, he went after Franek Gwiżdż for brewing moonshine, and he had his whole farm searched from top to bottom. After that Gwiżdż says to me, you son of a bitch, you came here drinking all the time, did I ever take a red cent from you, I'd even stick a bottle in your pocket for the road because I thought you were one of us. You just wait and see if you ever get vodka from me again, cause I'm still gonna make it, there's not a fucking thing you can do to stop me. The Germans could kiss my ass, and you can too. Luckily he hid it all underground somewhere so all we found were the traces of a fire pit in the elder bushes behind the barn. But he explained that by saying he sometimes boiled potatoes for the pigs back there when it was too windy in the yard. So there I was, neither here nor there, actually nowhere, with nothing but work in the fields from dawn till dusk.

I even thought about maybe taking up haircutting again. True, there was a barber in the village now, Jaskóła's brother-in-law. He'd moved here not long ago from the city because things hadn't gone so well for him there, and he opened a place in Niezgódka's outbuilding. Though before the war, when he married Kryśka Jaskóła, he was supposed to become a captain of horse in the uhlans. But no one brought that up. All sorts of changes happened to people through those years, what did it matter if a captain of horse became a barber. Though the farmers complained that he had a hand like a butcher, he'd put it on your head and it was like he was resting it on the block, you had to hold your neck firmly so he wouldn't break it. On top of that he was a tight-lipped son of a gun. He'd often not say a single word the whole time he was cutting your hair. What kind of barber is that? You don't go to the barber just to get your hair cut or get a shave, you go to sit and have a chat and listen to stories.

There were supposed to be buses that would start serving some of the villages and I thought about perhaps getting a job as a bus conductor. The work's not too tough, you ride around and sell tickets, and people get on and get off, people you know, people you don't, but the whole time you're among people. And among people life's always more enjoyable, especially if there's a fair and the bus is packed, you can have a joke, shout at folks, when there are people all sorts of things can happen. What can happen in the fields? A hare runs past, a lark starts singing, clouds come and it'll begin to rain?

Though on the quiet, most of all I was counting on Michał, that maybe he'd come visit finally, and he could give me some advice or maybe find me a job where he was. Because to tell the truth, I wasn't that fired up about being either a barber or a conductor. With both of those jobs I'd still have to work on the land every spare moment after work. And instead of making my life easier, I'd be worn out. Besides, at that time Stasiek was still at home and he was meant for the land. But for some reason Michał never came or got in touch, though he'd promised he would the last time he was home. He was even going to come stop for a while. He was going to take some leave. Because the last time, he only just swung by for a moment. How long had he stayed? Less than half a day.

We'd finished lunch and we were just sitting around the table, me and father were smoking while mother washed the dishes. It was Sunday. All of a sudden a black limousine pulls up outside the window. Mother took fright. Who are they coming to see? It was us. Jesus and Mary, it's Michał! Lord in heaven, Michał! Son! We thought something had happened to you! We didn't hear a word from you all these years. Then there was the war. So many people died, and now after the war they're still dying. So you're here! He was looking very smart, he wore an overcoat and a hat, leather gloves, a cherry-red scarf, the driver of the limousine followed him in with two suitcases. Father's voice trembled – Michał? Tears were rolling down mother's face. The cases were so heavy the driver staggered as he crossed the threshold, then he put them down in the middle of the room. But Michał told the man to go wait for him in the car, because they had to be heading back before long.

A whole swarm of kids gathered around the limousine like flies on shit, they touched it, patted it, stared through the windows. The driver just sat there stony-faced. In the end father went out and shooed them away:

"Stand back there. Stop patting it, it's not a cow. You'll scratch it if you're not careful."

Older people stopped to look as well, wondering who'd come to visit the Pietruszkas. No one would believe it was Michał. It was only when father sent Stasiek out to tell people it was him. No one in the village had ever seen a car like that. Before the war the squire had a limousine, but it was only half the size of this one and it had an open roof, this one was all closed in and it had windows like a house. One time the bishop came for a confirmation in a limousine, but it couldn't have held a candle to this one, even though it was all decorated and the bishop was in his purple.

The first thing Michał did was put his arms around mother and hold her for a long time, don't cry, mama, come on now, don't cry. Us he kissed just twice, once on each cheek. Then right away he started opening the cases. He'd brought all kinds of things for mother and father, though us brothers got our share as well. Me, I had socks, a tie, a scarf, some shaving soap. Mother got some material for a dress, a headscarf, needles and thread, cinnamon and pepper. Father, tobacco and cigarette papers and some winter gloves. Antek got a penknife with two blades and a corkscrew, Stasiek a mouth organ, and both of them got a shirt. Plus there were other things.

He said he was sorry to only come for a short visit, but he promised the next time he'd stay longer, maybe he'd even come for the harvest, because he'd not had a scythe in his hands all these years and he felt like doing some mowing, he wondered if he'd still know how. Today he'd just come by to see how we were all doing, how we'd gotten through the war. Since the end of the war he'd kept meaning to come see us, but something more important always got in the way. He'd not even had any time off till now, but he'd be back, for sure he'd be back.

There were some dumplings and broth left over from dinner, mother wanted to heat it up for him, but he said no, he wasn't hungry, and besides they'd had something to eat on the way. He only drank some milk, because mother had just done the afternoon milking and it was still warm. He knocked a whole mugful back in one, it must have been more than a pint, and he actually gave a sigh and said it'd been a long time since he'd drunk real milk like that, straight from the cow. He even seemed to be made sad by the milk, because he fell to thinking for a moment. Mother said maybe he'd like some more, or she could pour some off into a bottle and he could drink it on the way back.

He laughed, as if about the bottle, though there wasn't really anything funny about it. When he was apprenticed to a tailor and he'd come home every Sunday, mother always put milk in a bottle and he took it with him. But right away he hugged mother and kissed her on the forehead as if to say sorry for having laughed like that.

I found it hard to get used to the idea that this was Michał. Maybe it was because he'd dropped by so unexpectedly, plus he was about to leave again right away. It was another thing that it had been donkey's years since I'd last seen him, just before the war. That time too he came out of the blue, because it wasn't a Sunday like usual but the middle of the week, a Wednesday or Thursday. That time he'd been kind of bitter or sad. Father and mother both asked him, what's up, son? Tell us. But it was like he'd lost his tongue, he just sat there thinking and thinking, and it was only when he was leaving that he said there was going to be a war and not to worry about him if he didn't visit. Then later, after the war had started already, he came by wanting to see me because he had some important business, but he'd never gotten around to telling me what it had been.

I even thought about asking what he'd wanted from me that time during the war. Course, the war was over and there was no sense in going back to it. Still, it would give us something to talk about. But he looked at his watch, got up, and said it was time for him to go. All I said was:

"I thought we'd have a chance to talk, and here you are rushing off."

"We will talk one day," he said. "I'll visit for longer. Maybe I'll even come stay when I've got some leave. We'll see."

That time during the war we'd missed each other. I was in the woods with the resistance, though he must have been doing something as well, because he'd come and gone at night. He waited almost a week to see if I'd show up. He wouldn't sleep in the house, instead he stayed in the barn, he dug himself a hole in the hay. He didn't go outside at all, they brought him food to the barn at dusk each day. If anything happened, father or mother or Antek was supposed to go out into the yard and call the dog loudly three times – Burek! Burek! Burek! This was his first visit since then. After so many years you forget someone, even your own brother.

Though when you're a brother, it's for your whole life. And whatever happens to brothers, you can't change the fact that they're brothers. Of all my brothers he was the closest to me, closer than Antek or Stasiek. We'd gotten into all kinds of scrapes together when we were kids, we'd slept in the same bed. And I always defended him whenever anyone tried to hurt him, even if it was me against everyone else. Because even though he was three years older than me, I was a better fighter. That balanced things out. Sometimes I'd actually feel older than him, because I was tougher too.

He hadn't changed that much in appearance. Only his eyes had gotten kind of sharper, so it was hard to look straight into them, it was like he was cutting you down with them, while before his eyes had been gentle and blue. But everyone's eyes changed in the war, with some folks out of fear, others from lack of sleep, most from crying. On top of that those eyes of his darted to and fro like mice being chased. He wasn't even able to keep them on mother for long, though mother herself couldn't get enough of looking at him. She kept saying, Michał, Michał. Just the one time he got some warmth in his eyes, when a couple of chicks came out from under the brood hen in the basket. He even picked one of them up, but he put it down again right away as if it had scalded his hand. At another moment he lost himself in thought staring at the Last Supper, like he was remembering how he was supposed to become a priest.

I found him strange, sort of in a shell. If I hadn't known it was him, my brother Michał, I might not have felt it was my brother. I might have thought he was some distant cousin on father's side or mother's that we'd never met before but we'd just heard there was such a person, though no one knew what he did in the world, only that he existed. And here he'd shown up one Sunday afternoon unannounced, like a bolt out of the blue, and no one knew what to say, and he wouldn't even have anything to eat, if he'd eaten something it might have brought him closer to us. But he'd barely come in when he was hurrying off again, like the wind had blown him here by chance.

So there was no time to ask him what his job was, what he'd been up to, how things were going for him. You couldn't just ask him straight out when you hadn't known the first thing about him all those years. It was better to keep on not knowing anything. And the truth is, it's not right to barge into someone else's life right from the get-go, even if it is your own brother and son. I mean, who knows if you won't touch on something painful? Or even if it's still the same brother and son? To begin with you'd need to sit down quietly and stay there at least till the sun sets outside the window, to get used to that big gap of years. It'd be like taking a plow to land that's not been plowed in a long time. After that you might figure out where to begin, and begin from the beginning, the way God began the world.

The only thing father asked was whether there'd be collective farms here. But he didn't even answer that question, because the moment he was done unpacking the suitcases and handing out his presents, right away he started asking questions about what was going on with us here, and he asked and asked the whole time till he left. We couldn't get a word in edgewise. It was like he was thirsting to know everything. Like he hadn't come at all to see us after being away all those years, but that he was trying to grab as much as he could from us and take it with him. He hardly sat in one place for a moment, he kept standing up and pacing around, and there wasn't a single thing he wasn't interested in. He kept pulling things out of his memory like he was taking them out of a sack, anything he remembered, and he kept asking and asking. Sometimes he didn't even wait for the end of the answer before he asked his next question.

As for whether we were all well, mother, father, us brothers, only mother managed to tell him that the stabbing pains in her chest were getting worse. He nodded, then right away he asked how many acres we'd gotten in the land reform, which office we'd dealt with, whether anyone had tried to scare us into not taking it, then after that how things had been here during the war, who had died then, how our cattle sheds had burned down and whether we were planning to build new ones, whether they'd be wooden or brick, whether we'd roof them in thatch like before or put up a tiled roof, how many cows we had, two or more, whether we had a calf, whether we were planning to save it and rear it, whether we had the same horse or a different one, whether they were thinking of bringing electricity to the village, why the lampshade was so sooty, whether we used kerosene in the lamps or some other poor quality stuff, whether Franciszek the sacristan was still alive, whether the priest was the same or a different one and did he mix God and politics in his sermons, which farmers carried the baldachin over him on Corpus Christi these days, why it was still the same rich ones, whether the winter had been hard this year and had there been a lot of snow, whether the river had burst its banks in the spring and who we took water from when the spring flooded, whether we weren't thinking about digging a well, how the orchard was, whether that old *masztan* plum tree was still standing behind the barn, what had happened to it, whether father had planted any new seedlings, whether old Spodzieja was still mending shoes, so who'd taken over after he died, and the dog, was it still Burek, so what was this one called, Strudel, he laughed, Strudel, Strudel, and why had we given it such an odd name, whether mother kept a lot of chickens and geese, whether she had any trouble with polecats or hawks, or maybe with the neighbors, whether that old willow was still standing by the river, whether the blue tits still nested in it, where the girls and the young men went swimming these days, was it still down by Błach's place, was the water deep, what had happened to the tin crucifix with the broken arm that had always stood on the table, where we'd gotten such a fancy table, why there was nothing in our windows when there'd always been lots of flowers on the windowsill, whether we'd planted garlic this year, whether it had been a good year for garlic, and for onions, cabbage, carrots, beets, and that mother must have whitewashed the house recently because it smelled of lime, whether her cheese pierogies were still as good fried up with sour cream, did we do our threshing with a treadmill or still in the old way with a flail, whether old Mrs. Waliszka was still alive and did her son Mietek still drink the way he used to, whether the storks still came and nested on our barn, why father was wheezing like that, did he have to smoke so much, whether mother still baked bread or did we eat store-bought, had there been mines in our fields, whether our crop had been good this year, then he asked about each one separately, how was the rye, how was the wheat, how was the barley, how were the oats, where they were grown and how much there'd been of them, and why we didn't plant millet, whether people had stopped eating it in porridge, and what had happened to the steps that the stones were just lying there, whether I was still in the fire brigade and whether we had a motor pump, whether we had the same old fire engine, where they held dances nowadays, was it still in the firehouse, did people still have fights the way they used to or was there less of that now, and which grade was Stasiek in, was he a good student, did he have the books and notebooks he needed, whether there were partridges in the fields, or hares, or foxes, why the door to the hallway creaked so loud that when he was coming in he thought it was trying to stop him, who the mayor was now and whether we'd gotten our fair share of rationed goods, whether father wasn't thinking of keeping bees, a couple of hives at least, if he did that him and his wife would come for honey. You're married? He just nodded and right away he asked how Stefka Magiera was, whether she'd gotten married and who to, was she happy, was she still so good-looking, who had gone to high school from the village, who'd moved away and who was new, whether Mrs. Kasperek that used to teach Polish was still alive, who taught arithmetic now, who taught singing, whether there were still so many crows in the poplar trees up behind the mill, whether the boys still used to climb up there to knock down their nests, and who was best at it, because it used to be Szymek, and why were the tiles on the stove bulging out like that, were we still arguing with the Prażuchs over the field boundary, how had it happened that we'd stopped, but he wouldn't listen to the answers, he just kept asking more and more questions, did people still go sledging on Pociej's hill in the winter, did Pociej not chase them off, did the carol singers still go around into the New Year, who played Herod, and the devil, and who played death, and was the place by the willow tree at the footbridge still haunted, or maybe the devil had gone by now, whether Michał's godfather Skubida was still alive, so why was he killed, and his godmother Mrs. Kaliszyn, and did the swallows still nest under our eaves, how many nests were there, whether we joined forces with other people during the harvest or if we just brought in our own crop, why we wouldn't buy a clock, why mother was so thin, why father had gone so gray, why Antek, why Stasiek, why me, why this and that and the other, why, why, why?

In the end father couldn't take it anymore and he interrupted all the questions:

"We've told you everything, what else do you want from us?"

Mother pleaded with him:

"You might at least sit down and tell us what's going on with you."

It was like he suddenly woke up. He looked at his watch and said it was time, he had to be going. Right away he shook my hand, because I was sitting closest to him, then father's, Antek's, Stasiek's. He only said goodbye with a handshake, like we'd see each other again tomorrow, the day after at the latest, or like he was just someone we knew, not our brother and our son. Plus, while he was shaking hands he was looking somewhere else like he wasn't thinking about saying goodbye at all, but about God only knows what. It was only when he finally said goodbye to mother, and the poor old thing started crying again, he took her head in his hands, looked in her eyes and said:

"Come on, don't cry, mama. I'll come again, for sure I will. Maybe I'll even bring her. You have to meet her."

And after that we didn't hear from him again.

A year or so later mother sent him a letter, but he didn't write back. She sent another one and he still didn't reply. She was going to write again after a bit, but father got mad and said there was no point in writing all those letters, that he should answer the other ones first. Or maybe he was up to his ears in work, and she was just distracting him with all those letters of hers. When there's work, everyone knows it needs doing. Even here, when harvesttime comes you don't have time to so much as scratch your backside. Maybe it's his harvesttime. When it's over he'll come visit without writing a letter even. He was gone all those years and he came back then. It's not long till Christmas, he's sure to come for Christmas, maybe both of them, I mean he said they'd both come. Mother, you'd better start thinking about what cakes to bake. Letters won't do him any good, you can't make the days pass any faster with letters, let alone hurrying up harvesttime.

But father turned out to be mistaken, Michał never came either that Christmas or the next. Mother kept writing, though in secret now. One day I went into the barn to tear off some hay for the horse and I saw her kneeling at a stool by the back doors, at the far end of the threshing floor. Her glasses were perched on her nose and she was writing something. She was startled and she slipped the hand with the pen under her apron. It took her a moment to look up.

"Oh, it's you," she said relieved. "I came here to pray. It's hard to concentrate in the house, here's it's nice and quiet."

"Couldn't you go into the orchard? It's just as quiet out there, and there's more light," I said, staring at her and at the same time at the inkwell, that she hadn't managed to hide.

"There's plenty of light in here from the holes in the walls," she answered.

Another time I was going up to the attic to fetch something, I put my head through the trapdoor opening, and here I see mother sitting by a crack of light from the ridgepole with the chopping board on her lap, writing. I climbed back down as quietly as I could, making sure not to step on the creaky rung. It was the same after she was confined to bed, I'd often find her writing those letters, leaning over the stool with the medicines on it that stood by the bed. I'd try not to see, or leave right away pretending I'd just remembered something I had to do. Though I don't know who took her letters to the post office. Antek and Stasiek had left home by then. The other people who came to the house, I couldn't see her trusting any of them with her letters. Maybe it was father? He'd been opposed to her writing at one time, so perhaps now he was embarrassed to be seen with them and he mailed them when I was out. Because ever since it was just the two of them and me at home, he stuck to mother like a little child. He would have spent all his time sitting by her bedside telling her stories from the old days. Sometimes he didn't even tell stories, he just sat there like he was half asleep. Time was, he'd be the one chasing everyone out to work. Now mother had to keep reminding him about the jobs that needed done. Even the most everyday things. That he had to water the cows, or cut chaff, or lay down straw in the cattle barn, or even give the dog its dinner.

"Come on, get on with it," she'd often pester him.

But he'd just sit there waving her words away like pesky flies.

"What are you worried about? They'll get their water, the chaff'll get cut, the straw will get put down, the dog'll get its dinner. You just stay where you are, you're sick." And he'd go on sitting there.

Harvesttime would be right around the corner and he'd sit there like winter was coming.

"The rye must be ripe already," mother would remind him. "You might go take a look, see if it's time to mow."

"No way it's ripe yet. Last year at this time it was still green. When you're stuck in bed you think things are ripe already. But time in the fields is different from human time."

When he finally had to get up and go, because she wouldn't give him any peace, he was angry, he'd mutter something under his breath. Sometimes, out of irritation he'd grab the cat where it was curled up by the stove and chuck it outside.

"Go catch mice, damn you, instead of lying about indoors."

Or he'd clang the empty buckets because there wasn't any water and he was thirsty. One time he even kicked the door because the damn thing was creaking like it was ill.

Mother was finding it harder and harder to leave her bed. She'd only get up to cook something from time to time or to throw down some grain for the chickens when father forgot. When she did the laundry, she had to pull a stool up to the tub and wash the clothes sitting down. Father would heat the water, fill the tub then empty it afterwards, go down to the river to rinse the washing, and hang it out in the yard or up in the attic. It was only when Antek or Stasiek visited that she'd get better for the time they were here. She'd kill a chicken, cook up some broth, make dumplings, wash their dirty things that they brought with them. But after they left she'd get even sicker, and for a week or longer she wouldn't even get out of bed. Her heart hurt more and more.

"Death's on its way for me, you can tell," she'd complain to father.

Father would reassure her that if death was coming it would come for him first, and he didn't feel it coming yet. He gave her a rosary and told her to pray, that that would soon make her feel better. He'd take the prayer book as well and sit by her, but he wasn't so good at reading and he'd sometimes ask her for help.

"Read what it says here, this part. I can't see it properly."

And mother would read:

"'Conceived without the stain of original sin. . .'"

"That's how you write 'conceived'?" he'd say surprised.

She'd often get annoyed with him for interrupting her the whole time, she'd tell him to pray from memory, because what kind of praying was it when he didn't know what was written there. He explained that when he prayed from memory the prayers got muddled up with his other thoughts and God got lost in the thoughts, and after that he couldn't find him. He didn't take offense when she got angry, and actually she wasn't really that angry. Maybe they just grumbled at each other like that instead of sighing and complaining about being left alone. Or they had no need to talk any differently, because what was there to talk about, they'd already told each other everything there was to tell. Also, why use the same words when hundreds of thousands of them have already been spoken all through their life, and life had turned against the words anyway?

Sometimes I felt sorry for them. But I rarely went straight back home after work. I'd usually go out, either drinking or with girls. I'd often not get back till midnight, when they were long asleep. Many a time I'd just be going to bed in the morning as they were getting up. After you've been drinking, when you come back home you sometimes have trouble finding the door.

And a drunk man, as well as being drunk, he's a stranger even to his own kith and kin. They'd talk to me but my head would be humming, buzzing, I'd barely hear what they were saying. Or I'd have to remind myself who they were, that they were my father and mother, and that it was me they were telling off. Mother, like you'd expect, she'd be sighing and pleading with me, but at least quietly:

"Oh, Szymek, please, don't drink, you need to change. Change, son, stop drinking."

But father hadn't forgiven me for going to work in the registry office at the district administration, and the moment he saw me having trouble making it across the threshold he'd come down on me like a ton of bricks, that I was bringing shame on the family, that this had been a God-fearing family for generations, that they were born in God and died in God, that one of them had even planned to travel to the Holy Land, one of them had bought a picture for the church, one of them had held the baldachin over the bishop when he came to visit, Michał would have been a priest if we'd only been able to afford it, but I was a disgrace. I had no education, I had no holy orders, I had no God, and there I was giving ungodly weddings.

"I don't know what we did to deserve this. The devil's got you in his clutches, that much is clear, you monster."

"Well if you can't go with God you have to go with the devil, father," I'd answer him out of spite. "Besides, what do we know about the devil? No more than we know about God. Maybe God didn't insist on having the whole world, maybe he divided it up with the devil. What do we know? All we do is plow and plant and mow over and over, God's nowhere close and the devil's far away as well."

"But people are laughing at us, damn you! You wanted a priest in the family, you got one, that's what they're saying. You just need to buy him a cassock."

"I don't need a cassock, and people can kiss my ass. What are they, jealous that I work for the government?"

"Government, my eye. You're a bad seed. Maybe you should start giving confession? Baptizing children? Burying the dead? Get yourself a censer. Though you'd have to put vodka in it – holy water would burn you. Why God is doing this to us, I'll never know. What have we done? What have we done?"

"Stop doing all those things, son," mother would say to back him up. "You'll drive us to our graves. We've little enough time left as it is. Think about what you're doing. You ought to get married."

"How's he supposed to get married?" father would say sarcastically. "Priests aren't allowed to marry. They have to marry other people. Besides, who'd marry a no-good like him? He was so smart, he found a way to get out of working the land. You just wait, you good-for-nothing, you'll come back to the land."

Father's predictions went in one ear and out the other. I mean, why would I go back to the land. I wasn't wed to it and I didn't owe it anything, and at the registry office I didn't even work a quarter as much as I'd have had to on the land, because it was like Mayor Rożek had said, there was hardly any work. No one came to get married there, so all I did was sit at my desk and stare at the ceiling or go look out the window, chat with people that were waiting in front of the building, or read the newspapers. But you can't fill the day with newspapers, even a day divided in two like at the administration. Often I'd get a tad bored. Once I was done reading I didn't quite know what to do with myself. And so it went till four o'clock came around. Also, to begin with no one seemed to visit from the other offices. Maybe they were afraid of me, or were they deliberately keeping their distance? Only the district secretary would sometimes come by, his little eyes darting into the corners of the room, and he'd ask:

"How's it going there, pal, still no takers? You need to make more of an effort." Then he was gone.

Sometimes Mayor Rożek would call me in when he had a speech he needed to make at a farmers' meeting, or to the children at some school.

"Here, Pietruszka, read this through. If you can think of anything smart to add, write it in. You were in the police, you know how things are. It shouldn't be too antichurch, cause otherwise my old lady'll chase me out the house with holy water if she finds out, plus the farmers might take offense. And correct any mistakes."

Then he'd have me make a clean copy in good handwriting. Because he could read more or less okay, but his handwriting looked like chicken scratches. He couldn't even sign his own name properly. The district secretary showed him several times how to do it in a single go with a flourish underneath instead of printing one letter after another like a schoolboy, because no one's going to respect a signature like that. So whenever you went into his office you'd see piles of papers covered in practice flourishes.

"See, I'm learning. But I'm never going to get the hang of it, I can see that. Your hand would have to be born all over again. It wasn't like that for the mayors before the war. Back then, Kurzeja or Zadruś or whoever would just put three crosses and the thing was signed. Nowadays you can't get away with that. The nation's educated. Back then, what did they have to think about? Filling a hole in the road. Now there's politics as well."

It was hardly surprising. He'd been a wagon driver at the manor all his life till suddenly he became mayor, his hand was used to holding a whip, not a pen. But when the speech went well he'd always bring a half-bottle. And when it went badly he'd bring one also, to get over his disappointment.

"It didn't go off well, Pietruszka, it really didn't. There were barely two or three of them clapping, the rest just stood there with their heads down, staring like wolves. It wasn't like when I was a driver. You'd sit on your ass and the horses would pull the wagon. Plus, back then there were masters and so there was someone to rebel against. Who are you supposed to rebel against these days? Maybe if I rose higher, cause it's always easier when you're high up. The lowest place is always the worst, Pietruszka, and it's always worst nearest the earth. I'm telling you, a mayor's life is crap. And there I was thinking it'd be all sweetness. What do you reckon, maybe I could learn to drive a tractor? There aren't going to be any horses anymore. The horses around the villages are just gonna die off and then there'll be no more horses. The future is tractors."

But he didn't have time to learn. They shot him not long after that, no one knew why. He was going home on his bicycle like he did every day, because he lived in the old farmhands' quarters in Bartoszyce, and something went wrong with the gears on his bike, so he was pushing it through the woods. In the morning they found him on the road, he had three bullets in his chest and a piece of paper pinned to his jacket: Death to the red stooges. His bicycle was lying on top of him.

The first wedding I gave was for Stach Magdziarz from Lisice and Irka Bednarek from Kolonie. Irka wore a kind of green outfit, Stach had a brown pinstriped suit. Stach's mother was getting on, Irka worked at the mill. Stach hadn't gone to church since the war because the priest wouldn't give him absolution. It was because one time the priest had been on his way to administer last rites to a sick man, and here there was a fire at Sapiela's place in Kolonie. All the horses were out working in the fields and there was nothing to hitch to the fire engine. So without a second thought Stach flagged down the priest's wagon and hitched his horses to the fire engine, and off they went. It wasn't such a big sin, because the sick man was only at the end of the village and it wouldn't have hurt the priest to walk the rest of the way.

The mayor came, and the district secretary, and two other officials, to see how I did with my first wedding. I felt a bit awkward and a couple of times I got the words wrong, but it went more or less okay. Afterwards, Stach and I went to the pub and got so drunk we passed out. Because Irka would only have one drink, we couldn't convince her to have another. She sat there like she was all worried and kept asking over and over whether they were going to be happy now they were married. I had to swear at least three times that they would be. I even stood them a bottle out of my own pocket, for that happiness of theirs. And they were happy, till Stach got ulcers in his stomach and died.

Before you could say Jack Robinson I'd figured out how to give weddings, and soon marrying people was no harder than eating a slice of bread for me. Like I'd been marrying people since God knows when. Though really, what was the big deal. To start off you said a few official words. Do you, Piotr, Jan, Władysław, Kazimierz, take Helena, Wanda, Bronisława, or whoever to be your lawful wedded wife, do you swear to love and honor her till death do you part. I do. And do you, Helena, Wanda, Bronisława, and so on. I do. Then you put the rings on their fingers, if they had rings. You said that they were married in the eyes of the law. Then you added something from yourself. I wish you a life spread with roses, and you should respect one another, because from this moment on you're the closest one of all for each other.

I always spoke from the heart and the words pretty much flowed of their own accord, so whenever I was giving a marriage everyone in the offices would set aside their work and come down to watch and listen, even if it was through the half-open door. When the window in the room was open as well, it'd be lined with the heads of people listening outside, like flowerpots. Because the people that had come to the administration to get their business done, they wanted to see it as well. May you always help each other in hard times and in misfortune. May you never show anger, but always treat each other well, like land and sky. May you never be the source of worries for one another, because life itself will put enough worries in your way. Don't ever curse one another, don't insult each other, and may neither of you ever raise a hand against the other. If you do, may that hand wither. And not just because that's what people always say, but because you, husband, and you, wife, together you're like the hands of a single body, her the left, you the right. Your body is one. If one of you is struck down by illness, or is in pain, or if one of you weeps tears, it's all yours in common. You, wife, you'll never be able to say that you're not the one in pain. Nor you, husband, that you're not the one weeping. And may you both remember that you'll not be young forever. How much of life is youth? The tiniest part, less than springtime out of the whole year. Your woman will get wrinkles, you'll become an old man and go bald or gray, and then it's hardest of all to be husband and wife. At that time some couples are at each other's throats, though neither of them has done anything wrong. They'd kill the other one soon as look at them, though once upon a time they loved each other. Just remember that conflict never brought any relief to anyone, and you have to go on living till everything ends of itself. So it's better to live in harmony. Because you haven't gotten married only for a short time, till your youth passes, but until you stop being old as well. From now on you're like that tree outside the window.

In front of the offices there happened to be a huge maple that remembered the times when there was no district administration, just the four-flat buildings where they used to keep the cholera patients. In the summer people that had come to do business at the offices would wait in its shade, and you often had to tell them to be quiet because they'd talk as loud as if it was market day. Quiet there! There's a wedding going on! So then, you, husband, you're like the trunk of the tree, and she's like its branches. If you cut off the branches the trunk will dry up, and if you chop down the trunk the branches will dry up. I wish you good fortune, good health, and handsome children. Now you may kiss each other. Then I'd go for a glass of vodka with the newlyweds, because although it was mostly poorer folk that got married at the registry office, they'd always invite you for a drink.

For all the marriages I gave, there was only one time they had a proper wedding party afterward. The Kowaliks' son Józef was marrying Zośka Siekiera. His old folks slaughtered a hog and hired a band. They invited a few relatives and neighbors, and me as well. It wasn't about the young folks getting married, more that old Kowalik had too much land for those times and people were always accusing him of being a kulak and a parasite because he still kept a farmhand. Though the farmhand never complained, and when people asked him he even used to say he was better off with Kowalik than he would have been on his own. Actually Kowalik might not have had to worry about being called a kulak and a parasite, but when they started raising his quotas every year, in the end it was too much for him. He came running to the offices one day and said that either we should take his land from him, or he'd hang himself.

"I don't want any land!" he shouted, waving his arms. "I don't want it if all it's gonna do is bring me harm! Take it away from me! Plow it, seed it, mow it, set aside any amount you like! It said in the prophecies of the Queen of Sheba there'd come a time when the farmers would be giving back the land of their own accord! Now it's come true!"

At that time Mayor Rożek told him there was no need for him to give his land away like that or hang himself. Kowalik had a son, Józef. He should have Józef get married as soon as he could, because there were deadlines coming up, and he could divide his farm into two. Who should he marry? Anyone, whoever's available. Afterwards, if they don't hit it off they can get divorced. It won't be a church wedding because the registry office isn't a church and Szymon Pietruszka isn't a priest. But in the books it'll be written in stone that there are two medium-sized farms, and medium-sized farms aren't a problem for anyone. Because it would have been easier to get married and divorced three times over than reduce the quotas by a single hundredweight.

They chose Zośka Siekiera for the job, because she happened to live next door and she was poor as a church mouse. And she could only dream of marrying a rich man like Józef. For her it made no difference whether she had a church wedding or one in the registry office, whether it was for her whole life or just till they could reregister the farm, with banns or without, in a veil or in a regular dress, in front of a priest or in front of me. She would have stood before the devil in hell if only she'd been able to marry Józef.

Kowalik stuck five hundred zlotys in my pocket so I wouldn't make any speeches, just marry them and have done with it. Three months hadn't gone by when he was already trying to get them to separate. Except that at that point, Józef put his foot down and said no. He hadn't gotten married just so he could get divorced again right afterward. He'd taken Zośka to be his wife, not his serving woman, and he wouldn't let them do wrong by her. And now that the land had been reregistered, his father could kiss his backside. At most he'd stay on his land, and his father could work his own.

But as long as the old man lived, and he lived a long time, Zośka didn't have an easy time of it. Whenever he talked about her he'd only ever call her that beggar, that slut, that stray. He'd sometimes even kick her out of the house, he'd say, this isn't your place, get back over the fence, that's where you belong. Even when they had a child the old man didn't soften a bit. He never once minded the baby or played with it the way other grandfathers do, when they laugh with their grandsons and talk to them and tell them all sorts of wonders about the world. Plus he kept on saying bad things the whole time.

"It can't be yours, Józef, it doesn't look anything like you. When it laughs it's got the same beady little eyes as Heniek Skobel."

Zośka never so much as said to the old man, have you no conscience? At the most she'd run into the pantry or out into the orchard to cry, and Józef would follow and comfort her. What was he supposed to do – beat his own father?

It was only when death came for the old man and Zośka looked after him like he was her father, one time when she was straightening his pillows he took her by the hand and said:

"I've been a bad man, Zosia. And you've been a saint. I don't need God's forgiveness, I need yours."

After he died Zośka washed his body like it was her own father's. And she cried at his funeral like he'd been her dad.

I sometimes go over to their place to watch television and they sit there like two turtledoves, though they're gray now. Zosieńka, Józeńko, they call each other. They'd do anything for each other. They have grandchildren now. No, you just sit and rest, I'll do it, Zośka. You've done enough work today. I won't come to any harm. That's as may be. You've done just as much work as I have, Józef. Here, have some sour milk. And even at harvest-time, when people are sweating from the work and cursing left, right, and center, they're all, Zosieńka, Józeńko. Like they were singing along with life. Recently they even had a church wedding, because the priest had been pestering them about it, he wouldn't leave them in peace, he said what harm would it do if God joined in their happiness. He wouldn't get in their way.

Three years I spent giving weddings, then they transferred me to the quotas department where there was a huge lot of work, because it wasn't just grain but livestock as well, and milk, and there was all kinds of writing to be done, more every year. At the registry office, every now and then someone would come along to get married and that was it. Of course, once in a while they'd give me some other work so I wouldn't get bored. Correct something or write out a fair copy, or do some calculations. Or one time we got some books and the librarian had just gone on leave to have a baby, so the district secretary put me to work cataloging the books, putting plastic covers on them, sticking on the numbers and stamping them with the district administration stamp, then putting them on the shelves. Another time there was no one to supervise the workers mending the road to the mill. When the autumn rains came or a thaw in the spring you couldn't get through even with a pair of horses because the mud came up higher than the wheel hubs. So who could do the job? As usual everyone was up to their ears in work, while the "priest" was just sitting at his desk staring at the ceiling. Maybe you could go, Mr. Szymek. No one's going to be getting married today. And though supervising workers supposedly wasn't really work and you could go lie down in the shade of a bush, because the workers would get on with the job without anyone watching over them, the thing was that I'd gotten used to the office and being able to stare at the ceiling, and I didn't at all feel like I wasn't doing anything. You could have a nice little doze if the sun was hot through the window or if you'd been drinking the night before. Or someone would come by and you'd have a chat. Or you'd go and visit the other offices, or go flirt with the girls.

There were more girls in those offices than bees in a hive. A good few of them had only come to work at the administration so they could find themselves a husband quicker, and an office worker to boot. If I'd wanted I could have even gotten married, and more than once. But why would I, when I could have the same thing without getting married. In those days girls still used to like nylon stockings, and for a pair of stockings any of them was putty in your hands. You'd pull a pair out and show them and say, listen, Agnisia, Józia, Rózia, would you like these to be yours? So meet me this evening at such and such a time. Because there was something about those nylon stockings that the moment a girl set eyes on them she'd get this glassy look, her voice would soften, and she'd very near reach for your pants then and there. It was another thing that when one of them had crooked legs her legs seemed to straighten out when she was wearing stockings. They made fat legs look thin, and skinny ones look just right. When they were wearing those stockings even what their faces looked like wasn't such a big deal, their legs became the most important thing. And when one of the girls appeared in church wearing stockings, the whole congregation would look down instead of looking up. Mass would be ruined for all the other women, and a good few of the men only half paid attention to God.

I bought the stockings from this trader woman that would sometimes come to the village selling various things. I'd known her from when I was in the police, and one time I'd had her at the station because she was suspected of selling yeast to moonshiners. I searched her belongings and she happened to have one pair of nylon stockings that she was delivering to someone.

"Bring some more for me, I'll buy them off you. Maybe even a few pairs," I said. And since then she did.

One time I bought all the pairs she had, there must have been a dozen of them, all different sizes – large, small, medium – and in different colors, mouse gray, fox red, like scorched straw, like wholemeal bread, all as fine as gossamer.

"I'll take the lot," I said.

"Well she must be a real lady," she said. "All these pairs. Some girls have all the luck. What size foot does she have?"

"Who would that be?"

"The woman you're buying them for, your girlfriend or your wife, whoever."

"Don't know yet."

"The thing is, these are different sizes and they might not fit. And they're so fine you only need to scratch them with your nail and there'll be a run. She needs to take care of her hands. You ought to buy her some hand cream. I've got that as well. Otherwise she'll be bringing me stockings with runs in them, wanting her money back. And I won't take them. I can't be traveling all this way and come out at a loss."

"They'll be the right size. If not for one then for another. Why worry ahead of time."

"Well I guess it's none of my business. Shall I bring you more?"

"Sure, you do that."

I hid the stockings up in the attic, in the rye, in a plaited straw barrel. I pushed them as deep as I could into the grain so father wouldn't find them by chance when he went up to check that the rye wasn't getting damp. Though you didn't need to dig down deep to see whether it was damp, all you had to do was scoop a little from the surface or just put your hand in and hold it there a moment, when it was damp you could feel it right away, like putting your hand over steam. I was certain there was no better hiding place. In the old days people would keep whole fortunes in barrels of grain, dollars, rubles, and in wartime weapons. Because grain arouses the least suspicion. What could be more innocent than grain. And who would ever want to dig down to the bottom of those things when they held ten bushels or more each.

But one day I come home from work and I see my stockings laid out on the table like on a market stall.

"Where are those stockings from?" I asked. I was shaken.

Father was sitting by mother's bed, and he says calm as anything:

"You know what, they grew in the rye up in the attic. I went to check if it wasn't getting damp, and I picked some of them to show your mother. But she won't believe me. Maybe she'll believe you. Tell her they're stockings. What else could they be? Nylon ones. That's all they wear these days. I wonder how much one of them pairs costs? Probably as much as a bushel of rye. And see how many pairs grew up there. We didn't even sow or muck. Obviously it's not worth keeping rye anymore. We'll have to start growing stockings instead of rye, since God's blessed us this way. Since the beginning of time only rye has grown from rye, but we've had a miracle."

I was all set to grab the stockings, slam the door, and go wherever my feet took me. But I looked at mother. She was lying with her head turned to the wall as if she was embarrassed, and I suddenly felt sorry for her. I thought to myself, oh well. I took a bowl, poured myself some potato soup from the pot, sat down on the chair by the stove, because the table was covered with stockings, and I began to eat. Father was still going on about what had grown from what and how God had smiled on us, till in the end he got mixed up and forgot whether rye was growing from stockings or stockings from rye.

But I didn't say a word. What could I say? He knew what he knew, I knew what I knew.

I wasn't as young as I used to be and I wouldn't just go running after a pair of beautiful eyes. But the girls weren't as silly as before the war either. Not many of them went for you because of how much land you had. What kind of happiness was land? You work like a dog all the livelong day, day in, day out, and happiness only comes in the next life. And even that wasn't a sure thing. These days, people were taken at face value. So they preferred to dress well rather than parade their virtue. On top of that you kept hearing how people were having their land taken away from them, and what use was virtue with shared land?

I gave out so many pairs of stockings that if one girl had gotten all of them she'd have been able to wear them for the rest of her life, and not just on Sundays. And she'd always be seen in a fresh pair. I sometimes spent my entire salary on those stockings when the trader woman came by. All I had left was cigarette money. It was another matter that the pay was lousy and if I hadn't had meals at home I couldn't have managed on that income. But of all the pairs I gave out, only one let me down.

During the time I was still giving weddings they hired this one girl from Łanów. Łanów is a village about two and a half miles from ours. It's on the other side of the woods, but it still belongs to the Żabczyce administration. She worked in the tax department. Małgorzata was her name. To begin with I didn't pay much attention to her. Obviously we saw each other almost every day, because in the offices you couldn't help it, there was only one entrance and one hallway and everyone arrived at the same time and left at the same time. But I'd pass her just like one office worker passing another. Good morning. Good morning. Nothing more. She seemed somehow unapproachable. Any of the other girls, you could pat them on the backside or pinch them or rub up against them in the hallway and you knew they wouldn't take offense. With her, though, you'd be afraid she'd slap you. Maybe because she'd graduated from junior high. Back then, finishing junior high meant more than going to college today. There's a few folks from the village studying at college now, and what of it? They won't even take their cap off to an older person, they expect them to be the one to say hello first, because they're educated. Only one of them, Jasiu Kułag, he's nice and polite, he always stops and offers you his hand and asks how things are. He'll be a decent guy.

I admit I liked the look of her, plus she always dressed nicely, she always had a fresh blouse and dress and jacket. Plus, on rainy days she'd bring a little umbrella, she was the only girl in the offices that had one. That was probably how the rumor got started that she was living with the chairman, because how could she afford everything. They'd just changed from having mayors to having chairmen. Mayor Rożek was followed for a short time by Mayor Guz, then after him was the first chairman, a guy by the name of Maślanka. He wasn't from our village but his wife was, Józia Stajuda. No one knew where he was from. Whenever anyone asked him what he'd done in the war he'd squirm like an eel. They sent him from the county for us to elect as chairman.

I found it hard to believe she'd be living with Maślanka. She didn't look like that kind of girl. And I can say of myself that I know people, life's taught me who to trust and who not to. In the resistance I didn't trust a soul, and that mattered more than having a good eye or cold blood or a heart of stone. It might have been because of that that I survived. Because truth be told, you can only ever trust the dead. And not all of them, because with some folks even their death has something bogus about it.

Though on the other hand, why should I have trusted her. I didn't even know her, and there's always a bit of truth in gossip. Maybe she just knew how to cover her tracks. She wouldn't have been the first one to set her sights on the chairman. He was the chairman, after all, and he could always make life difficult for you if you weren't careful. What else could they have seen in him? Pudgy little guy, always sweating up a storm. But he knew how to turn on the charm. When he'd do his rounds of the offices in the morning he'd always have a nice word for each of them, smile at one, kiss the hand of another, stroke another one's hair like a father. And he wore this big ring with a red stone, supposedly it was a keepsake from his father, he'd flash it in front of every girl. Except that when someone came from the county administration he'd slip it off and hide it in his drawer. Some people said it wasn't anything to do with his father, that Maślanka had been a hog trader during the war and done well for himself. Whatever the truth was, after a guy like Rożek, whose every second word was "fuck," because with him what was in his head was on his tongue, the new fellow was almost like a squire. So she could have been one of those that gave in to temptation.

I thought to myself, give it a try, what do I have to lose. If that's what she's like it won't be hard. If he can do it so can I. We'll see who's better, chairman or no. When I put my Sunday suit on, you could never look as good, however many suits you were wearing. And you should see me in my officer's boots. Have you ever even worn officer's boots? You'd look like a bucket on a stool. Me, they said I could have served in the uhlans. Maybe I would have if things had worked out differently. So what if he was chairman. If the farmers had voted for you the way they used to choose the mayor, you'd have been village policeman at most. As for the ring, I used to wear one myself, and it was a whole lot bigger than yours, it had a stone like a twenty-pound carp. And it didn't come from selling hogs, I got it from my father and his father before him, it's been in the family for generations. You loser.

I got shot in the thigh during an attack on a mail train in Lipienniki. They drove me by cart to the manor, they said that was the safest place for me. They put me right under the roof in the attic, so I'd be hard to find if anyone came searching. I wouldn't have minded spending the rest of my life in a place like that. Their attic was bigger than our whole house. There was a carpet covering the entire floor, a chandelier hanging from the ceiling, elk and stag antlers on the walls. A whole family could have slept on the couch I was lying on. Plus I had a window right by my bed with a view of the grounds, so I could hear birds chirping close by from morning to night. It was like there was no war at all.

If anything happened, the story was that I was a cousin of the owners and I was sick with the consumption. Why not, I could be their cousin. I'd already been a chimney sweep when we had to carry out a death sentence on the mayor of Niegolewo. And a monk when I had to get out of the town and there were roadblocks everywhere. One time I was even transported as a dead man in a coffin, they were pretending to be taking me back to my parish to be buried in my own cemetery. Being the cousin of the owners of the manor was a piece of cake. Especially when all I had to do was lie there with only my face and hands outside the sheets. My face was fine, in fact it was a bit scrawny so it even looked right for the consumption. In addition they gave me a pair of glasses so if need be I could put them on and read a book. Except they made everything blurred, because even today I've got eyes like a hawk. I never opened the book once, though it lay right there the whole time on the nightstand. Right away a maid came in with water and soap and a towel, and to begin with she soaked my fingers for a long time, then she trimmed the quick around all my nails till they bled. I asked her why she was doing it. She said the mistress had told her to. Then she trimmed my nails so short they were almost even with my fingertips, and when I tried to scratch myself all it did was tickle. And on this finger, the middle one, they put a big gold ring with a huge stone like I said, big as a twenty-pound carp. With the ring on, my hand felt like it wasn't mine anymore, I was afraid to move it so I just kept it stiff on the quilt. They put one of the master's nightshirts on me and for the first night I barely slept a wink. How can you sleep in something that's more like a priest's surplice than a shirt? It had lace and frills, and there was so much material two people could have fit inside it. On the nightstand they put the master's gold watch. To my darling Maurycy, with love, Julia, it said on the cover.

To begin with I thought I was dreaming. But it didn't take long for me to get used to it, and then I regretted I'd have to go back to the woods. It wasn't going to be easy after I'd been lying there like the owners' cousin, having my food brought to me in bed. Having a gunshot wound would have been one thing, but it had to be the consumption. What kind of illness was that? Franek Marciniak had the consumption before the war. He'd eat slices of bread spread twice as thick again with butter, and he drank endless amounts of dog lard and ate eggs and cream, they took the food from their own mouths so he could have it, and the young Marciniaks would say they wanted to have the consumption too. Because he looked like a doughnut in butter.

I'd occasionally think I could actually be one of the owners' cousins, why not. For instance that Maurycy from the inscription on the watch. Though who had Julia been? Because neither the master nor his wife were Maurycy or Julia. Sometimes I imagined their life one way, sometimes another, but it was always a happy one. They wouldn't have given each other a gold watch if they hadn't been happy. And though they were probably long dead and in the ground, their happiness was still there, ticking inside the watch. When you listened carefully you could hear it clear as day, like far-off bells ringing over them in a dewy morning. I even wondered if time didn't move forward but instead turned in circles like the hands of the watch, and everything was still in the same place.

From all that lying I put on weight and they started worrying that I didn't look like I had the consumption anymore. Perhaps it'd be better if I was ill with something else. Except that nothing scared people off so much as the consumption, only typhus was better. But if they'd said it was typhus then word might get around and they'd come and take everyone to the hospital, and lock up the manor. On the other hand, I was looking more and more like I was their cousin. The maid, to begin with she treated me like I was just more work for her, when she brought my dinner she'd snap: "Dinner." Now, she'd say:

"Here's your dinner, your grace. Here's your breakfast. Here's your afternoon tea, see how tasty it is today. You're looking better, your grace. For supper it'll be butter rolls, tea, ham, cottage cheese, and plum tart."

I had the feeling she was staring at me more and more. Till I started thinking, maybe I am her grace, I ought to check. So one day when she was putting the breakfast tray down on the bedside table, I put my hand under her dress and moved it up her thigh all the way to the top, and the only thing that happened was the plates rattled on the tray.

"Oh!" she sighed in a squeaky little voice like a baby bird. "You're a quick one, your grace. Let me at least put the tray down." And like a little chick going out onto a branch for the first time and shaking because it doesn't know how to fly, she bent down over that hand of mine.

When I went back to the woods after that, for a while I lost the will to fight. I just kept thinking over and over, when it comes down to it, what's the point of fighting? Wouldn't it be better to just lie there in an attic like that? It was only when I got thinner from not eating so much that I started to feel like fighting again.

To begin with, one day I gave her a bolder nod than usual and instead of just good morning I also said Miss Małgorzata. Good morning, Miss Małgorzata. Then a few days later I added:

"You're looking nice today, Miss Małgorzata."

"Thank you," she said. "Nice of you to say so, Mr. Szymon." And though she was always so serious and she seemed to look down on everyone, you could tell I'd embarrassed her.

Some time later, it happened to be raining that day, the two of us stopped in the porchway to at least wait out the worst of it, because it was cats and dogs, and we got to chatting the way you do in the rain, that it's been like this for a week already, that if it keeps up all the crops'll rot. Since it wasn't easing up we kept talking, and I invited her to come by sometime and watch me give a wedding.

Not long after that, Wojtek Lis married Kryśka Sobieska. As usual, almost every woman in the place gathered to see it, and quite a few of the men, including the district secretary. And the window that opened onto the courtyard was so crammed with heads it looked like they were all growing from a single body. I didn't think she'd come. Then suddenly I saw her standing with the others in the half-open door, and my heart began to thump. I invited everyone to come inside, let Wojtek and Kryśka at least have a crowd of strangers at their wedding, since their parents weren't there, or any of their relatives. Actually I liked Wojtek, though he was a good few years younger than me, and Kryśka was in about her sixth month, she had a belly big as a drum, and she was a bit embarrassed. But I said to her:

"Don't be ashamed, Kryśka, you've got a person inside you, not a wild animal."

And I gave such a speech that almost everyone was in tears. The girls were one thing, but even some of the guys looked like they'd been staring into a bright light for too long. Kryśka cried, Wojtek cried. The people in the window cried. Though I wasn't saying anything sad. I talked about happiness. That you need to look for happiness inside yourself, not around you. That no one will give it to you if you don't give it to yourself. That happiness is often close as close can be, maybe in the simple room where you spend your whole life, but people go looking for it in all kinds of strange places. That some people search for it in fame and riches, but not everyone can afford fame and riches, while happiness is like water and everyone's thirsty. That often there's more of it in a single good word than in an entire long life. Kryśka's folks had disowned her and thrown her out of the house. Wojtek didn't have a father and his mother had died a year before. That a person could be famous and rich but not be happy.

I told them about a certain king who lacked for nothing, but who never had any dreams. Because of this he was afraid to go to sleep, because when he got into bed it was like he was lying down in his coffin. Though his bed was made of solid gold and he had a quilt of the finest down, and down pillows too. The greatest doctors on earth were brought in, they cast all kinds of spells on him, gave him different herbs to drink, they poulticed him with flowers and scents, they played music for him without cease and six naked women danced for him, but he didn't dream of so much as a daisy in the meadow. Nothing. Every royal night was an empty hole. He prostrated himself, he wore sackcloth, he even took off his golden crown set with diamonds and put on a crown of blackthorn. And he prayed endlessly, to different gods. Because some people advised him to pray to one god because that god was a king himself and he was more merciful than the others, while for another god faith was a great dream, and he might be granted some of that for one night at least. He built churches and almshouses, he washed the feet of the poor, anyone could walk into his palace as if it was his own cottage, and no one ever left empty-handed. In the end he grew thin as a lath and his brother started making secret preparations to take his place, because through all this time the kingdom had been shrinking like a fist. Just like one farmer will start plowing over another farmer's land, his neighbors were doing the same, plowing over his kingdom from every side, and not just in the spring and fall but all the time. He got sicker and sicker, his servants caught him talking to himself and laughing, shouting, threatening himself with his fist and stamping his foot. He thought about throwing himself off a cliff, because what kind of life was it when you didn't have any dreams, even if you were the king. It was like he was only half living, he lived in the day but he died at night. Imagine dying like that for years and years, when even dying once is so hard.

Then one day a certain peasant learned about the king's unhappiness. He wasn't a fortune-teller or a herbalist, just a goatherd that drove goats to market in the town. He came into the royal presence and said:

"Your majesty, there's a remedy to make you have dreams. Move into my cottage, you'll dream my dreams, and I'll live awhile in your palace without any dreams."

At the end I told them happiness is easier to find with a husband or a wife than on your own, and I wished Kryśka a son.

Where I got it all from I have no idea. What did I ever know about happiness, and today I know even less. But maybe happiness is only good for talking about, maybe it's not something you can ever know. In any case I could tell I'd done a pretty good job, everyone in the offices congratulated me. And one of the farmers that had been listening outside through the window, who'd come to pick up his benefit money, he asked me if I'd known that king, and he couldn't get over it:

"You've got the gift of the gab, son, you really have. If only everything you said could be believed. But even just listening to it is nice."

So then, I was certain she must have liked it as well. But she disappeared soon as the wedding was over. It was only the next day I ran into her in the hallway.

"That poor king," she said when she saw me. "Did he really not have any dreams?"

I couldn't tell if she was making fun, or if she just said it because she couldn't think of anything else to say. It hurt me a bit, but I let it go.

"I have something for you, Miss Małgorzata," I said, because I'd decided to use the opportunity and give her some stockings.

"What's that?" she said, intrigued.

"Come into my office."

She came in, she seemed a little excited from curiosity. I took the stockings out of my desk. I'd even wrapped them in colored paper.

"What on earth is this?"

"Stockings. Nylon ones."

She opened the package.

"They're lovely. Thank you. How much do I owe you, Mr. Szymek?"

"Nothing. They're a gift, Miss Małgorzata."

She reddened.

"Mr. Szymek, I can't. Please tell me how much. Really. No, in that case I can't accept them."

And she didn't.

It made me so mad that after work I went to see Kaśka that ran the grocery store and I gave her the stockings. Though she was the only one you didn't have to give anything to. You only had to go visit her, she always knew why you'd come. Because sometimes, when I didn't have anywhere else to go I'd go to her. Or whenever I needed to get as far away from everything as possible, I'd go to her. Or I was so frustrated that I didn't feel like going anywhere at all, I'd still feel like going to see her. Or when I didn't have the strength or the will to go see anyone else, I'd go to her and it would always be the same. Because with other women you had to spend time with them and flirt with them and walk them home and promise them things the whole time, and sometimes you still came out losing. But with Kaśka I'd swing by for matches or cigarettes, lean over the counter and whisper:

"Stay back in the store after work today, Kaśka."

With her, her heart was always on the outside.

"Just take your cigarettes or your matches, you don't need to pay. I bet one of those bitches of yours went and dumped you again. Office girls, big deal. Like they don't know what their body's for. It's for the same thing as all women. Either way you're gonna end up eaten by worms. They're not soap, they're not gonna wear away from being used. What the hell are they afraid of? That the priest won't give them absolution? So don't tell him everything. When you don't tell something it's like it never happened. If I were you, Szymuś, I'd find myself a nice ordinary girl. She doesn't need to be smart, the main thing is she should stand by you. You're smart yourself, any girl is going to look dumb next to you anyway. What do you need an office girl for? You can't even whack her one, she'd up and make a big fuss.

Those kind make all sorts of noise. I saw it at the pictures one time. He didn't even hit her that hard. She squealed so loud I had to cover my ears. What's the point in making a racket? Lie down, your man wants you to, and don't pretend you don't either. Or she'll start running around on you, and what're you gonna do, tie her down? When you have sit on your ass for eight hours a day your ass can go crazy. And when your ass goes crazy it's worse than when your head does. When your head gets like that, the worst it'll do is talk nonsense. But asses are trouble. You're getting old, Szymuś. Dear Lord. Though for me you'll always be a first class young feller. Tell me which one it is, when she comes in the store I won't sell to her, the bitch. Get out, slut! Go do your shopping in town! Office girl – big deal. She wants gingerbread. Not a snowball's chance!"

She was just a shop assistant, but she was a tower of strength. Sometimes she seemed dumber than a sack of rocks, but she had more wisdom in her than a hundred wise men. And her thighs, her backside, two women could have shared them and they'd still have looked good. When she took her clothes off you'd never know she was a shop assistant. Her breasts, it was like there were four of them. They stretched from one arm to the other, from her neck to her belly, like pumpkins in a patch. And whatever she was lying on, whether it was sacks of salt or sugar or buckwheat, or on the floor, she'd always lie down like she was in a made-up bed, she didn't like to do things any old how.

"Just a minute now, let me get undressed. I don't want to get my frock all crumpled." And she'd undress like it was her wedding night. "Touch my breasts first. I like it when I get gooseflesh. And I want us to do it for a long time. I'm not going to open up the store again anyway, so why do we need to hurry. It was open for hours, people could come buy whatever they wanted. There's always this big rush, then when it's over you regret hurrying. And you won't be back for a month or two, maybe even longer. They say I've gotten fat. No way, it's not true. What do you think? Tell me – am I fat?" Though sometimes it would be like she was suddenly afraid, and out of nowhere she'd ask: "Do you think there's life after death, Szymuś?"

"Come off it, Kaśka. You're a shop assistant, you believe in that nonsense? If there was it'd be the same as this life."

"You're a smart one, Szymuś. I'm glad you came today. Hee, hee! Just don't make me a baby, so I don't have to cry afterwards because of you. Though whatever you want. Oh, Szymuś. You're a one, you really are. Dear Lord!"

"I've got something for you, Kaśka," I said. "Close up the store."

"Are you nuts?!" she snapped back. "It's still early! Look how much bread I still have to sell. Almost two shelves' worth. What, am I supposed to sell it stale tomorrow?"

"If there's nothing else, they'll buy stale. Close up."

"What's your hurry? Can't it wait till the evening? It'll be evening soon. Do you want them calling me a whore again? That bitch Karaska's gonna come running and she'll be all, you whore, you closed up shop again yesterday and I didn't have any bread to give my man with his cabbage! Someone ought to report you, they ought to, it's downright ungodly. Whenever her ass starts itching she closes up, like she didn't have opening hours posted outside. So report me! I'll tell you where you can stick your complaint. Come and work here yourself, you old witch. Stand here on those skinny legs of yours for two hours and your ass'd start itching too. She ought to have kicked the bucket years ago, the bitch. Same goes for her old man. He won't eat his cabbage without bread, but that doesn't stop him from coming to the store and being all, how about it, Kaśka, eh, how about it? How about what, spit it out! What's under your dress. Buy some cigarettes, that's all you're getting. You think I don't get enough of that sort of talk? Sometimes I think I must have a hole in my frock. The women are even worse than the men. You've put on weight, Kaśka. The hell do you care if I sleep around and put on weight? What do you need? Get on with your shopping. Don't come hanging around here and complaining, it's not a waiting room, it's not a church. On top of that they'll tell you you're a lousy shop assistant. When the store's out of something it's your fault, because it says in the papers there's plenty of everything. You're screwing around instead of stocking up. How can there be no vinegar? How can there be no this, no that? Sometimes I just want to grab a broomstick and let them have it. I have to hand them such and such, measure something out, wrap it up. Or they take forever choosing, and all you can do is stand there waiting. Not this one, not that one, and inside you're all furious. If it were my store I'd chuck the whole damn lot of them out, go choose on your own time. But as it is I even have to make suggestions. What do you think, Kaśka? Which one is better? Do I get paid for handing out advice? Beside, what is there to choose from? Take what there is, even that's gonna be gone soon. With bread, one of them wants a well-baked loaf, the next one tells me to look for a lighter one. Sometimes they make me turn over every loaf in the place, because when they deliver it they're either all well-done or all not. And God forbid you don't have five groszes change, there'll be a whole line of moaners standing there looking daggers, come on, give her the change. I'm not budging from here till you give her the change! What, am I trying to stop you? It's not exactly a fortune. But am I supposed to give her the change from my own money? If I did that every time I'd be stone broke. And don't think they don't talk about me and you screwing. If you didn't have things so easy with me you'd have gotten married long ago. As it is you come here, do your business, what do you need to get married for. About today, go have a drink at the pub, the time'll pass quickly enough. I'll close up once I've sold the bread. You'll be even better if you've had a drink. Hee, hee! Not in such a hurry."

"Don't be mad," I said. "I brought you something."

"Me? Straight up? She must have really done a number on you. Or you're just teasing me."

"I'm not teasing. Here. Nylon stockings."

"Seriously?" She wouldn't believe me. "Oh my Lord! They're lovely!"

"The seller came by and I bought them for you. You can wear them to church."

She opened the packet and tried the stockings against her hair and her arms like they were ribbons. She hugged them and stroked them.

"Some of them already wear these to church," she said. "Plus in church there's always a crowd, you can't see people's legs. I'm going to wear them here in the store. It'll make those bastards' eyes pop out. They'll be all, hey, Kaśka, where d'you get them stockings? From my boyfriend. You have a boyfriend? Sure I do. Don't you think wearing them in the store is a waste? Why would it be a waste. If they get torn he'll buy me new ones. So he's rich then? He sure is. When we get married I'm not going to work in the store anymore. Even the richest women don't wear stockings like these every day, but I'm going to. To hell with the lot of them."

"But how are they going to see what's on your legs when you're behind the counter?"

"That's true. Silly me, I hadn't thought of it. In that case I'll come out and close the door each time, because hardly any of them close the door after themselves. All day long I'm yelling at them, close the door, close the door. My voice gets hoarse. Or I'll come out to chase flies. I know we already have flypaper up, but the stuff on it must be crap. Whenever a fly sticks to one of those strips it just buzzes its wings and it's off again. I think I'm going to shut up shop. You're worth it. Oh, Szymek, Szymek, what would I not do for you. But what sign should I put up? I can't say receiving new delivery, because next morning they'll all come running to see what came in. I'll say, gone to office."

With the other woman I went back to treating her like any other office worker. Good morning. Good morning. Nothing more. Till one day I'm leaving work at the end of the day and I see she's moving away slowly, holding back, like she was waiting for someone. I was all set to walk past her when she suddenly came to a stop and turned to face me.

"Are you mad at me by any chance, Mr. Szymek?" she asked, and her voice was soft as silk.

"Me? Mad? Of course not. At you, Miss Małgorzata?" I answered a bit too eagerly.

"Because it's like you've been avoiding me. I'm sorry if I hurt you with what I said the other day. But that story about the king amused me so much I couldn't help myself."

"There's nothing to talk about. It's forgotten already." I walked with her all the way to the footbridge outside the village. And since that coming Sunday the fire brigade was holding a dance in a clearing in the woods, I asked her if she wouldn't like to go with me. In the woods meant close to Łanów as well. I'd come pick her up and it went without saying I'd walk her home afterward. She agreed gladly, except that I shouldn't pick her up, she'd come on her own and we'd find each other at the dance.

I got hopeful again. I was a first-rate dancer and I'd won more than one girl over with my dancing alone. When it came to the polka and the oberek especially, no one else in the neighborhood danced them as well as I did. After the war there were a lot of younger dancers showed up at dances and they knew all kinds of fancy fox-trots and what have you, but when it came to polkas and obereks I was it. I was no slouch at the tango and the waltz either. My favorite was On Danube's Waves. But if it was a matter of coming to an understanding with a girl as fast as possible, the best thing was a polka or an oberek. With tangos and waltzes there was too much talking and making stuff up, when it was obvious what you were after. And if you didn't talk at all, she might think you were a dud.

Turned out she didn't like either polkas or obereks, so we danced nothing but slow numbers. On the other hand, she kind of held tight as we were dancing. Except what of it when there was some sort of strange force that wouldn't let me move my hand an inch on her back. She even had an opening in her dress below the back of her neck, I could have accidentally on purpose tried to stroke her on that little bit of bare skin, maybe that would have made her hold me even tighter, because touching bare skin is always better than through a dress. But it was like my hand was glued there on her back, stuck in the same place the whole time. As for the other hand, the one holding hers, it felt like I was holding a little baby bird, I was afraid I'd smother it.

I thought to myself, I gotta get a drink, because otherwise nothing's going to come of this. I was so distracted I even misstepped a couple of times, and that never happened to me. True, she told me she hadn't imagined I was such a good dancer. She wasn't bad herself. But what of it, when that wasn't what I was after. I went to the buffet and brought back a bottle of vodka and some open sandwiches. I was counting on her drinking a quarter of the bottle or so. Not too much, not too little, just enough, from what I knew about girls. I'd have three-quarters of the bottle and we'd be even. But it turned out she didn't drink vodka.

"Just half a glass, Miss Małgorzata," I said, trying to persuade her. "It'll do you good. What sort of dance is it when you've not had anything to drink? You might as well be at evening mass. Look, everyone's drinking. The girls too. Some of them because of their troubles, others for good health, plus everyone has their own reasons for having a drink. Vodka helps people get by. It makes you feel more like having a ball, and if it's time to die, it makes you feel more like dying. Because when you've had a drink of vodka, dying and having a ball kind of join into one. If I hadn't drunk in the resistance I doubt I'd be dancing here with you today. Once you'd had a drink you'd go out among the flying bullets like you were just walking through a stand of willow trees. Many a time, if you'd been sober your hand would have been shaking from your bad conscience. Once you had a drink your conscience did one thing and your hand another. See, you didn't bring a sweater, in the evenings it can be chilly. It'd warm you up. And it never hurts to make your head spin a little bit. There's no shame in having just the one glass. There's more shame in not drinking. Well then, Małgosia?"

But she dug her heels in, no. And right away she said she had to be going back because it was getting late, and I didn't need to walk her home if I didn't want to, she could go on her own. Let it be no, don't think I'm going to beg. Wonder if Maślanka has to beg as well. But I will walk you back, I know the right thing to do. I tipped back the bottle and emptied it on my own. Then I tossed the bottle and the glasses and the rest of the sandwiches into the bushes. Normally a bottle was nothing for me. We'd usually drink two bottles each, it was only after two that your soul became like a wide-open barn, like a stream from a spring, and you felt you could grasp your whole life in your hand.

One time, after two bottles I bet two more I could shave without cutting myself. We were drinking at Wicek Kudła's place. I'd managed to get Kudła's quota reduced, because by that time I was working in the quotas department. He didn't have a decent mirror, just a broken piece of an old one. And no one would even hold it for me, they were all drunk and they were afraid of putting their hand to some misfortune. They were babbling on trying to talk me out of it, but I sharpened the razor on the strop and lathered up, and I was ready. Don't be crazy, Szymek, no one shaves after a bottle of vodka, after two bottles all you're going to do is cut your face up, you don't mess with razors. Razors or scythes or God. God, you might be able to beg him to change his mind. But a razor, when your hand's shaking and your eye's iffy it's all up and down, and your face is nothing but ups and downs, that's just how it is. You'd think all you'd need would be an eye somewhere in the middle of your forehead, you could use it for seeing, drinking, eating, talking, sniffing, crying, whatever you needed. But you, on top of everything you've got a hole in your chin and your jaw sticks out. Just give him the other bottles, don't let him shave, I'd rather drink than watch someone bleed, it's okay watching a hog bleed but with a person every drop hurts. I was seeing double, at times I could hardly see myself at all, and the razor in that scrap of mirror was shaking like it was afraid as well. But I shaved myself and I didn't cut myself once. Give those bottles here.

But this time, that one stupid bottle went to my head and it was like I was walking up hill and down dale, and the ground under me was rocking into the bargain. At one point it must have rocked more than usual because I staggered and if she hadn't caught me I would have hit the deck.

"You're drunk, Mr. Szymek," she said. "I can get home on my own from here."

"It's just my legs, Miss Małgosia," I said. "My head's as clear as the moon up there above us."

The moon was like a cow's udder, if you'd pulled at its teats we'd have been covered in streams of moonlight.

"I could go all the way to the edge of the world with you, Miss Małgosia, we'd never lose our way. Wherever you wanted to go, nearby or far away, it'd all be the same to me, I could walk through the woods, I could walk forever."

Then I started going on about the resistance and how I had seven wounds. All healed up long ago, of course. But sometimes, like today, it's as if I can feel them bleeding. If she wanted I could show her and tell about each one. Then I tried to count how many Germans I'd killed. But for some reason I couldn't get past five. I checked them off on the fingers of my left hand, but when I got to the fifth finger the list broke off like the earth had swallowed it up. I couldn't make head or tail of it. All that shooting I'd done, and there were only five of them? Could they have risen from the dead?

Aside from that I could feel anger welling up inside of me. I was walking and walking, and all for nothing. She wasn't saying a word. It was probably the anger that made me think, so she'll go with Maślanka but not with me. How is he better than me? He wasn't even in the resistance, the loser, all he did was trade in hogs, other people spilled their blood for him. How do I know? People in the offices talk, you can't hide anything there. Though the people that talk do the same things themselves, there's nothing to get upset about. She wasn't planning on being a saint, right? Why would she? She'd get old and then regret it. What pleasure was there in being a saint? All you'd do is be in a picture on the church wall, or they'd hand you out during the priest's Christmastime visit or sell you at church fairs, or you'd have your name in the calendar. But you have to be a big-time saint for that. You'd have to kick another saint off, because there's already four or five of them for every day. Even the most saintly ones are going to get squeezed out soon. It's not worth the effort. On top of everything else, you never know if it's only down here you're considered a saint, but afterwards you're actually going to go roast in hell. How can we know what happens afterwards? So then, Miss Małgosia, is it far yet? We'll be through the woods soon. But I can keep going if you want. And if you want, I can marry you. It's high time I got married. People go on and on at me about how I ought to be married. Tell me, Miss Małgosia, would you be my wife? I can't promise you happiness because I don't have happiness inside me. But we'd get by somehow or other. I could even marry you tomorrow. I'll perform the ceremony myself. I'll make such a speech they'll remember us even after we're dead. At Mayor Rożek's funeral, the one that they shot, I gave this speech that had everyone in tears. The guy that came from the county offices, he just mumbled something, he didn't say a word about Rożek, he just went on about enemies the whole time. In the end Rożek himself rose up out of his casket and said, you, piss off, I want Pietruszka to make the speech. And no blubbering, I want to be able to hear it clear. That's how he was, he never minced his words, but he had a heart of gold. If you want, we can even get married in church. I don't know if God exists. But if he exists for you, he'll exist for me. The tailor could make me a suit and the dressmaker will sew a dress for you. What do you say, Miss Małgosia?

She was walking along like a shadow, still not saying a thing. I even had the impression that it wasn't her walking along but the woods, and I was talking any old nonsense to the trees. And maybe because of not knowing whether it was her or not, I suddenly put my arms around her and whispered:

"Małgosia."

She slapped me in the face, pulled free of my drunken embrace, and ran off.

"Małgosia, don't run away! I'd never do anything to hurt you! Don't run away!" I shouted. I started after her. But she ran like a roe deer. And me, the ground swayed underneath me and began spinning around. My legs got all tangled up. I tried to follow her, but I was pulled in every direction at once. I bumped into something once and twice, then in the end the road threw me to one side. Goddammit!

"Małgosia! Stop! Wait! I won't touch you anymore! I thought you wanted it too! Wait!" I had the feeling it wasn't just me shouting, but the whole woods were calling after her, and the moon over the trees, and the night. "Małgosia!"

Her shadow was getting farther and farther away, growing more and more faint, till it disappeared completely. I stood still for a moment thinking the road might stop dancing in front of my eyes and I'd be able to see her again and call her, and then she'd have to stop. Or maybe she'd get tired from all that running, or suddenly be scared. The road was lit up like a ribbon in the moonlight, but it looked even emptier. I didn't know if I should keep after her or not. I pushed on. You idiot, for a minute you thought she was Kaśka the shop assistant. With Kaśka you can talk any kind of nonsense you like and she'll still tell you you're smart. You're a smart one, Szymuś. If I was half as smart as you I'd have had my own store long ago. I could sell anything I wanted. I wouldn't sell bread or salt. They can go bake their own bread. Buy salt in town.

"Małgosia!" I started yelling through the woods again. "Don't be afraid of me! I'm not drunk anymore!"

All of a sudden, to my right I heard something like a tree crying. I don't know if it was an oak or a beech. I even reached out my hand, then I saw her pressed against the tree trunk.

"Oh, it's you," I said. "Come on, don't cry. There's nothing to cry about. We're not right for each other, that's all. Let's go, I'll walk you home then head off back on my own."

"I don't want you to walk me home. I don't want you to!" she said through her tears. "I thought that you at least, you were different. I thought you just seemed that way. I was close to trusting you." She broke away from the tree and ran off again.

But this time I didn't chase her. Run all you like, bitch, I've no intention of chasing you. They all want you to be different. How are you supposed to be different? Can a person be different from himself? He's the way he is, and that's how he has to be. I went back to the dance.

Now I really started to have a good time. Whoever showed up I bought them a drink, friends, strangers, enemies. Whether they wanted to drink or no, they had to. You won't have a drink with Szymek? I wouldn't even let the band go eat their supper, I brought them vodka and sandwiches and told them to keep playing. They played nothing but polkas and obereks, because that was what I wanted. Some folks were shouting that they were exhausted, they wanted a tango or a waltz. But I said no, polka, oberek, oberek, polka. And the band had to do what I said, here's another five hundred for you! The emcee came up and said what was I doing taking charge here, was it my party? So I grabbed the ribbon off his chest and pinned it on myself. I'm the emcee now, you scram! If you don't I'll make such a ruckus there'll be nothing to pick up afterwards. Count yourself lucky I'm feeling happy, because God forbid I'd be in a bad mood. Your whole dance would end up in the woods.

None of the girls would dance with me anymore, they all said they were tired and out of breath from all those polkas and obereks. Why was it all fast dances? Couldn't they play something slow? Polkas and obereks are old hat.

But I insisted they keep playing them. I could care less what you all think. Sit on your backsides, be wallflowers for all I care. I'll give you old hat.

"Come on, Ignaś." I pulled on Ignaś Magdziarz's arm. He was drunk and sitting on a tree stump swaying, looking like he was about to fall off any minute. "We'll show these bastards whether polkas and obercks are old hat. You be the girl and I'll be the man. Come on. If you get bored we'll switch, I'll be the girl and you can lead. Just don't step on my toes, and make sure you throw me up in the air at the right moment. Actually you can be two girls or two men if you like, makes no difference to me. One of them taller, one of them shorter, one fat the other thin, a red-haired one, a bald one, one of them blind, the other one lame, the hell with it all, Ignaś, I don't even need to be there, just so long as you'll party with me. I'll marry the two of you if you want. You think I can't? I can marry a guy to a guy, a woman to a woman, a dog with a bitch, an ox with a donkey, anyone I want, I can marry everyone to everyone else. If I want musicians I'll marry the fiddler to the accordion player, the clarinetist to the trombonist, the drummer to his drums. You don't believe me? Then drink up, cause you obviously haven't had enough to drink, and you have to believe it, Ignaś, you have to. Even if you've never seen it, you have to believe it. If you're drinking vodka and you don't believe you're drinking, it's like you're not actually drinking at all. People are hopping and jumping, but we need to party all the way around. The world turns around, life goes around, you need to drink around."

Ignaś just sat there rocking and crying and repeating:

"I can't, Szymuś, I can't. I can't be the girl or the man, not anymore. I have to puke. I've forgotten how to really party. Those were the days, Szymuś, those were the days. It was so fine back then."

I gave up on him and started dancing on my own. People were shouting, stop pushing! He's gone nuts! He's drunk as a skunk! Me, I had my arms up in the air like the branches of an apple tree, like the wings of an eagle, and hey-ho! hey-ho! I was shoved and yanked one way and the other, they tried to force me off the dance platform. But once I gave a good wave of those wings of mine, I had a space around me that was big as the whole dance, and so deep you couldn't see the bottom. All I could hear were squeals and shouts off to the side. I kept dancing.

I don't even know when the clearing emptied and the band stopped playing. What did I care, I had a band inside me, the fiddle was fiddling away under my chin, the accordion swung between my sides, the drum beat in my belly, the trombone blared in my ear, and the clarinet whined from my heart. Dawn was dawning through the trees, dew had fallen from the sky to the earth, the birds had woken up and the air was trembling with birdsong, and I was still dancing, all on my own in the clearing, all on my own in the world, like on a battlefield after the battle. Everyone had gone except Ignaś Magdziarz, who was lying drunk next to his tree stump. Otherwise there was nothing but empty vodka bottles, broken crates, smashed glasses, plates, scraps of paper.

Afterwards, at work I got hauled over the coals by Maślanka for supposedly disgracing the district administration. That was probably why I got transferred from weddings to quotas soon after. But the firemen were even madder at me, they were collecting for a motor pump and the dance was meant to bring in the rest of the money. Because of me they came out at a loss, I frightened people away and they ended up with most of the vodka unsold and half a cartload of sandwiches. Though how could they have lost money if I spent my whole month's salary there? On top of that, word went around I was getting married. One dance and I was already marrying. People! If that were the case I'd have been married a hundred times already. And this time things hadn't even started before they were over. But say what you like, say I'm getting married. If I deny it they'll just talk all the more.

It was another thing that I became a little bit meeker. People made jokes at my expense and I didn't do a thing. I didn't go around the other offices so much, I mostly just stayed at my desk. Besides, I didn't want to see her because she'd probably heard what I got up to at the dance. And I had no intention of trying with her again. It hadn't worked out, tough, let each of us go our own way. Good morning. Good morning. Nothing more. But more and more people seemed to be saying I was getting married. This person, that person, everyone I met. And that I'd changed, I was avoiding people, I didn't come by anymore, didn't visit with them. The girls were the worst of all. They're like a bunch of vipers.

So then – is a junior high graduate better than a girl who's only finished elementary school? Does she put out just the same? You always used to prefer them broader in the backside. Your tastes have obviously changed. And call that a bust? Her breasts look like they had the life sucked out of them by babies. Surely you can't be in love? You, in love! Unless it's like a dog in love with a bitch. Anyway, who'd believe you. You can't be believed even when you say good morning, the morning can still end badly. You're not to be trusted. And her, she's just a stupid girl and that's that. She'll be crying over you yet. You'd think school would have made her smarter, but she let herself get taken in like all the rest. You're probably just pulling the wool over her eyes with all your fine words, while she thinks you're going to marry her. You'll marry her for one night, till you go chasing after someone else. Besides, even if you did get married, what kind of life would she have with you? You're not a farmer, not an office worker either. Putting it in and taking it out, that's all you know how to do. That, you're good at. You talk away and before you know it, there you are inside. Where it's neither bitter nor sweet. And you can't be pushed out or pulled out either, it's like you've put down roots in her body. And afterwards, girl, make sure he hasn't left you with a baby in your belly. So you wait and see if the sickness begins. If you get a sudden yen for sauerkraut or sour apples. You run to the church to ask God for forgiveness. You beg him for your time of the month like you were asking for happiness. Lord, I'm suffering here, give me at least a drop of blood. Never, never again. But the moment it passes you take the bastard back inside yourself. Because fear is easy to forget, and God even easier. You're probably trying to win her over with those seven wounds of yours, aren't you, you weasel? Either way it'll end in bed, or some old place. I ought to scratch your eyes out. But let her do it for me. I've done enough crying. I'm such a fool.

Mother and father heard I was getting married, and it looked like I was hiding it from them. I could see them giving me funny looks. But I thought it was because I was coming straight home after work, that I wasn't drinking, and I'd stopped complaining about working in the fields. And maybe they were just waiting nervously to see how long it would last.

Till one day I'm sitting at the table having some cabbage soup, I was supposed go do some plowing, when suddenly mother pipes up from her bed that people are saying I'm getting married. That she was so pleased, so pleased, even if I was keeping it from them. God must have finally answered her prayers. Who was the young lady? Was she from a farming family? Was she a good person? And when were we planning to have the wedding, because she hoped she'd live long enough, so she wouldn't have to worry about me in the next life. From now on she'd be praying for both of us like we were both her own children. That the gold medallion she wore would be for my wife. And that now, death seemed just like falling asleep, and she could die without any regrets. After that, how could I tell her none of it was true. I said:

"It won't be that soon. It's going to take a while."

"Then bring her here one time so I can meet her. Maybe I'd be able to get out of bed and I could whitewash the walls."

As for father, he didn't ask about her. His only question was, how many acres do they have? It made me so mad, I was about to tell him they didn't have any land at all, that they worked as hired hands and they rented a room from someone else. But he was so fired up about the acreage that I told him:

"Fifty acres."

"Fifty?" He actually went pale. "Really! They're rich folks then."

"Yes, they are," I said.

"And they're fine with you marrying their daughter?"

"Why wouldn't they be? Don't you think your own son is worth something?"

"No one's saying you're not worth anything. It's just that rich folks are always drawn to rich folks, they look down on poor people. The Bugajs? Bugaj. Yeah, I've heard of them. But I had no idea they have fifty acres. They must have bought extra land. Is there many of them for it?"

"For what?"

"For all those acres."

"There's just her."

"She's an only child?"

"No, there's a brother, but he's sick with the consumption."

"Well if it's the consumption, nothing's going to come of him. Do they at least have a farmhand?"

"What would they need a farmhand for? They've got machines."

"True enough, these days even if you wanted a farmhand, where would you get one from? They've all gone off, damn them, they're all working in the factories, in town, in office jobs. You go there and even if you don't know two times two they'll take you on in an office. Back in the day they'd come begging for work. Now, you can't just hire someone for a day or two to help with the mowing. They don't even know how much they're supposed to charge for a day's work. And every one of them wants to be fed. Not just dumplings or buckwheat, no, they have to have meat, meat. Machines are definitely a lot better. How many cows do they have?"

"Five, maybe six. I've not been in the cattle barn. They might think I was only interested in their property."

"Good point. But it's always best to know from the get-go. With all that land you could keep ten cows. And not black and white ones, people say they give more milk but it's all watery. No, red cattle. The cows are smaller so they don't eat as much, but the milk they give is half cream. And it'd be good to have a bull. You can make a pretty penny off a bull. Maziarski had a bull before the war and he used to charge five zlotys for a covering, or four days' work for him. Whether the cow got pregnant or not. When there's a bull on the farm, people know you're doing well. Poor folks don't keep bulls. You should have lots of pigs as well. Pigs are the fastest way to make money. Though you need your own sow. Piglets are expensive to buy these days. Besides, why would you go buying them at market. That's a waste of time. You know where you are with your own pigs. You buy someone else's and they turn out to be runts, they won't grow. You never know what you're buying. They may look like piglets, then it turns out they're little devils. Instead of growing they get smaller. And you have to be careful no one's bringing the sickness into your sty. Don't let any outsiders in. You never know who people are. Even your neighbor, how can you be sure? He might have a nice look in his eye, but how can you be sure he isn't bringing death in? Death can be brought in with nice eyes, it can come in on your hands or on your boots, or even when you shake out your pockets. Think how bad it is when only one pig dies. But imagine what it would be like if all of them got the pest. Someone'll say to you, you've got some nice-looking pigs there. Then he'll do something to them out of envy, and afterwards it won't matter how much you feed them, they'll stay as small as cats. Because they will envy you, make no mistake. Rich folks are always envied. There's two sorts of people, the ones that are envied and the ones that envy them. It was envy that made Cain kill Abel, and you remember Wojtek Denderys before the war, that was why he set fire to his brother-in-law's place. All the evil in the world is from envy. Governments envy each other, one king envies another one, generals envy other generals, and so on down to ordinary people. Then if you look around the world you see mountains envying each other, and rivers, small things envying big ones, even one apple on the apple tree envying another apple. Of course people are going to envy you. Though you shouldn't hold it against them. They have to envy someone. You should keep bees as well, because with bees you have honey. And when you have honey you have everything. That's what they say, the land of milk and honey. Plus, the orchard looks more cheerful when there are hives between the trees. You're more inclined to drop by than when it's just trees. There'll be times you don't feel like visiting people, but you'll visit your hives. With bees you can talk to them, and listen to them as well. But don't plant plum trees. When they have a big crop the way plums do, who's going to pick them for you? They'll fall on the ground and make a mess of the whole orchard. You won't be able to pick them all even if you and her do the job together. Especially if she's an office girl like you say, she won't want to be getting all dirty with plums. You keep picking and picking and there's still just as many. You should only plant apple trees. At the most two or three pear trees so you'll have pears. Or if the priest comes and visits once in a while you can give him a pear. Priests like pears. Or you can just go and look among the leaves and see if any of them have turned yellow yet. It's nice when you pick the first one and bring it to your kid or your woman. Here, this is for you, it's ripe already. Don't plant oats. Unless it's for the horses. Because you have to have a pair of horses. Machines are one thing, horses another. On fifty acres both'll come in handy. Plus, what kind of farmer would you be if you didn't have a pair of horses. To at least go to the stable and look at them. The smell of sweat and manure tickles your nose, it's like something was growing. If the horse neighs you give it a pat and you feel better right away. You don't have to run to God with every little thing. And you'll probably have a chaise, right? So you'll need horses as well. If you've got all those acres you can't go walking to church on foot of a Sunday. Or if you get invited to a christening or a wedding. You will get invited. One time your woman will be the godmother, then you'll be the godfather. And with a chaise you can't get by without a pair of horses. With a wagon you can manage with one, a wagon's a different matter. But a chaise is a chaise, first of all you need a pair of horses, then you can have the chaise. And they have to match each other. Because a pair isn't just any two horses. A pair is two chestnuts or two roans. Or best of all one black and one gray. A black and a gray, that's a proper pair. They're like a wedding couple. The gray's like the bride, and the black is the groom. Or they're like day and night walking next to each other. But don't trim their tails, let them grow down to the ground. And leave their manes. A horse without a mane looks like an army recruit. A horse's whole strength is in the mane. And don't forget to buy them breast-harnesses, especially the kind that have studs! And a decent springy whip would be good. You'll probably give up your job at the administration? Why work in an office when you're going to be a rich man?"

"Let him be!" Mother had run out of patience. "He's not even married yet. He'll know what he has to do without being told. Just don't drink, son. And be good to her."

Father suddenly felt silly, he hung his head and sat there, half thinking about something, half just staring at the floor.

"Maybe I should go feed the dog?" he said after a bit.

"He just ate!" said mother, still annoyed.

So he took his tobacco from his pocket and started rolling a cigarette, and when he'd wet the paper he said:

"I'm not asking anything of him. I'm just giving him advice. He was never interested in the land, and here he's got fifty acres coming his way. Fifty acres, do you know how much that is? It's like if you took Socha's land, Maszczyk's, Dereń's, and Sobieraj's, and ours, and joined them all together. Five farms, and one farmer to run them. Who else is going to give him advice? Besides, do you think he'll listen? He'll do whatever he wants. He knows better than his mother and father. You say one thing, he does the opposite. You want the best, but he doesn't give a hoot what you have to say. Or he'll take the whole lot and let it all go to waste, and go off drinking and gallivanting. What does he care about the land. He never did what he was told even when he was small. Besides, let him do whatever he wants. We're going to be dead either way," he said angrily, as if we'd been quarreling.

But I hadn't said a word. I'd just been sitting there listening to his advice. I even regretted telling him they had so many acres. Where did I come up with that number? No one in our village had that much land. I should have said eight or ten tops, and leave out the brother with the consumption. Or there could have been a brother, but maybe a cripple that had to be looked after for the rest of his life. Mother would still have said what she said, but the most he'd have said would be:

"The Wronas have got that much. And they want you for their daughter as well. That way you could stay here in the village, you wouldn't have to move all the way out to Łanów. A person should die where they were born. They'll never get as used to a different place. Jagna's a hardworking girl. And they'll probably give her a cow, cause they have two."

I didn't think he'd believe they had so much land.

"That many acres," he'd say, "you'd have heard about it. Winiarski in Boleszyce, he has thirty-five and everyone knows him. And he was a councilman before the war. The priest and the squire would always be visiting him. At the harvest festival it was always Winiarski made the speech. He sent his son to study to be a doctor, and his daughter was a schoolteacher. Those people wouldn't want anything to do with you if they had so much land. The drink's making you imagine things. Keep drinking and you'll end up like Pietrek Jamrozek. He calls his own mother a whore when she won't give him vodka money. And his hands shake like leaves in the wind. The priest is always on at him from the pulpit. They take him away but then they bring him back and he starts drinking again."

But maybe it wasn't so much that he believed me as that he believed himself. And when he asked me how many acres they had, he only wanted me to agree with what he was saying. And I did, I said fifty acres, let him have that many if that's what he wants, let him at last have his fill of land, let him get dizzy from it at least once. I got carried away. I wanted to needle him, but the way it came out it seemed like God had finally answered his prayers.

In the end, though, he must have realized it was all made up, because from that time on he never once brought up those fifty acres. And he never asked once if I was getting married. Nor even if we were still seeing each other. Besides, it looked like he was starting to get a bit confused in the head, and after mother died he stopped talking almost completely, he'd only say something every once in a while. He didn't even worry about our fields anymore, what did he care about me getting married. There was just one time, when I'd stopped working at the administration, I came back from mowing and I was sitting there exhausted on the bench, and suddenly he asked:

"Is it harvesttime already?"

"Sure is."

"Are the children old enough to help yet? You should bring them one day. I'd forgotten they're my grandchildren."

And just like the time before, I had to nod and agree with him:

"Yes, I'll bring them."

WEEPING

People keep asking me, when are you finally going to get that tomb finished? You might at least roof it with tar paper, keep the water out. Well I would have finished it, I'd have finished it long ago, if that was all I had to worry about. But as if I didn't have enough on my plate already, here one of my pigs went and died. She was getting up close to her weight, she would have been a good three thirty, three fifty pounds. I figured, when I sold her I could get some more work done on the tomb. The walls have been up for a long time now, the partitions were ready even, all it needed was a roof and push comes to shove, people could be buried in it even if it was unfinished.

Chmiel was patient, waiting for when we'd start again, though he was getting old and bent over. Just one time he sent his old lady over to say his aches and pains were getting worse and worse, and by the way how were things with that tomb of mine, because he'd like to finish what he began. When I met him from time to time in the village he'd just nod back and walk on, or at the most he'd ask: so when? But like he wasn't asking about my tomb, just in general. He was content with any old excuse, it's because of this or that, Chmiel, though mostly it was, once I'm done fattening the pig. Everyone knows a pig's the fastest way to make a bit of money. So long as it doesn't get sick, you wait your eight months then it's off to the purchasing center. Fatten her up then, fast as you can, he'd say, cause you might run out of time. The fact was, whenever I did fatten a pig there were always more urgent things that needed paying. First it was taxes, next it was quilt covers, then winter clothes for Michał, one thing or another, or I had to order a supply of coal, and the tomb could wait, luckily no one was dying. Besides, I didn't rear that many pigs, one or two, as the chance came along. Because if you want to fatten a pig you need a woman at home, a guy on his own can't handle it. Though sometimes I thought about taking out a loan, building a pig shed for a hundred or so pigs and starting to raise them for money like some folks do around here. If it's not pigs it's something else, but only for money. Take Ciamciaga for instance, the man can't add three plus three but he started keeping sheep. No one had sheep in the village before. There were sheep once, but it was at the manor before the war. He even learned how to shear them. The first time he did it the poor creature was so cut up it looked like wolves had been at it. But now he shears, his old lady spins, his daughters knit sweaters, and everyone wears sweaters made of Ciamciaga's wool. Or Franek Kukla, he started an orchard and now he sells apples by the cartload. He's got apple trees all in long rows like cows in a big cattle barn. Plus each row is a different kind of apple. All the rows are straight and neat, all the trees are the same height. They're all as clean as if he combed them every day. I think they even all have the same number of branches, because where there used to be more, you can see they've been sawn off. And on each one it's like there's nothing but apples growing, no leaves, no branches, no trunk, no earth even. Except it's kind of quiet in his orchard, you don't hear bees buzzing or birds chirping, it's nothing but apple trees as far as the eye can see. I said to him one time:

"So you've got your orchard. But it's kind of sad in there."

He laughed:

"Ha, ha! What do I need a happy orchard for. All it has to do is make me money."

Maybe that's how things ought to be. Sometimes I've even seen myself going into that pig shed for a hundred pigs, inside it's white from all the animals and the only thing you can see is the rise and fall of fat bellies. And it's all mine. But I soon get over it. What do I need all that money for. I'm not planning to build anything. I don't have anyone to leave it to. So one or two pigs is enough. Pigs take work. You sometimes don't have time to cook your own dinner, you'll grab a slice of bread with milk or with a piece of sausage, but a pig has to have two meals a day. I might not even have reared the one or two, but someone's sow in the village would have piglets and they'd say, do you want one? Take it. They're a healthy size, they'll fatten up nicely. Or when I rode to market, coming home with an empty wagon seemed wrong somehow, so I'd ride back with a young pig at least.

One time Felek Midura convinced me to take one, he didn't even want the money right away but later, whenever I had it. Or we'd figure something out, I'd lend him my horse for plowing in the spring, because it was difficult for him with one horse on that hillside of his. Or I could pay him back in hay in the winter, since I had a meadow and he'd sold his. Or if not in hay then in potatoes. Come on, take one, they've got little short snouts and tiny ears, they'll be good eaters – even now I can barely pull them off the teat. So I took one.

But it had some kind of sickness in it. It ate enough for two piglets but it didn't get any fatter. A whole year I fed it and it never grew bigger than a cat. A pig like that is the worst, you don't have the heart to kill it but keeping on rearing it is a waste of time. Besides, what was the point of slaughtering it, you could hold the thing in your hands like a baby, why even bother. After a year I got used to having it around. I called him Squeals – the name just came to me. I kept saying to him, stop squealing, stop squealing, so he became Squeals. Besides, I'd started to feel he needed a name, I couldn't just keep calling to him, come and get it, especially as the eating didn't do any good. If I'd had more of them they wouldn't have needed names. But when there was only one, and there he was all alone between the horse and the cows, he had to be called something. Oftentimes I used to sit myself down in the shed and watch him feed. And however angry I was that he wasn't growing, I forgave him, because just watching him eat so healthily was a pleasure. Though one time I got so mad I grabbed him up away from the trough and hauled him over to Midura's.

"Here, take your crappy pig back, damn you. You knew, that's why you didn't want any money. Yours are all fattened up and sold, look at this one."

But the next morning I step outside and I see my Squeals running around the farmyard and grubbing about for food. It touched my heart.

"Squeals!" I called, and there he was trotting towards me at full tilt. It made me think. He was just a piglet, but he was capable of getting attached to someone. There had to be some intelligence there. Though it could also have been that Midura dropped him in my yard in the night to make it look like the pig had gotten attached to me. But I didn't take him to Midura a second time. Just so he'd come back or be brought back yet again? Luckily I'd not gotten around to thinking what I'd do with the money once he was fattened up, so it wasn't such a big disappointment. Because the one that died, ever since it was small that one had been meant to pay for the roof on the tomb. The moment I brought it back from market I put it in the shed, poured food in its trough, and said:

"Eat up and get big, you're going to pay for the roof."

Every time I fed it I repeated to myself that it was for the roof, that I needed to make sure it didn't go on something more urgent this time. And it was like it understood, because you could almost watch it getting fatter. Though for my part I never scrimped on the potatoes or the coarse-ground flour. And the whey was all for the pig. When there wasn't any whey I'd even give it milk. Sometimes I'd go pick nettles to fill it up even more.

Eight months hadn't gone by and it was ready to be taken down to the purchasing center. But I decided to hold on to it a bit longer, it ate like the devil and every day was a gain, every pound meant more money. Besides, a pig has to be at least three twenty, three forty, mother always reared them that big, it's only then that it's a real pig. After it's slaughtered there's less waste, with one that's not been properly fattened a good third of it can go to waste. Plus, when you take a big pig like that down to the center everyone wants to guess how much it weighs, everyone pats its back to see what kind of bacon it's going to give, sometimes the guys even get into an argument about whether it'll be three fingers or four. It makes your heart swell to think you've reared a pig like that.

It was almost there. I even stopped Chmiel of my own accord at the co-op one day:

"Not long now, Chmiel. In two, three weeks I'm driving that pig down to the center and we're on for the roof."

"You do that, make sure you're not too late."

Then one day I go in the shed and I see there's hardly anything eaten from the trough, and my pig's lying there like it's sleepy. I prodded it with my foot, come on, get up. It did, but it was kind of sluggish. I grabbed it by the tail and it didn't jerk or squeal. I pulled the trough closer and shoved its head in it, eat now. But it was like it didn't have the strength to open its mouth. I thought, maybe it's eaten a rat. Often when a pig eats a rat it can't eat anything else for a bit. Except that if it had eaten a rat it'd be thirsty, rats burn like fire. But when I brought it some whey it didn't even look up. I ran to the vet, but when he came all he could do was tell me to slaughter it and bury it.

The next day they came and sprayed my whole shed with something smelly. I had to take my cows and calf and horse and put them in the barn. Because when you went in there it made your eyes water. Even any of the chickens that got close to the cattle shed, their eyes watered too. And the dog, I thought he'd go mad. He sneezed and gagged, he foamed at the mouth and he clung to my feet so much I couldn't get rid of him. Have a bark and you'll get over it, I said, go on, bark like you were barking at a thief.

I even had a railroad rail ready to use for the ceiling, all I needed to do was go grease the right palm and drive up in my wagon. Because obviously you don't buy rails like that in the ordinary way, you need a special opportunity. And opportunities don't stand there waiting for you, you have to go after them yourself. I needed three lengths of about ten feet each. I went all over the place asking around, with no luck at all. Then one day I'm walking along the tracks and I see they're switching out the old rails for new. I started talking with the workers, were those old rails so used up they weren't any good anymore, or were they changing the railroad? No they weren't, but there was going to be an express train on this route. What's going to happen to the old rails? They'll be sent for scrap. Well, I'd buy one of those, I could use it for the roof in the tomb I'm having built. It could be cut into three pieces and there'd still be some left over. They didn't know about that, I should go talk to the stationmaster. I go to the stationmaster, I know him well, of course, and I say:

"Listen, Władysław, sell me one of those rails they're changing out, I need it for the tomb I'm having built. I hear the express train's coming through here. It can be the most worn-down one."

He can't do it. Why not, it's only going for scrap, the workers told me, and I'll pay however much I have to. He can't because it's government property, and government property isn't for sale. If it was his he'd give me it for free. But everything on the railroad is government owned. Even the red cap he's wearing isn't his, it belongs to the government.

"So what can I do? The ceiling won't hold without rails. What do you suggest, Władysław?"

"Hang on, just wait till this freight train's gone through. For a tomb, you say?"

"That's right. I've had the walls up a long time now, it's all partitioned off, there's only the roof left to do."

He took off that red cap of his and scratched behind his ear.

"Well everyone has to die sooner or later, that's a fact. And they have to be buried somewhere. Go talk to one of the switchmen, slip him something and he'll turn a blind eye, then you can bring your wagon in the night and take it away. Just remember, I wasn't the one that told you."

That's how it was with almost everything. Nothing would come easily. I had to have a pit dug so Chmiel could get in to do the building, ten feet by ten and five deep, and I lost a good few months on that. Time was I wouldn't have asked anyone, I'd just have dug it myself. But how could I do that with these legs of mine, and the walking sticks, and me just back from the hospital. I needed to hire someone for the job. So I got that swindler the Postman, because it's not so easy to hire a decent worker. His name's Kurtyka, but they call him the Postman. He lives with his sister, she's an old maid, they have three acres. The sister works the land while he gads about the village from morning till night, making some money here, stealing there, or someone'll buy him a drink. He's always drunk. And even when he's not, he pretends to be. He's so good at it that if you don't know him you can't tell he's not really drunk. But evidently he prefers living like that to being sober. Or maybe he's forgotten how to not be drunk. We've all gotten used to him always being drunk, he wouldn't be the same person if he tried to be sober. Because what is he, some Jasiek with three acres that he shares with his sister. As it is the other farmers laugh at him, the women feel sorry for him, the children chase after him down the street and shout at him: Postman! Postman! Postman!

I met him early one morning by the shrine. I was heading out to the fields to dig potatoes. He was standing there with his hands in his pockets. He was squinting in the sunlight like he was already drunk, or to fool someone into buying him a drink.

"Whoa." I stopped the horse. "Listen, Jasiek, maybe you could dig a pit for me for my tomb?"

He looked up and eyed me, smelling a half-bottle.

"What, are you planning to die?"

"One of these days I'll have to."

"They'll dig you a hole when you go, why worry about it ahead of time."

"I'm planning to build a walled tomb, the kind of thing you need to get done in advance."

"Do you think you're not going to rot in a walled tomb? You'll rot in there just the same."

"So will you do it?"

"I can dig you a pit, for a tomb, for potatoes, for slaking lime. Makes no difference to me, a pit's a pit. Just buy me a half-bottle."

"I'll buy you a half-bottle and pay you as well."

"But buy it now. A man's at his thirstiest in the early morning."

I gave him money for a bottle and we agreed that the next day we'd go to the cemetery and I'd show him where to dig. But the next day came, then the day after that, and three more days, and there was sight nor sound of him. I went down the village to look for him. I called in to see his sister. Is Jasiek in? He was here this morning but he went out. He might be at the pub. I went to the pub. Yeah, he was here, but he only had the one beer, no one would buy him a drink, so he left. He said he was supposed to go pick apples at Boduła's place, maybe look for him there. I hobbled over to Boduła's. Yeah, he was picking apples here, but that was last week, he barely picked any at all, no more than a basketful, and then he hits you up for a half-bottle.

In the end I saw him, he was walking up road toward me, but the second he spotted me he started reeling like he was half gone.

"You were supposed to come the next day, god damn you! And don't even try to act drunk in front of me."

"There's no need to shout, I'll be there. There's always a next day." And he leers at me with his supposedly drunken eye.

"Don't make me take this cane to you! Get a spade and come with me!"

He didn't even try to resist, and he stopped staggering. I got him a spade and we went to the cemetery. I showed him the place, I marked off from where to where, and I told him how deep it needed to be.

"Is that all? I thought you wanted something three times bigger. It'll be dug by sundown. Just have that half-bottle waiting, and a couple of pickles."

While I was still there he took off his jacket, rolled up his sleeves, then as I was leaving he even spat on his hands.

"Come by when you're done," I said.

I bought a full bottle instead of a half and I was planning on giving him the whole thing, because I thought he might come in handy again. I didn't have any pickles so I went over to Mrs. Waliszka's and she gave me almost a whole canful. But of course he never showed up that evening or any of the next days. It wasn't till a week later he came by, in the early morning. I could see he wasn't himself, or he was still sleepy or something.

"So did you dig the pit?"

"Sort of."

"What do you mean, sort of?"

"Well, it's not completely finished."

"Weren't you supposed to keep digging till the evening?"

"I would have, but I hit some roots. Must have been from that elm by Kosiorek's tomb. One of the damn things was thick as my leg. And the smaller ones, there were so many of them you couldn't even count them. I needed an ax. I was going to get my own, but I can't find it. You wouldn't have anything to drink, would you?"

I thought to myself, Kosiorek's tomb is over thirty yards from mine, and where is there an elm there? The elm's way over in the corner of the cemetery. Could its roots reach all the way across? He's pulling the wool over my eyes, the son of a bitch. But if I don't give him a drink he won't finish the job.

"Here, have one drink." I poured him out a quarter cupful. "Come back this evening after you've finished the job, you'll get the rest."

His face lit up like a little sun.

"The job'll get done. I'm telling you, there's no one in the village I respect like I respect you. Your health." He drank the vodka, made a face and shuddered.

"Off you go then," I said.

"What's your hurry? My word is my word. Let me have one more. After the work I don't need to drink. To tell the truth, after work I don't even like to. After work all you want to do is sleep."

I poured out another drink. He drank it. I poured another one. He didn't leave till he'd seen the bottom of the bottle.

"Right, now I'm gonna go dig your pit. Just hand me that ax."

And again he didn't show up for several days. I was all set to go looking for him. I thought to myself, I'll rip his arms off, the shit, because I had a feeling that once again he'd not finished the job, otherwise he'd have come for his money, and of course his booze. Then one day Michał and I are eating breakfast and he walks in.

"How long are you gonna string me along, damn you! Are you done or not?"

"Almost."

"What do you mean, almost?!"

"I just have one more spade length to go. I thought it would go quick as anything. The topsoil's fine, but lower down it's clay. I could've dug three pits in ordinary soil in the time it's taken to dig this one. You chose a bad place. It'll be damp there in the clay. Give me at least enough for a beer. I'm cruel tired."

"Where did you get so tired?"

"Where do you think? Working on your tomb."

I knew he was cheating me, but here you go, that's for a beer, just don't show your face again till the job's done. And so he didn't. Almost a full month passed. I thought to myself, I ought to at least go over to the cemetery and see how much he has left to go, maybe I could even finish it myself. I go over there, and my tomb hasn't even been started. Not even a single spade length. There's just the outline. I was furious. You lying bastard, you this, you that, I cursed him up and down and swore I'd get even with him. There I was giving you a half-bottle, giving you money for another, and for beer, and on top of everything you had the gall to make up stories about roots and clay!

For a whole week I went looking for him around the village, but it was like he'd moved away for good. Sometimes someone had seen him, but word must have gotten out that I was on the warpath and I was threatening to knock his block off soon as I found him, so he might have been hiding and sleeping during the day then coming out at night like a damn bat. Or maybe it wasn't me chasing him, but he was the one following me. There was a reason they called him the Postman. As for me, all that hobbling about on my walking sticks and my injured legs, to the pub, to the shrine and back, I'd soon had enough.

I needed to get started on doing the digging myself, because I could have spent another week looking for him and it would have been a waste of time. I never got my spade or my ax back either. I had to borrow a spade off Stach Sobieraj. Luckily I didn't find any roots or clay.

I was digging virtually with my arms alone, helping myself a bit with my stomach, because whenever I tried to push on the spade with my foot I got a pain that felt like it was coming up from deep in the earth. Though I often had to use my foot, because my arms weren't enough on their own, and my stomach was sore as anything from helping my arms. I was drenched in sweat, I saw darkness in front of my eyes, I could barely stand, but I had to keep on digging, because who else was going to do it, even half a spade length was good. And I went on like that day after day, like I was struggling with a huge mountain I had to level to the ground as some kind of punishment.

Many days I didn't even have the strength to walk back home. I'd go down to the road in front of the cemetery, sit by the roadside and wait to see if someone would be driving their wagon from the fields and could give me a ride part of the way. If no one came along I rested a bit, grabbed my walking sticks, put my spade on my back like a rifle, because I'd made a special cord for it like a rifle strap, and off I'd hobble. Some people even joked, they said, what's this, are you coming home from the wars?

Sometimes I'd had enough of that tomb. The hell with it, I thought to myself, what have I done to deserve having to slave away like this, will someone finally tell me? Father and mother were long since in the ground, my brothers can get buried wherever they like. I'll put Michał in an ordinary grave, in the earth, and me, when I die, at most the district administration will bury me. They owe me at least that much for all the years I worked there. I went on digging. I swore at the Postman, I cursed God, I cursed myself. And I kept on digging.

At times I regretted not having gone to my grave long ago, because I'd already dug a grave for myself one time, when the Germans took us into the woods to shoot us and ordered us to dig. I'd have been at peace now, I'd be nothing but dust and I wouldn't have to dig a second time. I'd be lying there and I wouldn't know a thing, I wouldn't feel anything, think anything, I wouldn't be worried about anything. And on the memorial it would say, Szymon Pietruszka, Aged 23, that's how old I was back then. These days not many folks remember the war, but if you just go to that place you'll see there's a nice memorial, it's clean and tidy and there's fresh flowers in a jar, who knows who brings them but they're always there, whether it's harvesttime or no, mowing, potato digging, spring, summer, fall, whatever happens to be in bloom. Then on All Souls' there's also a wreath with ribbons and lit candles, and always a few people standing at the memorial and crying. Who's going to cry for you when you're gone?

When they were building the memorial people even came to me from the Borowice district administration, because the bastards had taken us all the way out to the Borowice woods. Three of them there were, the head of the council, at that time he was called chairman, the district secretary, and another guy. They had briefcases and they were all dressed up in suits and ties, even though it was an ordinary weekday, a Tuesday. I'd just come in from mowing the meadow, I was fit to drop, hot, filthy, I was sitting on the bench in my undershirt and Antek's old pants that came halfway up my shins and had holes in the knees. I'd taken my boots off and propped my feet on them. But when they asked, are you Szymon Pietruszka, I wasn't going to deny who I was. Szymon Pietruszka. I was taken aback, because I mean, what could people from Borowice want with me? It's a ways away. I didn't even know any girls from over there. To begin with, all they said was they're from the district administration in Borowice, and they started smiling in this dopey way. Have a seat, I said.

"Would you have some glasses?" one of them said.

"Glasses? What for?"

The one who'd asked about the glasses turned to one of the other ones and said:

"Give it here, Zenek." The guy called Zenek started opening the brief-cases, out of one of them he took a quart-sized bottle of vodka and a loop of sausage, out of another one another quart and several dozen hard-boiled eggs, then out of the third another quart and half a loaf of country bread.

It was only then they said they'd come because they were putting up a memorial to us in the woods, at the place where we got shot, and they'd heard that one person got away, me, and they'd prefer it if everyone died and no one escaped. Because if one person escaped you'd have to write more about him than about the ones that were buried there. But otherwise no one escaped, this many men were brought there, this many men were shot. See, it's all on the memorial. From here to there, all squared away. To say no one, it was like a bell ringing clearly. To say someone escaped was like he'd knocked off a piece of the cross. Or at least spoiled something.

"But I'm alive. What does that mean?"

Had I dug a grave? I had. For myself? For myself. They even shot at me, I'd been wounded, right? So it was like I'd half died as it was. If the bullet had been just a bit more on target I'd be completely dead. Besides, years later who was going to remember that I'd escaped. Only the ones buried there would be remembered, because every last one of them would have their name written on the memorial. I'd be there as well. What was the harm in agreeing?

"So let's drink. Your health!"

But people see me, they know me, how would it look – here I am walking about alive, and over there I'm lying buried. Who knows, maybe it would've been better if I'd been killed with all the others back then. But I escaped, I can't go around claiming I died with them.

What difference did it make to me? I wasn't going to live forever either way, everyone has to die sooner or later, so eventually things'll even out. Memorials aren't built for the present. Now the people that remember are still alive. But they'll die as well one of these days, and after that the memorials will have to do the remembering on their own. And memorials don't like it when someone stands out. What did I care? The people that were killed and buried there, it'd be easier for them as well if one more joined them. And that way it'd be everyone. No one escaped. Your health!

"Here, have some sausage. It's homemade, not shop-bought. The bread as well. You know, what does it mean that one guy got away? Did anyone see it? No one did. The ones that saw it are six feet under. He could have escaped or not escaped. Maybe people just said he did. People say all kinds of things. Did anyone ever escape from a hellish situation like that? But folks like it when at least one person always escapes, and even if he didn't, they like to say he did. How could he have escaped? They brought them there, surrounded them, every one of them had a machine gun, plus they had dogs."

"There weren't any dogs," I said.

"So what if there weren't. There could have been. Besides, if death is staring you in the face it's death you see, fear, even if they'd had dogs you wouldn't have seen them. One time they came to Bolechów for this one guy, they had dogs and every one of them was trained like the devil, you couldn't take a single step. Even if he'd run away the dogs wouldn't have let him get far. They weren't village mongrels. And with a gunshot wound on top of that? He wouldn't have gotten more than a few yards. And those devils, once they smell human blood they'll bite you to death. Being killed by bullets is better than being killed by dogs. So then, are we good?"

They got me so muddled I didn't know whether I'd died or not. On top of that the vodka came over you in such a sweet way that you could have died and you wouldn't have known it. And I would have felt foolish drinking and eating with them and then saying no. But then all of a sudden mother called from the kitchen:

"Get away with you now, stop leading him into temptation. He doesn't need to be on a memorial, he's at home, thank the Lord. I cried my fill for him back then, why should I have to do more crying?" She turned to father to back her up: "You say something as well, father!"

But father had been drinking with us all the while and eating sausage and eggs, it would have been hard for him to be against it, and you could tell his head was muddled up pretty good as well, because all he said was:

"So how's the weather over in Borowice?"

"What kind of father are you!" Mother was so mad she clanged her ladle against the pot. "Here they are trying to convince your son that he was killed, and all you can do is ask about the weather!"

At this point, scared of getting in mother's bad books, he mumbled reluctantly:

"The thing is, if he thinks he was killed he won't feel like working. And there's no end of work around here. Harvesttime is coming. This year we planted three acres of rye alone. Then there'll be the potato digging. That's a big job as well. You came at the wrong time. You should have come after the harvest and the potato digging. In the winter would have been better."

Twenty-five of us they shot back then. They'd ordered a meeting on the square in front of the district offices. No one knew what they were capable of yet, they'd only been there a year, so the farmers all came in like it was market day, from our village, from others. Besides, there wasn't anything to be afraid of, just like always the local policeman had gone around with a drum announcing there was going to be a meeting, so at most we figured they were after meat and milk and cereals, what else could they want from farmers. Father was going to attend, but at the last minute he changed his mind and said, you go, because he might pick some clover for the animals. Or maybe take a nap, the whole previous night he'd had a stomachache, probably from the black pudding the day before.

There was already a crowd on the square in front of the building. An officer was standing on a table they'd carried out from inside, making a speech. Actually he was screaming, jumping up and down on the table and waving his right arm around, his left hand was tucked into his belt and it wasn't moving, like it didn't belong with the other one. Right next to him on the table there was a civilian that was supposedly translating, though the officer didn't give him much of a chance to translate. It looked like he missed about half of what the other guy was shouting about, because the other guy just kept on shouting and shouting. And he was having trouble with the translation, he stammered and stuttered and he was talking so quietly, like he was just telling someone in the next room. Maybe he was afraid, or he wasn't allowed to talk as loud as the officer. So I didn't even hear most of it, especially because the farmers were also muttering among themselves:

"Listen to the fucker yell."

"Keep shouting like that and your balls are gonna drop off."

"A dog can bark all it wants, it'll never talk like a human."

"Because you have to be born human to talk like a human, you can't learn it, Wincenty."

In any case, what I got out of it was that we needed to supply even more stuff, because the German soldiers were fighting for us just the same. At the end he screamed something so loud he almost rose off the table and floated into the sky. At that exact moment a whole bunch of soldiers poured out from behind the administration building. Where had so many of them come from all at once? Socha from Malenice pointed to where two trucks were parked in back of the building. They started to push us back against the fence with the butts of their rifles. The translator told us to form lines, because the officer was going to come talk with some of us one-on-one.

So we formed lines and the officer started walking around. But he evidently didn't have much to say anymore, because he just pointed at one or another of the men, and the soldiers pulled them out and had them stand in the middle of the square. He reached me and he might not have paid any attention to me, but he suddenly looked at my four-cornered Polish army cap and his face bulged. Because I wore a cap like that. I'd brought it back from when I'd been in the regular army, it didn't have the eagle on it and without the eagle it just looked like an ordinary cap, so what did I have to be afraid of. He asked me through the translator if I'd been in the war? I had. So I'd fought against him? I had. He smashed me right in the face. He was a stocky guy with a bull neck and a face like a cobblestone. My nose started bleeding. He hit me with his other hand, then punched me in the stomach for good measure.

Truth was I'd barely done any fighting at all back then, less than three weeks, and most of it we were just marching endlessly back and forth, then off in another direction till we didn't know which way was which. Then when we finally started to actually fight, right away the order came through to stop fighting and retreat. I shot my gun all of five times and I probably never killed anyone, unless God hit someone with one of my bullets. But I don't know about it if he did. On top of that I came down with the dysentery, and whenever we halted for a moment I'd have to run off into the bushes. I lost weight, grew a beard, got infested with lice, and that was my war. But I wasn't going to tell that bastard the truth when he asked if I'd fought. I had fought.

It wasn't enough that he knocked me around, he also pulled the cap off my head and stomped on it. And he didn't just point his finger at me, he used his whole hand. The soldiers grabbed me under the arms and dragged me out into the middle of the square with the other men that had already been picked out. Then a truck drove up and they ordered us to climb in.

To begin with it didn't occur to anyone that they were going to kill us. How could they go straight from a meeting to killing us? We weren't thieves or any kind of criminals, why would we have to die? Also, we were misled by the spades that were in the truck. If there were spades, that meant they needed laborers. Maybe they'd have us do some digging or fill something in. In wartime there's always digging and filling in to be done. It would have helped to know which direction they were taking us, but we couldn't tell because first, the truck was covered with a tarpaulin, and second, the sky was overcast that day and it seemed like the sun was on one side one minute, the next minute on the other, first in front of us then behind, like it wasn't really there at all. Stelmaszczyk from Obrębów even got into an argument about the sun with Wrona from Lisice. One of them said he knew the sun like the back of his hand, the other one said he did too. The first one said he got up with the sun every morning, the other one said he got up with the sun every morning as well. The first one said he had the sun in his blood, he didn't even need to look up in the sky to know where it was, the second one said he could have gone completely blind and he still would have known where the sun is in the sky. It's over there. In the end someone said that maybe the sun in Obrębów was different than the one in Lisice, because perhaps each village had a different sun, and so the sun over the truck was a different one again. It was only then they stopped arguing.

You could feel the potholes and the bends in the road. But potholes and bends won't tell you you're being taken to your death. Sure, there were four soldiers sitting at the back of the truck with their guns pointed at us, but that didn't surprise anyone, if they were taking us somewhere they had to guard us on the way. And even if we'd asked them where they were taking us they likely didn't know, because it was probably their higher-ups made the decisions. Besides, what language could we ask them in when they didn't know Polish. But Smoła couldn't take it, in the end he asked them:

"Excuse me, can you tell me where you're taking us? You probably need workmen, right? Am I right? We'll do it, why wouldn't we. Some of us were soldiers too, though in the old wars, so we even know how to dig trenches if need be. It's just a pity we didn't let the folks at home know we'd be gone a while. Because we haven't done anything wrong, have we?"

The soldiers didn't say a word. They just sat there all stiff with their eyes shining like cats' eyes under their helmets.

"What could we have done wrong? You don't need to go asking them, we know perfectly well ourselves," said Antos from Górki, bridling up. He was known for talking straight to anyone, even if it was the priest or the squire. Before the war he was always going around to political rallies everywhere.

"Or maybe there's no point in asking these gentlemen," said Sitek, like he was trying to excuse the soldiers so they didn't feel bad about not knowing. "They're probably country folks like us, they only know as much as we do. But I'm sure they won't hurt us, no way."

"You'll see, we'll be back home this evening," said Jagła, backing Sitek up. "There's twenty-five of us, we'll have the job done in two shakes. They'd have said if it was anything else."

"What do you mean, anything else?" said another guy, suddenly worried, and he leaned forward on the bench towards Jagła.

"They might say, they might not."

"Say what? What might they say?"

"Come on, what's the point of worrying ahead of time, when we get there they'll tell us."

"I don't like the look of this, I really don't. We're going somewhere and we don't know where. What can it mean?"

"Maybe they're going to kill us?" Strąk burst out, and everyone was suddenly terrified.

Strąk was the oldest guy in the truck, way older than Antos or Wrona. He could barely shuffle about, they'd had to help him into the truck because he couldn't have climbed up by himself. His son-in-law had sent him to the meeting just like my father had sent me. Why would they have chosen Strąk as a laborer when so many other younger, stronger men had been left behind on the square? If someone had thought about Strąk earlier, maybe we'd have figured out right away where they were taking us.

"Darn it!" said Kujda angrily, like it was Strąk's fault that they might be going to kill us. "You should have sat on your backside and not gone to any meeting."

"How was I supposed to know?" said Strąk, trying to defend himself. "The policeman said to go to the meeting."

But everyone started in on Strąk.

"Your son-in-law should have come. He's the head of the household, not you. You signed the farm over to him. You should stick to praying instead of going to meetings."

"Or if they start telling us to dig, and they will, because why else would there be spades here, we'll have to do your digging for you. No one's got four arms."

"He's got one foot in the grave already, goddammit, he smells death everywhere."

"You say they're going to kill us? Why would they do that? Why?"

"If they were going to kill us they wouldn't have bothered taking you. You dying doesn't mean shit to them. It'd be a waste of a bullet. Death'll take you without any help from them."

Strąk hunched over like he'd been swallowed up by the earth. He might even have regretted saying what he said about being killed, it came out like it was about everyone dying, when he was likely just talking about himself.

"But what if they are taking us to our deaths? What if they are? Maybe they're going to have us dig our own graves, that's what the spades are for? Lord!"

"In that case they'd have taken someone to fill the graves in afterwards. I mean, we couldn't do it ourselves. But they didn't."

"That can't be it. There's probably a dike burst somewhere, we had bad rains recently, it could have burst."

"Hey, hear that? Quiet there. Sounds like there's another truck behind us. I'm not just hearing things. My hearing's still good, even if I am getting on."

"What if there is, they're not gonna wait back in the village are they?"

"It's either the wind flapping the tarpaulin, or there's a mill somewhere close by."

"Do something, Lord. Make the axle break or whatever."

"A broken axle won't help you. One time my axle broke, I was taking rye to the mill, and instead of the miller I needed a blacksmith. A miracle'd be better."

"Sure, you just order us a miracle."

"There was a miracle over in Leoncin in the last war, but they didn't take us in trucks back then."

"I was supposed to go plow tomorrow, Stanuch and me were gonna team up our horses. You know, up by the hill."

"One time, this Gypsy fortune-teller told me I'd live a long life. Wish I knew where the bitch is now."

"Mind your language there, what if we are going to die?"

"What are you going to do about it? Run away? You can't run away. Besides, we have to die sometime."

"Dear God, the wife'll be left on her own with four kids! Though what does God care?"

"I didn't even say anything about what they should do at home if I don't come back."

"You'll go back, why wouldn't you. Błażek Oko came back from the war after twenty years, though no one ever thought he would. He was old and bald and his woman had gone to her grave, but he came back. And don't people come back from over the sea?"

"The storks came back this year, though I was all set to knock the nest off, what good is an empty nest to anyone."

"The moment we get back, I swear to God I'm gonna get legless. I'm gonna drink for three days. The hell with the horse and the cows and pigs and the land. There'll be no farmer for three days. I'll spend three days in bed with the missus, what do I care. We've got six kids, we'll have a seventh, what do I care."

"Hail Mary, full of grace . . ."

"Stop it, they're looking at us. Let them think we're not afraid of dying."

"But we are afraid, Bolesław, we are. Though if it has to be, it has to be."

"If you ask me, they're going to have us plant trees. Oleś the woodsman, he paid one grosz per pine sapling before the war. I wonder if there'll be a lot of soldiers."

"I hope to God it's trees."

"I'm telling you, lads, it's trees. I know trees. Can you hear the branches against the tarpaulin?"

"Listen, with lupin, is it better to plow it in while it's still in bloom or wait till afterwards?"

"It's better to make your confession."

"Without a priest?"

"Each of us to himself."

"How can you confess to everything on your own? Without a grille, without anything? Are the sins supposed to confess to each other? How will we know if they're forgiven?"

Suddenly we all swung forward like grain in a meadow and the truck pulled up. The four soldiers that had been guarding us quickly stood and rolled back the tarpaulin, then they jumped down, opened the tailgate, and all at once they're yelling, get down, get down, hurry! *Schnell, schnell!*

To begin with we couldn't see anything, the light blinded us like we'd just crawled out of a hole in the ground. I thought to myself that that might be what the light eternal looks like, except after that you can't see anything ever again. But right away we made out some woods, and Garus from Borzęcin recognized it was the Borowice woods because it was where he used to pick mushrooms.

Everyone got to their feet and there was a commotion in the truck like there was suddenly twice as many of us, but no one was in any hurry to climb out, they made like they didn't know if they should take the spades or not. On the way we might not have known, but now it was pretty obvious. I grabbed the nearest one and jumped to the ground. If I held back I'd attract their attention and they'd think I was up to something. Actually I was. I'd been thinking about escaping the whole journey, except there hadn't been any way to do it. But here I decided I had to. Even if I failed, either way it was death, and if I was running away I might not feel the bullets in me, maybe death would come right away.

It was a smallish clearing. The woods were dense round about. Oaks, beeches, spruce. Juniper and hazel too. The grass was like a carpet, and it was covered with heather. You could have sat yourself down, got some fresh air, listened to the birds or just watched the trees swaying in the wind. And if you happened to have a girl with you, it wouldn't be a forest clearing anymore but a little piece of heaven. You could imagine you were the first people. But we'd come there to die.

"You should've seen the agaric used to grow here, Lord those were some mushrooms." Garus had gotten out after me, he was full of regret for life. "And over there, among the oaks, there was boletus, ceps. There were so many you could have cut them down with a scythe, because hardly anyone knew about this place." He even started looking around for mushrooms, but a soldier thumped him in the back with his rifle butt and pushed him into the middle of the clearing.

They formed a wall around us and the same officer that had been screaming on the table outside the district administration started shouting again and waving his arms at the men that were still getting out of the truck. *Schnell! Schnell!* The younger guys jumped down without needing to be told, it was only the older ones that were left. For them, getting down off the bed of the truck was like jumping from the hayloft to the threshing floor. Plus there was nothing for them to hold on to or lean on, so it was no surprise they were afraid to climb down. Though why should they be in a rush? To go to their deaths? It wasn't even right to hurry to your own death.

In the end they all managed to get down somehow or other, only Strąk was left. He stood there at the tailgate, leaning on his stick and looking help-lessly from us to the ground and back again, like he was standing on the edge of a cliff. He realized no one was eager to help him and he shouted:

"Come give me a hand."

Guz stepped forward but a soldier stuck the muzzle of his gun in his belly and made him go back to his place. At that exact moment the officer shouted, *schiessen!* The soldier nearest the truck fired his machine gun at Strąk like he was shooting at a tree. Strąk dropped his stick but kept standing there. It was only a second later his body fell too and hit the ground with a thud.

Right after that they started pushing us with their guns toward the middle of the clearing. They marked out a pit about twelve yards long and two wide and ordered us to dig. Some on one side, some on the other, which meant we'd be falling in with our heads toward each other.

I dug away any old how, thinking the whole time about how I could get away, because death was galloping full speed toward me. Zioło from Bartoszyce was digging opposite me. Tears were already rolling down his cheeks and he was sniffling like a child. But if I just started running and headed for the woods I wouldn't even make it to the trees, the first shots would get me. It was no more than ten or fifteen yards to the edge of the woods. But those sons of bitches were standing right behind us, in a row, with their guns in our backs. I even heard one of them fart. I thought it was one of the guys out of nerves, but the smell definitely came from behind, it was like sour turnip.

I began to lose hope, because the pit was getting deeper and deeper. Everyone was whispering their prayers, you could tell from their lips, and every now and then you could hear the odd word over the rasp of the spades.

"What do you think you're doing? Dig properly." It was Antos to my left suddenly telling me off. I looked over. What was he saying that for? I always thought he was a smart guy, but fear had obviously made him stupid. At the same time I glanced at Kuraś, who was digging to my right. It took me aback, it was like I'd never noticed he was so short, even though I'd known the guy for years and I knew how small he was. But so what if he was short. It had never mattered. One man grows tall and another one's short, in the village you don't see it somehow, it's just how God measures things out. Besides, it often happens a little guy like that is stronger than a big one, and smarter. I thought to myself, God must have sent him to me, and on my right side too. If he'd been big like Antos there wouldn't have been any sense in even trying. I kind of felt bad for him, but they were going to kill him anyway, so he wasn't going to be out for revenge, while me, I might save myself.

It was only right though, to pray for his soul. So I started, but more in my thoughts than on my lips, so he wouldn't see. Forgive me, Antoni, may the earth lie lightly on you. Don't hold it against me that I made use of your death to escape. Just think how many of us are about to die, and every death a wasted one. Only your death will serve a purpose, Antoni. And if I make it, I'll take revenge for all of you, I promise. Look down from heaven and count every one of those bastards as I'm taking them out. Because each one of them will be partly for you. I promise, Antoni. Lord Jesus, who art in heaven, receive Antoni Kuraś, and not just his soul, but his body too if you can. Because even though he died in the woods, not on the cross, it's still a crucifixion just like yours. And forgive him all his sins, or give them to me and they can be mine till the end of my life and till the end of the world. Punish me for them, and save him. Antoni Kuraś is his name. Don't forget, Lord. And don't get him mixed up with anyone else. May he not have to wander around the woods for a long time after he's dead. Farewell, Antoni.

I grabbed him under the arms, he was light as a feather, and I threw him onto the soldier that was standing behind me. The soldier fired off a short burst then they both fell to the ground. Him underneath and Kuraś on top of him, already dead. First off they thought Kuraś was the one trying to run away, before they realized it was me I'd reached the nearest oak tree and gotten behind it, and it was only then they started firing and chasing after me. But beyond that oak tree there were more oaks, beeches, spruce, the whole forest. Plus, death was driving me along and I was running like a stag, dodging between the trees till they hid me completely. Though for the longest time it felt like they were right at my back, I could hear them running through the woods and shouting, and their bullets kept zinging around me.

I must have kept running for a heck of a long time, because I could barely breathe, I felt a stabbing pain in my chest, and it was harder and harder to swerve around the trees. I kept crashing into some obstacle, I'd fall over and get up, but it was all I could do to stay on my feet. Then I smashed into something again, fell over again, and this time I didn't have the strength to stand back up. Fortunately I couldn't hear anyone chasing me or shooting at me, all I could hear was silence surging through the woods. But I didn't want to live so much as just sleep and sleep.

All of a sudden I felt a twinge in my left side. I reached my hand down, and it came back covered in blood. The sleepiness passed instantly. I rolled my jacket up and saw that a part of my side had been almost completely shot away. There were lumps of half-dried blood in my torn shirt, blood all around my belt, and the leg of my pants was soaked in blood all the way down to the ankle. Though I hadn't even felt I'd been hit. I tried to stop the blood with my hand, but it kept running through my fingers. I struggled to my feet and set off again. But which way should I go to find people? Suddenly the woods spun around me like a merry-go-round, my eyes went dark, and I had to lean against a tree. I thought I heard a rooster crowing. I figured maybe I was dying and I was imagining things. But no, I heard it again, and it sounded like it was right close by, just beyond the trees. So I dragged myself that way, either holding on to the trees or on all fours. After a few yards, in a gap in the trees I saw a cottage with a roof of golden-colored shingles, smoke rising from its chimney. I passed out.

When I came round, a mongrel dog was standing over me yelping like I was a dead body. A farmer was walking toward me from beyond the trees, carrying a pitchfork at the ready like he was about to stick it in me, and at each step he was asking the dog:

"What is it, Mikuś? Whatcha got there?"

He wanted to hitch up his wagon and go fetch the healer right away, because neither him nor his wife believed I'd live, I'd lost so much blood. But I refused, let what was going to happen happen, the healer might turn out to be a snitch and I'd have run away in vain.

Luckily the bullet hadn't lodged in the wound. They washed it with moonshine, then they applied compresses of horsetail and coughwort in turn, and after a few days the bleeding stopped. After that they just put on badger fat, and slowly, slowly it started to heal. But the most useful thing of all was that I munched on carrots like a rabbit, that helped to make new blood. I'd sometimes eat half a basketful in a single day. Plus the farmer's wife grated carrot into a juice for me, and gave me boiled carrots for dinner. I ended up all yellow from the carrots, not just my face but my arms and legs and even my fingernails turned yellow, like I was covered in wax. My teeth, I had to clean them with ash to get rid of the color. So when I finally went to visit father and mother to show them I was still alive, a good few months had passed by then, father's first words were:

"Why're you all yellow? Are you really alive? Is it you or your ghost? We already mourned for you. We went gray because of you. But why are you all yellow?"

Mother sat up from her pillows and burst into tears. She couldn't get a word out at first, it was only when the crying eased off a bit that she defended me against father.

"What do you mean, yellow? He's thin and pale. Dear Lord in heaven. He's not yellow, he looks like he's just been taken down from the cross. You must be hungry, son? I'll heat something up for you. There's dumplings left over from dinner. I said so many prayers for you after they told us you were killed." She burst out crying again.

But father wouldn't give it up:

"Sure he's yellow. There's nothing wrong with my eyes. He's yellow as can be."

"It's from the carrots," I said.

At that moment he looked at me like I was making fun of him and suddenly broke off. He sat down on the bench, rocking and staring at his own bare feet. I was a bit surprised, because how could he have known I was yellow, it was dark in the house, the lamp was turned way down and there was no more light than you'd have from sunlight shining through a knothole, plus I wasn't all that yellow by then. Maybe he didn't believe it was me, but he felt it wouldn't be right to ask, is that you, my son Szymek, that they killed, so he just asked me why I was so yellow.

Because mother didn't need to ask anything at all, she cried her eyes out and everything was clear to her. But that's how things are in the world, for a woman, weeping is there to help when reason stops understanding. And weeping knows everything, words don't know, thoughts don't know, dreams don't know, and sometimes God himself doesn't know, but human weeping knows. Because weeping is weeping, and it's also the thing that it's weeping over.

When mother's tears eased off she still didn't ask me anything, she just started telling her own news. That her chickens weren't laying. Yesterday she only found three eggs. How could she expect them to lay, though? If they'd had wheat they'd be laying. But here all we had was potatoes and chaff, and nothing but what they could find on the ground by themselves. On top of that one of them got eaten by a polecat last month. And it had been the best one, it was going to be a brood hen. The speckled one, remember? I did remember, though there'd been more than one speckled hen. That was one smart hen. The second it caught sight of me it'd come pattering from the other end of the yard to see if I had any grain or bread crumbs to drop down for it. Why did it have to be that one the polecat killed. When it found something to eat on the ground it would rather let the other hens have it than get into a fight with them. It never squeezed through the fence into other people's farms, or onto the road. And it would always go roost at sundown of its own accord, when the other ones, you'd have to shoo them into the barn. It would have been a good mother to its chicks. I was so glad I had it, Lord I was so glad. But one morning I go into the barn and there's feathers and blood all over the place. She bled and bled. I've never seen so much blood from a single chicken. Another one they had to slaughter cause it looked to have some kind of sickness. It started keeping its distance from the other chickens. Then all it would do was stand by the barn, on one leg. I thought to myself, aha, there's a storm coming, just don't let there be lightning, Lord. Or maybe it was hail. That would have ruined everything. All it would do, once in a while it would go over to the water trough and drink and drink, then it would go back near the barn on its one leg. This went on for a day or two. I took a handful of wheat and put it right under its nose, but it never even poked its head out from its feathers. And at night you had to pick it up and carry it into the barn, because on its own it wouldn't have known it was nighttime. Then, at one moment I lift up its head and I see its eyelids are starting to close up over its eyes, that its eyes are like little tiny millet seeds. You poor thing, I can tell you're never getting better. Oh dear Lord Jesus!

"Leave him alone, you and your chickens!" Father had had enough. "On and on about them! Like there was nothing in the world except for chickens. I wish that damn polecat would just eat the rest of them. Or the sickness would kill them all."

At that point mother started crying again. But father must have needed her tears as well. Because he went off on her right away. What are you crying for, you silly woman? What are you crying for?

"It wouldn't be so bad if you had something to cry about. But what is there to cry over? Did someone hurt you? No, they didn't. So what is it? You've gotten so much into the habit of crying, your tears come whether you've a reason to cry or no. So then why? You'll cry yourself out, then something'll come along that you really need to cry your heart out over and you won't be able to. What will you do, cry with dry eyes? With dry eyes you can't even laugh, let alone cry. Crying's like money, you need to keep some back for a rainy day. Because a person doesn't have too much crying in them, that's a fact. And what they have is all there is. If a person cried like you, with or without a good reason, they'd run out of tears a quarter way through their life, when they need them their whole life through. When the bailiff came you cried just the same, you thought it would do some good. But all he wanted was your sewing machine, the bandit, he didn't give a tinker's damn about your tears. So what are they for? He was dead and you cried, now he's alive and you're crying. Those tears aren't worth a thing. That's what eyelids are for, you squeeze them shut and your tears go back inside. Because otherwise you'd have to cry every time you looked at the sun. Every time the wind blew in your eyes. Or whenever someone poked you in the backside with an awl. Cut it out, for goodness' sake! You've already cried your eyes out, all that's left are little slits. Then afterwards it'll be, come thread this needle for me because I can't see. How can you see when the eye of the needle's way smaller than a tear. Just so you know, I'm not threading any needles for you, you can do it yourself, go blind."

He was all riled up, he went to the bed and tugged at mother's quilt.

"Give it a rest. The polecats'll kill more chickens. That's what polecats do. The brown one will be just as good of a brood hen as the speckled one. I don't know why you think hens are so clever. How smart do you need to be to lay eggs. Sparrows do it, crows do it, everything does it. God told them to lay eggs so they do. Let them so much as try on their own. The only thing they're smart for is wheat grain. Go throw your tears down for them and see if they come running. For wheat grain they'd come. Though both things are like seeds. I'll turn down the lamp, maybe that'll make you stop. Tears like light. It makes them shine. If you must cry, cry in the dark. If we leave the light on now there'll be no kerosene left for when the cow's calving, you'll have cried it all away. Or someone'll see the light from the road and come running to ask what happened here. What could have happened? Nothing's happened. Szymek's back, is all. It's not the first time. How often did he come back from being with some young girl. From dances. In the early morning. Drunk, sometimes beat up. Mother's warming him up some dumplings from dinner. And she's crying because she happened to have just dreamed he was never coming back. But who believes in dreams in wartime, only one in a thousand comes true, and it's always the dream you didn't have. If you have to cry, you should cry yourself out in your dreams. Not now, waking up and then crying. Tell me, what are you crying for?"

He must have gotten cold, he was wearing nothing but his long johns and nightshirt. He was barefoot because he'd gotten straight out of bed to let me in, the night was a chilly one and the earth floor was cold. He tugged at the quilt mother was lying under.

"Come on, get up and heat him up those dumplings if you're going to."

The moment she got up, he slipped back into bed in the warm place she'd left. He asked her:

"Did I say my prayers this evening?"

"You never say them if I don't remind you."

"It must have been yesterday then." He covered himself with the quilt, even putting his head under.

He couldn't stand it when mother cried. And when nothing would work to make her stop, he'd do all sorts of strange things. He'd hammer on a pail with the masher, or open and close the door, clatter the pans in the kitchen, or stamp his feet on the floor. Or he'd take the broom and pretend it was a rifle and he'd drill himself, calling out orders to himself the whole time like he was the colonel of a regiment. He'd shout so loud the windows rang. Another time he'd march back and forth across the room with his broom-rifle on his shoulder singing army songs that he knew from long ago, and since he didn't remember all the words he'd hum and whistle and wheeze the other parts, because he didn't even have the voice for it. And if that didn't do the trick either, he'd pretend to cry along with mother, but much louder and more painfully than her. There were times he'd curl up and hide his face in his hands, he'd keep shaking his head and he'd start calling, Lord Jesus, my Lord Jesus, sometimes he'd even shed real tears.

We'd sometimes laugh so hard at father it made our bellies hurt. Though with me it didn't take much, I'd laugh at anything at all. It was like a pair of invisible hands were tickling me under the arms, and even if no one was in the mood to laugh, I'd burst out laughing out of the blue and for no reason. We could be sitting at the table and eating, there was nothing but the clink of spoons and the sounds of eating, and that would set me off. We could be kneeling at our beds in the evening repeating our prayers aloud after mother. Or even when father was sharpening his razor and had me hold the other end of the strop.

The laughter would first of all start pricking me with needles, then all of a sudden it would spread like fire though a haystack and there was nothing I could do to stop it, however much I might have squeezed my eyes and my mouth shut and held it inside with all my will. I could have scraped my fists against my cheeks and pulled at my hair and hunched over till my head was between my knees, the laughter would still bubble up and boil up and I'd curl over laughing. Then when father started in on me, saying, what are you laughing at, you twit, I'd laugh even more. And then, when he'd sometimes give me a whack across the head, then everything in me would be howling with laughter, my head, my belly, my legs, my arms. Worst of all was when it happened at a mealtime, because father would stop eating and wait furiously till I stopped, but I'd laugh so much I almost fell to pieces.

"Come on, eat up while it's still hot," mother would say to calm him down. "He'll laugh his fill and then he'll stop. Everyone has to go through their own foolishness. Did you never laugh when you were his age? He's still a child."

But often she didn't succeed in calming him, and when his fury got too much for him he'd jump up and grab me by the scruff of the neck and throw me out of the house, go do your laughing outside, damn you!

But I never got my fill of laughter as much as when father would make fun of mother crying. At those times he allowed us to laugh as well, he even encouraged us, go on, you keep laughing, maybe she'll stop. So we all laughed. Even Michał laughed, though he'd been a gloomy kid ever since he was little and he rarely laughed. Because of that I didn't like sharing a bed with him, because I could never have any fun with him before we went to sleep. He always either had a headache or a stomachache, or he'd tell me to stop because we'd tear the quilt, that we'd already said our prayers and God might get angry with us. When I tickled him it would sometimes make him cry. Even mother would say to him:

"You should laugh more, Michał, why are you so glum. See, everyone's laughing."

I mean, how could you not laugh when the mummers came by after the New Year, and Stach Szczypa was the devil with a black face, he wore an inside-out sheepskin jacket, he had a tail stuck to his backside and horns on his head, and he ran around the house like a madman sticking everyone with his pitchfork like he was taking them to hell. Anyone would have laughed at that. But Michał got all scared and went pale, he clung to mother and no one could explain to him that it was only Stach.

"It's just Stach Szczypa, son, don't be frightened. Tell him you're Stach Szczypa, Mr. Devil."

Antek as well, when father would make fun of mother crying he'd enjoy it so much he'd squeal and he'd laugh so hard he'd sometimes wet himself, though he was so small he was still crawling around on all fours. And Stasiek in his cradle, though he was too young to be able to laugh, he'd still try and gurgle in his own way. Even mother, you got the feeling she was only pretending to cry and that deep in her heart she was laughing with us and with father.

It was only much, much later, when I'd long gotten over the laughter, that I finally realized why father would make fun of mother crying, why he'd drill himself and sing army songs, why he'd rattle the pots and slam the door and bang on the pail with a masher and do all those crazy things. Because just like him, I couldn't bear it when mother would cry. I'd rather have mucked out the stable from dawn till dusk, or said rosaries for every one of us the way she did for us, than see her crying. In theory I could have just said, let her cry, crying is what mothers are supposed to do. But I couldn't. Often I'd be mad at myself that I didn't happen to be out in the fields at the time, or at the pub, or with a girl, or with the guys down in the village, there were so many places where no one was crying, but here I was sitting at home, letting her cry like a child. Every tear of hers caused me pain. I could have lifted up a horse, or a wagon, I had so much strength in me, but I didn't have the strength to raise my head and look into her teary face. I'd just sit there staring at the ground. I didn't even have the courage to say, don't cry, mother. I felt almost guilty for her crying, hurt by it, and I didn't hurt easily. Her crying fell on me like rain from a cloudy sky, and I just sat there meekly getting wet, like I'd deliberately gone and stood out in that rain of tears so it would fall on me.

Sometimes the crying did something to me, it was as if she was still carrying me in her belly, and together we were carrying something heavy, together we were picking up sheaves of hay during the mowing, and the sun was burning down on both our backs at the same time. I was bending over just like her and standing with her up to my knees in the river and we were washing clothes, beating them with the washing beetle, and the echo carried along the water all the way to the source of the river in one direction and its mouth in the other. Then when we went to the store to buy salt or kerosene or matches, I'd even hear the other women in there saying to her, so not much longer, huh, Magdzia? Any day now. And she would answer that it was still a long time yet, maybe it would never happen. And with my hands inside her hands she'd pick thyme and horsetail and chamomile, and all the herbs that grow along the field boundaries. And when she was kneading dough in the kneading-trough to make bread, I was in her and I was already the bread inside her. And after the whole day, when we were both exhausted, we would kneel to our prayers like a single body, me inside her knees.

Even at moments when she was weeping for joy, like now, I still felt guilty towards her, though I had no idea why. Maybe our wrongs are only known to our mothers, never mind what they say about only God knowing them. She must have known for me the things I didn't know myself.

Of the four of us brothers, I was probably the one mother cried over the most. Then Michał. But with Michał, obviously he's not going to understand any of it. Even if someone cried and cried. Because it wasn't anything that could be understood either through reason or through crying. Though you can sometimes understand things more through crying than with your reason. In any case it's a lot easier after you've cried your fill than after you've understood. Because it's only through crying that you can be with someone when you're apart forever.

As for Stasiek and Antek, of course she cried, that's how it is – you always cry for the ones that are gone. But I was there, except for the war I'd been at home all the time from when I was a kid till now, what was there to cry about? Unless she was crying for all of us and it just happened to be me that was there. The fact was, I lived however I could and however I had to, it couldn't have been any different, because no one lives the way they want to. Besides, even if you could live the way you wanted, would you be any the happier? You can never tell if the way you'd like to live wouldn't actually be worse. Maybe everyone has a different life than the one they'd want, but it's the best one they can have. When I was small she'd cry over me, but all mothers cry over their little ones. Not just people, cows do it, mares, bitches, she-cats.

We had a she-cat once, I drowned her kittens. She'd had five of them. She'd wandered off somewhere, the attic or the barn. She wasn't much of a mother. She'd sometimes leave those kittens all day long on their own, they'd mew for her so bad it wouldn't even help if you gave them milk in a saucer. Besides, she'd had so many kittens you'd have thought she would forget whether she'd had them now or another time. Towards evening she slunk up, she saw that the old sieve where the kittens had been was empty, and she started rushing around the room like a mad thing. She crawled under the bed, jumped on the stove, she even hopped into Stasiek's cradle and set him wailing. Father grabbed her and tossed her outside, but she started scratching at the door and mewing in this terrible voice so he had to let her back in. Mother gave father and me a telling-off for being so heartless, she took the cat on her lap, stroked her, and talked to her like one mother to another. But the cat soon jumped down and went back to the empty place where the kittens had been. She rolled into a ball there and we thought she'd gotten over it. Father even said that cats don't hurt for long, and they cry even less, but in the morning she was dead. Except that with cats, when they grow up they don't know each other, even a mother and her child, it's like they were strangers, just two cats. Whereas me, I was already a young man but mother still liked to weep over me. It was as if her tears had stayed with her permanently from when I was a kid. And even when she was dying, instead of at least one time thinking about herself, she took my head in her skinny hands and wept over me. Then she passed away.

Something took hold of my throat and I couldn't cry. The women that came to say goodbye to mother tried to get me to.

"You should have a cry, Szymek, you really should. A person ought to cry for their own mother. Even if they don't think they can. Especially a mother like yours."

But I couldn't. Father was crying, he cried any time anyone came, even Michał was looking at mother in this odd way like he didn't know whether he should cry, or instead not believe her that she was dead. But with me, something got stuck inside and I couldn't do it.

Come to think of it, when was the last time I'd cried? It must have been when the Kubiks' cow was calving on the meadow. I'd have been about ten years old. After that, never. I could say about myself that I'd gotten through life without crying.

Back then we used to graze the cattle on the meadow by the brick kiln. There was quite a band of us, and maybe three times that many cows, it was almost all the cows in the village. With so many cows it went without saying some of them had to be pregnant, because the pregnant ones were only kept back home a week before they were due to calve. Besides, no one worried whether they were pregnant or not. When your dads told you to take them out to pasture, you did it. You didn't whack them so hard when they were pregnant, but it had to be plain to see. With the Kubiks' cow you couldn't tell anything from looking at it. It may have been a bit broader when you looked at it head-on, but it could just have had more to eat than usual. Wacek, the Kubiks' boy, he didn't say anything either, plus he was a stutterer and he liked to shout louder than any of us, because for us it was all a big game, and he didn't give a second thought to his cow.

We played mountain. We'd shout, you, Fredek! Or, you, Kazek! Or, you, Jędrek! And whoever it was, he had to run away and the others tried to catch him. The first one that got to him jumped on top of him, then the others followed, till we made a mountain.

Władek Koziej was it, he was the smallest boy on the meadow. He didn't want to play. He begged us and cried and promised he'd bring us wild pears, that he'd steal tobacco from his father and bring it for us. Then, when we were all jumping on top of him he squirmed and shouted, let me breathe! Let me breathe!

Later on, when we were young men we served in the fire brigade together. One time, in the spring we went to a flood. Actually it wasn't even spring yet, it was just that the sun had been so warm for some reason that the ice had shifted and broken a dike over by Mikulczyce. Mikulczyce and Borek and Walentynów all got flooded out. As far as the eye could see, it was terrible. So much human suffering, it made you want to call out to God, where are you, Lord? We helped people down out of attics and trees and off roofs, they were mostly wet through and crying and half dead, because some of them had already given up hope of being rescued. We traveled by boat, but we couldn't always get where we needed to be, because either there were fences in the way or blocks of ice, so we had to wade through the water on foot, and push the ice aside with our bare hands.

I was fine, I knocked back a bottle right afterwards and that was the end of the flood for me. Władek drank too, but he had to take to his bed right afterward, he was white as a sheet and shaking. When they cupped him, the marks were like black stamps. Then he started coughing, and he coughed worse and worse.

"You'll get over it, Władek," I said to comfort him. "All the bad blood's been drawn out of you."

Then they applied leeches. Then he drank herbs. But he got weaker and weaker, you could see him fading away. One day they sent for me and told me he was dying.

"I can't breathe, you know, Szymuś," he whispered. You could tell it hurt for him to use what was left of his voice. "Just like that time on the meadow, remember? It's like you were all piled on top of me again. Let me breathe, just let me breathe."

Suddenly someone shouted that the Kubiks' cow had fallen over and it was grunting. The ones on top of the mountain jumped off and ran across the meadow, with me in the lead, because no one was faster than me. Behind me was Kazek Sroka and Stach Sobieraj, then all the others came after. But before they were even on their feet, we'd already reached the cow. She was lying there like something was pressing her down, she was rubbing her muzzle on the grass, and moaning the same way a person moans when they're writhing in pain.

"She's dying!" shouted Kazek, and he took off running. The others followed him like a flock of sparrows scared away, one after another, virtually racing each other. Even Wacek Kubik, he burst out crying but then he ran after them as well.

I started shouting, maybe she wasn't dying, maybe she'd just eaten something, but they were already quite a ways from me. I could have set off after them, I would have caught up with them, let her die. Wasn't my cow. But I wasn't going to be the last one to run away. Running away the last was like being the biggest yellowbelly of all. Or even worse, you're not running away because of your own fear but because of other people's. As for the cow, it wasn't mine, but it was still a cow. How could I run away from it? So I stayed. I just shouted after them:

"Cowards! Cowards!"

As for Wacek Kubik, I promised myself he'd get a knuckle sandwich from me later, because it was his cow, not mine.

All of a sudden the cow tossed her head, her side swelled up in a big lump, and inside the lump something started to move like it was trying to get out but didn't know how. I thought to myself, she's probably calving, and I got gooseflesh. I'd have preferred it to be dying. I'd never seen a cow calving from up close. Our cows had had calves, but father never let me into the barn when it was happening, he'd say I was still too young. Mother would bring him hot water, and he'd do whatever he did in the barn, behind closed doors. They'd only call me after the calf was born, to come take a look. One time I got angry and I told him I already knew everything, I'd seen a bull climbing on a cow, and a stallion on a mare, and a dog on a bitch, and everything on everything, I even saw Stefek Kulawik climbing on Bronka Siejka when she had no clothes on one time in the bushes along the river. But he told me those were dirty things, this was suffering and I'd have to grow up first.

I looked around for help, but there wasn't a living soul to be seen. The boys had vanished, they were probably hiding under the willows or in the gully. All I could see was a stork wandering about nearby, pecking at the grass. I suddenly wished I could be that stork, I'd even have eaten frogs. On the far side of the road someone was walking to the village or from it, but they were so far away I couldn't even tell if it was a man or a woman, and they wouldn't have been able to hear me if I'd shouted. Besides, they might not have known anything about cows. It could have been the shoemaker or the seamstress, or a rail worker, or the organist. The cow must have felt sorry for me, because she turned her head toward me, and even though her eyes were puffed up in pain, she looked at me like she wanted to make me feel better. She even tried to get up. All she managed to do was rise on her front legs, then she collapsed again like she was falling from a great height, there was a big thud on the meadow. That must have cost her all her strength, because she lay there gasping, her sides were working like bellows. You might have thought some bad person had been chasing her. One time the steward from the manor chased Karwacki's cow because it had wandered into a beet field that belonged to the squire. He was on horseback. When a cow runs it's like a woman, everything shakes. But he chased it and chased it till it died. He chased it out of the beets, then through the potatoes and the clover and the alfalfa. And the fields at the manor weren't like ordinary farmers' little fields, they went all the way from one end of the land to the other, and Karwacki only had that one cow. Fortunately the squire gave him a calf afterwards to make up, because the squire's wife stood up for Karwacki, and the steward was murdered by someone during the war.

All at once a terrible pain seemed to grip her, because she turned her head the other way so hard I heard a cracking sound in her neck. Her eyes were almost popping out, while I felt a tightening in my throat, half like tears, half not. I squatted down by her head and started stroking her. She was so hot my hand stuck to her skin.

"There there, there there, don't cry," I whispered almost in her ear. Though I don't know if she was crying. I was the one close to tears, maybe I was just comforting myself, because how else can you offer comfort, whether it's to a person or a cow. You can say to someone, let it stop hurting, and it won't do any good, unless it's God himself that says it.

She dragged her head back over the grass, heavy as a rock, and looked my way again. One eye, the one closer to the ground, was all covered with earth, and she probably couldn't see with the other one either, because it was all cloudy like someone had scrambled it up. Also there was a circle of flies that had settled all around the second eye that were stopping it from seeing. I waved my hand at them, but only a couple flew up, the others just stuck there. Flies are like that, they don't give a hoot about someone else's pain, they'll just stick where they are. It made me mad so I grabbed the cap off my head and knocked at the eye with it, and it got clearer straightaway. Except that at exactly that moment she tossed her head like she was trying to shake me off as well. Luckily I managed to jump back, because she would have knocked me over. She pushed against the ground so hard with her hooves there was a spray of earth. It looked like she was finally going to squeeze that mound of pain out of herself. But again it turned out to be beyond her strength, and again she collapsed onto the grass. She lowed, and the sound was so mournful all the other cows nearby raised their heads and looked nervously in her direction. The mound started swelling her out again, it got bigger and bigger, and all of a sudden I remembered that when a cow swells up like that and there's nothing else can be done, its side splits open.

I even had a penknife. On the meadow, not having a penknife was like not having a hand. And it wasn't just an ordinary knife, when you stuck it in wood it rang, and when you threw it at the ground it went in right up to the handle. Because of that penknife I was on good terms with boys much bigger than me. Some of them were four or five years older, almost young men. They knew everything that grown-ups know. It took your breath away sometimes to hear them, and they made you graze their cows for them if you wanted to listen. With the younger ones they'd tell them to go away or send them to bring some of their father's tobacco, it was only me they wouldn't do that to.

I took the knife out of my pocket, opened the blade, and stood over the cow with my arm raised. I knew where you made a hole, in the hollow by the hind shoulder. But I couldn't bring myself to say, all right, do it now. My hand was shaking, the whole of me was shaking inside. I just gripped the knife harder and harder. Suddenly the cow lowed again, just as mournfully as the first time, and I was choked with fear. And right where I stood with the knife, I dropped to my knees by her swollen belly and started praying out loud. Hail Mary, full of grace, the Lord is with thee, blessed art thou among women, and blessed is the fruit of thy womb. After that, I couldn't go on because I was crying. I pressed my head to her belly and tears flowed, not just from my eyes but from my whole face. They might even have dripped into the depths of her stomach. Because when a child cries, the whole world cries. And who knows if it wasn't from those tears that I became an adult. Though it might be that God gives a person one lot of tears like he has one heart, one liver, one spleen, one bladder. And you need to get those tears out so you can tell when you're still a child and when you've grown up. Otherwise they'll follow behind you all your life, and all your life you'll think you're still a child. Some people actually think that.

Though I wasn't any kind of crybaby. Even when I cried, it was usually only inwardly, so from the outside no one could tell by looking at me that I was crying. But that time, with the Kubiks' cow, something kind of opened up wide inside me, even the cow must have been surprised someone was crying over her, because who cries over a cow. Especially the Kubiks' cow, she was always covered in dried crap, no one ever bothered to even clean her. Because old man Kubik, when he wasn't at the pub he was at a rally, and Wacek only knew how to use a whip. Or maybe she was listening hard to see if the crying wasn't inside her, because she calmed down like she'd stopped calving.

Then something moved inside her and the mound I'd bent my head over when I was crying suddenly started to collapse. I jumped to my feet, and the cow jerked its head up almost vertically and started kind of dragging itself backward over the meadow. By now it wasn't grunting but rasping. I ran to its back, and there, the tip of a muzzle could be seen, and in a short moment a whole head appeared out of its backside like it was poking out of a hollow in a tree. I didn't know if it was the right thing to do, but I grabbed the head with both hands and pulled with all my might. And the calf was born. It was a roan like its mother, and it was all slimy.

After that, on the meadow they called me Godfather. It was Godfather this, Godfather that. The name stuck. I didn't mind, why should I. And as things turned out, up till now it was only that one time I was a godfather. Not that I wasn't asked. I've often been asked. I could have had any number of godchildren. Except what good would it have done them to have me as a godparent? What good did it do the Kubiks' calf? I couldn't even say what happened to it next, whether the Kubiks decided to keep it and raise it, or whether they sold it, or slaughtered it, or it died. And though it's not right to refuse when they ask you to be a godfather, I decided I'd never be one. If it were up to me I'd get rid of godfathers and godmothers altogether. You have one real father and one real mother, why do you need a pretend one too. They carry you to the altar for your christening, then after that you don't get so much as a stick of candy from them, they won't even pat you on the head, the one or the other of them. Or they could choose a godfather for you after you grow up. You call them godmother and godfather, but you're strangers to each other.

My godmother, she died young, when I was still in the cradle, I'm not talking about her. But my godfather, in all my life I saw him two times, not counting at my christening. The first time I was almost grown up. A man I didn't know came to our house one Sunday afternoon, I was getting ready to go to a dance and I hear father and mother saying, oh, it's Franek! This Franek says hello to them, then he gives me his hand, so I shake it like you do, but mother and father say, this is your godfather, kiss his hand. I didn't like that, I wasn't going to kiss some guy's hand. My godfather says:

"So this is my godson? He's grown some. He's a young man already."

He was from Zbąszyn or Suchowola, I couldn't even say. Father met him when he was looking for a stove-maker. Our stove was smoking, and for some reason none of the local stove-makers could fix it. They'd come, take the thing apart, put it back together again and it would still smoke. Someone told father there was a guy in Zbąszyn or Suchowola that there wasn't a stove he couldn't mend. Father went there and arranged for him to come. Then one day he showed up. He didn't take it apart or put it back together. He just poked around in it a bit and afterward it drew like no one's business. When the job was done the two of them were so pleased that they got drunk to celebrate and father asked him to be my godfather, because it was just at the time I was due to be christened.

The second time I met him was during the war, at the market at Płocice. We'd gone there to rub out this one bastard. Before, he'd been a bailiff at the court, then during the war he became a German. Every market day he'd swagger around the market in a German uniform with a gun in his belt, and he'd go up to the women that were selling things and take their eggs, butter, cheeses, chickens, poppy seed. When he was in a good mood he'd pay, at the official rate of course. And everyone knew what the official rate was. A whole chicken was the price of a few eggs. Though most of the time he wasn't in a good mood and he hardly ever paid for anything, the son of a bitch would even take the basket as well. And if one of the women tried to refuse, he'd just walk all over whatever she was selling and squash it with his boots, all the eggs and cheeses and butter and cream, he'd kick it all around and mess it up, he'd smack the woman around and call her a whore in Polish. When the women came back from market, instead of having a few pennies to pay for salt, thread, kerosene, matches, they'd be crying. We gave him a couple of warnings, he even got a beer mug over the head in a pub, he was hit so hard he was covered in blood. But it didn't help. He had to be killed.

Three of us went, me, Birchtree, and Sad Man. No, that's not right, Sad Man was dead by then. It must have been Rowan. Because Rowan liked going and carrying out verdicts. There aren't any dances these days, he'd say, it's good we at least get to take out some scumbag once in a while. His eye was straight as a pine tree. Whatever got in his sights – man, bird, hare – it was curtains for it. Except he didn't like taking orders, and for him there were no ranks or officers.

One time, after this one shoot-out he went missing. The guys went looking for his body, thinking he'd been killed and so he'd need burying. But they didn't find him. We thought, maybe he's been captured? But someone surely would have seen it. And it wasn't like Rowan to get caught. He always carried a bullet in his breast pocket, he'd take it out whenever he had nothing else to do and roll it between his fingers or toss it in the palm of his hand till it got all shiny like gold. He'd laugh and say it was himself he was polishing it up for, just in case, that he wouldn't let himself be caught. We started to think that maybe he'd been a spy. But Rowan a spy? In the end two men went off on bikes, because he had a wife and three kids and she needed to be told he'd died in action. They found her by the well, drawing water. But before they told her he was dead, just to be on the safe side they asked if she didn't happen to know where he was. She got all flustered, she couldn't tell who they were, and she started making stuff up, saying he'd been taken away to do forced labor, or he'd gone off after some hussy and left her with the children and the farm. It was too much for her on her own, she said. She even started to cry.

The guys didn't know what to say. But they heard someone threshing in the barn. So they asked who it was threshing. She said it was a relative, and she offered them a drink of sour milk in the house. The guys were no fools, they said sure, that would be nice, but first they'd go ask the relative if he knew anything. They open up the barn door, and it's Rowan doing the threshing.

"So you're threshing, Rowan?" they say.

"Like you see," he says.

"We thought you were dead, Rowan," they say.

"If I was dead I wouldn't be threshing," he says.

"It wasn't nice to run away from the unit like that, Rowan," they say.

"I didn't run away," he says. "I just came to do the threshing for the missus, who else is going to do it for her."

"Maybe you're a spy, Rowan," they say.

"If I was a spy I'd have a farmhand. The farmhand would be threshing, and I'd be informing on you," he says.

"Get your things, we're going, Rowan," they say.

"I'll get my things when I'm done threshing," he says. "I've got another couple dozen sheaves of wheat to get through. Oh, and these oats for the horse."

The men reached for their weapons, but Rowan whacked them on the head with the flail. Then he twisted their hands behind their back and took their guns away.

"Tell them I'm alive. And that I'm not a spy. Now go on up to the house, the wife'll give you a drink of milk. Then get the hell out of here. I'll come of my own free will, there's no way you'll make me."

We went into the pub to have one drink. Rowan was disguised as a wagon driver, he was carrying a whip and wearing a sheepskin hat. Birchtree had stayed at the market, he was going to let us know when that bastard bailiff showed up. We didn't want all three of us to be hanging around because it would have drawn attention. Plus, Rowan always had to have a drink when he was going to execute someone. He said it made his hand faster and his aim better, though he might not have been telling us everything. Actually, even when he wasn't killing he was fond of a tipple, though he didn't like to drink alone, and he always had to find himself someone that had some kind of problem, so he could act like a priest and find words of comfort for him. Because when you've got worries you have to have a drink, and at those times the comfort is surer as well.

That was how it was when Sad Man joined the unit. Rowan took to him like he was his own brother. Sad Man had only just gotten married and he'd

327 ·

had to run off to the woods to fight, and leave his young wife all alone at home. That was why his code name was Sad Man. He was a tall, strapping lad with black wavy hair and thick eyebrows, his wife must have been good-looking too. Some of the men envied him that young wife, though he never spoke about her, but Rowan started in right away comforting him.

"You'll have plenty of time to be with her, brother. I found it hard too. Sometimes I couldn't wait till nighttime. There were times I'd take her there in the fields, whether or not anyone was around. Sometimes people would even call and say hello to us. Now, when I go home sometimes I'll chop wood for her, check the horse's hooves to make sure it's not lost a shoe, currycomb it, tell her what needs sowing where, or planting, and she'll pull me to her, but I'll say, there's a war on, Waleria, we need to fight the enemy, let's leave lovemaking till afterward. It might be nice to do it with a different woman. It's basically the same, but a different one would always be a bit fatter or thinner, she'd make different noises. With your own woman the only thing you have in common is your worries. And it's a good thing God provides them, because what else would you do together? Even if you're not at log-gerheads, the two of you, all you do is turn your back on each other at night, you even keep the quilt between you so you won't get too hot. With your own woman, I'm telling you, brother, it's like being with yourself. You or her, you're one body, tired or not, bad or not. It's better to just have a drink, the result'll be the same. Also, we've already made three kids, do we really want a fourth? Who knows what would lie in its future. Maybe it'd be unhappy? You think I'd have joined the resistance if things had been different? The hell with that. I'm eaten alive by lice, I never get enough sleep, on top of that I could get killed. At home no one was chasing after me, no one came for me, I turned in my levies, hogs, earmarked cows. Windows always blacked out at night. Whatever they demanded, I never said a word. Even the military policeman said to me, Herr Sadziak, *goot, goot*. But I couldn't keep it up any longer."

Rowan died in an attack on the prison in Oleszyce. And Sad Man didn't let himself be comforted either. One night he took off to see how that young wife of his was doing all on her own. The boys advised him not to go, stay put, Sad Man. Rowan gave him the same advice, you want to know too much, brother, you might end up knowing what you shouldn't. You'd be better off just getting drunk.

It was a starry night. The dogs in the village knew him so only the occasional one barked in its sleep. Their dog had been shot by the military police during a search, a thief could have come and there wouldn't have been anyone to bark at him. He knocked on the window and waited for her to get up and appear there like a glowing light in her pure white nightgown, and she wouldn't believe it was him, she'd think he was a glowing light like her. Then she'd rush to the door and unlock it, and fall into his open arms. All around there'd be the smell of lilac from all the bushes that grew by the house.

He knocked a second time, a little louder, but nothing seemed to be moving in the house and no one appeared in the window. He stood a while longer and listened and watched, then he tried the door. It was unlocked. He went in and said into the darkness, Christ be praised, he said, it's me, are you there, Wandzia? But the only answer was a squawk from the brood hen in its basket under the table, because it probably thought someone was coming to take its little ones away.

He managed to find a lamp and light it, and he looked around. His Wandzia was asleep in bed with someone else. They were sleeping so soundly that when he held the lamp right over them, neither of them so much as stirred. The quilt was kicked off and the two of them were naked as the day they were born. The man at least had enough modesty to be lying curled up on his side, he must have been cold, or it was because he wasn't sleeping in his own bed. Sad Man recognized him as Felek, the head groomsman at his wedding. But her, she was lying belly up, her legs gaping wide, all crumpled and spattered, one breast one way and the other the other, the only thing she had on was the red bead necklace he'd bought her at a church fair when they were courting.

On the table there were two bottles of moonshine, one completely empty, the other half finished, and slices of sausage and pickled cucumbers and bread that was cut like for an engagement party. They'd also made themselves scrambled eggs and they'd evidently both eaten from the same pan, because there were two spoons resting against it. And their clothes were scattered all around the room. Her skirt was all the way over by the stove, it might even have been that she made the scrambled eggs without her skirt on.

He made the sign of the cross over them, pulled out his pistol, and shot her and then him right where they lay asleep. The cat mewed in the stove corner, so he shot the cat as well. Jesus was hanging over the bed with his heart on the outside, and he shot the heart. The chicks got out from under the brood hen, he stomped on the chicks and shot the hen. He shot out all the windows in the house. He shot all the pots and all the plates. He even shot at the water bucket. When he'd had his fill of shooting he sat down at the table and drank what they'd left him, then he sang a little. At my wedding they were breathless all, for my wedding party was an all-night ball, yes indeed, oh yes indeed, death was all around and pain was near, but I was smiling from ear to ear, and may the good Lord be with us here, yes indeed. Then he dragged Felek the groomsman's body off the bed, he lay down in his place next to his dead wife and he shot himself as well.

Rowan got up from the table to buy another drink, because for some reason Birchtree wasn't giving us the signal, and it could have looked suspicious to sit there with empty glasses. The pub was crowded, everyone was drinking, so there must have been spies there as well. All of a sudden someone grabs me by the elbow.

"Aren't you the Pietruszkas' kid?"

I don't look round, but the voice is somehow familiar.

"What, you don't know your own godfather?" He sits down in Rowan's seat, and he's pie-eyed. "You know, the Pietruszkas, that live past the co-op? You had storks on your barn. I mended your stove years back."

"Go away, you're barking up the wrong tree." The whole time I kept looking in the other direction. He turns around to the rest of the room, beats his chest, and says at the top of his voice:

"This is my godson!" And he claps his hand on my shoulder. "Except he won't own up to his godfather!"

At this the whole place went quiet and I felt everyone staring at me in disapproval, what kind of louse would deny his own godfather.

Rowan comes back with a half-bottle and says, who's this? I say, I've no idea, some guy's latched on to me, claims he's my godfather.

"What are you talking about, latched on to you, I'm your godfather! And you're my godson, the Pietruszkas' boy. Bring a drink for my godson!"

I could hardly control myself inside, I didn't know what to do. Finally I leaned forward and said in a friendly way:

"Shut your trap. I'm not any Pietruszka, the name's Eagle." The other guy ups and yells:

"What are you talking about, Eagle? You're the Pietruszkas' son, I carried you to the altar in these arms. Are you denying your own mother and father?"

"I'm not denying anyone, but these are different times, understand?"

He smashed his fist on the table so hard the glasses jumped.

"I don't care what times they are, you're a Pietruszka! And I'm your godfather!"

"If he's your godfather, ask him if he ever bought you anything," said Rowan, all riled up. "I bet you didn't get squat from him! Just like mine! Nothing, ever! They're all the damn same, those godfathers. Want me to slug him for you?"

"Give it a rest. Let him be my godfather." I even poured him a drink in my own glass, thinking he might calm down. But he got even more excited and started shouting again, blathering on about the Pietruszkas. I couldn't take it anymore, I grabbed him by the neck like a goose and shouted in his face:

"Eagle!" And I squeezed till his eyes almost popped out. A few folks jumped up from their tables, but Rowan blocked their way, watch it, he put his hand in his jacket and they sat back down.

"Pietruszka, you two-faced bastard!" He could barely breathe, but he grabbed hold of my coat and clung on like a drowning man.

"Eagle." I was so mad I lost it, I squeezed harder and harder. The barmaid screamed and threatened to call the military police.

"Smack him one. Let the godfather have it," said Rowan, egging me on.

At this moment Birchtree ran into the pub and signaled to let us know the bailiff guy was at the market.

"Let go of me, godfather!" I shouted. But he wouldn't. Without a second thought I punched him between the eyes. His nose started bleeding and those eyes of his went all cloudy.

"Pietruszka," he wheezed.

"Eagle." I whacked him again.

"Don't hit me. Don't hit me any more. You can be Eagle."

HALLELUJAH

I don't know if God died, if he rose again from the dead, if any of that is true, but blessed eggs taste different than eggs that haven't been blessed. And nobody's going to tell me it only seems that way to me. Ordinarily I'm not that wild about eggs, but blessed eggs, I can eat ten of them and still keep going. I don't need to even have them with bread, just a little salt, of course salt that's also been blessed. Best of all is with horseradish sauce, that ought to be not just blessed but so strong it knocks your socks off.

Mother would bake *babkas* for Easter. They were famous, those *babkas* of hers. The whole time before the next harvest there could be the worst shortage of flour, there could be no flour even to make the base for *żurek*, but when the harvest was done and the new flour was bolted she'd always set aside enough for her *babkas*, then the rest had to last as long as it could. And when she brought one of those *babkas* down from the attic, because that was where she kept them after they were baked, father and Michał and Antek and Stasiek would sit around the table like foxes round a henhouse, and their mouths would be watering as mother cut the *babka*. Me, I preferred blessed eggs even over *babka*. And usually we'd swap, I'd give someone my slice of *babka* and they'd give me their egg.

If it wasn't for the blessed eggs I could have done without Easter at all.

Because what kind of holiday is it actually? It's neither in wintertime nor in spring. Also, you never know when it's going to fall. You have to look at the calendar every year to see where it's marked. So you have to buy a new calendar every year if you want to know, like you couldn't just get used to the same day once and for all. I was born on Good Friday, but I can't say it was on Good Friday, because Good Friday is different each year. So maybe Jesus didn't die and rise from the dead after all, if it's a different time every year?

I like Christmas better. It's always in the same place. You don't have to check. Besides which, the year is finishing, and there never was a year you'd want to keep. And I love carols. Way back, when we'd all sing carols together at home, the walls would ring. Then when you went down to the village to hear them singing in other houses, you felt like the Star of Bethlehem that appeared over the stable was about to come to earth. Here there was singing, there there was singing, there was singing at all the neighbors' and at the edge of the village, and even far, far beyond.

These days too, when Christmas Eve comes along I like to sing a little. Because carols you can sing on your own and it sometimes still seems that everyone's singing along like in the old days. The one I like best is "God is born." I still have some of my old voice, and when I take a good deep breath I can make the walls ring like before. The neighbors stop their own singing to listen to me. Quiet there, Szymek's singing. On a frosty night they can hear me all the way at the end of the village. Even Michał's all ears when I sing, like he wants it to go on forever.

Sometimes I try and persuade him, if you want I'll teach you and then the two of us can sing together. Say after me, God is born. First the words, then later the tune. They're not hard. God is God, obviously. Is born, you know that too. I was born, you were born. A dog is born, a cat, a foal, a calf. Anything that wants to live has to be born. Remember, in the spring we had chicks, they were born as well, except from eggs. We used to sing this one every Christmas. We'd sit around the table, it was a different table back then, me, you, father, mother, and Antek, Stasiek would be in mother's arms. When mother was serving the food she'd always give him to you to hold, because he didn't cry when you had him. One time he peed in your lap. God is born, that's all there is to sing, don't be afraid.

Though when I was a young man I liked Easter too. In the fire brigade we'd always stand watch over Christ's tomb on Good Friday. In our uniforms with all the straps, with our axes at our side, we'd compete whose uniform shone the brightest. The whole week leading up to it we spent polishing our helmets and boots. A helmet like that, the best way to clean it properly was first with ash, then spit, then cloth, and it would shine like a monstrance, when you wore it you looked like Saint George, or maybe another saint, I forget which one used to wear a helmet. For the boots the best thing was a mixture of soot and sour cream, then rabbit skin to give them a shine. Though beforehand you had to go all over the place to try and borrow boots from someone. Because none of the young men had tall boots, only the farmers had them, and then only the better-off ones. Four of us stood watch so we needed eight pairs for the changing of the guard, plus everyone had feet of different sizes, sometimes we had to go all the way to other villages looking for boots, and they were rarely a good fit for everyone. You often had to stand there in boots that were too small for you. They'd pinch and chafe, your legs would go numb up to your knees, and on top of that people would come to look at the tomb, so they'd be looking at us as well, and afterward there was no end of gossip in the village, so-and-so was standing crooked, so-and-so was rocking from side to side, so-and-so was blinking like you wouldn't believe. But when it came to me they always said, he was standing straight as an arrow.

Then Easter Monday would come around and Dyngus Day, and we'd go from house to house from the early morning wherever there was a good-looking girl. We'd splash the parents a bit first, because you had to, then you'd throw more water over the daughter, though not too much, so you wouldn't get it on the walls after they'd been freshly whitewashed. Because if her folks got mad they might not invite you in for something to eat and drink. It was only later, once we'd gone around to a dozen or so houses and we were on the tipsy side, then we'd go all out. We'd toss whole potfuls, whole bucketfuls over them. Any woman that was on her way to church or from church, whether she was single or married, none of them was safe. Some of them we'd lure all the way to the well. Some of us would keep her there, others would draw the water, the girl would scream and we'd all have a good laugh.

One time Zośka Niezgódka managed to get away from us and ran off towards the river. Unluckily for her we caught up with her by the bank. She cried and pleaded with us, she said she had a new dress on, that she had new pumps, a new blouse, everything was new, because her aunt had just sent it from America, and she'd be afraid to go back home if it got wet. So we took all her clothes off. But she cried and begged even more, when she struggled her boobs jumped up and down, and down below she had red hair. Stand still, Zośka, or your maidenhead'll break and then none of us'll want to marry you. We grabbed her by the arms and legs and flung her in the river.

We'd always bless a whole *kopa* of eggs, five dozen of them. We'd color half of them red by boiling them in onion skins, the other half green with young rye. And it was always me that took them to be blessed, I never trusted anyone else to do the job properly. I'd squeeze through to the front when the priest got started so the most number of drops from the sprinkler would fall on my eggs, because farther back the priest just waved the thing and hardly any drops made it that far. I still did it even after I grew up. It was only during the war, after I joined the resistance, that Antek started going, and after him Stasiek. But they didn't keep it up for long. First one of them moved away, then the other, and once again it became my job to go get the eggs blessed, because what kind of Easter would it be without blessed eggs. I could go without cake, I could go without sausage, but there had to be blessed eggs.

When you eat one of those blessed eggs, even if you've got nothing to be happy about, it's always hallelujah.

It was only those two years I spent in the hospital that I didn't get my eggs blessed. But when I came home, the first Easter I boiled a whole *kopa* just like before. Though I didn't have any of my own, I had to buy stamped ones from the co-op, because my chickens weren't laying yet. Besides, I only had two chickens anyway, and a rooster. I'd just got the brood hen sitting on new ones, they hadn't even hatched yet. I colored them all red with onion skins, because I didn't feel up to tramping out to the fields for new rye, not on those lame legs of mine. I barely made it to the church. And I left home plenty early, if my legs had been healthy I could've gotten there and back again five times over. I thought I'd plop myself down in the pew and have a bit of a rest before the priest started the blessing, but I almost arrived too late, the priest was already going around doing the blessing. Fortunately he'd started from the side altar, and there was a whole crowd of people, in a lot of places they were having to stand, because our parish serves five villages, so before he got to my pew I'd already found a place between Mrs. Sekuła and some woman I didn't know.

Except that when I leaned over to untie the scarf, because the basket was wrapped in mother's old headscarf, the walking stick fell from my hand and crashed to the ground so loud it was like a thunderclap in the church. The noise went all the way up to the ceiling. Even the organ gave a groan in the choir stalls. Right away every head turned in my direction and frowned. The priest stopped the sprinkler in midair and followed where everyone was looking. I got all embarrassed, and for a moment I regretted wanting to get the eggs blessed. Why couldn't I have waited till next Easter, maybe I'd be walking better by then.

As if that wasn't enough, I couldn't loosen the scarf, because I'd tied the ends firmly so it wouldn't come undone on the way, and the priest was almost there. Plus I needed to kneel. How could I kneel when one leg was completely stiff and the other could barely bend either? All my efforts came to nothing, because the priest hurried by like a storm. And though Mrs. Sekuła helped me, and the other woman too, we didn't manage to get the scarf off in time, and I only got a few drops of holy water on my hands, none of it fell on the eggs and they didn't get blessed. So they didn't taste the way they should. They tasted like you'd just gotten them from the hen and boiled them and you were eating them. Though at least I didn't have to regret not having gone. There'd been worse times and I'd always gone, my legs weren't that much of an excuse.

When I worked in the district administration, the fact was I was a government worker, and the times weren't right for blessing eggs. Still, when Holy Saturday came around I'd leave work during the day, I'd say I have to go get my eggs blessed. I didn't hide it. And even when I got transferred to the quotas department it was the same, I'd say I need to go get my eggs blessed. Though the quotas department wouldn't employ just anyone, they were always holding meetings to get us to collect more and more. You often had to be hard as nails with folks. They hadn't even harvested their crop yet, it was still standing in the fields, and here we were sending all kinds of deadlines, provide your quota, provide your quota, anyone who doesn't is in deep trouble. But it all came from the higher-ups. Someone up there was setting the deadlines. It must have been someone that thought he was more important than the land. But only God is more important than the land, for anyone that believes in him. If you don't believe in God, then the land is the most important of all. And you can't hurry it either with deadlines or with whips. If you got mad at it for not obeying you it would just say, kiss my ass. But what could we do?

There were times my hand went numb from writing, because we'd write and write, directives, reminders, fines. My eyes would be red as a rabbit's. I'd get up in the morning and I could barely see. Mother would ask me, why on earth are your eyes so red. Why? From writing. Father would say, sure it's from writing. If that was the case no one would go to school, because there all they do is write. There wouldn't be any priests or professors. It's from drinking. Yesterday he barely made it over the threshold, then right away he crashed down on his bed like a hog. You were asleep, you didn't see it. You just keep drinking. At work they even told me I should go see the doctor, maybe he could give me eyeglasses. Some people at work had glasses. Sąsiadek did, and this one guy in the insurance department, I think someone in highways did, the local policeman used to sometimes put them on as well when he got a written order to go somewhere and he couldn't read where. And three of the women clerks wore glasses, but I didn't like the looks of any of them. I tried Sąsiadek's on one time, I actually looked pretty good, but it was like staring through fog.

Some people thought I'd taken the easy way out, but what was easy about it? After you'd dealt with them, people would come and curse me and the government to high heaven. At times my office would be bursting at the seams with all the papers I had to send out. And there was as much again stacked in the hallway or even outside. They'd bring in the letters they'd been sent and put them on my desk and say, you go and mow, and harvest, and thresh, you go collect it all. A good few of the women would point to their ass and tell me where I could stick my papers. All I could do was throw my hands up and keep repeating, it's not me, it's not my decision. Then whose is it? You're all the damn same, the lot of you!

Of course, sometimes I'd help people out. One guy, I'd move his deadline back a bit, another I'd reduce his quota by a couple hundred pounds, with someone else I'd at least advise them how to write an appeal and where to send it. Then people would want to thank me somehow. How does one farmer say thank you to another? He invites him for vodka. Vodka isn't a bribe. It isn't that one person gives and the other one takes, no – both of them drink. So I got to drinking quite a bit. Actually, in a job like that you can't not drink. Plus people think anything can be arranged with vodka, more than through God. And you never can tell. Sometimes it helps to have a drink, and sometimes even praying doesn't help. But if you want to live among people, you have to drink. Because then they accept you as one of them. And that means something.

In addition, the pub was virtually just over the road from the district offices, all you had to do was cross the road. And everyone knows gratitude isn't something you measure out, you do this much for me and I'll do this much for you, so it rarely ended with just a single bottle. Because gratitude isn't in the pocket, it's in the soul. And I don't care how much of a schemer a man is, after a bottle his soul has to come out. And at that point it's the soul that's standing the drinks, the soul that's paying, and moving from one soul to another is just like entering someone's house.

Also, someone or other always sat down with you, because even if he didn't have an actual reason to be grateful to you, he wanted to be grateful just in case. Then someone else would come along, then someone else again, often it was whoever found themselves in the pub at the time. Because who doesn't want to be a soul instead of just a body? When it came time to shut the pub, Jasiński, the manager, would lock up on the outside, and inside we'd carry on drinking. At most the prices would go up some, he had to earn a bit extra too on top of his salary. He'd go lie down on the chairs behind the counter and we'd drink on. I'm telling you, we drank like it was our souls celebrating because they were in heaven, and not us in a pub. Wake me up on your way out. Come off it, Jasiński, who's leaving, where would we go. We're not gonna come all the way down to earth again. We poured drinks left, right, and center, wake up Jasiński, we need another bottle. Because I was Eagle again. Come on now! You've abandoned us God, good job Eagle's here. Come on now! Soon as Eagle's here, every tear we shed is one dead enemy body! Come on now! Eagle's in the village with his men, they're drinking at young Marysia Król's, there's going to be a parade through the village, bring your flour and lard! Though it often ended sadly, one or another guy killed, a guy gets killed so many times and he has to keep on living. You were Eagle and now you're a piece of crap, not a government official. Wake up, Jasiński, another bottle!

The next day you'd be sitting half dead at your desk, your head would be splitting and your belly would be aching, and on top of everything you'd have to listen to folks complaining about how hard life was. No one cared that maybe you had it even harder, but you weren't going to take some form and go complain, who to? To God? Why is this happening to me, God?

Oftentimes I'd barely make it home when I had to be off to work, there'd only be time to have a quick mouthful of sour milk or cabbage juice. And though home was close by, once the devil began leading you astray he'd push you any which way, sometimes you even ended up back where you started. He'd mix your head up so bad you'd almost get lost in your own village. The only thing for it was to go from one house to the next. Luckily, in those days the houses were close together, like beads in a rosary, it was like they were only separated by the winter insulation on the outside, so you could count off the houses as you went, Hail Mary, full of grace, Our Father. Today almost all the houses are new, it's like someone snapped the rosary and the beads got scattered to the four winds, and you'll never be able to pray that way again.

When you get there, you still have to find the door, and find the handle in the door. There were times it was like searching for a needle in a haystack. I'd be looking and looking, and father would stand on the other side of the door and not open it.

"Open the door, father, it's me, Szymek."

"Open it yourself, you drunken lout."

"I can't find the handle."

"You hear that, mother? He can't find the handle."

"Come on, Józef, open the door for him, he's your own son."

"He's a devil, he's no son of mine. Do you hear him scraping his claws on the door? I'm not letting any devil into my house, not while it's still mine. Keep scraping, Antichrist, scrape till your claws are worn away."

"Open the door, Józef," mother would plead with him.

"Get up and open it yourself."

"I would, but I can't get up. Open the door, Józef. Even a prodigal son is still a son."

"I had sons, but they all left. Anything that's good, it either dies or it goes away, only what's bad stays behind."

One time when he refused to open the door for me, I somehow managed to find the handle, but it turned out he'd put the hook on inside. I started hammering with my fists, I knew he was standing right there, and in the end I was so furious I kicked at the door and I shouted:

"Soon as mother dies, I'm out of here! Nothing's gonna keep me!" And I walked off and sat on a rock outside the house. The night was maybe halfway through. I'd barely sat down when someone joined me.

"Shift up there a bit."

I looked, and it was Grandfather Łukasz, the one that had run away to America before the first war. The moon was bright as a shiny coin, the stars were like grains on the threshing floor, I couldn't fail to know him. It even made me sober up a bit. They say that in such cases you have to ask what their soul needs. But what can a soul from America need? It's only village souls that are always in need of something. Is it you, grandfather, I ask. Then greetings to you. How are things over there in America? They said you made a fortune, now I see you're back. Maybe it's true that when a person dies, his soul goes back to where he was born. Though why did you have to take it all the way to America in the first place? You paid its passage, and now it's back. You should have left it here when the Cossacks came looking for you, they wouldn't have harmed it, and people would have comforted it somehow or other. Then you wouldn't be drawn back here after you died. Was it so bad for you over there in America? If it makes you feel any better, you wouldn't have had it any easier here. Here it's the same as America, just on the other side of the world. Because America is anywhere we're not, grandfather. Tell me at least, what's it like in the next world? You killed the overseer, you know better than other people. You did the right thing, whether or not he was a bastard. A man often feels like killing someone, but these days there aren't any more overseers. It's a different system now. You probably don't know what a system is? You know, like a government. You killed an overseer and you had to run away, and your grandson's a government worker. You must have dreamed of having someone like that in the family? Here you are, he's sitting right next to you on a rock. He's a bit drunk, but that's because of you, grandfather. With you grandparents, whatever popped into your head you lost yourselves dreaming about it, and because of that, afterwards your grandchildren have to drink. You're all in the next world, your grandchildren are still in this one, and it's all one big circle. And circles can't be straightened out. So it's better to go to the pub than go away, because it's the same thing, just closer. Though sometimes, when there's a full moon like tonight, I feel like tying myself up on a chain and howling. I'd be a better dog than our Twisty. I'd smell thieves, and I'd smell your soul, grandfather. You wouldn't have to worry that no one would recognize you. Did you ever see a moon like that in America? You only ever get them here, over the village. Like someone took an ax and cut a hole in the sky. You could toss in a fishing net and catch yourself some fish. Do you know if fish from the sky are the same as fish from the river, grandfather?

We talked on and on, almost till sunup. He didn't say a word, while I talked about this and about that. In the morning father came outside and gazed up at the sky.

"This is quite some weather. I don't know why the sky looks so high up or so deep? Imagine having a farm like that sky. On a big plain. All you'd need to do would be pray, and everything would sprout and grow and flower. Not the tiniest cloud in sight. A sun like Jesus's eye. So then, maybe you could come do some work in the fields?"

"No way, not when I haven't slept. I'll do it tomorrow."

"Tomorrow, tomorrow, how long has it been tomorrow. Everyone else's fields are all plowed and harrowed, some folks have even done their sowing, and our fields haven't been touched since harvesttime. People are starting to ask if we're selling up, because the land's not being worked, and he keeps saying tomorrow. Tomorrow's good for the next world, in this one you have to plow and sow as long as the land'll produce. Because when it stops, you won't be able to beg it to start again. The land is good while it's good, but if it sets its mind to it, it can be stone."

"Grandfather was here with me all night," I said to try and change the subject. "He just disappeared a moment ago."

"So did he tell you where he buried those papers?" father asked, perking up.

"Not that one. Grandfather Łukasz from America."

He waved his hand.

"Him, he was a good-for-nothing. What did he want?"

"Nothing. He just came to talk."

"He must have needed to do penance. Was he barefoot?"

"I didn't look at his feet."

"He probably was. You always have to do penance barefoot."

One time I came back drunk, it was almost nighttime. For some reason I'd thought to slip a bottle in my pocket as we were leaving the pub. You might have said I had a premonition. But I didn't, it was just that I'd gotten paid that day, and when you got paid you sometimes took an extra bottle for the road. It came in handy in the morning when you couldn't get yourself together. I was a bit surprised to see a light still on in our window. But I thought, father's probably just soaking his feet. He had varicose veins and sores and when they were bothering him more than usual, he'd brew up herbs and soak his feet in them. He'd sit on a chair and put his feet in a pail till the cold woke him up or I got back.

I went in and I thought I was seeing things, it looked like Michał was sitting on the bench by the window. Except he seemed kind of sleepy, because he didn't even raise his head when I came in. But it was him all right. Maybe he'd been traveling a long while and he was tired? He never did have much staying power. One time he came back from market with father and the wagon kept bouncing up and down, it made him throw up. Or if he stayed up late one night, the next day he'd be all pale and have rings under his eyes.

"You're here, Michał," I said. And though my head was spinning, I was pleased to see him. "It's been years and years, we've been waiting all this time. Let's have a drink, brother. As it happens I've got a bottle on me. I took it because I had a feeling. How about that." I pulled out the bottle and stood it on the table. "Where are some glasses?" I ask. Father's sitting on a chair with his head down, like he's dozing. All of a sudden he jerks his head up and says to me:

"What, you want to give him vodka, you piece of work? Look at him."

"What do I need to look for? I can see it's Michał. Would I not know Michał? My own brother? He looks a bit older, but not even that much considering how many years it's been. Tell him, Michał, we're brothers, right? You're off away, and I'm here, and we don't know anything about each other, but you don't need to know anything to be brothers. Say, do you remember Franek Maziejuk? You were in the same class together. He hung himself. He was missing twenty hundredweight of sugar from his warehouse. What did he need all that sugar for? Course, the priest says from the pulpit, you mustn't sin. That's easy to say. As for me, I'm more or less alive here. But never mind that, you're here, you've come, that's the main thing. Now where are those glasses, mother?"

Mother didn't say a word. She was lying there with her eyes half closed, like she was asleep, though I knew she wasn't. I thought maybe she was in a huff because Michał was back and I'd come home drunk. Oh well.

"Do you know where they are, father?"

But father wasn't saying anything either. Besides, he might not have known if we had any glasses in the house. What would we have used them for? We only ever drank milk or water, sometimes herbs, and for that a mug was better than a glass. It's bigger and thicker, it's got a handle to hold it by, and mugs last much longer than glasses. There's one tin mug, I've got it to this day, it's my favorite thing to drink out of. Grandfather used it too and he said his grandfather did as well, show me a glass that'll live that long. Water never tastes as good as from that mug. Sometimes I'm not even thirsty, but when I drink from the mug it's like drinking straight from the spring. Or try picking up a glass with a hand that's tired from work, it's like picking up an egg with tongs. When you come back from mowing, whatever you pick up it's like you were grabbing your scythe.

"Let's look around then," I said. I took the lamp from the table so I could see better. "We can't go drinking from the bottle when my brother's come to visit. It's so good to see you, brother. At last we'll be able to talk and catch up after all these years. And you can tell me what it was you wanted from me back then, during the war."

I opened the dresser. Plates, big and little bottles, bags, it all began to dance in front of my eyes, but I didn't see any glasses in the dance. I wasn't sure myself whether there were any in the house, but I had this mighty urge to drink from a glass.

"How do you like that? Like the ground swallowed them up. Tomorrow I'm gonna go buy a dozen glasses and we'll keep them on display." I turned toward mother in bed. "Where are the glasses?" I tugged at her quilt. "Michał and me want a drink." Then I saw in the light of the lamp that her eyes were filled with tears. "What are you crying for? There's no reason. I've come home drunker than this many a time. I'm not that drunk tonight. Wicek Fulara had a baby boy. I married him and Bronka back when. You know what, tomorrow I'll borrow Machała's mowing machine and the whole lot'll be done in a day. I helped him with his application, he's sure to lend me his mower. Let him try not to, the son of a bitch." I was still standing over mother, holding the swaying lamp, and she was crying more and more. "Don't cry, mother," I said. "Father, what's up with mother?" I turned abruptly toward father and the lamp lurched in my hand like the flame had jumped out into the room. It went dark for a moment then got brighter again.

"Put the damn lamp down before you burn the place to the ground." Father raised his head and I could see he had tears in his eyes as well. He wiped them away with the back of his hand.

"Are you crying because Michał's here?"

"He's either Michał or he isn't," he said. "God alone knows."

"Why would God need to know if someone is Michał or not? I know I'm Szymek, you know you're father, Michał knows he's Michał. Everyone knows on their own better than God. Was he just born, that God has to know for him that he's Michał? Me, even if I didn't want to be Szymek there's nothing I could do about it. Even when I'm drunk I know who I am, because no one's going to be me in my place. Though you should have written to say you were coming, Michał. See, everyone's crying now."

"He didn't come, he was brought."

"By who?"

"His wife or whoever."

"You have a wife, Michał? You never said anything. We could have at least sent congratulations. All the best to the newlyweds. Or, may the sun never set on the road of your new life together. Or, here's wishing you health, happiness, good fortune, and your first son. You don't even need to make anything up, you can choose a greeting at the post office. Jaśka the postmistress, she just asks you which one you want, the number two or the number five?

Which one is cheaper? But for you I'd send the most expensive one. Maybe you did mention it? Maybe I forgot after all these years. Well now we really do need to have a drink. Father and mother, let them cry, that's their job. Ours is to drink. Don't you worry about them. I live here with them, they see me every day, and they sometimes cry over me as well. Not father, but mother does. And over you too, specially after you've been gone so long."

The tin mug happened to be on the table and I rinsed it out.

"You use the mug. I can drink from the bottle. Tomorrow we'll drink from glasses." I poured him out the bigger amount and left the smaller half for myself. "Here's to your health, because you came back, you didn't forget us."

I was just lifting the bottle to my mouth when father jumped up and covered the mug with his hand.

"Are you trying to get him drunk on top of everything, you damn godless animal? Drunken idiot, can't you see him?"

"Of course I can see him! He's my brother!" I slammed the bottle down on the table so hard the vodka splashed out of the neck. "Tell him you're my brother, Michał." I grabbed his head in both hands and jerked it up. He looked at me with eyes that saw almost nothing, had no life in them. "You're my brother. Always were, always will be."

At that moment mother got out of bed and asked him:

"Say something, Michał. Tell me, where does it hurt?"

"Where it hurts him is his business," I snapped at mother, though she hadn't done anything wrong. "He's here, he's back, that's all that matters."

"Well since he came back he's been sitting there not saying a word." Father got up from his chair and set off toward the water buckets, then when he got halfway he turned and went toward mother, then he turned back again, like he was cutting across a field but didn't really know where he was going. "She looked after him for a bit. But what could she do. Said he'd be better off here. We keep asking him, Michał, Michał, but it's like talking to a brick wall. Will you not tell your own mother and father? Even trees tell each other, any living thing will. A man'll talk to the earth beneath his feet if he's got no one else to talk to. You can't live and not talk."

"Have a drink, father." I pushed the mug of vodka into the hands he was holding out helplessly in front of him, like he wanted to lay them down somewhere, ease his troubles at least that much. "He doesn't need to talk. We can talk to him."

Mother died not long afterwards. Not from her illness so much as out of worry, because she kept crying and crying and saying, Michał, son, what's wrong? After she passed away father got sick too. Often he didn't hear what you said to him, like all his attention was focused on listening to the next world where mother had gone. So now everything was on my shoulders. He and Michał did nothing at all. They just sat there, one of them on a stool by the stove, the other one on the bench, waiting for me to come back from work.

I even thought about quitting, because it was getting too much for me. Right after mother died I still got some help from the women that lived nearby. One of them would cook for us from time to time, another one would clean the house, another one would do the laundry, and a fourth one would at least come and offer her sympathy. But as mother's death faded into the past, they stopped coming too. On the other hand I was reluctant to give up my job, because those few zlotys I brought in on the first of every month came in handy, you could always buy salt or sugar or a piece of sausage.

Then one day soon after Easter an inspector from the county came, and Chairman Maślanka showed him around the offices. This is highways, this is taxation, this is insurance, quotas, Mierzwa, Antos, Winiarski, Miss Krysia, Miss Jadzia. And I happened to be eating blessed eggs. In our offices we'd somehow gotten into the habit of always having a midmorning snack, Mrs. Kopeć, the caretaker, would even make tea and sell it for a zloty a glass. When I had something I could bring from home I did, so as to not be worse than the others. I mean, it wasn't for being hungry, I could stand being hungry, I could go without food for three days straight. When they came in I'd set the eggs out on the table on a piece of newspaper and I was peeling them, one of them was colored red and the other one green.

"What's this, you're eating blessed eggs, Pietruszka?" said Maślanka, half asking, half making fun of me, and the guy from the county smiled awkwardly.

"That's right." I went on peeling them.

"So what, blessed ones are better than ordinary hen's eggs?" says Maślanka.

"I think they're better. If someone else disagrees they don't have to eat them."

"I see! You must have blessed a whole lot of them if you don't have time to eat them all at home and you have to bring them to work?"

"A *kopa*."

"The thing is, the district administration isn't a church, Pietruszka!" he snapped like an angry dog.

"Right, but I'm not blessing them, I'm eating them."

He didn't say anything else, but I had the feeling he wasn't going to let me off lightly with those blessed eggs, and in front of the county inspector as well. I must have really made him mad, because he started bugging other people about eating. Antos was having bread and cheese. Bread and cheese doesn't have anything to do with God, except for saying, give us this day our daily bread, but believers and nonbelievers eat bread just the same. But he tore Antos off a strip, he said he had so many slices of bread he'd be eating for an hour, and the regulations specified fifteen minutes for the break.

A couple of days later he called me into his office, and though we'd been on first-name terms for a long time, he said:

"You drink too much, Pietruszka. It has to stop."

I was so mad, if I'd had something at hand I would have smashed his skull open. But all there was on his desk was an inkpot and a blotter, that wouldn't have been any good.

"Don't you Pietruszka me, you little squirt. The name's Szymek, in case you'd forgotten. And if I drink, it's on my own time. Don't think I don't know what's gotten your back up. It's not my drinking. Like you don't drink? I can't remember how many times I've seen you under the table. You're full of yourself because you're the chairman. What did you do in the occupation? Shit your pants is what."

A week later I lost my job. And it wasn't because of the drinking like he was trying to make me believe, because at that time I was already drinking less. In reality it was those blessed eggs that had scared him. He might even have liked the taste of them just like me, except that him, he'd hide under his blanket to peel them, and on top of that he'd send his kid out in front of the house to look out, pretend he was playing when actually he was making sure no one was coming. Then all of a sudden he sees a government worker in a government office eating blessed eggs like it was the most natural thing in the world, and it felt to him like they were hand grenades, not eggs. Besides, he wasn't just afraid of blessed eggs. He was afraid of everything. And God forbid you ever said in front of him, Dear God! He'd turn red as a beetroot and if he could he would've stuck the words right back down your throat.

"Save expressions like that for when you're at home, after work! This is the district administration! We need to keep superstition out of here!" But people say those things without thinking, they're just sighing. It's easier to change the words you use or your thoughts than those kind of expressions. But that's the sort of person he was.

When I started having a tomb built, all those years later, and I needed fifteen hundredweight of cement, he was still chairman, though his title had been changed to director. That was how much Chmiel had figured we'd need. And another two hundredweight on top, it might come in useful, we could at least make a couple steps so you wouldn't have to jump down with the casket. I could have bought cement off someone under the counter, and if it was for something else I might have done, but not for a tomb. First I went to the co-op. They had cement, but you needed an allocation order from the district administration. I went there. You could get an allocation order, but you had to sign an application. I signed it.

"What's the cement for?" the clerk asked me. She was maybe twenty years old, big blue eyes, she seemed a nice girl, a bit snub-nosed. But at her age even a snub nose looks pretty.

"I'm planning to build a tomb," I said.

"A tomb!" She almost burst out laughing, she had to turn her head and pretend like she just happened to glance the other way. Then she took a sheet of paper out of her desk and started following down with her finger to see what you were allowed to get cement for. House, cattle shed, stable, barn, silo, manure pit, for breeding rabbits, poultry, foxes, coypu, for a greenhouse to grow vegetables, flowers, potted or cut. Look, they even mention chrysanthemums, she said, pleased. But there was nothing about tombs. She asked a clerk that was sitting in the corner by the window:

"Mr. Władek, are there any official instructions about cement allocations for tombs?"

"Who's wanting to die?"

"This citizen here."

The guy gave me a blank look and shrugged.

"So what am I supposed to do?" I asked.

She smiled, but she spread her hands helplessly.

"You'd need to go talk to the chairman."

"Is he in?"

"He is, but he's busy."

"Then I'll wait."

Mr. Władek chipped in:

"If he's busy, he'll be busy till the end of the day."

"I used to work here years ago," I said. "This room was the tax department. It was before your time. They didn't have those desks either."

Mr. Władek seemed embarrassed. The girl hung her head too.

"Maybe I'll go ask." She looked at me, no longer with the eyes of an official this time, got up and went out of the room.

I didn't have to wait long, he saw me right away, though he'd supposedly been busy.

"Have a seat, Szymek," he said. I was surprised it wasn't "Pietruszka." He obviously remembered me, though a lot of years had passed. He'd really aged and put on even more weight, he was squashed against the arms of his chair. His nose had gotten lumpy as well and his eyes had a heavier look than before, or maybe he'd just been thinking hard about something before I came in. He gave a crooked sort of smile:

"So you're planning to leave for the next world?"

I sat down, struggling with my walking sticks. But it was like he didn't notice I had them.

"What's the hurry?"

"There's no hurry," I said. "Even if there was, I don't owe the government anything. Except for the taxes you let me pay in installments. But I'll pay it off before I die, don't worry."

"Who said I was worried? You want to die, be my guest. Anyone's free to die. It's no business of the district administration. But if you want cement, well that *is* our business."

"It's only fifteen hundredweight."

"Only fifteen hundredweight. It's not a question of how much, it's what it's for. What do you think, that I can give the stuff out for people to do whatever they feel like with it? It's written there plain as day in the regs what I can do. You want to increase your yield, by all means, that's economic development, I can give it to you for that. But if something's not listed it's not listed and that's that. What's the big deal about a tomb? You've got plenty of time. You'd be better off thinking about life while you can. I'm not saying you should get cows or pigs, cause they need a lot of work and I can see your legs are, you know. But maybe a chicken farm or a duck farm. We support those kind of farms. You'd make yourself some dough, and the government would get something out of it as well. We could give you a loan. No problem. Write an application and I'll sign off on it. The interest rate's low and the payoff period is long, later on we can cancel part of the debt. Then instead of being a dead man you're your own master. Your chickens are clucking, your ducks are quacking. All you do is swing by and feed them every so often, and the cash comes rolling in. If there's a blight you've got insurance, the government refunds the value of the stock and you get another loan. It's not like it used to be, when every dead hen was a cause for tears. The speckled one, the red one, the one with green legs. When one of them died it was like a person died, Walek or Franek or Bartek. You could even tell which egg came from which chicken. Now all the white ones are white, all the brown ones are brown. There's no more laying hens, friend, it's all just production. Or greenhouses. We support greenhouses. By all means. Cukes, tomatoes, chives, lettuce, radishes, it's a seller's market. You wouldn't have to worry about delivery. They'd come and buy the stuff up, in any quantities. They have their own crates. A tomb isn't a farm building, it doesn't increase productivity. All that cement, however much it was, just going into the ground."

"Fifteen hundredweight, like I said."

"Even fifteen hundredweight. How am I going to explain afterwards that I allocated it to build tombs instead of silos. It's a bad use of resources, a bad move. Or they might just come tell me I'm too old for the job. Believe me, there's no shortage of folks that would like to see me gone. They're starting to say it's time for me to retire. But I've still got four years to go, that's a long time. Other people say I never graduated from school, I just did some courses. I'm telling you, all the young folks these days have diplomas, and they're stuck up about it like you wouldn't believe. They don't give a damn about this or that or the other, all they care about is whether things are done scientifically. Every cow has to have six teats, two ears on every blade of wheat, four trotters on every pig. It won't be long before they start wanting to plow and plant in the next world as well. They won't even believe there was a war once. Where can you go study in wartime? In the woods, with the resistance. You know that better than anyone. A person's lucky to have a head on his shoulders and get by somehow. But times have changed, boy have they changed since you worked here. Nowadays, those ways wouldn't fly. These days every hundredweight of cement has to give an increase in the yield, in meat, milk, eggs, produce. They calculate everything. And it's always more and more. Then the farmers come along and they say, if you want more productivity I need cement. I can provide a hundred head like you want, director, but I'd need to build an extension on my hog shed. I could do this, I could do that, but I need cement! But we get a wagonload or two of cement and we've no idea when the next one'll come along. It gives me a headache trying to figure out who I should give the cement to and who not. I go visit my father-in-law's tomb on All Souls', and instead of thinking about him I keep thinking how many cattle sheds or pig sheds or silos you could have made from the cement that's gone into the ground there. It's heartbreaking. And there's one guy here in the building that's just waiting for me to trip up. He's always scheming against me. That director, he's too old, he's stupid, he's a lousy party member. Son of a bitch finished college on a scholarship we gave him from the district. But try getting him to actually do anything. Or if a directive comes through, he says it's dumb. For those people everything's dumb. But directives are directives. There aren't dumb ones and smart ones, you just have to obey them. Why do you think I went gray? Because of old age? No. I feel just as strong as when I was young. I sometimes have an urge to grab a tree and rip it up by the roots. I can do it with my Józka five times in a night. Except it's too much for her, all she wants is the usual once a week.

I'm too old for you, Leon, she says to me. If you'd married someone younger it'd make you younger as well. Well when we got married you were still young, I say, you can't change anything now. Though sometimes I think about it, getting married, know what I mean? Why not? The girls in the offices are younger and younger. Everywhere you look they're smiling and blushing, it makes your heart race. But just try getting married. Right away people'll be saying this, that, and the other. Because when you're in a position like this you have to be clean as clean can be. So let it be just Józka. Though it's a pity, friend. You, you're all set to head out for the next world, and you're not the least bit gray, you've just got the odd gray hair. Me, I'm gray as a mouse. Why? It's from all the thinking. And I have to think straight, think right, according to the instructions, not any way I feel like it. Think like a farmer. Be fair, think about the future. Imagine how much thinking that is. There's not enough hours at work, I'm telling you. I have to think at home as well. In your day things were different. You could even go over to the pub during working hours. Or not come to work at all three days running. Try that today. If they even caught a glimpse of the director drinking. Though I have to tell you, often I feel like getting so drunk I'd pass out. Forget about it all if only for a moment. Night comes, everyone's asleep, and I'm tossing and turning and thinking, for instance about who I should give cement to, and mostly who not to give it to. Because giving it, I could give it to everyone. Except how? People are crapping themselves over the new buildings they've planned. My Józka wakes up and says, lie still, can't you. You're thinking and thinking, but you're not gonna think up anything new. You'd be better off praying. It's true, I'd be glad to pray once in a while. But how can I pray when I have this job? You pray for me, Józka, maybe that'll help me feel better. You see, an old wife is good for some things, when times are hard. A young one'd only be interested in fooling around. Though don't think I'd be afraid to sign your application. I've been signing things all these years and so far I'm fine. It'd be different even if you only wanted to

· 356

cement your yard. I'd just sign and be done with it. Or build steps to your front door. I'd sign and take it on myself. Your legs are bad, we do what we can to help invalids, there's an explanation. Or even build an outhouse. I'd sign, it's God's will. You could argue whether it's a farm building or not. But a tomb's a tomb. Death, the next world, something to do with God. Well, not for everyone. For some people you're just there one minute, gone the next. Though I wouldn't trust anyone on that. People are complicated creatures, as they say. Not at all straightforward. You can never be sure they won't change at some point. But here it's all about life. You can hear it on the radio, they show it on the television, it's in the papers, they talk about it at meetings. You've chosen a bad time, friend. We're supposed to improve our lives. And rightly so. Because people ought to live better. We spent too long living in the next world, thinking we'd have it easier there. That there'd be more justice. And choirs of angels. It needs to be better here. And it will be! For instance, at the last meeting we passed a resolution to build a road through to Zarzecze, there'll be a bus line. And if there's going to be a road, there needs to be a bridge as well. No more wagons getting sunk in the river. The young folks want a soccer field so we'll make a soccer field as well, better they kick a ball around than go drinking. We could use a community center as well. We'll get one, not right away but eventually. And just so you know, we're also thinking about getting in running water. We've spent enough time lugging buckets from the springs. You'll just turn on the tap and water comes out. And if everything goes well, one of these days we'll even dam that little river of ours and make a lake. We'll build cabins and people'll come on vacation. You'll see what life's gonna be like! Maybe there'll even be fish. You and I can go fishing one day. And we're planning to have pheasants in the fields. We'll bring them in and set them free. You're mowing away, and here there's a pheasant in your field. It'll make mowing a whole lot nicer. Also they're working on getting rid of the potato beetle. They're gonna turn the pub into a bookstore and build a new pub. While the old road lasted the old pub was fine. But nowadays there's more outsiders passing through than locals, you have to think about them as well. Marzec already offered to donate his old wood plow. We'd hang it over the doorway and the place would be called 'The Wooden Plow.' And we're thinking of starting a choir. Why should everyone sing on their own in their own house. Plus, the old people are dying and the old songs are going with them. Then one spring we'll plant trees along the new road. We even thought of a slogan: Plant a Tree, Make Some Shade. We'll put in a whole bunch of trees. Elms, lindens, acacias. You'll see how green it'll be. And here you are talking about a tomb. I told you already, a tomb is a thing of the next world. Anyone that's in a hurry to go there, it means they've no wish to live in this one. It's worse than not paying your taxes. Your taxes can be canceled or at least paid in installments. But if someone doesn't want to live, it means they're being dragged backwards, it means there's something wrong with their consciousness. Szymek, Szymek, friend, when are you finally going to stop being a peasant? It's more than a hundred years since there was serfs. Hardly anyone even remembers Piłsudski these days. Before you know it they'll forget the occupation as well. And high time. The past has caused us pain for too long. We've gotten our tail mixed up with our head. It's time to think of the future. And you want to face the future with a tomb? You're not interested in anything else, cause you're just going to go off and die? And me, push comes to shove how am I going to explain I'm allocating cement for the next world? That would mean I believe in life after death, if I've started giving out cement for building graves. Whereas actually, you know best of all I never was a believer. You'd never see a Christmas tree or a nativity scene at my place. And carol singers, I'd run them off like dogs. I only ever believed in a better life here on earth. A better life here was my Star of Bethlehem."

He'd worked up a sweat and he was breathing so hard he had dried flecks of foam in the corners of his mouth. But you could see he was pleased with himself. It was like he didn't know whether to laugh or spread his arms to show the conversation was over. Or maybe he was just waiting for me to say something now. I tell you one thing, Leon, you've got your head screwed on right. All those years being director have paid off. Times change, people die but you're planted here solid as an oak tree. Not only that, you just saved fifteen hundredweight of cement from being put into the ground.

But I didn't say a thing. I just shifted my walking sticks to get ready to stand. At that point he jumped up, pushed open the door to the secretary's office, and called:

"Miss Hania! Two glasses and two coffees! And hold all my meetings for the rest of the day!" Then to me: "Wait up, what's your hurry? Let's have a drink. We haven't seen each other in years." It was like he was suddenly reluctant to part, not from me so much as from his own self-satisfaction. He even rubbed his hands and moved things around on his desk, and slapped me on the back. "I'm glad you came. Oh yes." He shuffled over to the cupboard and took out a stubby bottle. "I don't drink. Except sometimes, when the opportunity comes along. And this is something special." He held the bottle in front of me, turning it in his hands.

"What kind of vodka is that?" I asked.

"It's not vodka. It's brandy. You ever try it?"

"I don't recall. I've drunk all kinds of things, maybe I had this one time."

"You sip it. Not like vodka."

"Then I don't think so."

Miss Hania brought glasses and coffee on a tray. She passed right close by me, she sent a gust of air towards me from her body. She smelled of perfume and youth. I thought to myself, this isn't the same place I used to work. We ate on sheets of newspaper, and here they were bringing things in on a tray. She had slim hands. You could almost see through the skin, and her finger-nails were painted red. It was like she'd never worked the land, like she'd worked in these offices since she was a child.

"I made yours a bit weaker, director," she said with an ingratiating smile, putting tiny little spoons on the saucers next to the coffee cups.

"Good job." And he patted her on the backside like she was his Józka. She acted like she was embarrassed, but probably because it was in front of me, and she bounded out of the room like a deer. "Ha!" he laughed. "She's a cute one, huh?"

"Do you pat all of them like that?"

"If you were in my place you'd be patting them too. When you're in authority you have to pat the girls. You pat one of them, another one you don't, and you know everything that's going on in the building. Besides, they like it. You forget to give one of them a pat and she'll sulk. You should see her without her clothes on. It makes you want to live twice as long. The fact is, when they're properly fed everything else is the way it should be. Not like when we were young. Remember how many of the girls had crooked legs? They'd have the face of a Madonna and legs like a hoop on a barrel. These days it's all vitamins. And bread, friend, bread, no one has to go without, and so the young women grow up so fine all you want to do is climb on top of them. But what of it, when a guy's stuck with his Józka. And you might say it's all because of the reforms. Sometimes I might do the odd thing, but you have to watch out. Someone else'll knock her up and she'll say it's the director's. And even if it wasn't true they'd boot me out in a flash. Let's drink."

We clinked glasses. He drank a little bit, I did the same, because I was watching to see how much he took so I wouldn't come out looking like a bumpkin, since it was this strange kind of vodka that you only sip. It was disgusting, like moonshine watered down with tea and soapsuds. On top of that you had to slurp it like a bird. There's nothing like pure grain vodka, it slips down like a roaring stream. It makes you shudder and scrunch your face up, and it jabs you so hard you feel from the top of your head right down to your feet that it's you. And no one else has the right to be you. Not like with this pisswater.

"Well?" He looked down at me.

"Not bad," I said.

"There you go. You have to know what's what. And it's good for the heart. Do you take sugar? I don't. I learned to drink it without." He pushed the sugar bowl over.

"You've got a sugar bowl now as well."

"Life's not actually that bad when you think of it. And it's going to be even better. There'll be more cement, more of everything. There won't need to be allocations, or applications, or signatures. Remember way back when, it was the same with buckets. If you wanted to buy a bucket you had to buy a book as well. Nowadays you can buy all the buckets you want. Zinc-plated ones, enamel ones, plastic ones, yellow, red, blue. And the district administration won't care who's buying stuff or what it's for, whether they're building a silo or a tomb. All you need is what you might call the right attitude. Not demand too much. It's all right to complain a bit, so long as it's harmless. The most important thing is to look boldly into the future. Not backwards. Efficiency, plans, cultivation, investment, indicators – these are measures for today. Not blood and wounds. No one's yet lost out on the future, but the past has left a good many folks stranded. If you can get that into your head you won't come out the loser. Don't think I'm arguing for cooperatives. Even if that was what I wanted, this isn't the right moment. Today it's doing things of your own free will. Course, you have to help out when people want to join their farms, cancel someone's loan, or give them priority. But individual farmers count with us also. And they can do well for themselves. We're not standing in their way. Take Sieniak for instance. He has an apartment building, a car, his wife's got a fur coat, he's got a fur coat and his daughter too, and he's got two million in the bank. From what? Flax. No problem. The government gets a cut, let him have his share too. Kulaks and middling peasants and poor peasants, those labels don't hold anymore. Back then it had to be that way because of the dialectics, friend. You had to grab the peasants by the shoulders and shake them so they didn't sleep through the revolution. And also so they believed less in God and more in us. Besides that, we had to show people who was in charge. But that's all been and gone. There's no turning back. You have to change your soul, friend, your soul. These days you can't live with a peasant soul anymore. And things'll get even worse. They put aside class reckonings long ago. Now we're all children of the same mother again. There's no more orphans, no more stepsons, no one that doesn't belong to anyone. There's an enemy, of course. There'll always be an enemy. That's the nature of enemies. But it's not the same enemy that burned haystacks or that killed Rożek. That enemy, we could more or less live with them. These days people are their own enemy. And that's the worst kind of enemy, because he's hidden in your thoughts, in what you feel, he's tied up like a dog on a chain. In the old days, when someone had the devil in them it was easy to see. But how can you tell today, when there aren't any more devils? Me, if I'd been trying to live with the same soul as before I'd be long gone. Better folks than me lost the fight. But me, I sense things before they're even coming. I don't need swallows to know the spring. You just have to constantly believe, not just once in a while, but each day, every hour. And during working hours you have to believe twice over. Exactly what you believe in might change, but you just keep on believing. Because the worst thing of all is when you run out of steam, then it's all over for you. You're gone before you can say Jack Robinson. Looks like you're still there, but in reality you're not. My Józka says to me, Leon, it's like you were born a second time. You know everything in advance, you understand everything. Me, I keep praying and praying and I don't understand a thing, all I feel is regrets. You see? And you'd have thought she's just a dumb woman. Shall we have another? I'm glad you came. Ever since morning I've been feeling like having a drink with someone. Though I'm not supposed to. Because of my heart. Before you know it you're left behind. And you'll never catch up ever, friend. Because the peasant soul only ever travels by foot, or on a pony, it's never in a hurry, God forbid you should ever overtake the day. For the peasant soul every road leads to death, every life leads to the cross. These days people fly by jet, they overtake centuries, not just days. You ever been in a plane? I flew to France. I brought Józka a handbag back, got myself a pipe. Maybe I'll start smoking it. Pipes are fashionable these days. The trees, the fields, rivers, houses, it's all underneath you. It's so tiny you could take a whole village in the palm of your hand and watch the little people living there. You feel like you're an angel, or God himself. On top of that they give you things to eat and drink. Administrating from up there would be a piece of cake. All you'd need to do would be point your finger. This guy gets this, that guy gets that. And if you touched someone on the head he'd think he'd been struck by lightning out of a clear sky. If any of them complained you'd just squeeze them a bit, here, they could squeal away. Or when you needed to organize a day of community service, you could just drum your fingers on the village and it'd be like an earthquake, they'd all come rushing out of their houses. You wouldn't have to talk them into it, persuade them, beg them. You'd just grab them by the hair and here, here's your spade, here's your pickax. When you think how much time I've wasted on those kind of things. I'm telling you, when I get home from work all I wanna do is collapse on the bed and sleep. Just as well there's the television, it can talk to the missus for you, and the children, keep them entertained, do some of your worrying for you. Even better than you. All you do is press a button and you can go to sleep. Who'd've thought there'd be such wonders? People didn't believe there'd be the radio, or telephones. And here you have pictures flitting around your house like they were dreams. Yours, other people's. And you can watch. Maybe people'll stop dreaming one of these days? I mean, when it comes down to it why do they need to? You get all tired, all sweaty, you jerk about and run away and get scared, and on top of everything you never know what it all means. Back in your time what did they use to calculate on in the office? The abacus. There was only one in the whole building. It was on

Rożek's desk so you could tell he was the mayor. Now, you saw, there's a machine on every desk, and they do all the adding on their own. Hundreds, thousands, millions, in a split second – all it does is hum for a moment. That peasant soul of yours is applesauce, if I say so. It was thought up by the masters to stop the peasants rebelling. But the masters are all long gone. There's no more manor houses. Did we have a reform? We did. Did you get your five acres? You did. In other words, your hunger for land was satisfied. If it wasn't, we can give you another five. The Walichs' land is standing fallow, they handed it over to the government in return for a pension. If you want it it's yours, help yourself. But you ought to know that with a peasant soul, you could have a hundred acres and you'd still be eating *żurek* and potatoes and sleeping on a sheet of canvas. Because you can't bring yourself to use up anything you have. Anything except yourself. If the land produces, you'll take what it gives. If it doesn't, you won't. And you won't say a bad word against it, in case it punishes you even worse the next year. At most you'll have a mass said for it or you'll put up a shrine, a shrine to the holy earth, so it'll take care of you. You, Szymon Pietruszka. Except these days the earth doesn't believe anymore either. It needs superphosphates, lime, nitrolime, saltpeter, not superstitions. And you might say it's not even as attached to people as it used to be. If the farmer's bad at what he does the land'll just abandon him and move on to the next one and the next one after that, whoever can calculate better. The peasant soul doesn't like to calculate, it only likes to suffer. But why should you suffer when calculating is better for you. It's gotten used to it, suffering is its lot. And for the peasant soul the land is nothing but suffering either. And that's bad for the land. The land has to produce things, my friend. The world wants more and more food. Mountains of food. Bigger and bigger mountains. And the land has to provide it. It has to! Even if it spills its guts trying. And the peasant soul can go rest in the museum for all the centuries of work it's done. It deserves it. Let it remind people they used to be peasants. Young people can go take a look, or tourists. Tourism, I'm telling you, that's happening all over the world. More and more people are traveling all over the place and back again. Pretty soon everyone'll be traveling. Even old folks won't want to stay at home. You'll go knocking, and the place'll be empty. It's like people discovered that the world goes around, so they have to go around the world as well. Hardly anyone's capable of just sitting on their ass. Back in the day, someone went traveling it was either out of hardship or because they were going for a soldier. These days everyone wants to be a tourist, like there was nothing else they could be. Think of everything that's needed, all the trains, boats, airplanes, roads, hotels, stations, and of course all the sights. And the sights have to be there whether they exist or not. We thought about maybe turning the Bąks' place into a traditional cottage. It'd be perfect for it – it's got no soleplates, it has a thatched roof and tiny little windows like knots in trees. Bąk could be the farmer, and his missus would be the farmer's wife. We'd make them traditional costumes, we could round up some wooden spoons and dishes and what-have-you, they'd be paid. We'd put up signs, traditional cottage half a mile. But they won't agree, they want us to build them a proper house in return. They'd just go to the cottage during working hours. What else can tourists go see in a village? You can't show them rye growing, or wheat. It's just growing there, let it grow. Or cows being milked. Or calves putting on a pound and a half to two pounds daily. All they'd say would be, why are their eyes so sad? What kind of eyes are they supposed to have! They eat all they want, they don't care what they see or what they don't. People are no different, when they've eaten their fill they can't see much, on the outside they might even look happy. But if you really want to see their happiness, look in their bellies. With calves it's the same, their happiness isn't in their eyes. Or maybe they've just seen the people that are gonna eat them, and that's why they're sad. The thing is, that would never occur to those folks, they just go on about sad eyes. Damn philosophers. Try sticking a plate of meat in front of them, see if they complain about its eyes then. A peasant soul'd be just about right for them, they could get all sentimental over it as much as they wanted. And it would be a sight that had to do with class. Harmless, you might say. The burden of the ages. A thing to itself. As for you, friend, I mean good grief, you were a policeman but you still don't have the consciousness. I mean, you're not that old. Older people than you have started over. Take Boleń for example, going on seventy and he's building a farm. Maryka's planting flax, Janiszewski's switching to cauliflower. You'll have plenty of time to build your tomb! The job won't go away. Besides, maybe soon they'll stop burying people in tombs. They'll cremate them instead. That way you'd save your money. The land, there's less and less of it, not more and more. It's not such a problem when it's used for factories. But for cemeteries? There's more and more people. And everyone has to die sooner or later. Just think how much land you'd need if everyone was buried. And in walled tombs on top of that. The dead would take up all the land there was. Then where would we go – the moon? Besides, let me tell you, death isn't what it used to be either. You're here and then you're gone. There's a hundred others jockeying to take your place. They even occupy the memory of you. Back when, friend, when you died there was a hole left in the village, like in the road. But in those times, you might say death was attached to people. Everyone lived their whole life in one place, so the death of one person was kind of like the death of all of them. These days everyone's in motion, so death moves around as well. And moving around is like being in the front lines. They're attacking you left and right, and all you can do is keep pushing forward. People die of no one knows what, no one knows when, no one knows if it can still be called death. You don't even need to fall ill, there can be no reason at all. You get tired and bam, you're gone. Before, when you got tired you sat down on a field boundary, you took a breather and went on living. I'm telling you, the way we die you can't see we're dead after we're gone. Sometimes you can't even tell if someone's dead or they're still alive. And dying doesn't give you anything at all. It's only life that can still give you something. So live while you can. It won't be long. Few more years at the most, then maybe you won't need that tomb. They'll just slide you in the oven and all that'll be left is a heap of ashes. And it won't cost you a penny. The district'll cover it. You worked here for a good few years, you deserve it. The whole of you will fit in a clay jar. Would you rather get eaten by worms? That way's disgusting, friend. Even when a fly lands on you you brush it away. Down there there's masses of them. You've plowed, you know how much there is in the earth. They'll be tucking into you like you were shit, pardon my French, and you won't even be able to scratch yourself. Because how do you know you won't feel anything? Maybe death lasts a long time, not just a moment? Maybe it has no end? But what's left after fire? Fire is clean as can be. Cleaner than air or water. Even cleaner than conscience. You'd be the first in the village. The first in the whole district. Though I dunno why I'm saying all this to you. I know you're not going to agree. That peasant soul of yours mewling inside you, it won't allow it. And they don't do cremations here yet. Though you have to be able to see the future today already. Otherwise you'll go astray. Or go backwards. And what then? Start out all over again? That's not gonna happen, friend. I know life. You have to when you've worked with it as long as I have. At different stages. Here, there. And it's always been like a soldier in the trenches, so to speak. When it comes to life, I can say I'm something of an expert. I could run rings around a good few folks that are higher up than me. So what if I'm still here in the district administration. Do I have it bad here? If I fall, at least I won't fall far. And there's always those seven acres of mine. I've got my own potatoes, my own tomatoes, cucumbers, onions, carrots. I'm telling you, I know life better than almost anyone. And not from any school. The kind of life they write about in those schools, it's suckered all kinds of people. Ground them up like a machine. Forgotten they ever existed. But me, I'm still here, like you see. Sure, in school they teach you your multiplication tables, you need that, like they say. But they don't teach you life. You can fill your head with all sorts of stuff and you can know everything, but not know how to live. Because life, so to speak, isn't just living. Like you're just there, and life goes on regardless. Better or worse, uphill or downhill, it just keeps going. You're born, you'll die, and that's life. If it wants to knock us over it will, if it wants to set us up it'll do that too, it can cast us down or raise us up. And we just do what it wants, because either way we're alive. It's the wind and we're a feather in the wind. Oh no. No, no, friend. That's not it. That's all crap. Life is an occupation like any other. Who knows, it could be the hardest occupation of all. Because like, a doctor or an engineer, how much do they have to study? Or even a professor? Five years, ten, let it even be twenty. They give him his diploma, now he knows what he's doing. But life, how long do you have to learn it? There's no set number of years. And no diplomas. You can be a prophet with a long white beard and still not know how to live. Because it all depends on the person, whether they have the gift or not. Some folks would never learn even if they lived twice over. For some, eternity wouldn't be enough time. A dumbass is a dumbass. Though it goes without saying that I don't believe in eternity. It's just an expression, just a measure. Like people saying the sun rises, when everyone knows it doesn't rise, it's just the earth turning. Habit of speech. If it wasn't for habits like that, our steps would be longer, believe me. And we wouldn't be walking in the dark. I mean we're not blind, but sometimes we act like we were. Like we were walking along a milky way, when we need to be walking on the earth. We need to know how to walk. And of course something has to light the way. Because no one's got a candle inside them. Life has its twists and turns, its gullies, its cliffs, its whirlpools, its fine weather, all those things. Plus, as they say, it flows. Except some people think it keeps flowing in the same direction. Because that's supposedly how rivers flow. Time flows like that. And everything that flows, flows that way. But that's applesauce, friend. Because one moment it flows one way, the next it flows in a whole other direction, it even flows against itself, across itself, every which way. It's half like a whirlpool, half like mist, half like space. It doesn't have any fixed direction. When you don't know how to live, you take a step and you're a drowned man. Me, I could swim in it with my eyes shut. When it comes to numbers, I'm not disputing there are people better than me, I've never minded about that. But when it comes to life, they're all useless. Because with life, when you have to you need to move cautiously, but when the road is clear you gotta charge ahead. And before you hear what you need, you have to listen hard. When you see something, don't hurry up till you can see clearly what it is. But don't think things are always that way. This isn't like blackjack or poker where there's a fixed way to play. There are times when no one's said a word yet but you have to have heard them. You can't see someone, but you have to have seen them already. Because if you don't see them, they'll see you. And you need to know what might hurt you and when. And when you need to be healthy as a horse, however much you may be in pain. Though there's no point getting excited about good health. Obviously anyone who's constantly on the march here, there, and everywhere can't be completely healthy. I have a heart. I don't know if it's in good shape or not. But it works. If it needs to hurt it will, if it doesn't it won't. A hundred doctors could examine it and each of them'd say something different. It's just a heart. True, it's the director's heart. And sure, the district is big. But it's no more than a fingernail on the body of the district. In any case I'll tell you one thing, you have to know when to die as well. You, you've chosen the wrong time. Under the occupation, for instance, that was a good time. A historical moment, you might say. People died for a reason, even if a tree just fell on you. Or right after the war, that wasn't bad either. So long as you were on the right side, of course. But today, have you really given it enough thought? Sit on your backside and don't be in such a hurry. You wouldn't even have anyone to leave the farm to. The government would have to take it, which is to say the district administration. And all these farms that folks hand over in return for a pension, I don't know what to do with them. We'd have to arrange a funeral for you at our expense as well. You have brothers, of course, but they're in the city, they might come back or they might not. And since you used to work here it's only fair. At least get you a wreath. But where's the money supposed to come from? The librarian's on my case about how people are reading less and less, because the books are all old, and here we have youngsters growing up. I don't have money for that either. I even have to borrow gas money from the arts budget. Do you think there are times I don't howl inside? Damn right I do. Sometimes I go out into the fields and stare at the crops, it makes me go all soft inside. I could just sit there on the field boundary and listen to the larks singing. But I say to myself, where's your consciousness, eh, Mr. Director? You're supposed to be building a new life but you haven't uprooted the old one from inside yourself. Keep sitting there and you won't have a reason to get up again. Or there was a picture here in the offices, remember, in Rożek's time. A peasant plowing with oxen. I had to change it, because anyone who came to visit would just gawk at the picture. So I had a local guy paint me another picture, he charged ten thousand. See, now it's a tractor doing the plowing. Though between you and me, for some reason I can't get used to it. Everyone says they like it, but me, every time I look at it that soil causes me pain. It's like it was under attack. There are times I can actually hear it groaning and moaning, but the tractor's louder and when the driver steps on the gas he drowns out the noise. Try sitting for years under a picture like that." All of a sudden he grabbed the bottle, poured out another one for himself and for me, clinked his glass against mine and downed it in one, like he'd already forgotten you're supposed to sip it. "We've had quite a talk." He looked at his watch. "It's good to talk like that once in a while." He snatched a sheet of paper from a pile and started writing something. "You sure fifteen's enough? I'll give you seventeen just in case. Here." He handed me the paper. "Just be sure and tell Borek to take it from what's set aside for the creamery. Those are my instructions. And don't die on us just yet. Ha, ha!" He laughed and stood up. I rose too, though it's not so easy to get up from a chair when you have walking sticks. But he didn't come out from behind the desk till I was on my feet. Then he walked me to the door and slapped me on the back. "One more thing," he said, like he'd just remembered now. "It's too bad I canned you back then. Maybe you didn't drink that much after all."

I didn't say anything — what was the sense after all those years. I knew why he'd fired me. Besides, it was good it happened that way, I had to go anyway. How long was that job supposed to drag on? I mean, there was nothing keeping me there. Małgorzata had long left for the town, she was working in the county offices. I heard she'd gotten married, but maybe it was just a rumor? A year or so before mother died she'd come by our place to visit.

This nicely dressed lady in a suit and hat and with a handbag came to the house. She was pretty and a little sad. It was her. I was lying drunk in the other room. When mother heard she was asking for me she had her take a seat. And of course, being mother she says:

"Well, he's sort of here and sort of not, young lady. He's drunk in the other room, sleeping. Even if we woke him you wouldn't be able to talk to him. He only just got back. It's like this almost every day. I keep praying to God." The poor thing started crying. "Who are you, if I might ask?"

"A friend. We used to work in the district administration together." Her eyes got wet too. She took a handkerchief out of her handbag and made like she was wiping her nose. "I work in the town now."

"I don't think he ever mentioned you. But when he sobers up I'll tell him you were here. What's your name now?"

"Małgorzata. He'll know."

"You're so pretty, and I can see you're a good person. Come again sometime, maybe he won't be drunk. He doesn't always drink."

I even thought I heard her voice through the door with mother's voice as they were talking. But I was sure it was a dream. There was no point getting up for a dream. She never came again. Maybe that was finally the end.

Though I'd thought it was the end that time I walked her back home after the dance and tried to kiss her and she ran away. What did I want with a girl that goes to a dance with you then won't even let herself be kissed. When the next dance came I asked Irka Ziętek from the administrative offices. She didn't run away. And she had a drink. And ate a whole plateful of sandwiches. She kept sighing about how good the vodka made her feel, how good. During the dancing she stuck to me like glue. And it had only just started to get dark when we took a stroll. She was the one dragged me out, come on, let's go take a walk, I don't feel like dancing anymore. I feel like doing something else. Hee, hee!

Then a while later there was a dance in Bartoszyce and I even took two girls, both of them from highways. She didn't mean anything to me by then. We'd pass in the hallway like people that barely know each other. Good morning. Good morning. Like before. And truth to tell, it's a pity things didn't stay that way.

But one time, the workday was coming to an end, you could already hear the goodbyes in the next room, all of a sudden there's a knock at my door, come in, and it's her. She seemed a bit on edge as she entered. I'm not bothering you? Not at all. And she asks me if I could stay a little longer and help her, she has an urgent job she needs to turn in the next day and she can't handle it on her own. She asked her girlfriends but none of them can do it. I could see right away it wasn't a matter of helping her, she wanted to make the other thing right. Why did you put up a fight at the dance, you silly woman? I can stay behind. Why not. I often stay when someone needs help.

We were recording tax receipts, me on one side of the desk, her on the other. I arranged them in alphabetical order, each letter in a separate pile. She checked every receipt against a list to make sure the payments agreed with the invoices. Everyone had left the building already. It was starting to get dark. It was the end of September. She turned a lamp on. Then we had to transfer the payment amounts from the receipts to separate entries on a form. Serial number, family name, given name, village, acreage, land quality, to be paid, paid, installment amount, still to pay. Mrs. Kopeć, the caretaker, dusted quickly, emptied the ashtrays, swept the floor, then said goodbye and she left too. Then the amounts on the forms had to be added up to check they matched the receipts. Evening came. It got dark around us. When you glanced up at the room, nothing looked like it usually did. The desks, that during the day they pushed their way into the room so you could barely squeeze through, now they just stood there quietly like the coffins of dead clerks. The cupboards, that not long ago had just been cupboards, now they looked like old willow trees that someone had cut the tops off of. There was only us in the light of the desk lamp, we looked like we were inside a brightly lit sphere. Though just like two office workers working on receipts. Nothing more. But if someone had seen us through the window they could have gone telling people we were cuddling, because we were sitting right up close to each other and there was no one else in the building. Of course, from time to time one of us would say something, me or her, but only what was needed for the job.

"Could you pin those receipts together, Mr. Szymon."

"Is it Wojciech Jagła or Jagło?"

"Ten acres, class two land, do you have one like that?"

"How much do you make it, Miss Małgorzata? Mine comes out to such and such."

"This doesn't match up. We need to check it again."

At times a sadness passed across her face, but it was sadness from the receipts. The best medicine for that kind of sadness is an abacus. Immediately she started rattling away like a machine gun.

It was eight, maybe a little after. We were still deep in receipts. If only she'd once given me a warmer look, or if she'd gotten flustered when I glanced at her. Nothing. It was even like she was chiding me for those glances, she'd tell me to check something or other, write it down, add it up a second time. In the end I started to think about getting out my watch and saying, look, it's eight, nine, to finally make her lift her eyes from the receipts. Then I'd say:

"Let's take a bit of a break."

And she might reply:

"Maybe I'll make tea. Will you have some?"

I wouldn't have minded some tea. I started discreetly feeling my pockets for my watch. It was the same one I sold later to pay for the tomb. A silver one, on a chain. I got it off the Germans in a battle. Though truth be told, the men found it on a dead officer. It had slipped out of his pocket like it was trying to get away from the body, except the chain held it in place. It wasn't much of a battle. It only lasted half an hour or so, like it was all about the watch. On our side Highlander was wounded, on the other side they all died. Actually there wasn't really anything to fight about. Someone had told us there was a motorcycle and car with Germans coming down the road. We didn't even know where they were going or what for. Though for sure they weren't driving that way just for fun. We made an ambush in a gully that was overgrown on both sides with hazel and hawthorn and juniper. We blocked off the road in front and behind, we waited till they got close, then we let them have it from every side. There were a few bodies, a few guns, the watch, and that was the end of the battle. These days a watch doesn't mean a thing, every other person has one on their wrist, but back then it was still something, plus a silver one to boot. And the thing worked tip-top right till the end. I never once had to get it repaired. Whenever I checked it against the sun it always showed the same time. In the village, at twelve noon the sun's always right over Martyka's chimney, and the watch always showed twelve noon. It came in handiest when I worked in the district administration. As if the officer that let himself get killed by us back then knew that one day I'd be a government worker.

Except that it didn't feel right to be taking out my watch and saying, oh look, it's eight, or nine. She might have gotten embarrassed and started apologizing:

"Oh, I'm really sorry for keeping you so long, Mr. Szymon. But you've been a big help. Thank you. Please go now if you're in a hurry, I'll stay behind. I have to finish today."

There was still a big pile of receipts between us that needed going through. All I did was, whenever she'd lean over more than usual I'd pretend I was lost in thought and I'd secretly stare at her hair. It was like a field of grain, much brighter by the light of the lamp than during the day, I felt as if I was standing at the edge of a wheat field. She must have been tired already. A couple of times she asked, how much is such and such times such and such again? Another time she got annoyed at the receipts because they weren't written clearly. But they'd been like that from the beginning. Then she shifted the lamp over, saying it was too dark.

I was copying out a receipt from a Jan Bielak, village of Zarzecze, three thousand five hundred and eighty-two zlotys. Second installment. With her head bowed over the desk, she said quietly:

"Kiss me, Mr. Szymon."

I put down my pen. I thought she was making fun of me. Just in case, I answered as if I was joking as well:

"Maybe I'm not worthy of kissing you, Miss Małgorzata?"

"Please," she said even more quietly.

So I stood up, raised her head from the desk and I kissed her, but like I'd kiss a sister. Because I was more unnerved by her having asked for it than if I'd kissed her by force, but of my own free will. And I didn't enjoy it at all.

Anyway, she jumped up right away.

"It's late," she said in a kind of artificial voice, as if to show that nothing had happened. "We've been sitting over these receipts for hours. I didn't think it would take all that long."

"I'll walk you home, Małgosia," I said.

"No thanks, I'll go on my own. I'll be fine. I've often walked back at this hour. What's there to be afraid of? That bit by the woods isn't very nice, but I'll be all right. The moon's bright tonight. Then right after that is the village, the dogs'll be barking. No. Another time, when you feel like it. But please, Szymek, not today."

She's an odd one, I thought. She tells me to kiss her then she won't let me walk her home. Try understanding any of that. Go home on your own, be my guest! Except what kind of young man lets a young lady walk home on her own in the night. But go anyway! If something scares you in the woods you'll regret it. In the woods there are graves from the first war. Didn't old Pociej used to tell how one night he was coming back that way after walking a girl home, and all at once there's a soldier with a bullet hole in his head standing in his way saying:

"Stop this hole up for me, it's been all these years and it keeps bleeding."

Pociej never went back to that girl. He married someone else, from our village, from across the road.

I met her the next day in the hallway, she was coming from the other end. I stopped and gave her a big smile and said good morning. She nodded and smiled back. But she quickly went into one of the other offices, and I felt I'd been slapped in the face. Maybe those receipts yesterday had just put her in a funny mood, I thought, all those names, villages, acreages, installments, amounts, that was why she told me to kiss her. And today she'd had a good night's sleep and forgotten all about it. There was evidently no point in me worrying my head over it.

A few days passed, it happened to be a Tuesday and it was looking like rain. I leave the building and she's standing out there in front, seemingly looking at the sky to see if it's going to rain or not. The clouds are dark and swirly like they often are in the fall. I stopped next to her and I started looking at the clouds as well. All of a sudden, high up a wind appeared and began blowing the clouds and scattering them, driving them from the sky.

"You know, I think the rain'll hold off," I said.

She looked at me at first a little surprised to see me standing right by her. A moment later she gave me this nice smile.

"Then maybe today you'll walk me home, Szymek? If you feel like it."

She opened her umbrella and held it over the two of us. "Even if it rains we'll be fine."

"You can fold it up again," I said. "See, the wind's already blown the clouds away."

And luckily it didn't rain, because a little umbrella like that wouldn't have had a chance of protecting us. Even if we'd held close to each other our backs would still have gotten wet. Besides, who was supposed to make the first move? I didn't even have the courage to take her by the arm, and she didn't seem willing either. We probably would've ended up getting soaked, and the umbrella would have been folded up between us.

We walked the whole way like distant acquaintances that just happen to have met and be going the same way. As for talking, we pretty much talked about nothing at all, about the office, about the fall, she told me a bit about her girlfriends from school, and her teachers, and I told her about being in the resistance, though only the cheerier parts. And before we knew it we'd reached her house. Her mother was just lighting the lamp, because a glow like a will-o'-the-wisp started dancing about in the window, then the window lit up a moment later.

I said they had a nice house. It had a brick foundation, with an asbestic tile roof, wide windows, and a verandah. It looked like it was recently built. I said I was planning to build a house as well, except I didn't yet know when. First I needed to get ahold of the materials, then have someone make a plan for me, then hire masons, and these days there weren't any good masons except maybe in other nearby villages. After that there didn't seem to be anything else to talk about so I shook her hand.

"Good night, then. See you tomorrow at work."

"Good night," she said, but there was a quaver in her voice.

I'd gone maybe a dozen yards or so, in any case I'd passed the end of their fence and reached the edge of the field, when all of a sudden I heard behind me:

"Wait." She trotted up to me. "Aren't you going to kiss me goodbye?"

I had an urge to throw my arms around her and hold her close, and be held close, and maybe more, not to look at anything else at all, maybe even just pull her into the field that was there, just beyond the edge, because who was she, was she any different from the others, she was the same flesh and blood, I was the stupid one. But something held me back, no. No, Szymek, like it was her voice, but it was mine. If I'd at least been drinking, but no, I was stone-cold sober. I even regretted not going with Winiarski when he tried to drag me out for a drink at lunchtime. I kissed her goodbye, and I said again:

"Good night then."

Then two days later I walked her home again, and again, and then every day, and this went on for maybe three weeks. And each time it was the same:

"Good night then."

"Good night."

Sometimes she wanted me to kiss her, sometimes not. It was like there was a big bush growing between us that stopped us reaching each other. Though truth be told, I only had one thing on my mind. What she was thinking about, God alone knows. Maybe the same thing, though girls sometimes have strange ways of thinking. Here they put on all kinds of performances, and inside they're like a little trembling rabbit. Here they seem like they're going to live forever, and inside they only have a moment. Here there's a single drop, inside there's the ocean. Here there's a rose, inside there's a pitcher. In any case, with any other girl, after I'd walked her home that many times she'd have been mine long ago. And more than once. Apart from anything the road led by the woods, and the woods worked in my favor as well. The fall was well advanced, it was dark earlier and earlier, and it got so it'd almost be dusk already when we left work. By the time we reached her place it was nighttime. All the windows of the houses were lit up. And you could barely hear a human voice anywhere. Nothing but the occasional wagon that was late getting home. And the dogs would be barking the way they do in the night, in long howls.

I was surprised at myself for still being prepared to walk her home. After all, it was two and a half miles. Two and a half one way, two and a half back, five in all. If I'd only had a reason. But it was all just so I could say good night. Good night. And sometimes a good-night kiss. Kissing's fine for a beginning. Or when you're engaged to each other and you know that sooner or later you'll be together. But the only time we were together was from work to outside her house, from work to outside her house, and that could get boring. I never even took her arm because I thought she'd push my hand away and say, no, Szymek. Till one time she asked of her own accord:

"Maybe you could take my arm?" But then right away she added: "I've got new shoes on and they're a bit uncomfortable to walk in."

What was I supposed to do. I decided I'd walk her home a couple more times and call it quits. She wasn't the only fish in the sea. Even just at work there were plenty of girls that you'd only need to walk back home once or twice, girls from our village or other villages, girls that didn't even need to be walked home.

But that couple of times stretched out longer and longer, and I couldn't decide how many more times it ought to be. Even when we hadn't made any arrangement, at five to four I'd be looking out the window to make sure I didn't miss her, or I'd leave early and wait for her on the way, by the footbridge outside the church. Then once again we'd walk those two and a half miles from work to her house, step by step.

I figured it might be easier to put an end to it all in the spring. In the spring I'd have to plow and sow and there wouldn't be as much time for walking her home. Once and twice I'd not do it, I'd say I have to work in the fields, and maybe things'd finish of their own accord. Father was already going on about how the larks had arrived, the swallows had arrived, something or other had arrived. He started checking the plowshare, making sure it didn't need hammering out. Then he brought in some grain on a sieve and sorted through it under the lamp, figuring out which seeds were alive and which ones were dead, which ones would sprout and which wouldn't.

"Would you like to come in?" she said one day when we were standing outside her house. I was a bit taken aback, but I said yes. Why not?

Her father and mother were at home. They gave me a warm welcome, like they'd known me a long time. Her father even told her off for not being hospitable, she was their daughter, she should have invited me in long ago, we've been walking back together all this time, they can see from the window. He also knew that I was "Eagle." He took out a bottle and told Małgosia's mother to cut some bread and sausage. When we were already sitting, drinking and eating, he said to Małgosia:

"Listen, girl, do you know who Eagle was? Under the occupation he was the most famous of all of them. There was Tartar, Wheelwright. But they were amateurs compared to Eagle. One time Sokołowski the miller got robbed in the night, then in church someone recognized his daughter's fur coat on Gajowczyk's woman from the Colony. And Gajowczyk was in Wheelwright's unit. Who had it been? Their neighbors. But Eagle, he was the scourge of God. Am I right, sir?"

"I guess."

"Then here's to your health. You're a hero. Another thing I like about you is that you don't go around with your nose in the air like some of them that either carried a gun through the war or they didn't, but now you'd think they shot every German there was, single-handed. So you work in the district administration now?"

"That's right."

"With our Małgośka?"

"Yes, except we're in different departments."

"So the country at least showed its gratitude by giving you a government job."

We talked the whole evening, even into the night a bit. Whenever I started getting up to go it was, sit down, it's early yet. It'd be a sin to meet a fellow like you and not properly listen to him. Though actually I was the one doing the listening, while he talked about me. Here Eagle disarmed so-and-so, there he led an attack, here he set up an ambush, there he was surrounded but he got away. He just confirmed every once in a while that that was how it had been. That's how it was, sir, am I right? And though in some cases it was completely different, I just nodded, because the way he told it was truer than it actually was.

"Your health then."

Małgorzata and her mother were more bustling around the room than listening. Her mother would just sigh from time to time:

"Oh my Lord, the things you went through."

Małgorzata didn't say a word. I got the feeling she was mad at her father for talking so much, I don't think it could have been on my account.

At one moment her father got up, reached into the dresser, and brought out another bottle, this time of homemade honey vodka, because they kept bees. And when we finished it he insisted he had to drive me home, because how would it look for someone like me to go home from their house on foot. He stuck his cap on his head and set off to harness the horse, but he tripped over the stoop and Małgorzata and her mother eventually managed to convince him not to go. Because me he wouldn't listen to at all. He even hammered his fist on the table and said I had no say in the matter. It was his horse, his wagon, his idea. I was his guest. And not just any guest. He wouldn't have driven any old guest back home.

Małgorzata was embarrassed about her father getting drunk. But I took a liking to him. He was a straightforward guy, he said what was on his mind, and you could tell he was a good man. Her mother seemed a decent woman as well. A few days later I visited them again. Because since that time Małgorzata asked me in every day. Though I had the impression she didn't always want me to agree, just it was the right thing to ask. I didn't want to cause problems so I'd say, maybe not today, but inside I'd be hoping she would insist, please, do come in. But she'd say, as you wish. Or at most, my father would like it.

But one time I'd bought a bottle and I said, I have some time, I'll come in. It wasn't supposed to mean anything, it was just that I wanted to repay their hospitality. Because whenever I visited, the mother would always ask, maybe you'd like something to eat? And she'd slice some bread and bacon, make scrambled eggs. The father would bring a pot of honey from their larder, sometimes it was linden honey, sometimes heather, or acacia, or honeydew honey, and I'd satisfy my sweet tooth, and listen to him talking about bees, how they're smart creatures, a whole lot smarter than humans, though humans think they're the smart ones. He even encouraged me to do it myself, and I started planning to keep bees. A couple of hives to begin with.

But most of all I liked watching Małgorzata pottering about the place, among the chairs and table, the pots and plates and the washbowl, and the fire under the stove, and the curtains in the windows, and the pictures on the wall. It seemed so strange to me that this was the same secretary from the tax department at work. She somehow lost the unapproachableness that at work made her hold her head way up high and look down on everyone from above, and not smile too much, not talk unless she had to. And when she did speak, she chose her words carefully, as if they weren't words but secret signs. She even walked almost like her feet were hobbled, or as if she'd figured out those particular steps ahead of time for when she needed to cross the hallway to get to a different room or leave work to go home.

Here, the moment she crossed the threshold she took off her shoes and put on slippers. Her mother sometimes even told her off, you shouldn't be wearing slippers with a guest in the house. Or she'd put on an apron when there was washing or cleaning, peeling and chopping to be done, or if her mother needed help with something, though her mother used to shoo her away, she'd say, I can manage on my own, you take care of the guest. And though she wasn't all spruce the way she was at work, I preferred her here a hundred times more than there. I didn't mind at all that she didn't sit with me, that she left me to her father, or on my own when he wasn't there, because I was fine on my own. It was enough for me that she was bustling about and I was watching her. I wasn't bored in the slightest. I could have watched her like that all day and it wouldn't have gotten boring. My whole life. And I'd forget I was only going to walk with her a couple more times. Spring came, summer was drawing near, and I'd virtually made myself at home there, because I almost always went in.

Though sometimes I had the impression she was running away from me with all that housework. We'd go in, she'd say hello to her father and mother from the doorway, and they'd say, oh, you're back, what took you? Aha, Mr. Szymek's here, come in, come in. And right away she'd scuttle over to the window and draw the curtains and say, it's so dark in here. Or she'd go look in the pots and it'd be, I think you must've burned something, mama, it smells like it. She'd open the door and air the room. Or if the cat meowed she'd bend down and look under the table and under the bed, here kitty kitty. Then, when she got it out she'd take it on her lap and hug it and stroke it, you darling little thing, she'd talk to it in the sweetest words, just like to a baby, and she'd ask it if it had been hunting mice, if it had had some milk, and in the stream of tender words she'd throw out as if to keep me at bay:

"Have a seat, Szymek."

Her father sometimes got annoyed with her:

"Leave him alone, you mother cat. If you're not careful he'll go throw up on you. He drank all your mother's cream, there was no way he was gonna go mousing after that. Tell us what's going on at work."

"Nothing much. Szymek'll tell you. I'll tidy up a bit. Heavens, all these flies in here!"

At times, her first words from the doorway were:

"Heavens, all these flies in here!"

And the dance of the flies would begin. She'd open the windows and the door. She'd put a cloth in everyone's hand, and she'd direct us as we danced around the room with her. Her mother and father were supposed to mind the door and windows to make sure the flies didn't come back in again. Małgosia and me would be in the middle of the room, she'd do the walls and I'd do the ceiling and wherever else she told me to.

"Over there, Szymek! In the corner! On top of the picture! Above the stove! Over the cross! By the lamp! But don't squash it! Careful! Right there!"

Eventually, the moment she'd exclaim, heavens, all these flies in here! I'd go right over and take the cloth from the nail by the stove. I even had my own cloth, a red-and-blue checkered one that worked best for me. But the first time it happened I didn't know what to do with myself, I pressed against the wall so as not to get in their way. But she'd only taken a couple of swings and gone, shoo! shoo! when she turned to me and told me off:

"Come on, Szymek, don't just stand there, grab a cloth and help out!"

Her mother got all embarrassed and took my side:

"Małgośka, what are you saying? Mr. Szymek's our guest. You can't have a guest chasing flies!"

"He's no guest!" she shouted as she waved her cloth this way and that, but she probably only said it because she was carried away with chasing flies, she was all red.

"Well, I don't know anything about that. You all know better than I do," said her mother, as if she was caught off balance. "Maybe he could at least use this newer towel." She handed me a towel from over the washbasin.

I liked chasing flies with her. She'd get all hot and bothered, her clothes would be awry, her hair flying, but she seemed closer than when we were walking arm in arm from work to her house, when we were alone, without her mother or father around. And I liked it that the moment we crossed the threshold the jobs seemed to fall into her hands of their own accord. You might have thought the whole house was her responsibility alone, and the work was waiting for her to come back from work so she could do all the feeding and watering and washing and cleaning. Some days she didn't even have time to sit down. When she did, it was only for a moment, then she'd be up again to get back to work.

As I watched her I could barely recognize myself. When she was mixing food for the pigs in the buckets, with those white arms of hers covered to the elbows in potato mush like mashers, in her apron, with her old slippers on, it made me warm inside to see her that way. It was like she'd let me in on a secret of hers. I could watch her endlessly, it took the place of thinking or of words for me, and I wasn't at all distracted by what her father was saying to me, or what I was saying to him.

I sometimes had the sense that the work itself was passing her from hand to hand, that the furniture was moving her around the room. A bucket full of soapsuds is a heavy thing even for a man, but before I'd notice and jump up to help her she'd grab it by the handles and haul it out to the passage. Or when she was adding wood to the kitchen range, the kindling seemed to leap out of her hands into the fire all on its own. Or she'd be rolling dough to make dumplings, and she'd barely have sprinkled flour on the board when the flour was already shaped into a lump, then the lump was a patty, and the patty was cut up like a little sun. And when she was slicing the dumplings they'd fly from under her fingers, and her breasts would be galloping under her blouse like wedding horses, like any minute they were about to pop out onto the tabletop all naked. Or when she scraped carrots for soup. You'd think carrots were nothing special. But the whole room went red, like the sun was setting red when a high wind's coming. Actually all she needed to do was stand at the range stirring one of the pots with a ladle, even then the whole room was filled with her, every nook and cranny, while the rest of us, her father and mother and me, we were squashed into the tiniest corner. Or when she went outside, the chickens probably crowded around her even when she didn't have any grain for them. And the dog would bark for joy though she wasn't bringing anything for him. The cows mooed in the shed. The pigs grunted. Even the trees in the orchard were blooming. And so on and so forth, the way people tell these things.

It would seem she was just doing a simple thing like sewing a button on a pillowcase. It wasn't even just that the button seemed to slide onto the needle and thread of its own accord. More, I sometimes felt like putting my hand under the needle and saying:

"Prick me, let it bleed. Maybe the blood will tell our future." And the blood would drip and drip, then flow, then gush in a stream, a river, till death came.

Or when she wanted to sweep the floor she'd always herd her father and me into the other room. Even for that short time it seemed like it was going to be forever. And I'd say:

"We can stay here. Don't worry, you're not going to sweep us up by mistake. It's always nicer to sit in the kitchen."

At this her mother, who was watchful as a hawk, would say:

"Mr. Szymek's like our Franiu. The doctors wouldn't let him go out in the sun, he had to always stay in the shade, so he used to sit in the kitchen till the cows came home, he always said that was the best place for him. He'd probably have been about your age, Mr. Szymek. When Małgosia was born he was already big, he was already in school."

But Małgorzata didn't like her mother talking about Franiu and she'd interrupt right away:

"Maybe we could make fritters with apple, mama? Szymek, do you like apple fritters? They're really good, with cream and sugar."

Her father didn't like apple fritters and so he'd pipe up:

"What kind of an idea is that? Apple fritters. A man needs bacon or sausage, otherwise it's like he hasn't eaten. But as for Franiu, yeah, it's a pity. He was our son, whatever else you might say. Though it's been so many years now, you get used to it. I think there's still some bacon in the larder. Go fetch it, will you, mother. I'll see if there isn't a drop in the bottle still. Mr. Szymek and I could have a drink together, one glass at least. Małgosia, you cut some bread."

They baked their own bread. The loaves were big and round as cart wheels. One alone must have weighed fifteen pounds or more. Though why would anyone want to weigh it. You never weighed stuff when you loaned it to someone, or when they gave it back. It was your own bread, your own people, no one needed to know how much a loaf weighed. A loaf is a loaf, there's a half-loaf, a quarter, an eighth, a slice, those were all the measures you needed. She'd brace the loaf against her stomach, putting her left arm around it like it was a pregnant belly, lean back, and her right arm would bring the knife through the bread toward her like it was moving downhill. It looked like the bread was rolling toward her, straight into her arms, huge and happy. Though sometimes I'd get gooseflesh thinking she might not feel where the bread ends and her body begins, because the loaf was like a part of her body. Even her father, however carried away he was talking about the war or about his bees, he'd fall silent and watch her cut the bread.

"Those slices are too thin, cut thicker ones. Bread, you have to feel it in your mouth."

I was worried about something completely different, though it was about the bread also.

"Don't cut it that way, Małgosia," I'd say. "Lay it down on the table. The knife's sharp, it might not be able to tell between the bread and your body."

"We keep reminding her," said her father. "But these days, you know, Mr. Szymek, children won't listen to you. With me, it would've been enough for my mother or father to say something once."

"Give it here." I couldn't take it any longer.

"I'm fine." And she'd hunch over, like she was protecting the bread and the knife, almost afraid.

"Come on, give it to me, you can never be sure."

"Give it to Mr. Szymek if he's asking," her mother put in. "Better a man do the job."

I took the bread from her belly and the knife from her hand and I cut in the air over the table, holding the loaf in one hand, the knife in the other.

"You catch the slices."

"You're a strong one," Małgosia's father said in surprise. "I never saw anyone cut bread like that. Except maybe store bread. But not homemade."

It was a Saturday. Małgosia's father and mother had gone to their godson's wedding in Zarzecze and they weren't going to be back till noon the next day. I walked her home and we stood outside her house like we didn't know what we were supposed to do with ourselves without her parents. She didn't invite me in and I didn't hold out my hand to say goodbye. We were mumbling something or other, glancing to the side so as to avoid looking at each other, and every moment made us feel more uncomfortable. The sun was already dropping toward the west, and we stood in its rays as if we were at an open fire, so on top of everything else we were hot. I was just about to reach out my hand and leave, but she must have sensed it, because she looked into the sun as if she wanted it to blind her and she said:

"Won't you come in?"

"Maybe another time," I said. "I promised my father I'd run the lister plow over the potato field."

"As you like. But by the time you get home it'll be starting to get dark. And it's Saturday today." After a moment she fluttered her eyes and said: "We'd be alone."

"Maybe for a little while," I said, as if I'd let her talk me into it, though there was no truth in what I'd said about helping father with the potato field.

"I can do the job on Monday. Maybe I'll take the day off work, that way I could get started in the early morning."

But we'd barely gotten through the door when she exclaimed:

"Oh Lord, how dirty it is in here!"

I couldn't see any dirt. It was like it always was. Pots and plates were drying on the stove top. The bread on the table was covered with a white cloth. The bucket with soapsuds had been carried out to the hallway. The floor was swept.

"Where is it dirty?" I said.

But she insisted it was dirty.

"I have to tidy up a little at least. It'll be nicer to sit together when it's tidy."

She immediately tied on her apron, kicked off her shoes and put her slippers on. It was as if she'd suddenly taken fright at the fact we were alone. Because up till now, whenever I came by her parents were in, or at least one of them, like they were waiting for us, watching for us, like they'd stayed back from their jobs because of us. And really, the only time we'd been alone was on the road. But the road isn't home. There are trees, the sky, someone might always be coming. And here all of a sudden we had the whole house to ourselves. Plus, it was like the house was half asleep, not even the cat was mewing, they must have put it out as they were leaving.

"I don't see the cat," I said. And I bent down to look under the bed, here kitty kitty, because I felt odd too that her parents weren't there, just the two of us. "Well, if it's dirty then you should clean," I said, no longer putting up an argument. "Your mother was probably in a hurry, she mustn't have had time to clean. When you have a wedding to get to, that's how it is. You want to leave the place tidy, but you don't know where to turn. You've got to get yourself ready, but on top of that you can't let the animals go hungry. The chickens and the geese have to be rounded up and put in the shed. You have to check every nook and cranny. Close it all up. Otherwise you never know what you'll find when you come back home. The Kukałas in our village, one time they went off to a wedding, they came back the next day and their place was just a smoking ruin. The house, the shed, the barn, everything burned to the ground. Luckily they were all so drunk they didn't cry as much as if they'd been sober."

"Szymek, what's wrong?" She looked at me almost frightened.

"Nothing. I'm just saying what can happen sometimes."

"Are you angry at me for cleaning?"

"Course not. Clean all you like. I'll just sit here."

She carried the pots out into the passageway. She took the bread from the table and put it away in the dresser, then she gathered the crumbs and threw them into the firebox under the stove. Though I hadn't seen any crumbs on the table. The table stood by the window, the sun was shining in and you could see every smallest speck on the tabletop. She swept the floor. Then she opened the door and the windows. I thought to myself, any minute now we'll be chasing flies, but she let the flies be and just aired the place out. Then she started wiping the plates from the stove and putting them away in the dresser.

I sat there watching her and looking out the window, but I didn't say a word about her cleaning, I didn't tell her to hurry up. When she asked me to put the chairs back in their usual places, I got up and did it. She thought Jesus in the Garden of Olives was hanging crooked, so I raised it a bit on the left like she wanted. Though if you asked me, it was straight to begin with. Then she told me to check if the kerosene in the lamp was low. I checked. It wasn't. She didn't want anything more after that, so I lit a cigarette and started blowing smoke rings, watching them float away and break up and disappear. Maybe I wasn't even waiting for her to finish the cleaning. It was like it was always going to be that way. Me at the table blowing smoke rings, her drying dishes by the stove. Every now and then she said something, asked me something, nothing much, but for her it was like she'd almost become talkative. Or maybe she was just annoyed that I'd agreed so easily to her doing the cleaning, that I wasn't even asking if she'd be done soon. A couple of times she laughed, and it was such a joyful laugh I was taken by surprise, she never laughed like that. Maybe she wanted me to laugh with her. Except I wasn't much feeling like laughing, and I didn't completely believe in that laughter of hers.

The last yellow rays of the sun lay on the wall opposite the window, but the lower parts of the room were already getting dark. Where the water buckets stood in the corner, it seemed evening was beginning. All of a sudden there was a crash, she'd dropped a plate, the shards flew every which way across the floor.

"Oh, you clumsy thing," I said but in a well-meaning way, why would I care about a plate.

She gave me a bitter, reproachful look, hid her face in her hands, burst into tears, and ran off into the other room.

"Małgosia, what's wrong?" I called after her. "There's no point crying over a plate. We'll pick up the pieces and that'll be that!" I bent down and got to work. I gathered every last little fragment, put it all into the biggest piece, laid it on the stove, and went to ask her where I should throw it out.

"All done."

She was lying on the bed with her head thrust in the pillow, crying like a wronged child.

"There's no need to cry," I said. "A plate got broken is all. No big deal. Could have happened to anyone. One day I was taking myself some potato soup, the bowl knocked against the kettle and it shattered. Another time, I put a plate upside down on some cabbage to cover it and the plate slipped off and broke. If we cried over every broken plate we'd run out of tears to cry over people." I sat down on the edge of the bed, by her head, and started stroking her hair. "Don't cry now. Time was, when plates and bowls were made out of tin, a plate would last you your whole life. A young woman would get a set of six plates in her dowry, and on her deathbed she'd be able to leave them to her daughter. Some had flowers on them, some not. When one of those plates fell on the floor the worst that could happen was it would get dented. You'd eat and eat from it. And you could put it down on a hot stove top. When one of them got a hole you'd fill it with a rivet and hammer it out, or plug it with a piece of rag, and you'd keep eating from it. Then when it was really old the cat would eat from it, the chickens, you'd carry the dog's food out in it. Or you could give it to a kid as a toy to play with, it wouldn't do itself any harm with a plate like that. Come on now, don't cry."

For the longest time she wouldn't calm down, but gradually, gradually the crying eased off. Though she still lay there with her head in the pillow. I guessed she must be embarrassed because of her tear-stained face, worried that I'd think the crying made her look ugly. I got up intending to get rid of the broken plate.

"Where can I throw away the pieces?"

She didn't answer right away. After a moment, in a voice still wet with tears, she said:

"Just leave them there."

"It won't take a second," I said. "I'll get rid of them and that'll be the end of it."

I stood over her, waiting for her to say:

"Go throw them out then."

There'd be a bucket for rubbish outside the shed. Or under the verandah. Or by the fence. Or at the edge of the orchard, by the apple tree. Different people kept it in different places. They buried it, or tossed it in the river. I'd even have gone down to the river, but there was no river in their village. Otherwise I thought her crying would never end, it'd subside, but it wouldn't end.

It looked like she'd stopped crying, that she was just lying there hugging the pillow. But she was still full of tears. You could smell them in the air, like the smell of roasting salt.

"Don't go," she whispered. "I don't want to be left on my own."

"Fine," I said. "I just thought that you did all that cleaning, but there's still the broken plate."

"Sit by me. Where you were sitting before."

I sat down. Dusk had slipped into the room for good, like smoke from a bonfire. Underfoot you could barely tell whether the floor was boards or earth. The ceiling overhead, even though it was high and painted white, it looked like it was covered with mold. On the wall they had a stuffed hawk on a branch, in the daytime it looked like it was swooping down on a chicken in the yard, that it already had it in its talons, Małgosia's folks were running out and shouting, let it go, you bandit! Now, it was like someone had hung out a hawk carcass to scare off the other hawks. It was the same with the Apostles at the Last Supper. They were already old but the dusk made them even older, like they were tired of sitting at the same table for two thousand years, when would they finally be able to get up? And Małgosia's parents in their wedding portrait over the bed, they'd also gotten darker, as if they hadn't just gotten married but had just died, though her mother was still in her white veil like a bride.

"I want to be yours today," she said, suddenly raising her head from the pillow. She said it in an ordinary way like she was saying, the sun's rising. The forest is rustling. The river's flowing. "Do you want that?"

I leaned over and kissed her hair, because what could I say? It would be like someone asking, "Do you want to live?" And you answered: "I do." A better answer would be: "No, I want to die." So as to feel how painfully you want to live.

"I'll get the bed ready."

She got up, took off the bedspread, folded it in four and hung it over the armrest of a chair. She arranged the pillows, shook out the quilt. It was hard to believe she'd been crying just a moment ago. It was like she'd been making the bed for us every day before nightfall, and today another of those nights had come. And not even a Sunday night but a regular weekday one, like Tuesday to Wednesday, Wednesday to Thursday, and it was time to go to bed after a full day of life. It seemed like any minute now she'd go down on her knees at the bedside and start saying her prayers and telling me off, saying I should at least cross myself, because all the two of us had inside was exhaustion after that whole long day of life. Though it was the same as other days, no harder and no easier. Maybe I'd been mowing, and she was gathering. Maybe I'd been plowing and she'd been doing the laundry.

She took off her blouse and her skirt. She didn't tell me to turn around or not to look, she wasn't the least bit embarrassed. But why should I have been surprised, when you've gotten through a whole day you don't have the strength or the desire to be embarrassed. Your body's just an aching weight, and the eyes looking at it are blind. It probably would never have occurred to her that after all those years I could look at her any differently than the way I looked at the earth, at the landscape. After so many years I knew her body like I knew the earth and the landscape, and landscape and earth don't know what embarrassment is. I knew it in health and in sickness, in joy and in sorrow, in laughter and in tears, at every hour of the day and the night. What was there to be embarrassed about? How many times had I poured water over her to rinse off the soap as she crouched in the bathtub, and looked down at her naked body like the Lord God who made her looking down from above. How many times had I pulled off her sweat-soaked blouse when she was in a fever and too weak to even raise her arms. Why should she be embarrassed now. Or how often in the night had I listened so closely to her breathing that I even had the same dream as her, because when body lives alongside body for so many years, they dream the same dreams together too, why would they need two different ones. I knew the whole of her and every part. I knew her belly, her thighs, her knees, her elbows. I knew each of her arms and each of her legs, and all the fingers on her hands and the toes on her feet separately and together. I knew every vein under her skin, every scar and every spot. I knew her belly button had been poorly tied after she was born, and I knew she had a way of sighing that sounded like a sob. I sometimes thought she was all of life, I sometimes thought she was no more than a speck of grass in my eye. Sometimes I could see death within her, sometimes only a broken fingernail. So it was no surprise that she couldn't understand it when I still desired her. Something almost like fear came into her eyes. How could it be, her youth had passed and she'd even forgotten how to be embarrassed, why then? It's only in youth that bodies desire each other for no reason. And here we were after a whole day of life and I desired her, and it felt as if it was after an entire life. Sleep was weighing on her eyes, her arms and feet ached, her body felt like it had just been taken down from the cross, and here you were desiring her. And in an ordinary way, as if you'd come home from mowing and wanted a drink of water.

"Unfasten my brassiere behind," she said.

She bowed her head and as if she was afraid she waited to see whether my hands would touch her. There was only one button, unfastening it should have been the simplest thing in the world, I mean you fasten and unfasten buttons all your life. Yet that button kept slipping out of my hands like a fish. But she stood there with her head lowered and didn't so much as sigh at my clumsiness. Though her back was covered with goose bumps. She slipped the brassiere from her shoulders, threw it on the chair, then turned around to face me and said:

"See, I'm not embarrassed in front of you. I'm not embarrassed at all." Without warning she threw her arms around me. "Oh Szymek."

I put my arms around her too, but she pulled away and jumped into bed as agilely as a she-goat, snuggling deep into the puffy quilt so even her head was barely visible.

"Are you coming?" I heard her whisper anxiously.

It was already dark in the room, though the remains of the day were still lingering in the windows like in a puddle. We lay side by side without moving, under the heavy quilt, because she wanted us to lie awhile like that. I put my arm around her, her head pressed into my shoulder like in the pillow before. I was hot, I could feel my skin covering with sweat, but I didn't have the nerve either to move or to say anything. And she just lay there as well, she was just as afraid to move or speak. It was like we'd been scalded by our own nakedness, or as if being naked we only felt our own aches and pains, instead of desire.

She still smelled of her recent tears, I was on the verge of telling her she smelled of tears. But she must have sensed I was about to speak, because she put a finger on my lips to stop me talking. She told me to shut my eyes, and she shut hers too. When mine opened on their own, for the shortest moment, so I didn't even have time to make anything out except the darkness, right away I heard her telling me off in a whisper:

"Did you open your eyes?"

"Only by accident. But they're closed again now. What about you?"

"Mine have been closed the whole time."

Maybe because she was cuddled up to me so trustfully, she seemed as fragile as a roadside wildflower, that all it would take would be to reach over, pull it up, and throw it away. Her heart was humming right by mine, under the arm I'd put around her, and into the pillow, but it was so soft it wasn't like a heart. From that close up a heart usually pounds like a hammer, but hers was like the sound of grain being poured. Or maybe she was still nervous and she couldn't calm down. I took even tighter hold of her. She must have thought I didn't want to lie there anymore, because I heard another whisper:

"Let's stay like this a bit longer. Do you like it?"

"Yes."

The moon must have risen already, because the dogs began to bark, first the odd one, then more and more of them, howling, yelping, the way they only ever do to the moon, or when somebody dies. Someone was playing a harmonica far away, from time to time a couple of low notes reached us, sometimes part of a tune. There must have been a wagon on the road somewhere, because its axles squeaked. And we lay there like we were healing our aches and pains after a whole day of life or an entire life that we'd lived together, and the only thing left to do was die together. Except we didn't know how. I even tried imagining that we were lying there after death, under the weight of the quilt, that had lain on us so long it had turned to stone. But once it had been real feathers. Real geese had worn them as they lived and ate and grew and went down to the water, they had red beaks and cackled the way geese do. Then the women plucked the feathers from the geese. The women lived once just like the geese did. Those might even have been their happiest moments, when they gathered on winter evenings to pluck feathers, because why else would they have lived? If you listened really closely, you could still hear the sound of their hands in among the down, and the songs they sang. Though it might also have been that one of them was unhappy at the time and she put a curse on the feathers. And that curse caused our sudden and unexpected death, so we barely had time to cling to each other in a final attempt to save ourselves.

"Does it hurt?" I heard her whisper.

"What?"

"The first time."

"Everything hurts the first time." Because I was still seeing our death.

The harvest came a little earlier than usual that year. It was another matter that it had been dry for a long time, there hadn't been a drop of rain. Mother and father barely knew me. Mother thought God had answered her prayers, father reckoned I'd finally wised up, because everyone has to wise up in the end. I hammered out the blade of the scythe, cleaned out the mows in the barn, put new racks on the wagon. I went out to the field and brought back a handful of spikes, father crushed them on the palm of his hand, blew on them, studied them, put one grain between his teeth and bit it, bit another, and he reckoned we should wait another three or four days, but I said we should start right away.

We were among the first in the village to harvest our rye, people thought something must have happened, maybe my brothers had come to help? Małgorzata's folks got her to help in the harvest as well, because there are no indulgences for getting out of the harvest, just like there aren't any for mortal sins. So we didn't see much of each other during that time. It was only when I'd finished storing the rye in the barn that I walked her home again one day, but I didn't go in. She seemed odd to me, she wasn't saying much and she wouldn't look at me. I thought maybe she was just overworked, maybe a bit embarrassed too, because I found it hard to look her in the eye as well, I mostly looked at the sky or to the side, I just stole glances at her when she was looking the other way. Because with eyes it's often the way that it's easier to say a bitter word than look someone straight in the eye.

She complained a bit that her arms were all pricked from the harvesting, she had to wear a long-sleeved blouse, her back ached. But when we were saying our goodbyes in front of her house, she threw her arms around me even though it was still light out and her mother could have been standing in the window.

"Oh Szymek," she sighed. But she often sighed like that. I said:

"Soon as the harvest's done, Małgosia."

Then I mowed the barley and brought it in, then the wheat, though there was only a couple of acres of that. Then right away I began the plowing. As I was plowing the last part, behind Przykopa's place, the storks were gathering in the meadows getting ready to fly away. They're strange birds. They clattered their bills for the longest time, then they all walked off in different directions and started preening, then they picked out one of their own kind and went for it with their bills. I ran at them with my whip, because they were going to peck it to death. But before I reached them they took off and flew farther away down the meadow, including the one they'd been attacking. Then they finished it off. Afterwards Bida found it dead when he was grazing his cows.

All I needed to do now was harrow and I could get on with the sowing. But it was dry, the earth was all clumpy, I thought I'd wait a few days and see if it rained. So at work I arranged with Małgosia that I'd walk her home. We walked slowly, dragging our feet, we even held hands and we looked each other in the eye this time, and she talked willingly, and laughed, she was the way she always used to be. But as we were saying goodbye outside her house, it was only then she seemed to remember she had something to tell me, and almost in a hurry she started explaining that she'd be gone for two, maybe three weeks, because she was taking some leave from tomorrow, she had to go visit her cousin, she'd gotten a list from her and the cousin was begging her to go and stay. She didn't tell me sooner because we hadn't seen each other, and she'd only gotten the letter the day before yesterday. The cousin was only a distant relative, the daughter of her father's cousin, and Małgosia's mother was her godmother, but they were as close as sisters, and they hadn't seen each other in three years. Before she got married she'd come to stay with them in the country every summer. Then her husband had gone off with another woman and left her with two small children, plus the younger one, Januszek, had been born with a crooked head and he was having an operation, so she had to go.

I was a bit angry, she could have told me on the way at least instead of waiting till we were outside her house. We'd have sat down somewhere and said our goodbyes properly, not just any old how. Though I had no doubts it was all true. Everyone has cousins they sometimes don't even know, they don't remember them, they don't know they exist, then all of a sudden they show up like ghosts from the underworld. She must have felt I was mad, because she clung to me and asked me not to hold it against her. She had to go. She even had tears in her eyes.

"I'm going to miss you," she said. "Believe me."

My anger passed, but I was a little sad, as if she was leaving for the next world, not to stay with her cousin for a couple of weeks.

"Go then," I said. "But come back quickly."

"It'll be no time," she said.

"Of course it will," I said. "Maybe I'll take some leave too. I could fix the roof on the barn. I never have time to get to it."

"Will you think of me? Think of me. Please. It'll make it easier for me."

It rained, I harrowed and sowed, I fixed the barn roof and the time passed like the crack of a whip. I wanted to walk her home the first day she was back, but she said she was in a hurry because her mother was baking bread and she had to get home quickly to help. The next day she left work early and I didn't see her. This went on for a few days, if it wasn't one thing it was another, forgive me, I'm sorry, I'm in a hurry, I have to be back earlier than usual, I have an errand to run. Till one day, as we passed each other in the hallway I said:

"You've changed since you came back, Małgosia."

"Why would I have changed? You're imagining it." She disappeared into her office.

I wasn't going to force myself on her. Though various thoughts started rattling around in my head. But one day I leave work and I see she's walking slowly in front of me, eventually she stops and smiles that sad smile of hers and asks if I'm mad at her. Me, mad at you, of course not. Then could I walk her home maybe? And, like nothing had happened, she starts telling me how she and her cousin hadn't been able to get their fill of talking, every day they'd gone to the cinema, to visit her friends, on walks, sometimes to a café, but she didn't like the taste of coffee, she preferred tea, and most of all she liked some of the cakes, she even said the name of them but it was something strange. She could have eaten four at once, except apparently they make you fat. But I haven't gotten fat, right? She gave me a flirtatious look.

"What about Januszek?" I asked.

"Januszek?" She seemed flustered. "You know, it turned out he was too small, so he didn't have the operation after all."

And again I believed her. If that's what she said, that's how it must have been.

Some time passed, I'd almost forgotten about her leave and I was even thinking it was time to ask her seriously if she'd be my wife. I mean, how long would we be walking from work to her house, over and again? She was still young, but I was getting on for a bachelor. I decided that at Christmas I'd have a talk with her, and before then I'd think everything through. Because strange to say, up till then we'd never talked about what was going to happen with the two of us in the future, it was like we were unsure of each other the whole time or we were hiding something from each other.

It was November, gray and cold and windy, put your arm around me, she said. We happened to be by the woods when at one moment she slipped out from under my arm and stood still and said:

"Szymek, I have to tell you after all."

"So tell me." I was sure it wasn't anything important, I didn't sense anything from her tone of voice.

"I was pregnant," she said.

My heart started pounding so hard it almost jumped out of my chest. But I stayed calm, like I was just a bit surprised, and I asked her:

"What do you mean, *was?*"

"Because I'm not anymore. That time, when I took time off, I went to a doctor. That was why I went away."

"Why didn't you tell me?"

"I didn't want to worry you."

It was as if the woods that were rustling all around us started to fall on me. Rage flooded through me. I didn't know what was happening. Maybe that's what it's like to die a sudden and unexpected death.

"You whore!" I howled, and somewhere deep inside, tears began to choke me. Maybe I had to be furious to keep myself from crying.

"Szymek, forgive me!" She cowered, put her hands together like she was praying. "I was sure you wouldn't want it!"

"You're no different from all the other whores! Whores I can have as many as I want, as many as these trees! You, I wanted you to be the mother of my children!" I grabbed her by the hair and twisted my hand, she sank to her knees.

"Forgive me!" she sobbed.

I started hitting her in the face, on the head, wherever the blows fell. Inside myself I no longer felt rage, only tears like a flooding river, and it was the tears that hated her like nothing else in the world. I dragged her across the grass by the hair like a tree branch.

"Forgive me," she begged. "Forgive me or kill me."

I left her like that, weeping and beaten on the ground, and I set off walking quickly as if I was escaping, faster and faster.

"Szymek!" I heard her calling in despair. "Come back! We can still have children! As many as you want! I didn't know! I was afraid! Come back! Szymek!!"

It was nearly night and a drizzle had started by the time I reached the village. The first house was Skowron's cottage, crooked with age. It had a thatched roof and no soleplates. I dropped onto a rock by the wall to try and pull myself together. Skowron came out. He wasn't even surprised to see me there. He looked at the sky:

"Well, it's finally started. It's gonna be raining a week or more, you can tell. Come inside or you'll get wet."

"No, I'll be off in a minute, I just sat down for a moment. You wouldn't have a glass of something, would you, Skowron?"

"There was a bit left over from Easter, but my old lady rubbed my back with it one time. It's been aching like the blazes, evidently from the rain."

I had the impression there were swallows chattering in the empty nests under the eaves, though how could there have been swallows at that time of year. I must have been imagining it. I was imagining all sorts of things that seemed to exist and not exist at the same time. The rain, the village, even Skowron standing on the stoop. The rain had set in for good, but I couldn't feel it falling on me, I couldn't feel anything at all. All I wanted to do was get drunk. But for that I'd have had to get up off the rock outside Skowron's place and go somewhere. That's easier said than done when you don't know where to go. I didn't want to be in the pub. The pub was good for drowning your everyday sorrows, when a hog dies, or hail flattens your crop, or you lose a court case and you need to tell someone about it. But here, if God himself had sat by me I wouldn't have said anything to him. At most it would have been, it's raining, Lord. But he'd know that already.

I remembered that Marcinek used to sometimes have vodka. Back when I was in the police I even searched his house. I didn't find anything, but there was an old milk can in the pantry. What's that, I asked. Kerosene, he says. I smelled it, pure moonshine. But let it be kerosene. You have to get along with folks.

Marcinek was sitting by the stove in his long johns and shirt putting kindling in the firebox. His missus was feeding the baby, but it might have been sick, because it was screaming to high heaven and she had to force her nipple into its mouth. The three other kids were already in bed all in a row, propped against the wall, and they all seemed sleepy though they weren't actually asleep, because when I came in they all looked at me with blue blue eyes. This wasn't Marcinek's whole family. His eldest, Waldek, worked in

Lasów minding cows for Jarociński, and the next one down, Hubert, had been taken in by his grandmother. But they all had strange names like that: Rafał, Olgierd, Konrad, Grażyna.

"Let me have a quart," I said.

At first he didn't speak, he just kept putting sticks in the stove, then after a moment he said:

"Where am I supposed to get that from?"

"Come on, I'm not here to spy on you."

"Go to the pub. It's still open. I don't sell vodka anymore. I work on the railroad now."

"Give him it, Jędruś," his old lady spoke up. "Don't you see he's all wet? He can't go to the pub looking like that. Don't you remember that milk can? You have to help people."

Marcinek gave his woman an angry look.

"Don't you know how to feed a baby, dammit? All he does is scream and scream, it's more than a man can bear!" He went on feeding the fire.

"You got a bottle?" he said gruffly.

"No."

"Then what? You want me to pour it in your cap? You don't even have a cap."

But he got up and left the room. The baby started screaming again in its mother's lap.

"Hush now, hush, you'll get some dill leaves, just suck a little longer." She took her other breast out of her blouse. "Maybe there'll be more in this one." The baby tried it but started up again. "Little thing like this doesn't even know he's alive, but he's already done more than his fair share of crying. Are you not going to get married, Szymuś? It's high time, life on your own's no picnic."

Marcinek came back with a quart bottle under his shirt. He'd filled it right up to the top.

"Though I don't have anything to stop it with," he said. "Unless I make a cork out of paper."

"There's no need," I said.

"Why don't you wait awhile," said the wife. "Potato soup's almost ready. You could have something to eat."

"Why would he want potato soup," Marcinek interrupted her. "His folks are probably waiting for him at home, they'll have sausage."

I took my first drink right outside the door. Then a second at the gate. On the other side of the road, at the crossroads there's the shrine, and I collapsed on the steps under the Lord Jesus. The rain not only didn't let up, it fell harder and harder, or maybe that was just how it appeared in the darkness, because in the darkness all sorts of things seem to happen that you wouldn't see with your eyes in the daylight. So I sat there in the rain taking swigs from the bottle, and I even started feeling good. I talked a bit to Jesus, who was sitting above me under his little roof, his chin resting on his hands, pondering. And he talked to me. And so we talked to each other, till I'd finished the bottle and there was nothing left to talk about anymore. I said:

"I'll be off, then, Lord, because otherwise I'll start pondering like you, when you and I aren't equal. I'll just leave you this empty bottle, maybe it'll come in handy if someone brings you flowers."

I set off, though I wasn't entirely sure where to. It suddenly occurred to me that maybe Kaśka was still in the store. I hadn't been to see her for a long time. I'd just drop in there once in a while for cigarettes, though I preferred to buy them at the pub. When I had to go buy other things, I would just be going to the store, not to see her. One time she even asked me, are you ever gonna come see me again? Swing by sometime. Swing by, you won't regret it. Maybe you could come today, I could stay late.

I stood in front of the door, it was locked up already. I called out, Kaśka, open up! Open up, you hear? Bitch isn't there. She was supposed to stay late. I got so mad I started hammering on the door with my fists and kicking it.

Open up! But on the other side it was quiet as the grave. I was all set to plop down in front and wait for her till morning, when I heard her voice from the other side of the door, she was all in a huff:

"Who's there?"

"It's me, Szymek. Open up!"

She gave me an angry welcome:

"Could you not find a worse time to come? The bastards are doing an inventory starting tomorrow. And here I've got half a sack of sugar too much and I've no idea where it came from. My mind's on other things, I don't have time for fun and games today."

"Do you want me to go?"

"Never mind what I want. Get yourself inside, since you're here already." She turned the key in the lock behind me and slid the bolt shut. "You look for him the whole year and he's nowhere in sight. Where did you get so drunk?" She took a strong hold of me under the arms and led me through into the storeroom. The light was on there. She sat me on a sack of sugar or salt. She exclaimed:

"Dear Lord in heaven, you look awful! Were you trying to drown yourself or something? You're soaked to the skin. Were you with some slut? You should have just stayed with her. Why did you have to come bothering me? I've thought and thought, the moment I closed up today I counted everything over and over, but I still have half a sack too much. And that bitch in accounting's just waiting for a chance to kick me out and put her bastard boyfriend in my place. Whenever she visits the store she always finds something to complain about. There's too many flies. You've got flypaper up, right? Sure, but the stuff they put on it is crap. Plus the store's in the country, not the town, there have to be flies. Or the next time she says the floor's not been swept. Sweep it yourself, bitch! Doesn't say anything in the contract about sweeping. Or have people wipe their shoes before they come in, then no one'll need to sweep the floor. Is it my fault her fella's got the hots for me? He can have the hots for her as well, did I say he couldn't? Though with a face like hers the devil himself wouldn't be interested. He's all, here Miss Kaśka, there Miss Kaśka. And when he laughs it sounds like someone stepped on a rat, the prick. Go to hell, Mr. Marzec, this is a store, not whatever you think it is. He forgets there are other people there. That old witch Mrs. Skrok pipes up, for goodness' sake, Kaśka, all those men, you'll end up in hell. I'll see you there then. I'll tell you where you can stick that hell of yours." All of a sudden she grabbed me under the arms and tugged so hard I lurched toward her. "Come sit over here, that sack's got sugar in it, it'll get wet and lumpy. If you weren't such a bad boy I'd buy you an umbrella. You could carry it around with you. Have you seen the priest's umbrella? He follows behind a coffin, it's pouring, everyone's looking like scarecrows, but him, he's dry as a bone. He even has the sacristan carry it for him. And you, you're not just anyone either, you're a government worker. Even Smotek's got an umbrella. His son-in-law gave it to him. He wandered in here one time with the umbrella open. I say, it isn't raining inside. I just need mustard, he says, it's not worth folding it then having to open it again. Maybe you wanna take a nap?"

"I didn't come here to sleep."

"You can barely stay upright you're so drunk. And sopping wet into the bargain."

"I'm not sleepy."

"Then let me at least dry your hair, the water's dripping in your eyes." She snatched a towel from a hook and started rubbing my hair so hard I thought she was dragging me down the road. But I had no wish to stop her, let her drag me, maybe she'd fall down a hole and then she'd stop of her own accord.

"Your hair's like a horse's mane," she said. She wasn't angry anymore, she was even being nice. "I'm not sure I'd like you as much if you didn't have hair. I can't stand bald men. I'd never sleep with a bald guy, whoever he was.

One time Kuśmider wouldn't leave me alone, he kept going on about how he'd come by. Come by where? To the store, Kaśka, to see you. Then go buy yourself a rug first. You can wear it in the winter instead of a cap. You won't even have to take it off in church. Your hair's all wet, but it's so thick. If you keep chasing after the other girls and ignoring me, one of these days I'll pull it all out. Though chase whoever you like, I could care less. Men are like cats, they'd die if they only had one place to go poking. They have to run around. But if one of them took you away from me forever, I think I'd kill her. Then you, then myself. With that butcher's knife up there, see it? Imagine how people would talk in the village. Did you hear what that Kaśka went and did? Who'da thought. There she was selling sugar and soap and salt and candies, and she had it in her to kill? Then that piece of work in accounting could give the job to her son-of-a-bitch boyfriend, let him come work here. I mean, what is there to sell? Sugar, salt, soap, candies, matches. Over and over. Sometimes I've had it up to here. One time they delivered a barrel of herring. My hands, my apron, face, hair – I was covered in herring. On top of that people almost broke down the door buying them. Everyone was taking five pounds, ten pounds. Have you all gone nuts? Fighting over fish? I felt like knocking them over the head with those herring. It'd be nice if I got a delivery of chocolate one day, or raisins or almonds. In town people drink coffee, they could start drinking it here as well. Instead of just vodka the whole time. But instead of that the bastards have me doing inventory every other day. Couldn't you have called by this morning, let me know you were coming? I'd have gotten the job out of the way. Now what am I supposed to do?"

"What do you think? Get undressed."

"Oh, you." She pressed my head against her belly. "You're a bad one, but I don't know what I'd do without you. Things might be worse or they might be better, but they wouldn't be the same. I'd probably give up the store. Maybe I'd go become a nun. I'm telling you, life in a nunnery isn't bad. They feed you, and all you have to do is pray. When I reached old age I'd be all set. Duda wanted to marry me. But what would that mean? Dirty dishes and dirty kids. He can hire a maid."

She took off her apron. She was wearing a green dress with white dots, it looked nice on her. I thought she looked like a green tree covered in snowflakes that were falling from the sky. But she got all riled up again and started shaking the snowflakes off.

"They can kiss my you-know-what!" she exclaimed. "I'll put a sign up to say I'm sick. They can come do the inventory next week." She reached around and started unbuttoning her dress. But suddenly something seemed to stop her, because she frowned and her hands fell to her sides.

"Your eyes are closing, Szymuś," she said. "This isn't gonna be any kind of loving."

She stood there for a moment helpless, looking at me as if in reproach, then she said uncertainly:

"So shall I take all my clothes off?" But she didn't seem to expect a reply, because she sat down on a sack with a sigh: "Oh, you."

She kicked her shoes off.

"I need to take them to the cobbler, have him put taps on. They're getting worn down," she said, and she pushed one of the shoes toward me with her foot as if to show me. She unfastened her stockings. She took the left one off, then got up, pulled the chair closer and hung the stocking over the armrest, and only then took the other one off. But with her dress she hesitated, she unfastened it at the back, but it was like she couldn't decide whether to take it off or not. In the end she did, and she slipped off her blouse as well. Then she got mad again:

"God damn them! How long is it since the last inventory? No more than a month. And I've not taken so much as a zloty's worth of anything. But the heater, I've been asking and asking and they don't have anyone to repair it. I could've turned it on, you would have dried out a bit. How will you manage all wet like that?" She took off her brassiere, her breasts seemed to jump out toward me. She stood there with the brassiere in her hand, she gave me a kind of tender look and said:

"Szymuś, you're so drunk you won't be able to get it up."

"I will, Kaśka, I will. When you touch it it'll get up. The worst thing is, I don't even feel like living."

"What are you saying, Szymuś!" She stepped back like she'd been burned, and tossed the brassiere on a pile of sacks. "Did you hear that? He doesn't want to go on living! Spit and cross yourself!" She dropped down onto her knees by me and held my head against her huge breasts. "Maybe you killed someone, Szymuś? What is it, tell me! You can tell me. I won't breathe a word. Oh, my darling. Even if you've killed someone." She started to cry.

"What are you blubbering for, you silly thing? I haven't killed anybody."

"Then you must have had a bellyful." She pushed my head away from her breasts and instantly stopped crying. "Maybe someone slipped something in your glass? Cigarette ash or something worse. You should at least have eaten. Even if you didn't want to, you should have forced yourself. Next time don't drink with just anyone. You're a government worker, respect yourself. God damn them, to your face they're the Angel Gabriel, but behind your back they'd pull you down to hell and convince you you were in your own home. Getting pie-eyed like that, dear Lord. I knew right away you'd only come to me cause you were drunk. He doesn't feel like living. Who does? Ask around the village, no one does, but they're all living away, stuffing themselves with food. And buying anything that comes along, whether they need it or no. And me, do you think I feel like living? What kind of life do I have? It's just as well you remember me once in a while and come visit. Or when one of those bitches of yours won't give it up for you. Otherwise it's nothing but the store. From morning to night I'm wondering and wondering, will he come by or not. I play games, I say, if the next customer's a woman he'll come. Then the next customer's a guy or a kid. Sometimes I even run out onto the road and ask, don't you need anything, Mrs. Oryszko, or you, Mrs. Stefańska? Just so it's a woman. What's gotten into you today, Kaśka? they say. Have you been to confession? Come on by, I just got some new baking powder in. I got this in, that in. I pray, the moment I open up the shop, even before I sweep it out, come by, Szymuś, come by, my sweet one. You might at least come for cigarettes. But evidently the pub's closer. He must have bought them there. I think to myself, I'll go over to the pub and talk to Irka, tell her not to sell him cigarettes, she should say only my store has Sports. Don't be so silly, she'll say, he'll just buy some other kind. Holidays or some other brand, they're just as good. It doesn't make any difference to them, so long as they can have their smoke. So what am I supposed to do, curse him out? Have a mass said? Or have him make me a baby? What if he says it isn't his? He'll end up hating the baby as well. How can you hate a little thing like that? Maybe it'd come to love its mother in time. It's your own fault, I say to myself. You slept around, it could be anybody's. Well, I did sleep around, but I know whose baby it is. What was I supposed to do, wait till you showed up whenever, or not at all? Blood is thicker than water. And what am I a girl for? Am I supposed to touch myself? I know you won't marry me either way. But while I'm young I can't help it if I want it. Sometimes I even wake up at night because I think someone's on top of me. But whoever it is, it's you, Szymuś. I close my eyes and I see you, I smell you. I ruffle that big mane of yours. And I say to myself inside, it's Szymuś, I'm so glad. I thank the good Lord that you exist. Like if it's Stach Niezgódka or Franek Koziej, he does his business, fastens his pants, and leaves. At most he'll say, you're a good kid, Kaśka. And it's on the tip of my tongue to say, where's Szymek? Szymek was here. I thought you were Szymek. You tricked me, you whoring son of a bitch! I'll scratch your eyes out! Get the hell outta here or I'll start shouting, I'll say you were robbing the store! You thought you had me? The hell you did! You were just screwing someone's hole, you fucker! Kaśka may be a whore, but she's not just anyone's. When she wants she's a whore, and when she wants she's a virgin. If I wanted, I could even be a princess. Miss Kaśka, you're like a princess, one guy said to me once. They were mending the railroad. If only I was a prince, he said. I'd dress you in furs, in a hat, in shoes with those big heels, and I'd drive you to church in a carriage! And you all think I'm just a shopgirl and anyone can have their way with me. All you village big shots. No damn way! Only Szymek has had me. You can tell whatever stories you like. Where I've got a beauty spot. Who enjoyed me more. I'm his whore. Only his. I'm almost like a wife to him. The Lord God, he knows how it really is. I don't have to take a vow. He'll still join us together forever when we're dead, it'll be the same as if it was here on earth. He'll ask, Szymon, do you take Katarzyna to be your lawful wedded wife? She ran the store in your village. You used to buy cigarettes from her. People said different things about her and some of them were true, but her soul was faithful as a dog to you, and her body's already rotting. And you, Katarzyna? I do, Lord. That's what I died for. Because I could've gone on working in the store for a long time to come. It wasn't so bad. Once in a while I'd get a delivery of something good. One time I got lemons, Lord. People were in such a rush to get them they almost killed each other. Over lemons. People are so dumb. I'd understand if the things were sweet, but they were sour as hell. Or I'd take a bread crust and keep chewing it till I stopped feeling weepy. Or when I'd get so mad I didn't have the strength to cry. Or I'd think, maybe he'll come tomorrow. I dreamed I saw him on his way somewhere, I thought, maybe he's on his way to me? I'd look out the window the next day. Szymek! Szymek! I dreamed about you! But you didn't even wave, you just kept on walking. You were probably going to one of those tramps of yours. I hope you break your leg and never make it, and her, I hope she goes bald. Do you think I don't know? People tell me everything. A shop is like a church. I set aside a loaf or something for somebody and I know everything, what you did, where you went. If you're drinking in the pub they come tell me right away, he's drinking in the pub. When you were going with that redhead, before anyone else managed to tell me she was in here herself boasting about it, the slut. I wouldn't sell her a damn thing. I'm going to complain, she said. Complain all you like, go see the district representative for all I care. We'll see whose side he takes. It was only after that that people told me, he's with that redhead, Kaśka. The redhead. They were standing together down by the footbridge, laughing up a storm. You should go down there and push her in, the bitch. The water under the bridge is deep, it's just waiting for folks to drown in it. You're a damn fool, Kaśka, you're dumb as a doorknob. You might be the dumbest girl alive, in this village at any rate. But I never ask myself if I want to live, Szymuś. What would be the point? Ask a stupid question and you'll get a stupid answer. And how much life do we have? No more than a thimbleful. Even if the thimble was full of bitterness, it's not enough to poison you. I've told you time and time again, give up that damn office job. It's not gonna make you any smarter. All that writing, even the smartest guy would go dumb. So what if you're a government worker. Did government workers ever come up with anything smart? My shop always used to close at six in the evening, now they've decided it's going to stay open till seven. What do I sell that I need to stay open till seven for? It was probably one of those tramps of yours. You should dump that one too. She should go down on her knees, damn her, beg you not to leave her, instead of breaking up with you. I'd rip her hair out if I knew which one it was. They say it's some floozy from Łanów. What, is she the only woman in the world? They're common as flies, all they do is wiggle their asses and flash their teeth, their tits are out on display almost, it's an embarrassment. Ugh! Every one of them just looking for someone to leech on to. If it's not Jaś then it's Staś. Plus, they think they've found the key to happiness. Think again. He drinks and he beats her and all he wants to do is make babies. Chasing happiness is a waste of time. Even if you catch it, who knows whether it's really happiness? There's a good many of them have had more than their share of that kind of happiness, but they all go on and on about being happy. You know why someone's happy? Because they're dumb. Maybe you're the only one made to be happy, Szymuś? If that's it, you need to find a woman you can be happy with. I'm not going to stand in your way. If you have to you can say, that Kaśka, she's real stupid. What kind of shopgirl nonsense has she gotten into her head. Just look at her. There's nothing worse than a whore that takes to dreaming. Pity, she was a really good lay. God shouldn't allow just anyone to have dreams. If someone's running a store they should run their store. You'll find yourself someone at a dance one of these days. She'll come fluttering up to you of her own accord. There's no shortage of dances, they hold them all the time, and the dresses are getting shorter and shorter. Pretty soon a guy won't need to put his hand up a girl's dress, there won't be dresses anymore. What'll it be like walking around then, what do you think, Szymuś? To have no shame? It's easier somehow when you're ashamed. It's often the way that the more shame you feel, the more enjoyable it is. You can slap his wrist. That's enough of that, big boy. Keep your hands to yourself. Reach for your fly if you can't reach for heaven. Tomorrow I'll run over to Zośka Malec's, see if she's got anything new. I could have one of those dresses made. I'm no worse than those other girls. Except I've got fat knees. See how fat they are? It's not so bad when I stay behind the counter. But you wouldn't want to take me to a dance. You need a girl with knees like little apples. That don't always make you look at them when she bends them. Maybe you'll find yourself a woman like that. You'll dance a polka together, you'll stamp your foot down and her dress'll fly up, you'll see if she's the one for you. Just don't let anyone make a fool of you, Szymuś. She may be meant for you but you're not meant for her. You think she's an angel, and those kind are the worst. Afterwards she'll be sickly, or she'll never want to do it with you. What can you do with yourself then? You'll be running to the john all the time. That's not heaven, Szymuś. You'll spit on your happiness then. You'll say, the hell with this kind of happiness. Come to Kaśka then. Even if you're as drunk as you are today. But come here, I mean it. Even when it's raining like it is now. Or worse. At midday. In the early morning. Anytime. You just need to say, shut up the store, Kaśka, and I'll do it. Of course I will. It's not a drugstore where someone needs medication or they'll die. You can buy your salt tomorrow. It won't hurt you to eat an unsalted dinner for once. Can't you read, damn you, I'm doing inventory. I've gone to the office, read what it says. Closed for delivery, it's written plain as day. Delivery of what? Nothing, I'm just getting it on with Szymek. We were just feeling frisky for some reason. Couldn't you find a better time, dammit? We have things we need to buy. Well I could, but he came by and told me to close up shop. Did he have to come to you of all people? Aren't there other girls, even rich ones? But who else can he do whatever he wants with? Come here all wet and drunk and say he doesn't feel like living. And Kaśka's just a hole in the fence, she has to comfort him, who else will? If he wants he can come in the morning, afternoon, evening, or in the middle of the night. If he wants, he can come for the rest of my life. I could do it with him in the dew, in the thistles, on the threshing floor, on the stubble field. If he wanted we could do it on a bed of nails and it would be like a king's bed, so long as it's with you, Szymuś. I wouldn't mind. Why should I? It's only the kind of women that go on about happiness, they think they're still in the Garden of Eden. Every one of them wants to be tempted by the serpent. They should all damn well stay there! You should just spit on all that, and come to me. You don't need any temptations with me. Just say, take your clothes off and I will, for you. Or say, just lift your dress up, I'm in a hurry. I'll do it. It makes no difference to Kaśka one way or the other. I want things to be good for you, Szymuś. I'll be good enough to make up for all the other girls. I'm not overworked here, what is there to do. All I do is sell stuff. I've got plenty of energy. I'll never tell you I'm exhausted, not today, Szymuś, another time. I'll always want to do it. Why wouldn't I. There'll be all the more to remember in the next world, make the angels blush. And when God calls me and says, why are you making the angels blush, I'll say, it's not me, Lord, you created me for Szymek. I'm just the rib that was meant for his comfort, that's me. And if you get bored with me, Szymuś, don't come here anymore. But if you get dumped again, come even if it's only because you're hurting. Just don't say you don't feel like living. Because I won't feel like living twice over. And then who'll run the store? Unless it's the accountant's bastard boyfriend. But come even if it's just because you're hurting. Whether you're hurting or not, say, get undressed, and I will. Sometimes it's even nicer when you're hurting. As long as I'm able to, come, Szymuś. And when I can't anymore I'll tell you myself. Don't come any more, Szymuś. My boobs are sagging. My skin's starting to come off my body. See how my belly button's all spread. I'm going gray, Szymuś. Even the old guys that come in the store have stopped their sweet talk, they don't call me Kaśka anymore but that old hag Kasia. She moves around like a fly in honey but she's still got a mouth on her. Find yourself a younger woman, Szymuś. You need someone younger. For me it's time to start praying, begging God to forgive me. Just buy me a rosary in return for everything. When you're with one of your floozies at a church fair, you can buy it there. It doesn't need to be an expensive one, so long as it's strong. So it won't fall apart in my hands. Because I've got a good few rosaries I need to say. Do you not know how many, Szymuś? I never held back with you, you should know that. And I don't regret it. But now my back's killing me from working in the store, Szymuś. The veins in my legs look like ropes. Sometimes I think about what it's going to be like to die. And that I'd like to die with you, Szymuś. Let it be the next life already. Maybe you'll come there one time and say, close up the store, Kaśka. But till then, you have to live, Szymuś, you have to live. What else is there that's better?"

BREAD

When we'd break the earth for the first time with the plow in springtime, we'd lay a slice of bread on the first piece of ground to be plowed. It goes without saying it wasn't just a regular slice like you cut to eat with a glass of milk or a pickled cucumber, or on its own, without anything. It had to have been cut from a new loaf on Christmas Eve.

Mother would already have set the table for the Christmas Eve dinner without meat. Father would light the lantern, take the ladder from the hallway, and go fetch a loaf from the barn, because we kept our bread on the roof beams in the barn. There was a fresh draft in there so it didn't go moldy, and it was high up. It was hard to get to without a ladder. We tried sometimes, me and Michał, we'd attempt to shimmy up the post the middle of the beam rested on, but we never managed it, and the ladder always stood out in the hallway.

There was *żurek* soup with buckwheat, noodles and poppy seed, and pierogies stuffed with cabbage, but we waited for mother to cut the bread like that was the most special dish. And dinner would start with the bread. Mother would rest the loaf against her stomach, she'd make the sign of the cross over it with the knife, she'd first cut a big slice that was going to be for the earth in the spring, then just a regular slice for each of us, according to our place in the family, first for grandfather, then grandmother while she was still alive, then father, us boys, and for herself last of all. Father would get the lantern again and put the first slice in the attic, he'd stick it way up high on a rafter beneath the thatch, usually in the darkest place. And there the slice of bread would wait for the spring like a sleeping pigeon.

And with each of us boys, the moment we were out of the cradle and could more or less keep on our feet, father would take us with him when the spring came and he went out to plow. He'd unwrap the bread from its white cloth and tell us to put it on the ground. Then he'd put our little hands on the handles of the plow, take hold with his own hands, and we'd plow over the bread. He did this with each of us in turn, Michał, me, Antek, and Stasiek. Right away he'd start teaching us how to plow. Don't hold it like that, keep it tight, walk in the middle of the furrow, it needs to go deeper when the earth is dry, when your hands get bigger you'll be holding the reins in this one and the whip in the other, as well as the plow. And don't try to scare off the crows that are following behind you, let them be, because when you're on your own out in the field with no one but the horse the crows'll keep you company, and whatever they eat will grow again. And each time you turn, always let the horse have a little breather. Now what's that singing in the sky?

"A lark, daddy."

"That's right, a lark. Do you know where the lark came from?"

"It flew here."

"That's true. But one day the Lord God was walking over the fields, and there was a farmer plowing. Is the work hard, God asked the farmer. I'll say, Lord, answered the farmer. So God took a clod of earth and threw it up into the sky and said, let it sing for you, it'll make the job easier."

When we were a bit older we'd ask father what would happen if we didn't put the slice of bread on the earth at first plowing. He'd frown and look at us like we'd been tempted by Satan or something, and he'd call on mother as a witness:

"You hear what ideas they've gotten into their heads, the little good-for-nothings? I ought to take a stick and knock those devilish thoughts out of them. Cross yourselves right now, or else!"

We'd be all scared and cross ourselves. Michał would often do it three times, but it didn't calm father down and he'd take it out on mother:

"You're their mother, why aren't you saying anything!"

"They're kids, they're still allowed to ask about anything. You're their father, you should explain it to them."

"I never asked my father about anything. Nor did he ask his. You had to listen, not ask questions." Angry that mother hadn't taken his side, he'd turn to grandfather: "Did I ever ask you anything, father? Did you ever ask your father?"

But grandfather was really old by then, and often he'd be rubbing his feet, because they were always aching, and he didn't quite get what father was after, whether he was supposed to nod or disagree with him, and he'd mostly give a vague answer:

"Well, when you didn't know something, you'd ask. But back then children were different, they're not the same these days."

"What do you mean, not the same!" said father, turning on grandfather now. "Didn't people plow and plant and harvest on the same land? You don't know what you're saying. Old age is starting to get to you, I can see."

Because grandfather was the one father got mad at most often of all. For the slightest thing, sometimes without any reason at all. If the rain set in he'd complain that grandfather's feet kept hurting and they wouldn't stop. One time the wind blew down a poplar and it fell on the barn, and he went after grandfather about that too, he said why hadn't he planted an ash or an elm, no, he had to go and plant a poplar, and poplars aren't good trees at all, they're crap, you can't build anything with the wood, and you can't burn it because it burns like straw. Or another time he stepped on a chick, because the chicks had gotten out of the basket where the brood hen was and they were pattering around the room, that was grandfather's fault too because grandfather was sitting on the bench instead of by the stove where he always sat, and father had had to go around him. It was probably all because of those papers that grandfather had buried somewhere and couldn't remember where. Or maybe because grandfather never got upset when anyone got angry at him. You could be as mad as you liked at grandfather, he'd just look at your anger like he was staring into space or he couldn't hear anything. So us boys would get mad at him sometimes too, because we knew he'd never grab a stick and come after us, or tell on us to mother or father, or hold it against us. Sometimes he'd even take a pear or a greengage out of his pocket and he'd say, here, Szymuś, here, Michał, they're sweet as sweet can be, have one and don't be so angry.

Though just as father could suddenly get angry, the anger would pass equally as quickly. He'd reach for his tobacco pouch, roll himself a cigarette, and start to tell us what would happen if we didn't give that slice of bread to the land:

"There'd be misfortunes." And he'd start explaining what the misfortunes would be, starting with the land getting covered with weeds, then there was rains, hail, heat waves, drought, mice, vermin, and other plagues, all the way up to the most terrible possibility, that the land might stop producing anything at all, because it would have turned to stone. Then grandfather would add his own misfortunes to the ones that father said. Because grandfather knew even more than father about misfortunes that can happen to you. And not just because he'd lived longer. He'd worked on the squire's land and he'd served in the tsar's army, and one time everything he owned had been swept away in a flood, another time it had all been burned by lightning. So earth, water, sky, war, it was all the same to grandfather. But father didn't like grandfather topping him when it came to misfortunes. Grandfather would barely get out the words:

"Back in the day – "

When father would immediately jump in with:

"Never mind back in the day. Misfortunes back in the day aren't the same. You were working the squire's land, so they were the squire's misfortunes. It was the same in the army, the bread was rations, whether there was any or no the soldiers had to have some because otherwise they wouldn't fight. Here the land is ours. If you treat it badly it won't forgive you. There can be misfortunes like in the Holy Bible, or in the Queen of Sheba. The prophecies weren't for nothing."

Mother sometimes had to step in and protect us from all those misfortunes:

"Stop frightening them. They're just children. When they grow up they'll have their own misfortunes, what do they need yours for. All you'll do is keep them awake at night."

Sometimes Stasiek would wake up in his cradle and scream the place down like he'd been dreaming one of father's misfortunes. It didn't help to rock him, he'd just cry even louder. The only thing that worked was for mother to stop up his mouth with her breast.

At that time I didn't know a whole lot about bread except that sometimes we had it and sometimes we didn't, and that when we had it it was good, and when we didn't it got even better. While we still had it we knew that when we finished one loaf father would go to the barn and bring another. And mother would ask while she was cutting it, how much shall I cut you? Because sometimes your eyes are bigger than your stomach and you end up throwing it to the dog.

But it also happened that spring would be a long way away and father would bring the last loaf and he'd say, this is the last one. Then we wouldn't see bread for weeks on end. Not till Easter, because mother would always leave enough flour for one or two loaves at Easter, you couldn't have Lord Jesus rising from the dead and us without bread. Then there'd be one or two loaves for the harvest, to keep the mowers' strength up. The whole time in between you'd be living by the old taste of the bread. You'd dream about bread when you were asleep and when you were daydreaming. You'd miss it like it was someone close to you. Worst of all was in the evening, because in the evening it'd appear to you like a ghost. All of a sudden there'd be the smell of bread, like someone had walked past the window with a big loaf under their arm, or the neighbors had just taken bread out of the oven. You couldn't stop yourself saying:

"There's a smell of bread from somewhere."

But father was always keeping an eye on our thoughts to make sure we were thinking about anything but bread, and he'd disagree right away:

"What are you talking about? The Maszczyks are probably just burning straw, they must be out of firewood. Or maybe Dereń was mucking out this morning, manure sometimes gives a smell like bread. Especially horse manure." He'd sniff and make like he couldn't smell anything himself. He'd even go over, open the door and let the air in, and he'd say he couldn't smell a thing. To prove his point he'd sometimes ask grandfather:

"Can you smell anything, father?"

And grandfather wouldn't smell anything either and he'd nod to say he couldn't smell anything.

"There must be a thaw on the way. I've had ants crawling up my legs all morning, the little buggers. Biting ones. The weather must be about to change. Did you see there's a wind blowing up? The wind often brings new weather. If anyone was baking bread it could only have been the Wronas, and they're east of us, but when the wind blows for a change of weather it's always from the west. One time the Turks were eating bread in their trenches, and we could smell it so plain in ours it made our bellies hurt from hunger. You can smell bread from miles away."

Mother was the only one that believed I must have smelled bread, because otherwise I wouldn't have said anything, and she started sending me to bed right away:

"It's bedtime, you need to go to bed and get to sleep. Don't think about bread, son."

Because her too, when she was clearing the table, she'd often cup her hand and make as if she was gathering bread crumbs, she'd even cross over to the range and toss the crumbs into the firebox.

One time, despite myself I blurted out:

"Mama, there isn't any bread!"

Father was sitting at the table staring out the window, he came down on me like a ton of bricks:

"What are you shouting about, you little nuisance? Let her throw it on the fire! If she's swept it up let her throw it in! Crumbs always have to be thrown into the fire! It's a sin to do otherwise!" He was so mad he actually stood up and walked back and forth across the room, then in the end he went outside.

I don't know what could have ruffled his feathers like that, I hadn't said it so loud. But maybe it was just the fact that it was bread? Because after the bread ran out, everyone would avoid talking about bread as well. No one actually said not to talk about it, but still it was as if we'd forgotten the word "bread." Even grandfather, he'd be talking about what they ate in the different wars he'd been in, he'd mention beans and cabbage, kasha, noodles, sometimes meat, but he never mentioned bread. It was the same with us kids, when we were kneeling by our bed saying our prayers out loud, and mother was standing over us making sure we didn't miss out any words, when it came time to say, our daily bread, we'd drop our voices and mother would let it go. Though there was even something about our prayers that bothered father, he'd say to mother:

"They ought to say a Hail Mary instead. Our Lady's more likely to grant children's wishes. She had a child of her own."

Father seemed to be just sitting there and thinking, he rarely said anything, but he didn't trust a soul. He must have known that at a time like that the slice of bread wedged up there on the rafter was like the apple in the Garden of Eden, it could have tempted anybody. Most of all he didn't trust me. Whenever he watched us all, his gray eyes drilled into me more than any of us. But he didn't even trust grandfather. Though grandfather didn't have a single tooth in his head, how could he have been tempted by bread that had been there since Christmas Eve and had dried as hard as stone. Even when he had fresh bread he'd only pick out the inside, and he'd have to chew every mouthful forever before he swallowed it.

With Michał and me it was different, we had teeth like wolves, as far as we were concerned the bread could have been drying for a hundred years and it would still be bread. The best bread of all, that mother had held against her stomach and as she cut it she asked us how much we wanted. Your gums itched when you remembered about the bread that was up in the attic. Though you didn't need to remember it, you always had it before your eyes. Half the time, hunger would stir you so your mouth watered, the rest of the time you'd be tempted so hard by the idea of being full that you could almost feel the bread filling your belly. It tempted you all the time, from morning till evening, and even for a long time into the night, after we'd gone to bed, it still wouldn't leave us alone.

I shared a bed with father and Michał, I was next to father. Michał slept crosswise at our feet, because he didn't thrash around in his sleep, and also he was shorter than me, because for the longest time he didn't grow. The moment father got into bed he'd turn his back toward me, maybe mutter something about me not pulling the quilt off him, and he'd be snoring right away. I didn't need to wait much longer for Michał either. He'd dig around with his legs a bit at the beginning, because he could never find the right place for them. But once he'd found it, his legs would twitch a couple of times then he'd sleep like the dead. After that, by the bed under the window where mother slept with Antek, Stasiek's cradle would stop rocking, sometimes Stasiek would whimper some more, but mother didn't hear him now.

As for Antek, even if he'd heard something he would just have pretended all the more to be asleep, more than if he'd actually been sleeping. Our grandparents slept in the other room across the hallway. Also, grandmother would go off to bed the moment it got dark, and grandfather would just sit on a stool for as long as he could, dozing. So when he finally went off to bed he was already as sound asleep as if it was the middle of the night. Mother would have to help him over the doorstep, because the threshold grew bigger under grandfather's feet, like he was already dreaming that he was trying to cross over into his own house but he kept not being able to do it. Though as it happens the actual threshold was quite high. Because thresholds were made not just for the sake of it, but so there'd be somewhere to sit when you had more people than usual.

The roosters were already crowing for midnight. Father would turn on his other side so he was facing me. Then he'd turn his back again. Michał would move his legs because they'd gotten stiff. Stasiek would squeal in his sleep, and the cradle would start to rock. But I'd still be seeing that slice of bread high up on the rafter, it'd be shining there like the brightest star, and the picture wouldn't go away. At times it ached like a sore tooth, other times it nagged at me like a bad conscience. If I could have wriggled around a bit it might have gone away. But there was no room in the bed, and right next to me was father's back, big as a mountain. He could have woken up at any moment and asked:

"Are you not asleep yet?"

Just in case, I'd decided I would say the fleas were biting. But I don't know if he would have believed me, because we didn't have fleas in our house. Mother would air the sheets outside every day, and underneath she'd put dried thyme. When I finally managed to get to sleep, I could never tell whether I was dreaming or awake, because I still had the slice of bread before my eyes. One time I dreamed I went to the attic, and propped up the ladder, but the ladder was too short, so I climbed a poplar tree, but the poplar turned out to be too short as well. It could have been the same whether it was a dream or waking. In the morning father asked me:

"Why were you squirming around so much? Were you having a dream?"

I got out of it by saying it was probably from the cabbage and beans I ate the day before, because with dreams you can get out of it by saying anything at all. Luckily father wasn't in the dream, so he believed me without a problem.

It was worse during the day, when he happened to be sitting in the main room. Sometimes he was just across the table from me. And it was like someone had deliberately pushed the bread into my mouth and told me to eat it in front of him, because it was only bread. And bread is there to be eaten. My whole head filled with the sound of me crunching the dry bread between my teeth. I looked around terrified, because I was sure everyone could hear. Father, mother, Michał, Antek, even Stasiek in his cradle. And grandfather seemed about to open his mouth and say:

"Listen, everyone, there's some kind of crunching sound. Michał, go check under the bed, see if that damn cat's eating a mouse under there."

And father, it would be like he'd been waiting for exactly that:

"Cat? What cat? I put the cat outside! Come on, fess up, which one of you is it? Is it you, Szymek? Open your mouth this instant, you little pipsqueak!"

Because I think father suspected something as it was, he'd sometimes look at me like he was about to ask:

"What are you eating there?"

I'd cringe under his gaze, and I'd repeat to myself in my head, I'm not eating anything, I'm not eating anything, I'm not eating anything. Or, I'm just having a plum, because I was thinking how we had plums at the priest's house in the fall. Or I was remembering how we went picking hazelnuts at the manor before the Assumption, I'm eating one of those. But they weren't ripe, daddy. And the steward chased us off.

One time he stared and stared at me and then all of a sudden he asked:

"What are you thinking about?"

At first I froze, I couldn't get a word out. It was as if my mouth was still full of bread. I was like a mouse being chased by a cat. So I pretended I thought he was asking Michał, not me. I looked at Michał like I was expecting him to answer. Michał looked at me. But father wasn't fooled:

"Not Michał. I know what Michał's thinking. Michał's thoughts are clear as springwater. I mean you."

"Me?" I said with a surprised look, buying myself a few extra seconds to decide what I was thinking about. Before he said anything back, I already knew.

"I'm thinking about Lord Jesus," I got out in a single breath.

Father's eyes opened as wide as they would go, he straightened up and looked at me like a blind man looking at the sun. He didn't know what to say. I thought he'd leave me alone now. Maybe he'd get up and say:

"I have to go check on the horse."

Or start to ask grandfather:

"So did you remember yet? Maybe you buried them under that wild pear behind the barn? Remember there was a wild pear that grew there?"

"Of course I remember the wild pear. It was taller than the barn, the fruit was sweet as honey." Because the fact was, grandfather remembered absolutely everything, his whole life was written in his memory day by day. Except for that one matter of where he'd buried the papers. "But it wasn't under the pear. More likely it was under the apple tree. There was one apple tree had apples that were half red and half yellow. But one day there was a storm and it got blown down along with its roots."

Father narrowed his eyes again, he might have been wondering whether or not to believe me. Then, as if he wanted to hear one more time what I was thinking, he said:

"So you're thinking about Lord Jesus?"

"Lord Jesus." I nodded eagerly, and even grandfather was touched:

"You're wanting to send Michał for a priest, but it looks like Szymuś is the one God's chosen. Little kid like that, and see what ideas he's got in his head. Lord Jesus, how do you like that. Even grown-ups might not think of that. I'm telling you, he's the one going to be a priest."

I bit my tongue to stop myself saying I wouldn't be. I couldn't see myself as a priest. Doing nothing but saying mass all my life, and on top of that having to wear a dress like a woman. Though the other boys said that under the dress the priest wore pants like any man. But what kind of pants could they be that he had to cover them up. Plus, I already liked Staśka Makuła. She grazed cows with us on the meadow, and even Wicek Szumiel, who was the oldest one of us, he couldn't take her because she was too strong, even though she was a girl. And she cussed better than many a grown-up, however mad they might get. Her though, she'd not be mad at all, she'd be laughing and skipping about, but she'd be swearing up a storm. Come on, Staśka, let it rip, we'd say to egg her on, and she'd curse so much even the cows turned their heads to look. And when she ran off to bring the cows back in, her boobs would bounce up and down like pears in the wind. We'd chase behind her like dogs after a bitch, hoping they might pop out. Look at Staśka's titties! Like you could already see them white against the grass.

We sometimes tried to get her to show us what she had under her dress, but she wanted a zloty to do it. So we scraped together a zloty, everyone put in what they could or pinched some change at home, and we gave it to her and said, okay, Staśka, show us what you've got there. But then she said that for a zloty she could only show us what she had up top, if we wanted to see more it would be another fifty groszes. Where were we supposed to get fifty groszes? Fifty groszes was what young men got from their fathers when they were going out with a young lady. But luck would have it that Kazek Socha's father came back from the fair rolling drunk, they had to lift him down off his wagon, and Kazek swiped fifty groszy from his pocket. So now we had it. Come on, Staśka, show us. But she put the price up again, she said two zlotys, because she needed new silk stockings, like Tereska the miller's daughter had. We were so mad we threw ourselves on her, we'll take your clothes off ourselves, goddammit, but she got free of us, and she took out her penknife and stood there with her feet planted:

"If anyone comes closer I'll cut their weenie off, you little bastards."

It was only when we grew up that she didn't ask for anything.

The only thing I liked about a priest's work was confession. It must be great to sit there in the confessional behind the grate and listen to the sins of the whole village. Boy would you learn some stuff. And forgiving sins or not forgiving them, ordering penance. Most of all I'd have scared people with hell, I'd make their hair stand on end and their blood curdle, I'd make their teeth chatter and their eyes weep endless tears. Though I'd need to invent a different hell, because people have stopped being afraid of the old one. Perhaps it ought to be that it's not just the soul that suffers, but the body along with it? Or that people wouldn't be together, but each person would be alone? Maybe there shouldn't even be any devils, just people and their own torments.

I'd give the longest confessions to three young women from our village: Kryśka Latra, Weronka Maziarz, and Magda Kukawa. And among the married women, Mrs. Balbus. Because before she married Balbus, she had more boyfriends than you could shake a stick at. Every evening her father would chase her around the village with a whip, and she'd be running away. People even said she'd had a bastard child, but that she'd drowned it. Though when she was with Balbus it didn't change anything. But to find out if what people were saying was true, I'd have to give her confession. I wouldn't confess old women or old men. The curate could do them. Well, maybe old Mrs.

Przygaj, to find out if girls slept around in the old days as well. Because who would know better that Mrs. Przygaj. Apparently she never let an opportunity go by. The village mayor, a farmhand, the miller, a neighbor, whoever came along. And most of all with the soldiers that used to be stationed in the village. They had dark blue jackets and red pants, people said that was what drew her to them. Her husband would pray to God that he'd drive the demon out of her, and she'd just laugh at him. One time she brought three soldiers home at the same time and partied with them naked, and her husband had to look on. He beat her afterwards with a wet rope, so she arranged for him to be drafted into the army and he never came back. Though would she be willing to admit to all of that in the confessional?

"Michał or Szymuś," said mother, "God grant it'll be one of them."

"I'm telling you, it'll be Szymuś," grandfather insisted. "Maybe he could serve right here, in our parish. I won't live to see the day. But you could move to the presbytery. It'd be heaven there. The orchard alone must be four acres. And you've got the church right there."

"What exactly were you thinking about?" Father didn't let all that about the priest distract him from asking me more questions.

"I was thinking . . ." I tripped over my tongue, because I wasn't entirely sure what I'd been thinking.

"What was he thinking about?" Grandfather came to my rescue. "He was thinking about Jesus, he already said. He's hanging on the cross right up there, you only need to look, there's nothing else to think about."

I looked up at the cross in panic, and it was like something opened up inside of me.

"I was thinking," I said, "about how he suffered for us and how he died on the cross."

"He truly did suffer, that's for sure," mother put in from by the stove. "But people are the same as they always were."

"Maybe they'd have been even worse," grandfather suggested.

"Even worse?" Mother shuddered.

"Think about it, what if everyone was like that no-good Marchewka. Could you stand that? Think about all the chickens he's stolen from you."

"What else?" Father wouldn't give it up.

"What else?" Grandfather bridled because he thought father was on at him. "He cut down those willows on your pasture. And he gave you an earful for good measure. Is that not enough for you?"

"I'm not asking you, father, I'm asking him."

"Szymek? What on earth's he done to you?"

"Not what he's done, what he's thinking about. Out with it." It was like he was driving a horse uphill with a whip.

I got this sinking feeling in my belly. Out with what? On top of everything else it was lashing down outside, so there was no chance father would leave the house, a dog wouldn't want to go out in that. He could keep grilling me all afternoon. I rooted around desperately among my thoughts, but my thoughts were like mice, they kept running away. All of a sudden grandfather got up, took a step toward the middle of the room, and sighed:

"When you're old, taking a single step is like walking to Calvary."

At that very moment it came to me.

"I was thinking," I quoted from memory, "about how when Jesus was carrying his cross to Calvary and he fell, there was a farmer walking by on his way back from the fields, and he helped him carry it."

"Not a farmer, Simon of Cyrene. What's that damn priest been teaching you!" father said, getting all testy.

"I said so right from the beginning," grandfather agreed with father. "The moment he first came here I said, he's supposed to be a priest? He's got a face like a little girl. He can't even grow a beard, he's just got fuzz here and there. How could he know anything. He doesn't know the first thing about Jesus, just like he doesn't know the first thing about people."

"People are one thing, Jesus is another," mother objected.

"What do you mean, another thing?" grandfather said, bridling in turn. "Was Jesus not a person? It was only after he died he became God."

"Of course he was, he even let himself be crucified because he couldn't take it anymore."

"It wasn't that he couldn't take it anymore, he wanted to redeem people."

"And in return they gave him something bitter to drink, and stabbed him in the side, am I right? I'd never have saved those villains. I'd have sent them to hell, let them roast down there, let them howl like wolves! Let them tear their hair out and shout for God's mercy! Let them weep and weep till the darkness covers them over!" Mother was like a wasp with those villains, she wouldn't leave them alone and she probably would have gone on longer if father hadn't roared:

"What else?!"

My heart missed a beat. Luckily mother was still filled with anger at the villains that killed Jesus, and at that moment she started taking it out on father like he was one of them:

"Leave the boy alone, will you! He's told you almost the whole gospel and all you can say is, what else, what else! Show me another child that knows that much. They can't even tell you the ten commandments."

Something came to me again.

"I was thinking, daddy, that he was proclaiming the ten commandments," I threw out breathlessly, like I was trying to get this piece of good news out before mother.

But father bristled like a turkey-cock.

"Who?"

"You know, the Lord . . . God," I said, though less surely, because I sensed something bad in his voice.

"Which one?" he asked with a frown.

"There's only one Lord God, father. That's what the priest told us. And there's only one hanging on the wall there."

"But in three persons! In three persons, you little twit!" He was shaking with anger.

I was all set to burst into tears. But something told me father wasn't entirely on solid ground with Jesus. I pretended to be upset that someone had gotten it all muddled up, and I asked hesitantly:

"What do you mean, daddy, that there's only one but in three?"

"Because it's in three persons!" His chin twitched. "The Son of God! The Holy Ghost! And God the Father!"

"So which one of them is God?"

"They all are!"

"How can all of them be when there's three of them, not one?"

"There's only one!!" he roared. He grabbed a piece of kindling from the floor and chucked it at me, but I dodged and it hit Michał. Michał burst out crying and mother shouted:

"Have you gone mad?"

Even grandfather, though he didn't like getting on father's bad side, mumbled to himself:

"That's not how you explain it. That's not how you explain it."

Father was so furious he grabbed the slop bucket with such a jerk that it splashed on his pants, and he charged out to take it to the cow.

Then there came a year that was worse than any other. First of all, during the entire spring not a drop of rain fell, then the whole summer it wouldn't stop raining, and it kept up almost till autumn. The river, even though it had been just a little stream, it burst its banks, it grew to be the size of ten rivers and it kept on swelling. People were fretting, what's going to happen, what's going to happen? And the roosters went on crowing to show it wasn't going to let up any time soon. Some folks spent whole days just standing at their windows staring out to see if they couldn't spot at least a tiny bit of blue sky to give them hope. Other people were expecting the end of the world, they thought there was going to be another flood like the one in Noah's time. They'd even gather at Sójka's place in the evening and read the Bible aloud to see if it was the same or not. At the church there was one special service after another. And anywhere there was a cross or a chapel or a wayside shrine, people would gather to pray or sing or at the very least cry together, instead of everyone on their own in their own house. As for confession and communion, there were lines like never before. Kruk the unbeliever even let himself be converted, because his old lady and his daughters kept on and on at him about how it was all because of him. He had five daughters, three of them were already old maids but two were still marriageable. Though why would God want to punish the whole world on account of Kruk. Afterwards the guy regretted it, because he still got no peace at home just like before, and outside the rains went on and on.

People even made the priest lead a procession out into the fields, they thought maybe that would help. But they didn't get very far. Just beyond Midura's place, where the road turns toward the fields, Franciszek the sacristan, who was carrying the cross up front, he got stuck in mud almost up to his knees. The banners got bogged down with him. Mrs. Karpiel and Mrs. Matyska ended up in it too, because they were tertiaries and they'd wanted to be in the lead. The priest got stuck, even though Skubida and Denderys had been holding his arms. They had to stand on either side of him and drag him out and carry him over to drier ground, he wouldn't have been able to get out on his own. As it was, one of his shoes came off in the mud, and one of the women had to fish it out and put it back on his foot. Because Franciszek the sacristan was wearing tall boots, and he'd gone marching on ahead without looking back at the rest of the procession. People called to him, hey, Franciszek, wait up there! But he just kept going, and it was only when the mud reached up over the tops of his boots that he realized he was all on his own. Luckily he had the cross with him, so he leaned on it like a shepherd's crook and managed to get clear. Though the priest gave him a telling-off once he was on the drier ground, for abusing the cross like that. So that was the end of the procession. They prayed a bit and sang a bit at the edge of the fields, then they went back to the church.

Some of the better-off farmers took holy pictures out onto their land and made a little hut for them like a sentry box. But that did no good either. After all, it couldn't have happened that the sun shone on some folks' land while it rained on other people's, when it rained it rained everywhere. Everyone went out to the fields and gathered what could be gathered in the rain and mud. There wasn't much, because what hadn't dried up in the spring had gotten waterlogged in the summer and the start of autumn.

We only picked three wagonloads of potatoes, after we'd planted a big stretch of field. And they were all the size of walnuts. Father came back with the third wagonload and said that was the lot, and grandfather came out, and mother, and us children, and we all cried. Father couldn't even bring himself to get down off the wagon, he just sat there with the whip and the reins in his hand and watched grandfather crying and fingering the potatoes. All he said in consolation was:

"Well, there's nothing to be done about it. Whatever the land is like, the potatoes are like that too. And the land is rotten. I just hope it recovers from all this."

During the threshing, when he took a full sieve and winnowed it there was nothing but chaff, and the grain at the very bottom. He left what he needed for the next sowing, he barely had half a sackful to take to the mill for grinding, and that was the end of the rye. Mother baked bread out of it just the once, she set aside a few measures for an emergency.

The bread from the one baking lasted us a month, month and a half, and it wouldn't even have been that long except father took some of the loaves while they were still hot and hid them somewhere. Michał and I searched the whole barn, we even jabbed the pitchfork into the hay in the bins, but we couldn't find it. It had to have been hidden in the barn, but we would have needed to turn the place upside down. Michał wasn't the person for that. The whole time I had to keep reassuring him that looking for the bread wasn't a sin. When he stuck the pitchfork in, he'd only just go in with the very tips of the prongs, as if he was afraid that, God forbid, we might actually find the bread. He kept asking me:

"What'll we do if we find it?"

"Eat it."

"On our own?"

"Who else are we going to eat it with?"

"Are we not going to give any to father and mother?"

"Take them some, you'll see what'll happen. You'll get a hiding for being so good."

Then he remembered a story grandfather had told about how once during the uprising the Cossacks had been looking for rebels and they'd made grandfather stick a pitchfork into the hay. And grandfather had hid them himself in that hay. But what could he do, they ordered him to stick his pitchfork in, so he did. All at once he saw blood on the tip of the pitchfork. Right at that moment, pretending he'd stumbled on the sheaves, he rammed the pitchfork into his own foot with all his strength and started screaming to high heaven. The Cossacks all burst out laughing. But they didn't make him search anymore.

"Idiot," I said to him, "we're looking for bread, not rebels. Bread doesn't bleed."

But he wouldn't search any longer.

I even thought about following father out when he went to bring a new loaf. But each time he did, he'd tell mother not to let us out till he came back. Or he'd say he was going down the village to see the blacksmith, or one of the neighbors, and he'd appear afterwards with a loaf under his arm. He'd give the loaf to mother, and she'd padlock it in the chest. Then each day she'd cut one slice each for us in the morning, another in the evening.

Thanks to that, the bread lasted till Saint Blaise's Day in early February. From then on we only ate potatoes. In the morning it was *żurek* with potatoes, at midday potato soup or potatoes and milk, in the evening potatoes baked in the ash pan, with salt. The ones from the ash pan were best. We wouldn't light the lamp, we'd just sit around the stove in the kitchen with the door of the firebox open, and whatever light it gave would light the room. We were eating more salt now so we didn't have the money for lamp oil, and besides, lamp oil would have been wasted on plain potatoes. True, father had sold the heifer because we didn't have anything to feed it with, but almost all the money had gone on paying taxes.

Mother would bring the potatoes from the cellar gathered in her apron like eggs. She'd lay them down on the ground at father's feet. Father would take a burning ember from the firebox so he could see what he was doing, and he'd divide the potatoes into the same number of piles as there were people at home, except for Stasiek, because Stasiek was still at the teat. Then he'd even out the piles, moving bigger and smaller potatoes around, so they were all equal. Then mother would tell him to take two from her pile and give me and Michał an extra one each, because we were still growing. Grandmother said the same, that she didn't have long to live and it was enough for her to say her prayers before she went to bed, she didn't need to eat. So he'd rearrange the piles yet again.

Sometimes he'd take so long organizing the piles of potatoes that he'd be covered in smoke from the ember he was using as a light. One time he even singed his eyebrows. Even so, the potatoes would get all mixed together when he put them in the ash pan and covered them with ash. I could never figure out how he knew which one belonged to who when he dug them out again afterward and put them back in the same piles, putting a name to each potato. This is Szymek's, this is father's, this'll be mine, this one's Michał's, this is mother's, Antek's.

When he'd shared them all out, without waiting for them to cool even a bit he'd take the first potato from his own pile and, as if it wasn't burning his fingers in the slightest, he'd peel it and begin eating. Right away he'd start saying how good it was, that it was nice and well done, and what would we do if we didn't have potatoes, and generally he'd talk and talk like he was describing some strange world. That though meat provides strength, potatoes give you patience. That you can find any kind of food you want in potatoes, if you only know how to eat them. Because eating is a skill just as much as reading and writing. But some people eat like hogs and for that reason they don't know a thing. Or they only eat with their mouths and their bellies. Whereas you need to eat with your mind as well. That everything comes from the earth, and the earth has the same taste in all things. So potatoes can be beans and crackling, they can be cabbage and bacon, pierogies with cheese or with sour cream, even a chicken leg big as a mangel-wurzel. Even badness and goodness come from potatoes, because they come from the earth.

During the daytime he was gruff and tight-lipped, but over those baked potatoes he'd talk till he was blue in the face, he sometimes even forgot to take salt and mother would have to remind him:

"Put some salt on it."

My grandparents had lived way longer than he had, and they must have eaten way more potatoes, but they paid attention just the same like they were listening to some kind of prophecy. Though one time grandfather interrupted to back father up, he said that potatoes are eaten by kings just as much as by their servants, by generals and ordinary soldiers, by priests and paupers, because potatoes make everyone equal. And that death makes people equal too, but it doesn't taste nearly as good. At this father jumped on grandfather, what did death have to do with potatoes. Death was death, it had to come to everyone. Potatoes grow so people can have food to eat. Grandmother didn't much like what grandfather had said about equality either:

"What a lot of nonsense you talk sometimes. Kings eating potatoes, when they have to rule the world." But she evidently started feeling sorry for the kings, because she added: "Unless maybe they're in a sauce, something you can't even imagine is poured over them. And as much meat as there are potatoes, to go with them. With meat they could eat them."

"They eat them with whatever they eat them with," father barked at grandmother. "People don't need to know everything about kings. People don't even know everything about their neighbors, even though they live right there. And that's how things should be."

One day father went off to see the blacksmith and get the plowshare hammered out, because there was a breath of spring in the air. Someone had said they'd heard a lark singing, though there was still snow on the fields. Mother was out too, she'd gone over to the neighbor's to borrow some sifted flour to make żurek. Grandmother was rocking Stasiek, and grandfather was dozing by the stove, though his sleep was shallow because every so often he'd open his mouth and mutter that it wasn't spring yet, not by a long shot. Potato soup was making on the stove top.

I hadn't gone to school because I'd said I had a stomachache. The whole time I sat bent double so it looked like it was true. Grandmother had given me some mint drops and every now and then she'd ask, how are you feeling, does your tummy still hurt? I groaned and said it did, but I'd been thinking about how to get out of the main room, because since early morning that slice of bread on the rafter up in the attic had been tempting me, it might even have made my stomach hurt a little. I didn't have any bad intentions. I just wanted to look at it, to see what bread looked like.

"It's a little better," I said when grandmother asked me for the umpteenth time. Because I figured it had hurt enough by now, and besides, any moment mother could come back from the neighbor's or father from the blacksmith's and I'd have to stay sitting there bent in two with an aching stomach.

It was like grandmother had been waiting for me to say it, she started singing the praises of the mint drops. And when she was about to get carried away and say that sometimes the pain would just vanish as if by magic, I told her it had stopped hurting now, and I grabbed the bowl with the chicken feed and said I'd go see to the chickens. I put the bowl down in the passageway and quickly climbed up to the attic. At first, before my eyes got used to the dark, it looked like the thatched roof had collapsed onto the attic floor, it was so black up there. But I knew by heart the place where the bread was. I'd snuck up there a good few times when I had a particularly strong yen to take a look at it. Besides, all you had to do was tip your head back, open your eyes wide, and wait like that for a short while, the roof rose higher and higher, and the place became much much bigger, like you were standing in the middle of a church at dusk. Then it would gradually come into view out of the darkness, way up a height, like a sleepy pigeon huddled behind a rafter. It was gray like a pigeon. It even poked out from behind the rafter like a pigeon's head, a little grayer than the gray of the thatch.

I suddenly had an urge to touch it, stroke it, on its head at least. But how could I get to it? Father must have pulled the ladder up into the attic when he put the bread up there on the rafter. I tried climbing up the crossbeams. It was hard, though the beams were no farther apart than the rungs of a ladder. The thing was though, they were planted tight against the thatch like feet on grass, and each time I took hold I had to push my hand under the thatch with all my strength to get a decent grip. If I'd let go I would have come down on the attic floor like a ton of bricks. Then it would have been judgment day downstairs. I could just see grandfather starting up out of his seat saying, what's that, is the house falling down?! And grandmother would shout, Jesus and Mary! And Stasiek would burst out crying. And mother would happen to come back right at that moment and she'd be wringing her hands saying, where's Szymek? And father would be back from the blacksmith's and he'd be going, where's that little monkey gotten to?

But I managed to clamber up to right by where the bread was, and hanging from a beam with one hand, with the other one I snatched the bread from the rafter and put it in my shirt. Getting down was easier. I sat down by the chimney flue, but for some reason I didn't have the courage right away to take the bread out. I listened carefully to check there weren't any suspicious sounds coming from downstairs. But all I heard was grandmother singing to Stasiek, "Oh my people, how have I wronged you?" I looked around nervously. Everything was quiet as could be, even the mice seemed to have gone from the attic for the moment. The only sound was my heart hammering so hard it felt like it was outside my body. I put my hand cautiously under my shirt and, first of all, felt the bread while it was still in there. It was all dry and cracked, not like bread at all. And I couldn't tell if it was my heart or if the bread itself was pounding. I took it out carefully with both hands. I bent my head to get a better look. But all I could see was a rough gray piece of something that was supposed to be bread. What was so special about it, I asked myself, that the land couldn't do without it?

I got the urge to break off a piece and try it. Maybe when it was in my mouth I'd taste whatever power was in it? A communion wafer isn't anything special either, just flour and water, no taste at all, but it still contains Lord Jesus. Just a tiny bit. Father'll never know. How can you remember a slice of bread from Christmas Eve till the springtime? It had been bigger and now it was dried up. People dry up in their old age as well.

I stuck just the very edge between my teeth and bit down not hard at all, but all of a sudden there was a snapping sound like something had broken, and a piece came off that was half the size of my hand. I was terrified. My first thought was to get the heck out of there. But where to? I felt like I was choking. I'd have knelt down in front of that dried-up slice of bread and begged it to let itself be put back together. I could sense someone already hurrying up the ladder. Someone was coming from behind the chimney and stretching out their arms to grab me. The front door slammed. I seemed to hear voices, father and mother and grandfather and grandmother, calling, Szymek, what have you done! Szymek, for the love of God! Szymek!!

And all at once, like I was trying to eat up the great guilt inside of me, I started biting on the broken-off piece. It crunched in my mouth so loud you could hear it across the entire attic. It felt like it could be heard downstairs, in the yard, in the whole village. People were coming running from all over to see what was happening at the Pietruszkas'. It prickled against my tongue and my gums and on the roof of my mouth. But I bit down like mad, in a rush, as if I was worried I'd run out of time. Because of that I didn't taste the bread at all, all I could feel was my mouth being scratched inside, it was like I had a wound inside my mouth.

Then I ate the rest of the bread as well, because I didn't know what else to do with it. At that point something strange happened, my fear suddenly passed and I felt something like bliss coming over me. I could even have gotten up and gone back down, except I didn't feel like it. Quiet and calm came back to the attic, and after a moment I was overcome with sleep. I dreamed of our fields, cracked with dryness, overgrown with weeds, horsetail and wheatgrass and pigweed, while right next door, on other people's land there were handsome crops of rye, barley, wheat. But none of it made me sad at all, even father, who was walking across our fields and calling in a tearful voice, how wretched I am, and how wretched you are, land!

I was woken by scuffles and shouts. Father was standing over me. He was furious, in a rage, like he'd lost his reason. He was waving his arms and screaming:

"You monster! You animal!" And other names. "Dear God, hold me back or I'll kill him, I'll kill him like a dog! I wish you'd died before you were ever born! What are we going to do now? The land'll never forgive us! Get up!!"

I still had the sweetness of sleep and the bread inside me, I threw myself at father's feet and started yelping:

"I couldn't stop myself, daddy! I must have the devil in me! Take me to the church, I'll lie down with my arms spread the whole day! Maybe the devil will go out of me!"

"I'll devil you! Get up!" He kicked me in the stomach so hard I folded in two. Then without warning, as if he'd been overcome by an even greater attack of fury, he grabbed me by the waist and lugged me down the ladder like a sack of flour. Without putting me down he carried me all the way across the yard to the barn wall. He set me down and ordered me to stand there, while he started feverishly looking for something on the ground.

Mother came out of the house and said:

"What's he done that's so terrible?"

Father was marching back and forth digging in the hay with his boots, muttering to himself, he seemed to have gone mad. Finally his shoe hit something that made a clinking sound, he bent over and pulled out the dog's chain. We'd set the dog free halfway through the winter so it could feed itself, we didn't have anything to give it.

Mother asked again from the doorstep:

"What has he done that's so terrible?"

But he probably didn't hear her, he was busy untangling the chain. He pushed the barn door open furiously, grabbed me by the arm, and yanked me inside, though I didn't resist. He pushed the door to behind us, gave it a couple of kicks because it wouldn't close properly. He was shaking like he had a fever, it even made the chain rattle in his hand. He put the chain around my neck.

"I'm going to hang you, you animal," he muttered. "I don't care if God won't forgive me. You and I'll go to hell together. But I'm going to hang you."

He was fiddling with the chain around my neck, and the chain was jingling like bells on a horse. I even had the impression father was putting bells on me like he was getting me ready for a sleigh ride, not for death. And maybe it was because of that that I wasn't afraid at all. I had an ache in the pit of my stomach, but it wasn't from fear of dying, it was probably from the bread. Because I didn't yet know what it meant to die. I'd seen dead bodies, of course. All kinds. People that had died of old age, of illness, who'd drowned or been hung. There was even one, Paluch his name was, he'd been bringing in his crop, he'd slipped off the sheaves and a wagon wheel had run him over. He was already dead, but he was holding on to the wheel so hard they couldn't pry his fingers off. Or Kurzeja the miller, he got dragged into the belts at the mill, he didn't look either like he'd been killed or that he'd died naturally. Or another time Sylwester Sójka killed his brother, Bolesław Sójka, with a flail, in a fight over property. It looked like it had been an accident, that they'd been doing the threshing together and they'd either been standing too close together, or their flails had been too long. He even cried over his brother's body, he was shouting, get up, Bolesław, come back to life, brother! Like he was calling him to get back to the threshing. You felt that the other guy would just wipe his eyes and stand up, because who wouldn't react when their brother was calling. Or Kułaga beat his old lady up so bad she ran out of the house onto the road completely naked, then she dropped down dead in the road. Actually it was hard to say exactly what had really happened, because some people said she'd dropped dead, others that she was a tramp. Or Rżysko, one time he was at the pub and he drank so much he never got up from his drinking. A drunken dead body looks like it's just drunk. The Jew was pulling his beard out because no one would pay for what the man had drunk. He'd even owed him from before, he was going to settle up with him that day. But they went through his pockets and he didn't have a red cent on him. Or my school friend Jędrek Guzek, when I saw him in his coffin he was dead and all, but he was dressed in a brand-new suit with brand-new shoes and a new shirt, and his hair was cut and combed, I'd never once seen him like that when he was alive. I even thought to myself, seems like it's not such a bad thing to die. He'd made a bet for a penknife with Jaś Kułaj that without using a strap he could climb all the way up the highest poplar tree over on the far side of the dike behind the mill. He'd almost made it to the top when he fell. We took him to his mother so she could put him to bed, because there was something wrong with him. She cussed us out, called us the worst names. It was only later she started wailing, Jędrek, Jędrusieniu!

I could go on and on. But I'd never yet seen what it was to die on your own. I might not know even today. Though when it comes to the dead my memory is good. I could even write them all down in a list in order, starting with Wróbel, when I was three years old and mother took me with her, saying, let's go say goodbye to Wróbel, because he's dying. I was a little afraid because I thought death would be sitting at Wróbel's side. I'd never seen death, except with the Christmas carol singers of course, but that was always one of the young guys dressed up. We went in. Mrs. Wróbel was stirring something on the stove. Their Józef was sitting on a bench by the window mending some reins, and in the corner of the room, high on white pillows, was Wróbel's head with his big mustache spreading like the branches of a tree. We went up to the bed, mother crossed herself and knelt and told me to kneel down as well. Then the mustache on the pillow moved, and a scrawny hand reached out from under the quilt and rested a moment on my head. Then we got up, and mother asked:

"Has the priest been yet?"

"He has," sighed Mrs. Wróbel, and at the same moment she started in on Józef: "Józef! Józef! You need to be going! I keep asking him and asking him."

I was about to say to mother:

"Mama, where's death?"

But she tugged me by the hand and we left. Outside, the sun was nice and warm and Kozieja was leading a calf up the road, and the calf was prancing around in such a funny way that I started to laugh, and mother did too, and anyone that was coming down the road stopped and laughed as well.

"Kneel down," father grunted.

I dropped instantly to my knees, the chain rattled around my neck.

"Say all the deadly sins," he said. "Beat yourself on the chest. Ask God to forgive you. And say three Hail Marys so Our Lady will help you as well." He knelt next to me. He clasped his hands on his stomach, half closed his eyes, and started praying. The sparrows were chirping above us all around the barn, as if they were mad at being disturbed. I repeated all the seven deadly sins like father told me to, but none of them resembled the sin I'd committed. I wondered to myself, what's father hanging me for if it's only the deadly sins that God doesn't forgive?

All of a sudden the barn door creaked softly. I turned my head and in a patch of light at the edge of the threshing floor I saw mother. I looked over to father, but he seemed not to have heard her, he was still praying, his hands on his stomach, his eyes half closed.

"There's no wrongdoing so bad you can't forgive your own child," said mother. "And he's your child. Bad or good, he's yours."

I suddenly twisted my whole body around toward mother, the chain rattled again, and I called out:

"Mama, what's father hanging me for? I can just go climb the highest poplar across the dike and throw myself off!"

"Even if you kill him, he'll still be yours." This time it was like she hadn't heard me. "Except you won't be his father anymore, you won't even be a human being."

At that moment father's hands parted on his stomach and came to rest heavily on his knees. He seemed to be holding back tears under his half-closed eyelids. After a moment he wiped his eyes and said in a tired voice:

"Take him away. I'm going to kneel here awhile yet."

Another time, mother took me with her on a pilgrimage after the harvest.

A whole crowd of people went from our village and from other villages. Old folks, children, men, women, young girls and young men, married folks, single family members and whole families. The priest was there, and the organist, and Franciszek the sacristan. There were banners and the picture of Our Lady from our church. We walked from dawn till dusk with two breaks for a rest and one for dinner. Though some people wouldn't have rested at all, they'd have just kept on walking and walking. At night we mostly stopped in the villages, though one time we slept in the woods in the open air, and another time in haystacks that belonged to a manor. The breaks were also breaks from singing, because they sang the livelong day. Some folks even ignored the organist, who was supposed to be leading the singing, and they sang on in the breaks, mostly the people up front.

People went hoarse from all the singing, and after a couple of days it was nothing but rasping and croaking and barking till it hurt your ears to listen. The organist, it was like one of his lungs had dried up, he kept ordering more and more frequent breaks and he'd cough longer and longer after each hymn. But people didn't pay any mind to his coughing either and when he didn't begin the singing they'd start up themselves, and the organist had to join in whether he wanted or no. The keenest singer of all was Zdun. Maybe because people said he should have been the organist, if he'd only been a bit younger. Because apparently it used to be that if someone wanted a Veni Creator to be sung at their wedding so you could hear it all around the church, they'd always pick Zdun, and only the organist would accompany him. On the way back home Zdun actually lost his voice from all the singing and he had to communicate with people in sign language. My mother went hoarse as well, for two months afterward she kept drinking chamomile tea for her throat. It wasn't really surprising, given that the whole way we were walking in a cloud of dust. Twice there was a bit of drizzle, otherwise it was nothing but sunshine, and people got lumps in their throats from the dust and dryness.

I didn't sing because I didn't yet know the hymns, but my throat was dry as well and I kept spitting the whole time. Mrs. Orysz was walking in front of us and she moved farther forward because she said the Pietruszkas' kid wouldn't stop spitting. Mrs. Waliszyn actually got into an argument with mother, saying I'd spat on her skirt, she showed it and said, see, are you telling me the little brat didn't spit on me, take a look. Then he'll try to tell me I sat in some shit in the dust. I spat on Mikuta's boots as well because he happened to be passing by and he got in the way of my spit. But it hit the tops, he didn't feel it and he just carried on walking.

Mother gave me a rosary so I could say a few Our Fathers and Hail Marys instead of daydreaming. To begin with I carried it in my hands. But it felt awkward, like I had my hands tied together. Besides, even if you carry a feather for long enough it starts to feel as heavy as a whole chicken, or a goose or duck. So the rosary got to feel as heavy as a chain. I hung it round my neck and my arms immediately felt like wings.

We happened to be walking past a fruit orchard. There were raspberry apples shining in among the leaves. I could see mother was lost in song, her head held high, her eyes half closed, because we had the sun in our eyes. Below, the cloud of dust came up over our knees. To make matters worse Kolasa was walking next to us and he had a stiff leg from the war, it was like he was dragging that leg deliberately through the dust. Everyone was always moving away from him and telling him to go walk at the back, but he insisted on being in the middle.

To begin with I drifted away a bit so I wouldn't be right next to mother. Then I moved to the edge of the procession, and from there I slipped into the orchard. At that moment they were singing O Mary, we greet thee, and no one noticed me. Besides, everyone had gotten used to people disappearing off to the side to go to the toilet, they could have thought that's what I was doing. I ran to the apple tree with the most fruit and started picking as fast as my hands would go. I'd gotten an armful when I suddenly heard a shout through the trees:

"Get him, Azor! Catch the thief! I'll teach you to steal apples, you little bastard!"

But before Azor could reach me I was already back in the pilgrimage. The dog ran to the edge of the orchard and stopped in its tracks dumbfounded, because he'd been chasing one person and all at once he saw a whole swarm of people, all of them singing into the bargain. Instead of barking, he started this terrible howling. A moment later the farmer appeared out of the orchard, he shouted something and waved his walking stick and I thought he was about to chase me through the procession. I decided that if push came to shove I'd shelter under the banner. But all of a sudden he came to a halt too and fell silent, maybe it had occurred to him that he ought to go on a pilgrimage as well, because he'd racked up a whole lot of sins, that was for sure.

"Quiet, Azor, quiet," he said, calling the dog to heel. He took his hat off, and we walked on.

Later, two women up front started an argument, one of them said the other one had stepped on her heel so hard she'd made it bleed. Actually you couldn't even figure out who'd done what to who, they were jabbering so loud you could barely hear one of them saying the other one walked like a cart horse, the other one said the first one waddled like a duck, one of them sang like she only wanted Our Lady to hear her, the other one sounded like kasha boiling in the pan. The first one said the other one's husband ran around after other women, but you couldn't blame him because who could stand being with a dragon like her. The other one said the first one went chasing after other men herself. They were virtually at each other's throats, so maybe it wasn't just because of one stepping on the other one's heels. People from way the other end of the procession started calling out:

"Hey, quiet down at the front there! We can't hear ourselves sing! You ought to be ashamed of yourselves!"

One guy with a pockmarked face lifted up his walking stick and started pushing his way forward shouting:

"Get out of here! Get out! Damn nuisances! Witches!"

Other folks got mad with him in turn, asking him what he was doing pushing through like that. The way to God was the same whether you were at the front or the back. The important thing was to have a pure soul.

"Jesus and Mary!" someone yelled. "Goddammit! Are you blind?!"

"Stop cussing!" people told them off. "We took an oath there wouldn't be any bad language!"

I took advantage of the commotion and made my way back to mother.

"Where were you?" she asked me sharply.

But right at that moment, in an attempt to calm the procession down the organist started singing:

"Sing out, our lips, and tell the Virgin's praise! . . ."

The rest of the hymn followed from the crowd:

"Sing of her glory to the end of days! . . ." Mother joined in too.

I took an apple from inside my shirt and started eating. I ate four of them or more before the hymn ended. I was just finishing the last one when mother asked:

"Where did you get that?"

"From the orchard. We passed by an orchard, didn't you see, mama?"

"Throw it away," she snapped.

"It's ripe, mama!" I said almost in a shout. "Do you want a bite?"

"I said throw it away. And where's your rosary?"

It turned out the rosary had ended up on my back when I'd run from the orchard to get away from Azor. Or maybe I'd twisted it back there when I was sticking apples under my shirt.

"You should be embarrassed," she said, all upset, though she was talking in a whisper. "You're on a pilgrimage to repent your sins, and here you go stealing. He's a punishment from God, this boy. Are you ever going to mend your ways?"

Luckily Duda and his daughter were walking right behind us. Duda was as quarrelsome as the worst old woman, in the breaks between hymns he was forever arguing with someone, even his own daughter if there wasn't anyone else. She was an old maid and ugly as sin, but she was a real angel. It rarely did her any good though. Duda started grumbling again now:

"This isn't the right way. I'm telling you, we've been on the wrong road the whole time. This isn't the road. It's nothing but dust, and there's sight nor sound of the highway."

No one wanted to get into it with Duda about the road, because it wasn't the first time he'd said it. Besides, there was nothing but women around, the men were all closer to the back where they could at least have a bit of a natter. The women, even when they weren't singing they were whispering prayers or saying them in their heads, or counting their rosaries that they wore wrapped around their hands. But one of them couldn't take any more of Duda's griping and she said the priest was leading the pilgrimage, not Duda, and the priest knew which way was right and which way was wrong better than him. He wasn't going to get us lost, after all. Duda should cut it out or go take his own route if this one was the wrong one. But it didn't do any good, she just spurred Duda into attacking her and the priest as well, he said he's just a boy, not a priest, he's still wet behind the ears, all he knows is book learning. Her he went after for defending the priest, she was a young'un just like him, she was probably always hanging around the presbytery trying to get in his pants. How was a priest any better than a regular guy? The woman went red, she lowered her head and started quickly saying her rosary. The other women lost themselves in prayer the same, because none of them felt like tangling with Duda. Mother was the only one that told him off:

"Shame on you, Duda. There's a child present." This was meant to refer to me. She hugged my head to her side, forgetting about the apples.

Duda carried on bellyaching about the road, saying it was the wrong way.

"Whether it's the wrong one or the right one, it's leading us to God, daddy." His daughter Weronka tried to cheer him up. "Why don't you think about what you're going to ask him when we get there? Or would you like some bread and cheese?"

We stopped for the night in some village and we were already lying on hay in a barn when mother remembered about the stolen apples. Had I thrown them away? But she wasn't mad.

"It's just that my throat is dry," she said.

I still had four. I pulled one out of my shirt and pressed it into her hand in the dark.

"Here, mama," I said. "It was such a big orchard, the wind'll blow down more than this, or they'll fall on their own."

She took the apple, but it was like her hand was lifeless.

"It's a sin, Szymek," she said.

"Then let it be my sin," I said. "You can eat it, mama." To encourage her I took out another apple and started crunching away loudly. But I didn't hear her eating. Though maybe she just ate real quiet, or after I'd fallen asleep.

It was black as pitch in there, but you could hear absolutely everything, even from the farthest corners of the barn, who was doing what. Some people were eating, others were rubbing their aching feet, others still were saying their prayers, and some were already snoring. It was only the young folks that evidently weren't tired from the journey, and they were messing around like there was no tomorrow, every other minute you could hear a squeal from one of the girls accompanied by guffaws from the guys. In the end someone couldn't take it any longer and they shouted from the thresh-ing floor down below:

"Get to sleep, damn you! Or if you have to fool around, go outside!"

Silence filled the darkness for a moment, then things slowly started up again. Close to us some people took out a bottle of vodka, because as well as the smell, they were given away by the sound of the bottle as they pulled it from their lips. You could even tell if it was a man or a woman drinking. From time to time there was a gulping sound when someone must have taken too big a swig, or maybe their throat was sore from singing and the drink wouldn't go down smoothly.

For the longest time I couldn't get to sleep. The hay was prickly, and folks were snoring on every side. I could never have imagined that people snored in such different ways, even when they were all together in one big group. Some of them were quiet as anything, like they were just whistling a little under their breath to show what a good sleep they were having. Some were a little noisier, but it was still just as if they were spitting out the last remnants of their singing in their sleep. With others it came from the lungs, but it was still bearable. Worst of all were the old men, it was like they were struggling through a thicket of blackthorn and juniper and haw, or they were crossing pastureland and getting deeper and deeper into mud. At times one of them would make a cracking sound like he'd just torn down the trunk of a willow tree, then sat on the trunk and he was gasping. Though it could also have been a woman. On the pilgrimage there were women built like men, women like stoves, like barrels, sacks, drums, not just the skinny quarrel-some ones, or the spitfires or the painted young things. Some people in the corner nearby started giggling in a funny way, as if they were trying to be as quiet as they could, almost secretly, but you could tell they felt like laughing so loud the whole barn would hear them, maybe even the whole world. I thought they must be tickling each other, probably under the arms, because when you're tickled under your arms you want to laugh so bad you feel like jumping out of your skin.

"Mama, people are tickling each other over there," I whispered in mother's ear, not knowing she was barely awake.

"Don't listen, son, go to sleep," she sighed, and pulled me closer to her.

But how could I sleep when it sounded like at any moment one of them was about to jump up and run, probably the woman, run off over the hay and the other people, because it sounded as if they were short of breath. A short time later they started groaning and making a rustling sound. Mother was dog-tired and she fell asleep for good, the whole barn was asleep, and those people just kept groaning and groaning. Then every so often the woman said, oh Jasiu, oh Jasiu. And he'd say, shh.

The next day we were walking down a gravel road lined with acacias and suddenly someone said it was this road where bandits robbed farmers when they were on their way back from the market at Kawęczyn. At that, one woman burst out saying that it wasn't bandits, they just drank all their money away and afterward they blamed it on bandits. The farmers from our village used to travel to the Kawęczyn market, even though it was a long ways from us. They'd leave by night so as to arrive in the morning, then they'd travel back the whole of the next night and again arrive in the morning. And it also happened that someone would come back without two cents to rub together because he'd been robbed by bandits. Franek Szczerba's father came back one time on foot, without his horse and wagon, a week later, aching and hollow-cheeked. After he got back he didn't have the will to do anything, all he wanted was to sit around all day at the pub and drink, supposedly out of bitterness at having been robbed like that, and it goes without saying, on credit. But Franek let on to us that it wasn't bandits, his father had spent everything on an "auntie," but she'd dumped him anyway. Because Szczerba had had a lady friend in town in Kawęczyn. Franek had been at the lady's once when his father took him to market, and the lady had stroked Franek's hair and made him shiver. Then she gave him an orange and said:

"You have a nice son, Ignacy. All right, go play outside awhile, kid."

So maybe she was right, the woman that said it wasn't bandits, because what would bandits be doing on an ordinary road like this one. We took a break and sat on either side of the road in the shade of the acacias, and right away we felt sleepy. It hurt to think we'd have to be setting off again in just a moment. Plus, birds were chirping so nicely among the leaves. Not far away there was a manor house, you could see its roof peeping out from the grounds. Some people started talking about what life must be like in a manor like that, on its grounds. But the organist got up, and the priest, and we had to set off again.

I might not have remembered that road, it was just a road like any other, there are roads like that everywhere, if it hadn't come back to me several years later. A couple of miles from Kawęczyn, in the Kawęczyn woods, it was September, my unit was stationed in the village of Maruszew. One day, out of the blue we were surrounded by Germans. Someone must have informed on us, otherwise how could they have known? The village was right in the middle of the woods, and the woods were huge. Beyond the village there was a river and more woods. There was one guy, maybe he'd been the one? But if it wasn't him, may God strike me down. His code name was "Prosecutor." Truth be told, I didn't like those kind of names. I liked "Honeybee," "Birchtree," "Mint," "Goldfinch." But he picked Prosecutor, let it be Prosecutor. When I asked him why that name, he said he wanted to study law after the war.

"Putting all this on trial. Measuring out punishments. There'll be more work than you can shake a stick at," he said.

"Who's going to believe in the law after the war, are you daft?" I tried to convince him. "And what kind of profession is the law. All they'll do is curse you out. Even being a farmer's better than that, though that's no profession either. But at least you don't get in anyone's way. You'd be better off being a dentist. People's teeth are going to be all messed up from the war, then you'd really have all the work you could handle. And Dentist sounds better than Prosecutor."

Before the war he'd worked for the town hall. He'd graduated high school, he was a smooth talker and he had nice writing. So I thought to myself, he could write the death sentences, if he's so keen on being Prosecutor. Because no one was willing to write them. And there were orders from above, you weren't allowed to kill even the biggest bastard without a sentence. No one knew why, because why did a son of a bitch like that need a written judgment, but that's how it was. His eyes sparkled and he got to work right away. We were supposed to rub out this restaurant owner in Tylice, because he'd turned out to be a snitch. So write it down, Prosecutor. He brings it to me, I read it and I can't tell if it's a sentence or a sermon.

"Make it shorter," I tell him. "Write it again."

He brings it again and it's the same thing. I start explaining to him, but I'm already getting annoyed.

"When you're killing someone, there's no time to be reading stuff. Why would you even want to? He's not gonna remember it. Write it again."

He brings it once again, and this time I'm really pissed off.

"Are you nuts? We're just going there to kill him, what the heck have you written here? Who's even going to listen to any of this? God? Not the guy, for sure! Even a son of a bitch like him, when he's about to die death'll stop up his ears and his eyes. What the hell are you talking to him about Satan for?! Have you ever seen Satan? No! Then don't talk bullshit! When someone doesn't see the person inside them, they're not going to see Satan. They'll either go to hell or they won't. You don't know, and neither do I, even though I'm your commanding officer. No one knows. There are times you could be sent there for less, then for worse things you repent and you're not sent. Piece of work like him, he could have all kinds of ways to get out

· 456

of being sent. If he wants he'll pull the wool over God's eyes, and Satan's as well, and he'll do a bunk while you lot are still reading to him. Plus, how do you know a guy like that isn't going to be better off in hell than in heaven. I mean look, we've got hell on earth down here but him, the scumbag, he's opened a restaurant and on top of that he's selling people out. Besides, what's it to you whether he goes to hell or not? Hell or heaven, he just needs to be gone from here. Got it? Hell doesn't have to be what you think. You can spend your whole life working in the fields or going to your office with your briefcase, and that can be hell. Did you used to have a briefcase? There you go then. Write it again."

But nothing came of it even though he kept trying and trying, and in the end we had to kill the restaurant owner without a sentence. Afterwards Prosecutor moped around all dejected, and in the end I felt sorry for him and I called him in again.

"Try writing a couple more," I told him. "Make up some bad guys. You'll get the hang of it, you will."

Maybe I'd been wrong to throw him in at the deep end like that, I thought. Doing anything well takes hard work. Sometimes you need to go one small step at a time, for years sometimes. Take mowing, no one's born knowing how to pick up a scythe and just start mowing. Their father has to teach them, they have to watch other people doing it, they have to make a mess of a good few swaths, even bang up their scythe. I think I gave him good advice when I said to make up bad guys as an exercise. What else was I supposed to tell him? He was an office worker that had graduated high school, I'd barely finished seventh grade. Also, in the spring of seventh grade father took me out of school for good because he'd started the plowing, he happened to be doing the hill up by the woods, and he didn't have anyone else to lead the horse by the head to make sure the furrow was straight. Of course there was Michał. Except Michał was afraid of the horse's head, and besides, he always got headaches from the sun. But it didn't matter, no one ever went anywhere after seventh grade, they just kept working the land, so leaving school a couple months early made no difference. So he says to me, I have a request. Go on? He says, if he had a typewriter he'd learn to write sentences in two shakes of a lamb's tail. He just couldn't get the hang of it when he wrote in longhand. Besides, what kind of sentence is it when it's written by hand.

"A typewriter?" I was taken aback. But he used to work in an office, I guessed he must know what you could write on a typewriter and what you could write by hand. "Well, if we can get one somewhere it'll be yours."

A short time later we organized a raid on the Arbeitsamt in Kołomierz. We were after the lists of people being sent to do forced labor. He was supposed to just take a typewriter, but he also got writing paper, carbon paper, paper clips, pencils, erasers, other things as well, even a hole punch. He carted a whole sack full of stuff into the woods. He was as pleased as a little kid with a bag full of toys.

After that he'd take the typewriter off into the woods, hide himself away in the bushes, and write. He'd put it on a tree stump and kneel in front of it. Often you could hear him, it was like a woodpecker pecking away far off in the woods. The lads made fun of him, they said he must be writing love letters to his girlfriends or maybe poetry, and some of them wanted him to write a poem for them so they could send it to their own girlfriends. Because other than me, no one knew what he was actually writing.

In the end, curiosity got the better of one of the men, he took the sentences out of the other guy's knapsack while he was asleep and he brought them straight to me to read. I started reading and my hair stood on end. Every one of them was for someone in the unit. Carp, Rowan, Honeybee, Pinecone, Birchtree, Stag, Cricket, Burdock, Knothole. There was one for me too. On every one there were crimes like the worst son of a bitch. And every one of them was sentenced to death. The higher ranking ones were sent to hell as well. Naturally that included me. I thought to myself, that damn typewriter's driven him insane. Maybe there's something inside a machine like that, if it makes a man stop trusting his own hand.

"Get Prosecutor in here this second! What the hell have you written here, you bastard? Who told you to do this?"

"You did, sir."

"Me?! I told you to make up some bad guys! Dear God, if I wasn't your commanding officer I'd smack you in the face!" I ripped up all the sentences. "From now on, no more writing!" I changed his code name from "Prosecutor" to "Skylark," and I ordered the typewriter to be smashed against a tree, who needed a typewriter in the woods.

After that he went around with a wild expression in his eyes, like he was looking but not seeing. He didn't talk to anyone. They even said he wasn't eating much, he'd just poke his spoon in his mess can a bit then throw the food out for the birds. A few days later he disappeared from the unit and we never heard from him again.

Dawn was just breaking when first from the river, then from the woods, we heard shots, and the dogs in the village started barking. To this day I can't figure out how it could have happened. We had lookouts posted, and for several days before there hadn't been any outsiders in the village, no one from the village had left. It was another thing that they took us from the woods, and from the south side at that, where no one would have expected them. There wasn't even a cutting through the trees that way. And the Germans were scared to death of the woods. Especially woods like around Kawęczyn, where there was no telling where they began or where they ended. Maruszew was surrounded by woods on three sides, and half on the fourth. There was just the one road led there, and that was only a track. It was a good three and a half miles to the dirt road and twice as far to the highway, and you had to ride a whole day by wagon to get to the railroad stop. No German had ever appeared there, they might not even have known there was such a village. God himself seemed to have forgotten about Maruszew. As well as being far away from the rest of the world, people had a poor life of it there. The earth was sandy, and what can you grow in sandy soil. Rye, oats, potatoes, and that was how they lived out their days. Though in front of every house there was a little garden, and in each garden there were sunflowers, so you could have thought people led happy lives there. Because the sunflowers shone like little suns, even when the big sun went behind the clouds.

Whenever we wanted to clean up and wash our clothes, lick our wounds and get our strength back, and live like humans at least for a bit, we'd go to Maruszew even just for a couple of days. They'd take us in and share whatever they had with us, and though they didn't have much, when you were there you felt the war wasn't happening. You ate potato pancakes, drank homebrew vodka, and slept in beds. I even had a girl there. Tereska was her name. She was pretty as a picture and the kindest soul you could hope to meet. Her parents never said anything, even though when I was there we'd live like husband and wife. I never said anything about marrying her. Sometimes I'd promise to visit after the war if I lived, but maybe they didn't believe I'd survive, and they preferred me to leave their daughter sinful and single than a widow. I still have the little religious medal she gave me one time so I'd always come back safe and sound. I'd often not see her for half a year or more, but every time she'd greet me like the dry earth greets the rain. Right away she'd bring the bathtub, set the water to heat in the kettles, and make the bed. Her parents would go off without a word and busy themselves with something, or go in the other room, and she'd tell me to take my clothes off and get in the tub. She'd soap up my back, pour water over me out of a mug, then help me dry myself. Who knows, maybe I might have married her after the war, but they burned her along with the whole village. She had broad hips, breasts like cabbage heads, she would have made children, two, maybe three.

I pulled on my pants and boots in a flash, grabbed my Sten from the chair, and put my jacket on as I ran. As I was crossing the hallway, behind me I heard her sob, Szymek! But there wasn't even time to turn around and say, Tereska. I rushed outside. A few of the lads were crouching and moving along outside the house, firing straight ahead. But there were furious bursts of machine-gun fire coming at the village from every direction, from the fields, the woods, the river. I tried to give orders, but there was no one to carry them out and no one to pass them on. The village wasn't at all big, but in the confusion everyone was trying to escape however they could. They fired every which way, without rhyme or reason, from attics, round the corners of houses, the men were pressed against the ground, against walls, a tree, a fence. Some of them I had to shake, I gave an order, didn't you hear? No firing at random! Retreat to the end of the village! We'll take up positions there! On top of it all, the villagers starting running out of their homes. What's happening?! It's the end of the world! Jesus and Mary! There was shouting, wailing. Women, men, mothers with babies, children woken from their sleep.

There was some witch of a woman in a long nightshirt, her hair like a crow's nest and holding a crucifix, she started going on about how the whole world was taking revenge because of us, it was all our fault, because we kept coming here to have our way with the local girls and do bad things, because we'd made whores of them all. Maruszew had become Sodom and Gomorrah! And now God was sending down a punishment! But why Maruszew of all places? Lord, why Maruszew?!

Someone galloped by on horseback shouting, run! run! They'll burn the place down! They'll throw people into the flames! Someone herded their cattle out from the farmyard into the road and drove them along, lashing their backs and legs. Two small children in ragged hemp shirts ran by hand in hand, crying. They were followed by their mother, her hair all awry, she was crying even louder than them and shouting, Iruś, Magda, come back! Where do you think you're going, you little fools, come back! The first house at the edge of the village by the woods was already on fire.

Finally I managed to gather together some of the unit. We divided into three groups that were supposed to follow each other, and I gave the order to try and break through towards the river. I was in the last group. It was a good ways down to the river, plus the fields were bare because harvesttime was long past. Luckily it was just before the potato digging. We could crawl along the furrows in the potato fields, or at the very least hide our heads among the stalks. The nearest and surest way would have been to the woods, but they'd closed the woods to us like a barn door. In the first moment a dozen or so of the men had headed for the woods, with Sorrel in the lead. They'd been mowed down, hardly a handful made it back. It seemed like there wouldn't be as many of the Germans around the fields, because that was the direction they'd least expect us to take. And in the fields they could be seen just like we could.

The last group started shooting first so we'd draw their fire, they immediately let loose a vicious barrage of shots. During this time the first two groups were crawling across the potato field. When they were about halfway the second group suddenly started firing, and under their cover the first group got even closer. Then, when the first group let them have it from right close up, you could even move forward in jumps. We started lobbing grenades. And we made it out. The only thing left was for us in the third group to provide cover for the other two groups to cross the river.

Suddenly, I felt a jolt in my stomach and my eyes went blank. It was even good not to feel or see anything. I don't know how long I lay there, but when I opened my eyes I thought I was in the next world. And maybe the lark in the sky was Tereska's soul that had risen from her burned body and was singing over me so as not to let me die. And the farmer that way far off in the distance was plowing something that seemed half like earth, half like sky – maybe that was her father, and he was only a spirit as well. And maybe only her mother was in this world, keening, "Lord Jesuuuus!"

Almost a third of our unit perished, including the ones they caught alive, and the wounded. They packed them into trucks, threw in the menfolk from the village they'd not already burned or shot, and on the same Kawęczyn road we'd taken that time on the pilgrimage, they hung them from the acacia trees. They didn't have enough nooses so they took all the halters off the cows in the squire's herd. They didn't have a high enough ladder so in Wicentów, where the procession had spent the night that time, they sounded the alarm and stuck the firefighters and their ladder in another truck. And once they started hanging they couldn't stop, it was like when a drunk starts drinking and he just can't stop himself. Actually they were also drunk, some of them couldn't stand up straight, and one of them, when he clambered up the ladder to tie the noose to a branch, he fell off with a crash. The whole way there they were singing dirty songs. When they ran out of our men to hang and there were still some trees left, they hung whoever came down the road.

There was a doctor from Młynary came along in a wagon, he was on his way to a woman that was about to give birth. He even knew German but it didn't do him any good, the bastards still hung him. They hung him higher up and the guy that had been driving the wagon, who was the husband of the woman having the baby, they hung him lower down on the same tree. Some musicians came up the road on bicycles on their way to play at a wedding somewhere, an accordionist, a fiddler, clarinet, trombone, and drums, five of them. First they made them play something. When they started up, the trees actually shook, though there was no wind at all. Truth be told, they couldn't play as well as they played that day, because they weren't the best musicians in the world, like Bargiel from Oleśnica, for instance, or Wojcieszko from Modrzejów. When Kużyk's daughter over at Stary Bór got married, Wojcieszko's band played at the wedding for three days without sleeping. They just kept their eyes open, ate, drank, and kept playing. But maybe the Lord God helped them out, or they were so afraid of death that they played better than they were really able. And they were probably already thinking they'd play for a while then hop back on their bikes and ride off on their way. But those sons of bitches were enjoying it so much they stomped their feet and shouted, more, more! Turns out you can keep death away with music.

There was an accordionist lived in our village once. Grab was his name. He was a band all on his own, all he needed extra was a drum. He could make that accordion sound like a fiddle, a clarinet, a trombone, even a church organ. He didn't stretch it out, he just ran his fingers over the buttons and played. His fingers bent both ways, like they were made of wicker. You couldn't find another musician to equal him in the whole neighborhood, probably even farther. When he finally took to his bed, because he was really old, he put his accordion on a stool right by the bedside and whenever death drew close to him, he'd play. And death would go away again. He'd probably have lived till he got tired of life. But something went wrong with his accordion, the buttons still kind of worked but the bellows were somehow short of breath. And he died. People said that the kind of music he played for death, no one had ever heard it in their lives, there may never have been music like that ever before. It gave you gooseflesh, cats would run from the house, dogs would howl, horses would rear up as they were pulling their wagons. And if anyone happened to be passing by his house when he was playing they couldn't help but stop and stand there like a dead man.

But that was long ago and there hadn't been any war, maybe death liked listening to music. In wartime, though, death has no hearing. All that came of their playing on the Kawęczyn road was that they hung them on a single tree. They didn't smash their instruments, they just hung them along with the musicians. The accordion with the accordion player, the fiddle with the fiddler, the drummer with his drum on his belly, and so on. One of the soldiers even took a picture of them, another one let off a round at the drum.

A farmer came by taking his cow to be serviced, they hung him too. One idiot went out in front of his house to watch them drive by. Actually they might not have hung him, because he was standing behind his fence and there was only his head sticking out. But he wanted to make a good impression so he took off his cap and bowed. And that evidently made such a good impression they hung him. Another guy, they asked him where the village chairman lived. The guy didn't understand, and he shook his head and shrugged to say he didn't. How could he understand when our language comes from the earth and theirs comes from iron. Earth can't understand iron. They hung him too.

They also hung the squire from Jasień, the same one that they took the halters off his cows. But him they hung from his gateway, not from a tree. There were three gates into the manor, two ordinary ones for everyday use, and a third one that was only used once in a blue moon, as the expression goes. The other two were on the side facing the village, the third one opened onto the road with the acacia trees. From there there was an avenue lined with lindens that led directly to the courtyard in front of the manor house. The third gate was usually closed, they'd only open it on special occasions, a ball, or if an important guest was coming. Even when the squire and his lady drove to church on Sunday, they'd just use one of the regular gates. But when the squire's daughter Klementyna was coming home from her studies for the summer vacation, the big gate would stand wide open all day. All the boys from the manor and from the village would climb the trees along the road and watch to see if they could spot the carriage with the young mistress coming into view. They'd get twenty groszes for their pains. When the carriage appeared, they'd pass word from one tree to the next, all along the acacias, through the gate, along the lindens, and across the grounds to the manor, to say she was on her way. Every living soul would come out of the manor onto the courtyard, not just the squire and his wife and their relatives, but the footmen and the chambermaids and cooks. When the carriage pulled into the courtyard they wouldn't let the young lady get out on her own, but they'd pluck her from her seat like a flower and stand her on the steps in front of her parents. The young lady would be all happy and smiling at everyone, prattling away, and throwing her arms around some of the servants so her hat fell off and rolled down the steps, and everyone chased after it. It sometimes happened that dinner got burned, but no one was punished, since it was because of the young mistress.

They started hammering on the gate with their rifle butts. First, one of the servants came out, but he didn't have a key. They shot him dead. Then the squire came with the key, but he couldn't get the gate to open, he tried every which way but nothing worked. In the end he managed to unlock it. But they were furious at having had to wait so long, so they hung him. Though was it his fault the gate wouldn't open? They hadn't unlocked it since the war began. The young mistress had come back from her studies for good and now she just stayed home, which is to say at the manor. And when someone important came it would be on the quiet, and they used one of the side gates. So apparently the big gate was so rusty they couldn't open it even after it was unlocked, and the hinges creaked so loud the bastard soldiers held their ears and stamped their feet. People said that God was protesting that way. But what could even God do about it when there were twenty truckloads of them, all armed to the teeth.

The gate is actually still standing today, except it's in the middle of fields and it doesn't lead anywhere. Because when they divvied up the manor lands after the war, there wasn't so much as a fence post left. Folks cut down the trees in the grounds for building houses or for firewood. The same went for the avenue of lindens that led down to the gate. The manor house was demolished down to the foundations. And now it's just fields like everywhere else. Wherever you look there's rye, wheat, clover, barley, potatoes, beets, carrots. And the gateway, standing in the middle of the fields like someone just stuck it there because otherwise things would be too flat. Two tall gateposts joined at the top with a half-rounded arch where there used to be a lamp on a wrought-iron chain. That was where they hung the squire. The gates themselves were wrought iron as well, they had twisted designs with lilies and bindweed and vines or something. They always had to be opened by two men at once, one wouldn't have been able to do it. And since then they were locked for good. Because when they took the squire's body down someone locked the gate again, and the key disappeared.

After the war all kinds of people tried to open it. Some blacksmith guy, some cooper, a tiler, even a fellow that mended radios. Mechanics from the farmers' circle, tractor drivers, all kinds of folks. It's only natural, there's never any lack of people that want to know what's on the other side. One time somebody's relative from America came and offered a hundred dollars to whoever could get it open. People started trying again. All sorts of different types rolled in from far and wide. To begin with, none of them had any luck. The relative from America was convinced it couldn't be done, and he upped the offer to a hundred and fifty, then two hundred. And they got it open. What can money not do. Except that when they saw on the other side of the gate there was just grain and beets and carrots like everywhere else, they took fright and locked it up again so hard that the key twisted in the lock, and it stayed that way. And now it's shut forever.

Not long ago a foreign tour was on its way to Kawęczyn by bus. When they saw the gateway in the middle of the fields they had the driver stop, and they got out and started laughing and laughing, saying what a strange country we were, building gateways in the middle of fields as if they led to mansions, when people could go any way they wanted around the gate. Kuśmierz from Jasień was plowing near the gateway, and they started taking photographs of him from every side as he worked. Then one of them gave him a pack of cigarettes. Kuśmierz didn't want to take them because he didn't know what he was being given them for, but one of the guys from the bus said:

"*Gute Zigaretten.*"

So he took them, but he lit up one of his own. Then they asked him:

"What's this gateway? Did someone build it at the entrance to their field?

Do you have to go through it when you're sowing? Is that maybe a custom in these parts? Does it make your crops grow better? How much do you get per acre?"

But Kuśmierz didn't tell them the truth. He thought to himself, they came all this way to visit us, they even gave him a pack of cigarettes, he'd feel kind of foolish telling them the truth. So he told them that no one built the gateway, that it grew there of its own accord. Because gateways like that, they grow around here, some places are thick with them. No one plants them or sows them, they just grow there like trees. The soil is rich, all it takes is for the wind to bring a seed or a bird to drop one from its beak. Around here you can find whole stands of gateways.

Three days they all hung there on the acacia trees, because the local village chairmen were forbidden to take them down for three days, the same for the squire in the gateway. Their hands were tied behind them with barbed wire, their feet were bare, all they had on were pants and shirts. Luckily it was a warm September, day after day the sun shone in a clear sky, there was gossamer floating in the air and the nights were mild. So at least they didn't freeze like they would have if they'd been hanging in the rain and cold, at least they weren't swung back and forth by the storm winds that often blow that time of year.

For the longest time after the war no one took that road to get to the market in Kawęczyn. They'd go through Zawady, though it was an extra four miles. Because all sorts of things happened to people when someone dug their heels in and insisted on riding that road, or taking it on foot. Sometimes, in the middle of the day they'd chance to look up and they'd see bare feet dangling among the leaves, or a rope with a big noose hanging from a branch. Or even the horses, you'd think they wouldn't care about humans or the things that go on among them, but who knows if they don't think humans are just like horses for them, just like they're horses for people, in any case they'd prick up their ears and snort, and toss, and strain in the traces.

One farmer from Mikulczyce had a stallion black as a raven, with white fetlocks and a white flash on its forehead. Everyone envied him that stallion. When it was pulling his wagon it would hold its head up high and take short steps, like a young woman that's trying to please the boys. The farmer never had to use the whip, he never had to call, whoa! or giddyup! like with other horses. He'd just hold the reins in his hand and give a slight tug, and the horse knew which way to go, left or right or straight on, at a trot. So the farmer reckoned a horse like that could go through hell and back, not just down the road to Kawęczyn. But when he started on that road, the horse suddenly reared up, and it wouldn't budge an inch. The farmer gave it the whip on its legs and its back, god damn you, you this and you that, you think you're getting any more oats you're mistaken, it'll be nothing but chaff from now on! But the horse just set off headlong across the fields. It tipped over the wagon, broke the shaft, the farmer messed up his back, and the horse ran all the way through one village and then the next and it probably would have kept running even farther, but its heart gave up and it fell down dead. Another guy rode that way on a pregnant mare, and everyone knows a pregnant mare is patient and obedient, it'll go anywhere you tell it to. So it went down the road, but later it gave birth to a dead foal.

Or years after the war, the Sputnik was flying across the sky with a dog in it, when Drzazga was coming back from the district offices in Daszew. It was around noon. He was exhausted, because he'd waited forever at the offices and still not gotten what he wanted, so he sat under one of those acacia trees for a moment. Next to it there was the stump of another tree that had been cut down because it was too old. At one moment he looked over at the stump, and sitting on it there was a guy with a halter around his neck, barefoot, in pants and shirt, his hands tied behind with barbed wire, and he says to Drzazga:

"Do you know how far it is to Wólka from here? They cut down my tree, my land's gone, and I don't know where I am."

Wólka? Wólka? Drzazga thought and thought and he was on the point of asking him, which one? Because Wólka's a common name, there's one in every district. Then all at once the guy jumps up and rushes off. All he remembered was he was really young and his hair was blond.

Blond and really young, it must have been "Grasshopper." The hair on his chin was just beginning to sprout, he envied "Kuba" because Kuba had a beard like a dog's coat, plus he shaved with a razor. He always held Kuba's mirror for him when he was shaving, and in return Kuba would shave Grasshopper once a week. He'd lather him up nice and thick from his throat to his nose, almost up under his eyes, so it would look like he had a full beard like a grown man. Then he'd strop his razor, and he'd go about it wholeheartedly, like he was shaving a real man. He'd even pluck a hair from his own mop and use it to test whether the razor blade was good and sharp. And though the razor didn't scrape against Grasshopper's beard, like it was just wiping off the lather, Kuba would say to make him feel better:

"There, you hear it scraping? It's starting to grow in. You're gonna have a fine beard, thicker than mine."

But Grasshopper never lived to see his beard. In return for shaving him, he'd taught Kuba how to make the sound of a turtledove. After Grasshopper died, Kuba would make turtledove noises over and over till it drove you nuts. Kuba had wanted to learn how to sound like a turtledove because he had an ash tree in front of his house that turtledoves nested in. And he figured that when he got home he'd be most likely to find out from the turtledoves what had really been going on while he was gone – in the village, at home, with his wife and children. Grasshopper wanted to teach him the stork as well, when you're down you can cheer yourself up by clattering like a stork, Kuba. But no, he was only interested in turtledoves. He wanted to teach him the skylark, you can sing to yourself while you're plowing, Kuba. No, only the turtledove. What did you need to know the truth for, Kuba?

Because there wasn't a bird Grasshopper couldn't imitate. He could do a blackbird, a cuckoo, a kite, a nightingale, an oriole, a starling, a woodpecker, a roller, a bullfinch, whatever you wanted. He could do a magpie when it was going to rain, and a different magpie when it was a sign of something bad about to happen. A rooster, he crowed better than a real one. We'd be stationed deep in the woods but you'd think there were houses close by, because roosters kept crowing. And they crowed one way for midnight, another way when they'd been with a hen. He could croak like one crow or like a hundred when a flock of them roosts in the tops of the poplar trees, and like a thousand when they're gliding across a deep blue sky at sunrise. Sometimes the guys would name birds that I didn't even think existed. He could do every one. One of the men in particular, "Pistol," he was a biology teacher. He'd come up with all kinds of weird names, I'd sometimes say to him, shut the hell up, Pistol, those aren't real birds. I know a good few kinds of birds myself, but those ones I'd never heard of. Stuff like whimbrel, godwit, ruff, bunting. He swore they lived in the woods in Poland. Maybe they do, why would you not believe a teacher.

I was shot three times that day, twice in the side and the third one in the belly. They weren't deep wounds, fortunately, they mostly just grazed the skin. I holed up in the attic of the presbytery at Płochcice. Not many people thought I'd pull through. They came to visit me, the doctor and the priest in turn. The doctor just shook his head like he couldn't believe I was still alive, while the priest kept checking to see if it wasn't time for last rites. It made me so mad that in the end I started making nice with the priest's housekeeper. She gave me one of his old cassocks, a cloak, a hat, shoes, shirts, pants, even a prayer book, and one day at dawn, when everyone was still asleep I slipped out of the presbytery dressed as a priest.

I'd been home not so long before, in the summer during the harvest, so they weren't expecting me. But they could have heard what went down in Maruszew. Besides, I had a yen stronger than ever to see mother. It was thirty-five miles or more from Płochcice to our village, plus I had to choose a route so I'd meet as few people as possible, I had to avoid forest roads and paths and other villages. And it wasn't enough that I was all bandaged up, I also felt awkward in the priest's outfit. I regretted not having dressed as a regular person, it's just there weren't any other clothes at the presbytery. As it was, the housekeeper had given me all that stuff in fear that she was committing sacrilege. It was only when she saw me dressed up that she said:

"May God lead you, and may he forgive me."

It was another matter that the priest was a bit shorter than me, and bigger in the belly, but in that place I couldn't tighten the clothes because that's where my wounds were, so I looked a bit like I'd borrowed an outfit from my younger brother. The sleeves barely reached past my elbows, the cassock came halfway up my shins, and the tightest part of all was across the shoulders. By the time I'd gone a few miles I was as exhausted as if I'd been carrying a heavy weight. On top of that, at every step it felt like someone was sticking a bayonet in my side, from the wounds. So I couldn't even concentrate and think about the things a priest ought to think about. And all the while I had to hold myself straight like a priest, and have a cheerful expression on my face, like I was thinking about God. Plus, every other minute someone came along and greeted me, Christ be praised, and you have to raise your hat every time and answer, for all time. Though somehow I managed. What was worse, quite often when someone saw a priest coming toward them they'd immediately stop and wait, they were pleased as punch that chance had plonked a priest in their path for them to talk to. What do you think, father, how are things going to turn out for us? Did you hear what those villains did over at Maruszew, father, they hung them all along the Kawęczyn road. Where's God in all that, father? How can he look down calmly on such things? And you'd have to make stuff up, tell lies about God when you had no idea what you were doing, say that his judgments are inscrutable, that all we can do is pray for the folks from Maruszew. Or someone asks you, I guess you're from a different parish, father, or have they sent us a new curate.

One farmer came by in his wagon, I even turned my head away, but he pulled up, whoa, and said he'd give me a ride, because he couldn't allow a priest to go on foot. Whether I liked it or no, I had to get in. Then in the wagon he asks, have you come from far? Actually your face is sort of familiar, you look a bit like this guy that they say died at Maruszew. The parish ought to be ashamed they can't afford a decent cassock for you.

The whole thing tired me out even more than the wounds. I got as far as Mierniki, there I went to a fellow I knew and changed into ordinary clothes. Besides, what would mother have said if she'd seen me dressed as a priest? I spent the night there and continued on my way. The man I stayed with wanted to give me a bicycle. I tried, but riding was worse than walking. A couple of times someone gave me a ride a bit of the way. I wasn't a priest anymore so I wasn't afraid to talk about why I was on the road. I'd say I was going to see about a horse, that most of all I was hoping for a dapple. Another time I said I was setting up as a beekeeper and I was looking for a good queen.

It was late when I found myself in our yard. The dog recognized me at once and started whimpering and rubbing against my leg. I took hold of its snout and said, quiet, Burek, I'm not here, you're a dog but you have to understand, I'm nowhere to be seen. Like a person he understood and wagged his tail, and slunk back to his kennel.

There was a bit of a frost and maybe because of that I started getting the shivers, because as long as I'd been walking I was too hot, I'd been drenched in sweat. I crouched behind the corner of the barn and decided to wait there for mother to come out for the evening milking. I looked up at the sky, nothing had changed, the stars were still in their same places for that time of year. The Big Dipper was over the poplar tree at Błach's place, the Little Dipper a bit farther. Maybe it was from staring at the sky that my head suddenly started to spin. For a moment I thought I was going to pass out, but it gradually passed.

I didn't want to go into the house so as not to get into an argument with father like last time. It wasn't for that I'd come all this way on foot, and wounded. I just wanted to see mother and tell her I was alive, because she could already be praying for my soul after what happened at Maruszew. Besides, that earlier time I'd come at the wrong moment, during the harvest. Everyone knows that during the harvest a person can only understand himself. They'd been getting ready for bed, mother was in her nightshirt kneeling by the turned-down bed, saying her prayers. Father was soaking his feet in a basin. He could at least have said:

"Thank God you're alive."

Or:

"You're not looking so good."

Or:

"So how are things?"

Mother started giving vent to all her grievances as she heated up some pierogies for me in the frying pan:

"It's enough to make you dizzy, he disappears all this time, dear Lord. Then yesterday a magpie perched on the ash tree and it kept cawing and cawing, it set my heart pounding, something must have happened to Szymek. I said to father, Józuś, shoo that evil bird away, something bad must have happened to Szymek. In the end I threw a rock at it myself and chased it away. I pray so much for you, I ask Jesus and Mary to keep you in their care. Every night you're in my dreams. One night I dreamed you brought a cross into the yard. I asked you where you got it and you said it was lying by the roadside when you were coming back from the fields. And you asked me, mama, where should I put it? I said, put it in Sekuła's yard by his wagon barn. It'd be a waste, mama, you said, the wood in a cross like this must have a lot of resin in it. Szymek, I don't think I could live if they killed you "

All father did was take his feet out of the basin and rest them on the rim to let the water run off. Then all at once he yells at mother:

"Come on, give me something!"

"What do you want?"

"I need to wipe my feet!"

She threw him a cloth, and as he bent down he said:

"Why would they kill him. You think he has it so bad. I'm telling you, they made up that resistance stuff to get out of doing any work. They left their fathers and mothers, what do they care about anything. And you, you don't even have time to scratch yourself on the backside, but you're always praying for them, crying for them. There aren't any dances for them to go play at, so now they're playing at soldiers."

"It's not exactly a game, father," I said, but without taking offense. "The work's just as hard."

"And what work do you do exactly?" He was so furious he was hissing.

So I got riled up as well and I said:

"We kill people."

"You kill people? Not every day you don't. If you were a good son you'd show up once in a while and do some mowing. Or I don't have anyone to help me bring the crop in. Antek's still little, all he does is run around among the sheaves!"

"Every day, father. Sometimes the day's not long enough." I could barely hold my rage in check.

"Then once in a while, hold off with the killing and come help out." He stopped wiping his feet, looked at me, and asked as if he was surprised: "And your hand never shakes when you're doing it?"

"No."

"Then you're not our blood anymore."

I leaped up and slammed the door so hard it groaned. Mother ran out after me, but I rushed off into the orchard and headed down toward the river.

This time, the front door creaked and the pale light of a lantern appeared on the threshold. Mother's shadow moved off toward the cattle shed. It seemed smaller than usual, or maybe the night was bigger. In one hand she was carrying a pail for the milk, the other hand held the swinging lamp. The frozen ground crunched under her feet. I was about to go out to meet her, but it occurred to me that if I rose up in front of her out of the blue like that she might think it wasn't me but my ghost. Because it was a starry, moonlit night, a night that seemed made for souls to do penance. And the dog was sitting quietly in its kennel, because dogs can't smell ghosts. She went into the shed. I could still see a faint light from her lamp through the half-open doorway.

"Come here! Move back a bit!" I heard her say to the cow.

I looked over at the kennel to check whether the dog wasn't going to jump out and give me away. But no, it evidently still got what I'd told it. I started creeping along the wall toward the light, and when I reached it I quietly stuck my face in the doorway. I felt a waft of warmth, animal sweat, manure. And I suddenly reckoned I understood why God wanted to be born in a cattle shed. Slow as anything I opened up the lighted crack. The door creaked, but mother seemed not to hear. She was sitting hunched over beneath the big belly of the cow, as if she was lost in prayer, with only her hands working somewhere in the belly's depths. Milk was squirting from those hands of hers into the pail she held between her knees. The milk splashing into the pail was the only sound in the whole shed, maybe even the whole world.

"Mama," I whispered.

At that exact moment the milk came to a stop in her hands. She raised her head slowly, looked around the roof and the walls, and asked softly:

"Szymek?"

"Not there, mama. Here," I said more boldly, and walked into the shed, closing the door behind me. She looked at me unbelievingly. It was like she didn't have the strength to get up from her stool. The cow even waved its tail a couple of times, asking why she'd stopped milking it.

"So, mama. How are things with you all?"

"You're alive?" she said. And it was like her entire body burst out crying, not just her eyes.

"Careful, or it'll get in the milk," I said, and took the pail from her. "It'd be a pity to have to throw it out."

All at once she stopped her crying, like biting off a thread in her teeth. She wiped her eyes on her apron.

"Wait now, I'll finish the milking," she said.

"I have to be going right away," I said, because what else was I supposed to say.

"Won't you even come in the house?"

"I can't. They're waiting for me."

"Then at least drink some milk."

I lifted the pail to my mouth and tipped it.

"You've gotten thin, you're not looking well, son," she said, starting her lament. But my head was almost completely stuck in the pail, and her voice sounded like it was coming from far away. "Michał was here. He had something he needed to see you about. He looked bad too." I guzzled the milk like it was the juice of the earth. "Forgive your father, those things he said only came out because he was angry." I felt the milk giving me back my strength with every mouthful.

GATEWAY

Not a cross, not a Lord Jesus, not a propeller. So what should I put on the tomb? I even thought about maybe building a gateway like the one out in the fields. A lot smaller, of course, because the one in the fields could be the gateway for the whole cemetery, not just a single tomb. Except these days who could make iron gates like that, there isn't even anyone to shoe horses, you have to go all the way to Boleszyce. While Siudak was still alive he shod horses, did all the ironwork on wagons, whatever anyone wanted, plows, grates, grapnels for the fire brigade. For Pociejka the miller he made a whole iron fence for around his house. He was getting well on, but he kept working. Someone would be passing by the smithy, they'd stop for a while, operate the bellows for him, hold something for him, and he went on working almost till the very end. And the things you could learn from him, he knew more about iron than folks that lived all their lives in America could tell you about America. He'd say, for instance, that iron gets old just like a person, and it has a soul just the same. There ought to be a smithy if only for the sound it makes all through the village. But here the smithy's stood empty a good few years now, since Siudak died. It's going to ruin, and for some reason no one's interested in being a blacksmith. Even Siudak's sons got into mending televisions, and however much you asked them they couldn't even repair a simple lock. And what would a gateway be without gates?

One time I had a dream about it. A huge crowd of people was cramming between the gateposts, it was as if there was no other way through, though all the fields were wide open. They milled around and squeezed together and cussed each other out, they were clambering over each other's backs, it was exactly like people getting on the bus on market day. You could barely even see the gateway itself, there were so many people surrounding it they formed a big pile, and at the very top of the pile, among all the heads and backs, stood Wojtek Kubik with his arms stretched out, shouting: one at a time, one at a time! Stop pushing! Where do you think you're all going, damn you! I'm over here, dad! Give me your hand, which one is yours? The one with calluses, Wojciu! They've all got calluses, which one is yours?! Then Mrs. Waliszyn pipes up, look at him, he's standing on all our heads and he can only see his own folks! At that point I shouted to Wojtek as well, Wojciu, have you seen my family, did they go through already? No one's gone through at all, Szymek, not the least little bug has passed, it's empty as the fields.

But I probably needed to ask someone if it was right to put a gateway on a tomb. It's another thing to have one out in the fields, anything can be there. On top of everything people'll say I've got a screw loose. You put a gateway on your tomb? You don't even have a gate into your yard. You ought to put new doors on your barn, the old ones are falling to pieces. You ought to mend your front door. One time they used to put a gateway up for the harvest festival, or when the *starosta* of the district was going to visit, or when newlyweds were coming back from the church they'd put one up so the young couple would buy them a bottle. For a barracks you need a gateway. Gate of Heaven you say in the litany, but that's not a real gateway, it's Our Lady. The best person to ask would be the priest, priests know about these things. But we've just gotten a new one and he's a bit strange, he plays soccer

479 ·

with the boys, one time he brought the harvest in with Sójka like he was a farmhand, or he'll go out in front of the presbytery and play the fiddle. His housekeeper says she's going to quit, he's such an oddball. You can't ask someone like that for advice about what to put on your tomb.

The last one, if he'd still been alive he would have given me advice. He taught me religion way back in school, knew me since I was little. He knew everyone, he'd been in the village for years. But he passed away not long after I came back from the hospital. I just had time to go buy the plot for the tomb from him. Though he didn't look at all like he was about to die. Sure he was getting on, but he had a good firm step and he held his head up straight. He even recommended that I choose a place closer to the wall, said it'd be quieter there, because these days on All Souls' it gets like market day at the cemetery, people pushing their way around, trampling across the graves, they've no respect for anything. Though they bring ten times as many wreaths and flowers as they used to, and there's enough candles to light the whole village. Best of all would be if I wanted to be right in the corner, where there's that old oak tree, the only one that survived the war. But I happened to be fond of the propeller on Jaś Król's tomb, and I wanted to be near him.

"As you prefer," he said. "Your tomb, your wishes."

I didn't expect him to receive me in such a friendly way. When I went to him I was all set for a fight, in my head I was figuring out what to say to him when he asked questions. Because things weren't as good as they might have been between us. A couple of times he'd singled me out during his sermon, when he needed a bad example that wasn't from the Bible but from the village instead, so he could get through to people better. Because they were quite happy to hear about Judas or Mary Magdalene or the prodigal son, but then they'd go off and do whatever they wanted. On top of that, while my old folks were still alive he kept visiting them, scaring them, lecturing them, nagging them to get me to change. After every visit I'd get it at home even worse than in the sermon. I'd come through the door and right away father would be:

"I never thought I'd live to see the day. The priest criticizing our family from the pulpit. Like we're no better than thieves. One of these days I'm gonna take my ax and smash your head in, you animal. Or you should leave this world of your own accord, then finally there'd be peace."

When I went in he was sitting at his desk writing. He didn't even raise his head, though I made a lot of noise, what with the legs and the walking sticks and all, also I struggled with the door. When I greeted him with "Christ be praised" he barely nodded. It was only when I clattered a bit more with my sticks that he glanced up over his eyeglasses and muttered something that was supposed to be:

"Oh, it's you."

I started in right away telling him why I was there, but he interrupted me.

"Are you still a wild one? It's high time you settled down. Wait a minute while I finish." He went on writing, his big gray head almost leaning on the desktop, as if he was writing something that took a huge effort.

"It's a funeral oration," he said when he finally stopped. A guy by the name of Molenda from Lisice had just died, and though he knew the man well, he knew all the parishioners like the back of his hand, still he didn't have the memory he used to. He'd sometimes use the wrong name for the deceased at the graveside, and even get his life mixed up with someone else's life. Though if you ask me, mixing up lives isn't as bad, because either way it's all the same water flowing into the same world.

But to get a person's name wrong, it's like that person never even existed, and there was no telling what you were burying.

He set aside his pen and took off his glasses. From the folds of his cassock he took out a handkerchief big as a headscarf and wiped the sweat off his forehead.

"I'm not as young as I used to be," he said. "Time was, I could bury three or four, one after the other, and I'd have something different to say about each one of them. And from memory, I didn't have to write anything beforehand. But back then one life seemed so different from the next." He blew his nose into the handkerchief so loud that the glasses in the dresser jingled. He put the handkerchief away and said with a sigh: "So what, you're finally giving it up? You thought you'd live forever. All those years fighting, and where's it gotten you?"

"What do you mean, fighting, father," I said as humbly as I could, because I thought to myself, if I start arguing with him he'll just go and jack up the price of the plot. "I was living, is all. Better or worse, it wasn't up to me. You can't always live the way you'd like to, you live the way you have to. A person doesn't choose their life, father, life chooses the person according to its will, depending on who it needs for what. One person's good for one thing, another person for another, and someone else again isn't good for anything. There's no telling how it decides that one man's a general, another's a judge, a third one is a church man, that you're a priest, father, for example, and as for me, I don't even know what I can say about myself."

"Come off it, you were a priest as well!" He gave a big grin from ear to ear. I was all riled up inside, but I said to myself, think your own thoughts but sit still and be good, and all I said was:

"When people have to, they can be anything, father. Even a bandit or a robber."

"All right, all right," he interrupted. "Tell me though, when was the last time you made confession?"

"Confession?" I felt like he'd called on me in the back row in religious instruction, behind Stach Niezgódka's back, because I always sat in the back row. "Must have been after the war."

"What do you mean, after the war?"

"You know, when it ended. I'd killed all those bad guys, I had to confess it so they wouldn't come haunting me at night. Though if you ask me, father, you shouldn't have to confess those kind of things. Course, there could have been an innocent guy among them. There were a few other sins that had mounted up a bit, the way they do in wartime, so I had to get clean."

"So you cleansed yourself and went back to sinning, is that it? Do you at least come to church? Because I somehow don't recall seeing you."

"The last two years I was in a hospital bed, father, I couldn't exactly go to church."

He narrowed his eyes in a strange kind of way, as if against the light, though he was sitting with his back to the window. In order not to come out looking like a nonbeliever, I added:

"But before the war I never missed mass. Mother wouldn't have let us. I'd sometimes go to the evening service, May Day services, the rosary. And I used to sing in the church choir. Maybe you remember me? Though it's been donkey's years. Kolasiński the organist even used to say that if they sent me to school I could sing in town at the opera. I was a bass. I often sang solo. But the land wouldn't let me go. You can't reconcile singing and the land. The land needs work, father. As for singing, it's mostly good for making the work go easier, or for after work, on Sundays. Though even on Sundays you can't have a good sing, because God sends rain clouds, and here your crop's in sheaves still out in the fields."

"Don't you start talking to me about God!" he said, interrupting me with a sour face. "Hiding behind God. Do you even remember his ten commandments?"

"Of course I remember them. You taught us religious instruction at school, father."

"So tell me, what's the third commandment?"

"The third commandment?" I hesitated. "I think it's, thou shalt not steal," I said. It was mostly a shot in the dark, because at my age how are you supposed to remember which one is third, fourth, tenth, your memory doesn't remember them all in the right order. People can't even live in the right order, let alone remember things.

"The third is to keep the Sabbath day holy." He pointed his index finger at me as if he'd suddenly spotted me in the congregation from the pulpit. "I see you're a bigger sinner than I thought," he said with a bitter sigh, though a bit indulgently as well.

"I won't deny it, father, I'm no saint," I said a little more boldly. "Though in my view sins oughtn't to be connected to a person so much as to their life. For a person it's often too much just to have to live."

"But they have to die as well, and then what?" This time he was seriously upset. I regretted annoying him unnecessarily, because as well as raising the cost of the plot he might stick me next to some guy that drowned or was hung. Not long before, Bolek Brzostek had hung himself. He worked in the warehouse at the co-op, there'd been an inspection and it turned out he was a million zlotys short. The Brzostek women had so many clothes they couldn't decide what to wear, they were constantly heading into town to go to the pictures, because his old lady liked the pictures so much she used to say she could spend her whole life there. He had a new house built, bought a car, people couldn't figure out how they did it on that little salary. You've got a head on your shoulders, Bolek. Your Dziunia's a lucky woman.

"Well, when you have to die, you have to," I said, humble again. "But death knows best of all when to come, father, there's no point hurrying out to meet it."

"Maybe you're in no hurry to meet it. But it might be in a hurry to meet you. How can you know?"

"I guess I can't."

"Is it not said, 'ye know neither the day nor the hour'?"

"It is."

"You see then. And you also remember 'memento mori'? You used to serve during holy mass, you'd have picked up a bit of Latin there, Franciszek the sacristan used to teach it."

"Kind of, though he mostly had us scraping the wax off the candlesticks. *Saecula saeculorum*, forever and ever. *Dominus vobiscum*, the Lord be with you. And *ite missa est*, the mass is over. That's all," I said, because I was afraid he'd start asking me questions about the mass as well. "Other than that he just made sure we knew when to carry the missal from one side to the other."

He gave a good-natured laugh:

"Oh, that Franciszek. As for you, don't worry, I've no intention of taking you on as an altar boy. Besides, these days it's all in Polish. I had to learn everything all over again myself. Though I still can't get used to it. It sounds funny to me. There are times, may God forgive me, when I feel it's like a whole other faith. But enough of that. So you say you need a place for a tomb?"

I nodded. He started getting up from behind the desk, his head shook a bit, maybe from all that writing, because sitting like that with your head down, you couldn't have held it up for long even in two hands, let alone just having it on your neck. It was another thing that he seemed to have put on weight, not that much, it was just that back in the day he was thin as a rake. All these young newlywed women, unmarried women, probably even old grannies would come flocking in for every service just for his sake, they'd compete with each other who would bring the most flowers for the church, till there were times he'd tell them to stop, he'd say it's too much, too much, ladies. God doesn't like too many riches, he was poor himself, remember. They may even have believed more strongly in God for his sake than they would have if it'd been someone else.

I braced myself to see how much he would say, because I was convinced he was standing up so as to tell me the price, and he wasn't on the cheap side, oh no. He always said, it's not me you're paying, it's God, so don't sell God short.

"Will you have a glass of wine?" I was floored at first, I would have expected all kinds of prices rather than wine. He looked at me in a mock-angry way. "Surely you won't say no to your religion teacher?"

"I wouldn't want to take up your time," I stammered, because I didn't know what else to say. "I'm sure you've got as much work in the church as we do in the fields. I still have my potatoes to bring in. And you have that funeral."

"Don't get all concerned about me." He walked over to the dresser. "What a hypocrite," he said, pretending to be in a huff. "You never bothered about my feelings before, you just did whatever you felt like. That vulture, that greedy pig with the big belly. Have you forgotten the things you used to say? And where's that big belly of mine? I was always skinny, still am. When you passed me on the road, I wouldn't have expected a 'Christ be praised' because it wouldn't pass your lips, but you might at least have said good morning. Yet all you'd do was look down and scowl like there was no tomorrow. Or start gazing at the sky as if you'd heard an airplane. I was the one that taught you God's ten commandments. You're not going to try and tell me they never came in useful? For each of my students, good and bad, every day I say at least one Hail Mary." He put a bottle of wine and two glasses on the table. "And don't you worry about my time either. My time is for God and for my parishioners. Your potatoes can wait awhile too. The Lord's given us a mild fall, thank goodness, you'll have time to get them in." He seemed to lose himself in thought for a moment. "Though I'm not sure I have the right to say this is still my time. I sometimes have the feeling I'm living at the expense of eternity. Come on, take a seat."

He gestured to an armchair that happened to be right beneath a huge larchwood cross that took up almost the whole wall from ceiling to floor. It was like it was fresh from the ax, none of it had been planed, there were splinters everywhere. If you'd touched it you'd for sure have gotten a hand full of spelks. I was about to say that the carpenter that made the cross, I wouldn't hire him to build a cattle shed, how could he leave so many splinters, but he spoke before me:

"You're looking at the cross? It was made by someone special."

"I can see," I said, and dropped into the armchair. I sank into it like it was a pile of hay.

He took my walking sticks from me. One fell on the ground and he picked it up himself, though you could tell it was an effort for him to bend over, and he grunted and turned red. He looked around to see where to put the sticks, and in the end he hung them over one of the arms of the cross. He poured out two glasses, a full one for me, just a little for himself, explaining that he still had to lead the rosary because the sacristan was sick. He handed me the glass so I wouldn't have to get up, because he'd put it down a short ways away. I tried to stand, though I don't know how I would have managed it without my walking sticks. But he put a hand on my shoulder to tell me to stay seated. He took the armchair opposite.

The wine was so sweet it was sickly. Truth be told, I'm not a big fan of wine. When it's sweet I can hardly get it down, I don't know how people can drink the stuff. But I couldn't tell him that. I said it was nice.

"Must be foreign."

"No, it's made with blackcurrants," he said. "You like it? Helenka, my housekeeper, she makes it. She'll be pleased when I tell her you said it was good. She adds a little rose hip, juniper seeds, something else besides. Though she won't say exactly what, she treats it like a big secret. She won't even tell me exactly what she makes it from. If you like it, father, she says, then drink it and don't ask questions. There's no need to know everything right from the get-go." He raised his glass. "Your health, then." He barely touched the rim of the glass, smacked his lips, and set the wine aside.

I raised my glass too.

"Your health, father." Again I started worrying about what he'd charge for the plot. Because he suddenly started staring at the wall, like he was bothered by the same thought, how much he should ask. Or maybe he was just looking at the larchwood cross. He suddenly broke off staring and sighed:

"So are you not afraid of death?"

I gave a sigh of relief that he hadn't been thinking about the price.

"What's there to be afraid of? A person's only afraid when they're not certain about something."

"All the same, everyone's afraid of death."

"Because that's how life is, father, the fear comes from life. A person's afraid of storms. He falls asleep and he's afraid. He's afraid of the next person. He's constantly afraid. Even yesterday, it's already past and it's no threat to him, but he's afraid of it. And it's not just people. Animals, the land, water, everything's afraid. Or take trees for instance, do you think they're not afraid? They won't say it because they can't talk, they can't cry, they just stand there. But why is it an aspen's leaves shake the whole time? Even when there's no wind. With oaks, of course, it doesn't show. They're hard as rock. And they live for centuries. But when an oak tree finally falls, the whole forest is terrified. And what's a human next to an oak tree, father?" I grabbed my glass from the table and knocked it back in one. I felt like I'd just swallowed a frog, but I made sure it didn't show.

"Will you have some more?" he asked, and without waiting for me to at least nod he filled my glass again. "That's for sure," he sighed, as if lost in the deepest thought. He might not even have been listening to what I was saying, because after a moment he said: "The thing is, I thought you needed me to comfort you. Forgive me, though – put it down to priestly weakness."

I didn't know how to respond, so I took another sweet mouthful of frog juice.

"I'm not sure if a person can comfort another person, father." It came out too arrogant, but the sweetness was making me sick to my stomach. "It's a bit like a blind man leading another blind man through the woods. One's as unfortunate as the other, and the woods are dark and unknown. You have to live alone, for yourself, and you have to die the same way, no one can die for someone else. Besides, people have tried to kill me so many times that when I come to die it won't be the first time. As for living, I've done a good bit of that too, enough for three men. In the resistance I was wounded seven times. Once I even thought I was in the next world. No one believed I'd pull through. But here I am."

"Has it not occurred to you that maybe God wanted you to live?"

"It's hard to say whether it's God, father. I was always strong. Before the war, at dances we'd sometimes stick each other with knives, I'd bleed so much another guy would've been dead, but me, I'm still alive. It's only now that our wounds become so unforgiving, the slightest thing and you're a goner. You might not believe me, but I've never had so much as a cold in all my life. Though in the resistance we often slept on the bare ground, in rain and mud, on moss, on snow. You'd wake up frozen to the earth, like you'd become part of it. You couldn't open your eyes, the frost was so heavy you'd have ice in your mouth and your arms and legs would be stiff as boards. But we always had vodka with us, a mouthful or two and it would all thaw out. Or this accident of mine. The doctors were shaking their heads saying there was nothing they could do to save my legs. They explained they'd have to be amputated. First they said both of them. Then, that I'd lose at least one. I refused, because how can a person live without legs. And here I am walking."

"You certainly are a tough nut, my son," he said like it was part of a mass or service or confession that he'd memorized – he knew all those things by heart. "But that's pride, believe me, it's pride. Beware of pride. It can destroy the human soul worse than anything else. Don't try to be strong at any cost. Strength separates us from other people. Remember that Jesus was God but he allowed himself to be crucified so he could experience human weakness. You have to admit to weakness as well, because it's in you, it really is. It may even want you to weep over yourself. Weep, even if you have to force yourself to. Otherwise you'll never understand yourself, or other people."

"Is it my fault I had to be strong, father? That's just how my life was, and maybe those were the times also. You said Jesus was God. But with people, a single moment of weakness can sometimes cost you your whole life, and without salvation. You say I should cry. But life made me forget how to cry, father. Life can make you forget how to do various things, and not teach you anything in return. Course, they say life teaches. But it's not true. Besides, however much someone wants, he still has to do what he has to do. He's got it written somewhere in that book of his that he has to be strong, so he has to be. Just like another guy has it written that he has to be bald, or another one that he has to marry a particular person, and he has to, even though she's a real vixen. That he's going to be born in this village here, in this house, and not a hundred years earlier or a hundred years later, because from long ago all the way to the end of the world everyone has their assigned time, their place, their life. What's there to cry over? Crying over yourself is like crying against yourself. People always cry to someone, father. Even when you're crying over yourself, you're crying to someone. However deep it is inside you, however secret, it's always to someone. And me, I don't even know if there's anyone inside of me."

"But God is standing over you, have you ever thought about that?"

"If he is, he sometimes lets himself be forgotten. It may even be wisdom on God's part that when there's nothing he can do, he lets himself be forgotten."

"Now you're blaspheming, my friend, you're blaspheming terribly." He raised his hands as if he wanted to push away from me. He made the sign of the cross. "But may he forgive you in his great mercy." He hung his head as if he was praying silently. Also, our conversation might have tired him a bit, he was old after all, sometimes he'd fall asleep during confession. All of a sudden he started and gave me a sort of kindly look. "You're going to stand before him as well one day, what will you say to him then?"

"I won't say anything. When your lips are dead your words are dead as well, father. Whatever you may or may not have said here on earth, you won't say it up there. God too, what he had to say to people, he said it all here, on earth. Up there he became a mystery and he keeps his peace."

"I truly feel sorry for you, my son. But perhaps one day you'll understand, if only in your final hour, that you too, you were only human. A lost, stray human being like every one of us in this vale of tears. And that strength of yours you keep going on about is nothing but ordinary human weakness that you won't accept, that you hate so much in yourself."

"What do you mean?" I was upset, who was he to talk to me that way, even if he was a priest. "Do I not know who I am? I paid a heavy price for that knowledge. It didn't come for free."

"Right, my son. Perhaps you hated it within yourself more than others do. Perhaps you were harder on it than others. Perhaps it hurt you more than it hurt other people. But believe me, it's only thanks to our weakness that we're connected to other people, that we recognize ourselves in other people, and they recognize themselves in us. And that's how our human fate is shared. It has room for everyone. In it our humanity is fulfilled. Because we don't exist outside of our fate. We belong to human fate through weakness, not strength. And it's in this weakness of ours that God manifests himself in every person, not in their strength. So you too, be forbearing toward it, don't shield yourself from it, submit to it, because otherwise you'll have a hard death. And that's not the same thing as having a hard life. And who knows, you might take months and years to die, the way God sometimes tests people, they're confined to their bed by some terrible illness, their death has no end. The sight fades in their eyes, their ears stop hearing, their mind stops understanding, and they lose all feeling except pain. How are you going to die then, if you can't come to terms with yourself, or at the very least understand yourself?"

"Death'll come somehow or other. Death isn't anything special, father. People aren't just living from cradle to grave, they're also dying from cradle to grave. Dying isn't something you do just the one time. Who knows, maybe dying takes longer than living. I mean, dying goes on even after you're dead. You continue to die among the people that are still alive. That one time, maybe it's only the end of dying. But before a person reaches that end, how many times do they have to die first. The truth is, father, with each person that dies in our life, those of us left behind die a little bit ourselves. The person goes away and they leave us their death, and we have to shoulder it. They just lie there rotting in their grave and they don't know, they don't feel that they're rotting because they don't know anything or feel anything at all, not even that they left someone behind. And even if there's no one close to follow them in death, still those further from them die, their neighbors, people they know, even strangers, though the strangers might not even be aware of it. You see, father, it's enough for us to be surrounded by constant dying for it to shape us. Or say a cow dies, or a horse drops dead, or a hawk gets in among the chicks. Those are our deaths as well. Maybe it's from those deaths, when too many of them collect inside you, that your own death comes. I sometimes even have the feeling that I come from the dead. I seem to be alive, but it's like death is just letting me be so I can bury the last ones. And as if that's to be the end of something ending forever."

"But what about the next world? Has it ever occurred to you that you'll have to go on living there? Eternity's promised to everyone, after all. Whether it'll be good or bad, that God has to decide."

"Has anyone ever come back from there, father, so we can believe something's there? We only die in the one direction, not the opposite one."

"And what about hell? Are you not afraid of hell?" he exclaimed in a bitter tone.

"What's hell to me, father, after I've been on earth."

His head drooped, he folded his hands across his stomach and froze like that without a word. I began to regret getting drawn into the discussion. Stach Sobieraj was supposed to give me a hand bringing in the potatoes. In return I was going to lend him my horse the next day. What could I tell him now? That I'd been at the priest's all this time? What, were you making confession? No. Then what on earth were you up to?

He said in a voice that seemed to emerge from his thoughts:

"I knew you'd come one of these days. If not of your own free will, then because of the tomb. You have no idea how much I was looking forward to this moment. How long is it since I came to this parish. Half a century it'll be. I can still remember you running around in short pants. Your hair was the color of flax. And I seem to remember that for the longest time you wouldn't grow."

"That wasn't me. Maybe you're thinking of Michał, father. Michał didn't grow for a long time."

"Come on, don't try to wriggle out of it. I remember I used to make fun of you, so when do you finally plan to start growing, Pietruszka? See, Bąk's already getting a mustache. And Sobieraj's going to start chasing after the young ladies any day now. Now what's the seventh commandment, Pietruszka? Do you know or don't you? Tell him, Kasiński. Because Kasiński couldn't contain himself, he knew. That Kasiński, he always knew everything. That's why he rose so high. I can't remember if the two of you sat side by side at the same desk or if he was right in front of you. But when it came to picking apples from my orchard, I remember, the two of you went together. Except you never wanted to even repeat after Kasiński. You'd stand there like a post, your eyes on the floor. By the end the whole class was prompting you, but you, it was like you'd set your mind on not knowing. And when Franciszek the sacristan and my dog Flaps caught you in the apple tree, remember? Kasiński got away, and you were left in the tree and you wouldn't come down. Flaps was barking at you, Franciszek was shouting, get down this minute, you little monkey! In the end I heard the ruckus in the orchard and came out, I pleaded with you, threatened, come down, Pietruszka. Come down or in school I'll make you recite the ten commandments and the seven deadly sins and the six articles of faith. And you'll have to stand in the middle of the classroom, not just say them from your seat. Come down. In the end Franciszek had to go get a ladder and bring you down by force. He was so mad he was all set to thrash you then and there, he'd already taken his belt off, but I stopped him:

"'Beating's wrong, Franciszek. He'll come to confession tomorrow morning and confess his sins. You will come, won't you, Pietruszka?'

"'He needs a good hiding,' he said, angry at me as well. 'He'll come to confession and you'll absolve him, father, is that it? He ought to go picking apples at Macisz's place, that's no church orchard! Macisz never so much as shows his face in church! On top of that he goes around saying there's no God, that everything came from water. Heretic. See, the apple tree was bent over it had so much fruit, look at it now. And all you'll do is give him three Hail Marys to say, for all those apples. You punish people more when they only sin in their thoughts. Twelve or more – and litanies, not Hail Marys. One litany is like five Hail Marys. What's a Hail Mary? Hail Mary, Mother of God, that's it. And sins in your thoughts are no sins at all, those people aren't going to go stealing somebody else's apples. You even make me bring apples to religious instruction, father. The last priest, Father Sierożyński, he had this oak ruler and he'd whack the little monsters on the hands till they swelled up and they weren't even able to pick apples. But you, you tell me, go get a basketful of the raspberry apples by the fence there. I've got religious instruction tomorrow, let God be good to those little kids of mine if he can't be good to everyone. And God is good, Franciszek is bad because he's the one that has to chase after the little buggers. When one lot grows up, another bunch comes along, it never stops, your whole life chasing and minding. And they're worse and worse behaved. Not one of them's ever going to learn properly how to serve at mass. All they want to do is dress up in their surplices. But carrying the missal from left to right, for that they need a shove in the back from Franciszek, go on, now's the moment. See, another broken branch.'

"I waited all morning for you back then," he suddenly said in a resentful voice. His resentment seemed so old it was like it came from another world. Half a century is a long time. "I would've forgiven you. I even came much earlier to the church, though I hadn't intended to take confession that day. Franciszek wasn't there yet, and he usually came right after sunrise. I truly don't know why that youthful confession of yours was so important to me. Over a handful of apples from my orchard. But God must have known. All I remember is that when I was already sitting in the confessional I suddenly felt crushed by the great silence in the church. I had the impression the church was built of that silence. And it was strange, but I had no desire to pray, though praying's in a priest's blood, it's a matter of habit, anywhere and anytime. Perhaps I didn't want the words of the rosary to give away the fact that I was there. Even to myself, even to God. I just leaned my head against the grille and surrendered to the silence that was still dark from the night. It was like I was curled up in its darkest corner, like I was hiding, not there. It was only in the depths of my soul I heard something like the soft sound of a barely smoldering hope that you would come, that any minute now in the silence I'd hear your nervous steps, like drops of water falling on the floor of the church. At the same time I was worried that God would see that hope in me, because it could be the shadow of a sin I didn't know to confess. That hope has smoldered in me all my life now. Often afterwards I'd come much earlier to the church, just to sit in the confessional and listen to the silence of the dark building. Besides, when you're in the confessional it's as if it forces you to listen hard, and you listen even if you don't hear anything, even when there's nothing but complete silence on the other side of the grille you can still hear the whisper of people's confessions. And still in your helplessness you never know how to tell sins from sufferings. At a certain moment the door would creak and I'd look out to see if it was you. But it would be Franciszek arriving.

"'You're here early, father,' he'd grunt. You could tell he was annoyed. And he'd set about sweeping the floor. Out of irritation he'd not sprinkle water on it and he'd end up brushing big dust clouds through the whole church. You could barely see him through the dust.

"'You're spreading it around, Franciszek,' I'd tell him off. 'You need to sprinkle some water.'

"'You're wasting your time, father! He's not going to come!' he'd call back, and carry on what he was doing. 'He'd come for apples! You'd be better off taking a stroll and getting some fresh air instead of sitting in all this dust! The sun's shining, the sparrows are chirping, it'll do you good! A church needs to be properly swept so people don't say afterward that it's the house of God but it looks like a pigsty in there!'

"'Leave off with the sweeping, Franciszek! Come over here, I'll confess you.'

"'Me?' He was so taken aback he stopped sweeping. 'My sins are old ones, father, and they're always the same. You gave me confession just last week. This week all I've done is dig potatoes for my sister. What new sins could I have committed?'

"'We'll always find something or other. Come on.' It was ever so easy to comfort Franciszek. He was a simple, trustful soul, and he'd spent his whole life around the church. Though I may have been a bit too generous with the Kingdom of Heaven when I offered consolation. Perhaps I promised folks too much in return for everything they lacked, for all their wanderings and despair and fear. After all, I've been providing consolation here for so, so many years. The world passes by me, but also through me, time passes, people pass, and I keep on and on giving consolation. I sometimes wonder if

I ever really succeeded in comforting anyone at all, if anyone fully believed me. I mean, how much do I actually know about what the Kingdom of Heaven is like, what hell is like? What do I actually know about where one person or another is going to end up, what his fate in eternity is going to be? Whether it won't just be a continuation of his life here? Because if we take our souls from this world, maybe we take our fates as well? These are probably sinful thoughts that I'm admitting to you here, may God forgive me. But I sometimes think that the only wisdom life has left us is to be horrified at life. And despite that I offer comfort, because that's the kind of service I chose to perform. Though when I realize that the people I've offered consolation to might be damning me and cursing me, I don't know if God might not tell me I made the wrong choice. Of course, it's said that whoever you absolve, their sins will be absolved, whoever you deny, they'll be denied. But can I really be certain who deserves forgiveness and who doesn't? What I'd most like to do is to absolve everyone, because I feel sorry for everyone. But do I have the right to use God's mercy as my own mercy, even when I feel great pity toward someone? Does God also feel that pity? It's true his mercy is without limit. But I have no idea how what I'm allowed to do relates to that boundlessness. I'm just a human among other humans, everything connects me to them. So I absolve them, perhaps in vain, I deny them absolution when I'm no longer able to absolve them, but I wander among these mysteries the way only humans can wander, not knowing in the painful way only humans can not know, taking other people's sins on my own conscience and being sinful myself. But perhaps my calling isn't to know but to offer comfort? It's truly a hard way to earn your daily bread, spending your whole life comforting those without comfort, the helpless, the lost. Hard and so very bitter. You have to be one of them yourself, perhaps even the poorest of the poor, lost in uncertainty about this world and the next, maybe even as sinful as them, in order for the comfort you provide to be more than just words, for you both to share your comfort the way you share your fate. I sometimes wonder if in all the hopes I've tried to stir in human hearts, all those hopes of others, I wasn't seeking consolation for myself. It's just that the longer a person consoles others, the less he finds for himself, and the worse he's prey to doubt. So you see, that's why I'm a sorry kind of priest. Or perhaps it's old age. Yes, it's probably old age. All that's left for me is solitude with God." He lost himself in thought for a moment, but he livened up right away. "So who's going to be building the tomb for you?"

"Some folks have suggested the Woźniaks," I said. "But I was thinking of Chmiel."

"Go with Chmiel," he said abruptly. "The Woźniaks are bunglers."

I knew they were bunglers, I only mentioned them so he'd recommend Chmiel. Because I wanted it to look like I was choosing Chmiel on his say-so, so maybe he'd charge me less for the plot. But he didn't charge anything at all. When I asked him, so how much will that be, father? he just waved his hand.

"I hope that there at least you'll be able to lie at peace. It won't be anything."

Truth was, I'd already gotten Chmiel to agree to do it. Right after I got back from the hospital, straight from the bus I went to see him. He lived just beyond the bus stop, so I thought to myself, I'll swing by and find out now what I'm going to need for a tomb like that, and if he'd do it, and when. There was no sense putting it off, you put it off once and twice and after that it never gets done. But Chmiel was out. Only his missus was there.

"Goodness me, you're back!" She seemed genuinely pleased to see me. "He's gone to see his brother in Boleszyce. Why do you want to have a tomb built though? You're not so old. Are you sick maybe?"

"No, I'm not sick. Tell him I'll come on Sunday. Do you know how things are looking at my place?"

"Have you not been there?"

"I came here directly from the bus, I thought I'd swing by, talk to him on the way."

"Well you can imagine, you'll see for yourself in a minute."

"How's Michał?"

"Oh, I saw him by here one time, would have been a month or so ago, he was standing outside the co-op. I said to him, how are things, Michał, are you not missing Szymek? One of your cows is with Borzych, I believe, Talar took the other one. Can't tell you who's got your horse. They did say, but I don't remember. There's always so much to keep in your mind."

Sołuch had my horse, Stach Kwiecień told me on the way. "They've starved it so bad you won't recognize it. Theirs stayed in the stable while they used yours to do all the work. So are you going to be lame for the rest of your life?"

Aside from that he told me old Mrs. Waliszyn had died, that No-Hope Jasiu had killed himself on his motorcycle. And that I no longer had a dog, though he couldn't say whether the dog had gotten free from its chain on its own, or whether someone had let it loose, you know how it is with dogs. Besides, I could get a new puppy from Mikus, his bitch had just pupped. He'd seen Michał, but when was it now, when was it? Oh yeah, he'd been sitting on the steps one time scraping carrots with a piece of glass. Those are good carrots, huh, Michał? You make sure you eat them, carrots give you more blood. Look, Miętus is coming, he might have seen him. Say, Miętus, you seen Szymek's Michał by any chance?"

"Is he not at home?"

"I don't know, I just got back from the hospital, I'm on my way from the bus."

"He's probably at home. Where else would he be. So you're walking with sticks now, is it? Will you always have to from now on?"

"There's not so much of that 'always' anymore, Walerian."

"Maybe, maybe not, but it'll feel like you're doing more walking now in a day than you did before in a month. You could well have a long road ahead of you. Because me, I'm almost there."

"You look okay."

"Maybe on the outside, but inside I'm like that old willow that used to stand by the footbridge. I want to go see my sister in Zochcice one more time, then I think I'm going to die."

Michał wasn't at home. I went around the yard, the barn, the cattle sheds, I called, Michał! Michał! Everything was in ruins. I started digging around, I thought maybe there'd be a little grain left in one of the sacks, I could take it to the mill to get it ground and make some bread. Bread would be a beginning. But there was only one sack left, with bran. I'd had three before. There was rye in the first one, the second had wheat. I went into the orchard. Some of the trees had withered, others were looking crooked and sick, and all the earth there was trampled flat as a threshing floor. After that I went to the attic. Getting up there wasn't actually that hard, though climbing down was worse. Then I sat and thought awhile in the main room, although there wasn't really all that much to think about, either way I had to start from scratch. But before I did anything else I got up and headed out to the village to track Michał down.

I went around the nearest neighbors. One place after another was closed up, everyone was out in the fields because it was harvesttime. At the Kuśmiereks' only Rysiek was in.

"Say, Rysiek, you haven't seen Michał have you?"

"What Michał?" His hair was all matted and his eyes were red, you could tell he must have been drinking the day before. It was vacation time and he wasn't going to his technical school.

"You know, my brother."

"Oh, the old guy."

"He's not exactly old."

"What do you mean not old? He's got a beard down to here, like what's-his-name, Lord Jesus, or that other one."

"He's got a beard? I didn't know."

"Yeah. Will you have a drink, uncle? My head's splitting, plus father's making me go help him in the fields. I told him, don't sow rye. Turn the whole thing over to corn, and get into rearing livestock. Beef cattle, hogs – do you have any idea how much money you can make off those things? I could buy myself a motorbike. A car even."

I went by Kałuża's, two doors beyond Kuśmierek's, but only his old lady was there, she was sitting outside on the bench feeding the chickens.

"You haven't seen Michał have you, Mrs. Kałuża?"

"Oh, you're back, thank heaven! We didn't think you'd come back. Michał? I don't go anywhere these days, sweetie. My legs won't carry me anymore. Sometimes just down to the road. When did you get lame now? And in both legs as well? Our Irka's got another little girl already, but that ne'er-do-well still won't marry her, can you imagine. And her pretty as a picture. Never were such times."

I remembered Mrs. Chmiel saying Borzych had my cow. Maybe Michał was at their place as well. But only the cow was there. Michał had used to visit, but he'd not been since spring. Only one time he'd come by there recently, Borzych's wife had given him a bowl of cabbage, he'd wolfed the whole thing down in a flash so she gave him seconds, plus he ate like half a loaf of bread. Ask Koziara maybe. They were saying he'd helped Koziara bring his hay in. All right, let me have my cow. I put the halter around the cow's neck, I'm leading it out of the cattle shed and Borzych pipes up, says he's owed something.

"For what?"

"What do you mean, for what? For the cow. It's been here a whole year, since Prażuch died."

"You son of a bitch!" I was furious. "You must have milked it! I used to get two bucketfuls every day, how much cheese and cream and butter have you had from that?!"

I took the cow into my shed, tied it up, and went back down to the village to continue looking for Michał. Kwiatkowski was driving his wagon to go gather his sheaves.

"Have you seen Michał maybe?"

"Whoa." He stopped his horse. "Michał?"

"You know, my brother."

He took his cap off and scratched his bald head.

"I think I saw him somewhere or other. Hang on. Might it have been at the church? Or maybe at the shrine outside Myga's place. Hop in, I'll drive you over to Myga's and you can ask him."

At Myga's no one was in, there was only his dog minding the door. I whacked it with my walking stick.

"They must be out in the fields!" shouted Kwiatkowski from the wagon. "Maybe Michał went with! Come on, let's have a smoke!"

"Which fields, do you know?"

"Across the river, or the old manor fields. They've got rye both places. Too bad I'm not headed that way or I'd give you a ride. Best of all would be to wait till they get back in the evening, then they'll tell you."

Where was I supposed to go, across the river or to the manor fields? The manor was closer so I went there. As luck would have it, that was where they were mowing. Their rye looked good, it was just a little bit laid down on one side. Edek was mowing, Helka was gathering.

"God bring you happiness!"

"God give you thanks! Oh, Szymuś, you're back? Just in time for the harvest. Your rye's on the far side of Przykopa's place, the farmers' circle sowed it for you. Though how are you going to bring it in on those sticks, you poor thing? We'll give you a hand once we're done with ours."

But Michał wasn't with them and they didn't know where he might be. He'd visited them a month or two before. He wasn't hungry, he just wanted a drink of whey. He helped them do their threshing. They didn't make him, he did it of his own free will. He's a strong one, he is, Edek could barely keep up with bringing him hay. They told him to come for dinner the next day but he didn't show up. Maybe go ask the Pająks. Mrs. Pająk sometimes used to take him something to eat after he stuck a pitchfork in his foot last year. From the ankle down to here, it almost went right through. He was bleeding so bad they couldn't stop it, till in the end Pająk poured spirit on it and dressed it. He'd been going around the sheaves in the farmyard sticking a pitchfork in them like he was looking for something. One time Mrs. Pająk swept your place out and cleaned up in there, and she washed all his clothes. Mrs. Błach met her when she was rinsing them down at the river. Apparently they were crawling with lice. She changed his bedding, and she gave him one of Pająk's old shirts and a pair of pants. And Pająk went there every day and changed the dressing. There are some good people in this world."

"I won't bother you any more. I'll go down to the road, see if someone's passing in a wagon and they can give me a ride."

"Come visit sometime."

But no one came along. My right leg was hurting and I had to sit down, take a rest, I rubbed it a bit. It was only when I got close to the village that Kudła came by. Can I get a ride from you? Hop on. Even a short way helps. No, he hadn't seen Michał or heard where he could be. He lives beyond the mill, it's kind of outside the village, all he knows is when his old lady goes down the store and hears this and that. They do have a radio, but it broke and now it's just been sitting there silent for a year or more. The Siudaks' kid promised to come fix it, but he's hard to get ahold of, and when you do meet him he scratches himself on the back of the head and all he'll say is, yeah, I'll try and call by sometime, I will. You had to go build your house so far away, if you were closer I might come sooner. Now it's harvesttime, the missus doesn't have the time to listen to what all they're talking about. Besides, you won't learn the truth, but it's nice to at least have a bit of a gab."

"Pull up here, by the shrine, I'll swing by Florek Zawada's."

Florek and I had sat next to each other at school, then the whole time we were young men we'd gone out on the make together, gone to dances, we'd been in the fire brigade together, so I figured he'd probably know something. He'd visited me a couple of times in the hospital and he always brought something, cigarettes, a cake, another time some sausage and a bottle of vodka, and each time he'd say, what are you worried about, what are you worried about. Michał's not gonna die. Concentrate on getting out of here. He was pleased to see me, we exchanged kisses and he clapped me on the back, commiserated about my walking sticks, told me who had my horse, who had my cows, he wanted to share a bottle with me. His Magda tried to get me to stay for dinner, though they'd both just gotten back from the fields when I arrived. But where Michał was they didn't know. He'd been there the previous Sunday. They'd given him dinner, he ate it and stayed awhile, but he didn't come again after that. They even wanted him to stop with them. They said, stay here, Michał, we have to go get the harvest in, you can mind the place for us. You don't need to keep going from one house to another. Maybe you should try Żmuda the barber, he cuts people's hair, shaves them, he knows more. Plus his window looks out onto the road, he can always see who's coming along, which way they're headed. Us, these days we're in the fields all day long. I think he was supposed to cut Michał's hair and give him a shave, the district ordered it. Someone was saying about it, you remember who it was, Magda?"

I went by Żmuda's. So you're back, Mr. Szymek? How are things? Are you always gonna have to be like that? No, it's true, I had instructions from the district administration to cut your brother's hair and give him a shave.

Someone brought it up at a meeting, that it reflected badly on the village. It was embarrassing that someone should go without being looked after. But you understand yourself, Mr. Szymek, I'm not going to plonk him down in the chair by force. Getting your hair cut, having a shave, those are matters of free will, so to speak. If someone wants to, be my guest. Just like they ask for it to be shorter, longer, crew cut, down to the skin, sideburns straight down or angled, cut wet or dry, would you like aftershave. By all means. I don't impose myself on anyone. If they bring him here and sit him down I'll cut his hair and shave him like anyone else. Whenever he walked past I'd run out, Mr. Michał! Mr. Michał! But I never managed to get him to come in. Maybe now that you're back. By all means. I'm here."

Zdun came by. Hey there, Zdun, you haven't seen my brother Michał anywhere have you? Let me see, your brother? Has he gone somewhere? Well, yeah. If he's gone then he'll come back. But what's up with your legs there? You fall off a ladder?

I went to see Fularski. They don't have any land, they gave everything to their sons-in-law, all that was left was the orchard and the beehives out among the trees. So they were probably home and they might know where Michał was. But they didn't. He came by one time, but it was last year, Fularski was fumigating his bees. He came up and stood right by one of the hives. Step away or the bees'll sting you! He didn't move. The bees were crawling all over him and he didn't do a thing. Either he didn't feel anything, or they didn't sting him. Because you should know that bees, they can tell a good person from a bad person. The bad person they'll sting to pieces, the good one, they'll crawl around all over him and not one of them will sting him. Go try Wrona or Maciejka maybe, they live closer to you and they're more likely to know something, we're right at the edge of the village.

Wrona said yeah, he'd met him a couple of times. He was walking through the village. But where was he going? He didn't want to ask, because why would you ask someone where they were going. If someone's walking then they're going somewhere, they know best of all where, it's not necessary for everyone else to find out.

My legs wouldn't carry me any farther. The right one felt like it had a nail stuck in it, the pain was shooting all the way up to my armpit. I could barely put weight on it, so I mostly just dragged it along the ground. My hands were swollen from the sticks. I thought I'd go by Wojtek Kapustka's. It was unlikely Michał was there, but theirs was the closest house. Oh, you're back, they'd say, and I'd at least sit and rest up awhile, get a drink of water, because my throat was dry. But as if out of spite they weren't yet back from the fields. The only person there was their boy, he was bringing in the cows. I asked him, you haven't seen my brother Michał have you? Guy with a beard down to here? He looked at me like I was trying to strangle him and didn't say a word. Was he a mute or something? He'd been able to speak when he was little. So what grade are you in these days, Iruś? Still not a word.

His grandfather appeared out of the barn all covered in chaff and straw. Michał? I was looking for eggs, cause those damn chickens, they lay them and you can't find them afterwards. They lay them in the nettles, under the raspberry bushes, then later that dragon of a daughter-in-law of mine says I stole them and sold them to buy cigarettes. I don't even smoke, hand to God I've not smoked these fifty years. I couldn't breathe, couldn't sleep nights, so I quit. Plus, all this used to be mine. Mine, not hers, damn outsider. I could throw eggs at the fence, at the barn if I wanted. It was mine, as God's my witness. He was an important guy, that brother of yours. I saw him, but way back when. He came here once in this big black limousine, I remember that. Big important fellow, but he still recognized me. Shook my hand. Asked how much I got out of the land reform. If things were fair now. Two and a half acres, Michał. Other people got eight, ten. It's hot, he could have gone down to the river. Look, Kulawik's coming up the road. Ask him. Hey, Sylwester, you've not seen Michał anywhere have you? Szymek's brother?

Michał? Oh, your brother, Szymek. So you're back. Praise the Lord. And you still have your legs, they didn't take them off. Thank God. I saw him standing in the window one day, be a week or two ago. I was on my way to the co-op, he was standing there just watching the world go by, it looked like. I was going to ask him, how are things, Michał? But how could I ask through the glass. Besides, he was looking in sort of a funny way, maybe he wasn't watching the world. Go try Wojcio Zadrożny. One time in the pub he said he'd seen him at Macała's place, he was cutting the tops off beets. We were having a beer.

Zadrożny got all mad and started swearing and fuming, he hadn't said anything of the kind, Kulawik had gotten it all mixed up. Maybe Mielczarek had told him. Besides, you cut beet tops in the fall, it's summer now. He wouldn't even have remembered from last fall till now. That time in the pub there were twenty guys or more, not just him. And beer, he could swear he hadn't been drinking beer, he didn't even like beer. He drank lemonade. He'd been talking about how they needed a new director of the district administration, because the one we had now had been doing it for too long, and he was the biggest crook. That's what we were all talking about. But how could he be replaced? Everyone was thinking about how to do it, and saying their ideas. In the end one of them upped and stood us a bottle, they said that without vodka it was even less clear how to get the job done. Then another bottle. Then everyone stood us a bottle, so how could he remember if Michał had been cutting beet tops at Macała's. Once we saw him here, we were on our way back from church, when was that? Zośka, you remember by any chance when that was? Back in May. May, that's right, because we were surprised it was still May and he was barefoot already. Why don't you have any shoes on, Michał? It's only May, the ground's still cold.

I went out onto the road, but I had no idea where to turn next. Maybe I should try Macała? But I see Dereń coming along. You've had more than your fair share of suffering for your sins, you poor guy! Was Michał at your place maybe? If not today then yesterday or the day before? If you want the truth, he wasn't. And I'll tell you another thing, he's a stubborn bastard, even if he is your brother. One time in the winter I went to see him, the missus made me go over there and check he wasn't sick in bed, there was a frost like you wouldn't believe. And if I'm to be honest with you, that place of yours was like an animal's den. The windows looked like someone had put lime on them, it was freezing cold in there. And he's sitting on the bench blowing on his hands. Do you not want to come over to our place, Michał, I say, you could get warm, have a hot meal. Do you think he came? No. I tell you one thing, you're gonna find it hard to mow or do the plowing with those legs of yours. People were saying they were going to amputate one of them. But I see you got both of them. You'll need to get some hired help. You any idea what they're asking for day work these days? And it's hard to find anyone. They'd rather go work in the factories. Look, Mrs. Antosz is coming. Her head's all messed up these days, but what does it hurt to ask, sometimes fools know better.

Have you seen my brother Michał? Why, have you lost him? You should keep a better eye on him. I've been gone two years. If it's two years then you'll not likely find him. Dear Lord, the folks that have died these last two years. Jadwisia Oko? Wasn't a moment ago the two of us were little girls scattering flowers on Corpus Christi. I remember she had these pinker-than-pink ribbons in her hair. And there you have it, she's gone. What's up with your legs there? Nothing really. I just need to walk with sticks. You look like those guys on stilts. It is more comfortable that way? Yes, it is. God bless.

Szymek, you're back! Stach Sobieraj came running out of his house when he saw me through the window standing by his gate. We were going to come visit you Sunday! Tereska was gonna kill a chicken, make you some soup! Here, come back up the house. So here you are. I was even going to bring a bottle. We didn't think you'd be back till the fall. Sit down, tell me how things went there. Maybe another time, Stach, right now I have to go look for Michał. I can see he's not at your place. He was here, he's come by from time to time, quite often actually, he'd always eat something and sit awhile. One time he spent the whole day chopping wood. We didn't tell him to, he did it of his own accord. He took the ax, it happened to be lying by the chopping block. Have you been to Borzych's? He's got your cow. I was there, the cow's back in my shed already. Then try Zadrożny. I've been there. Maybe Kapustka. Been there too. Tell you who's most likely to know, Żmuda the barber. He cuts folks' hair, does shaves. I've been there as well. Oh well, I'll just keep looking. Swing by maybe Sunday, we'll have a drink to celebrate you coming back.

Franek Duda drove by in his wagon bringing sheaves from the fields. You haven't seen my Michał anywhere have you, Franek? What, is he missing? Yeah. I'm telling you, pal, right now even neighbors don't see each other. Everyone's in the fields, they're mowing, gathering, they leave before dawn and don't get back till it's dark again. He might be out in the fields with someone and you'll never find him here. Giddyup! Hang on a minute. Whoa! I think I might have seen him. It would've been last week, I was going over to the pub for a beer, he was sitting under an ash tree at the Malec place rocking a stroller. Their girl Elka had a baby. Go try them.

I hobbled over to the Malecs' place, Elka Malec was actually there, she was giving her baby the breast. You had a baby, Elka? Boy or girl? A boy. When did you get back, uncle? Mama cried when she heard you were going to lose your legs. She was beside herself. She kept saying, dear Lord, dear Lord, a man like that. Does he have a name? It's Miruś, Mirosław. That's what Zenek wanted to christen him. Because my dad was all, call him Walenty. But that's no kind of name for a child. Miruś, Miruś, you're a pretty little boy. I heard Michał was here, Franek Duda told me, I'm looking for him. Yes, he was, just yesterday. He's been here a lot. He often looked after Miruś when I had an errand to run. He'd take him out in the stroller, rock him. One time they went all the way down to the river, I couldn't find them. They say he can't talk, uncle. But he talked to Miruś.

I went out onto the road. I thought, I'll knock my sticks on Malec's ash tree, maybe it'll tell me. Goddammit! Evidently I was going to have to go from house to house. Only, in which direction? Toward the co-op? Or was it better to go toward the mill? No, the co-op. The mill. Co-op. Mill. It was like the road had a hundred directions. I called by Bąk's. They'd not seen him. I went to Sójka's. They hadn't seen him. Sobczyński's. There was no one in and the place was padlocked. I was shocked. They'd padlock the door when they were out working in the fields? No one ever used to lock their door. Unless these days you need to. At Madej's I shouted, Walek! Walek! Because since they built their new house you have to go up some steps, and by this point I could barely walk on the level. I even thought I saw a curtain twitch in the window, either that or my eyes were starting to play up.

Heat poured down from the sky, and the earth was hot underfoot. I could feel it, not just in my feet and through the sticks, but even up under my ribs. My back was in agony. I'd never had any problems with my back before. I could lift all I wanted, walk anywhere, didn't feel a thing. I needed to rest up at least a short while.

"Afternoon, Seweryn!" Old Grabiec was sitting on the bench outside his house. I'd been sure he was dead already. I don't know where I got the idea. It was another matter that at his age he could have been dead three times over. Perhaps someone told me in the hospital. "I'll join you for a minute."

"Help yourself, there's room enough for the both of us. And who are you?"

"Don't you know me? It's Szymek Pietruszka."

"Right, Szymek. My eyes are going dark, son, I can only half see. But now I see you. You used to be quite the fighter at the dances, you put on a show. And you used to like to drink. Are you coming from the fields?"

"No, I'm looking for my brother Michał. He's gone off somewhere."

"Doesn't he know where he's gone?"

"He probably does, but in his own way."

"How else is he supposed to know? Everyone knows in their own way. Is he older than you or younger?"

"Older."

"Then he'll know better than you. Are your folks still alive?"

"No, they died a long time ago."

"They did right. There's no sense living too long. One war for one life, then a person should move on. Not like me, four of them. Were you in a war as well?"

"I was. But that was a while back."

"I thought you might have been, cause you've got walking sticks."

"That's not from the war. It was on the road."

"You fell off a wagonload of sheaves."

"Kind of."

"There's no point taking too many at one go. The wagon can rock. And it's harder for the horse. It's better to make two trips. Tell me now, is it true about them Sputniks?"

"Well, they're flying up there, it must be."

"I guess, though who's actually seen them. You can see the stars on a clear night. And the dogs would bark."

"It's too high for dogs."

"The moon's even higher, and they bark at that. Have you heard anything about a war, maybe? Are they getting ready to fight?"

"Why are you so interested in war? It's not been that long since the last one."

"Because the powers that be have to go head-to-head. Otherwise they wouldn't be powers. At least I might get out of paying my taxes. It's got to the point I owe thousands, dammit. They keep adding penalties. And I've got nothing."

"No one does, Seweryn. One harvest goes well, then the next one rots. How's your grain been?"

"Like everyone else's."

"Kernels big?"

"Neither big nor small."

"Why aren't you mowing yet?"

"I'm waiting for one of them to bring their wagon."

"What did you sow?"

"Nothing. What's the point in sowing when there's no one to get the harvest in."

"Doesn't it pain you that the land's just lying there?"

"Why should it pain me. Pain doesn't feel pain. The world was there, then it went away. You have to accept it."

"Get your scythes! Get your scythes! Get out into the fields! Another day or two and the weather might turn." Gula had appeared in front of us, his missus had sent him out to buy salt for their dinner and he was on his way back from the co-op.

"Say, Marian, you haven't seen my Michał anywhere, have you?" I was only asking, because I knew he wouldn't know. And Gula just casually says:

"Yeah, he's mucking out at Skobel's place."

"Mucking out at Skobel's?" I jumped up and grabbed my walking sticks. "Damn, and here I am looking all over the village for him!"

"What were you looking for him for? You should have just gone straight to Skobel's."

Luckily Skobel's place wasn't far, he lived right the other side of the co-op, it was just a bit downhill, closer to the river. It would never have occurred to me to go ask Skobel if Michał was there. No one ever went to Skobel's even to borrow a whetstone for a scythe, or leaven for bread, base for *żurek*, you wouldn't borrow his plow or wagon or horse, not to mention money. I walk into his yard and his dog comes out at me, it won't let me take a step farther, just stands there yapping at me. I whacked it on the back with my stick like it was Skobel himself. Get lost, you little sod! It yelped and slunk back. Skobel came out of the barn.

"What's the dog ever done to you?"

"Where's Michał?"

"What are you all upset about? You're supposed to say, Christ be praised, when you go visiting someone. He's in the cattle shed, he's mucking out."

I hurried into the shed and I saw Michał, my brother, barefoot, up to his ankles in manure, working a pitchfork like he was Skobel's farmhand. He was skin and bones. His beard reached his chest, his hair was all the way down his back. I barely recognized the brand-new dark blue suit with white stripes that I'd bought him the Easter before I went into the hospital. Thirty-five hundred zlotys it cost me. And it looked like he was wearing the same cherry-red tie with white dots I'd gotten him at the same time, since he had something tied around his neck. But I was just guessing, because he was covered in filth from head to foot like some animal.

"Michał! It's me, Szymek!"

He looked in my direction, but only as if to say, who's blocking the light in the doorway there, then he lowered his eyes again and dug the pitchfork back into the manure.

"You bastard, Skobel! How you could let him do the mucking out? A guy like him!"

"Keep your shirt on. You think this is the old days? Not anymore, things are different now. Was I supposed to feed him for free? Wasn't for me, he'd have starved to death. Everyone else is only good for feeling sorry. But looking after him, feeding him, all of a sudden they don't feel so sorry anymore. Let God look after him. One time I found him here in the orchard, he's eating green plums."

"So in return for a bowlful of food you make him your farm boy! You're a piece of work! And him, do you know who he was?"

"Everyone knows. Like people don't talk? But they forget when some-one's down on their luck."

"People don't know squat!"

"People know everything!"

"Michał!" I snatched the pitchfork from his hands. "Home now! Come on, on the double! You miserable shit, Skobel, I'd like to give you a taste of this!" I jammed the pitchfork in the ground inches from his feet, it made him blanch. I pushed Michał out ahead of me.

He walked in front obediently, with me barely limping along behind. Maybe he thought another farmer was taking him to a new job. He never asked questions about who and where, you could lead him anyplace. They could have led him to his death and he never would have even asked, why? It was like there was nothing inside him except the fact that he was walking. I was seething with anger. It was like someone had taken a big stick and stirred me up inside all the way to the bottom, like a pot filled with bubbling kasha. I felt I needed to do something to make him understand that I was back, that I was his brother, that I was taking him home and no Skobel or Macała or anyone else would ever take him again to tie up sheaves or cut beet tops or muck out the cattle shed.

"Hurry up." I prodded him in the back with one of my sticks, though I couldn't go any faster myself. My legs were fit to drop off, my hands were wet and stinging from blisters that had burst.

We came into the house.

"This is your home," I said. "Sit down."

I went to the cattle shed and took the halter from around the cow's neck. It was too long so I folded it in four. I returned to the house. He was sitting there like I'd told him to, resting his forehead on his hands and staring at his feet. He stank so bad the whole place smelled of Skobel's manure. I stood at arm's length from him. I put the right-hand stick aside and leaned on the left one alone, broad and firm, so as not to lose my balance.

"I have to beat you," I said, and with all my strength I struck him on the back with the folded-up halter. I did it so hard it made me stagger. He didn't so much as flinch, or look to see who was hitting him or why. All that happened was a cloud of dust went up from him and there was an even stronger smell of manure. I had to straighten myself because the stick had slipped in my hand, then I whacked him again, and again, and one more time. He didn't react. Though he'd only have had to give me a slight push and I would have gone crashing to the floor. He was still a strapping guy just the same, even though he was underweight, and I was leaning on a single walking stick with a red-raw, swollen hand, and on a pair of exhausted crippled legs, and I had nothing to prop myself up with. Plus, with every blow the halter shook me like a reed in the wind, when for a beating like that you need to be planted foursquare like a table, your feet rooted to the ground, and the ground afraid to shift beneath you. Then you can give a beating. Not just with the halter but with your whole body, with all your pain, your rage. Then you could even make a rock shed tears. Though it would've been easier to make a rock cry than him. All of a sudden he took his head from his hands, put his palms on his knees and leaned forward, like he was trying to make his back as broad as possible for the beating. I started beating that back, gathering myself for every blow like I was passing sacks of grain to be put on the wagon. My whole body twisted with each swing. The rage grew within me. It would have been enough for a dozen halters. I felt it around me even, like the room was furious along with me, the whole house, the cattle shed, the barn, the farmyard, the whole village, the land. It was the rage helped me forget that me, a brother, I was beating my own brother. And what was I beating him for? Truth was, I didn't really know, and I don't think I ever will. Only he knew. But not the slightest murmur passed his lips. His beaten body didn't even groan of its own accord, the way bodies do when they're being beaten. Even a tree, if you hit it it'll groan, a rock will make a sound. But here, only the halter moaned. The halter was doubled up with pain. If it could have, it probably would have leaped at me and at the very least stayed my hand to stop me beating any more. Or it would have wrapped itself around my neck like a snake and hung me from the ceiling.

I was breathless. I felt like I'd climbed a high mountain on those crippled legs of mine. I felt I was stopping. My arm weakened and the halter was just flopping from my back to his. All at once the stick, which for a long time had been shaking under me like a willow branch, fell out of my hand when I took another swipe. I staggered so bad I would have fallen over if I hadn't grabbed the side of the table at the last moment. My first reaction was to bend over and pick up the stick. But I was stopped by a terrible pain in my right knee. I broke out in a cold sweat, and something popped in my lower back. Ever so slowly, one hand holding on to the table, the other reaching toward the floor like a rake, I bent over farther and farther. Finally I got ahold of it. Except that when I straightened up, I got dizzy. I barely made it to the bench, and I dropped down exhausted, like I'd just come back from the fields after a whole day bringing in the harvest.

"You're not to muck out at Skobel's ever again," I said.

He sat there with his head drooping on his chest and his hands on his knees, like he hadn't even noticed I'd stopped beating him. From outside there was a constant creaking of wagons, everyone was bringing in the harvest. By now almost everyone had rubber tires on their wagons, and you couldn't hear them the way you used to with iron rims. Now you could hear the horses more. They were walking slowly, like they were carrying the wagons on their backs.

I suddenly wished that one of the neighbors would come by, someone from the village. Or a stranger. I had no business with anyone, nor anyone with me. But I wanted someone to come, maybe it would be on his way, or he was coming home from the fields and he heard I was back. Or just like that, because he didn't have anyone else to visit. Kuś, or Prażuch, they'd have come for sure if they'd still been alive. Because the ones that were dead were the ones you could most rely on. I even started listening to see if I couldn't hear steps in the passage. Maybe the door handle would rattle. The door would open. Someone would stand at the threshold, they'd say, Christ be praised, or just, good afternoon.

"What are you sitting like that for, like you were perched on a field boundary outside? Have you just come in from the fields, or did someone die?"

"Neither the one nor the other. I was just giving Michał a beating. With this halter, see?"

"A beating? A brother giving a brother a beating? You're grown up, the both of you. Brothers mostly only fight when they're young."

And maybe it was from waiting in vain that it occurred to me to give him a bath. I'll cut his hair and give him a shave, then someone can come. I got up from the bench. I put the walking sticks in my raw hands. It stung all the way to my elbows. I could barely stay on my feet.

"You stay put," I said. "I'm going to give you a bath." I shuffled off to find a bathtub. Luckily they had one at the Pajaks', so I didn't have to go far. Pajak even brought it to the house for me. He set it in the middle of the room and wedged it in place with laths so it wouldn't wobble. Then he brought two bucketfuls of water from the spring, filled some pots, and put them on to heat.

"People should help each other in their misfortune. You helped me in my bad hour. Remember the oration you made at our Włodziu's funeral?"

"How long ago was that, Bronisław. I'm amazed you still remember."

"Course I remember, I'll remember till the day I die. The priest said what he had to to be over and done with it. All he was thinking about was how to get back home to the presbytery soon as he could, he was stamping his feet. It made no difference to him whether it was our Włodziu or somebody else. Son of a bitch didn't even say he'd been blown up by a mine, it looked like he'd just died of typhus or dysentery. Don't go there, Włodziu, I said to him, the sappers'll come and clear the mines from our land. But no, off he went.

And you, you didn't care that there was a frost, though it was so cold everyone's tears froze. You didn't miss anything out, you said he was a good child, he respected his parents, and he was like a grain of wheat sprouting from the seed, but that he never grew to be a spike. Because it was like someone cut him down deliberately with a willow switch. You hear, mother, I said to my old lady, you hear what kind of son we had? And God took him from us."

I gathered a few sticks around the yard and lit the stove. The fire took, and right away it was like something came to life in the house. Soon steam started rising from the pots.

"Take your clothes off," I said. I set a chair between the stove and the bathtub. I leaned with all my weight on the stove. I put one pot first on the chair, then from the chair onto the ground right next to the tub, and only then I leaned over and poured it out. My face covered with condensation from the steam. I added a little cold water from the bucket. "Come on, it'll get cold. Take your clothes off."

He didn't respond, he just sat there. As best I could I undressed him with one hand, because I had to hold on to the table with the other one. Luckily he didn't resist. He still stank so bad from Skobel's manure it stung my nose. It was only when I pulled off his underwear that he suddenly curled up and started shivering, like he was ashamed of being naked.

"There's no need to be embarrassed in front of me," I said. "I'm your brother. There's no one here but you and me. Pająk went home. Come on." I took him by the hand and led him to the tub. He stood there, hesitating. "Don't be afraid, it's only water," I said.

He squeezed my hand and wouldn't let go, as if I was leading him into a deep pool, though it barely came up to his ankles. As he stood in the tub he reminded me of someone, but I couldn't figure out who. Maybe it was the hair falling down his back and the beard that reached down to his waist. He was so skinny his bones almost poked through his skin, and also the skin hung from him the way snow sometimes hangs from a branch when there's a thaw. His back was covered in blue welts from where I'd beaten him. The hair between his legs was gray as a mouse, though on his head he only had the odd gray hair, same with his beard. Usually your private parts are the last to go gray.

"Sit down," I said. "First of all I'm going to soap you up."

I'd brought myself a piece of soap from the hospital. Someone had left it in the washroom and I took it, like I had a feeling it'd come in handy. I moved the chair up to the tub, sat down, and poured water all over him out of a mug so he'd soak a bit. Then I lathered up some soap in my hands. And carefully, so as not to hurt him, I soaped up his back, his chest, his arms, everything. His skin was twitching like a rabbit's when you stroke it. I could feel the trembling pass into me as well, though I was barely touching him, more with the lather than with my hands.

"Stop shivering," I said. "I'm not doing anything bad to you. I'm washing you. You always liked to get washed. Remember when mother would give us a bath for Christmas or Easter, you'd never want to get out of the water? While me, father would sometimes have to chase me into the tub with his belt because I'd be pretending to still be asleep. Or the water would be too hot for me, or the soap got in my eyes. Or when we'd go down to the river to wash, remember? First you'd soap my back, then I'd do yours. Then we'd scrub our feet with a rock or with sand. When we didn't feel like washing we'd scare each other with ghost stories. Mostly I'd scare you. Look, Michał, there's something standing over there. See, there by that willow tree. It's white, like it's dressed in a sheet. It's a ghost! And we'd take to our heels. Me first, you behind. Mother and father would say, what's happened? We saw a ghost! You're just trying to get out of bathing, these boys are a cross to bear! Mother was always like that. And you're going to get into bed with those dirty feet? If it was down by the river it must have been the Bartosz girl's ghost, father would say. He was always more likely to believe us. You should have said to it, in the name of the Father and the Son, what is it your soul needs? The Bartosz girl wouldn't have done anything to hurt you. She used to like going down to the river when she was still alive, seems she still does now. She'd sit on the bank and stare at the water. What on earth do you see out there, Agata, I asked her one time, I'd gone to fetch water from the spring. Oh, it's always something different, Józef, always something different. Though what could she see there, sand, mud, rocks, and the river flowing."

I took the chair and moved to the other side of the tub, because it was hard for me to reach all of him from the one place.

"Do you remember that time we went swimming by Błach's place on Saint John's Day at the end of June? Because swimming would start on Saint John's Day always. That's the day Saint John blesses the rivers. Though I often used to go swimming before Saint John's Day, even in May sometimes. It was so hot that year the leaves were curling up. There were hordes of boys and girls, more bodies than water. Even the willows along the bank were wet from all the splashing. Fredek Zięba brought their horse down, as many of us as could fit climbed up on it, and it was giddyup! into the water. There were kids hanging from its neck, clinging to its tail. Shouts and screams, you'd think the heavens were coming down. But you were sitting on the bank, by the osier bushes, and you were trying to stop yourself from crying, because you couldn't swim. I kept trying to persuade you, come on, Michał, you'll learn, hold on to the horse's tail and kick your feet as hard as you can. Come on! Everyone was encouraging you. You should just jump in headfirst, Michał! Put your hands together like you're praying, stretch them out in front of you, and jump! Go for it! Or, let's throw him in, that's the fastest way to learn! Let's get him! You ran away, we chased after you. We caught up with you in Mrs. Machała's field, you slipped and fell in a furrow. You fought, spat, bit our hands. But there were four of us. We carried you down to the river, swung you by the arms and legs, and boom! The splash was so big we got soaked. Wave your arms, Michał! Wave your arms and legs! But you, as if to spite us you didn't move either your arms or your legs, and you went straight to the bottom. I had to dive in and fish you out. You'd swallowed so much water you couldn't catch your breath, and afterwards you had hiccups for the longest time. Later on father gave me the belt for trying to drown you. But that was the quickest way to learn! That's how everyone was taught, they'd take your arms and legs and wham! Save yourself or you'll drown! Me, they even threw me from a willow tree so it'd be from even higher. And that was exactly the right thing for me. When I was in the resistance, one time I had to jump from a bridge. I was being chased from behind, ahead of me the road was blocked, there wasn't any other way out."

I got up and added more hot water from the pot. I stirred it around his body.

"And remember before the war when you came home one time wearing a hat? You stood on the doorstep, it was like you were embarrassed about having the hat on. And we just stared at you. Is it Michał or isn't it? You quickly pulled it off, but father says, put it back on, let me take a look. Actually it looks good on you, it's just you don't look like yourself. It cost a lot? Mother says, you shouldn't have spent so much on a hat, son, you could have bought a whole suit for that much money. It was a Sunday. Father wanted us to go take a walk through the village, maybe we'd bump into the priest. He's always kind of asking after you. But we were young men, the two of us, what did we care about the priest, plus it was so hot, so I dragged you down to the river. The girls had grown into young ladies by then, and the river was filled to bursting. I stripped off my clothes and dove right in. You sat on the bank, in the shade of the bushes. Stefka Magiera swam up to you and tried to get you to come in, won't you get undressed, Michał? It's hot as anything, take your clothes off and join us. Her breasts looked like they'd been drinking the water in the river. You look nice in that hat. Will you be staying for long? The Magieras thought you'd marry her. But you wouldn't have been happy. During the war she hooked up with this one guy that used to come buy flour, and she went off with him. Left her man and her baby. Michał! Michał! Come in and have a swim! Everyone was calling to you. In the end the guys actually got jealous. Leave him be! He must have the consumption. They're not allowed to go swimming. Look, he went and bought himself a hat so he wouldn't look like someone from the village! He looks like a tush behind a bush! One of them ran up from behind, snatched the hat off your head, and tossed it into the river. The whole mass of them jumped in after it. Someone scooped water up in it. Another one plopped it on his head and started swimming in it. I jumped in to fetch it back, but he threw it into the crowd. They pulled and tugged at it and grabbed it from each other. Stefka Magiera was so upset she started crying. You're horrible! You're horrible! she shouted. None of you's ever going to have a hat like that! One guy dove down and got a rock from the river bottom. They put it in the hat so it would sink. In the end I managed to get it off them and I tossed it far downstream so I'd be the first to swim there and reach it. And I was. But Bolek Kuska jumped out onto the bank and got there before me. He grabbed the hat and ran even farther to where there was a shallow stretch. He went in and there, in the mud and sand and rocks, he started stomping the hat into the water. I beat him up so bad he couldn't close his mouth for a month. He looked like he was smiling the whole time. I cut holes in his shirt and pants with my penknife, and I tossed his shoes into the river. Him and his brother Wicek came to our house afterwards with their old man to make a fuss, and I gave the old man a hiding as well. You, you didn't do anything, you just watched them messing with your hat, then you got up and said, come on, Szymuś, let's go. Leave them the hat, let them play."

I got him up from the bathtub and dried him off. I didn't have anything to put on him so for the moment I wrapped him in a sheet. Where I could I tied it, in other places I fastened it with safety pins. I managed to find three of them in the drawer of the sewing machine.

"Now I'm going to cut your hair and your beard."

Turned out I still had the knack. I could cut hair and give a shave just like in the old days. Though there probably weren't many people remembered I used to do it. Maybe just some of the older guys. But most of the old ones were already dead. Now the young people were the old ones. And after them the next young ones were already waiting to be old in their turn. They were younger and younger when their hair became speckled with gray, their foreheads got bare, and their faces started to sag and get furrows and pits. Though from day to day you couldn't see old age passing across people. It was like old people had come to the village from somewhere else, while young folks had left and then come back when they were already old. It just sometimes seemed strange to me that they were the same people. But I guess they were.

I had to rest my backside against the table because otherwise I wouldn't have been able to stay in place. His hair was thick and strong, he had that from mother, like me. Because Antek and Stasiek got their hair from father, Stasiek was already almost completely bald, while Antek had bare patches that looked like holes in a thatched roof. I gave him a buzz cut, because his hair was crawling with lice. Then I washed his head.

"All right, now let's eat."

From the hospital I'd brought half a packet of tea, a little sugar, half a loaf of bread, a bit of cheese, and two pork chops. Jadzia the auxiliary had given it all to me as a parting gift. She came out into the hallway with me when I went to say goodbye.

"Here, take this." She thrust a package into my hands. "You're not going to go buying things at the store right away, but you'll need to eat when you get home."

I felt silly, because I'd not told her that much about home and what I did tell her mostly wasn't truth, the way you talk to a woman, or a dead person. I was even going to tell her they'd probably have dinner waiting for me. I'd let them know I was coming home. But she knew I didn't have anyone, so who could be waiting for me. Besides, she didn't let me hesitate very long.

"Just take it. For your own good." I wanted to kiss her hand, but she hid both of them behind her back. "You can't go kissing an auxiliary's hand, Mr. Szymek. You know what, come visit us sometime, if you're here for the market or something. It was fun being around you. I had a good laugh. Because mostly people just die."

I didn't even tell her about Michał. All I said was that I have three brothers, that much I told her, and that all three of them are in the city. Besides, Antek and Stasiek she'd met when they came and visited a week or so after the accident. I've no idea how they found out, because I didn't let them know. They were dressed up to the nines. Spanking new suits, shirts, ties. It actually made me feel good to have brothers like that. But after an hour I'd had enough of them, though we hadn't seen each other for two years. They barely even asked if one leg or both had been run over, or how long I was going to be in there, then already they started arguing with me, trying to say it was my fault. Because instead of sowing rye and wheat I should have started an orchard, kept bees, or shifted to raising cattle like they'd kept telling me to. That way I wouldn't have had to hurry before the rain and bring the crop in on a Sunday. Sunday's for resting. Sitting at home with your wife and kids. Or if the weather's good, going for a ride in the car, to the woods or down to the river. But I imagined I'd be forever young. This girl wasn't right for me, that one wasn't either, and there you have it. Luckily Jadzia came in and I introduced her to them, these are my brothers, Antek and Stasiek, this is Miss Jadzia the auxiliary.

"Mr. Szymek, he's a trooper," she said, like she sensed they were quarreling with me. "He's in all kinds of pain, but he doesn't breathe a word of complaint. He even likes to joke around."

It was only then that they stopped. Though Stasiek evidently hadn't had enough, because when she left he said:

"Or you should marry her. She works in a hospital, she's used to hard work, she'd be able to help you in the fields as well."

Dusk was gathering in the windows, it was getting dark in the room. We sat there drinking tea and eating bread and cheese. I'd left the chops for the next day. You could still hear wagons loaded with sheaves creaking on the road. Occasionally someone would shout, giddyup! Other times a horseshoe would scrape against a rock. On someone's wagon the perch was rubbing against the bodywork. There was a squeak of axles that needed oiling, the rattle of traces against the shaft. I was waiting for him to at least ask:

"So where were you all this time?"

If he was a cat he'd have jumped up into my lap right away and nuzzled me like it hurt him not to be able to say a word in human language. If he'd been a dog he probably would have been straining at his chain, he'd be so pleased to see me back. Everyone that met me at the very least said, oh, you're back. And here he was, my brother, and he wasn't saying a thing.

"Did they tell you I was in the hospital?"

He lifted his mug to his lips and opened his eyes so wide they were round as little coins, but you could never have guessed anything from them. You couldn't tell whether they were looking, thinking, or whether they just wanted to die and not know anything. Also, he was holding the mug in a kind of odd way, with only two fingers round the handle. I even checked to see if I was holding mine the same way. But I was holding it normally, with my whole hand round the middle. With his bread and cheese he broke it into crumbs in the palm of his hand and only then picked it up and ate it, like he was picking seeds out of a sunflower. Actually he'd always eaten differently than other folks. When we had *żurek* with potatoes in the morning, my spoon would be half potatoes and half soup, I could hardly stuff it in my mouth it was heaped so full. Him, he ate the potatoes and the soup separately, a tiny bit of potatoes and no more than a mouthful of liquid, on top of which he barely moved his jaws. That way he could scarcely eat his fill, and he was doing twice as much work with his hand. You eat so your belly will be full. It's your belly that gives you strength. And strength lets you work. I sometimes asked him, when you eat like you do, does it taste better, does it make you fuller, or what? Tell me. Surely it isn't a secret? Not that I wanted to learn how to eat that way, I was fine as I was. But I figured I could learn at least that much from him, because you can learn a lot from how someone eats.

Or when he cut himself a slice of bread, it was so thin you could see through it. And even if he was eating it without anything on it, he'd still always hold it flat on his spread fingers, as if it had slices of sausage on it that he didn't want to drop. Or when he had an apple, he'd always first cut it into four equal-sized pieces, dig out the pips, peel the skin, and only then eat the pure white quarters. Or even when he drank water, you never heard a sound from his throat like thirsty people usually make.

But maybe over those two years I'd gotten unaccustomed to him. Now it was hard for me to go back to knowing that this old man in a white sheet was my brother Michał. Maybe he'd also forgotten we were brothers. What does that mean anyway, to be brothers? When we were kids I didn't even like him that much. I preferred playing with other boys. He couldn't swim, couldn't shoot a catapult, couldn't climb trees. When he crossed a stubble field barefoot he'd complain that it prickled. Whereas me and the other boys, we'd have races to see who could make it to the far edge of the field first. We'd even choose stubble that had been cut with a sickle instead of a scythe, because it pricked even more. Or where there were the most thistles growing in among the crops. It was usually on Waliszka's fields or Boduch's because their fields were long and thin like sausages. When you ran the length of a field like that your feet were covered in blood, but you wouldn't dare let it hurt.

True, he was the best student of the four of us brothers. One time he even got a book as a prize for being the best in the school. They wrote on the book, For Michał Pietruszka for outstanding achievement and exemplary behavior, with gratitude also to his parents. It was because of the parents being mentioned that father often let him off working in the fields. When we went to church he'd give us one coin to give for the collection from the four of us, except Michał was the one who had to put it on the plate. When mother was carving up the chicken of a Sunday, father would supposedly make sure everyone got the same amount, but it would always turn out Michał had less, and father would tell her to at least give him the neck or the stomach as well. Michał could read his book late into the night and it was never a waste of oil. It was another matter that I didn't like books. You had to read whatever they told you to at school, but that was all. I could never figure out why people read at all, it seemed a waste of time. Father would explain to me:

"You little monster, it's so you can at least praise God with your reading."

So one time I told him that when I grew up I wasn't going to believe in God. Then I ran out of the house. I didn't actually know what it meant to believe or not believe, I was just trying to needle him. The moment I stopped attending school, my books were thrown in the corner and I started going to dances. After the first dance father gave me a hiding. The same after the second one. After the third I grabbed a pitchfork, come on, father, just you try. That time he beat me with a chain off the wagon. I was covered in welts, mother had to dress them.

"What did you do this to him for?" she said tearfully. "Beating your own child like that, dear God in heaven!"

"He's no child. He's a bandit! He'll throw you out of your own house in your old age."

But Michał read. The years passed and he kept on reading. Then one day a distant cousin of mother's came from the city, a tailor he was. Mother begged him to take Michał on, and he agreed. Let him at least learn tailoring, because what could he do here at home. Antek was already minding the cows, Stasiek looked after the geese. And there wasn't so much land they couldn't work it without him. Tailoring was a good trade, you're sitting down, you have a roof over your head, and you can make your own clothes. There wasn't any tailor in the village, so if he learned how to do it he could come back and be the tailor here. We could set up a room for him, maybe even buy a new sewing machine. For the moment he could use the one we already had.

"You won't regret it, cousin. He's a good boy, and he'll be a good tailor. He doesn't have a yen to go wandering every which way like the other boys. All he does is read books. We'll make it up to you, in flour or with a chicken."

"You know, being a priest would've been even better," father said to back her up. "We were planning for him to be a priest. But we can't afford it. Like you see, we still have three of them left at home. There won't be enough land to go around. That way, we'd have one less mouth to feed."

So off he went to mother's cousin to learn to be a tailor. He was there three years or so. Every other Sunday, sometimes even every one, he'd come home. And for each harvest or potato digging. He'd always bring mother at the very least a reel of thread, some needles, cigarettes for father, candy for Antek and Stasiek, a bottle of beer for me. Except he got really close mouthed. He wouldn't say anything about what things were like for him there, good or bad, whether they fed him properly, how the cousin's wife treated him. Father would ask:

"So do you know how to make pants yet?"

He'd never give you a straight answer yes or no. He'd just shrug and you couldn't tell if he knew or not.

"Being a tailor evidently takes as much learning as being a priest," father would have to say in answer to his own question.

Each time he went back, mother would give him whatever she could so he wouldn't arrive back at her cousin's empty-handed. Flour, kasha, peas, a slab of bacon, some cheese, sometimes a chicken. And eggs, every one we had she kept for when Michał would come. Us, we ate any old stuff, boiled noodles on their own, kasha with milk, because everything else was for the cousin. Once I caught a jackrabbit in a snare, that went to the cousin as well. Oh, he'll be so pleased. We'd never dried our plums before, but now we did, so we'd have something to send to the cousin. We'd had that cousin up to here. Stasiek was little and he didn't yet understand anything, one day he asked if mother's cousin was a dragon, since he needed to eat so much. Even father would let out a sigh every now and then and say, a priest would have been better. But mother would just say, quiet now, hush, she'd calm us down. Sometimes you need to take the food out of your own mouth, when Michał is done learning he'll make clothes for Stasiek, and Antek, and Szymuś, and for you too, father.

Then one Sunday he came and said he wasn't at the cousin's anymore, that he was working in the factory now, and mother didn't need to get anything ready because he wouldn't be taking anything from us anymore. It made us sad, because all that flour, kasha, peas, eggs, cheeses, everything had gone for nothing. Father just said:

"I thought we'd maybe buy some drill and you'd make me a new suit. But obviously it's God's will. This suit's still fine."

From that moment on he came less and less. Once a month, once every two months, for Christmas, Easter, harvest. Though he had problems mowing. He'd jerk the scythe and move forward too quickly, and he'd take such big swings you'd think he was trying to cut down a whole acre at one go. He ended up jamming the scythe into the ground a couple times, it got blunted a bit, then after one swath he was as tired as if he'd mowed the entire field. Though the fact was he'd never been that good a mower. When could he have learned? They'd been going on about him becoming a priest from when he was tiny, and a priest has a farmhand, he doesn't need to do his own mowing. Though if you ask me, I don't think he'd have made much of a priest either. To be a priest you need to have a calling, you need the gift of the gab. A new sermon each Sunday, plus for every wedding, every funeral. And all those people you have to remind in the confessional, don't sin, don't sin, God is watching you. God died for our sins. It'll all be reckoned up on Judgment Day. Where could he find the talking for all that?

Also, if you're a priest you need to believe in life after death. But here, one Sunday there were a few of the neighbors round, and father and mother, and they'd gotten to talking about life after death, one of them had seen one thing, another one something else. Michał was getting ready for the train, he was fastening his suitcase, he was running late and as if out of spite his case wouldn't shut. All of a sudden he exclaims, there's no life after death! All there is is what's here, that's what you have to believe in! The neighbors' jaws dropped, mother and father went red as beetroots. Michał just grabbed the suitcase, even though it wasn't properly closed, he charged through the door, and only from the hallway he threw out:

"Goodbye."

I had to go with him whether I liked it or no, because I'd agreed to walk him to the station. But he didn't utter a word to me the entire way. Though the fact was we were walking as fast as our legs would carry us, because the train had already whistled on the far side of the woods. It was only at the station, when we were quickly saying our goodbyes, that he muttered:

"Tell father and mother I'm sorry."

He didn't come again till Christmas, then after that only at Easter, and from then on that's how it always was. And when he did come he never said much, he'd just sit there thinking and thinking. Father asked him:

"So what is it you do in the factory?"

"What people usually do in factories. Different stuff."

"Do they pay you well?"

"Not that much, but it's enough."

"And where do you live?"

"With this family."

"Are they at least decent folks?"

"They're okay."

Mother asked him:

"Do you have a young lady? Just don't worry about whether she has money, son. Take the poorest one, even if she only has the shirt on her back, so long as she's an honest woman."

"This isn't the time for young ladies, mother, there are more important things."

After that I didn't ask him any more questions, because for me young ladies were the most important thing. What could be more important than that? You send a guy like that off to the city and he just goes strange on you. If it was me there, I'd for sure know how to enjoy life in the city. You heard various things. Sometimes Gienek Woś would come home on leave, he was a professional soldier, boy did he have stories to tell. It gave you gooseflesh. Florek Sójka would get so excited he'd jump up and down:

"Fucking hell! What are we waiting for! This I gotta see!"

"They stand on the sidewalk in the evening like street lamps. They give you a nice friendly smile as if they've known you forever. And they're all dressed up like royalty, their dresses barely come down over their asses. Some of them have this fox fur thing on, and under that they're bare. You take the fur off and she's yours. You don't even have to go far, round the corner where it's dark, just make sure the cops won't see you. Some of them stand there in their underwear or in their stockings, everything's on view. You can get ahold of their tits like you'd take a cow by the udder, and all you do is ask, how much? Their perfume takes your breath away. Whatever you want, a short one, a tall one, a thin one, two at once if you like. You say, come on, and they go with you. Plus they're not afraid you'll make them a baby. They don't ask you if you'll marry them. They don't give a damn who you are. But it's best not to say you're from the country. And it's not wham-bam, you on her, her under you. There's all kinds of different ways. Left, right, and center. Any way you want, I'm telling you. There's any number. Though those ways cost more. Or there's others that wait in horse-drawn carriages, except they charge even more. You get into the carriage, it sets off, it's a ride to heaven. The most expensive are those that one of them takes you one way, one the other, and you have three more of them at your feet."

"Christ, how much would that cost? How much would it be, Gienek?"

"You'd need maybe a couple hundredweight of rye per person. Not that much actually. But you could enjoy it all for yourself. What's there to enjoy out here?" Gienek would try and get us going when he'd had a few. Because for the time being we'd just gone to the pub to get drunk. "Though it depends. Bondarek now, he'd have to pay one and a half times that much cause he's a redhead and a shortass. You, Szymek, it would only cost you half. Come visit sometime, the two of us'll go out have some fun. I know this one carriage driver. He'll take us all over town."

The dark was growing denser and denser in the house. In the gloom his face looked like it had gotten darker. People were still bringing in their crops.

"Remember," I said, "there was a time you were supposed to come stay longer. We were going to talk. But don't say anything if you don't want to. If you want to live like that without a single word, be my guest. Though how would it be if everyone in the village fell silent? All they did was plow and plant and mow and bring in the harvest, and no one would say so much as a God bless you in greeting. And what if along with the people the dogs and cats went quiet, and all the other animals, and the birds stopped chirping and the frogs stopped croaking. Would there be a world? Even trees talk if actually you listen to them. Each kind has its own language, the oaks speak oak, the beech trees speak beech. Rivers talk, corn. The whole world is one big language. If you really listened carefully to it, you might even be able to hear what they were saying a century back, maybe even thousands of years ago. Because words don't know death. They're like see-through birds, once they've spoken they circle over us forever, it's just that we don't hear them. Though maybe from God's heights every person's voice can be heard separately. Even what I'm saying to you now. What they're saying at Maszczyk's, at Dereń's, in every house. If you leaned your ear close to the world, who knows, you might be able to hear people whispering and make out what they're thinking, what they're dreaming about, whose house a cat is purring in, whose stable a horse is neighing in, whose child is sucking at its mother's breast, whose is just being born, all that is language. God tells people to pray in words because without words he wouldn't know one person from the next. And people wouldn't be able to tell each other apart either if they didn't have words. Life begins with a word and ends with words. Because death is also just the end of words. Start maybe from the first ones at hand, the ones that are closest to you. Mother, home, earth. Maybe try saying, earth. I mean, you know what earth is. Where do you spit? On the earth. You know, what you walk on, what houses are built on, what you plow. You've done your share of plowing. Remember father teaching us to plow? He taught us one by one, you, me, Antek, Stasiek. Whenever one of us had barely grown taller than the plow, he'd take us with him when he went out to do the plowing. He'd put our hands on the grips, then put his hands over ours and walk behind, like he was holding us in his arms. You could feel his warmth at your back, his breath on your head. And you'd hear his words like they were coming from the sky. Don't hold it like that, it needs to be firmer, follow the middle of the furrow, it has to go deeper when the earth is dry, when your hands get bigger you'll also be holding the reins in this hand and the whip in that one. You'll learn, you will, you just have to be patient. Moles, they know how to dig in the earth, trees put down their roots in it, men dig trenches in it in wartime. Springs rise up out of the earth and people's sweat soaks into it. It's this earth, no other, that every person is born in. And remember when anyone was leaving the village, they'd always take a little bit of earth with them in a bundle. Or sailors, when the land's still way far away, they say they want the earth under their feet again. And God came down to the earth. And when people die they're buried in the earth. We'll be put there too. I'm planning to have a tomb built. Eight places, so there'll be room for all of us. Maybe Antek and Stasiek will agree to be buried with us. There's a saying, may the earth weigh lightly on him. So wherever it'll be lighter for them. They say that when a person's born, the earth is their cradle. And all death does is lay you back down in it. And it rocks you and rocks you till you're unborn, unconceived, once again."

F
Mys

Mysliwski, Wieslaw

Stone upon stone